PRAISE FOR
AVA'S DEMON

"AVA'S DEMON is a gripping and exciting story, halfway between fantasy and science fiction, with a unique narrative, complex characters and a really stunning, breathtaking art and color palette."
— **MÍRIAM BONASTRE TUR** (*Hooky*)

"I started reading and I couldn't stop! It's very fun to look at!"
— **BABS TARR** (*Batgirl*)

"The sheer amount of dedication and work put into AVA'S DEMON is evident in every single page, every layout...I just cannot get enough of it."
— **IRENE KOH** (*The Legend of Korra*)

"Reading the dark and colorful AVA'S DEMON feels like watching a TV series...all I want to do is binge it!"
— **SWEENEY BOO** (*Over My Dead Body*)

"Lots of mystery, high quality sci-fi, creepiness, a touch of humor, and...amazing colors! It seems AVA'S DEMON has everything. A real pearl!"
— **MIRKA ANDOLFO** (*Unnatural*)

"The art is gorgeous and spellbinding and the story is hypnotic...it's not hard to read the whole thing in a single sitting, you get so wrapped up in it!"
— **VITA AYALA** (*New Mutants*)

"A beautifully illustrated journey into the battles we have with our inner demons as well as some very literal ones. A story that kept surprising me and taking unexpected twists at every chance."
— **JORGE CORONA** (*The Me You Love in the Dark*)

"Every drawing Michelle makes hints at a deeper, richer world behind it...it's beautiful to look at and makes you want to know more."
— **LOIS VAN BAARLE** (*Loish*)

For my husband Krzys, who has always been
an incredible source of love and support.

Colorists: ARSHA, FOCH FLOS, MINH MA,
NAVA, NICOLE SANDS, RACHEL TIBBS

Edited by ALEX ANTONE
Book Design by CARINA TAYLOR
Production by ANDRES JUAREZ

Teaching Guide by Creators Assemble, Inc. | Lexile Measure: HL470L

ISBN: 978-1-5343-2438-1 | B&N ISBN: 978-1-5343-9941-9

SKYBOUND COMET™

SKYBOUND ENTERTAINMENT
ROBERT KIRKMAN | Chairman
DAVID ALPERT | CEO
SEAN MACKIEWICZ | SVP, Publisher
SHAWN KIRKHAM | SVP, Business Development
ANDRES JUAREZ | Creative Director, Editorial
ARUNE SINGH | Director of Brand, Editorial
SHANNON MEEHAN | Senior Public Relations Manager
ALEX ANTONE | Editorial Director
AMANDA LAFRANCO | Editor
BIXIE MATHIEU | Editor
JILLIAN CRAB | Graphic Designer
RICHARD MERCADO | Production Artist
MORGAN PERRY | Brand Manager, Editorial
KEVIN BIDES | Brand Coordinator, Editorial
SARAH CLEMENTS | Brand Coordinator, Editorial
DAN PETERSEN | Sr. Director, Operations & Events
Foreign Rights & Licensing Inquiries:
contact@skybound.com
SKYBOUND.COM

This graphic novel has been adapted for print
from a multimedia webcomic.

For the original experience, please visit www.avasdemon.com.

® IMAGE COMICS, INC.
ROBERT KIRKMAN | Chief Operating Officer
ERIK LARSEN | Chief Financial Officer
TODD MCFARLANE | President
MARC SILVESTRI | Chief Executive Officer
JIM VALENTINO | Vice President
ERIC STEPHENSON | Publisher / Chief Creative Officer
NICOLE LAPALME | Vice President of Finance
LEANNA CAUNTER | Accounting Analyst
SUE KORPELA | Accounting & HR Manager
MATT PARKINSON | Vice President of Sales & Publishing Planning
LORELEI BUNJES | Vice President of Digital Strategy
DIRK WOOD | Vice President of International Sales & Licensing
RYAN BREWER | International Sales & Licensing Manager
ALEX COX | Director of Direct Market Sales
CHLOE RAMOS | Book Market & Library Sales Manager

EMILIO BAUTISTA | Digital Sales Coordinator
JON SCHLAFFMAN | Specialty Sales Coordinator
KAT SALAZAR | Vice President of PR & Marketing
DEANNA PHELPS | Marketing Design Manager
DREW FITZGERALD | Marketing Content Associate
HEATHER DOORNINK | Vice President of Production
DREW GILL | Art Director
HILARY DILORETO | Print Manager
TRICIA RAMOS | Traffic Manager
MELISSA GIFFORD | Content Manager
ERIKA SCHNATZ | Senior Production Artist
WESLEY GRIFFITH | Production Artist
IMAGECOMICS.COM

AVA'S DEMON

BOOK ONE: REBORN

MICHELLE FUS

CHAPTER 1

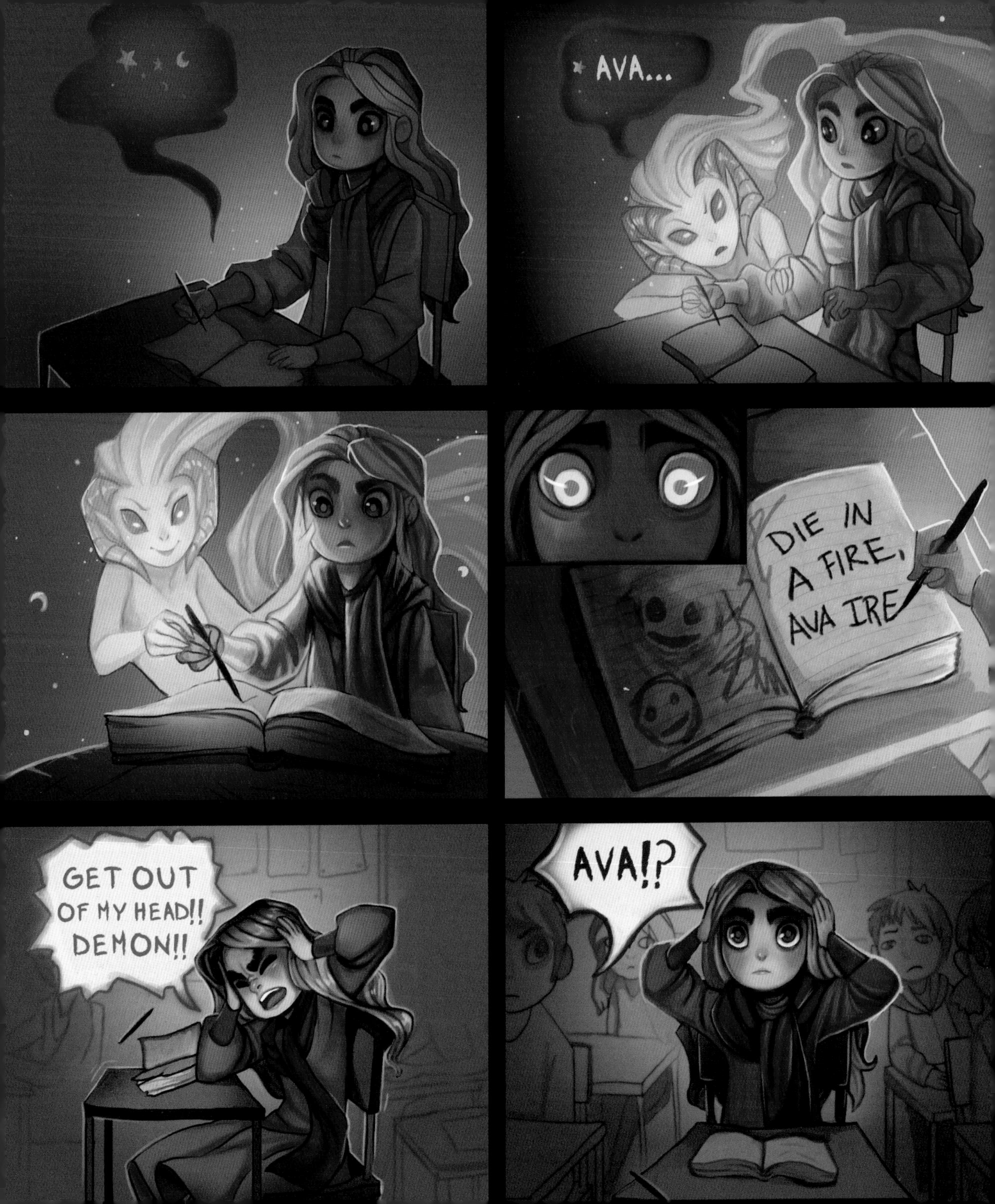
AVA...
DIE IN A FIRE, AVA IRE
GET OUT OF MY HEAD!! DEMON!!
AVA!?

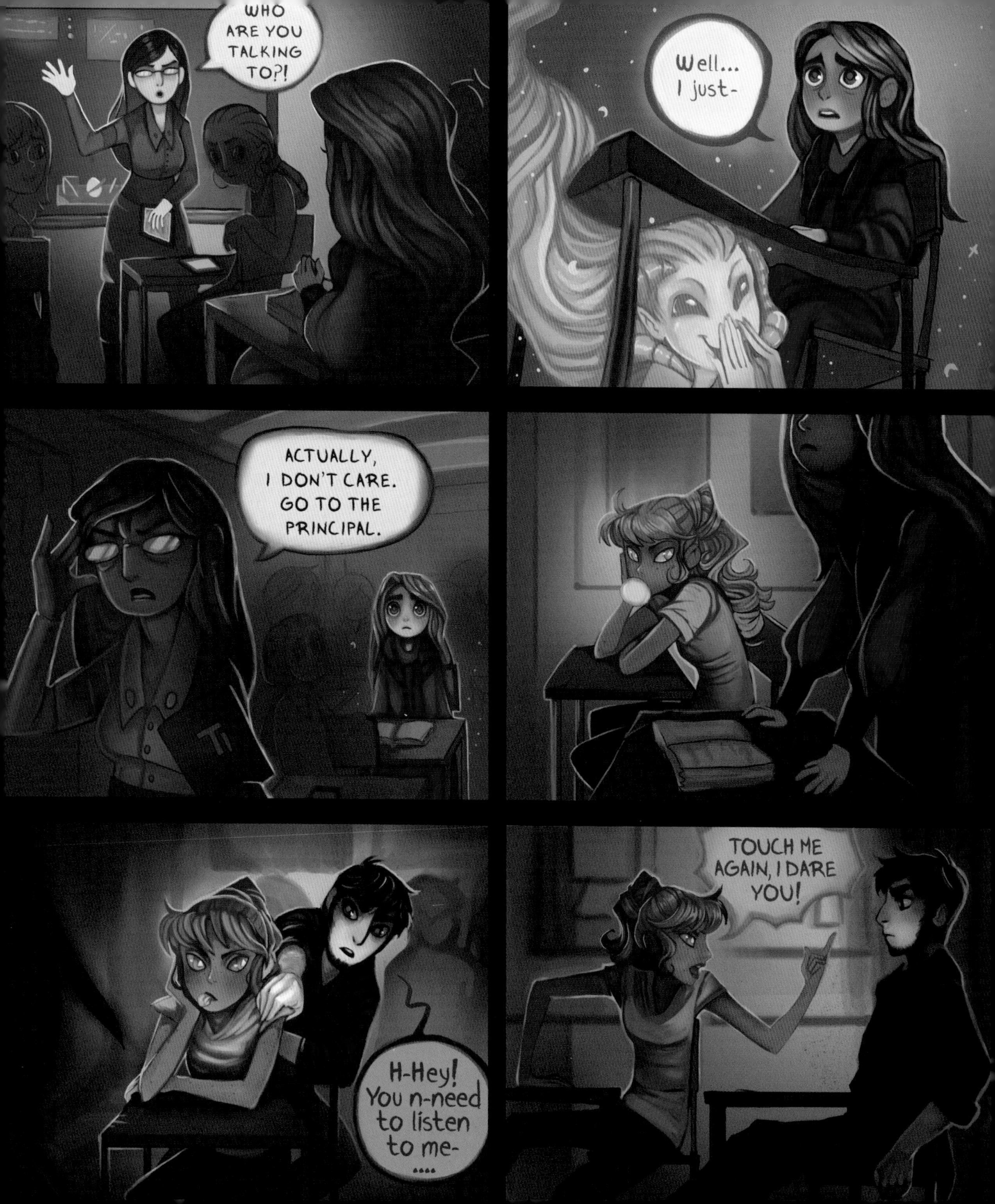
WHO ARE YOU TALKING TO?!
Well... I just-
ACTUALLY, I DON'T CARE. GO TO THE PRINCIPAL.
H-Hey! You n-need to listen to me-
....
TOUCH ME AGAIN, I DARE YOU!

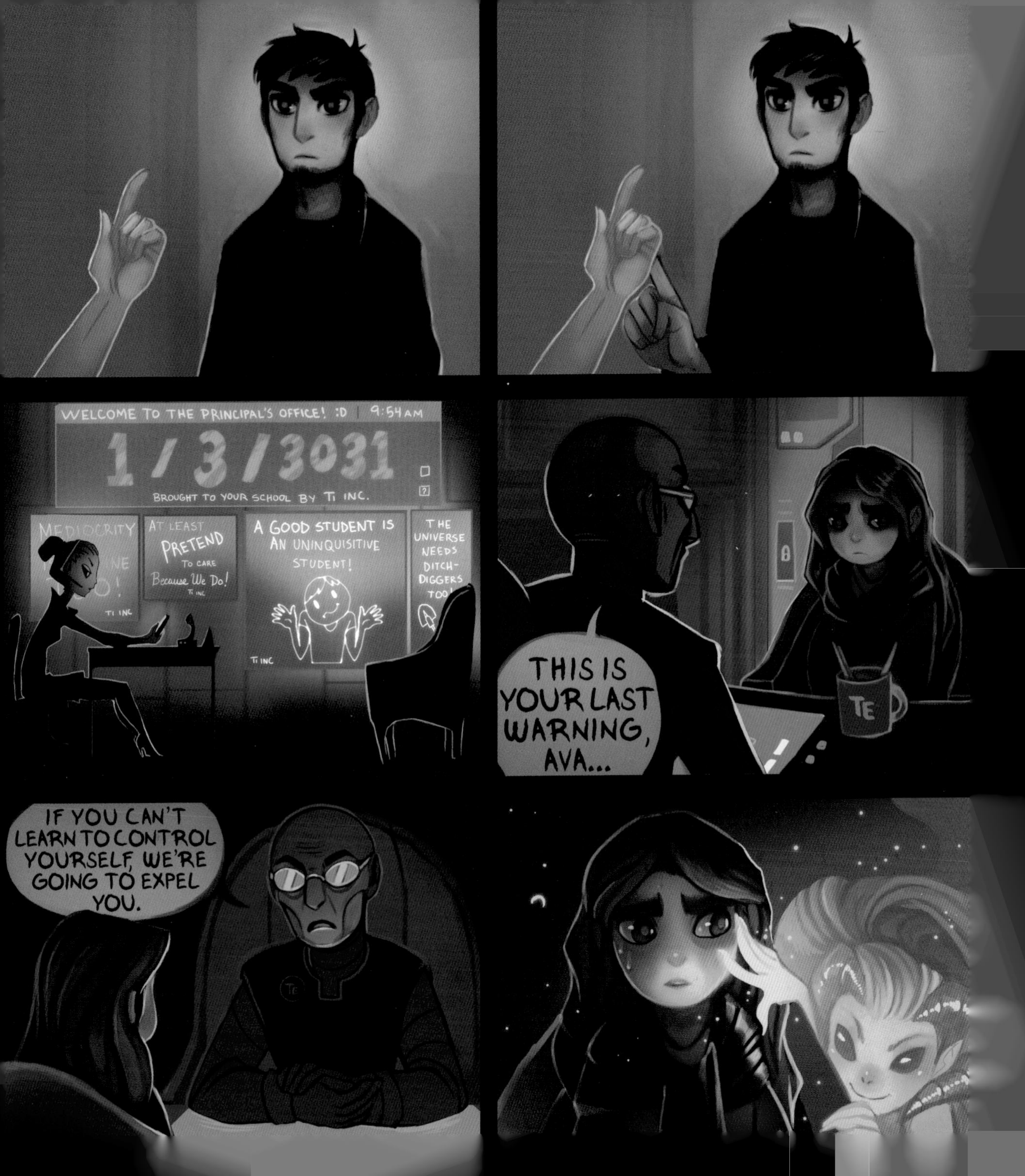
WELCOME TO THE PRINCIPAL'S OFFICE! :D 9:54 AM
1/3/3031
BROUGHT TO YOUR SCHOOL BY Ti INC.
MEDIOCRITY
Ti INC
AT LEAST PRETEND TO CARE Because We Do!
Ti INC
A GOOD STUDENT IS AN UNINQUISITIVE STUDENT!
Ti INC
THE UNIVERSE NEEDS DITCH-DIGGERS TOO!
THIS IS YOUR LAST WARNING, AVA...
TE
IF YOU CAN'T LEARN TO CONTROL YOURSELF, WE'RE GOING TO EXPEL YOU.

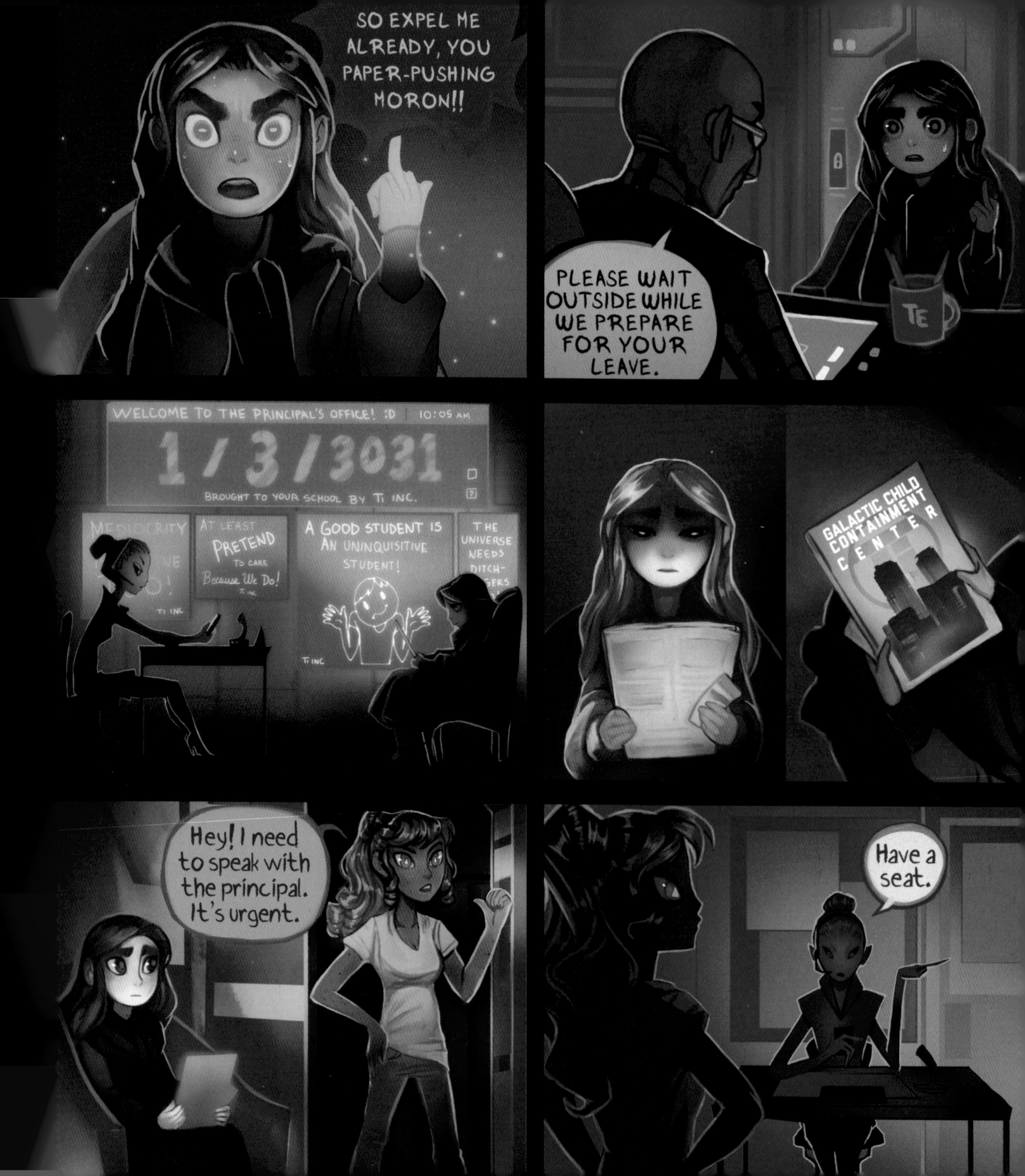
SO EXPEL ME ALREADY, YOU PAPER-PUSHING MORON!!
PLEASE WAIT OUTSIDE WHILE WE PREPARE FOR YOUR LEAVE.
TE
WELCOME TO THE PRINCIPAL'S OFFICE! :D
10:05 AM
1/3/3031
BROUGHT TO YOUR SCHOOL BY Ti INC.
AT LEAST PRETEND TO CARE Because We Do!
A GOOD STUDENT IS AN UNINQUISITIVE STUDENT!
THE UNIVERSE NEEDS DITCH-
Ti INC
GALACTIC CHILD CONTAINMENT CENTER
Hey! I need to speak with the principal. It's urgent.
Have a seat.

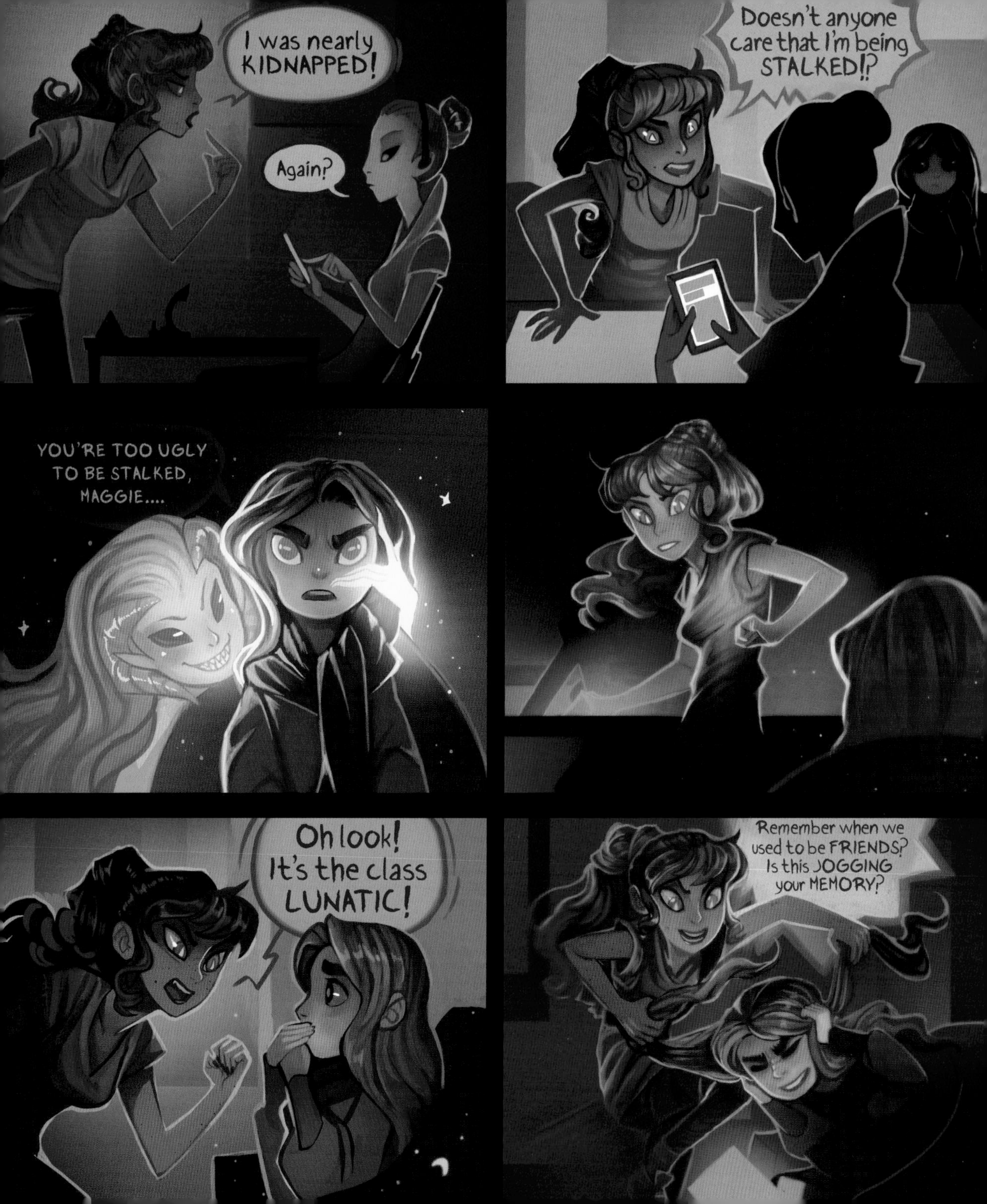
I was nearly KIDNAPPED!
Again?
Doesn't anyone care that I'm being STALKED!?
YOU'RE TOO UGLY TO BE STALKED, MAGGIE....
Oh look! It's the class LUNATIC!
Remember when we used to be FRIENDS? Is this JOGGING your MEMORY?

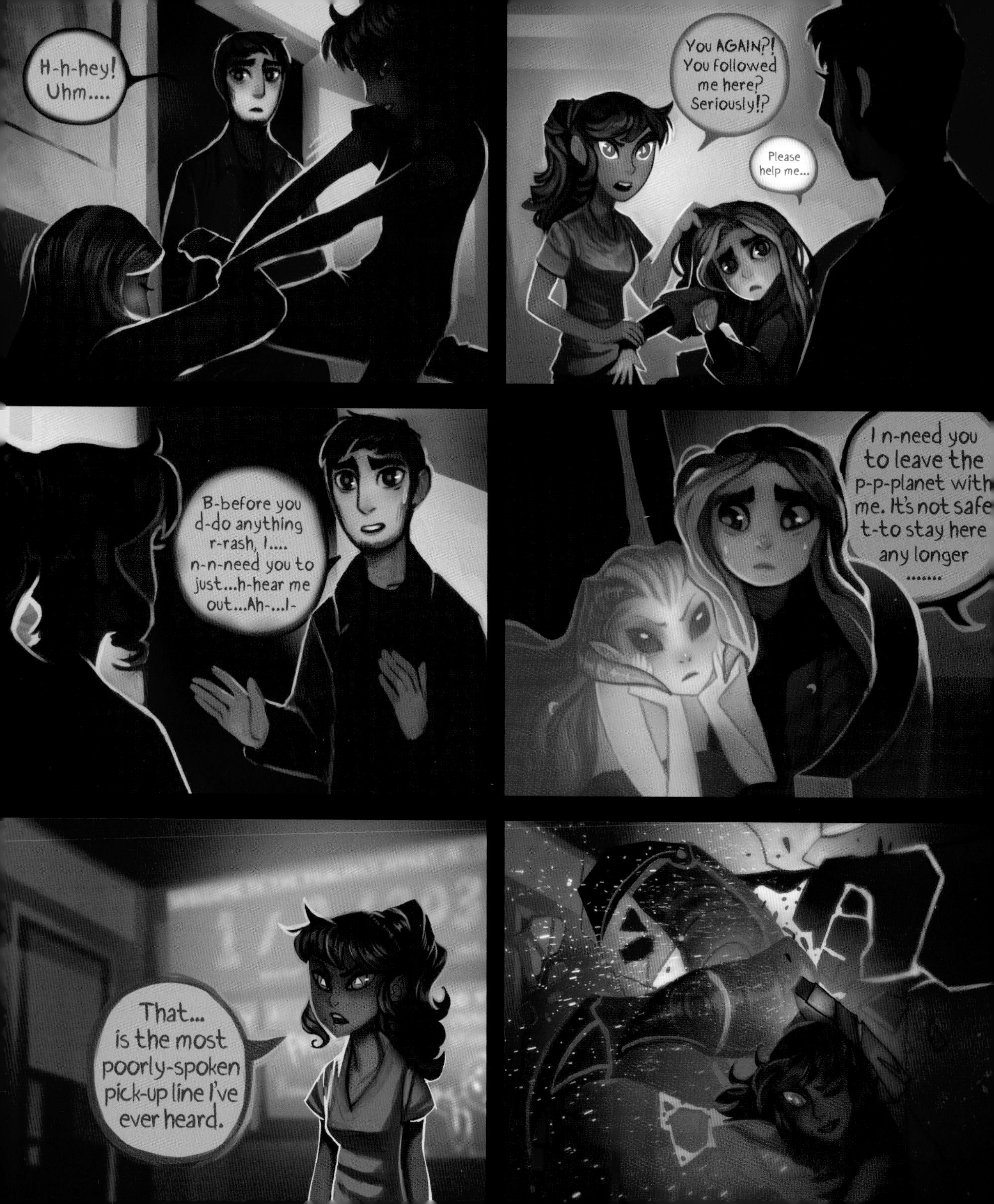
H-h-hey! Uhm....
You AGAIN?! You followed me here? Seriously!?
Please help me...
B-before you d-do anything r-rash, I.... n-n-need you to just...h-hear me out...Ah-...I-
I n-need you to leave the p-p-planet with me. It's not safe t-to stay here any longer ....
That... is the most poorly-spoken pick-up line I've ever heard.

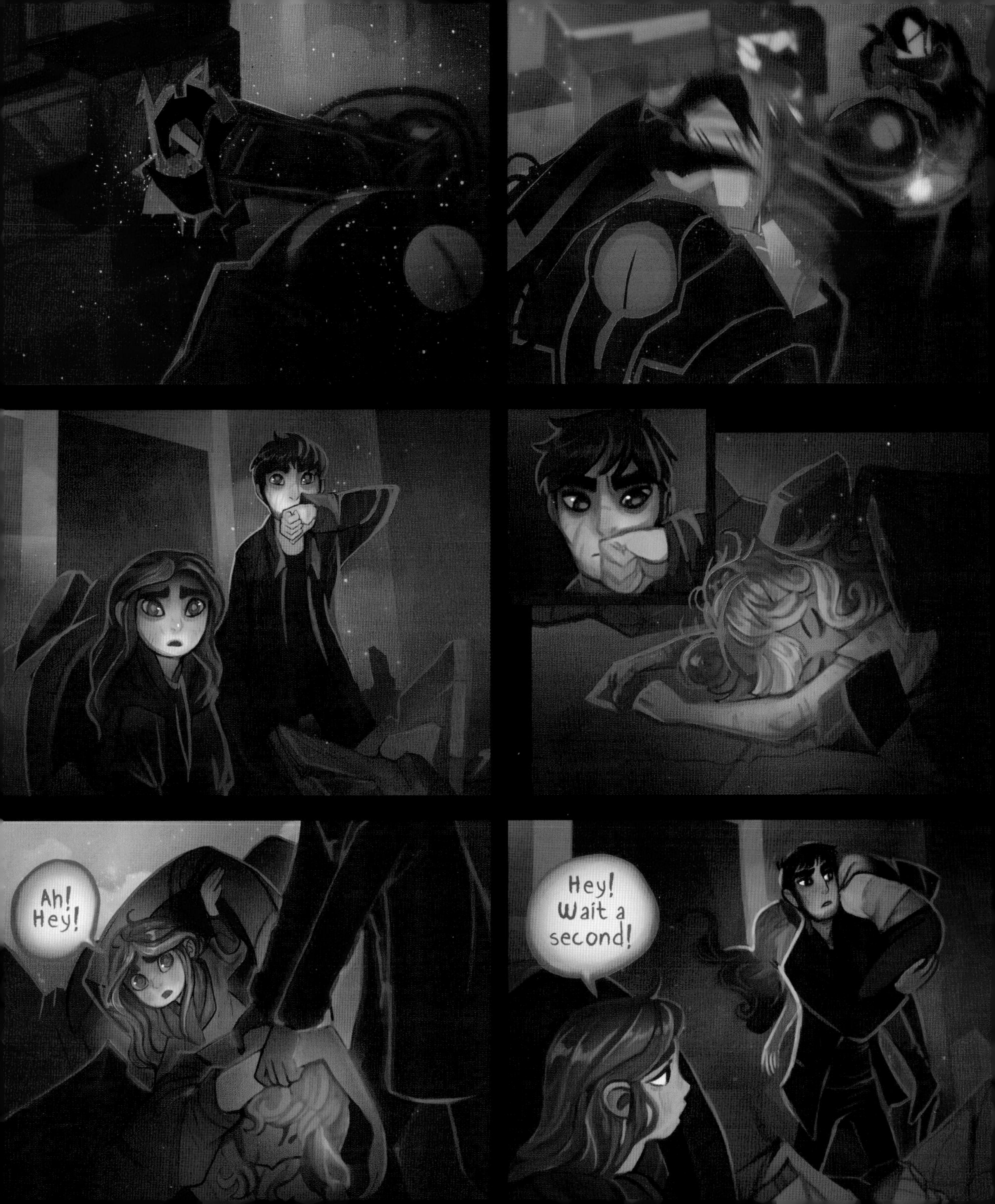
Ah! Hey!
Hey! Wait a second!

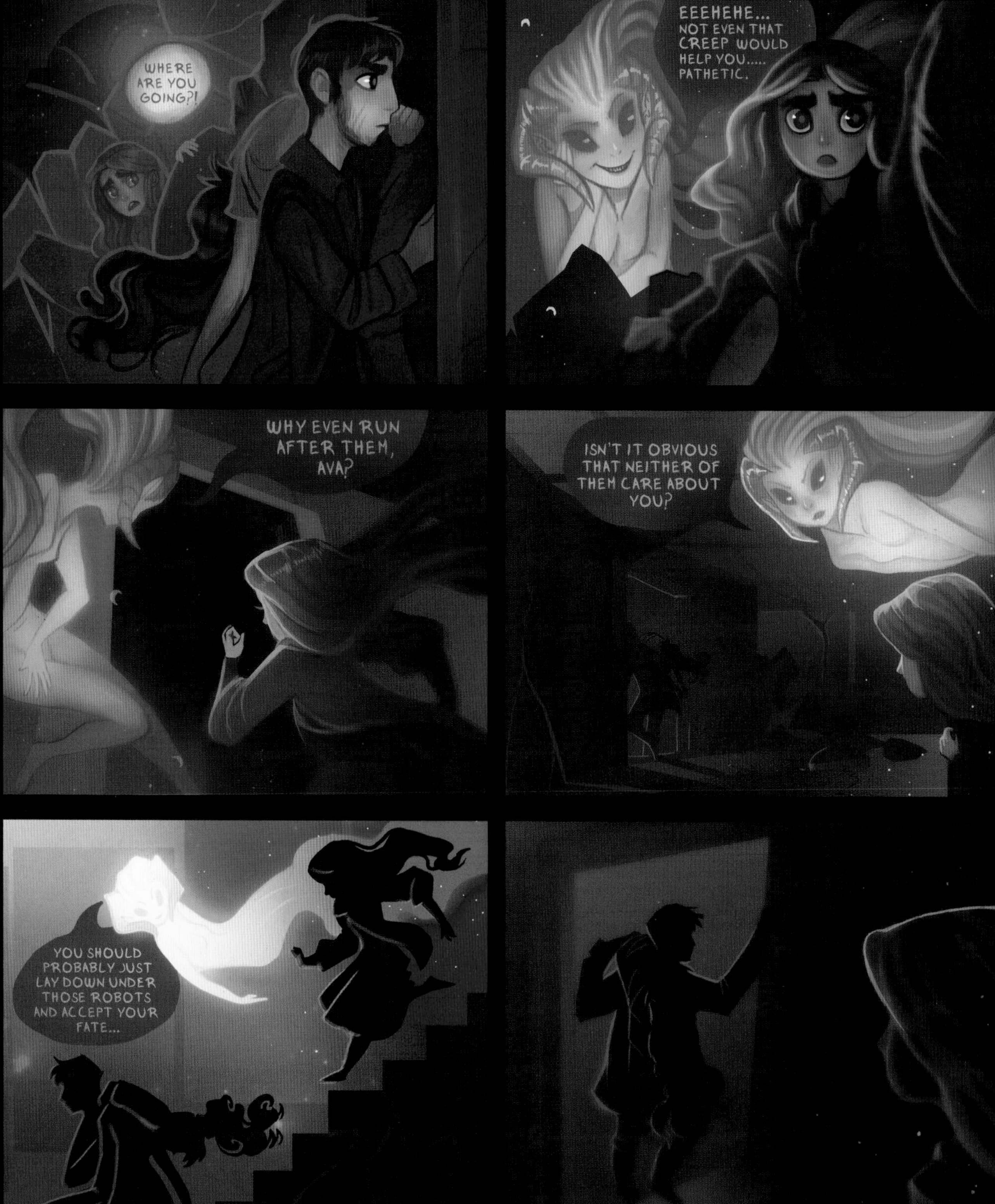
WHERE ARE YOU GOING?!
EEEHEHE... NOT EVEN THAT CREEP WOULD HELP YOU..... PATHETIC.
WHY EVEN RUN AFTER THEM, AVA?
ISN'T IT OBVIOUS THAT NEITHER OF THEM CARE ABOUT YOU?
YOU SHOULD PROBABLY JUST LAY DOWN UNDER THOSE ROBOTS AND ACCEPT YOUR FATE...

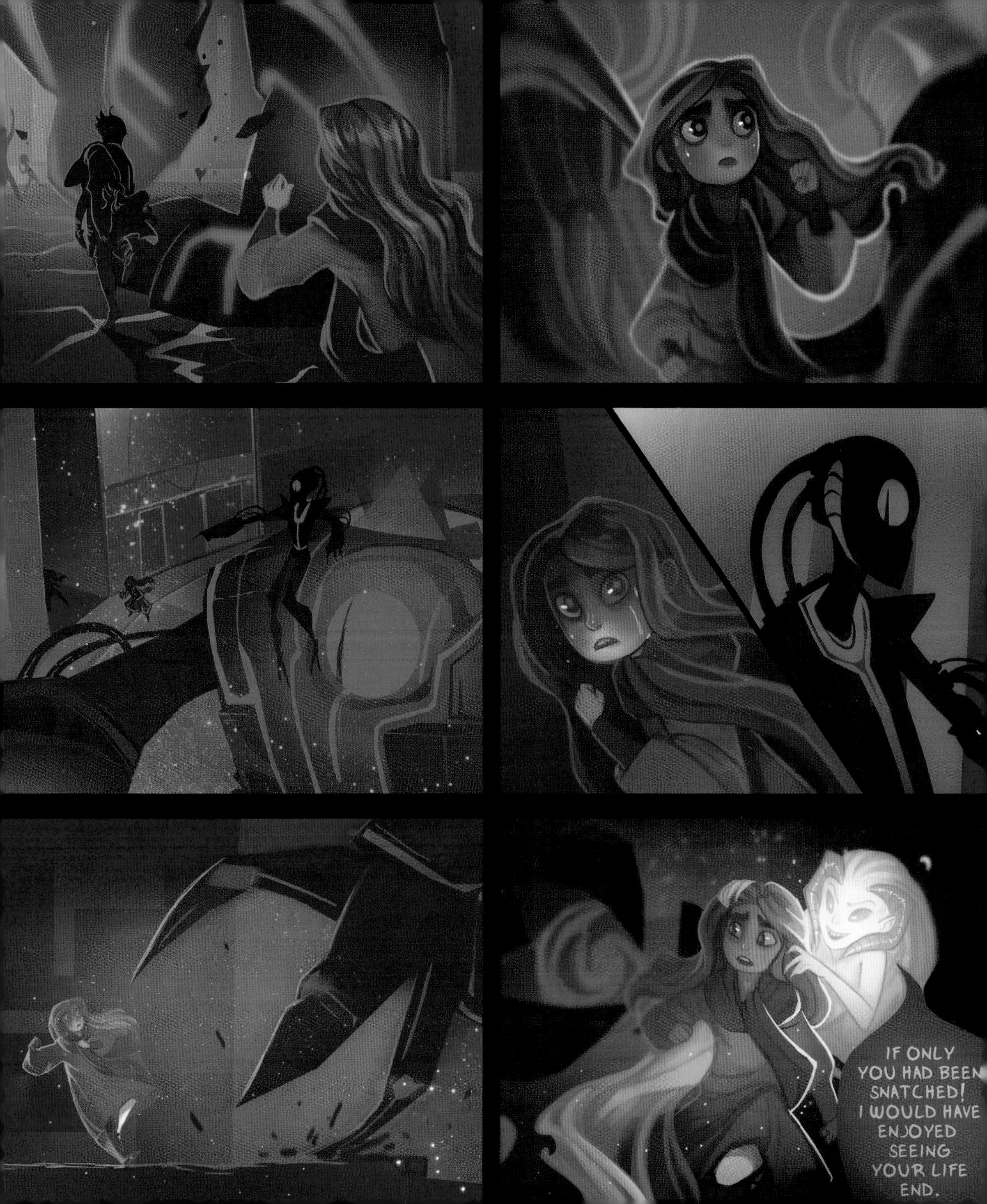
IF ONLY
YOU HAD BEEN
SNATCHED!
I WOULD HAVE
ENJOYED
SEEING
YOUR LIFE
END.

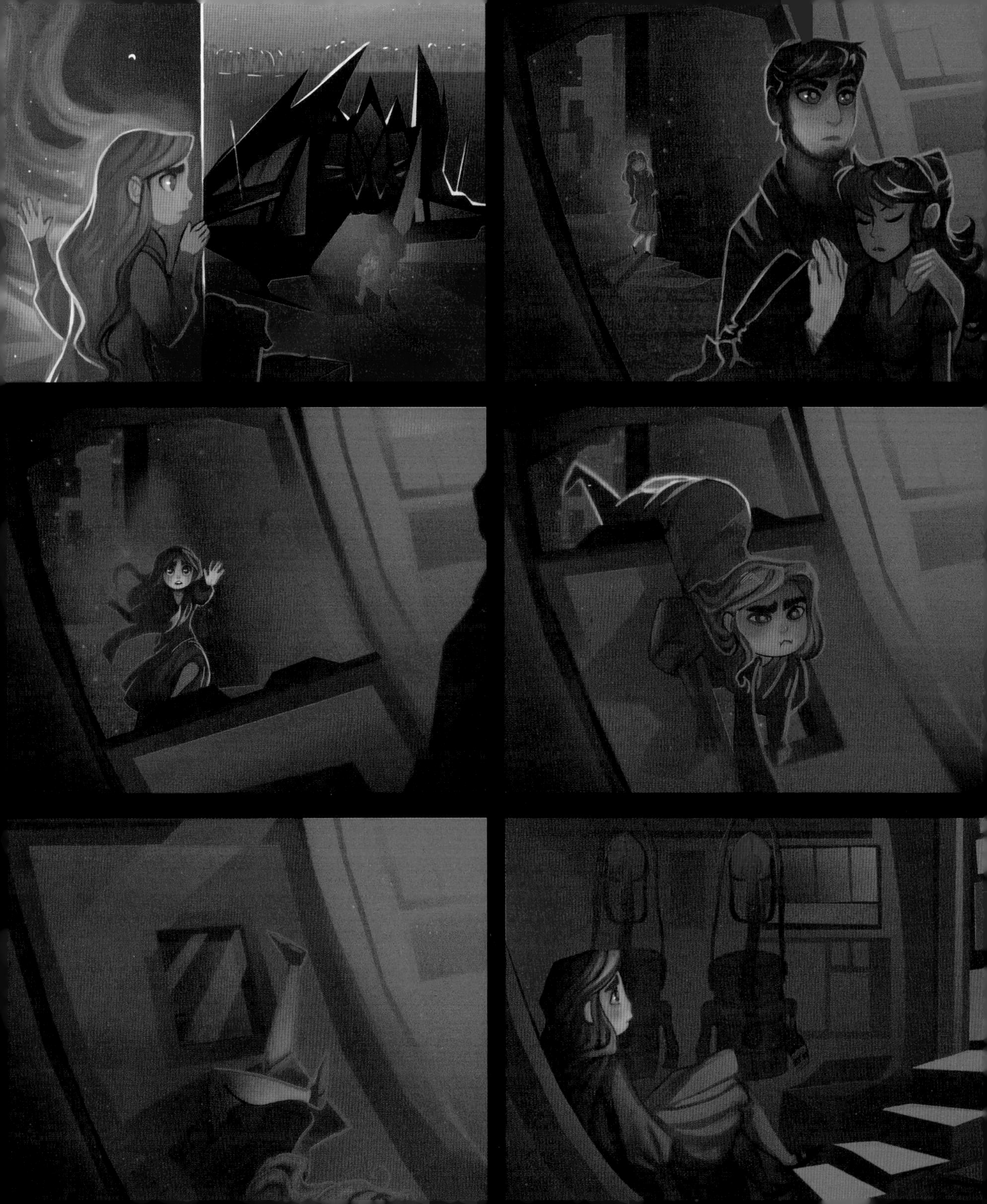

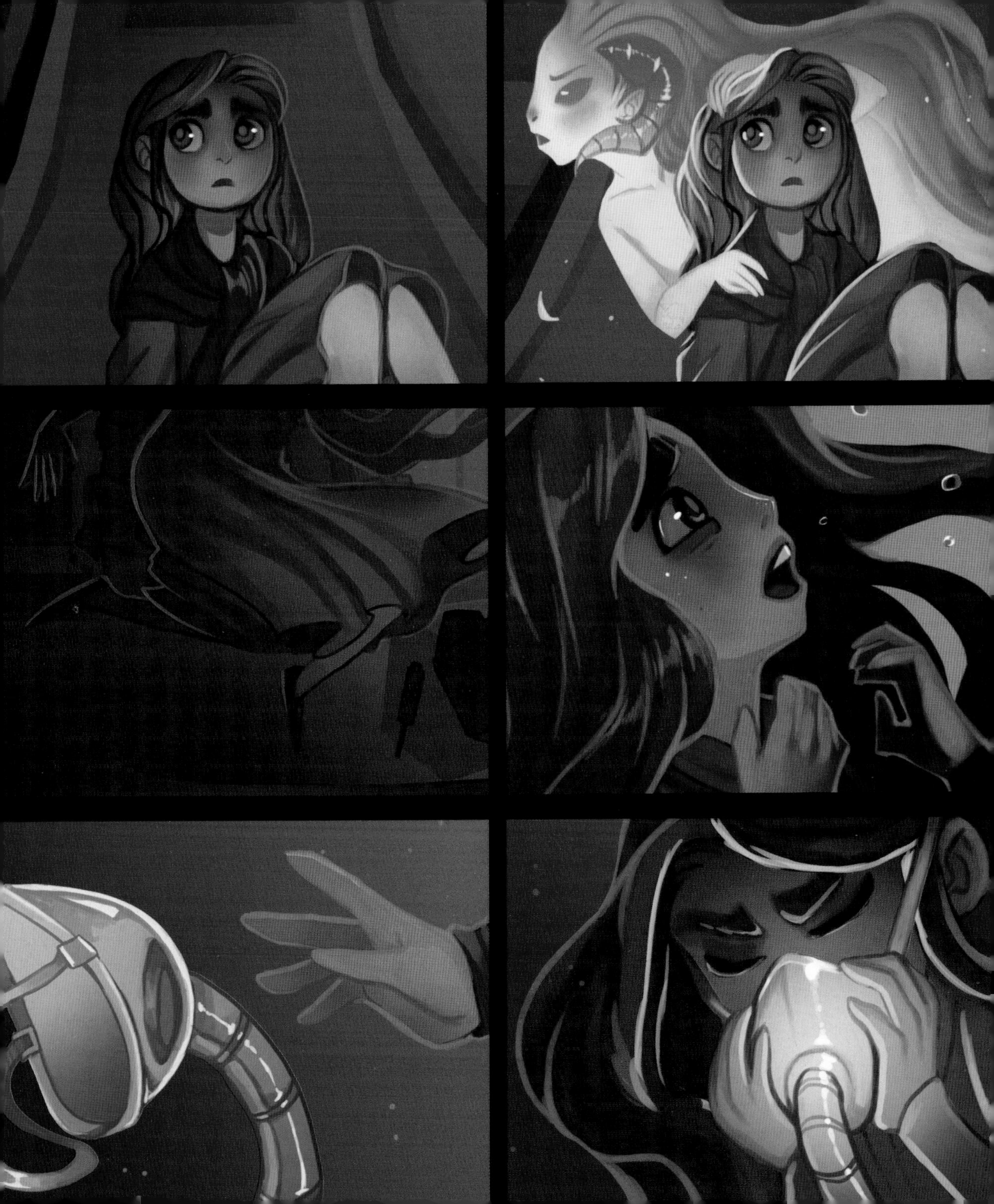

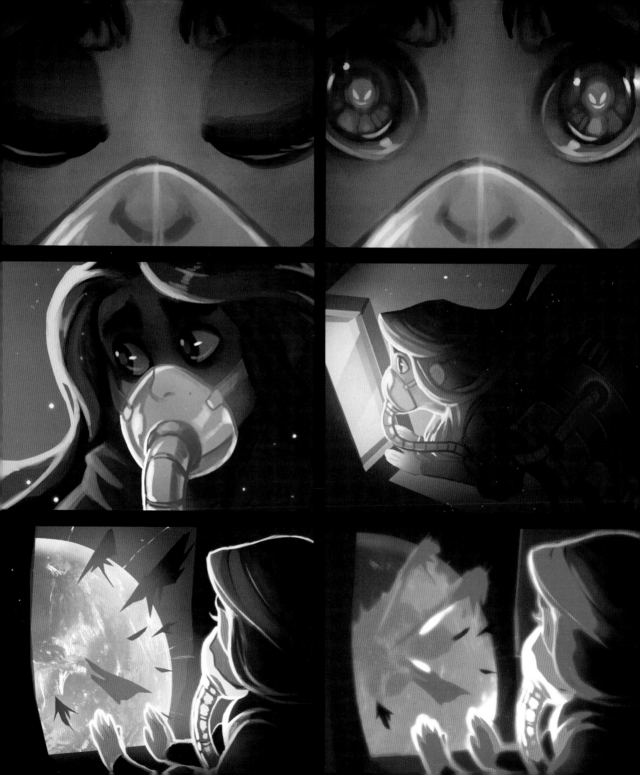

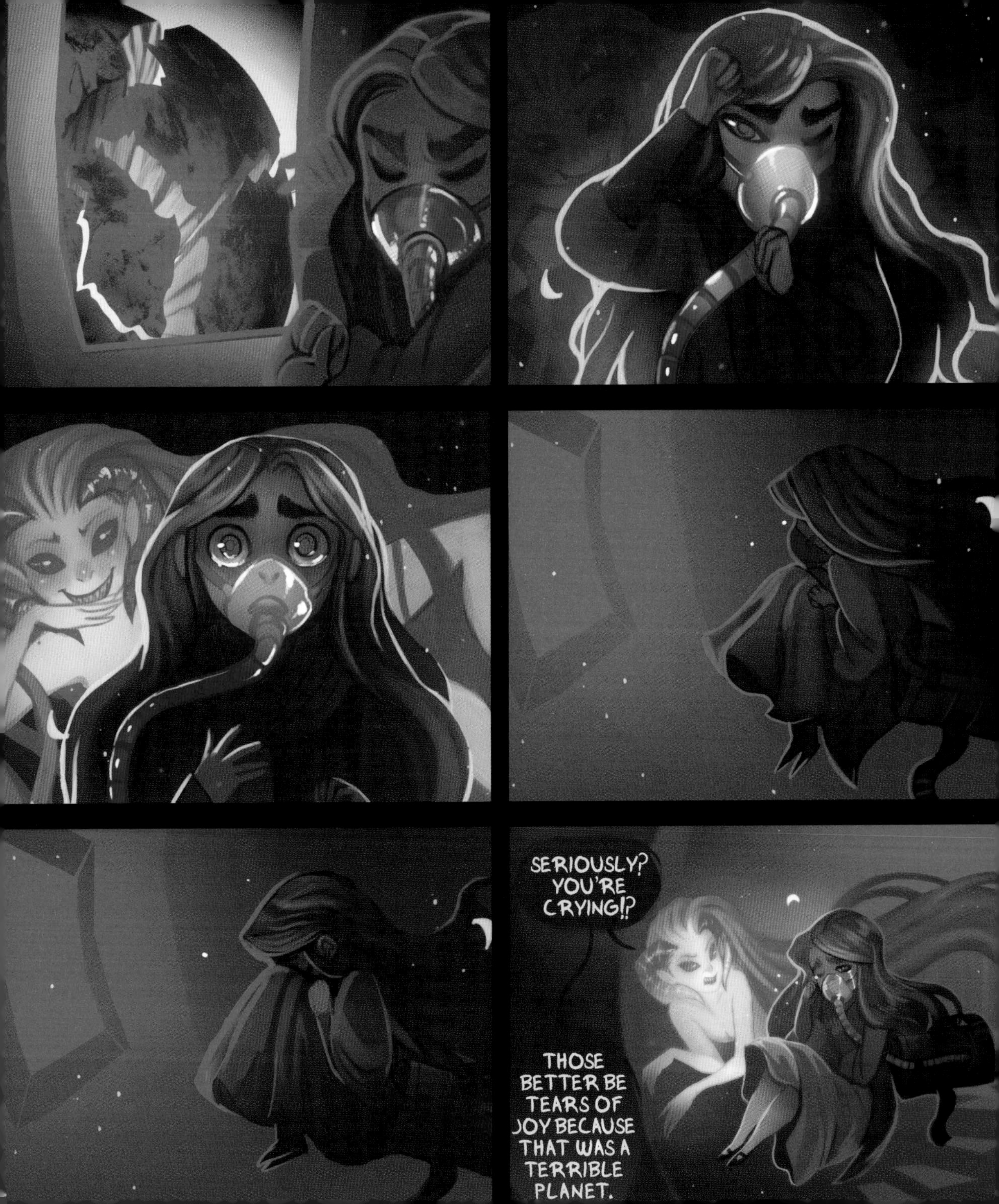
SERIOUSLY? YOU'RE CRYING!?
THOSE BETTER BE TEARS OF JOY BECAUSE THAT WAS A TERRIBLE PLANET.

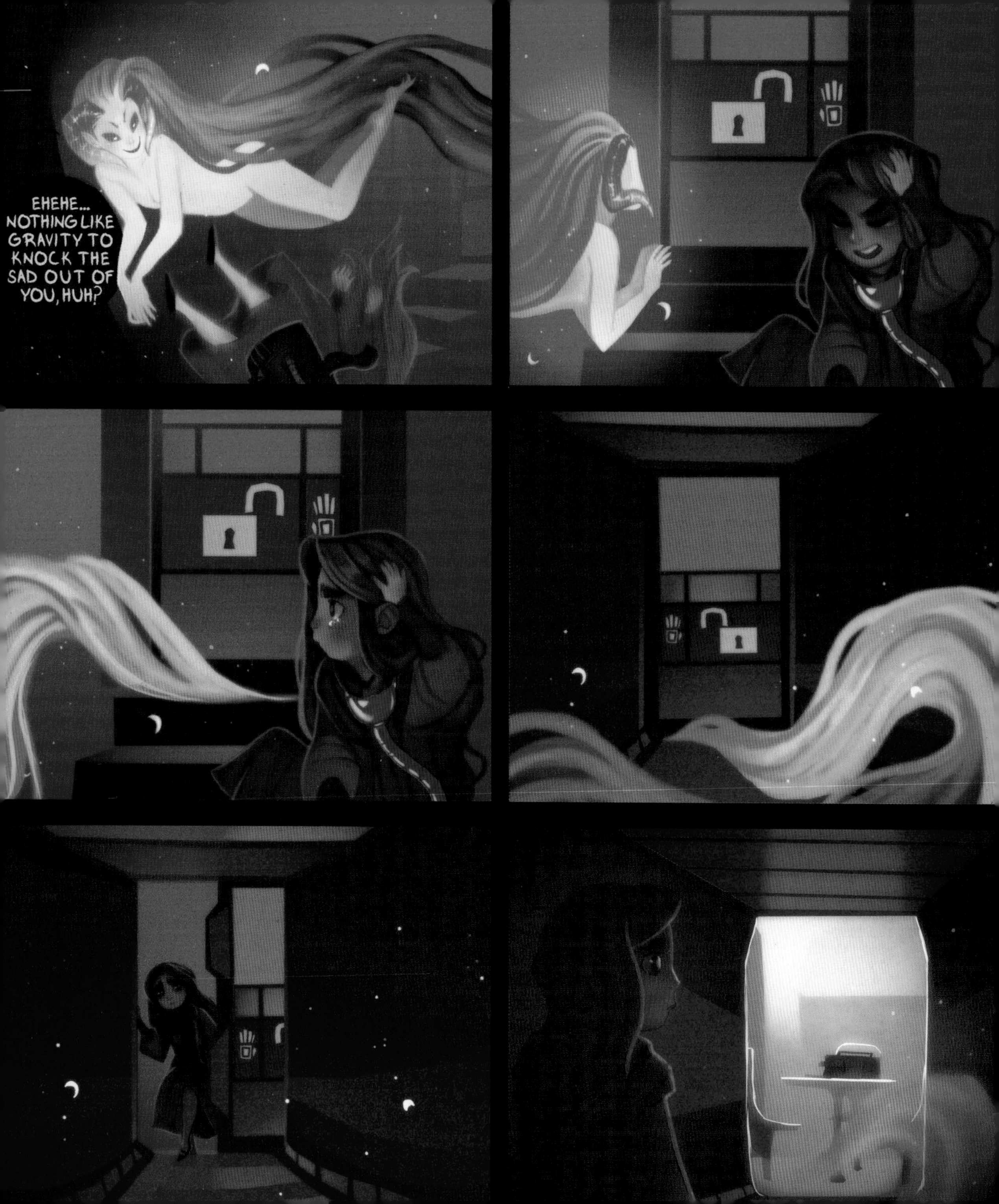
EHEHE... NOTHING LIKE GRAVITY TO KNOCK THE SAD OUT OF YOU, HUH?

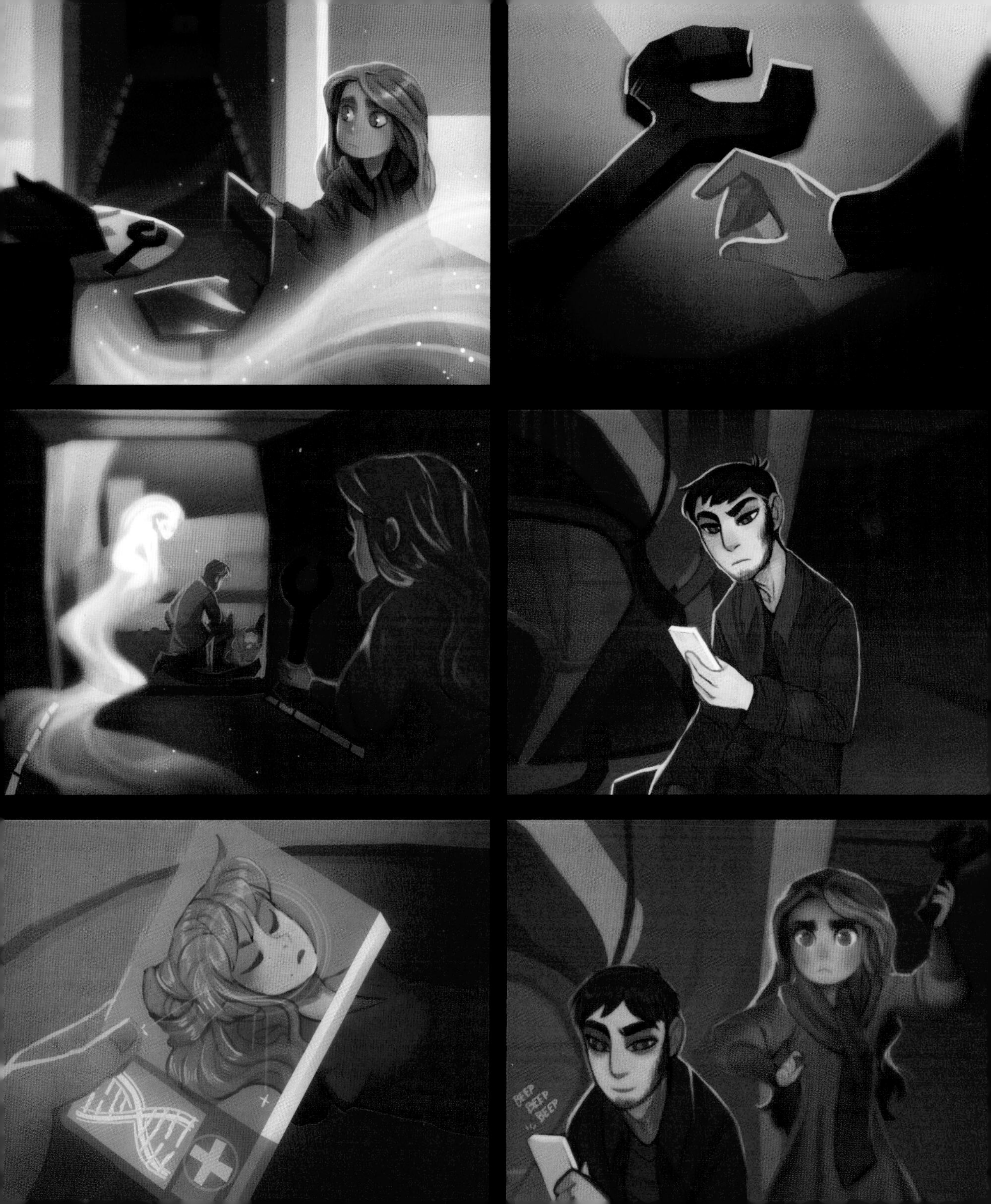
BEEP
BEEP
BEEP

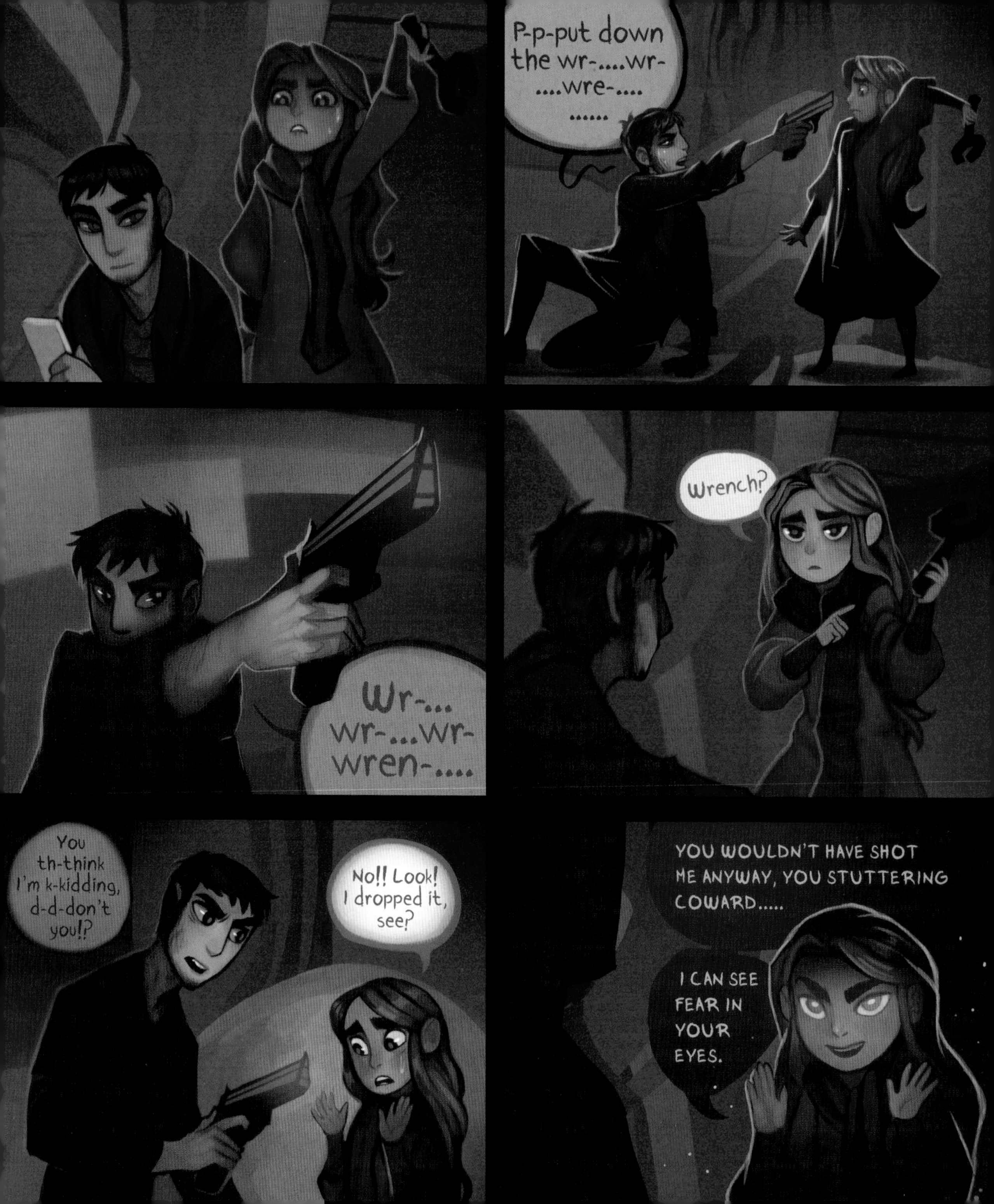
P-p-put down the wr-....wr-....wre-.... ......
Wr-... wr-...wr-wren-....
Wrench?
You th-think I'm k-kidding, d-d-don't you!?
No!! Look! I dropped it, see?
YOU WOULDN'T HAVE SHOT ME ANYWAY, YOU STUTTERING COWARD.....
I CAN SEE FEAR IN YOUR EYES.

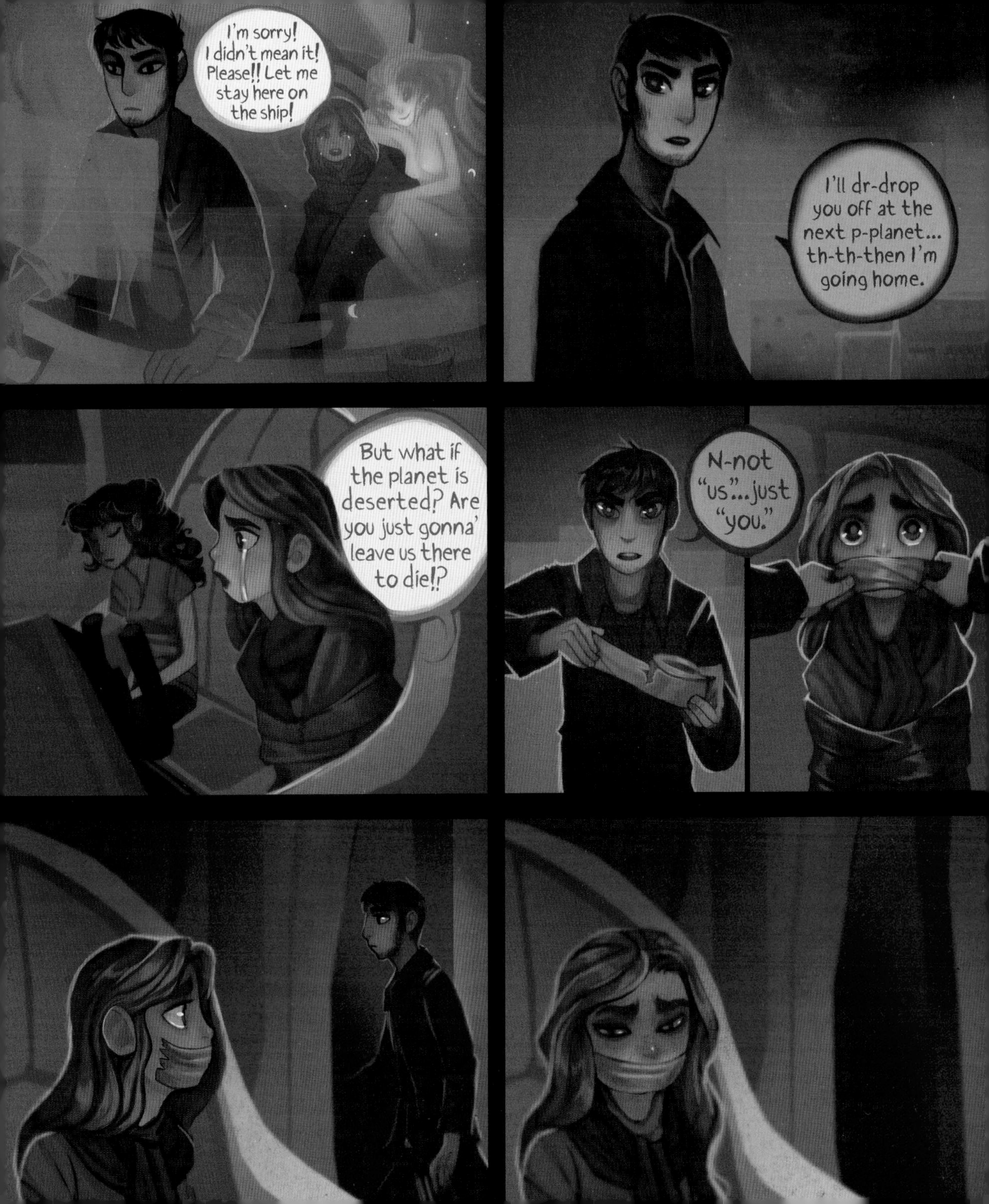
I'm sorry! I didn't mean it! Please!! Let me stay here on the ship!
I'll dr-drop you off at the next p-planet... th-th-then I'm going home.
But what if the planet is deserted? Are you just gonna' leave us there to die!?
N-not "us"...just "you."

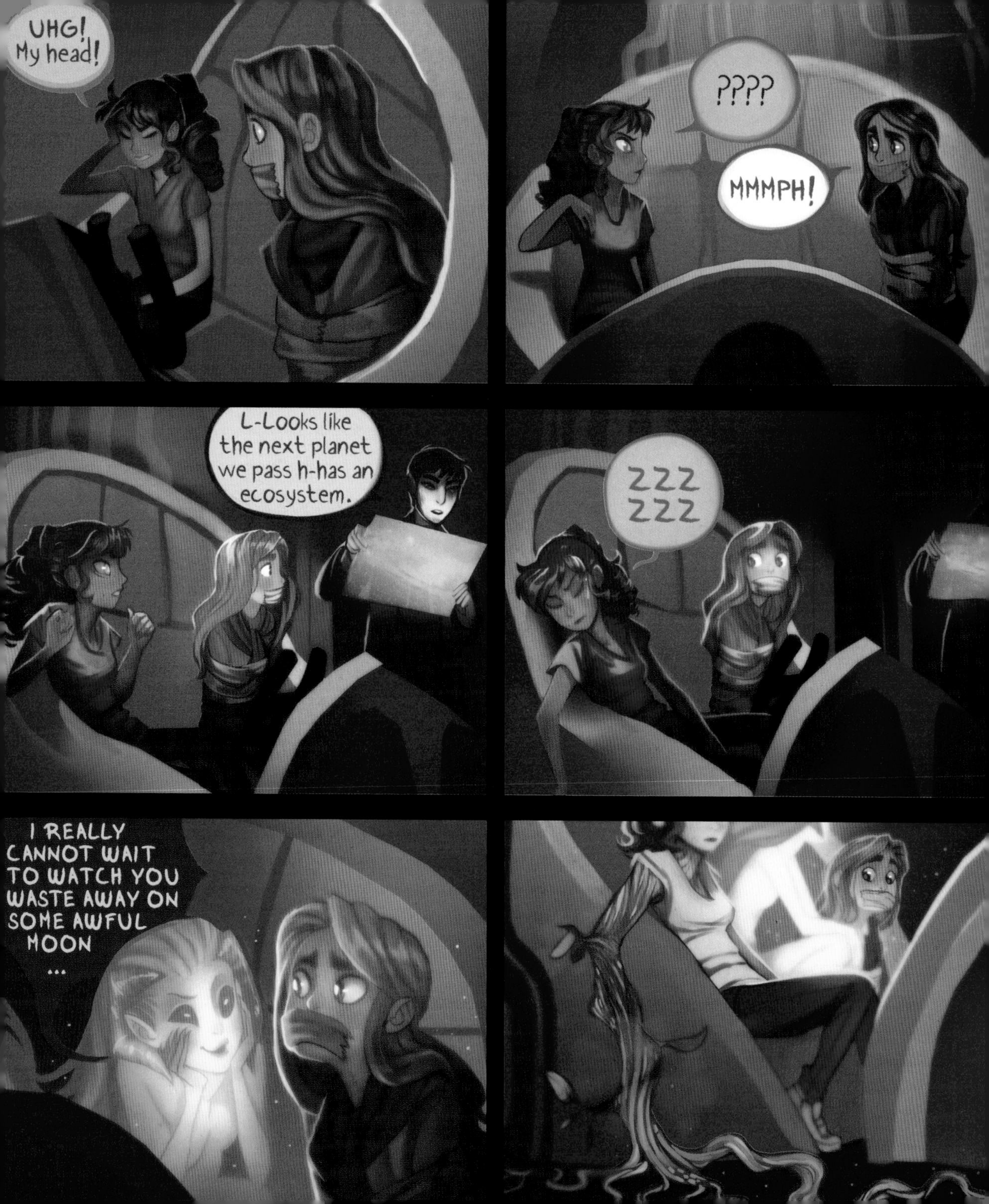
UHG! My head!
????
MMMPH!
L-Looks like the next planet we pass h-has an ecosystem.
ZZZ ZZZ
I REALLY CANNOT WAIT TO WATCH YOU WASTE AWAY ON SOME AWFUL MOON ...

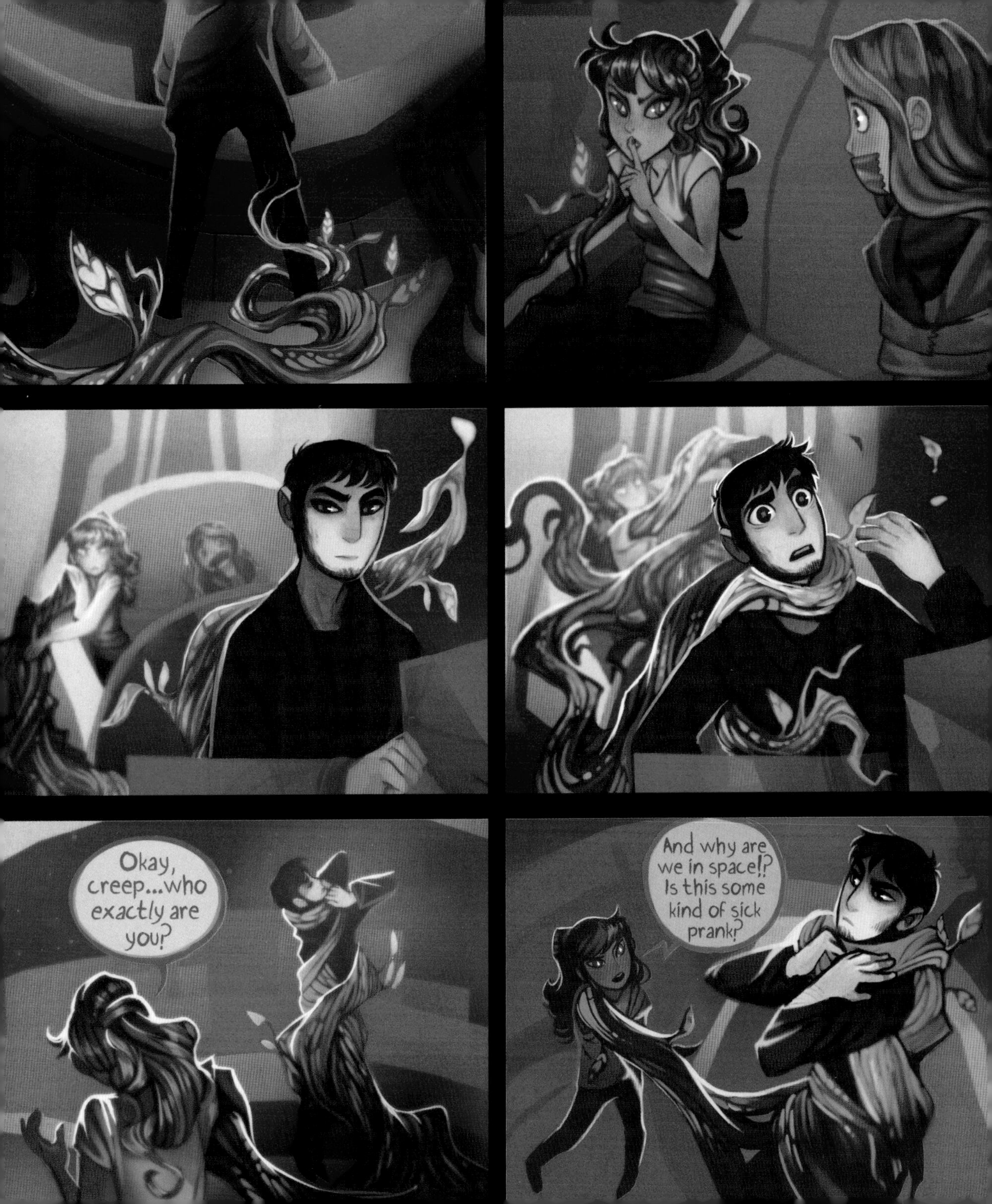
Okay, creep...who exactly are you?
And why are we in space!? Is this some kind of sick prank?

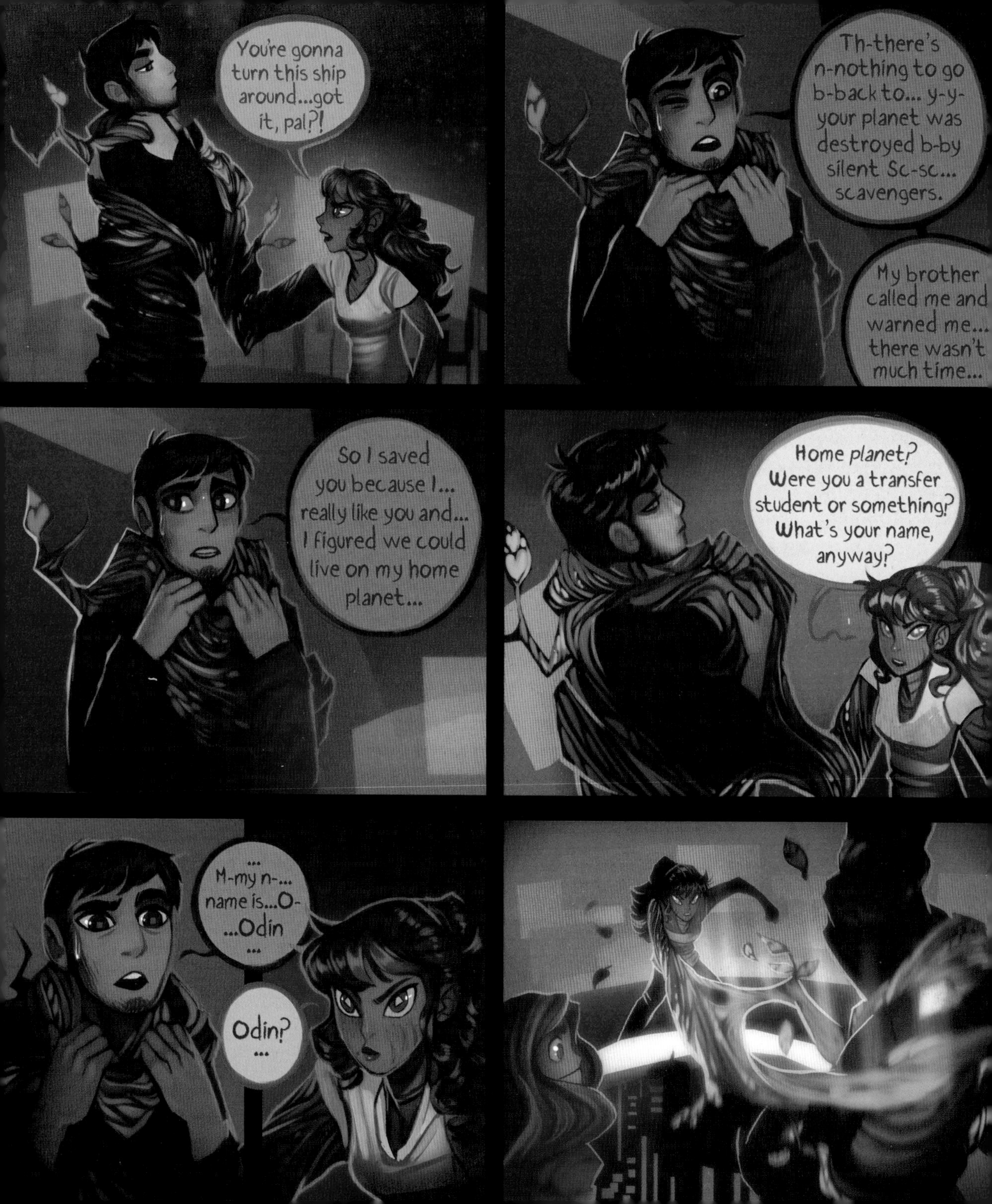

You're gonna turn this ship around...got it, pal?!
Th-there's n-nothing to go b-back to... y-y-your planet was destroyed b-by silent Sc-sc... scavengers.
My brother called me and warned me... there wasn't much time...
So I saved you because I... really like you and... I figured we could live on my home planet...
Home planet? Were you a transfer student or something? What's your name, anyway?
... M-my n-... name is...O- ...Odin ...
Odin? ...

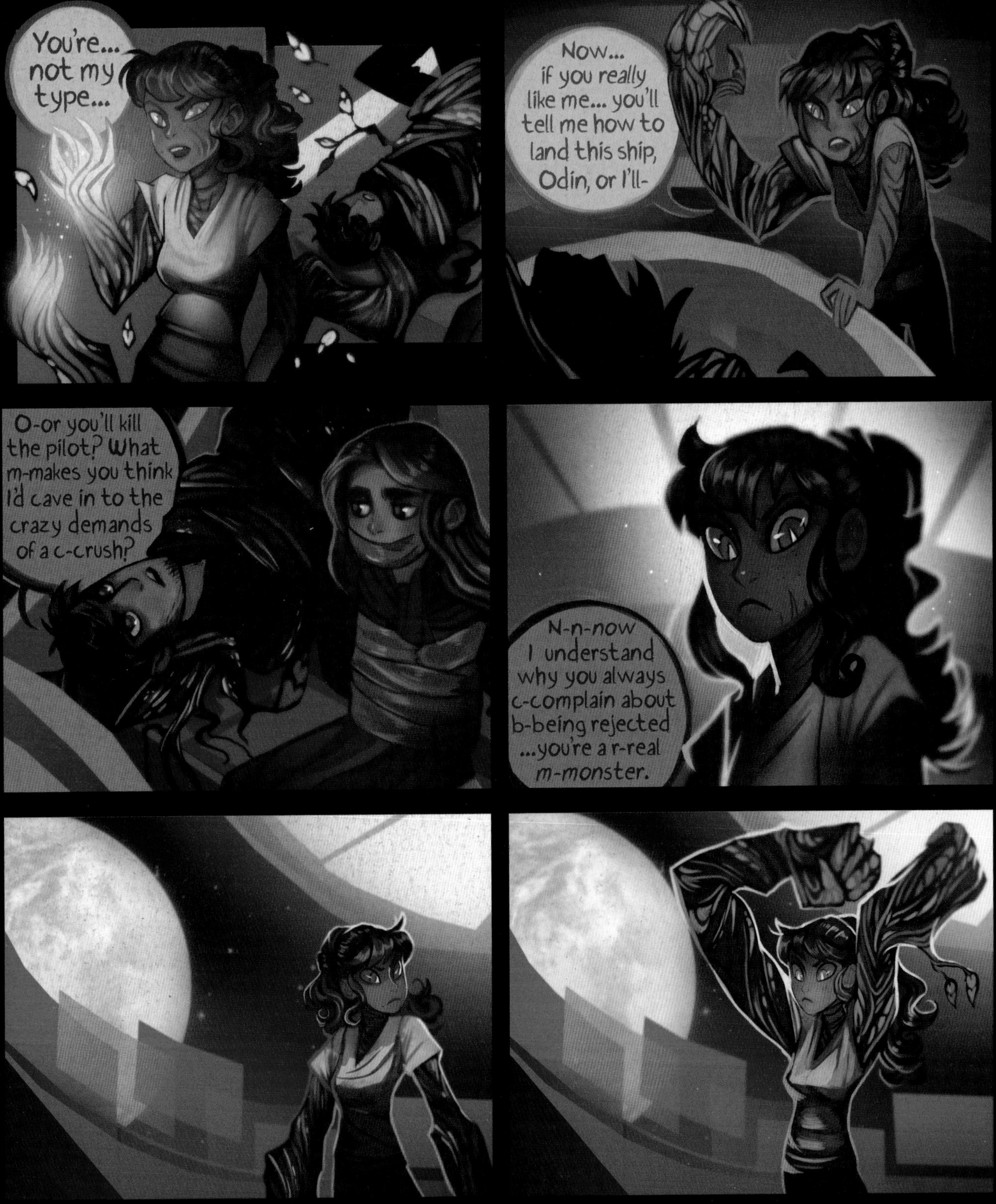
You're... not my type...
Now... if you really like me... you'll tell me how to land this ship, Odin, or I'll-
O-or you'll kill the pilot? What m-makes you think I'd cave in to the crazy demands of a c-crush?
N-n-now I understand why you always c-complain about b-being rejected ...you're a r-real *m-monster.*

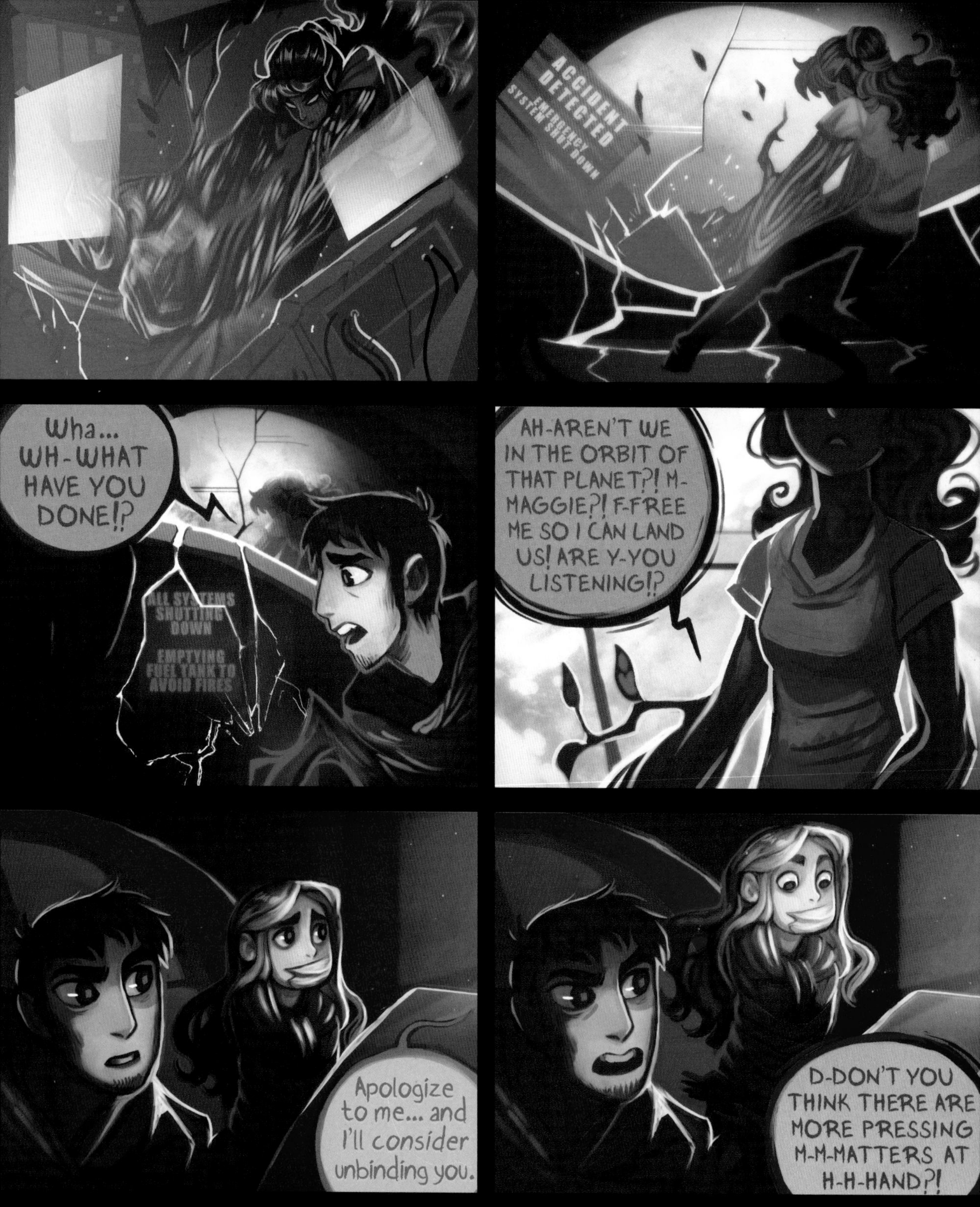
ACCIDENT DETECTED
EMERGENCY SYSTEM SHUT DOWN
Wha... WH-WHAT HAVE YOU DONE!?
ALL SYSTEMS SHUTTING DOWN
EMPTYING FUEL TANK TO AVOID FIRES
AH-AREN'T WE IN THE ORBIT OF THAT PLANET?! M-MAGGIE?! F-FREE ME SO I CAN LAND US! ARE Y-YOU LISTENING!?
Apologize to me... and I'll consider unbinding you.
D-DON'T YOU THINK THERE ARE MORE PRESSING M-M-MATTERS AT H-H-HAND?!

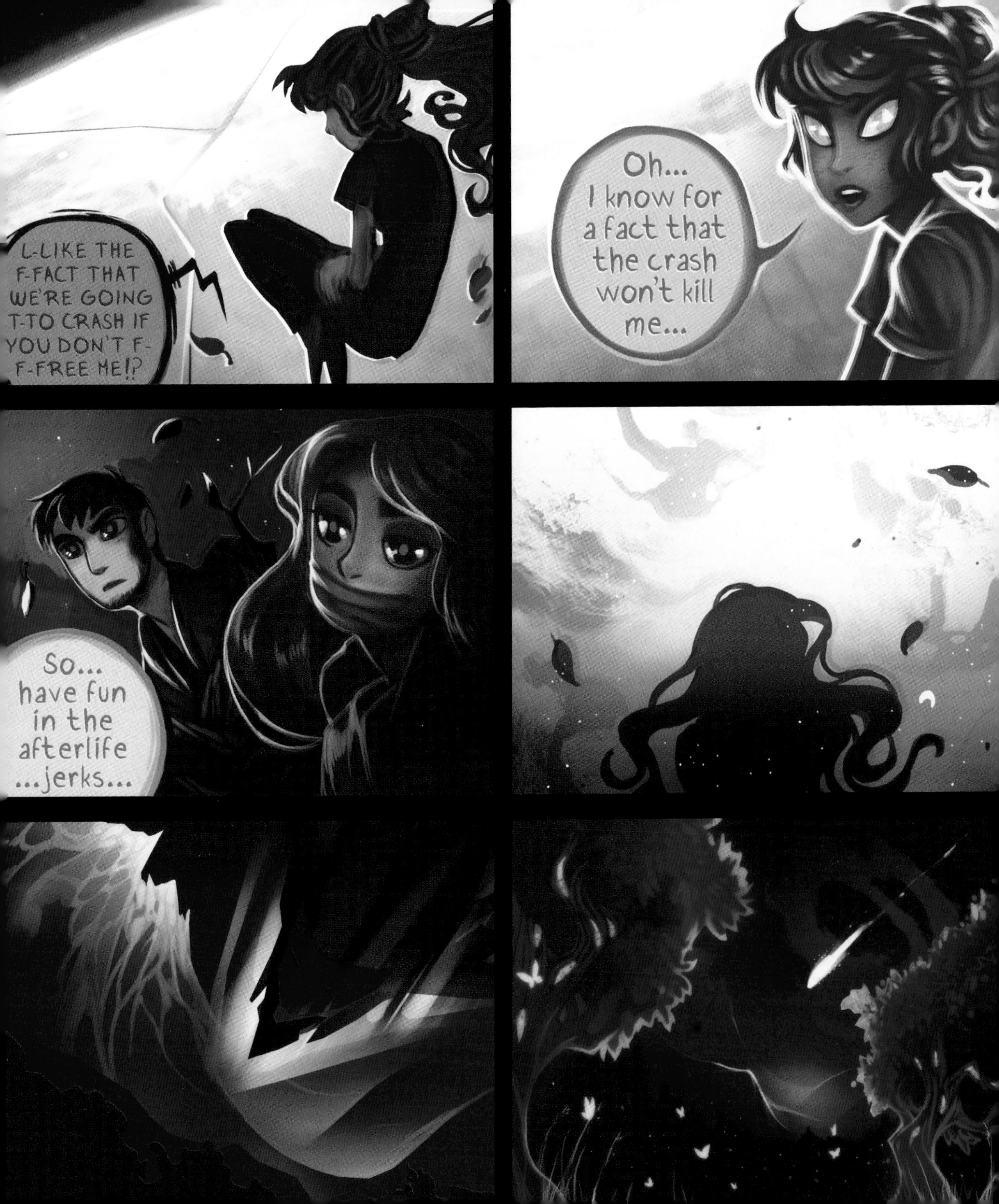
L-LIKE THE F-FACT THAT WE'RE GOING T-TO CRASH IF YOU DON'T F-F-FREE ME!?
Oh... I know for a fact that the crash won't kill me...
So... have fun in the afterlife ...jerks...

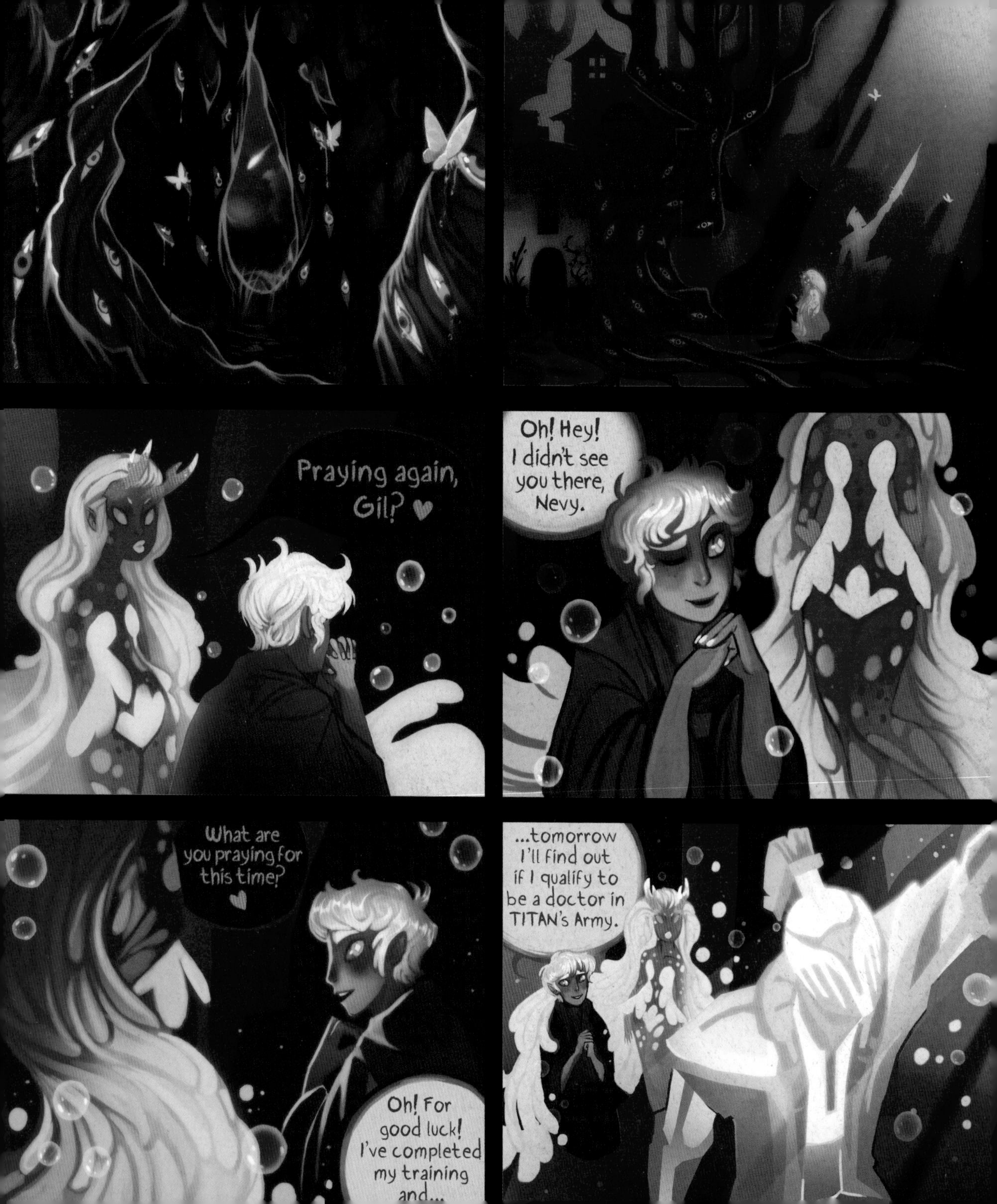
Praying again, Gil? ♥
Oh! Hey! I didn't see you there, Nevy.
What are you praying for this time? ♥
Oh! For good luck! I've completed my training and...
...tomorrow I'll find out if I qualify to be a doctor in TITAN's Army.

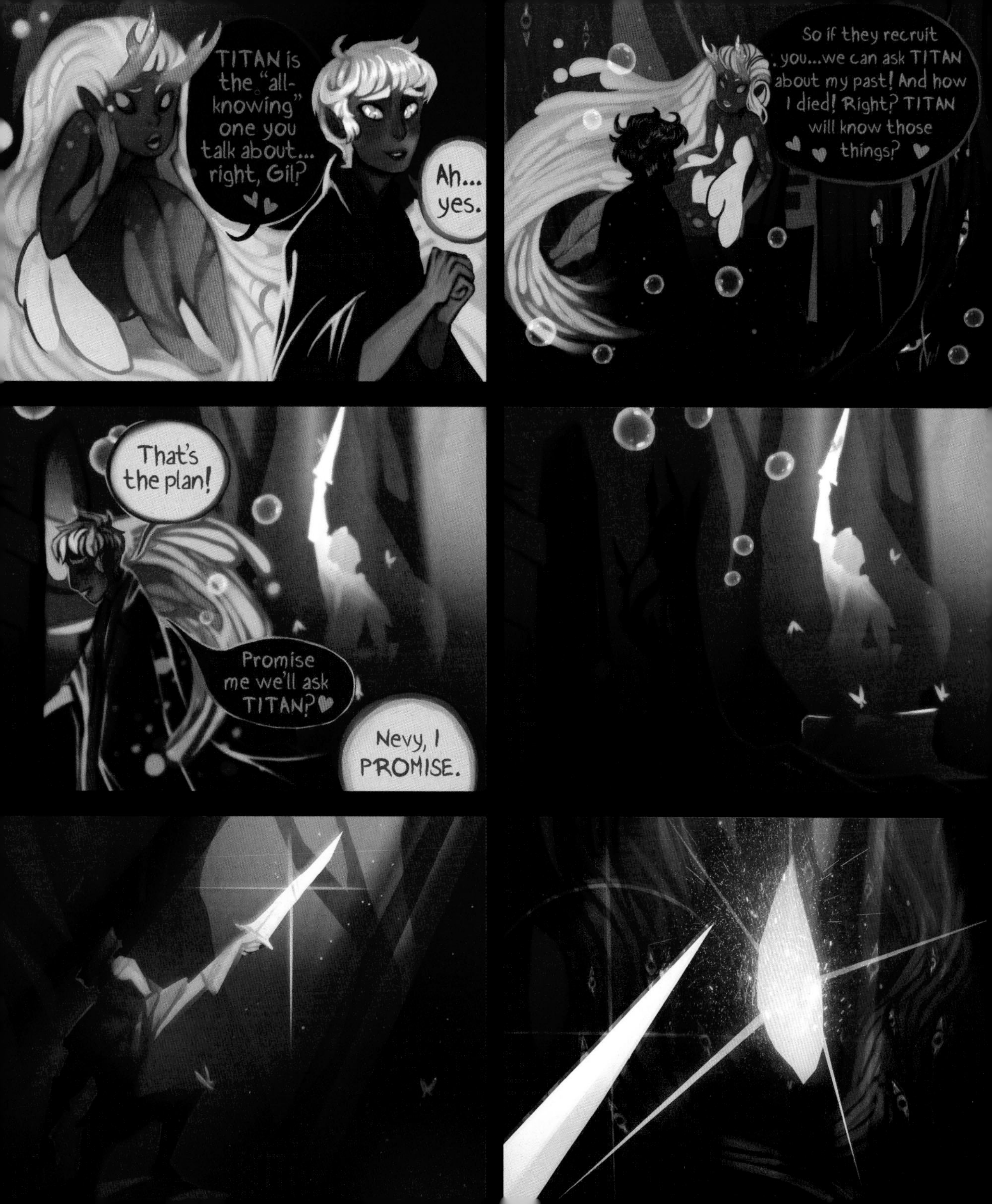
TITAN is the "all-knowing" one you talk about... right, Gil?
Ah... yes.
So if they recruit you...we can ask TITAN about my past! And how I died! Right? TITAN will know those things?
That's the plan!
Promise me we'll ask TITAN?
Nevy, I PROMISE.

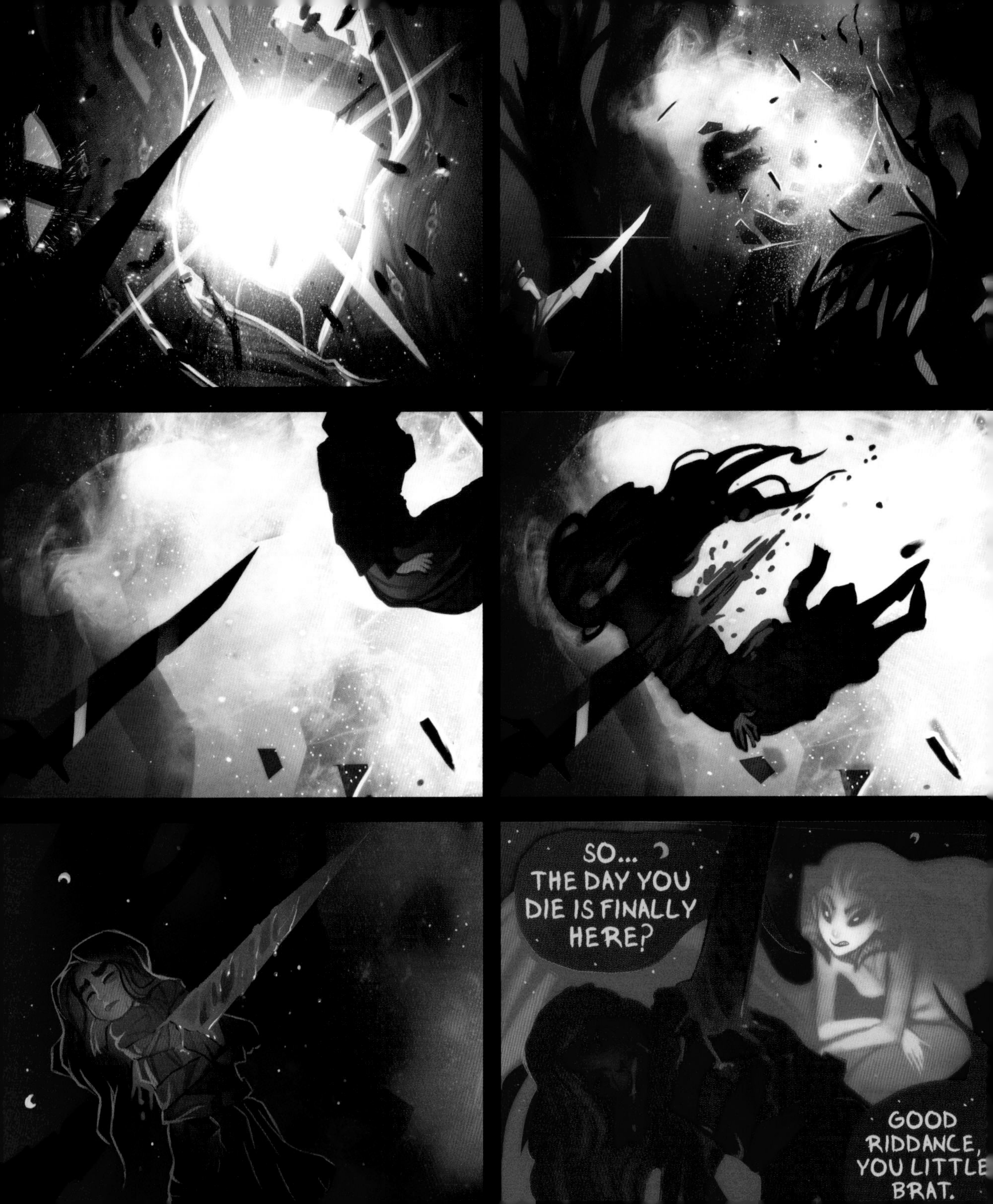
SO... THE DAY YOU DIE IS FINALLY HERE?
GOOD RIDDANCE, YOU LITTLE BRAT.

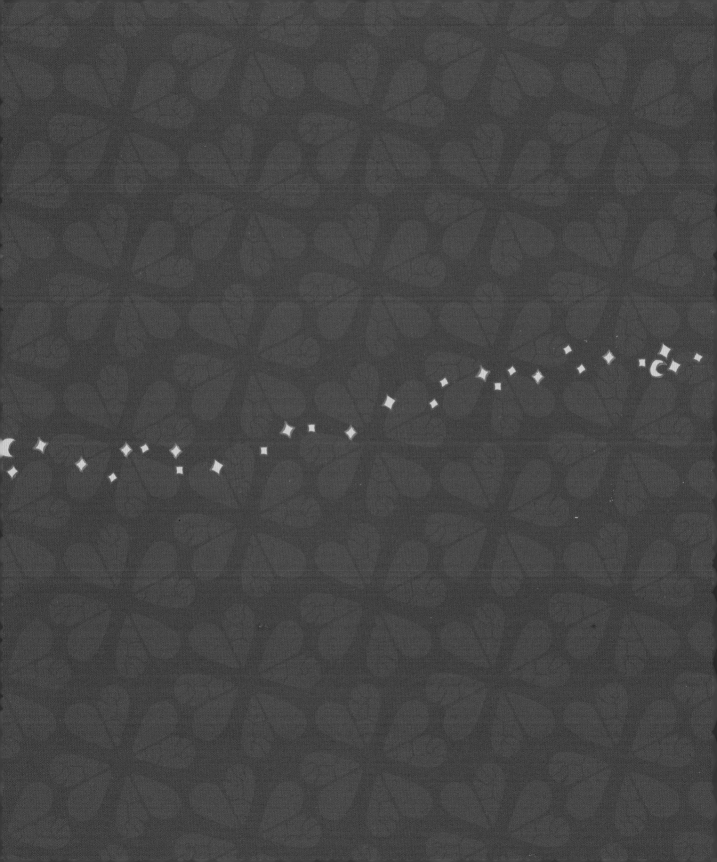

CHAPTER 2

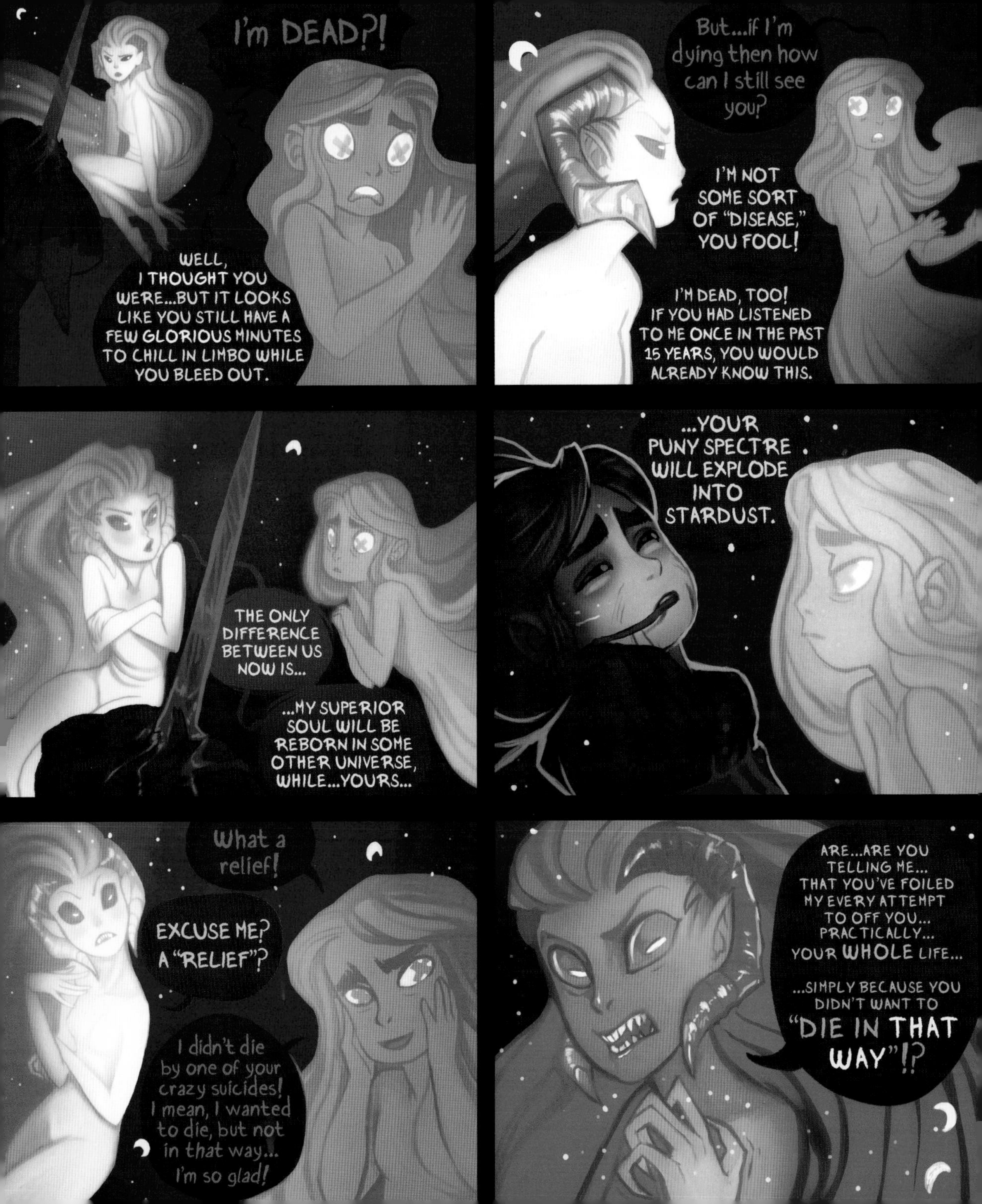
I'm DEAD?!
WELL, I THOUGHT YOU WERE...BUT IT LOOKS LIKE YOU STILL HAVE A FEW GLORIOUS MINUTES TO CHILL IN LIMBO WHILE YOU BLEED OUT.
But...if I'm dying then how can I still see you?
I'M NOT SOME SORT OF "DISEASE," YOU FOOL!
I'M DEAD, TOO! IF YOU HAD LISTENED TO ME ONCE IN THE PAST 15 YEARS, YOU WOULD ALREADY KNOW THIS.
THE ONLY DIFFERENCE BETWEEN US NOW IS...
...MY SUPERIOR SOUL WILL BE REBORN IN SOME OTHER UNIVERSE, WHILE...YOURS...
...YOUR PUNY SPECTRE WILL EXPLODE INTO STARDUST.
What a relief!
EXCUSE ME? A "RELIEF"?
I didn't die by one of your crazy suicides! I mean, I wanted to die, but not in that way... I'm so glad!
ARE...ARE YOU TELLING ME... THAT YOU'VE FOILED MY EVERY ATTEMPT TO OFF YOU... PRACTICALLY... YOUR WHOLE LIFE...
...SIMPLY BECAUSE YOU DIDN'T WANT TO "DIE IN THAT WAY"!?

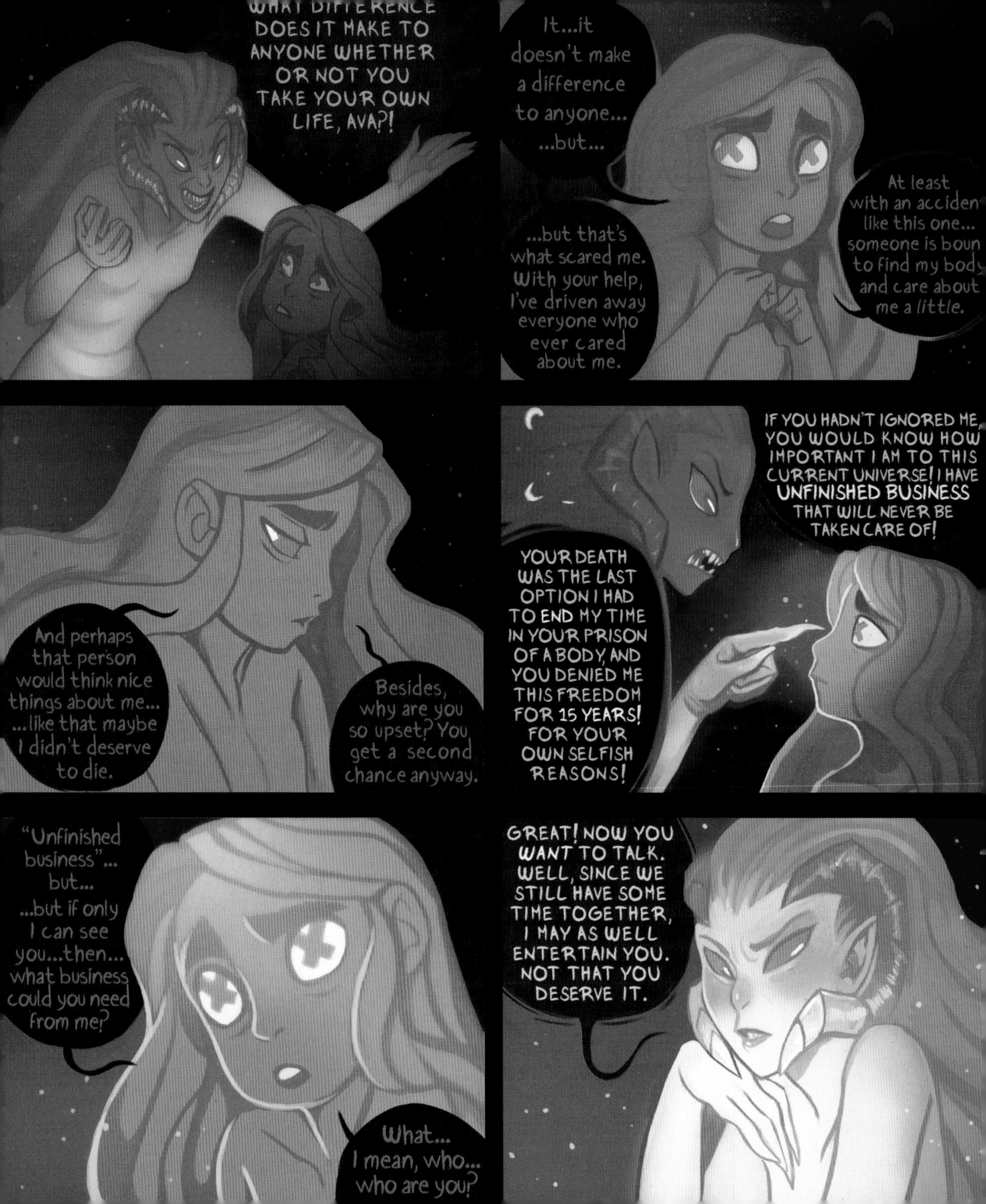
WHAT DIFFERENCE DOES IT MAKE TO ANYONE WHETHER OR NOT YOU TAKE YOUR OWN LIFE, AVA?!
It...it doesn't make a difference to anyone... ...but...
...but that's what scared me. With your help, I've driven away everyone who ever cared about me.
At least with an acciden like this one... someone is boun to find my body and care about me a little.
And perhaps that person would think nice things about me... ...like that maybe I didn't deserve to die.
Besides, why are you so upset? You get a second chance anyway.
IF YOU HADN'T IGNORED ME, YOU WOULD KNOW HOW IMPORTANT I AM TO THIS CURRENT UNIVERSE! I HAVE UNFINISHED BUSINESS THAT WILL NEVER BE TAKEN CARE OF!
YOUR DEATH WAS THE LAST OPTION I HAD TO END MY TIME IN YOUR PRISON OF A BODY, AND YOU DENIED ME THIS FREEDOM FOR 15 YEARS! FOR YOUR OWN SELFISH REASONS!
"Unfinished business"... but... ...but if only I can see you...then... what business could you need from me?
What... I mean, who... who are you?
GREAT! NOW YOU WANT TO TALK. WELL, SINCE WE STILL HAVE SOME TIME TOGETHER, I MAY AS WELL ENTERTAIN YOU. NOT THAT YOU DESERVE IT.

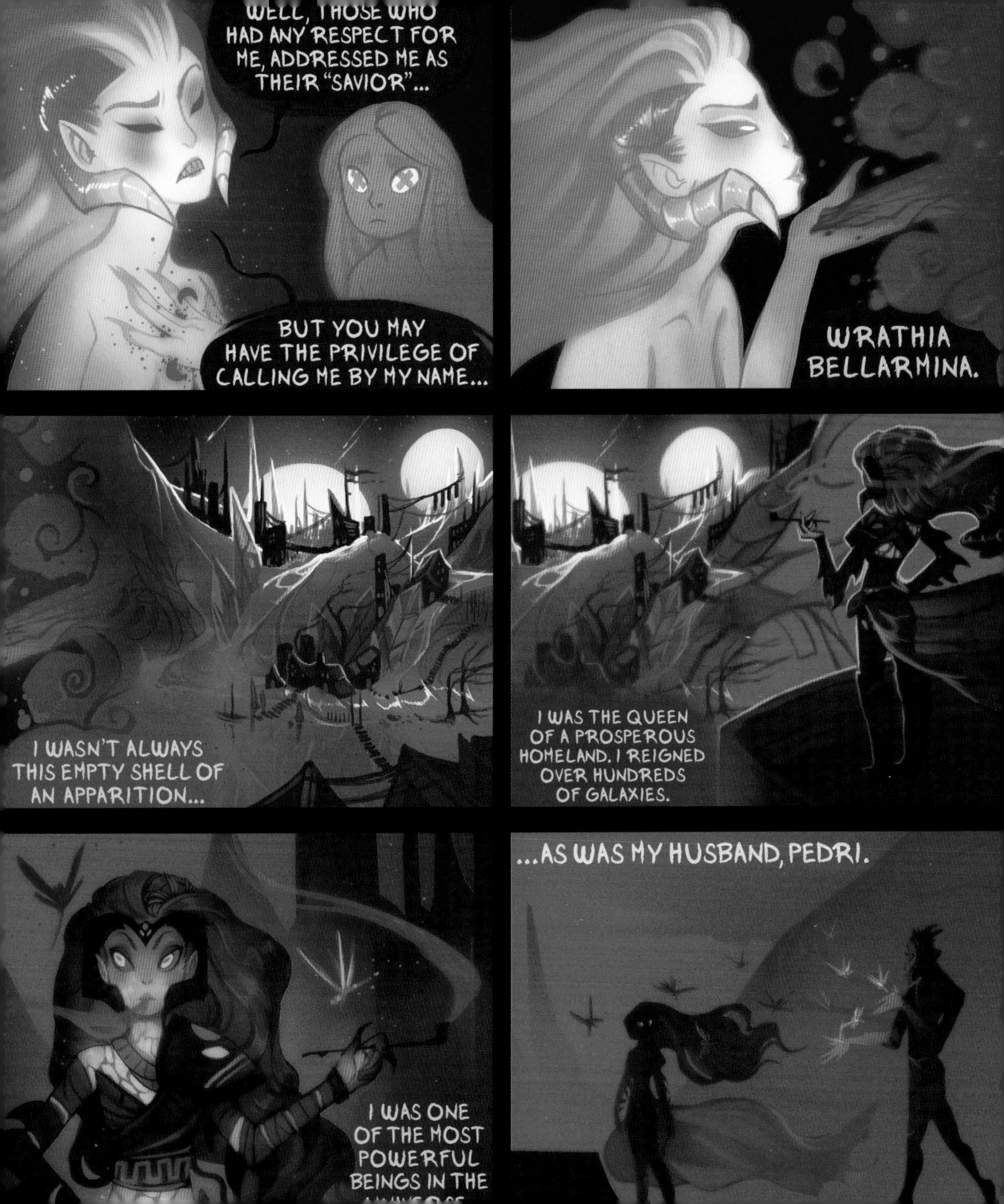
WELL, THOSE WHO HAD ANY RESPECT FOR ME, ADDRESSED ME AS THEIR "SAVIOR"...
BUT YOU MAY HAVE THE PRIVILEGE OF CALLING ME BY MY NAME...
WRATHIA BELLARMINA.
I WASN'T ALWAYS THIS EMPTY SHELL OF AN APPARITION...
I WAS THE QUEEN OF A PROSPEROUS HOMELAND. I REIGNED OVER HUNDREDS OF GALAXIES.
I WAS ONE OF THE MOST POWERFUL BEINGS IN THE
...AS WAS MY HUSBAND, PEDRI.

WE WERE...

ALMOST...
...UNSTOPPABLE.

WE EVEN HAD AN HEIR TO OUR THRONE.

IT WAS PARADISE UNTIL...
THAT FATED DAY WHEN WE WERE FINALLY CHALLENGED
...

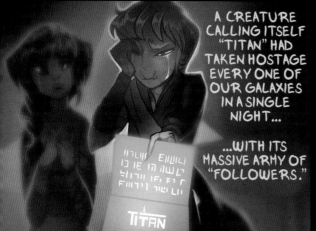

A CREATURE CALLING ITSELF "TITAN" HAD TAKEN HOSTAGE EVERY ONE OF OUR GALAXIES IN A SINGLE NIGHT...

...WITH ITS MASSIVE ARMY OF "FOLLOWERS."

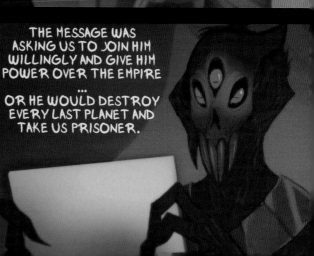

THE MESSAGE WAS ASKING US TO JOIN HIM WILLINGLY AND GIVE HIM POWER OVER THE EMPIRE
...
OR HE WOULD DESTROY EVERY LAST PLANET AND TAKE US PRISONER.

I WAS LIVID WITH THE IDEA OF SURRENDERING. BUT IT SEEMED I HAD NO CHOICE IF I WANTED TO KEEP OUR EMPIRE ALIVE.

AMIDST MY RAGE...

...MY HUSBAND SAID SOMETHING ALARMING...

BE SMART... SURRENDERING WILL NOT GUARANTEE OUR SURVIVAL.

SO I CAME UP WITH A PLAN.

IF WE COULDN'T CLAIM VICTORY IN LIFE...

...THEN WE WOULD CLAIM VICTORY IN DEATH.

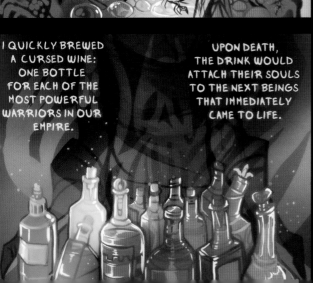

I QUICKLY BREWED A CURSED WINE: ONE BOTTLE FOR EACH OF THE MOST POWERFUL WARRIORS IN OUR EMPIRE.

UPON DEATH, THE DRINK WOULD ATTACH THEIR SOULS TO THE NEXT BEINGS THAT IMMEDIATELY CAME TO LIFE.

MY PLAN WAS TO HOPEFULLY POSSESS A BEING STRONGER THAN MYSELF. PERHAPS THEN I WOULD BE POWERFUL ENOUGH TO BEAT TITAN.

PERHAPS OUR FRIENDS WOULD DO THE SAME. WE COULD BE REUNITED WITH THEM AS AN ARMY. WE COULD ALL HAVE OUR REVENGE AND TAKE BACK OUR HOMELANDS.

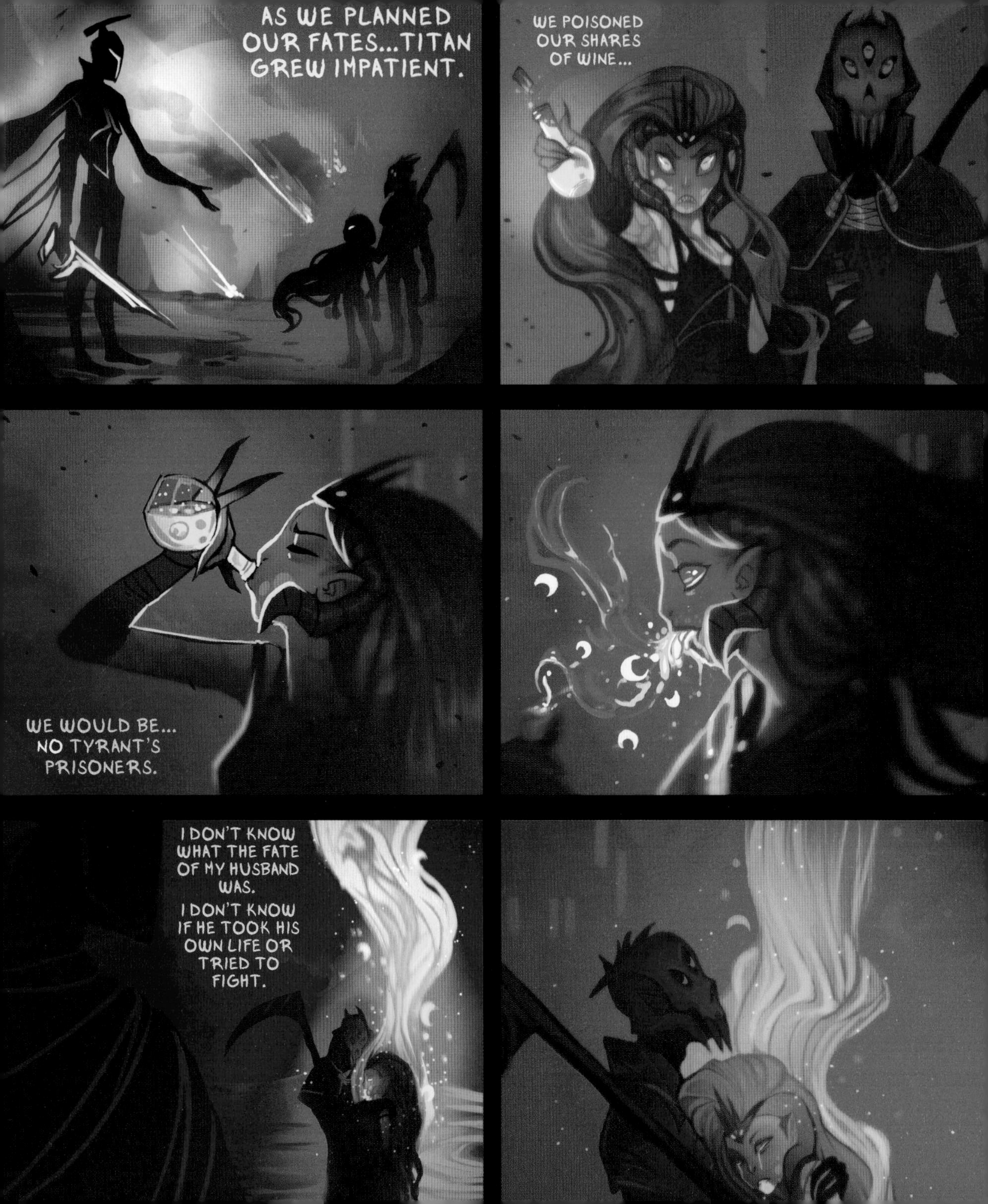
AS WE PLANNED OUR FATES...TITAN GREW IMPATIENT.
WE POISONED OUR SHARES OF WINE...
WE WOULD BE... NO TYRANT'S PRISONERS.
I DON'T KNOW WHAT THE FATE OF MY HUSBAND WAS.
I DON'T KNOW IF HE TOOK HIS OWN LIFE OR TRIED TO FIGHT.

...AND SMALL.

I ONLY REMEMBER FEELING WEAK...

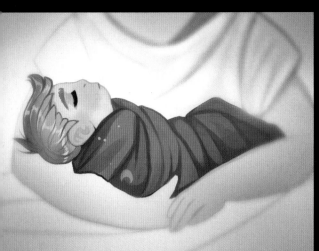

AND I GOT STUCK.... WITH YOU.

I WAS FURIOUS.

I COULDN'T FATHOM GETTING REVENGE WITH SUCH A WEAK CREATURE!

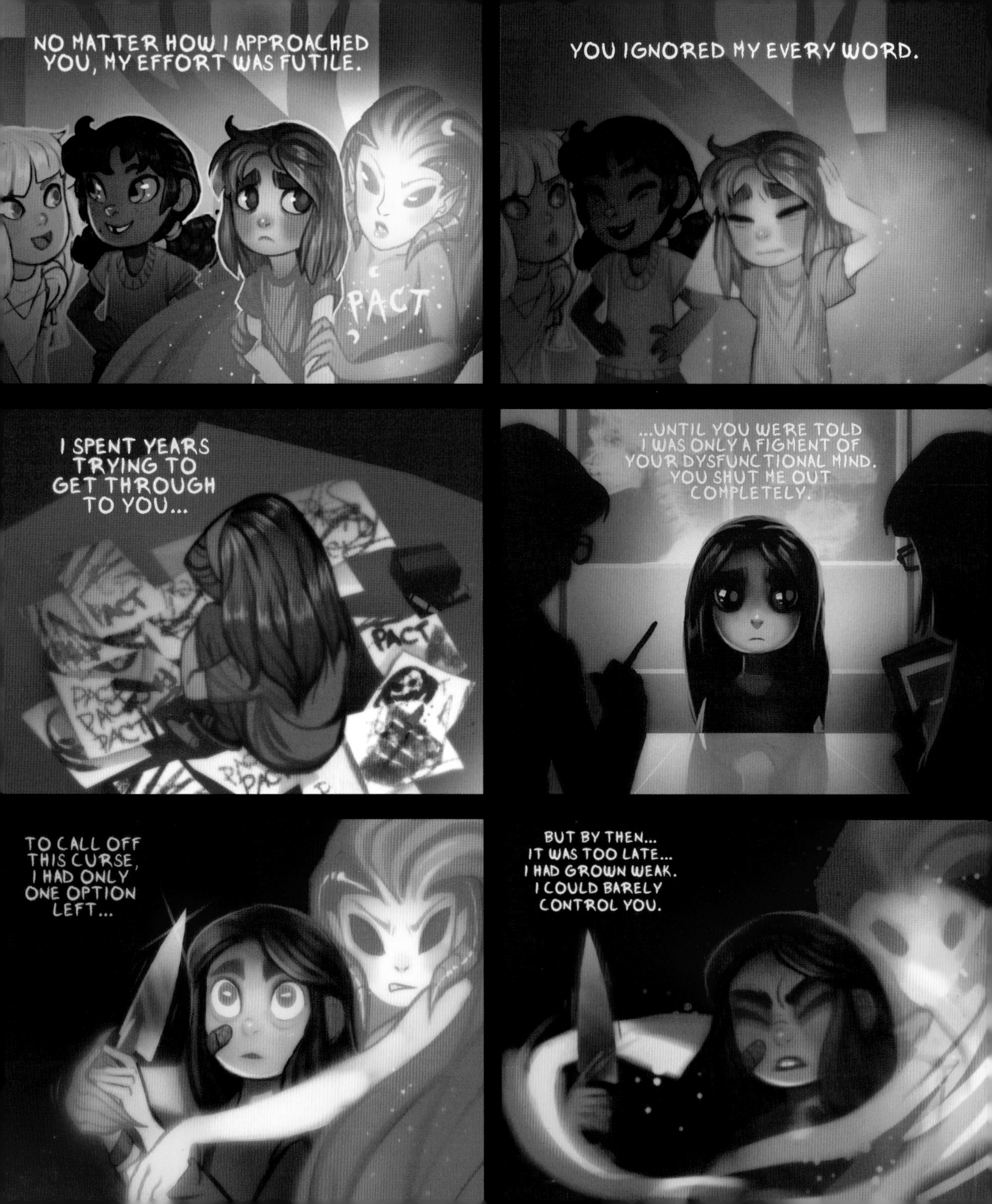
NO MATTER HOW I APPROACHED YOU, MY EFFORT WAS FUTILE.
PACT
YOU IGNORED MY EVERY WORD.
I SPENT YEARS TRYING TO GET THROUGH TO YOU...
PACT
PACT
...UNTIL YOU WERE TOLD I WAS ONLY A FIGMENT OF YOUR DYSFUNCTIONAL MIND. YOU SHUT ME OUT COMPLETELY.
TO CALL OFF THIS CURSE, I HAD ONLY ONE OPTION LEFT...
BUT BY THEN... IT WAS TOO LATE... I HAD GROWN WEAK. I COULD BARELY CONTROL YOU.

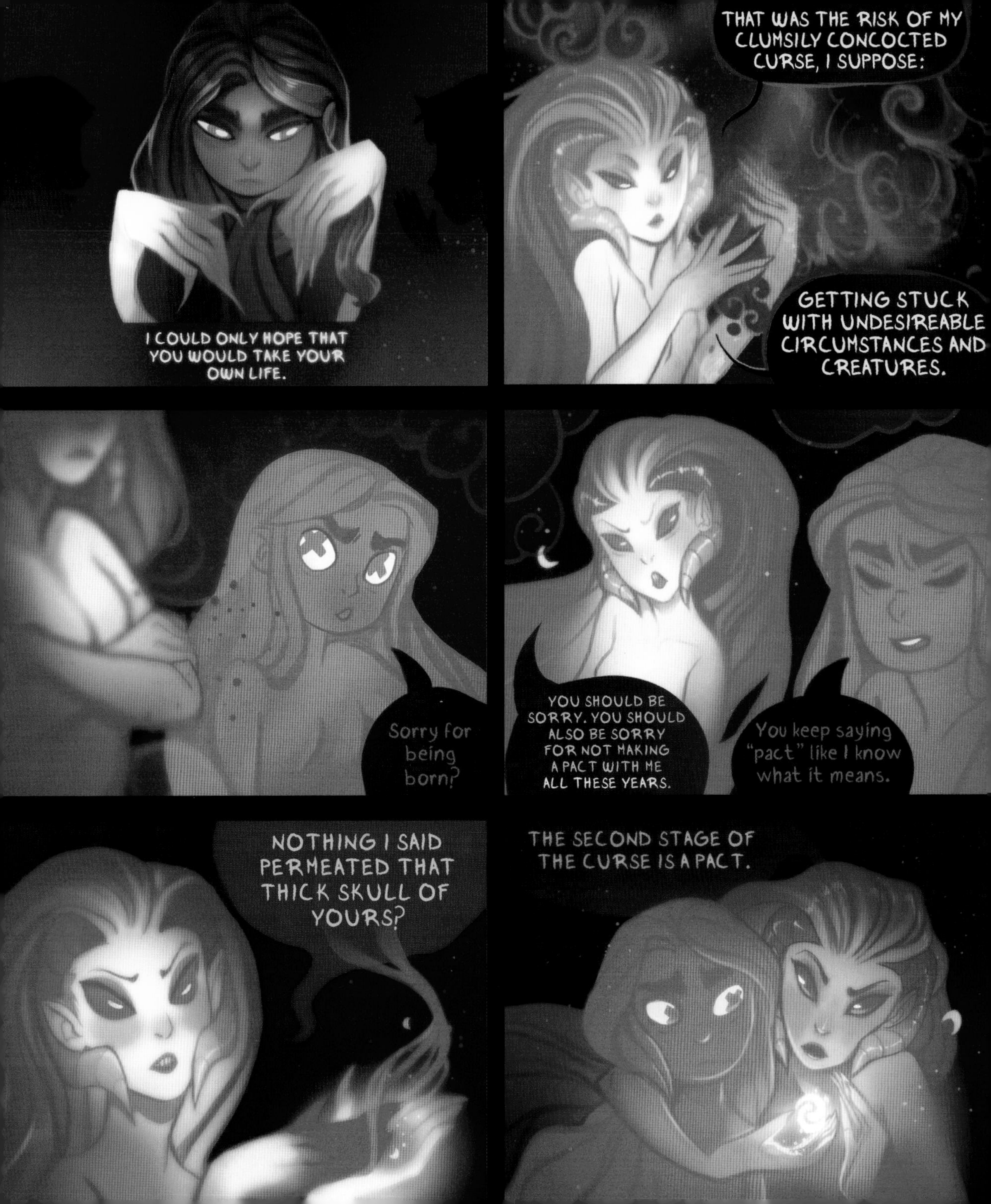
I COULD ONLY HOPE THAT YOU WOULD TAKE YOUR OWN LIFE.
THAT WAS THE RISK OF MY CLUMSILY CONCOCTED CURSE, I SUPPOSE:
GETTING STUCK WITH UNDESIREABLE CIRCUMSTANCES AND CREATURES.
Sorry for being born?
YOU SHOULD BE SORRY. YOU SHOULD ALSO BE SORRY FOR NOT MAKING A PACT WITH ME ALL THESE YEARS.
You keep saying "pact" like I know what it means.
NOTHING I SAID PERMEATED THAT THICK SKULL OF YOURS?
THE SECOND STAGE OF THE CURSE IS A PACT.

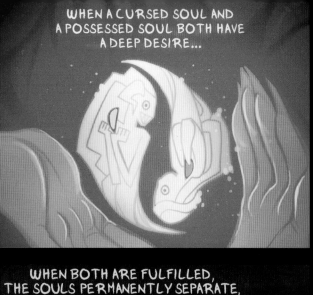

WHEN A CURSED SOUL AND A POSSESSED SOUL BOTH HAVE A DEEP DESIRE...

...THEY CAN FORM A PACT TO COMBINE THEIR POWERS AND FULFILL THOSE DESIRES.

WHEN BOTH ARE FULFILLED, THE SOULS PERMANENTLY SEPARATE, AND CONTINUE THEIR LIVES AS NATURE INTENDED.

Well that SUCKS because I have no desires...except maybe to get rid of YOU.

A LOT OF THINGS "SUCK" AT THE MOMENT, SO YOU CAN SPARE ME YOUR NEWLY-DISCOVERED SNARKY ATTITUDE.

IT FIGURES THAT MY BEST ATTEMPT AT BEING A GOOD LEADER WOULD END WITH ME LOSING EVERYTHING!

MY CHILD WILL BE ASHAMED TO LEARN OF ME... IF IT'S STILL INTACT.

Intact? You mean the egg?

WE HID IT.

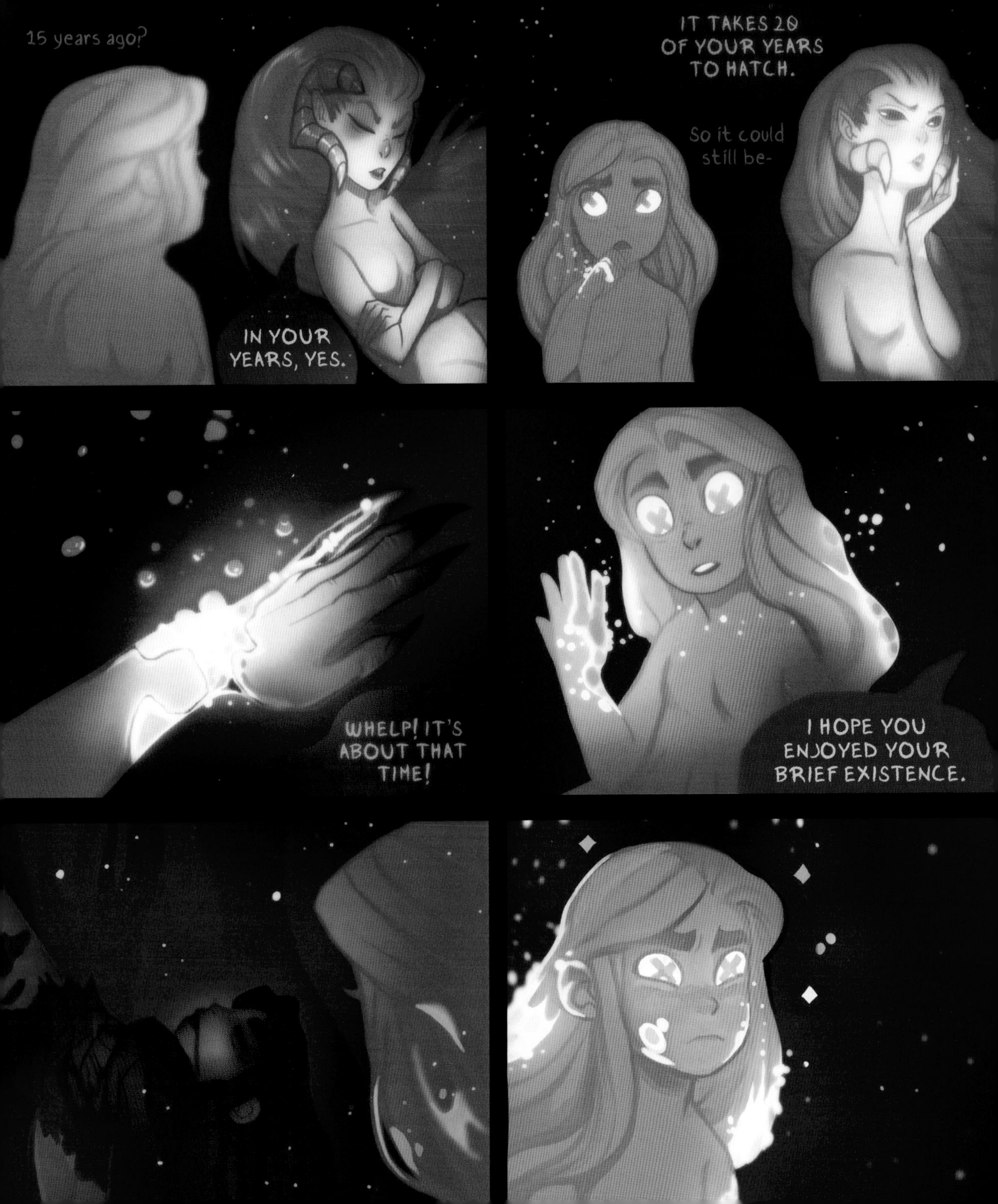
15 years ago?
IN YOUR YEARS, YES.
IT TAKES 20 OF YOUR YEARS TO HATCH.
So it could still be-
WHELP! IT'S ABOUT THAT TIME!
I HOPE YOU ENJOYED YOUR BRIEF EXISTENCE.

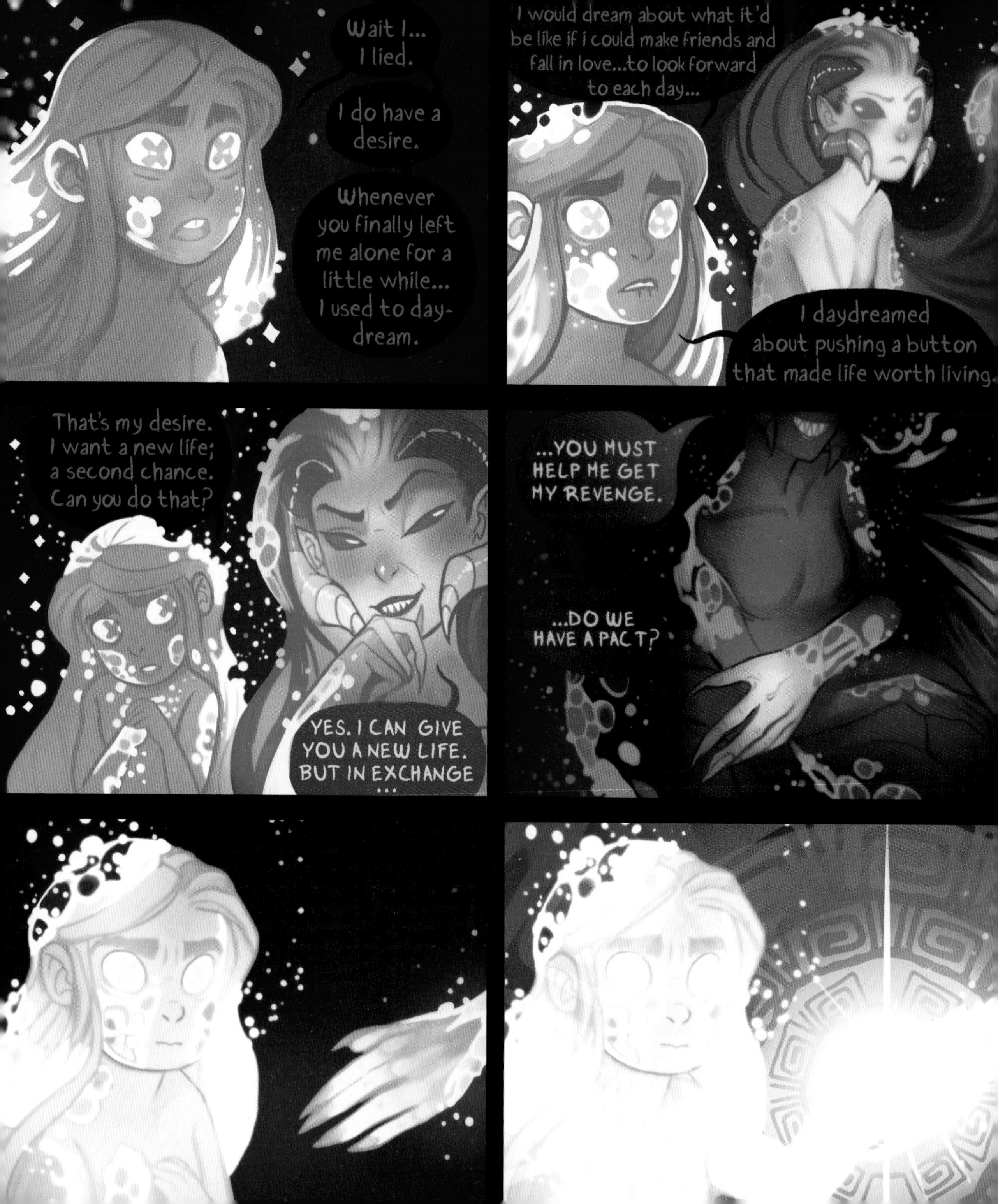
Wait I...
I lied.
I do have a desire.
Whenever you finally left me alone for a little while... I used to day-dream.
I would dream about what it'd be like if i could make friends and fall in love...to look forward to each day...
I daydreamed about pushing a button that made life worth living.
That's my desire. I want a new life; a second chance. Can you do that?
YES. I CAN GIVE YOU A NEW LIFE. BUT IN EXCHANGE ...
...YOU MUST HELP ME GET MY REVENGE.
...DO WE HAVE A PACT?

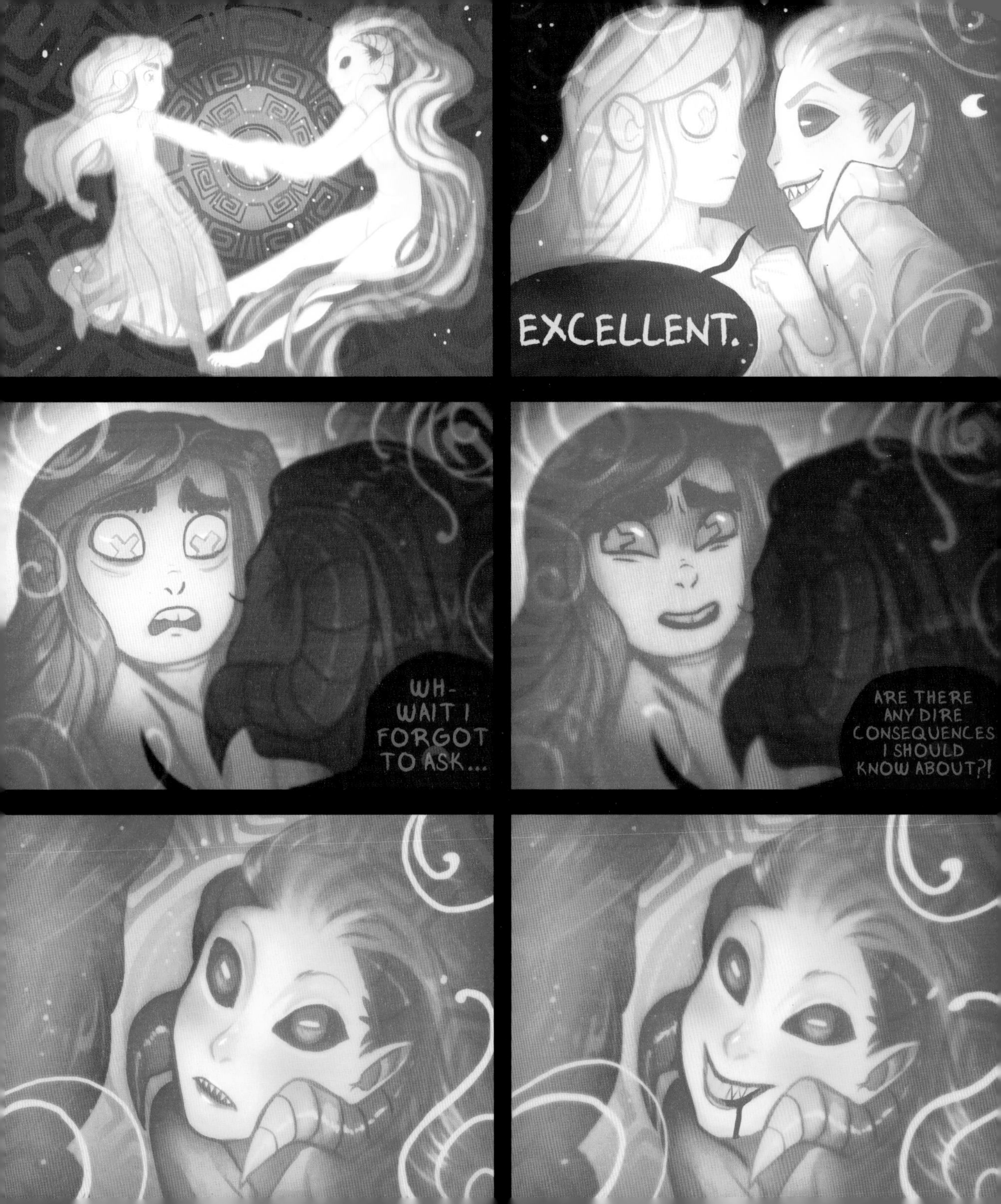
EXCELLENT.
WH- WAIT I FORGOT TO ASK...
ARE THERE ANY DIRE CONSEQUENCES I SHOULD KNOW ABOUT?!

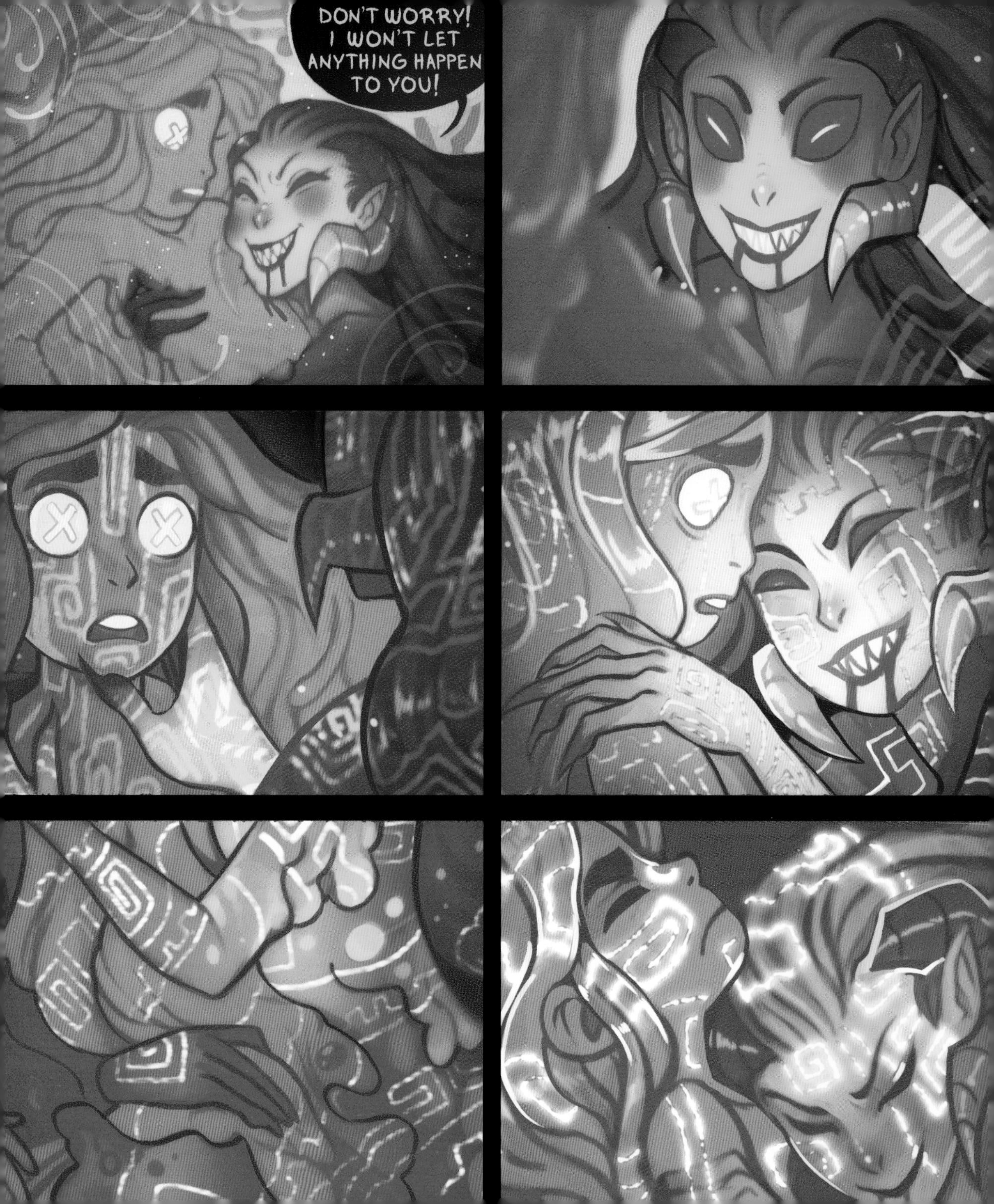
DON'T WORRY! I WON'T LET ANYTHING HAPPEN TO YOU!

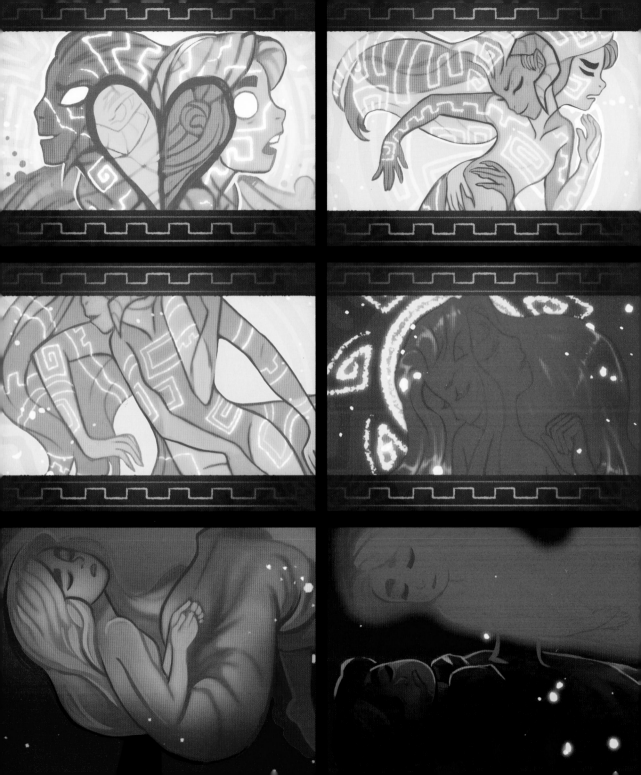

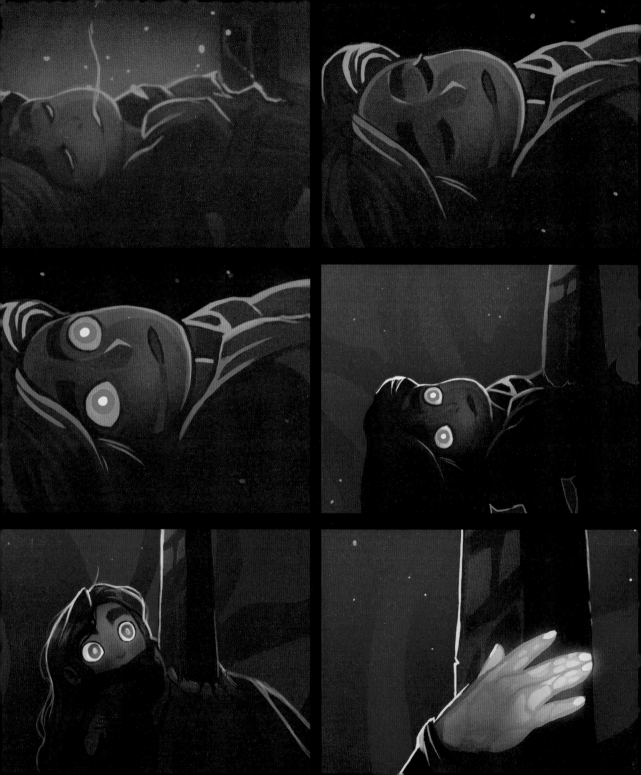

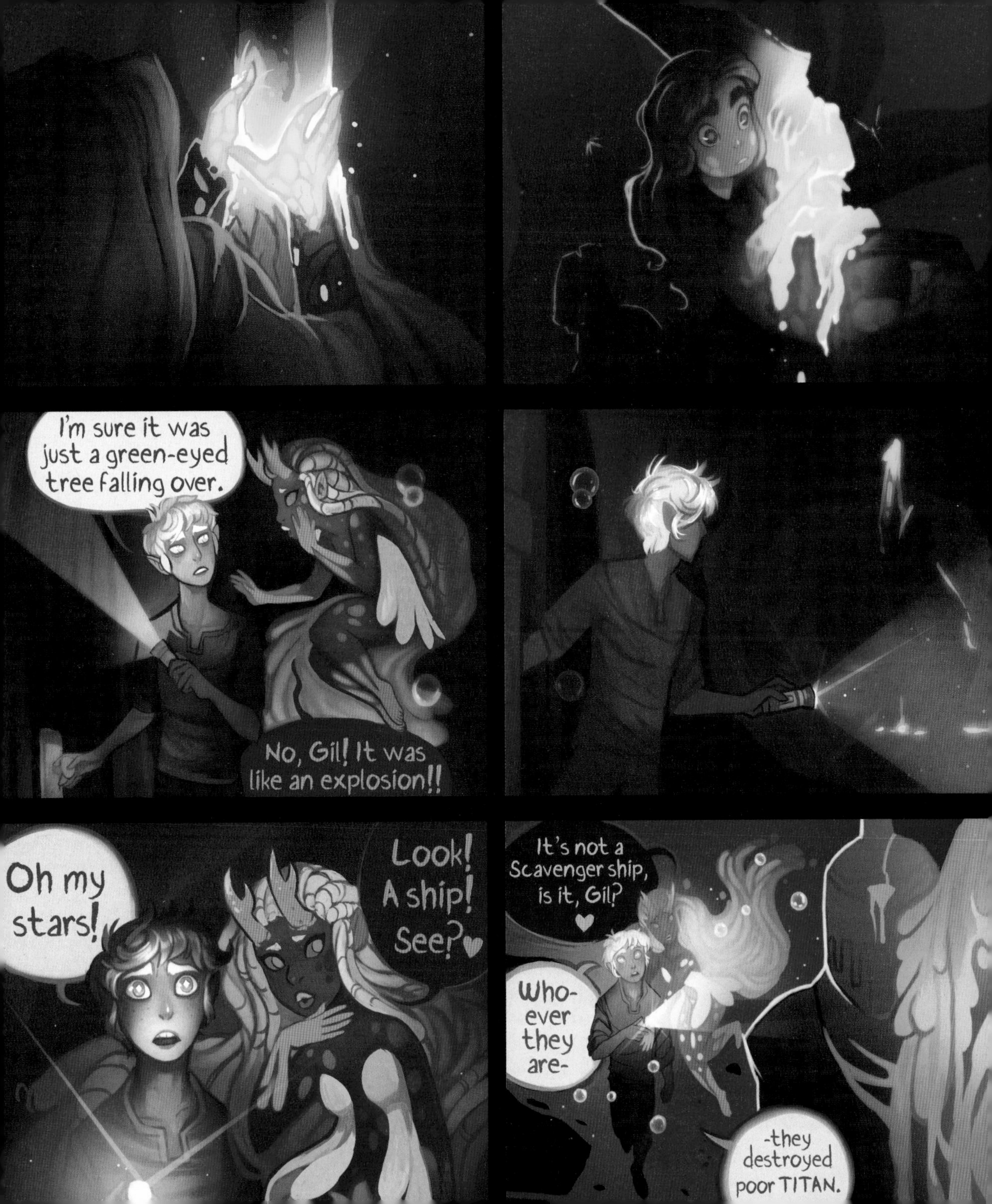
I'm sure it was just a green-eyed tree falling over.
No, Gil! It was like an explosion!!
Oh my stars!
Look! A ship! See?♥
It's not a Scavenger ship, is it, Gil? ♥
Who-ever they are-
-they destroyed poor TITAN.

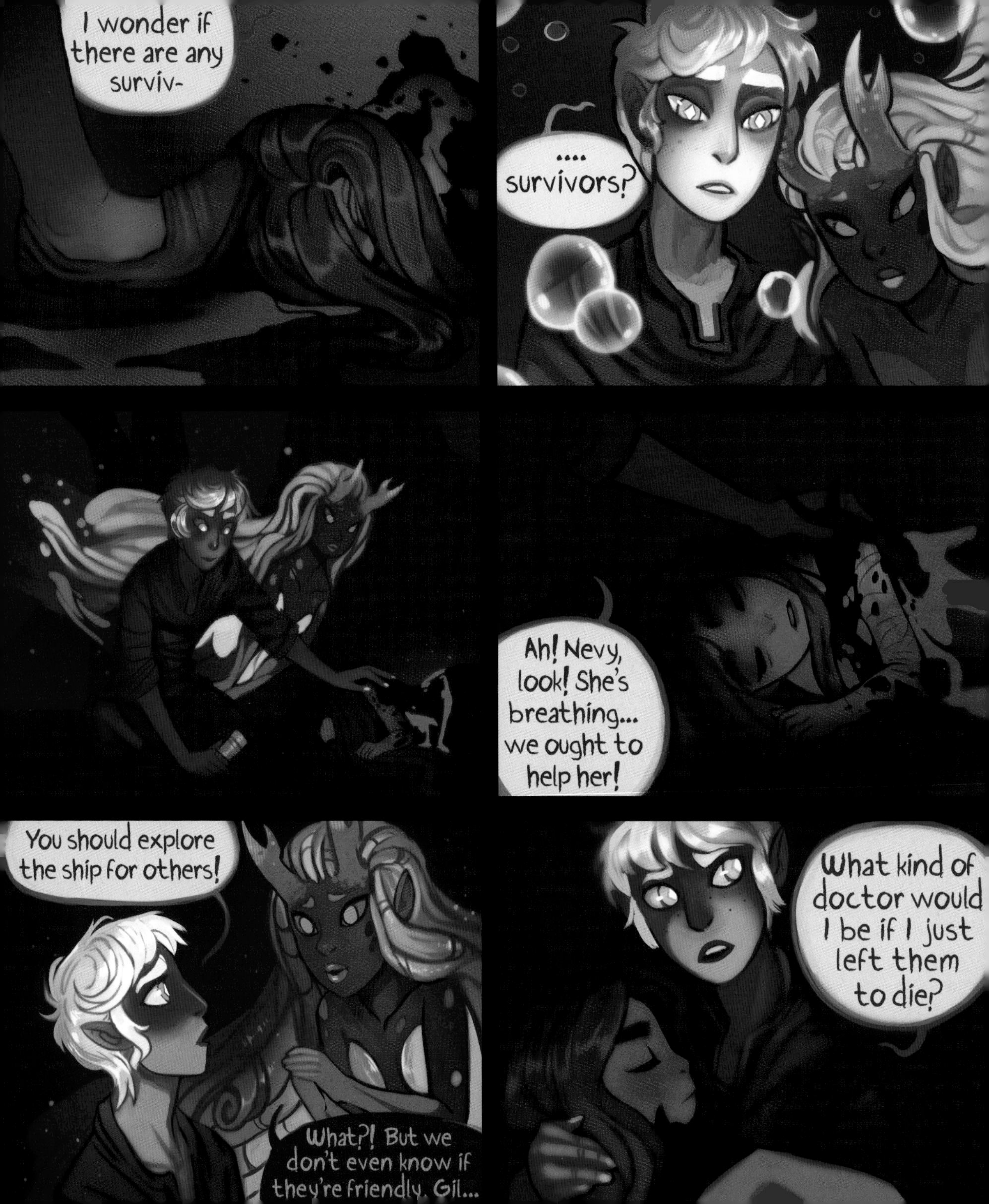
I wonder if there are any surviv-
.... survivors?
Ah! Nevy, look! She's breathing... we ought to help her!
You should explore the ship for others!
What?! But we don't even know if they're friendly, Gil...
What kind of doctor would I be if I just left them to die?

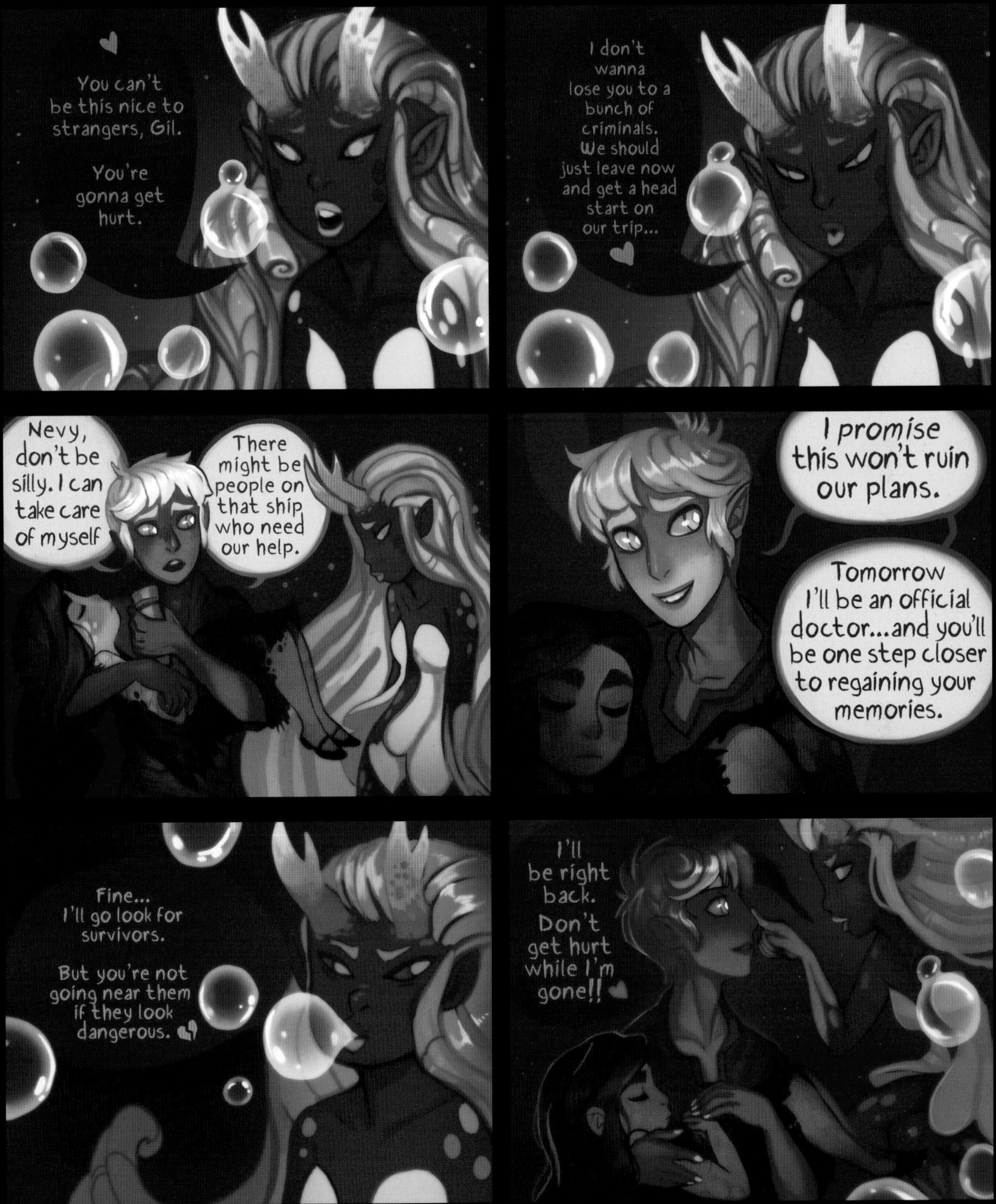
You can't be this nice to strangers, Gil.
You're gonna get hurt.
I don't wanna lose you to a bunch of criminals. We should just leave now and get a head start on our trip...
Nevy, don't be silly. I can take care of myself
There might be people on that ship who need our help.
I promise this won't ruin our plans.
Tomorrow I'll be an official doctor...and you'll be one step closer to regaining your memories.
Fine... I'll go look for survivors.
But you're not going near them if they look dangerous.
I'll be right back.
Don't get hurt while I'm gone!!

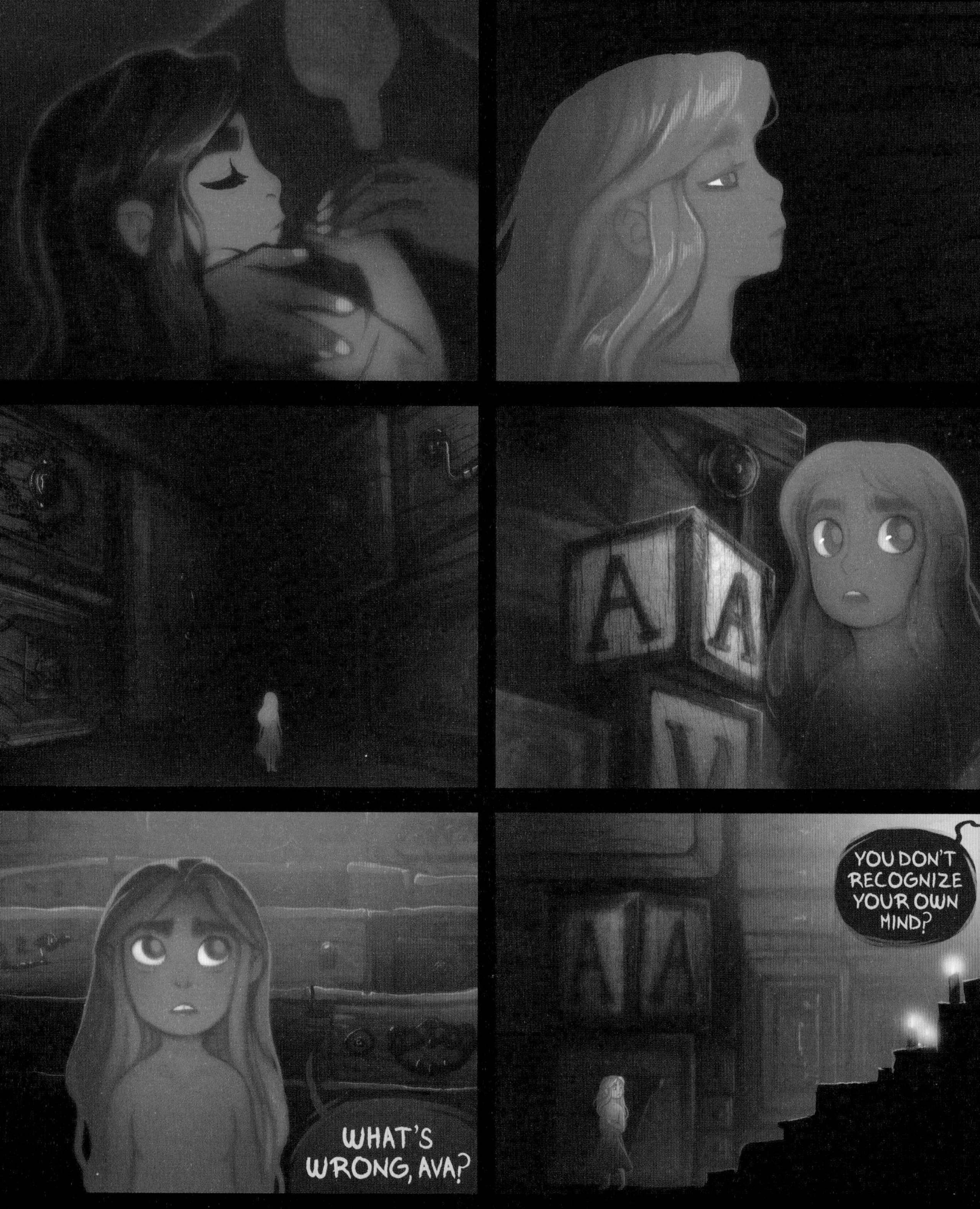
WHAT'S WRONG, AVA?
YOU DON'T RECOGNIZE YOUR OWN MIND?

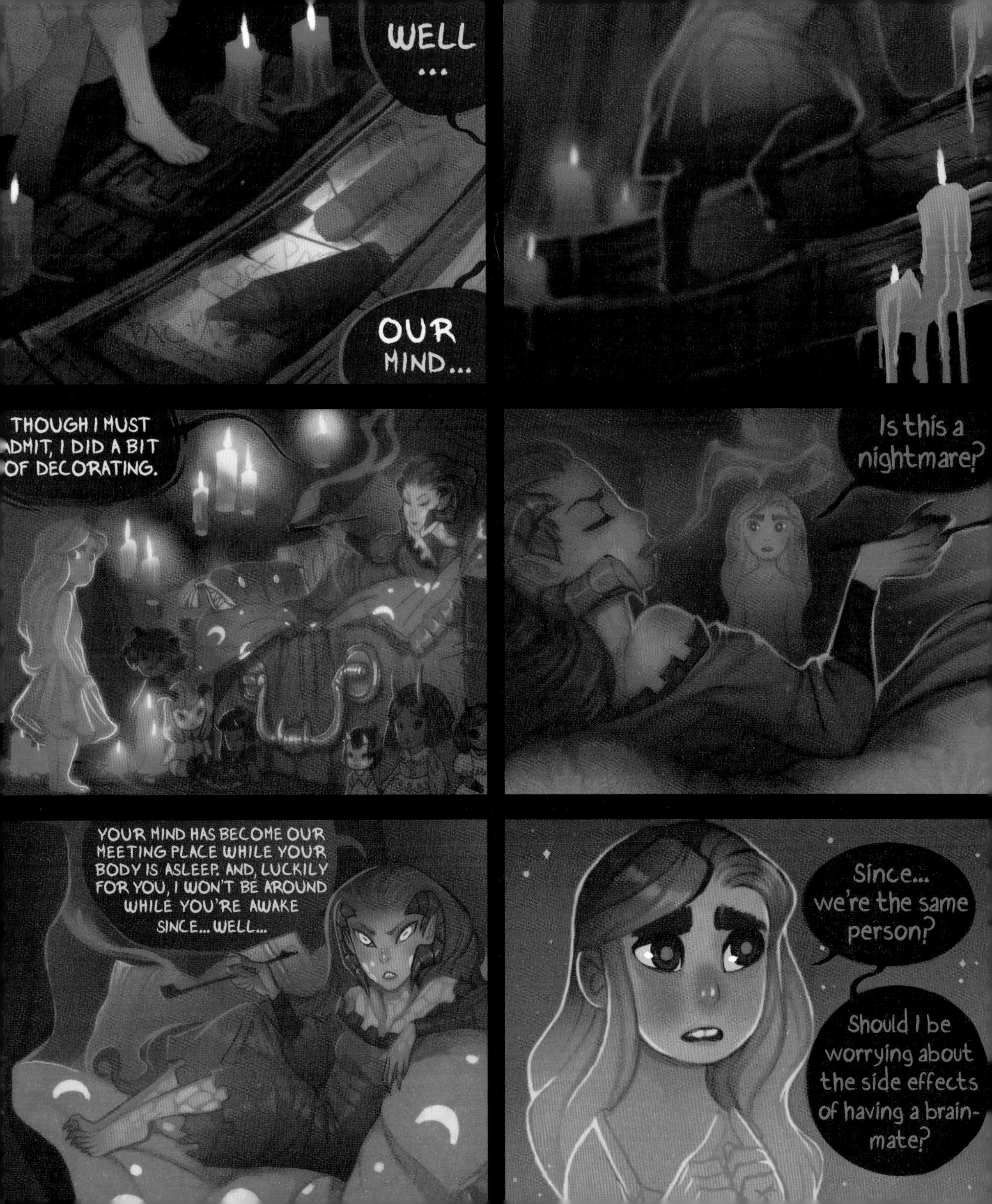
WELL ...
OUR MIND...
THOUGH I MUST ADMIT, I DID A BIT OF DECORATING.
Is this a nightmare?
YOUR MIND HAS BECOME OUR MEETING PLACE WHILE YOUR BODY IS ASLEEP. AND, LUCKILY FOR YOU, I WON'T BE AROUND WHILE YOU'RE AWAKE SINCE... WELL...
Since... we're the same person?
Should I be worrying about the side effects of having a brain-mate?

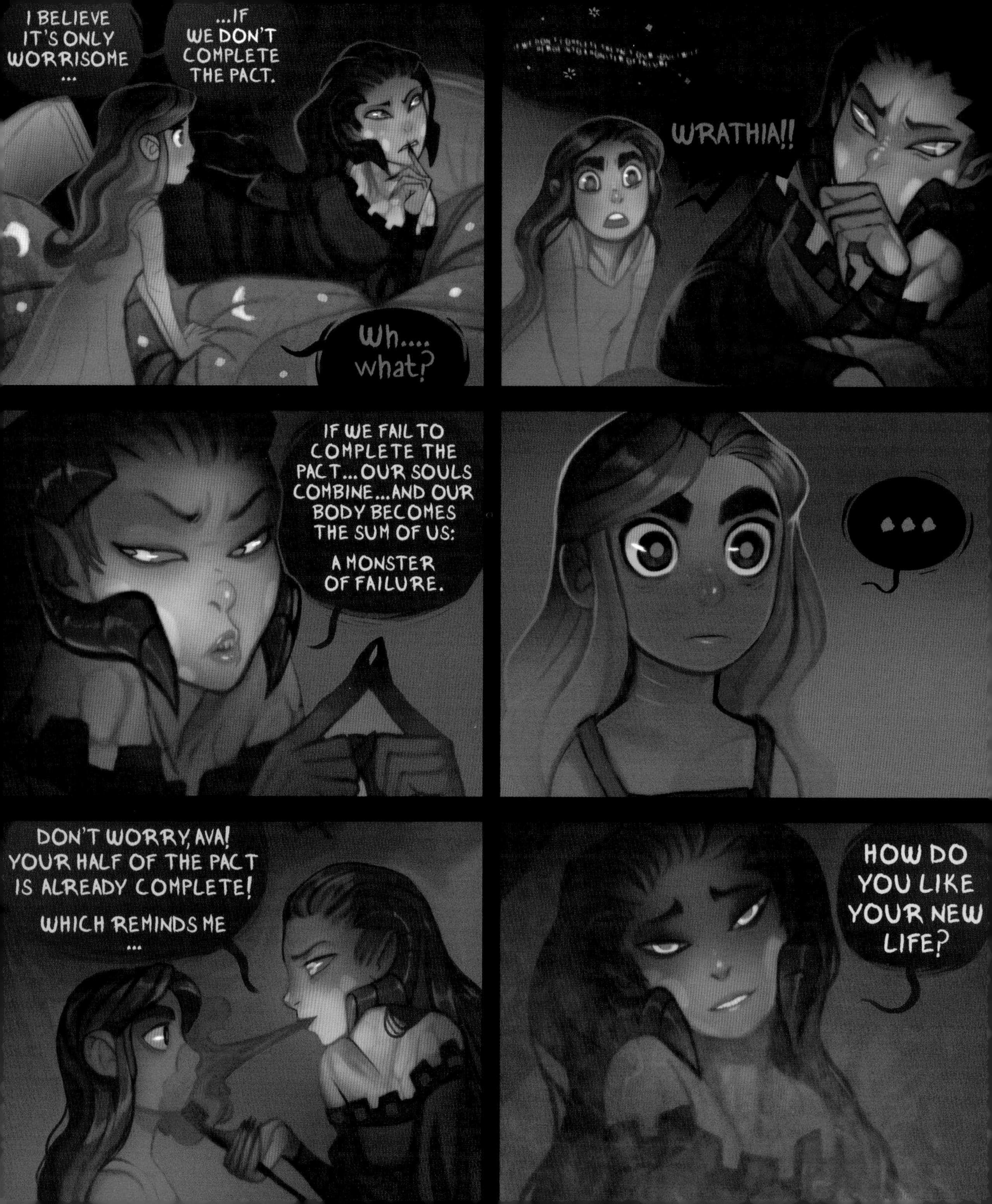
I BELIEVE IT'S ONLY WORRISOME ...
...IF WE DON'T COMPLETE THE PACT.
Wh.... what?
WRATHIA!!
IF WE FAIL TO COMPLETE THE PACT...OUR SOULS COMBINE...AND OUR BODY BECOMES THE SUM OF US:
A MONSTER OF FAILURE.
...
DON'T WORRY, AVA! YOUR HALF OF THE PACT IS ALREADY COMPLETE!
WHICH REMINDS ME ...
HOW DO YOU LIKE YOUR NEW LIFE?

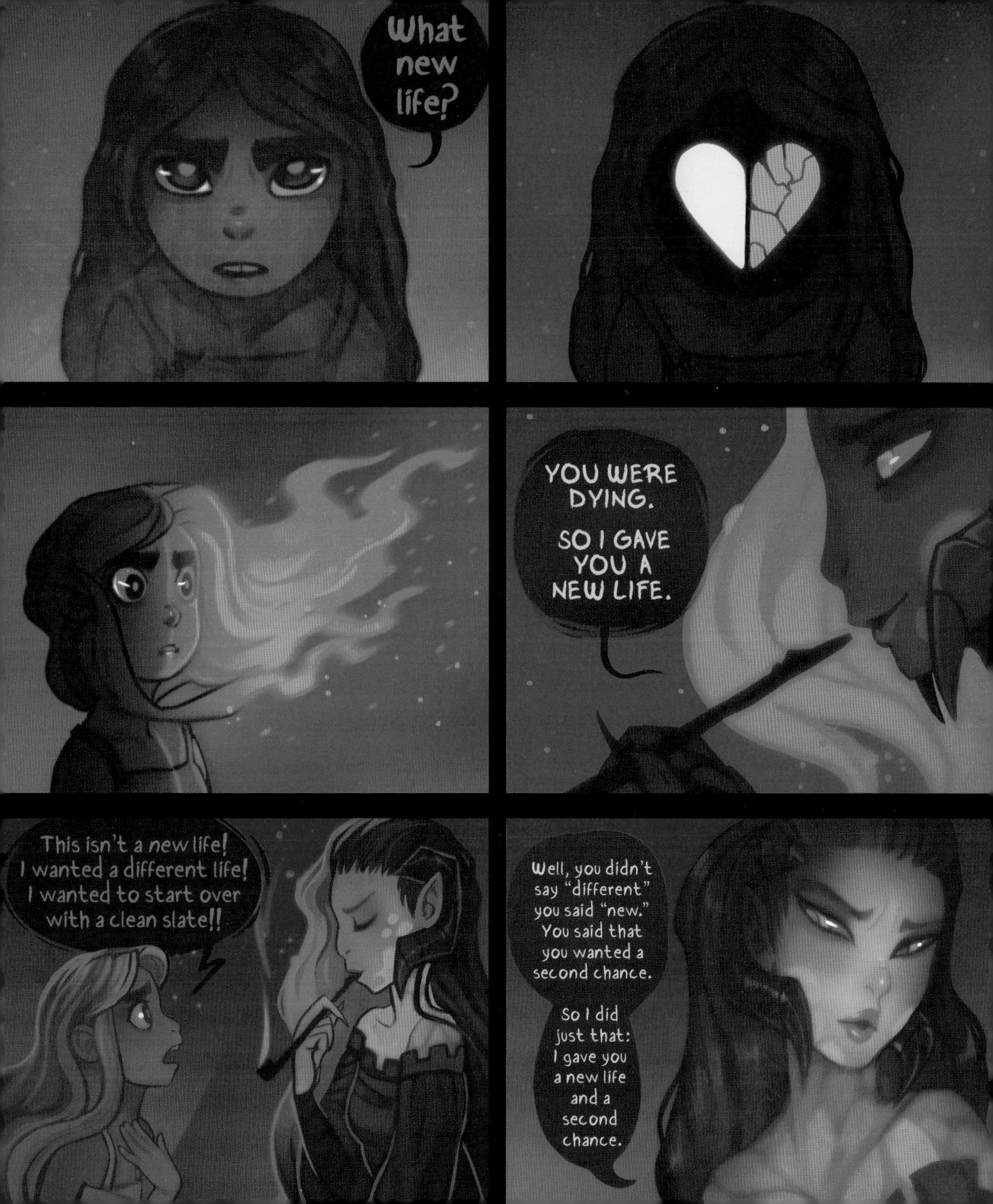
What new life?
YOU WERE DYING.
SO I GAVE YOU A NEW LIFE.
This isn't a new life! I wanted a different life! I wanted to start over with a clean slate!!
Well, you didn't say "different" you said "new." You said that you wanted a second chance.
So I did just that: I gave you a new life and a second chance.

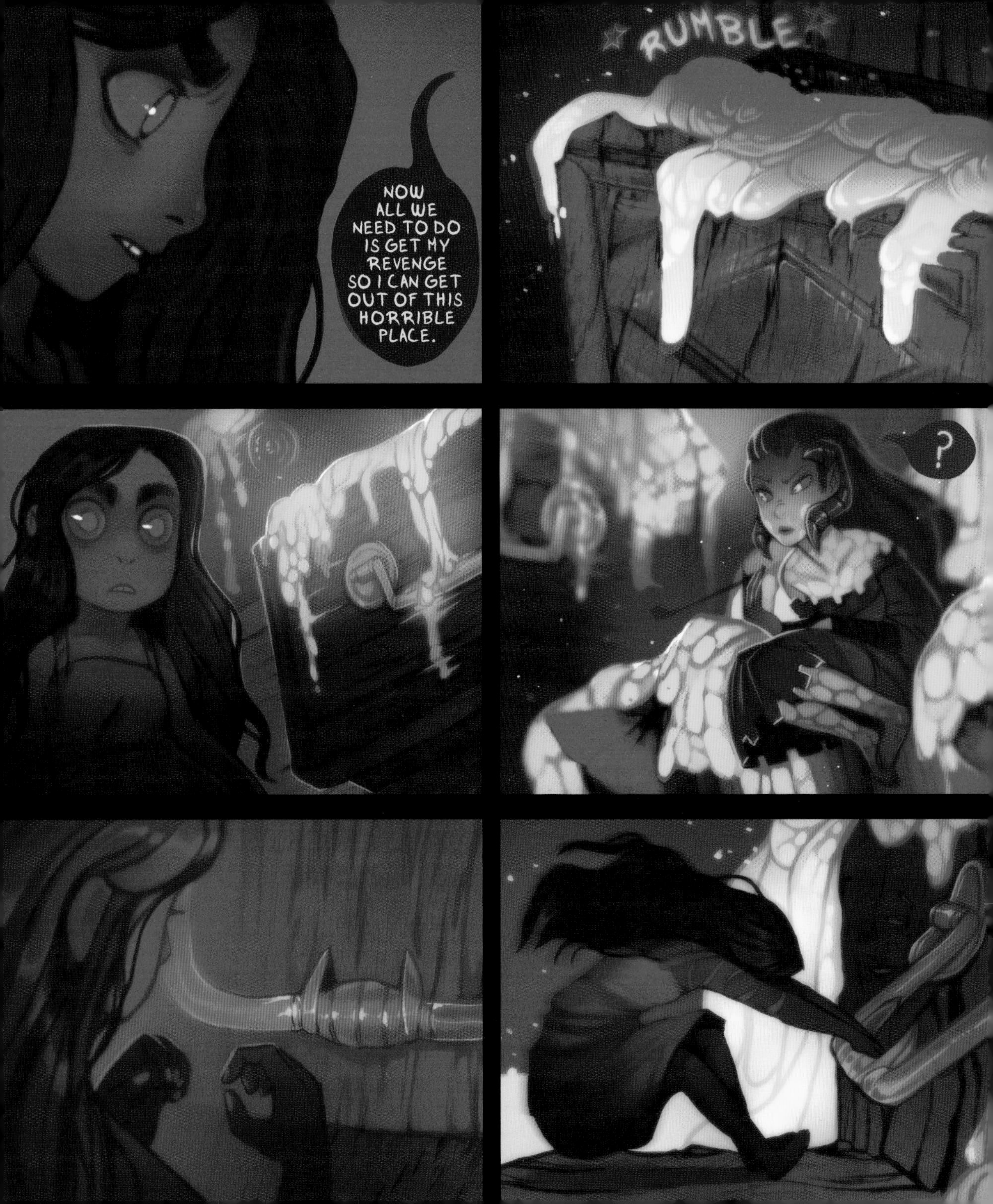
NOW ALL WE NEED TO DO IS GET MY REVENGE SO I CAN GET OUT OF THIS HORRIBLE PLACE.
RUMBLE
?

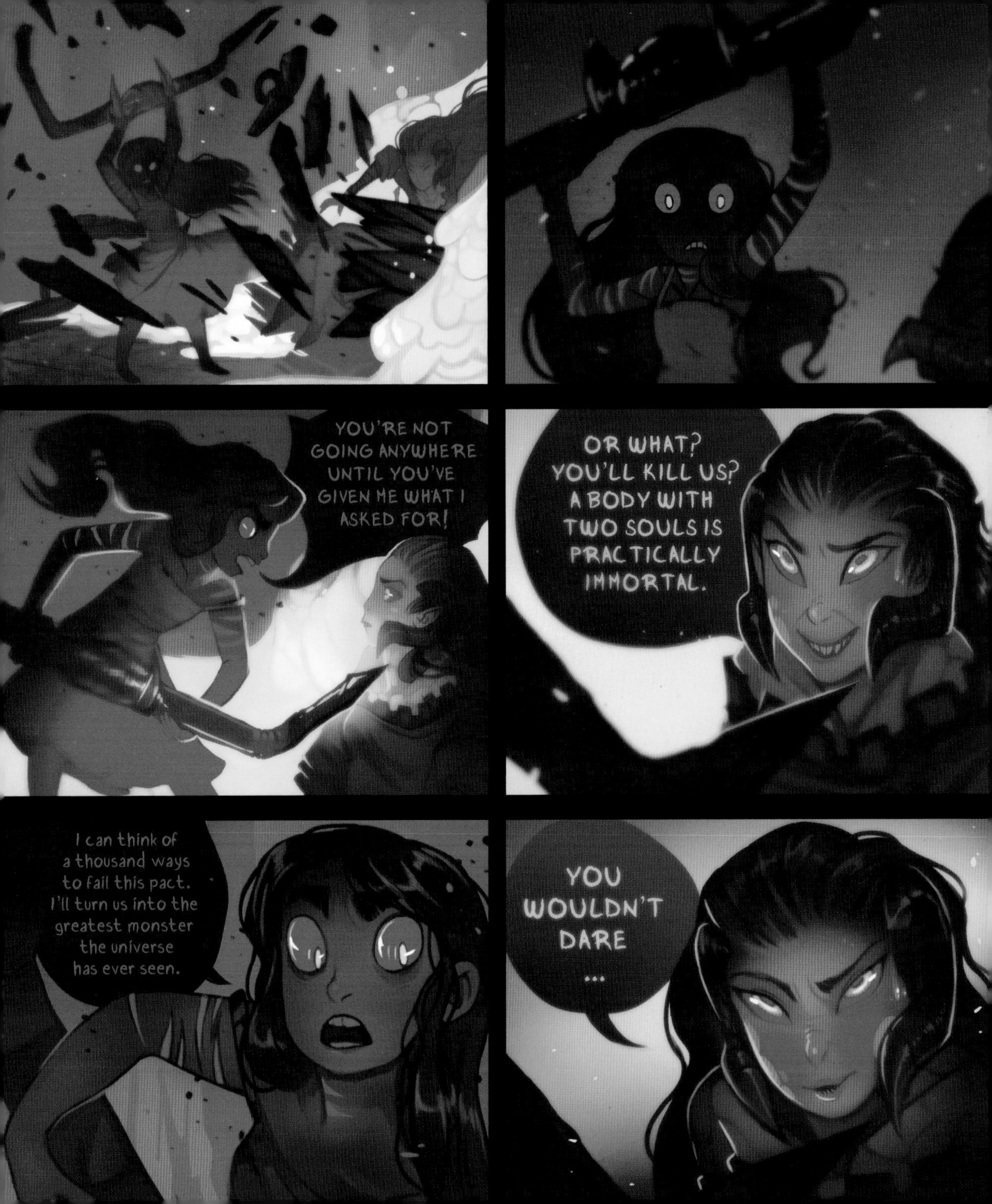

YOU'RE NOT GOING ANYWHERE UNTIL YOU'VE GIVEN ME WHAT I ASKED FOR!
OR WHAT? YOU'LL KILL US? A BODY WITH TWO SOULS IS PRACTICALLY IMMORTAL.
I can think of a thousand ways to fail this pact. I'll turn us into the greatest monster the universe has ever seen.
YOU WOULDN'T DARE ...

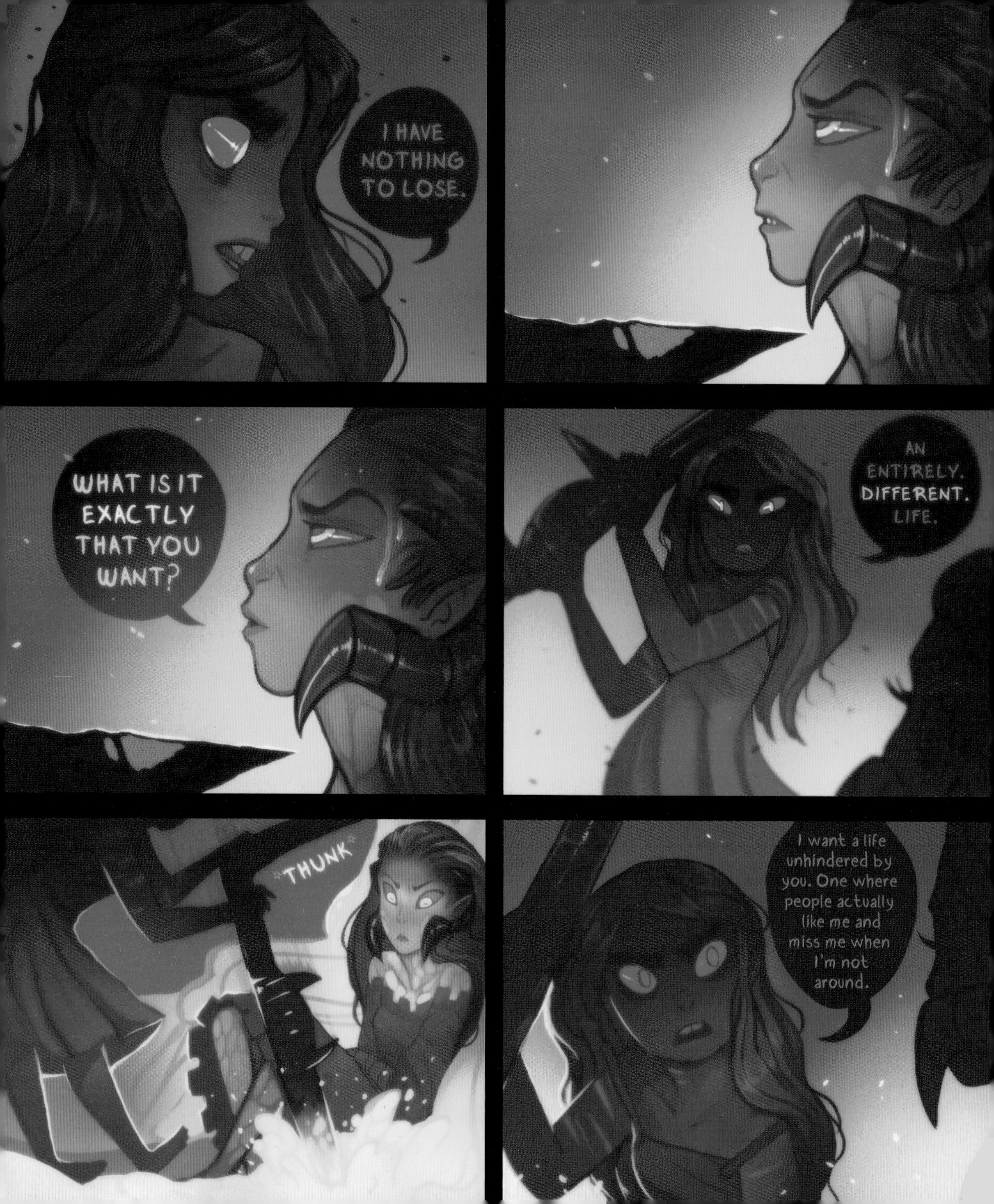
I HAVE NOTHING TO LOSE.
WHAT IS IT EXACTLY THAT YOU WANT?
AN ENTIRELY. DIFFERENT. LIFE.
THUNK
I want a life unhindered by you. One where people actually like me and miss me when I'm not around.

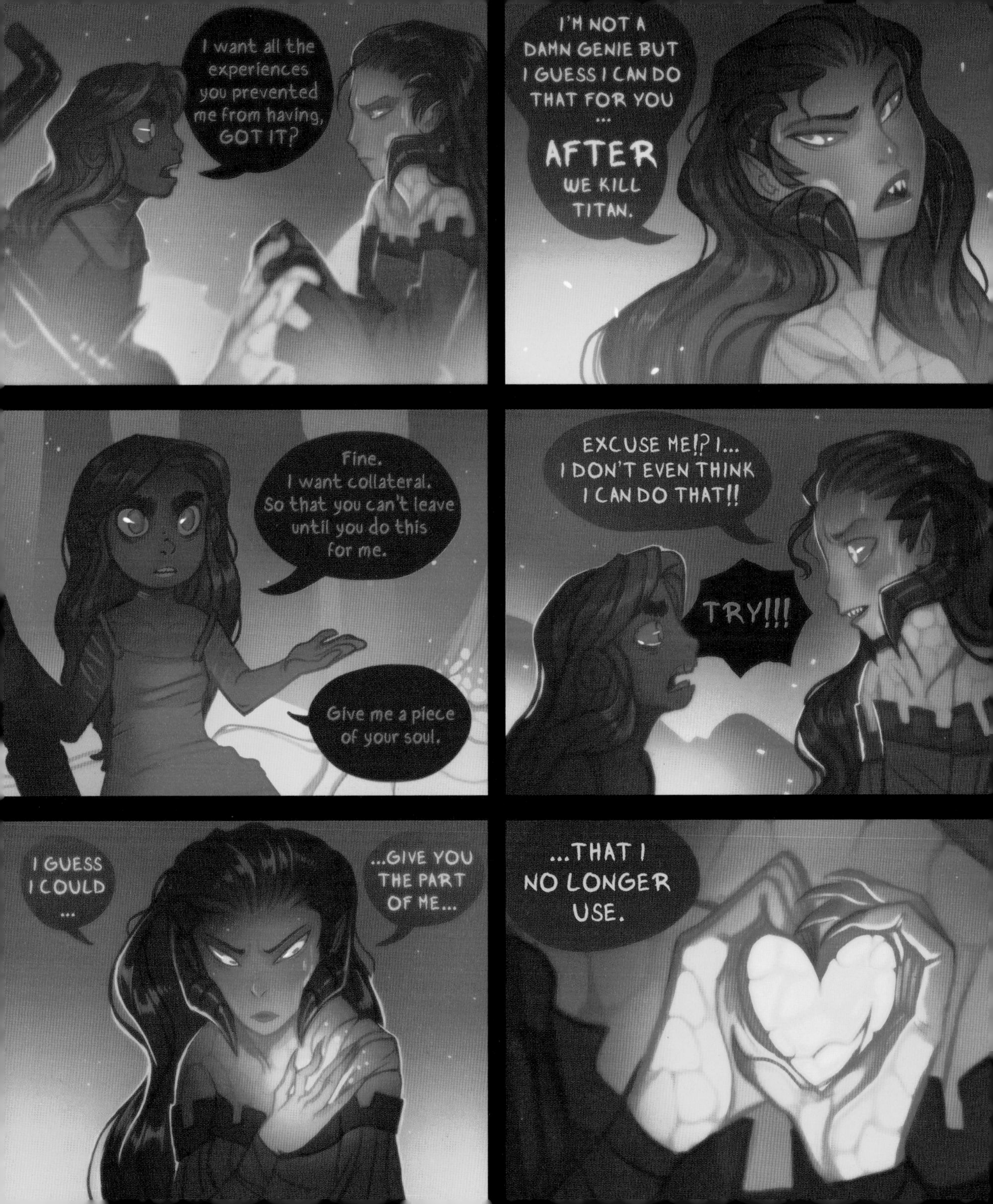
I want all the experiences you prevented me from having, GOT IT?
I'M NOT A DAMN GENIE BUT I GUESS I CAN DO THAT FOR YOU ... AFTER WE KILL TITAN.
Fine. I want collateral. So that you can't leave until you do this for me.
Give me a piece of your soul.
EXCUSE ME!? I... I DON'T EVEN THINK I CAN DO THAT!!
TRY!!!
I GUESS I COULD ...
...GIVE YOU THE PART OF ME...
...THAT I NO LONGER USE.

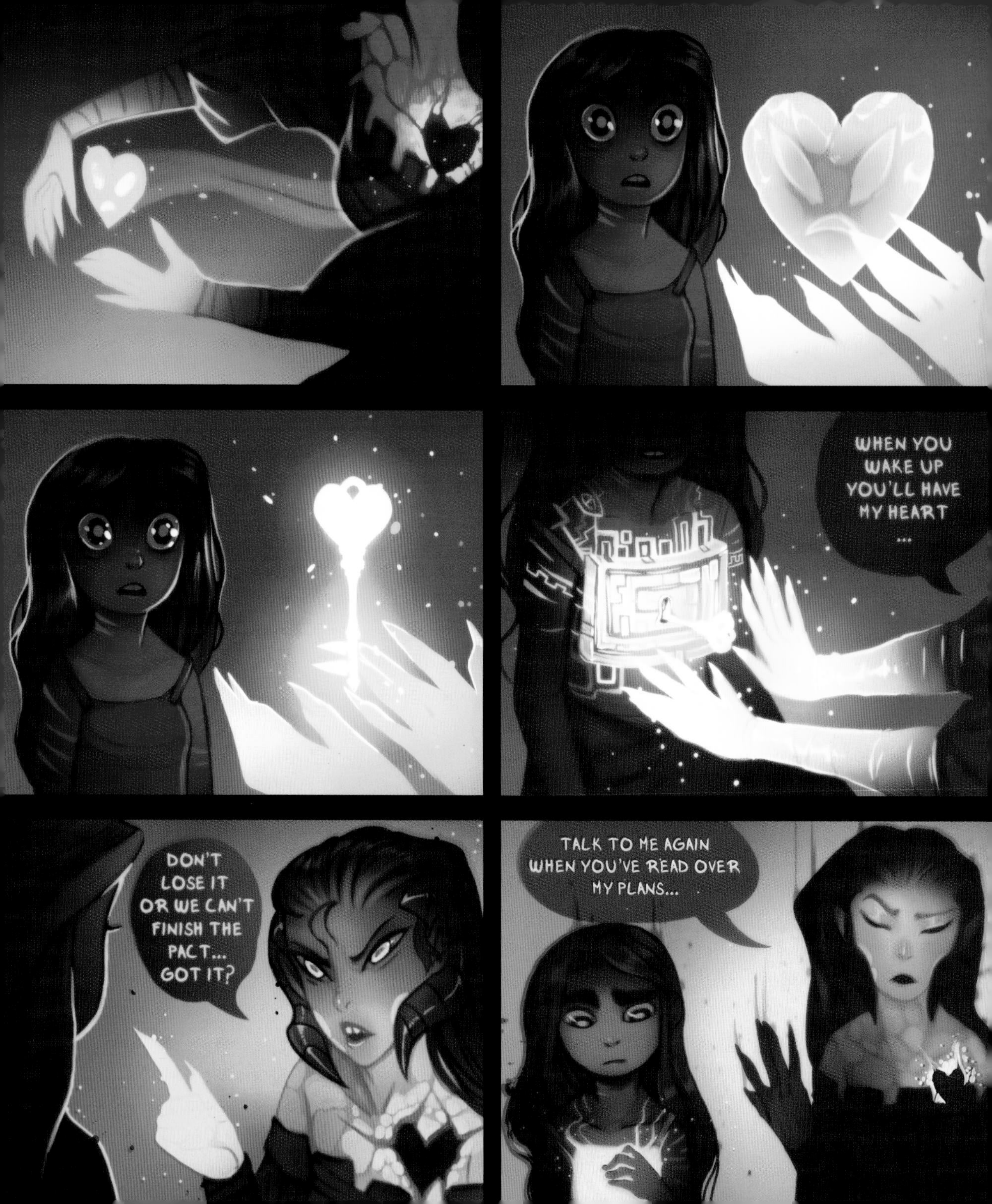
WHEN YOU WAKE UP YOU'LL HAVE MY HEART ...
DON'T LOSE IT OR WE CAN'T FINISH THE PACT... GOT IT?
TALK TO ME AGAIN WHEN YOU'VE READ OVER MY PLANS...

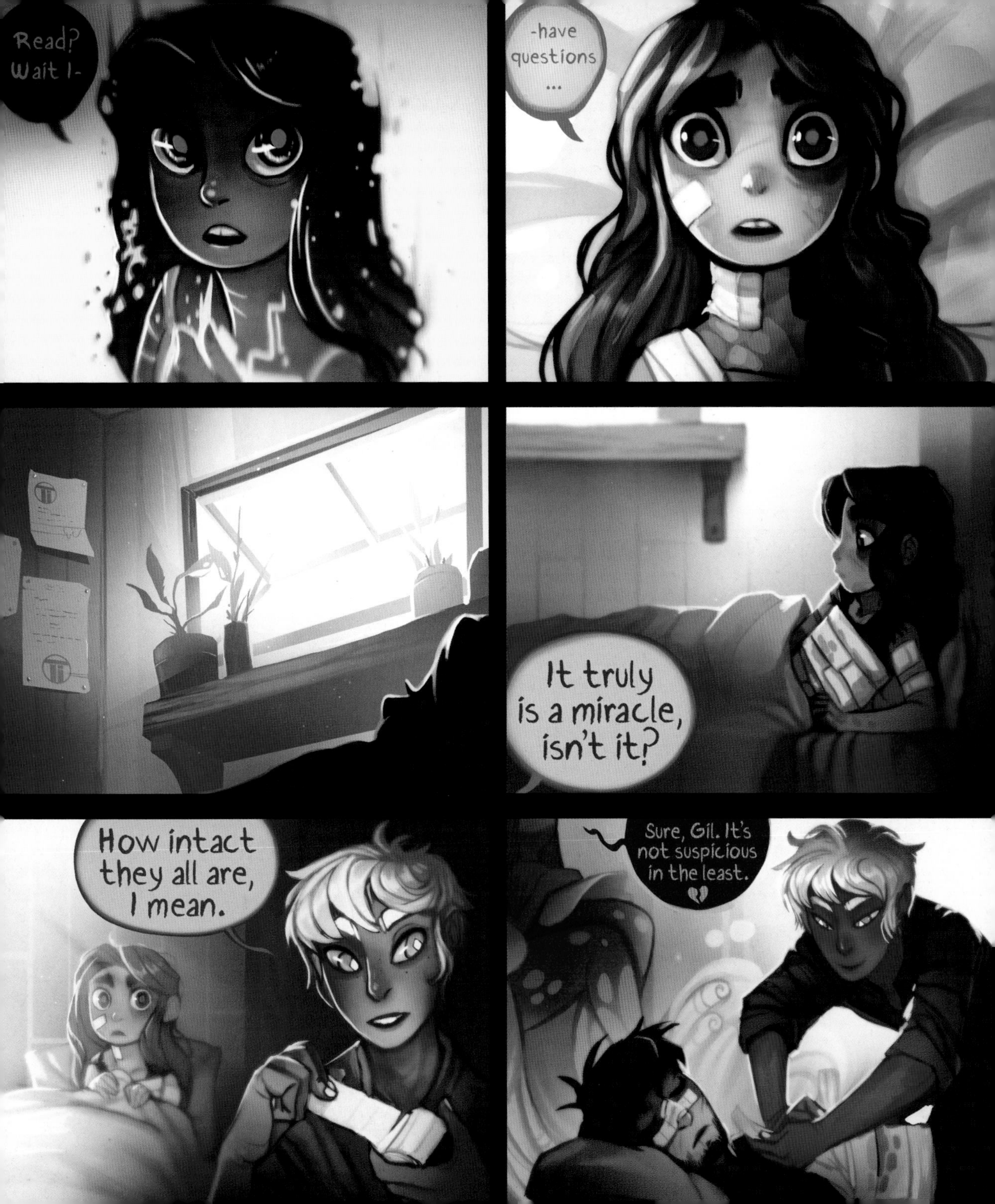

Read? Wait I-
-have questions ...
It truly is a miracle, isn't it?
How intact they all are, I mean.
Sure, Gil. It's not suspicious in the least.

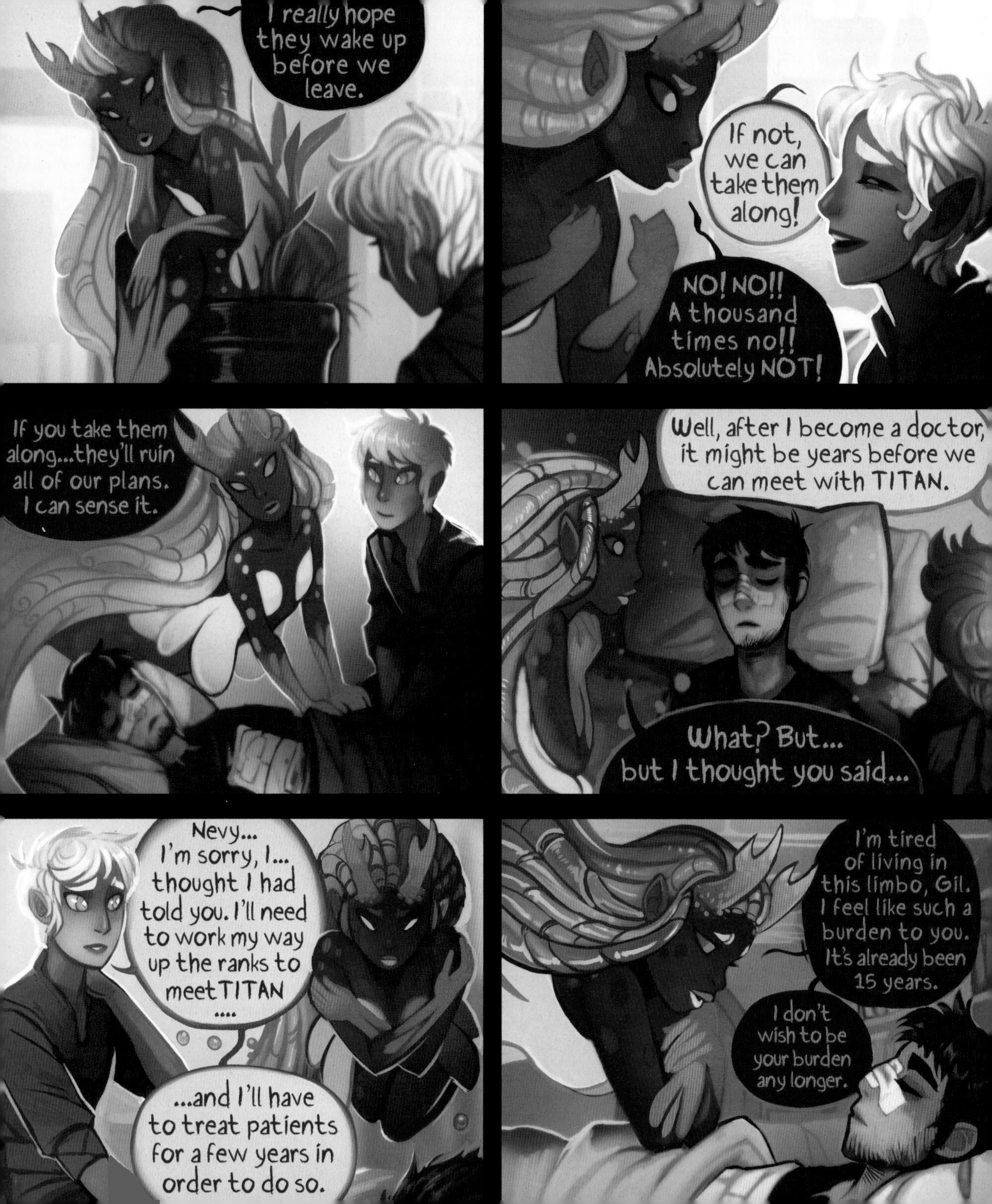
I really hope they wake up before we leave.
If not, we can take them along!
NO! NO!! A thousand times no!! Absolutely NOT!
If you take them along...they'll ruin all of our plans. I can sense it.
Well, after I become a doctor, it might be years before we can meet with TITAN.
What? But... but I thought you said...
Nevy... I'm sorry, I... thought I had told you. I'll need to work my way up the ranks to meet TITAN ....
...and I'll have to treat patients for a few years in order to do so.
I'm tired of living in this limbo, Gil. I feel like such a burden to you. It's already been 15 years.
I don't wish to be your burden any longer.

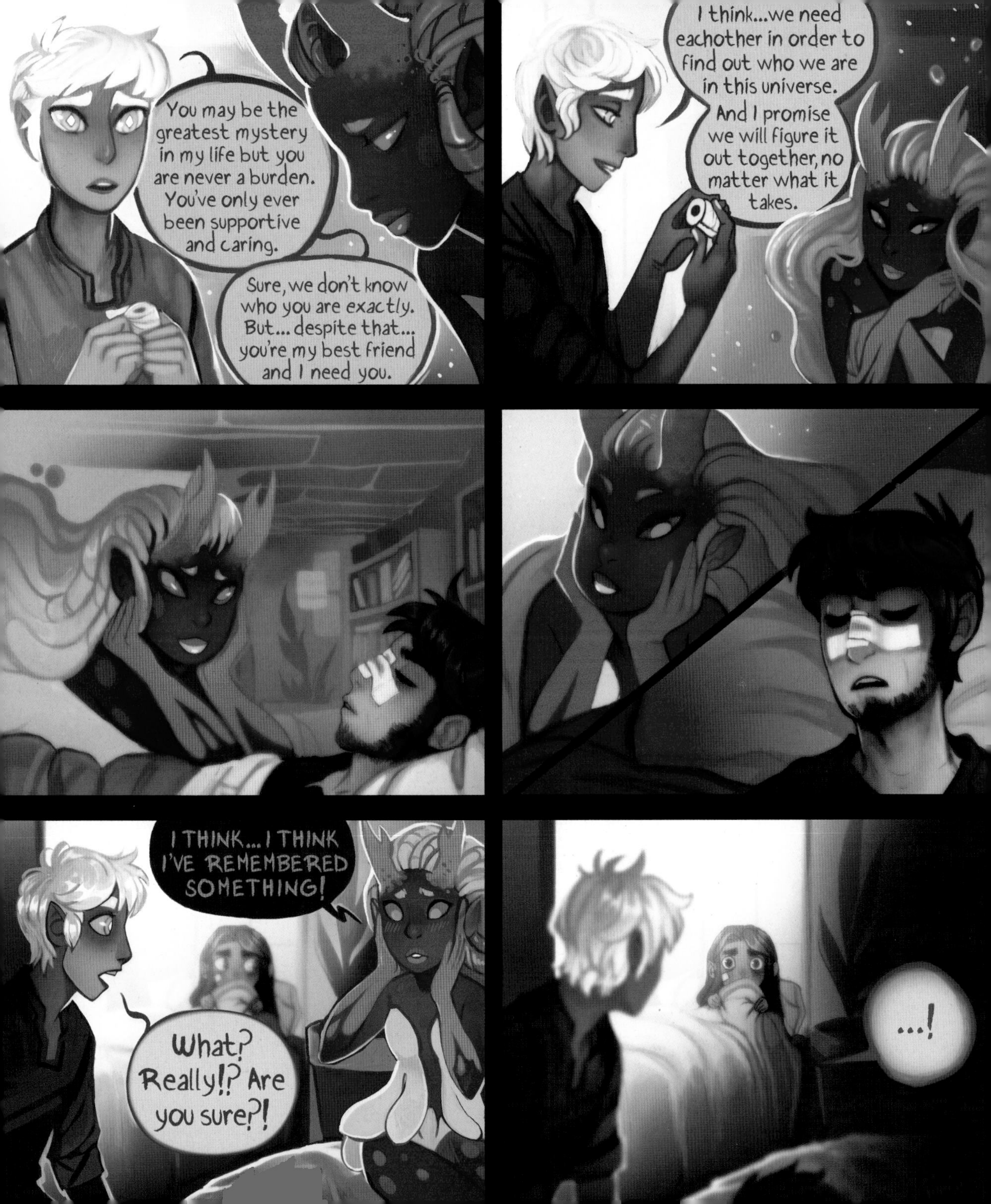

You may be the greatest mystery in my life but you are never a burden. You've only ever been supportive and caring.
Sure, we don't know who you are exactly. But... despite that... you're my best friend and I need you.
I think...we need eachother in order to find out who we are in this universe.
And I promise we will figure it out together, no matter what it takes.
I THINK... I THINK I'VE REMEMBERED SOMETHING!
What? Really!? Are you sure?!
...!

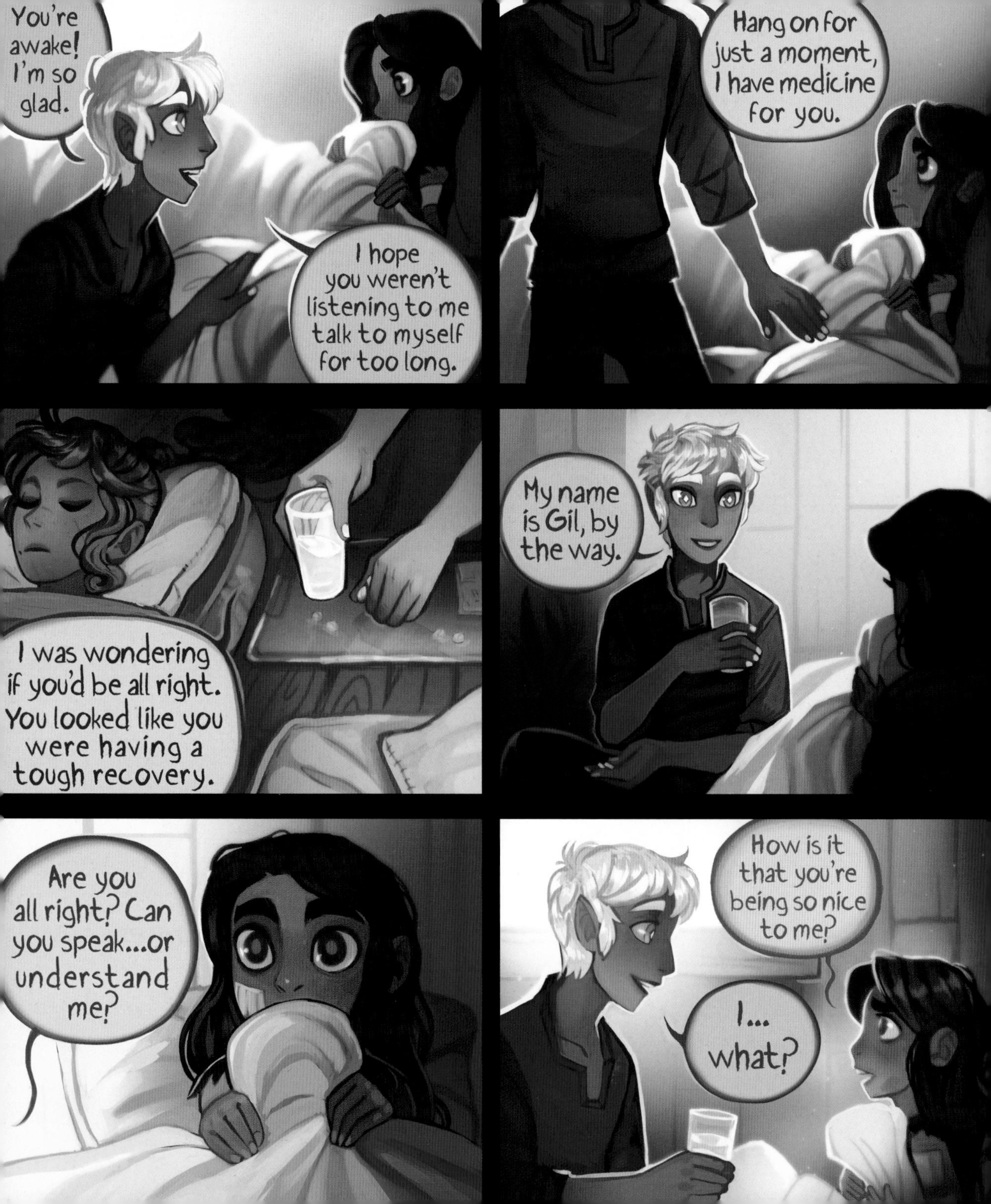

You're awake! I'm so glad.
I hope you weren't listening to me talk to myself for too long.
Hang on for just a moment, I have medicine for you.
I was wondering if you'd be all right. You looked like you were having a tough recovery.
My name is Gil, by the way.
Are you all right? Can you speak...or understand me?
How is it that you're being so nice to me?
I... what?

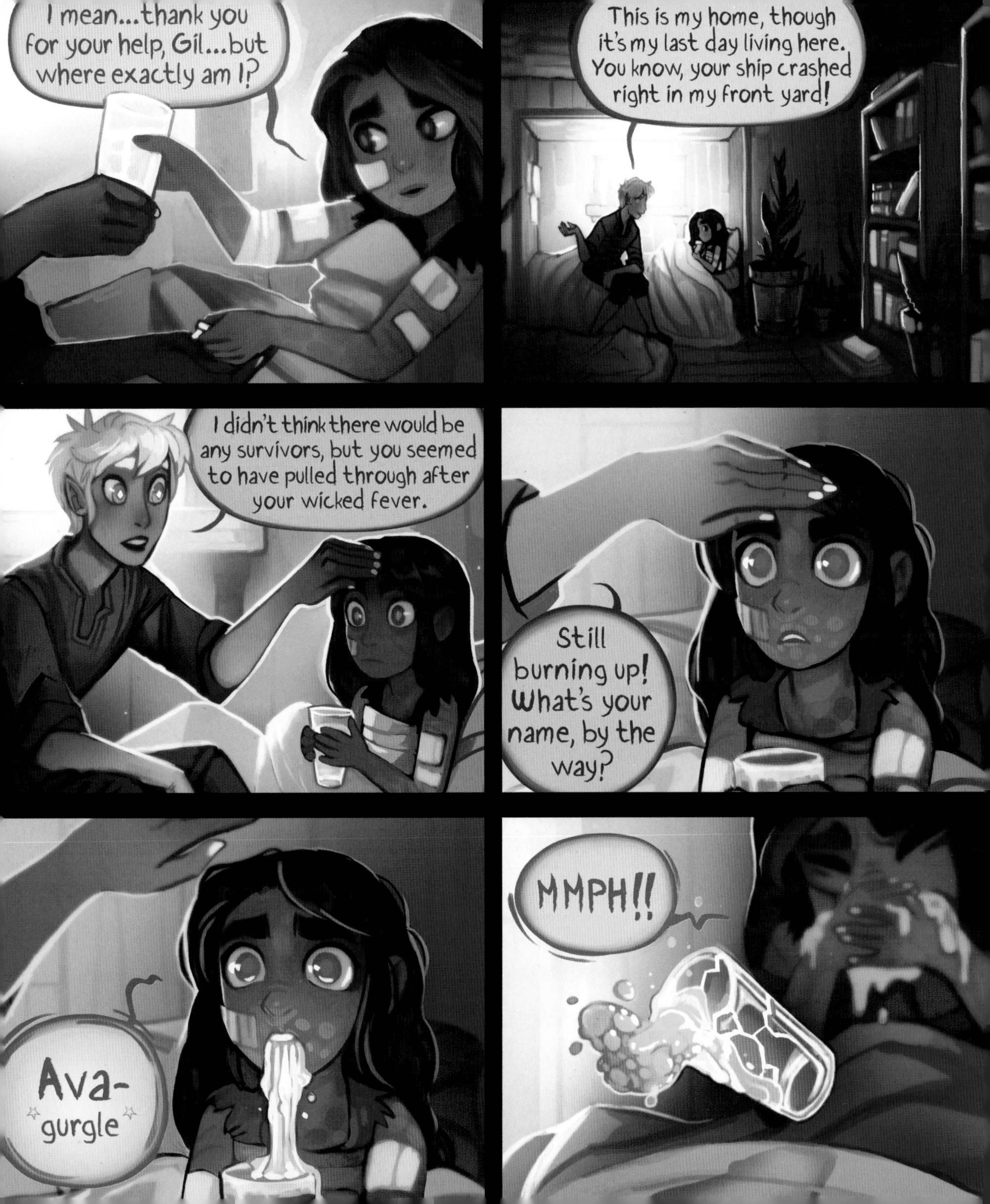
I mean...thank you for your help, Gil...but where exactly am I?
This is my home, though it's my last day living here. You know, your ship crashed right in my front yard!
I didn't think there would be any survivors, but you seemed to have pulled through after your wicked fever.
Still burning up! What's your name, by the way?
Ava-gurgle
MMPH!!

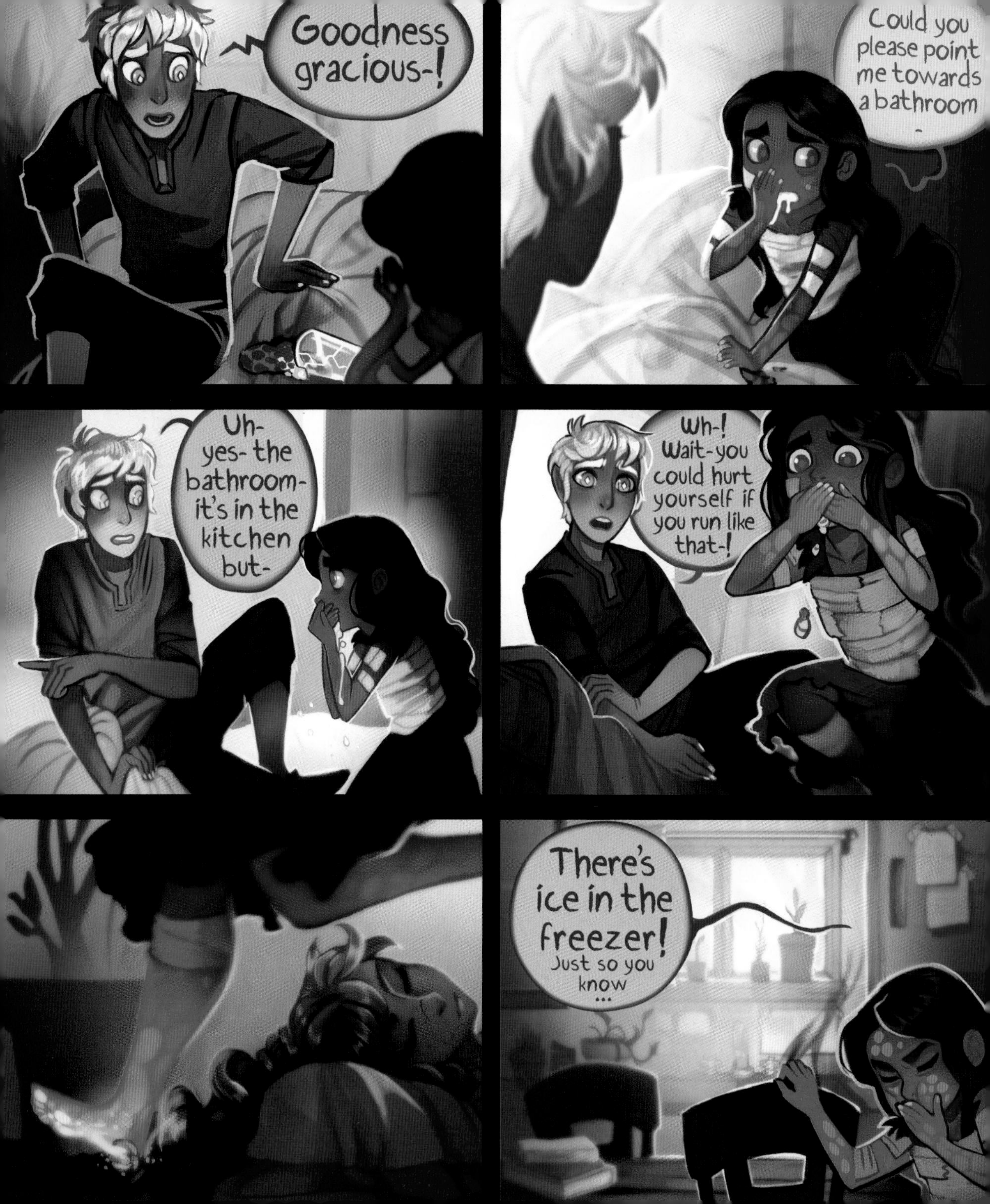
Goodness gracious-!
Could you please point me towards a bathroom -
Uh- yes- the bathroom- it's in the kitchen but-
Wh-! Wait-you could hurt yourself if you run like that-!
There's ice in the freezer!
Just so you know ...

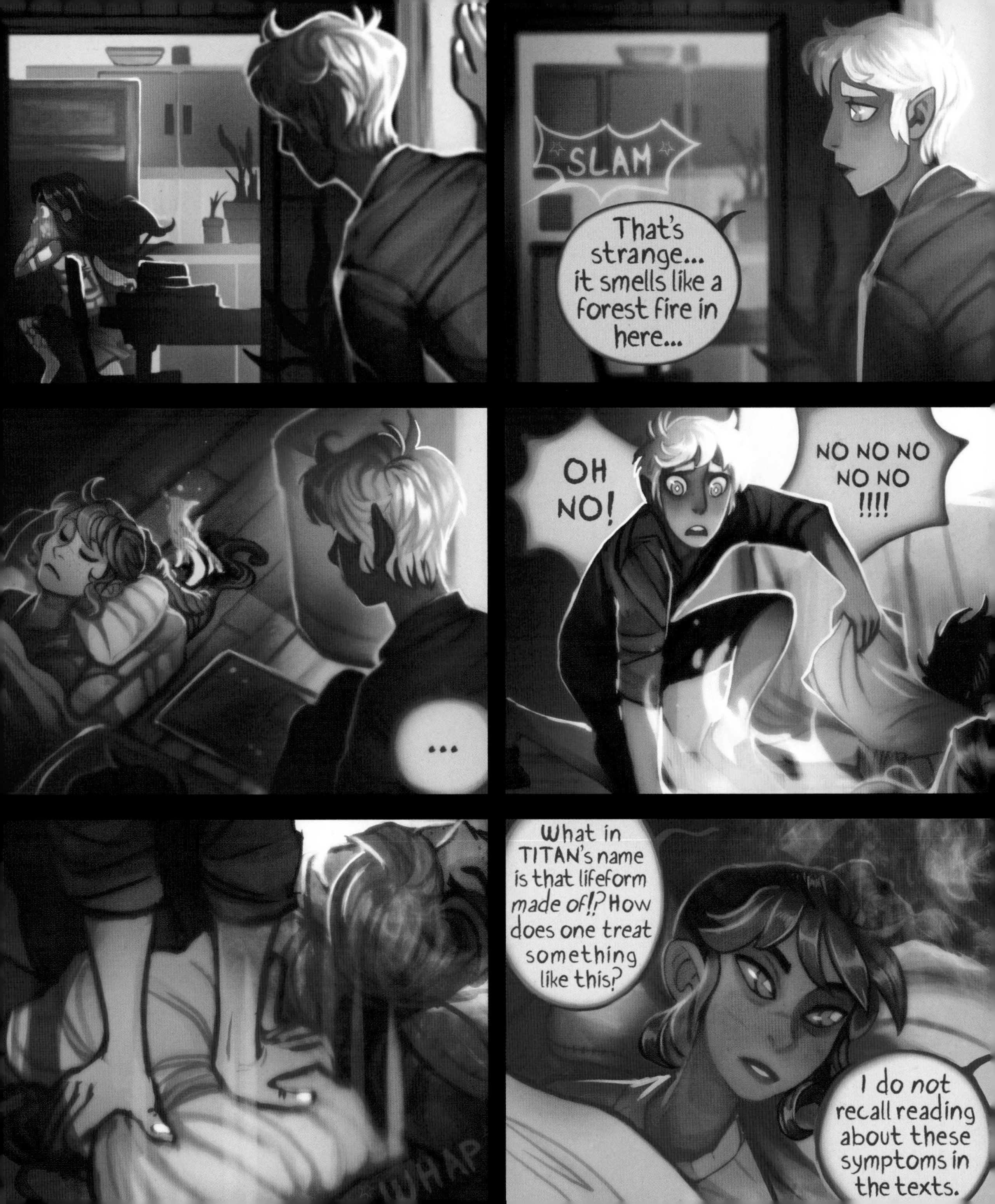
SLAM
That's strange... it smells like a forest fire in here...
...
OH NO!
NO NO NO NO NO !!!!
What in TITAN's name is that lifeform made of!? How does one treat something like this?
I do not recall reading about these symptoms in the texts.

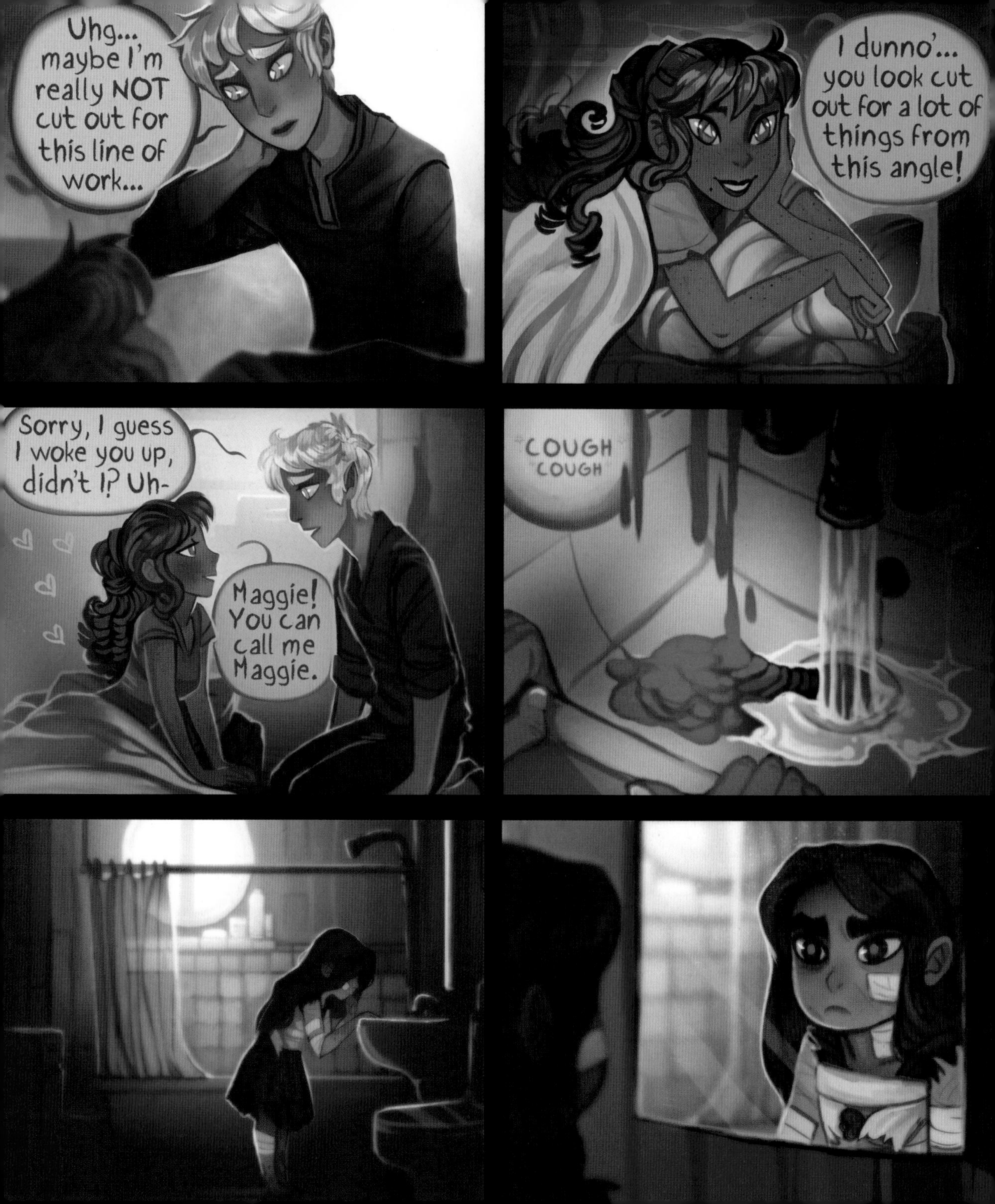
Uhg... maybe I'm really NOT cut out for this line of work...
I dunno'... you look cut out for a lot of things from this angle!
Sorry, I guess I woke you up, didn't I? Uh-
Maggie! You can call me Maggie.
COUGH COUGH

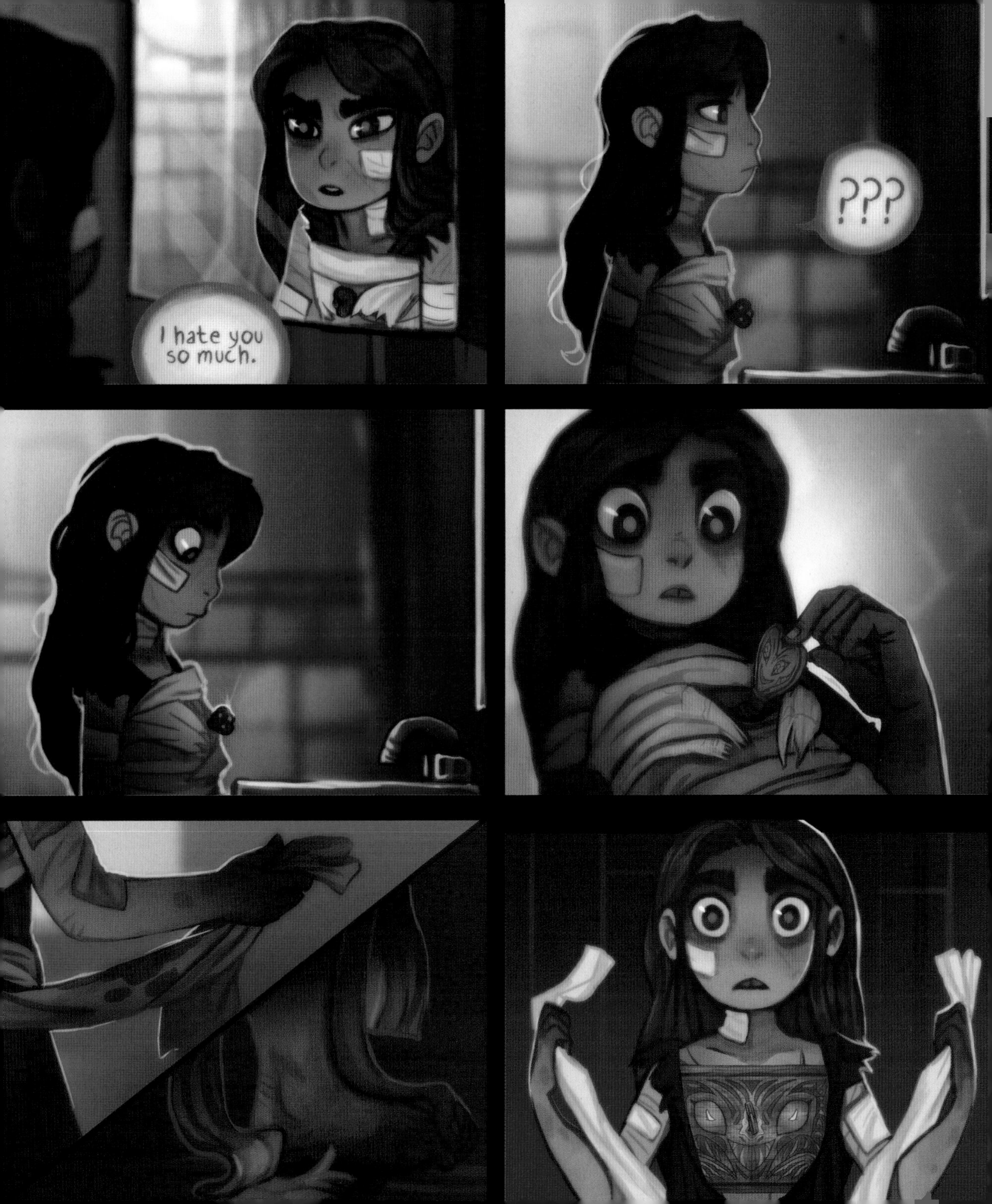
I hate you so much.
???

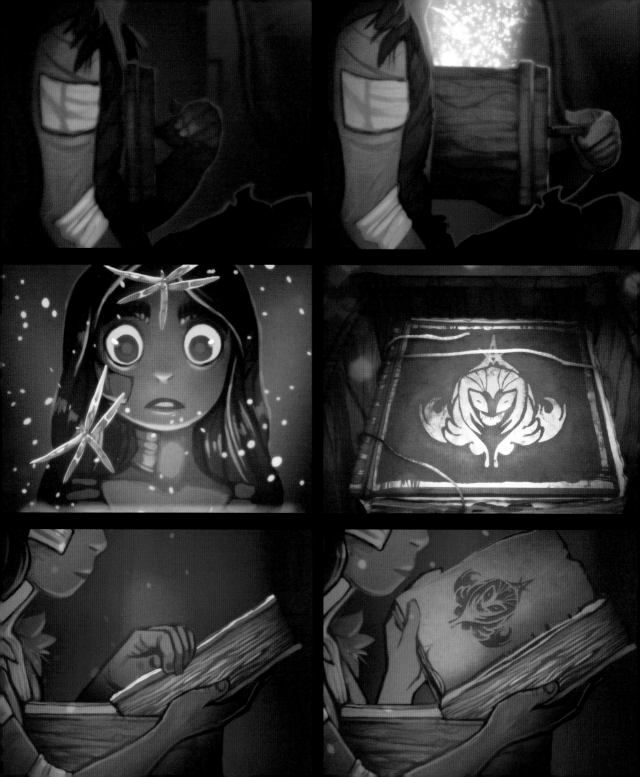

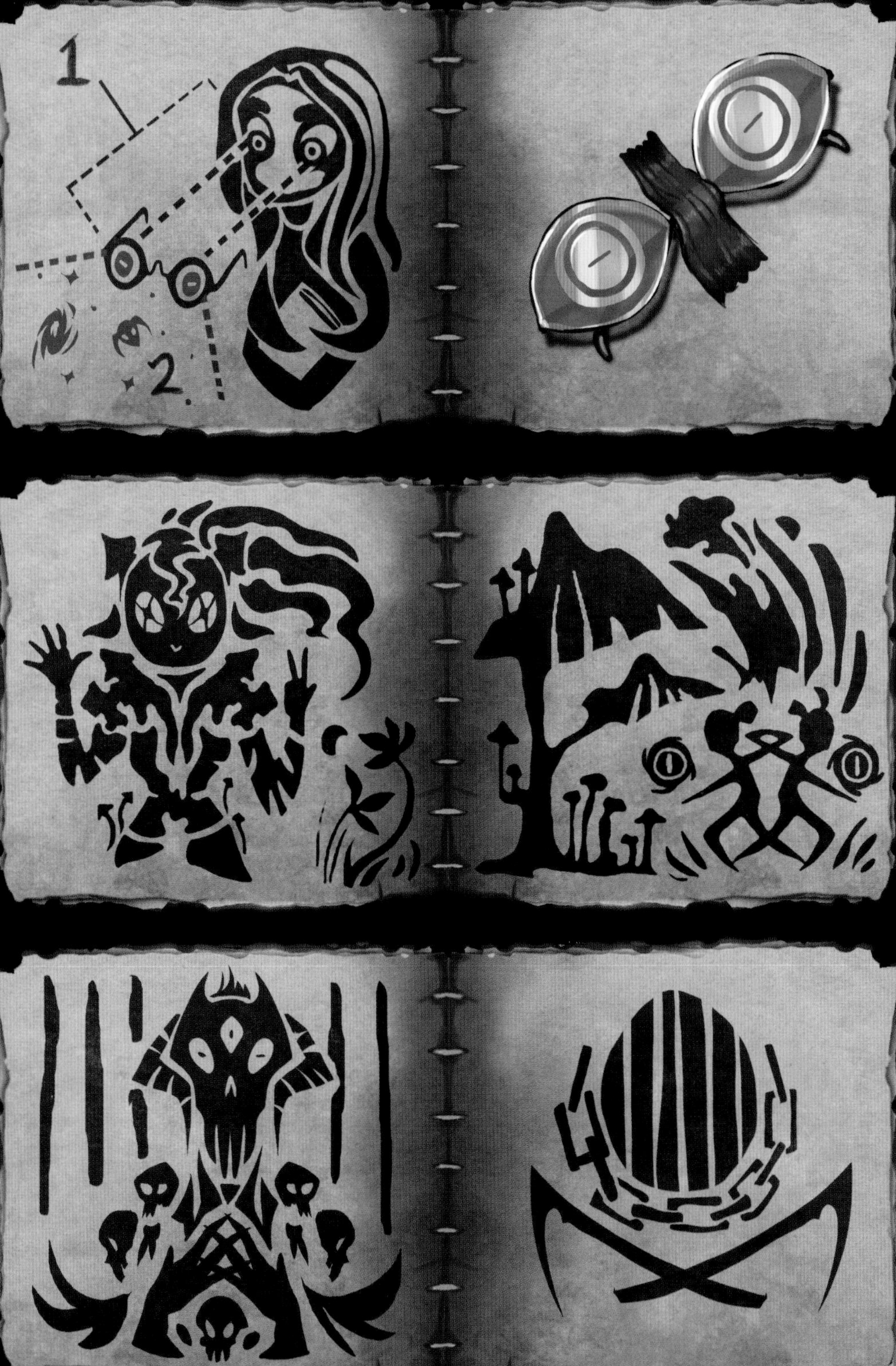
1
2.

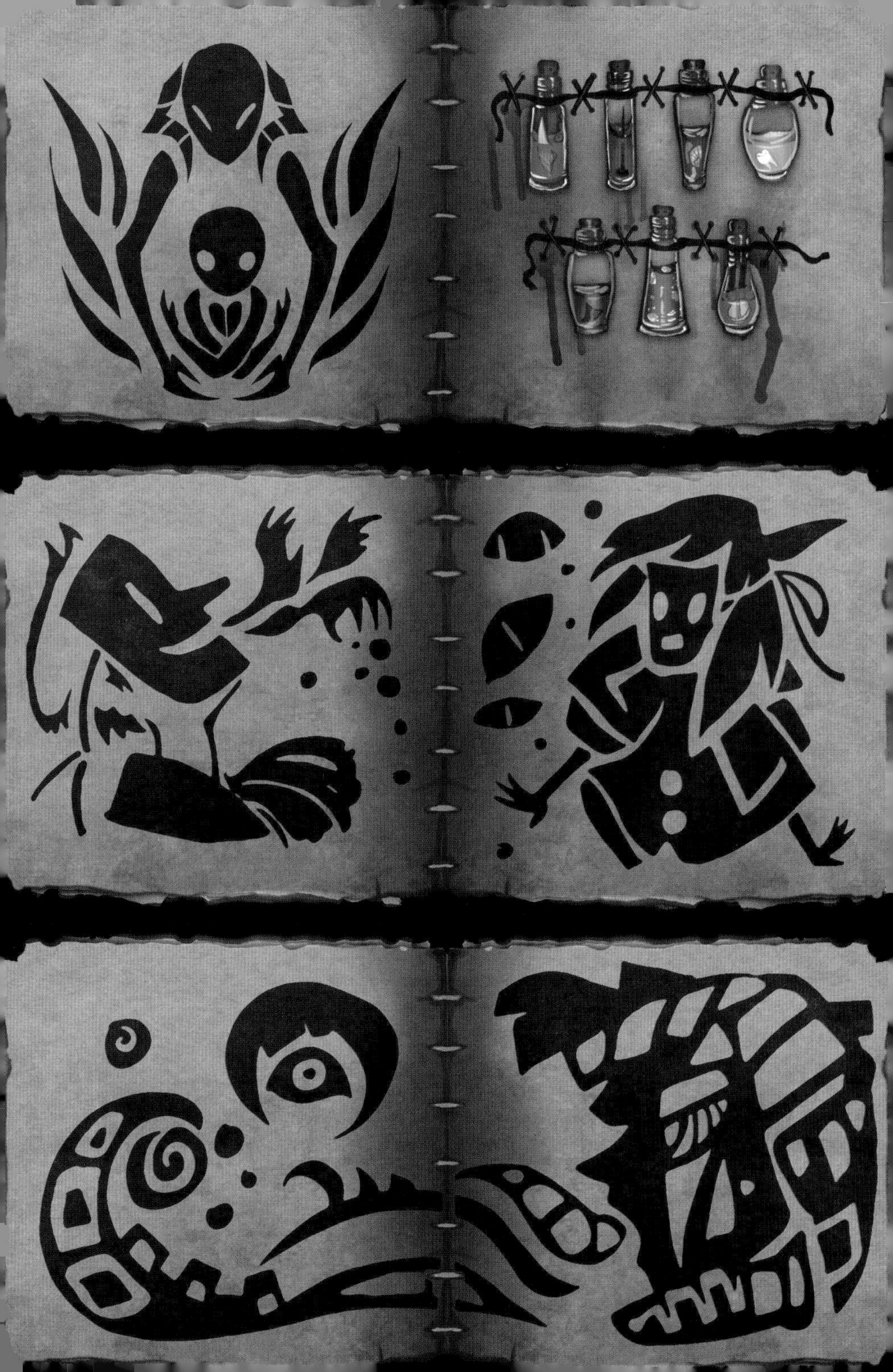

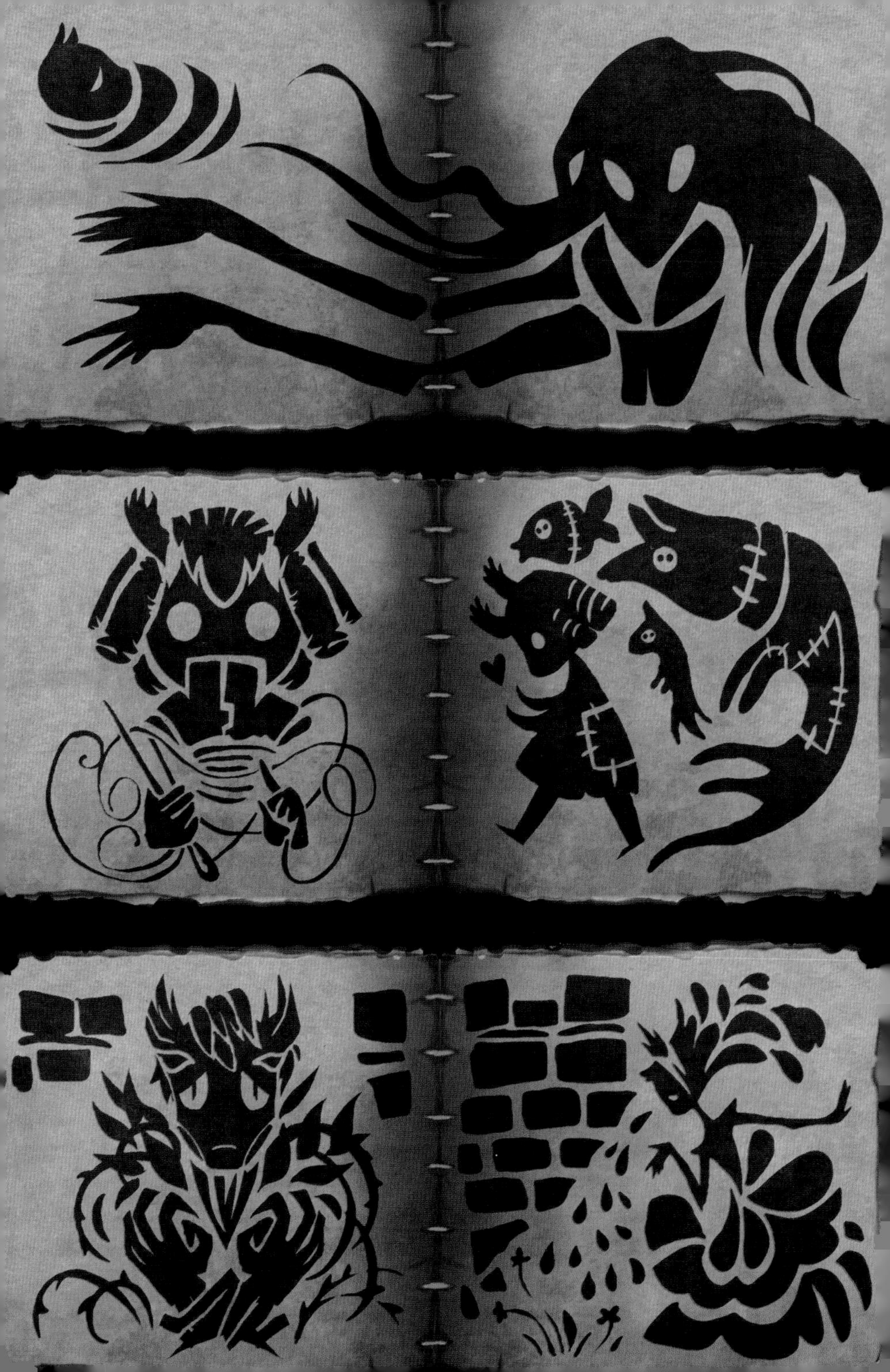

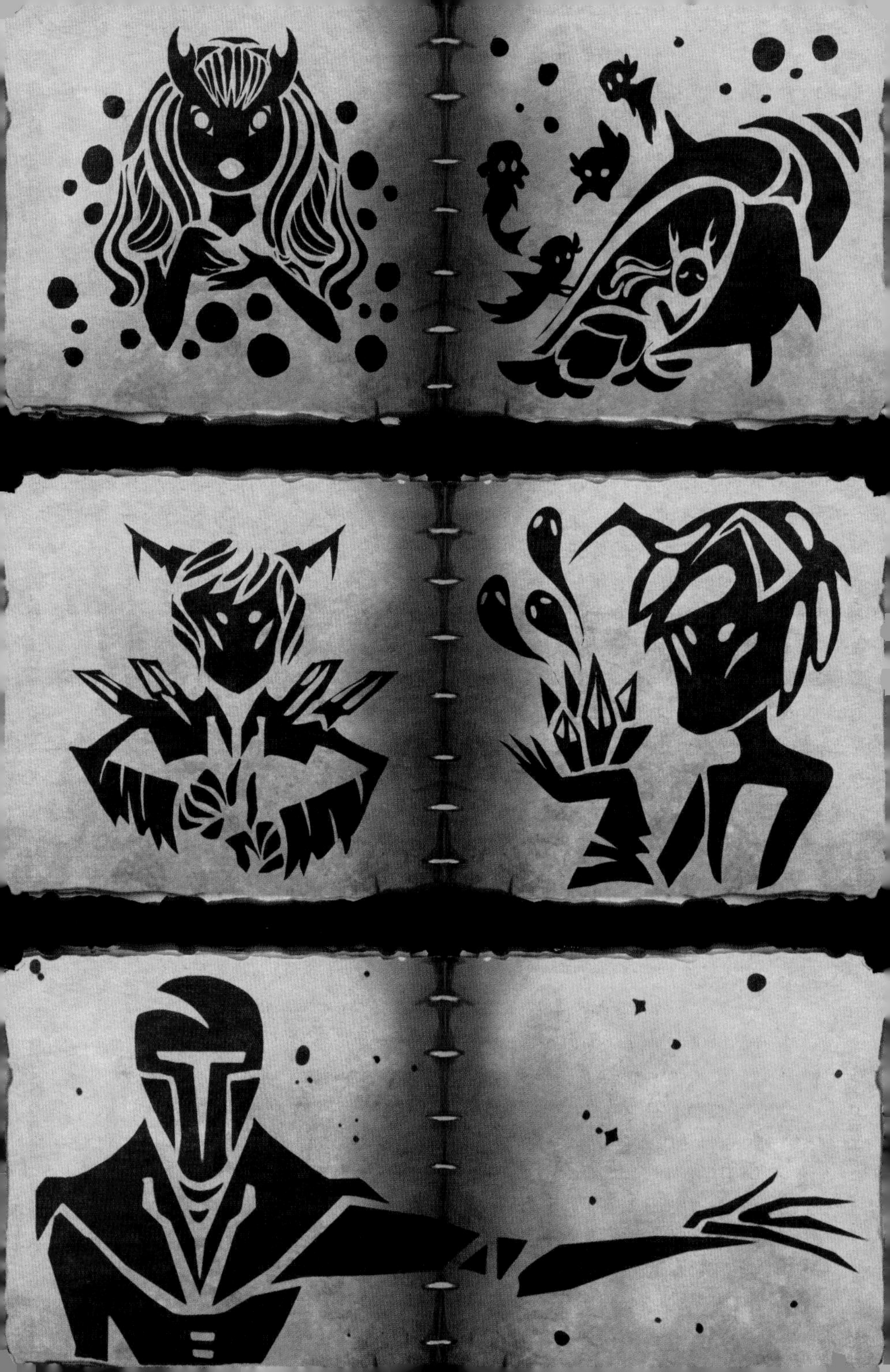

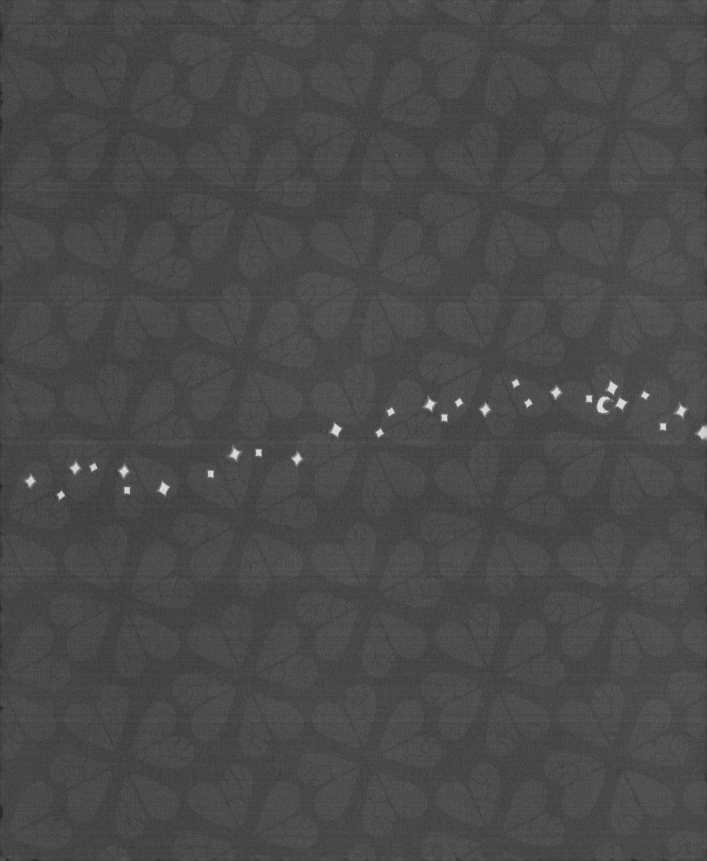

CHAPTER 3

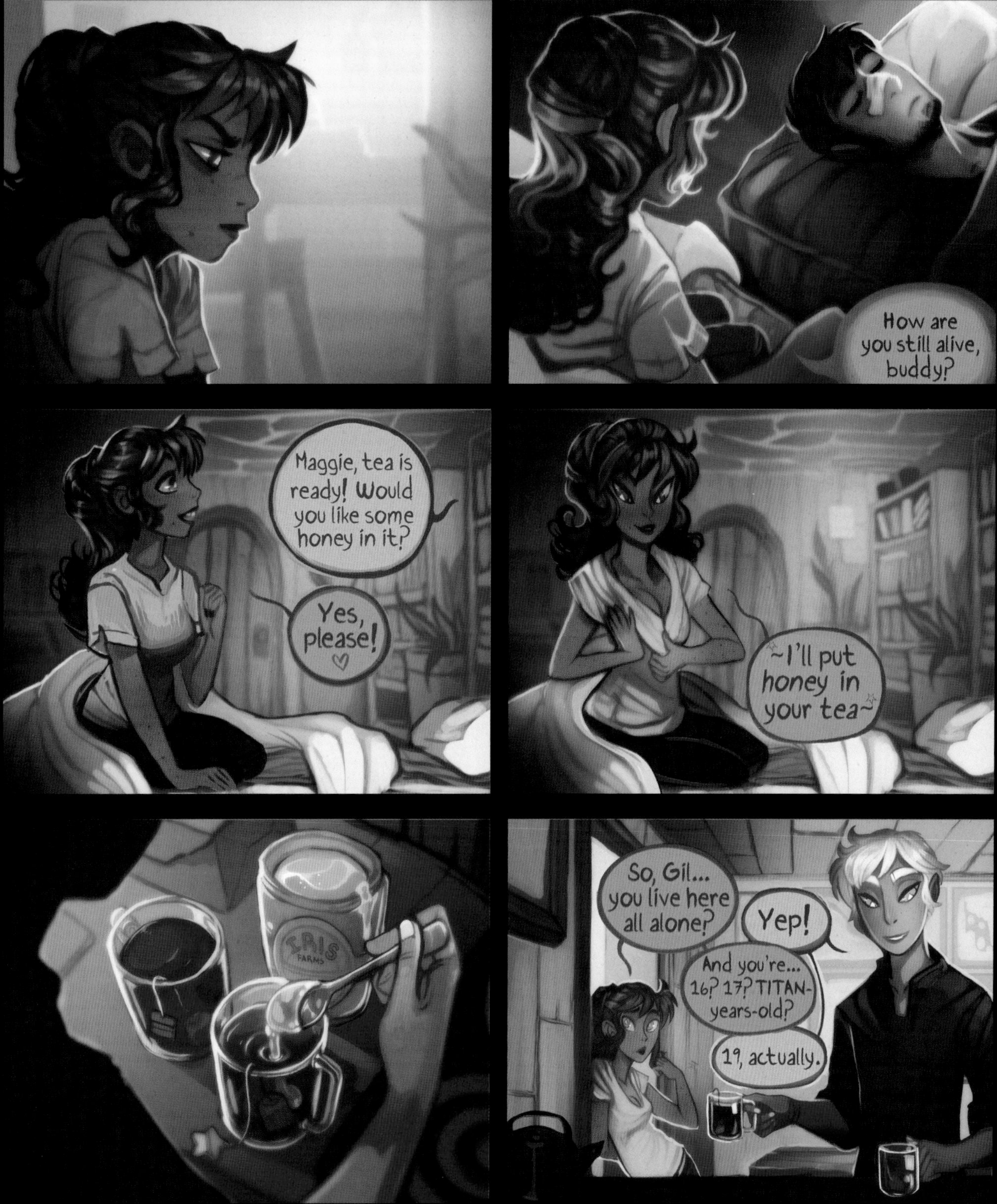
How are you still alive, buddy?
Maggie, tea is ready! Would you like some honey in it?
Yes, please! ♡
~I'll put honey in your tea~
IRIS FARMS
So, Gil... you live here all alone?
Yep!
And you're... 16? 17? TITAN-years-old?
19, actually.

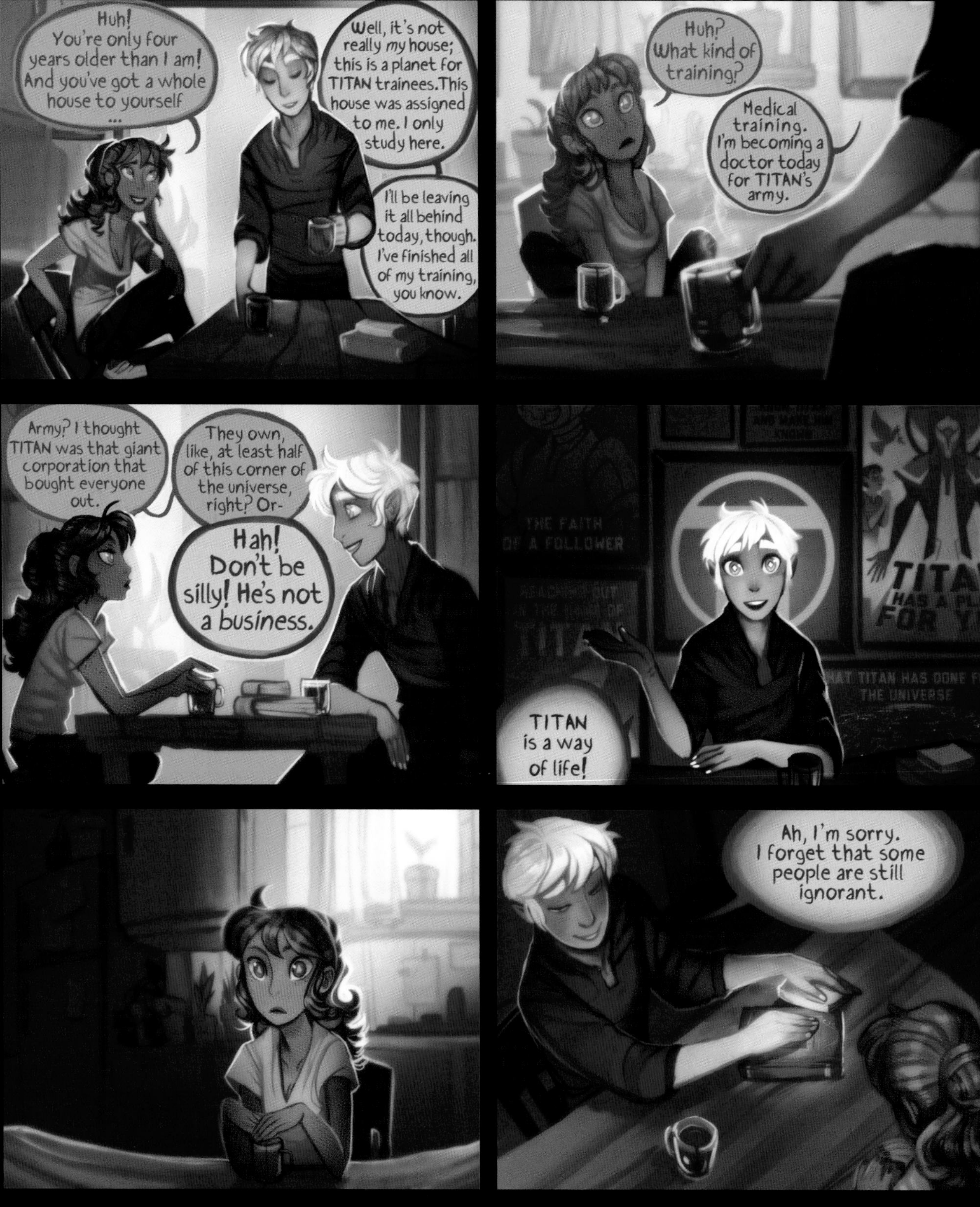
Huh! You're only four years older than I am! And you've got a whole house to yourself ...
Well, it's not really *my* house; this is a planet for TITAN trainees. This house was assigned to me. I only study here.
I'll be leaving it all behind today, though. I've finished all of my training, you know.
Huh? What kind of training?
Medical training. I'm becoming a doctor today for TITAN's army.
Army? I thought TITAN was that giant corporation that bought everyone out.
They own, like, at least half of this corner of the universe, right? Or-
Hah! Don't be silly! He's not a business.
THE FAITH OF A FOLLOWER
TITAN is a way of life!
Ah, I'm sorry. I forget that some people are still ignorant.

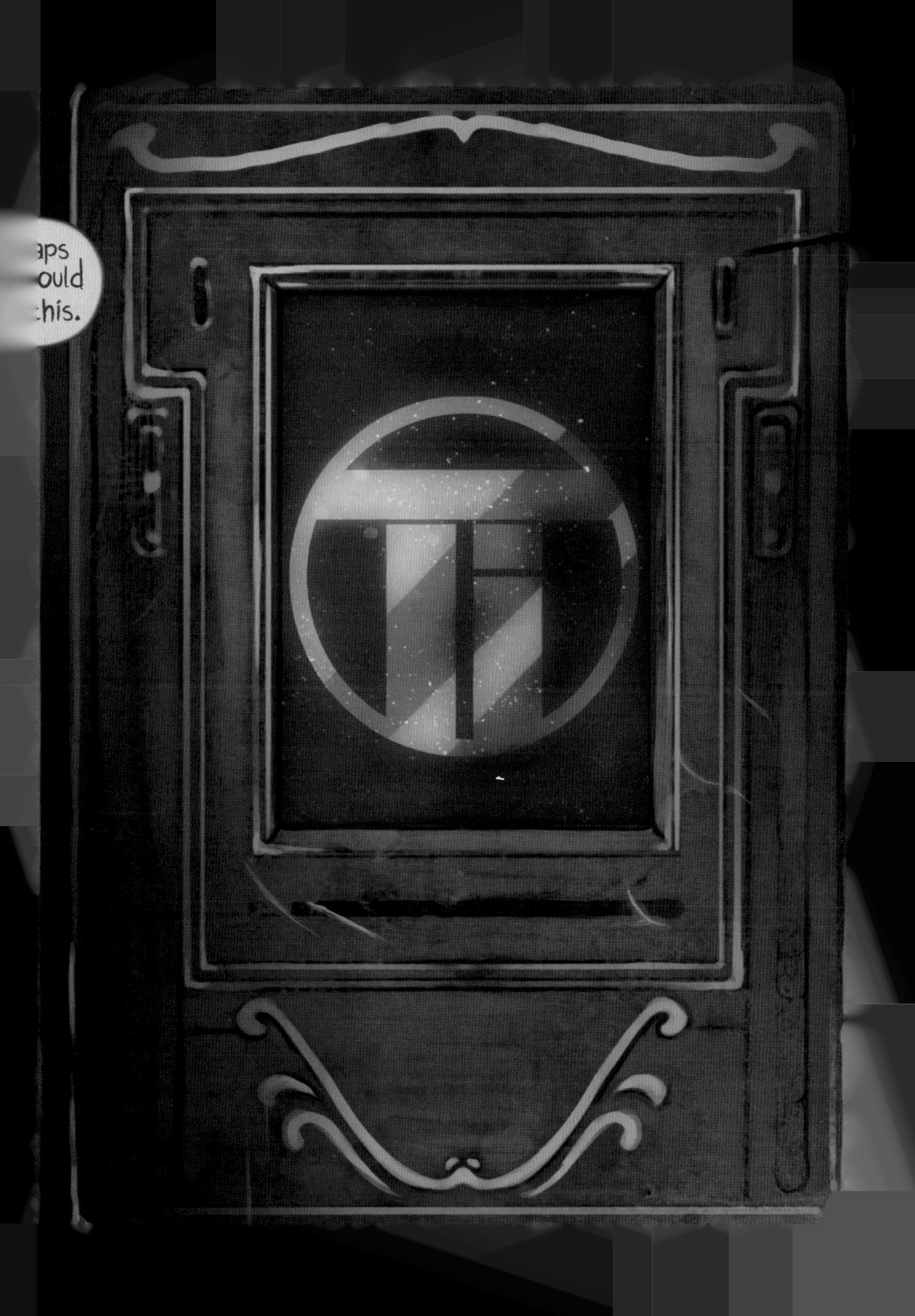
aps
ould
this.

HE CREATED
THE BEGINNING
OF EVERYTHING

AND CRAFTED
TIME AND SPACE
WITH A KNIFE

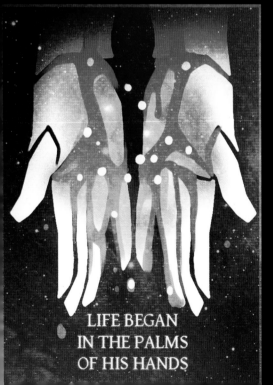

LIFE BEGAN
IN THE PALMS
OF HIS HANDS

AND WHEN YOU LOOK
DOWN HIS THROAT
YOU CAN SEE THE ENTIRE
UNIVERSE

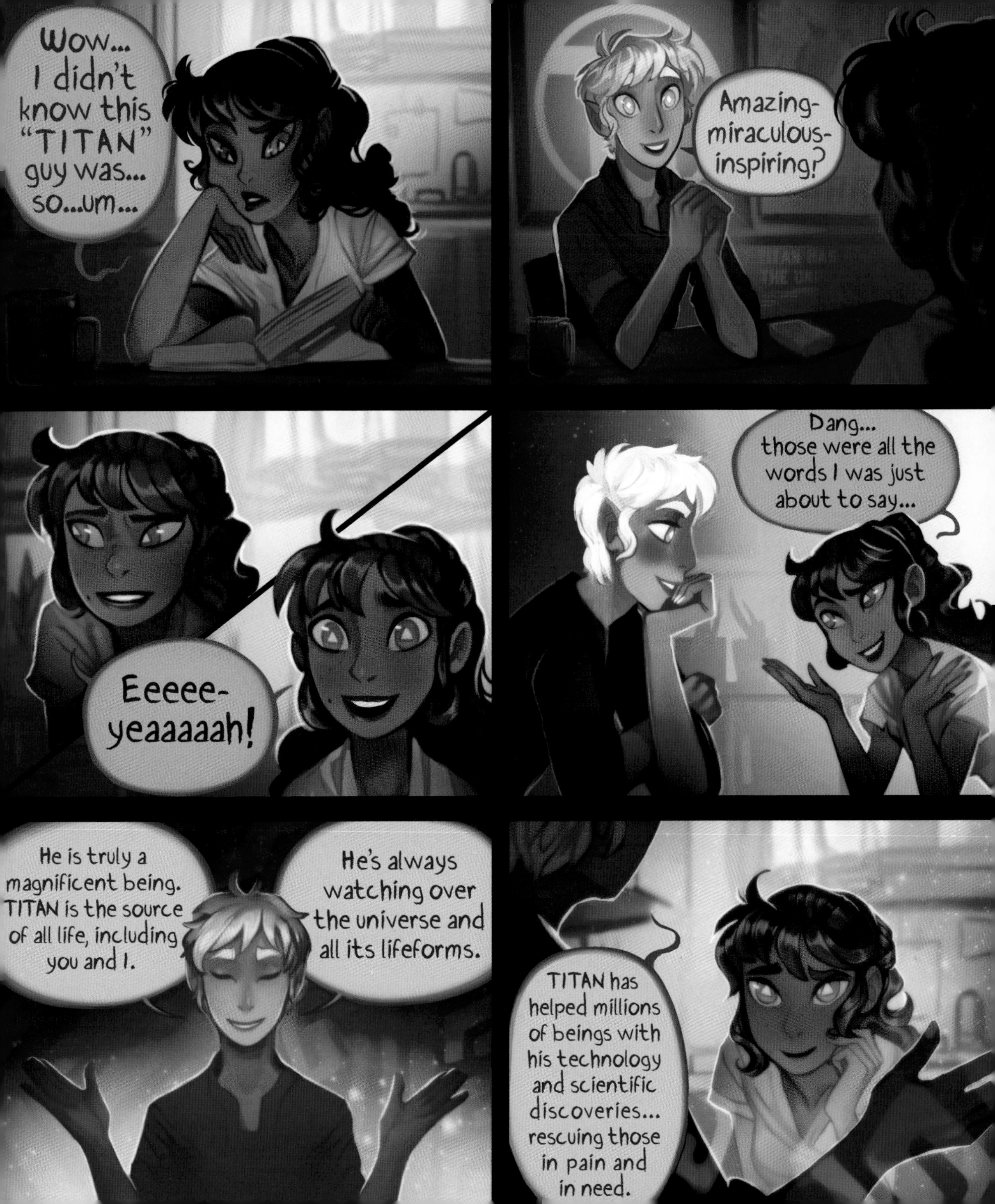
Wow... I didn't know this "TITAN" guy was... so...um...
Amazing-miraculous-inspiring?
Eeeee-yeaaaaah!
Dang... those were all the words I was just about to say...
He is truly a magnificent being. TITAN is the source of all life, including you and I.
He's always watching over the universe and all its lifeforms.
TITAN has helped millions of beings with his technology and scientific discoveries... rescuing those in pain and in need.

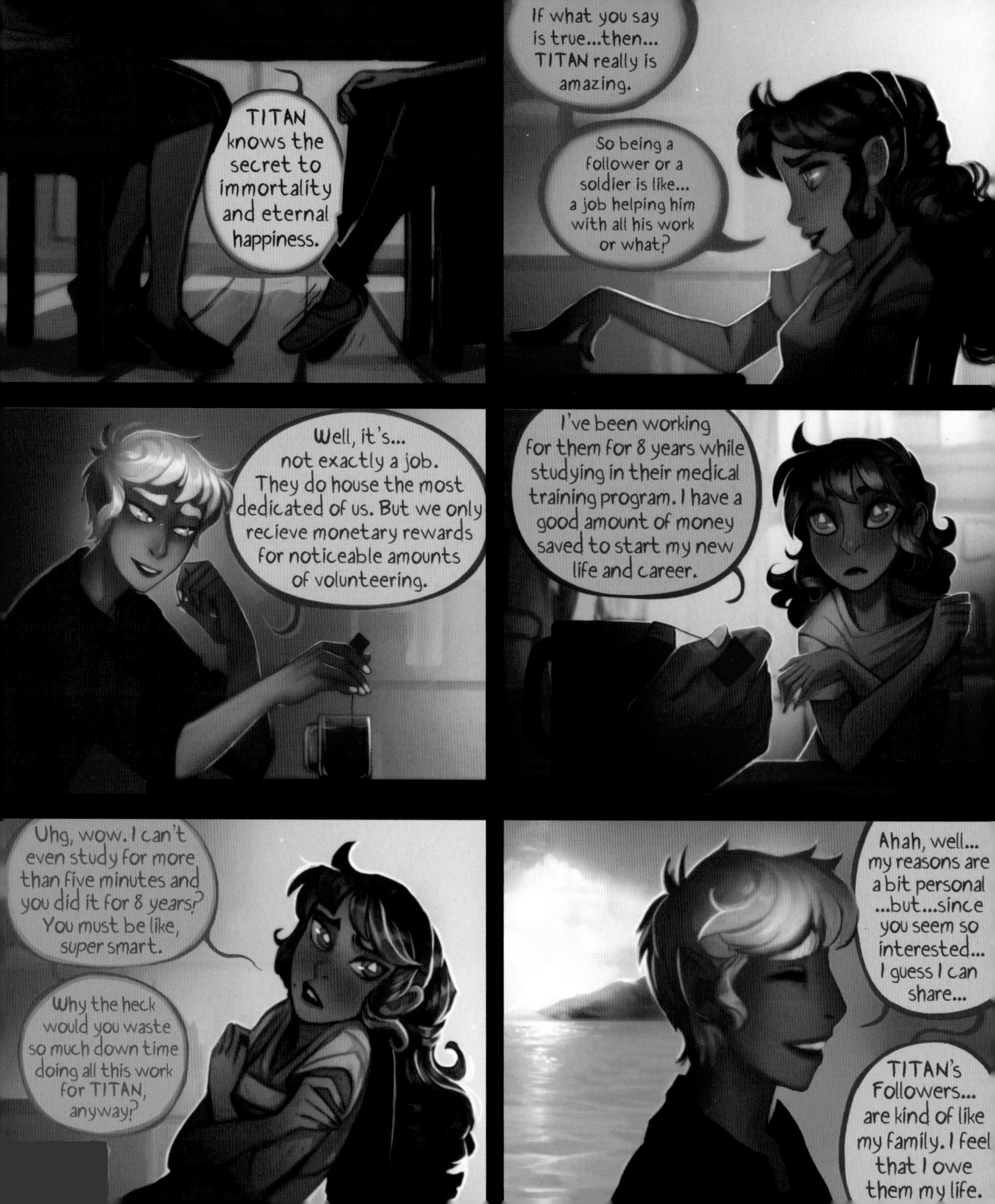
TITAN knows the secret to immortality and eternal happiness.
If what you say is true...then... TITAN really is amazing.
So being a follower or a soldier is like... a job helping him with all his work or what?
Well, it's... not exactly a job. They do house the most dedicated of us. But we only recieve monetary rewards for noticeable amounts of volunteering.
I've been working for them for 8 years while studying in their medical training program. I have a good amount of money saved to start my new life and career.
Uhg, wow. I can't even study for more than five minutes and you did it for 8 years? You must be like, super smart.
Why the heck would you waste so much down time doing all this work for TITAN, anyway?
Ahah, well... my reasons are a bit personal ...but...since you seem so interested... I guess I can share...
TITAN's Followers... are kind of like my family. I feel that I owe them my life.

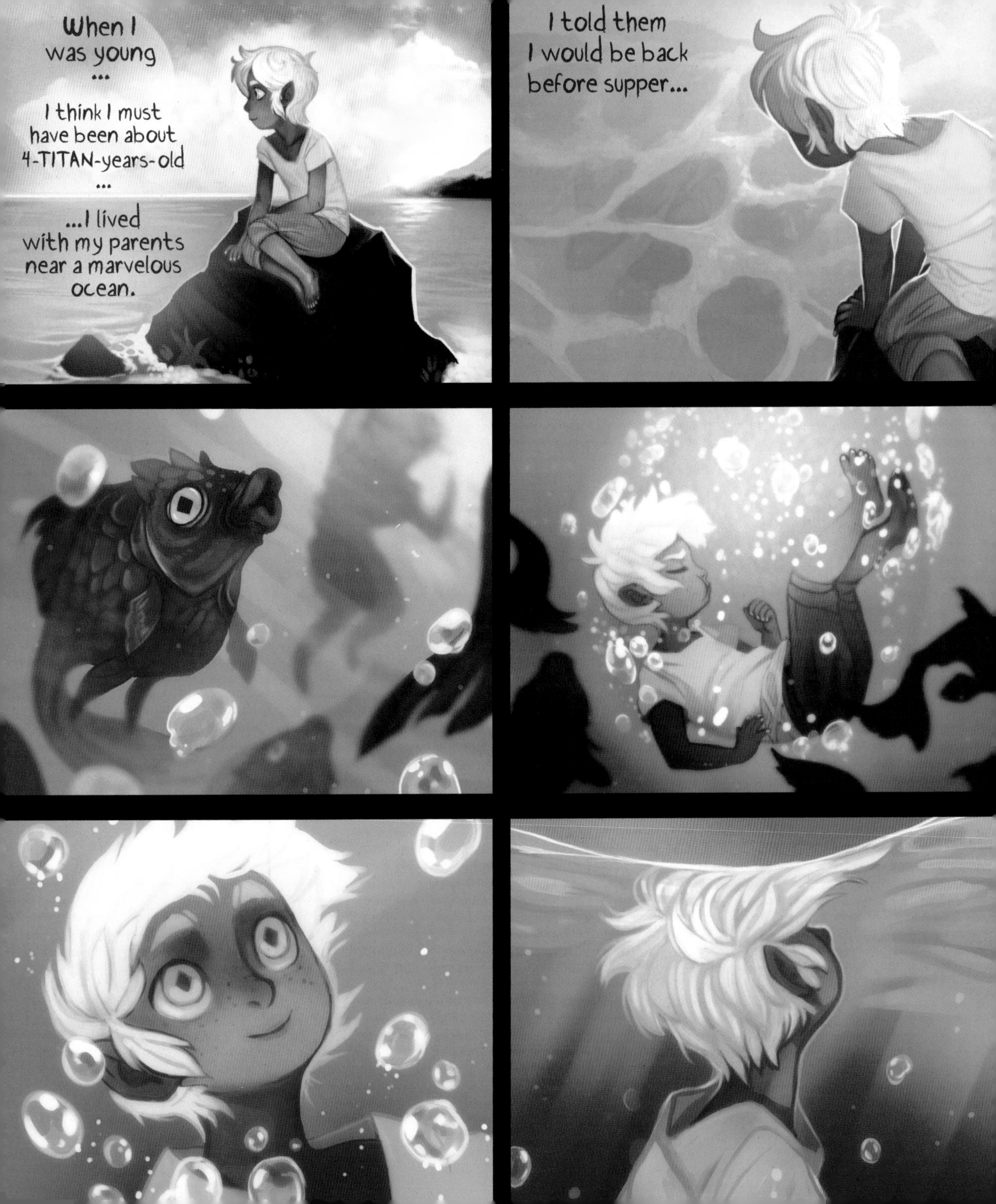
When I was young
...
I think I must have been about 4-TITAN-years-old
...
...I lived with my parents near a marvelous ocean.
I told them I would be back before supper...

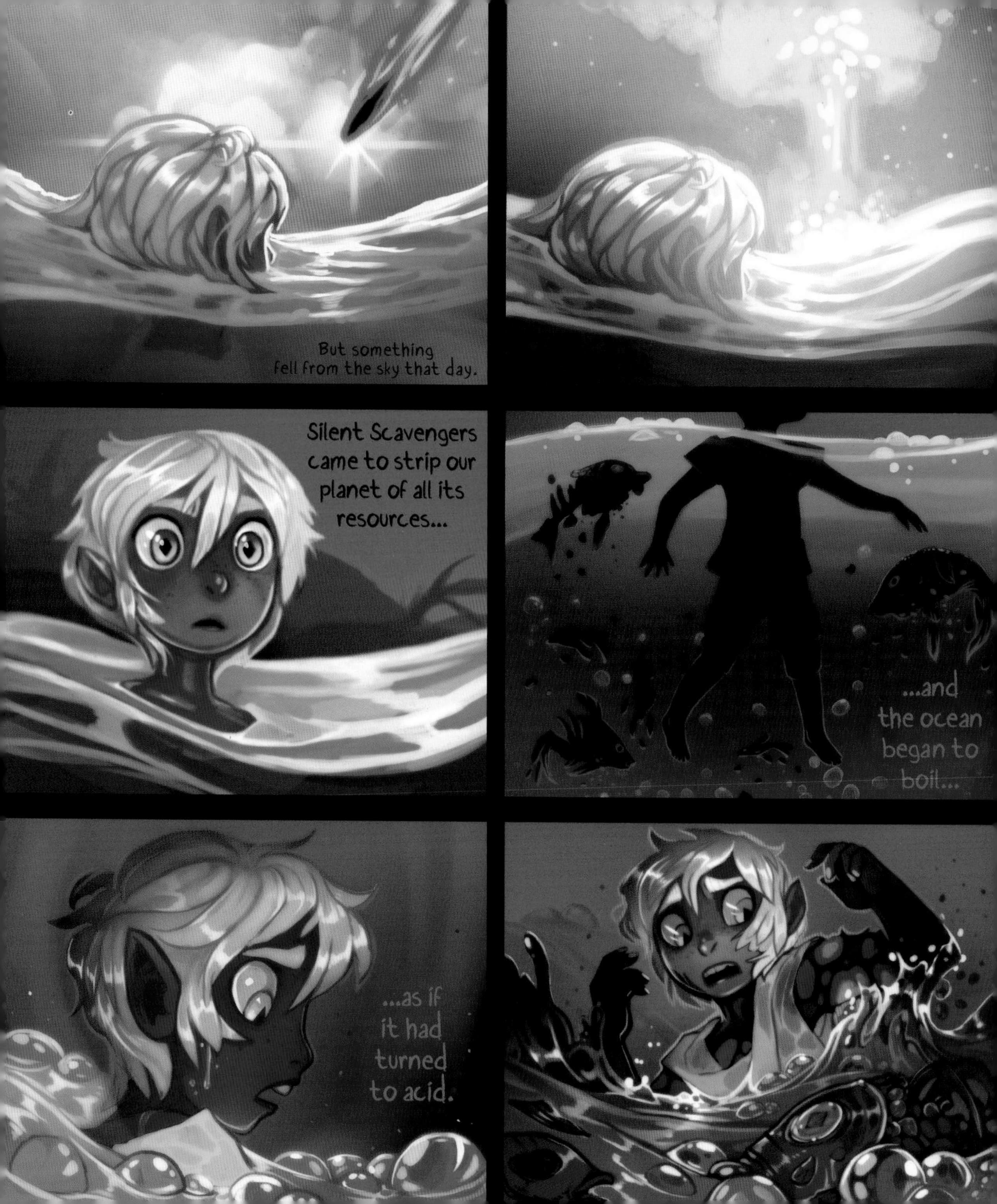
But something fell from the sky that day.
Silent Scavengers came to strip our planet of all its resources...
...and the ocean began to boil...
...as if it had turned to acid.

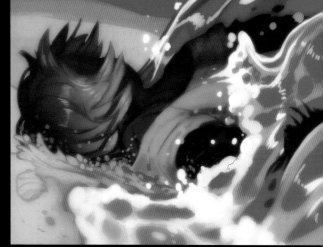

I died
that day.

I watched
myself as
I died.

I thought
it would
be the end
of me.

I was
wrong.

My whole world turned dark.

But it wasn't long before
I saw a light.

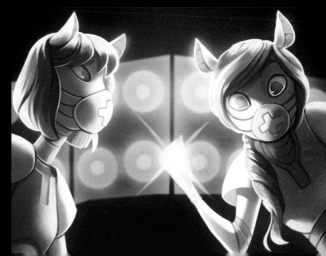

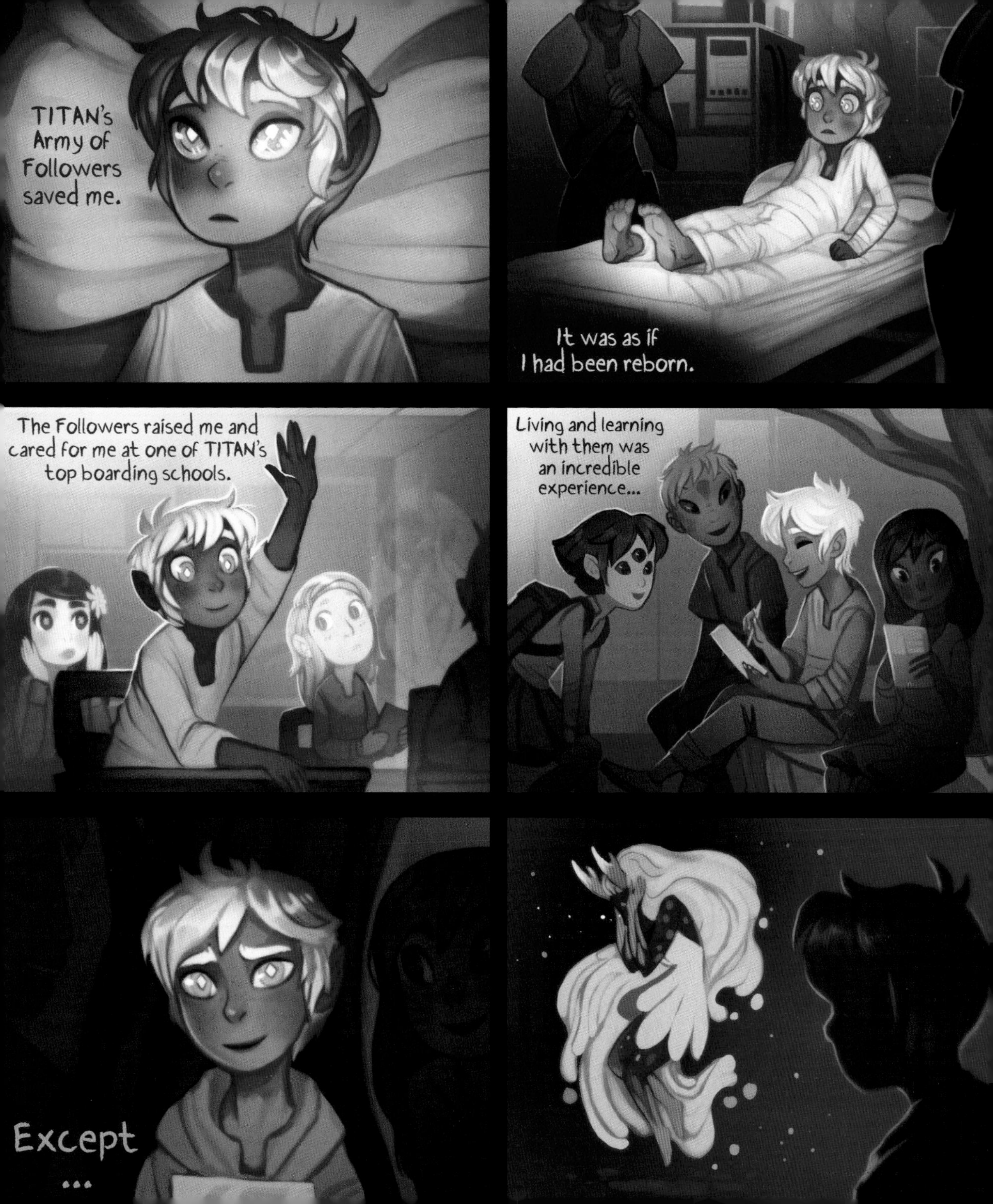
TITAN's Army of Followers saved me.
It was as if I had been reborn.
The Followers raised me and cared for me at one of TITAN's top boarding schools.
Living and learning with them was an incredible experience...
Except ...

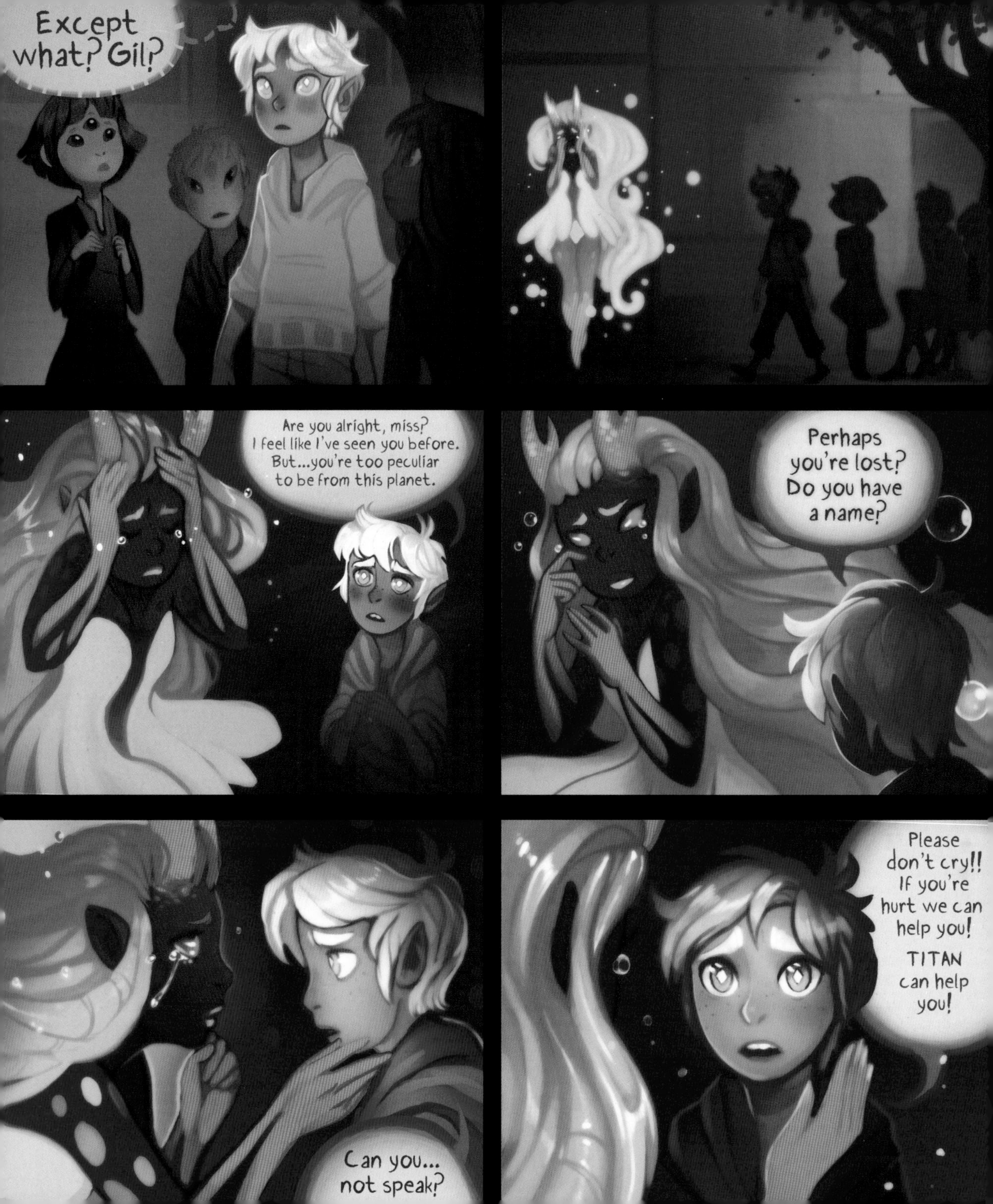
Except what? Gil?
Are you alright, miss? I feel like I've seen you before. But...you're too peculiar to be from this planet.
Perhaps you're lost? Do you have a name?
Can you... not speak?
Please don't cry!! If you're hurt we can help you!
TITAN can help you!

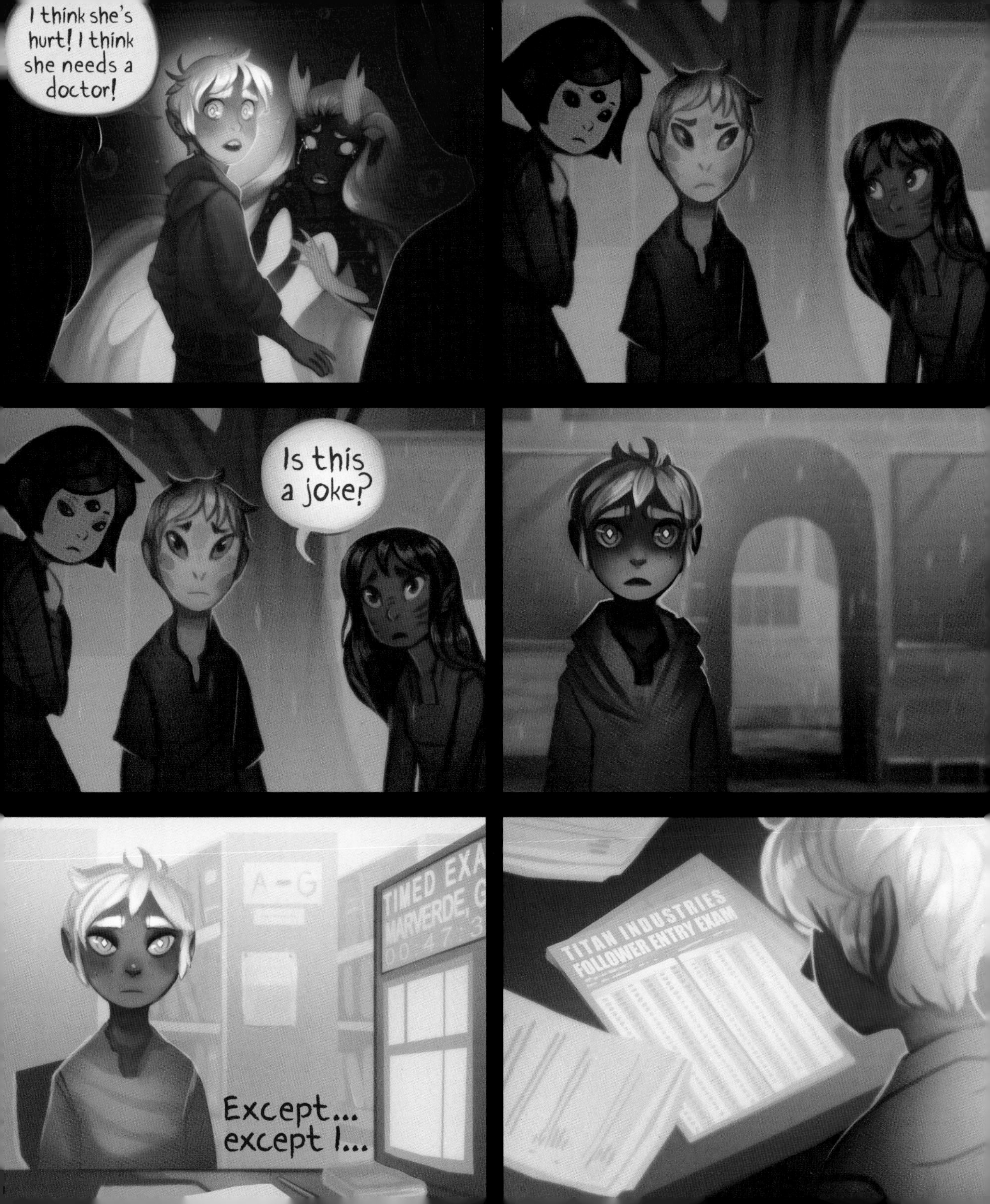
I think she's hurt! I think she needs a doctor!
Is this a joke?
TIMED EXA
MARVERDE, G
A–G
Except... except I...
TITAN INDUSTRIES
FOLLOWER ENTRY EXAM

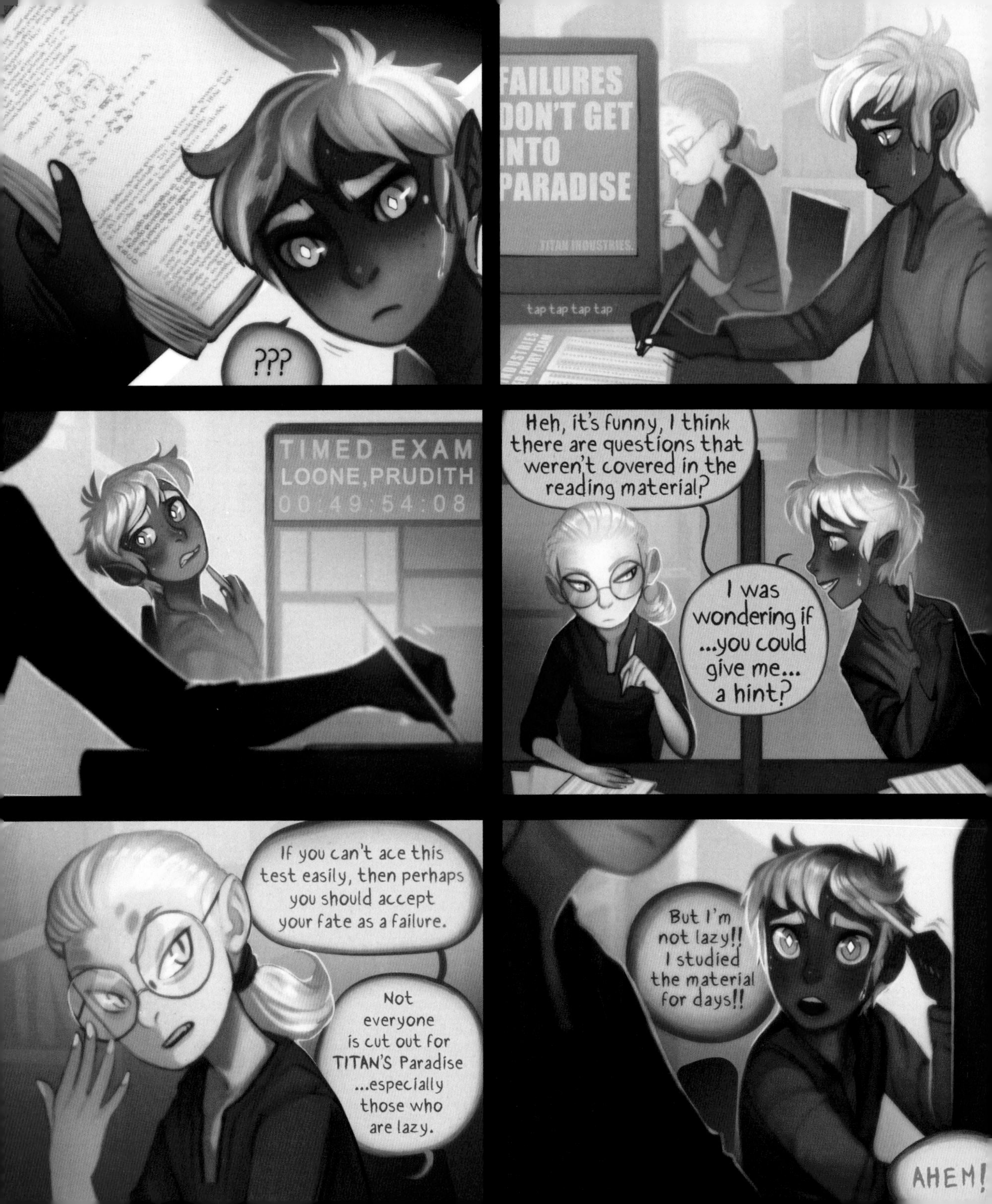
???
FAILURES DON'T GET INTO PARADISE
TITAN INDUSTRIES
tap tap tap tap
TIMED EXAM
LOONE,PRUDITH
00:49:54:08
Heh, it's funny, I think there are questions that weren't covered in the reading material?
I was wondering if ...you could give me... a hint?
If you can't ace this test easily, then perhaps you should accept your fate as a failure.
Not everyone is cut out for TITAN'S Paradise ...especially those who are lazy.
But I'm not lazy!! I studied the material for days!!
AHEM!

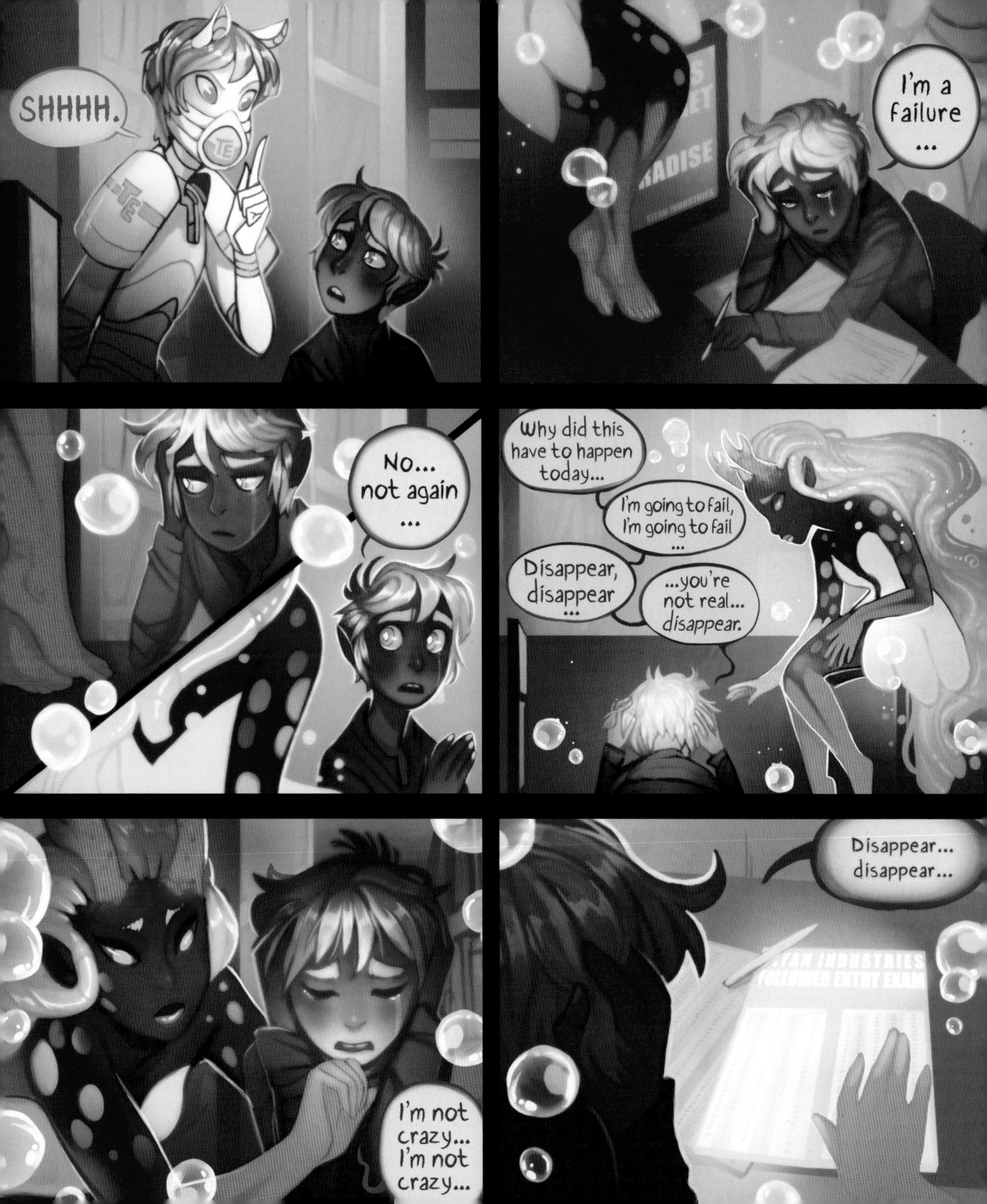
SHHHH.
I'm a failure ...
No... not again ...
Why did this have to happen today...
I'm going to fail, I'm going to fail ...
Disappear, disappear ...
...you're not real... disappear.
I'm not crazy... I'm not crazy...
Disappear... disappear...
TITAN INDUSTRIES FOLLOWER ENTRY EXAM

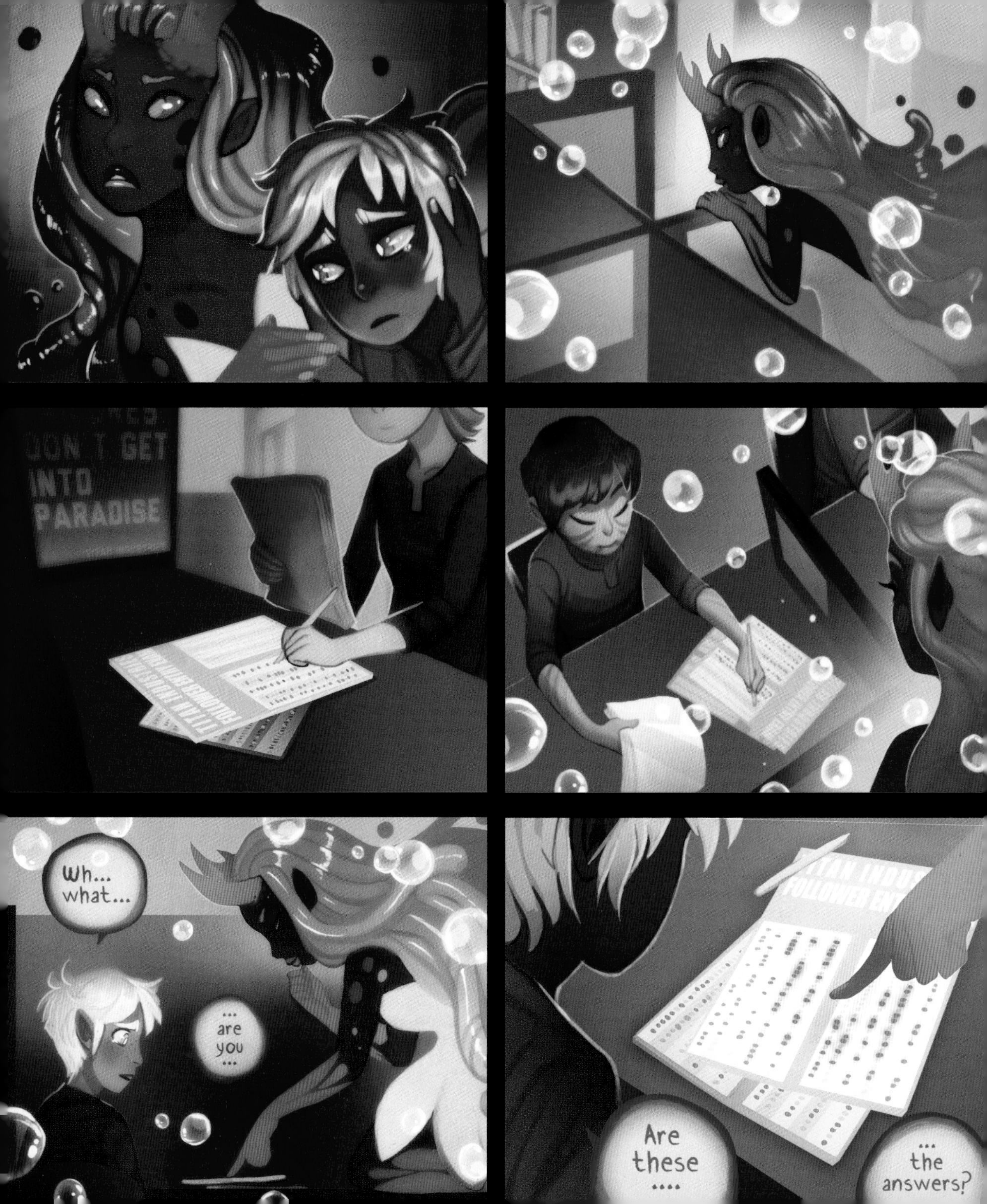
DON'T GET
INTO
PARADISE
Wh... what...
... are you ...
Are these ....
... the answers?

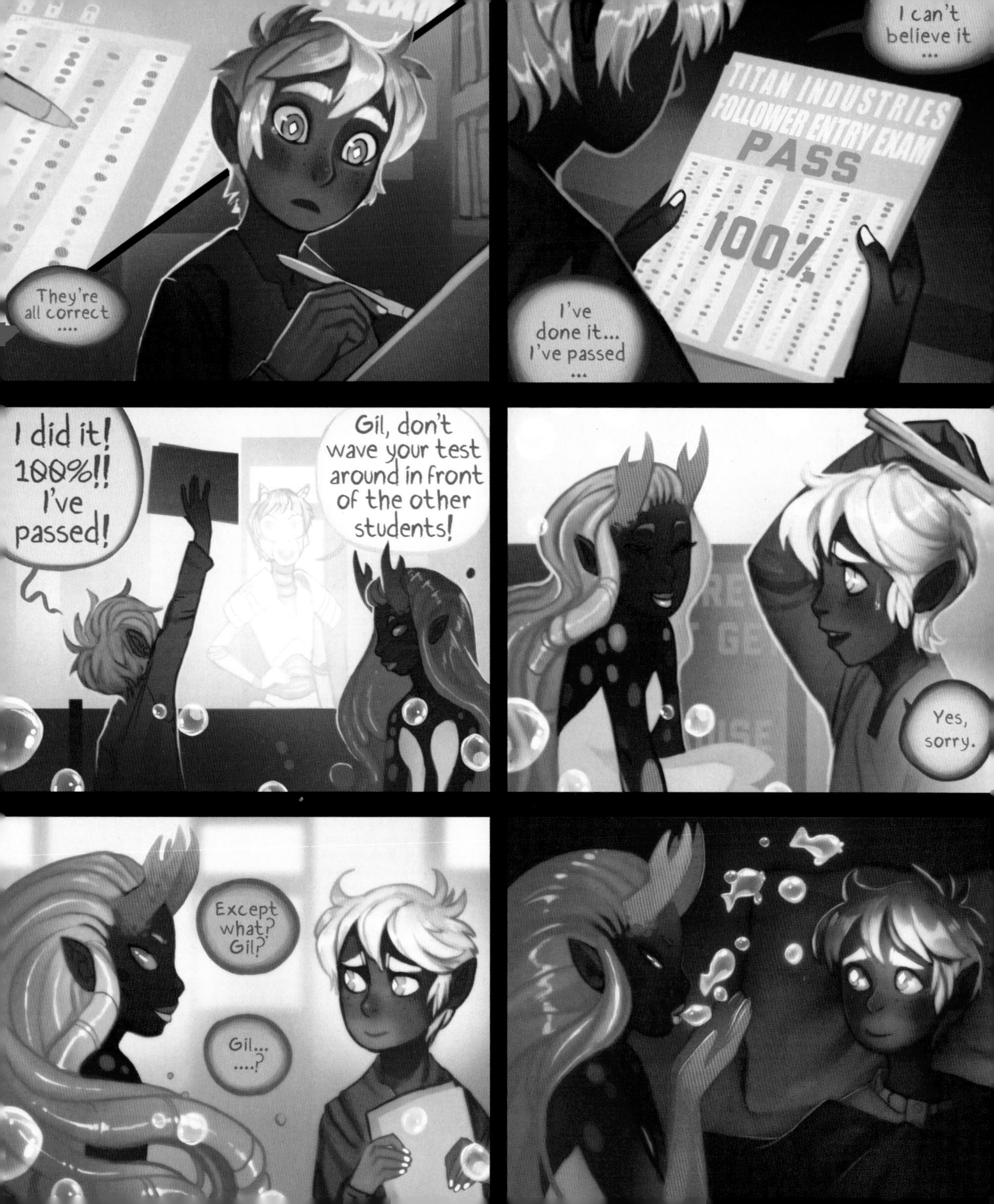
They're all correct ....
I can't believe it ...
TITAN INDUSTRIES FOLLOWER ENTRY EXAM
PASS
100%
I've done it... I've passed ...
I did it! 100%!! I've passed!
Gil, don't wave your test around in front of the other students!
Yes, sorry.
Except what? Gil?
Gil... ....?

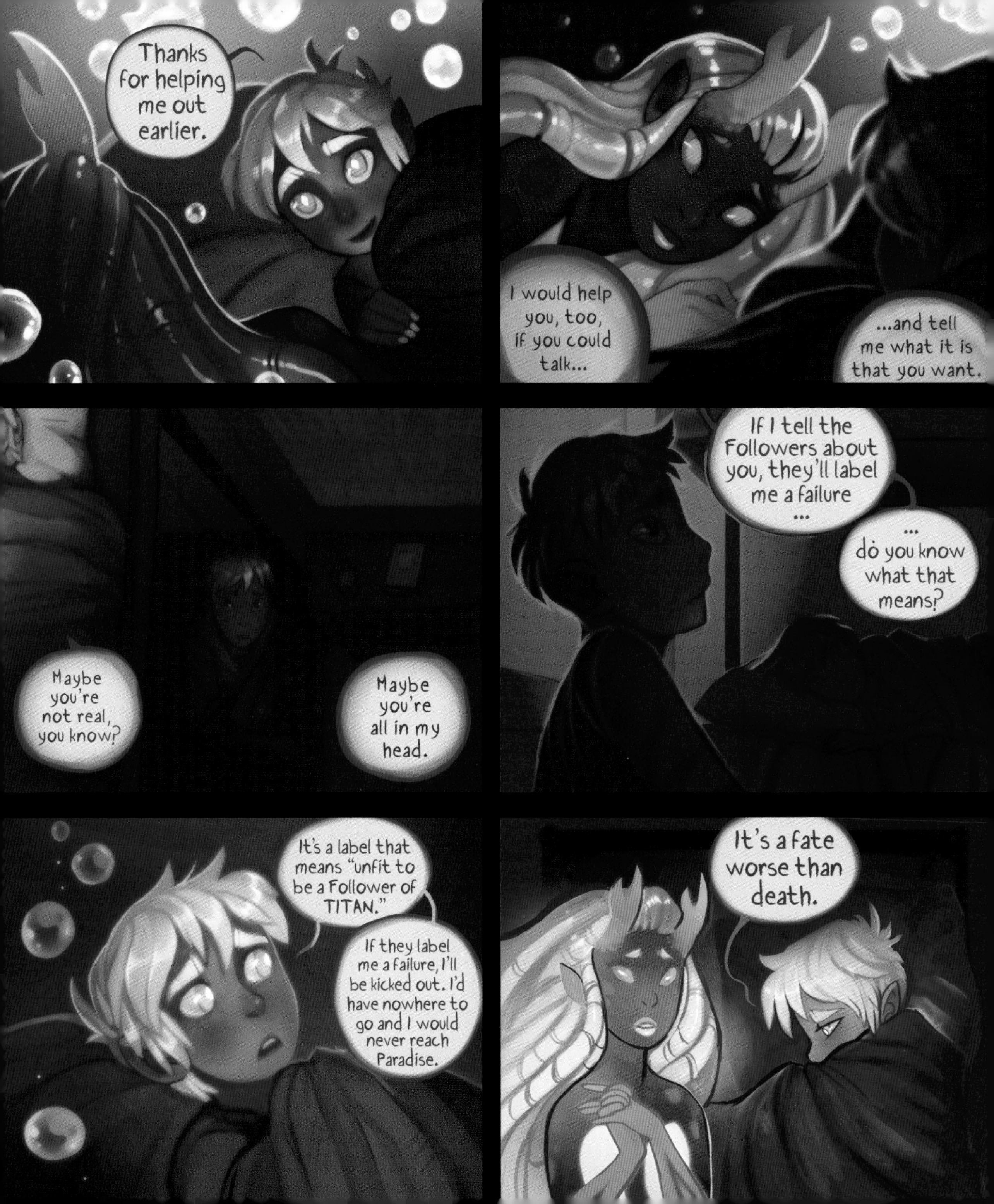
Thanks for helping me out earlier.
I would help you, too, if you could talk...
...and tell me what it is that you want.
Maybe you're not real, you know?
Maybe you're all in my head.
If I tell the Followers about you, they'll label me a failure ...
... do you know what that means?
It's a label that means "unfit to be a Follower of TITAN."
If they label me a failure, I'll be kicked out. I'd have nowhere to go and I would never reach Paradise.
It's a fate worse than death.

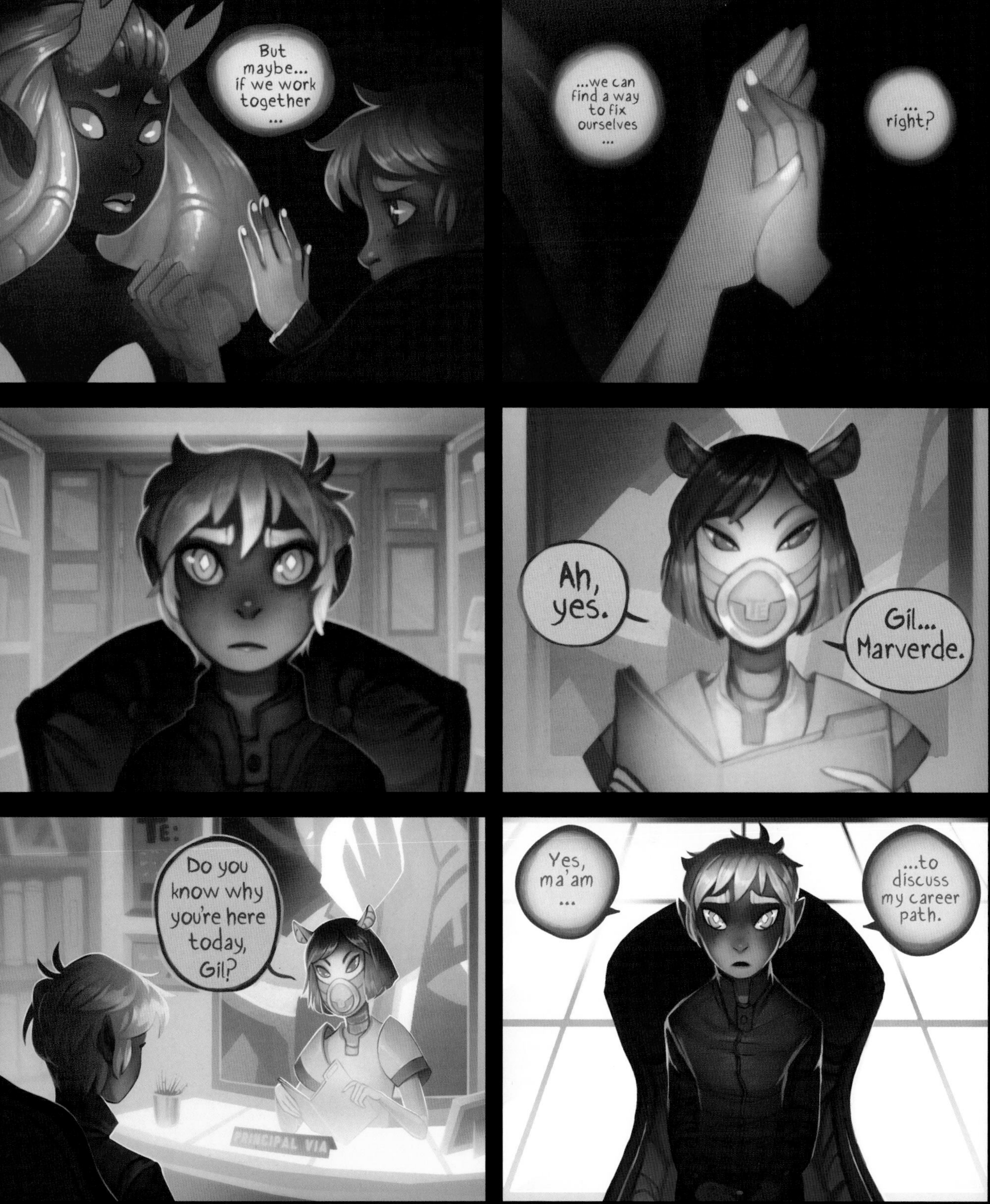
But maybe... if we work together ...
...we can find a way to fix ourselves ...
... right?
Ah, yes.
Gil... Marverde.
Do you know why you're here today, Gil?
PRINCIPAL VIA
Yes, ma'am ...
...to discuss my career path.

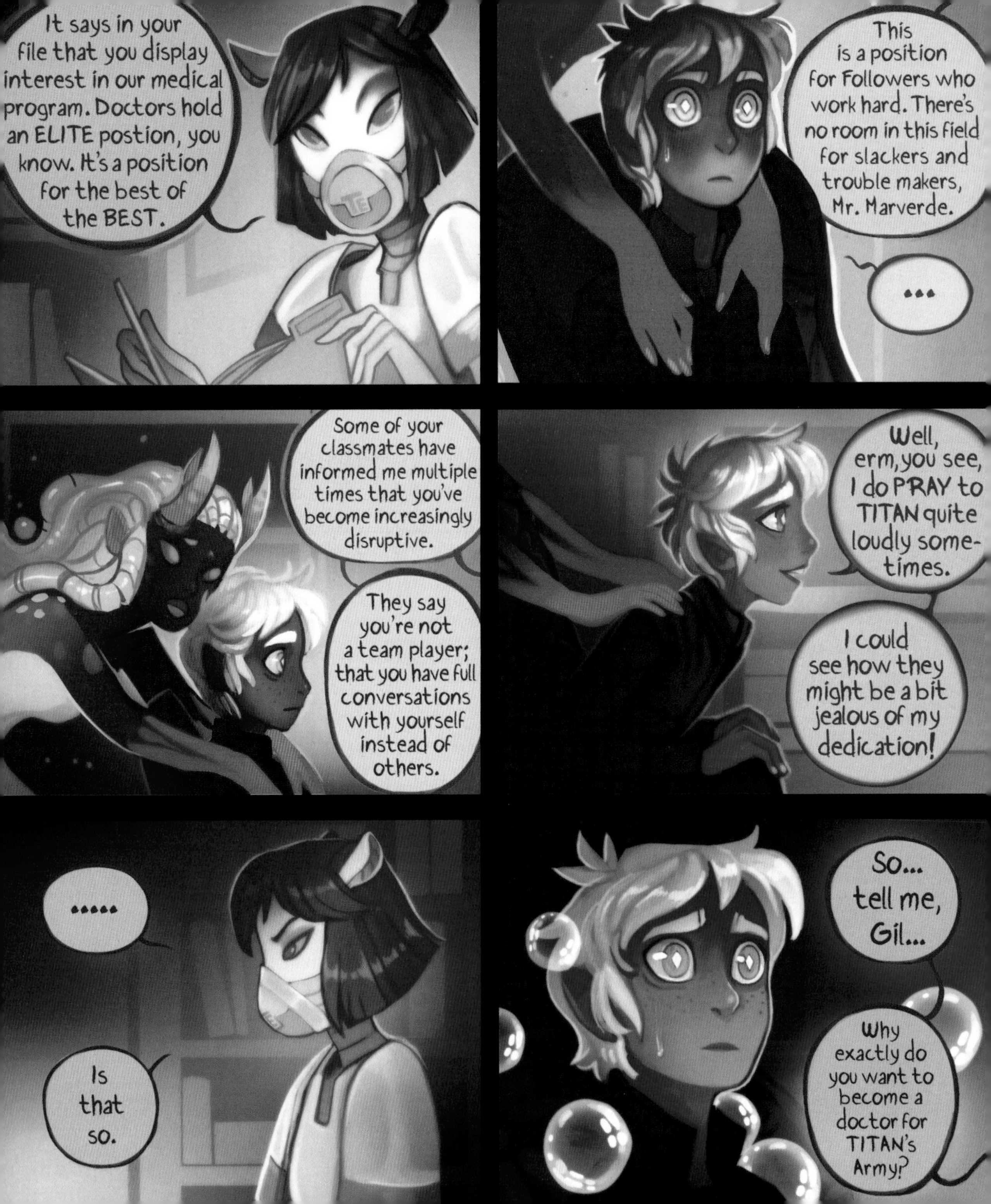
It says in your file that you display interest in our medical program. Doctors hold an ELITE postion, you know. It's a position for the best of the BEST.
This is a position for Followers who work hard. There's no room in this field for slackers and trouble makers, Mr. Marverde.
...
Some of your classmates have informed me multiple times that you've become increasingly disruptive.
They say you're not a team player; that you have full conversations with yourself instead of others.
Well, erm, you see, I do PRAY to TITAN quite loudly some-times.
I could see how they might be a bit jealous of my dedication!
.....
Is that so.
So... tell me, Gil...
Why exactly do you want to become a doctor for TITAN's Army?

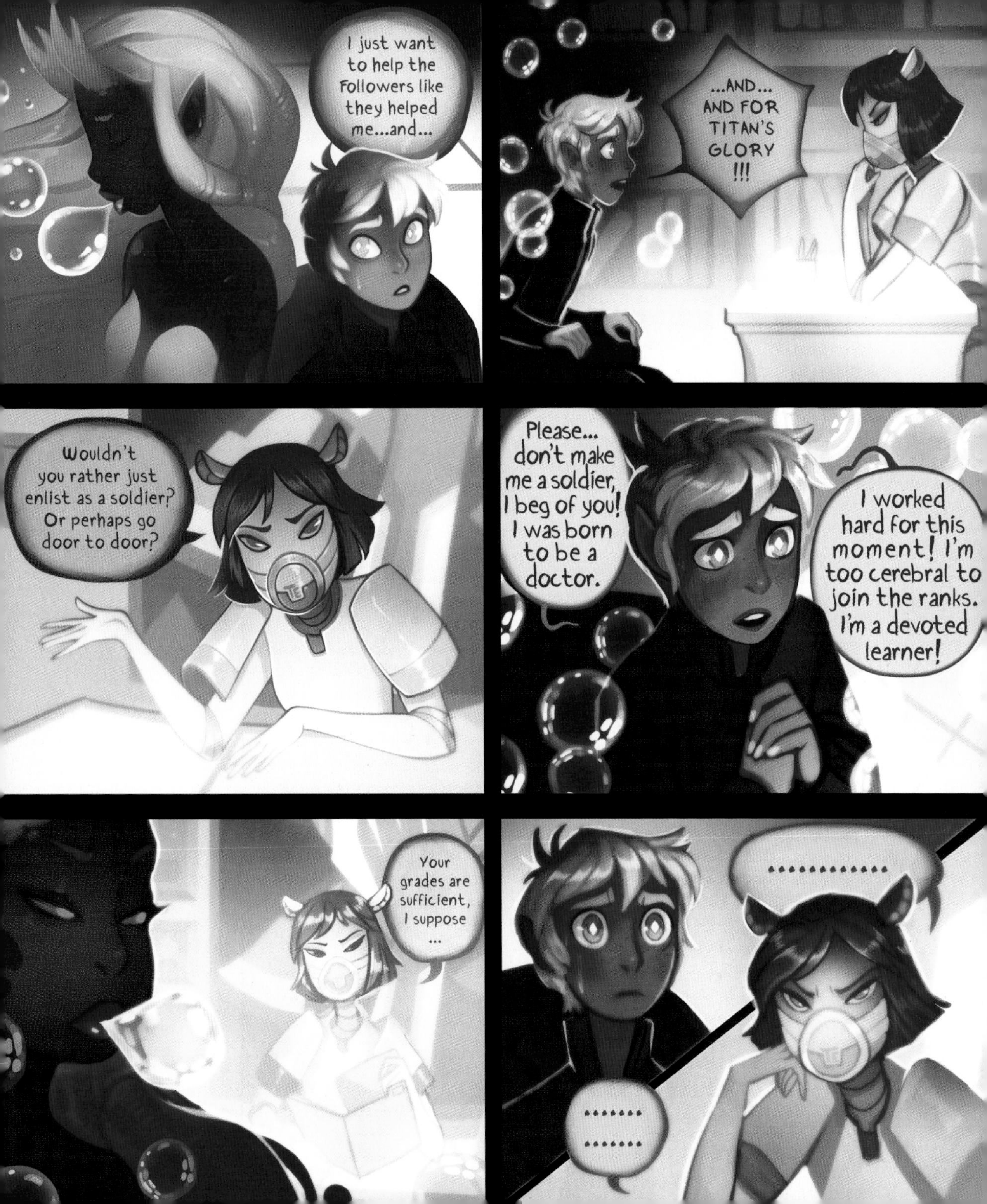
I just want to help the Followers like they helped me...and...
...AND... AND FOR TITAN'S GLORY !!!
Wouldn't you rather just enlist as a soldier? Or perhaps go door to door?
Please... don't make me a soldier, I beg of you! I was born to be a doctor.
I worked hard for this moment! I'm too cerebral to join the ranks. I'm a devoted learner!
Your grades are sufficient, I suppose ...
....
......
......

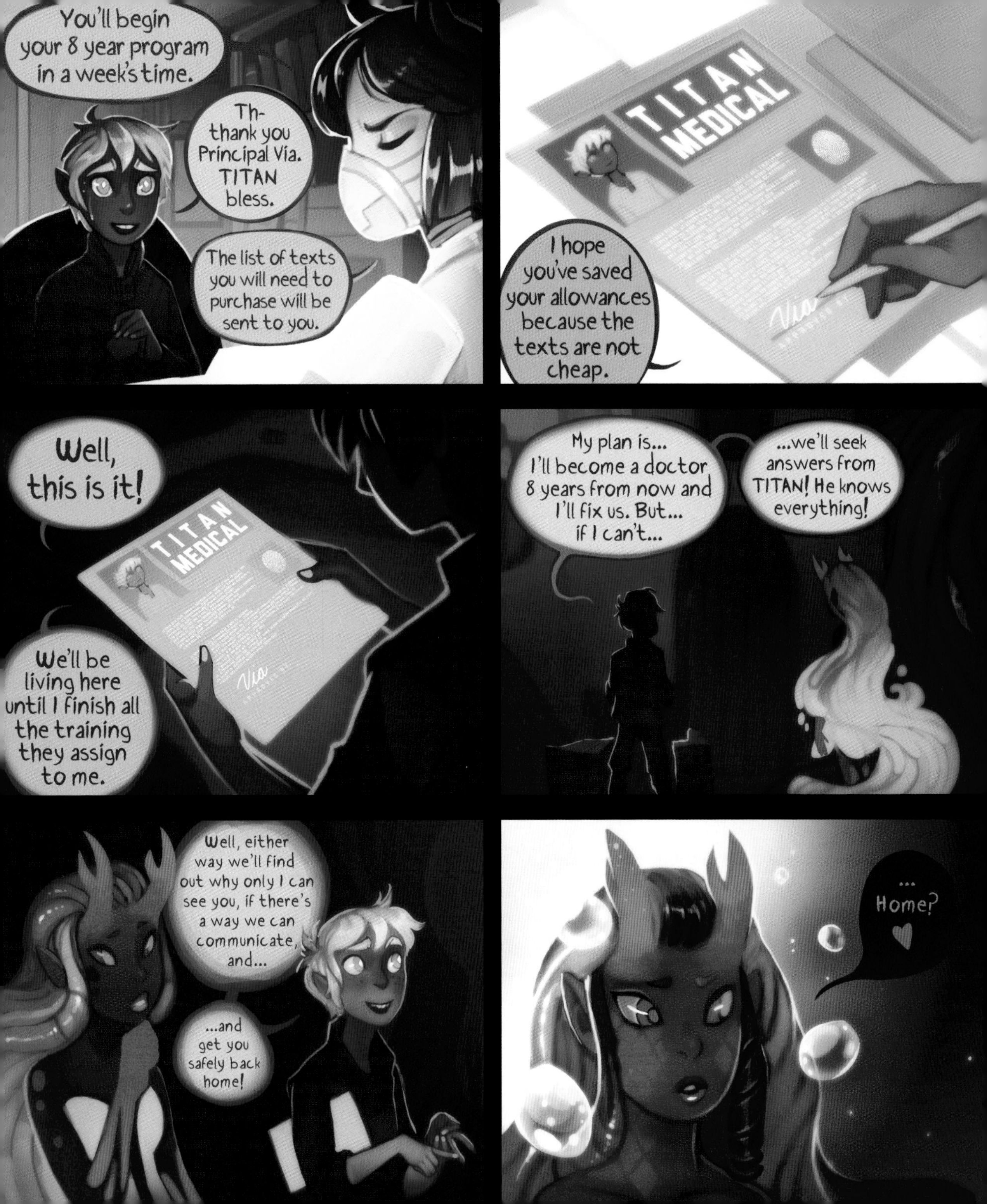
You'll begin your 8 year program in a week's time.
Th- thank you Principal Via. TITAN bless.
The list of texts you will need to purchase will be sent to you.
TITAN MEDICAL
I hope you've saved your allowances because the texts are not cheap.
Well, this is it!
TITAN MEDICAL
We'll be living here until I finish all the training they assign to me.
My plan is... I'll become a doctor 8 years from now and I'll fix us. But... if I can't...
...we'll seek answers from TITAN! He knows everything!
Well, either way we'll find out why only I can see you, if there's a way we can communicate, and...
...and get you safely back home!
... Home?

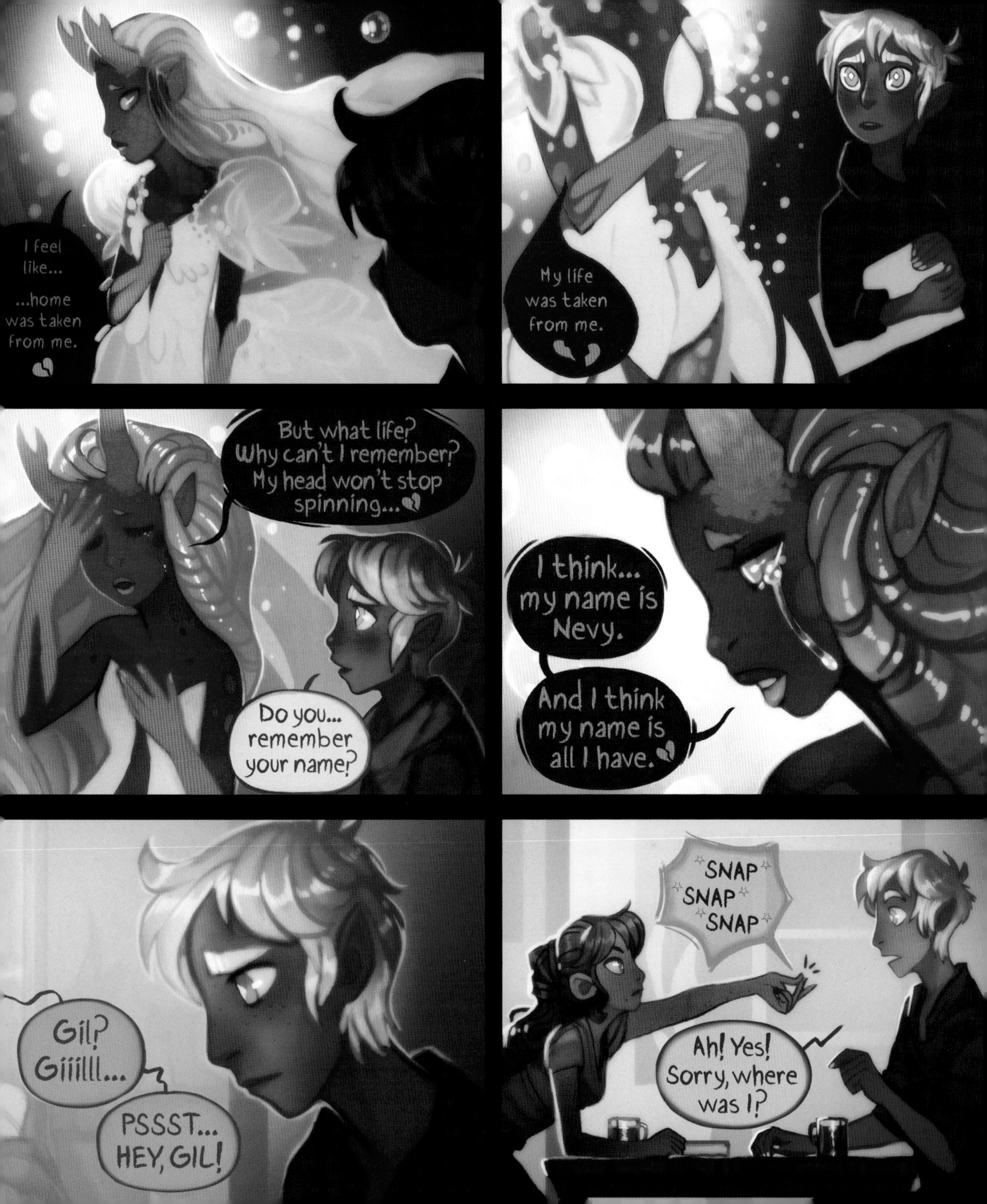
I feel like...
...home was taken from me.
My life was taken from me.
But what life? Why can't I remember? My head won't stop spinning...
Do you... remember your name?
I think... my name is Nevy.
And I think my name is all I have.
Gil? Giiilll...
PSSST... HEY, GIL!
SNAP SNAP SNAP
Ah! Yes! Sorry, where was I?

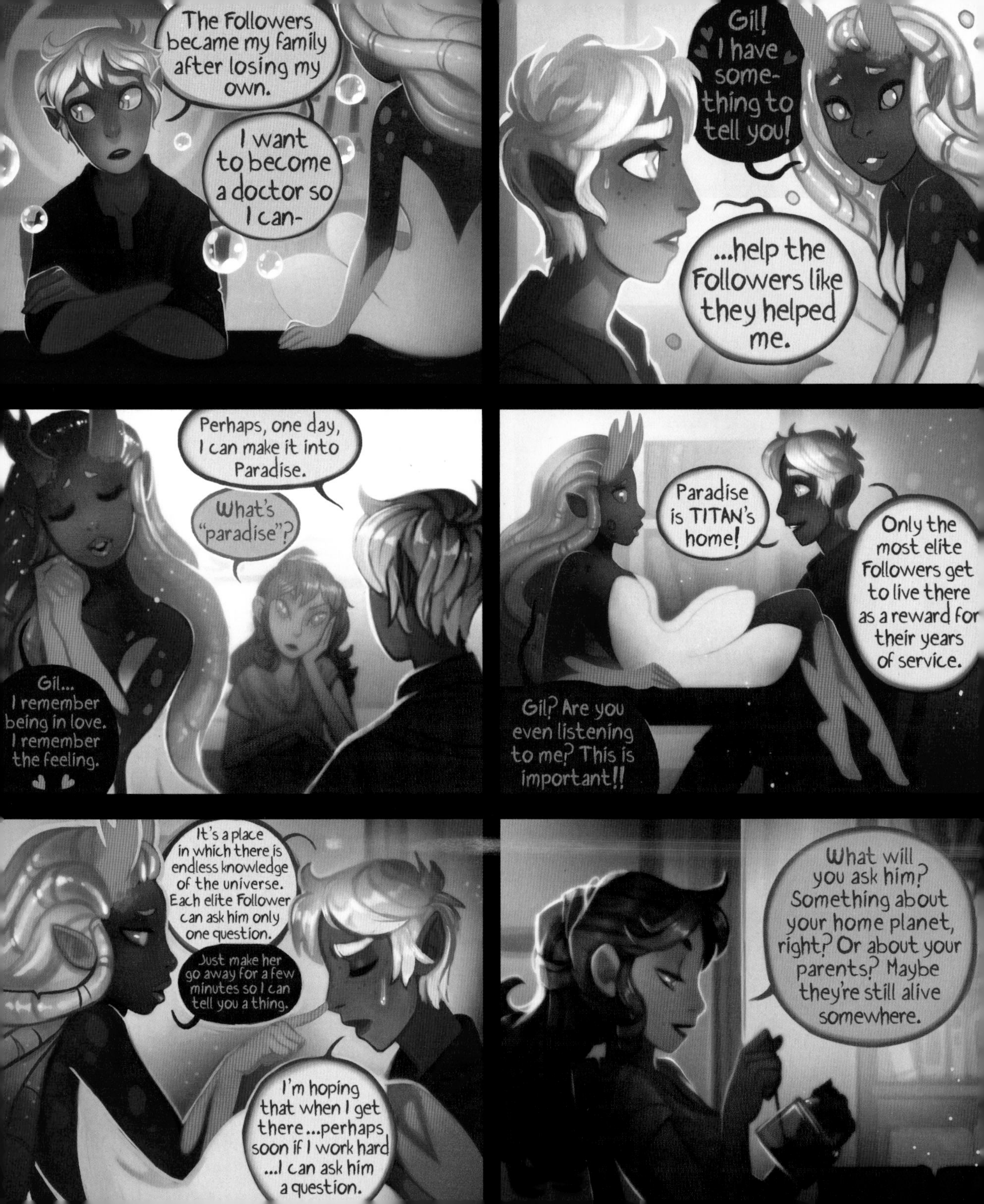
The Followers became my family after losing my own.
I want to become a doctor so I can-
Gil! I have something to tell you!
...help the Followers like they helped me.
Perhaps, one day, I can make it into Paradise.
What's "paradise"?
Gil... I remember being in love. I remember the feeling.
Paradise is TITAN's home!
Only the most elite Followers get to live there as a reward for their years of service.
Gil? Are you even listening to me? This is important!!
It's a place in which there is endless knowledge of the universe. Each elite Follower can ask him only one question.
Just make her go away for a few minutes so I can tell you a thing.
I'm hoping that when I get there...perhaps soon if I work hard ...I can ask him a question.
What will you ask him? Something about your home planet, right? Or about your parents? Maybe they're still alive somewhere.

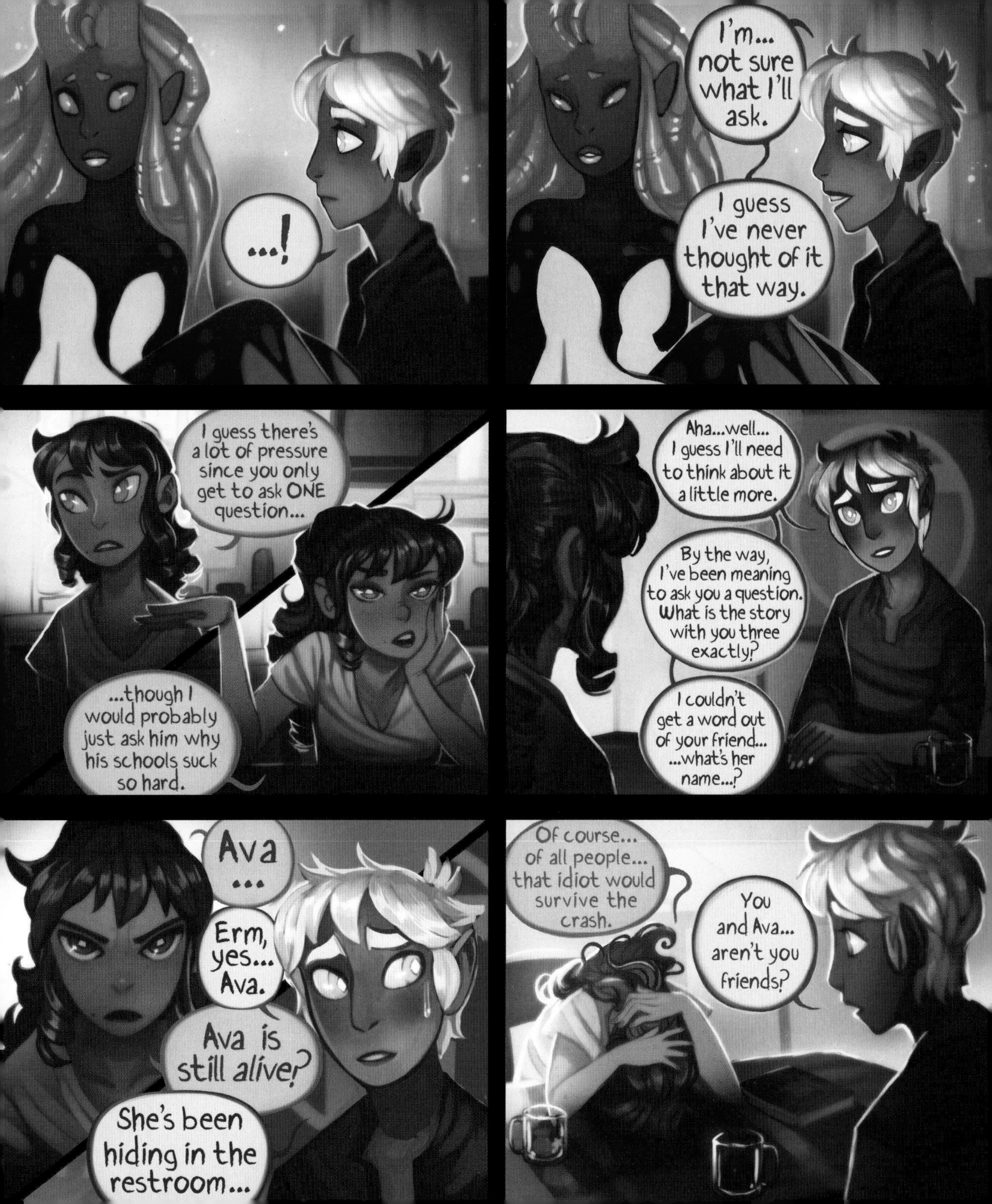
...!
I'm... not sure what I'll ask.
I guess I've never thought of it that way.
I guess there's a lot of pressure since you only get to ask ONE question...
...though I would probably just ask him why his schools suck so hard.
Aha...well... I guess I'll need to think about it a little more.
By the way, I've been meaning to ask you a question. What is the story with you three exactly?
I couldn't get a word out of your friend... ...what's her name...?
Ava...
Erm, yes... Ava.
Ava is still alive?
She's been hiding in the restroom...
Of course... of all people... that idiot would survive the crash.
You and Ava... aren't you friends?

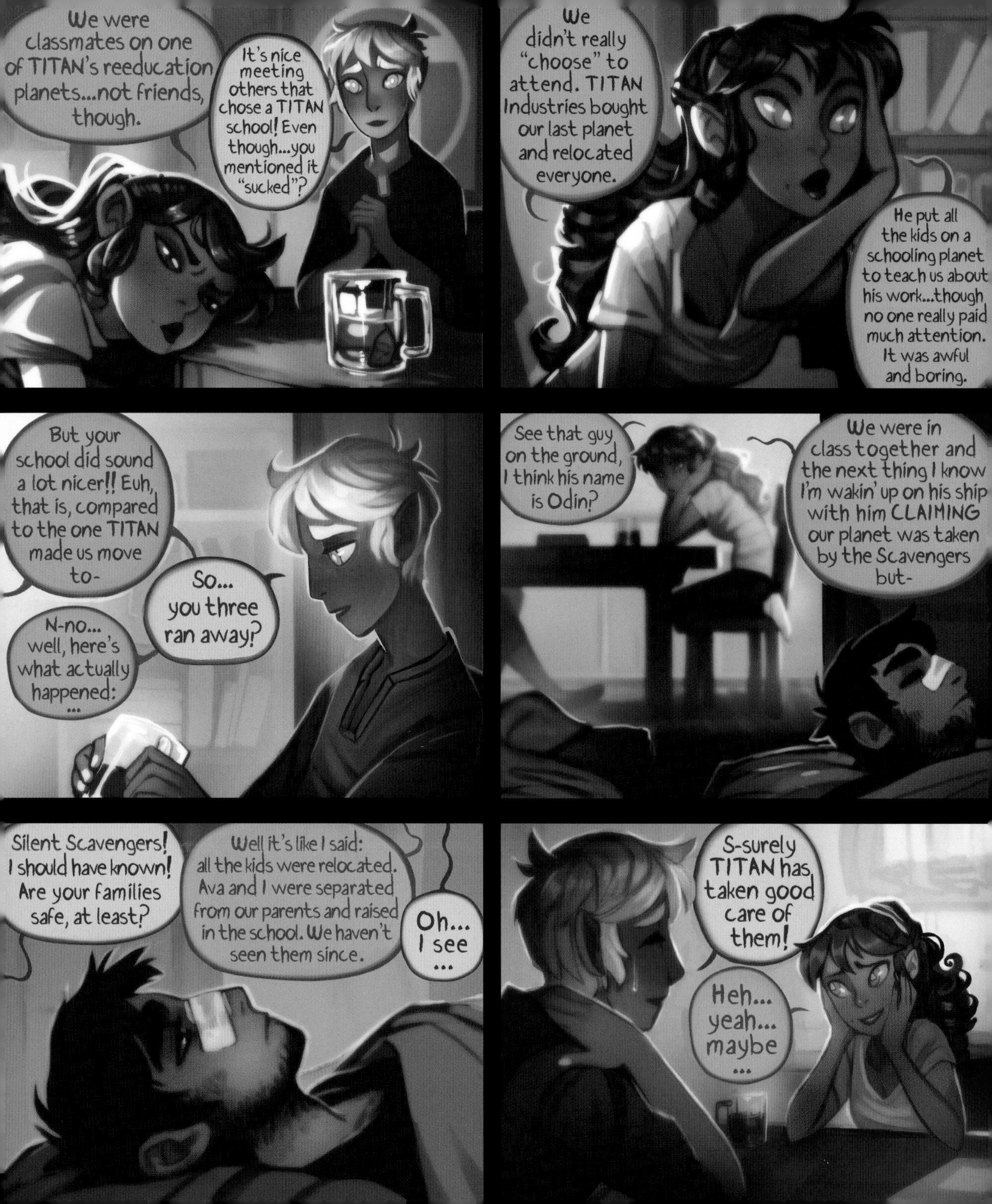
We were classmates on one of TITAN's reeducation planets...not friends, though.
It's nice meeting others that chose a TITAN school! Even though...you mentioned it "sucked"?
We didn't really "choose" to attend. TITAN Industries bought our last planet and relocated everyone.
He put all the kids on a schooling planet to teach us about his work...though no one really paid much attention. It was awful and boring.
But your school did sound a lot nicer!! Euh, that is, compared to the one TITAN made us move to-
So... you three ran away?
N-no... well, here's what actually happened: ...
See that guy on the ground, I think his name is Odin?
We were in class together and the next thing I know I'm wakin' up on his ship with him CLAIMING our planet was taken by the Scavengers but-
Silent Scavengers! I should have known! Are your families safe, at least?
Well it's like I said: all the kids were relocated. Ava and I were separated from our parents and raised in the school. We haven't seen them since.
Oh... I see ...
S-surely TITAN has taken good care of them!
Heh... yeah... maybe ...

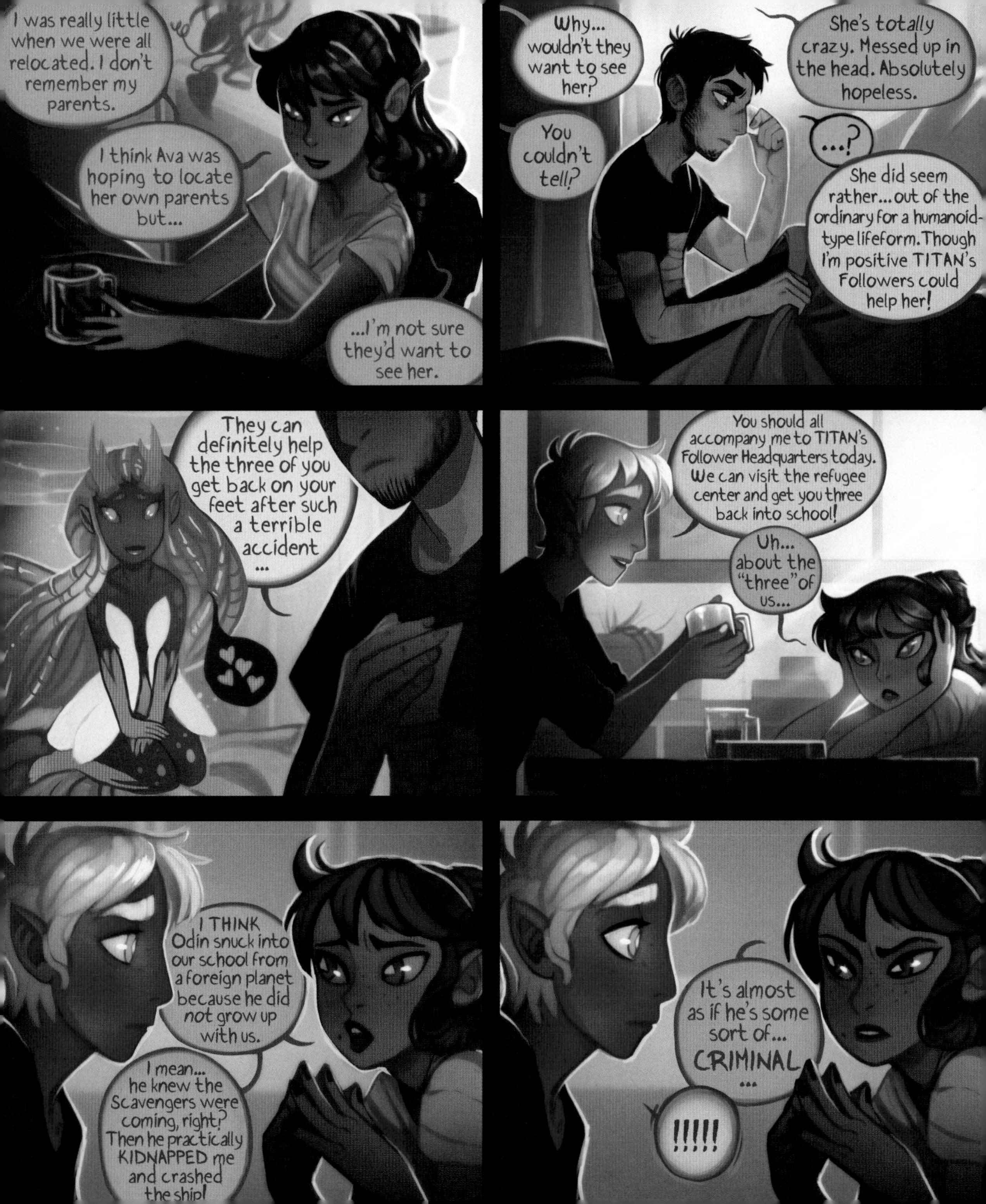
I was really little when we were all relocated. I don't remember my parents.
I think Ava was hoping to locate her own parents but...
...I'm not sure they'd want to see her.
Why... wouldn't they want to see her?
You couldn't tell?
She's totally crazy. Messed up in the head. Absolutely hopeless.
...?
She did seem rather... out of the ordinary for a humanoid-type lifeform. Though I'm positive TITAN's Followers could help her!
They can definitely help the three of you get back on your feet after such a terrible accident ...
You should all accompany me to TITAN's Follower Headquarters today. We can visit the refugee center and get you three back into school!
Uh... about the "three" of us...
I THINK Odin snuck into our school from a foreign planet because he did not grow up with us.
I mean... he knew the Scavengers were coming, right? Then he practically KIDNAPPED me and crashed the ship!
It's almost as if he's some sort of... CRIMINAL ...
!!!!!

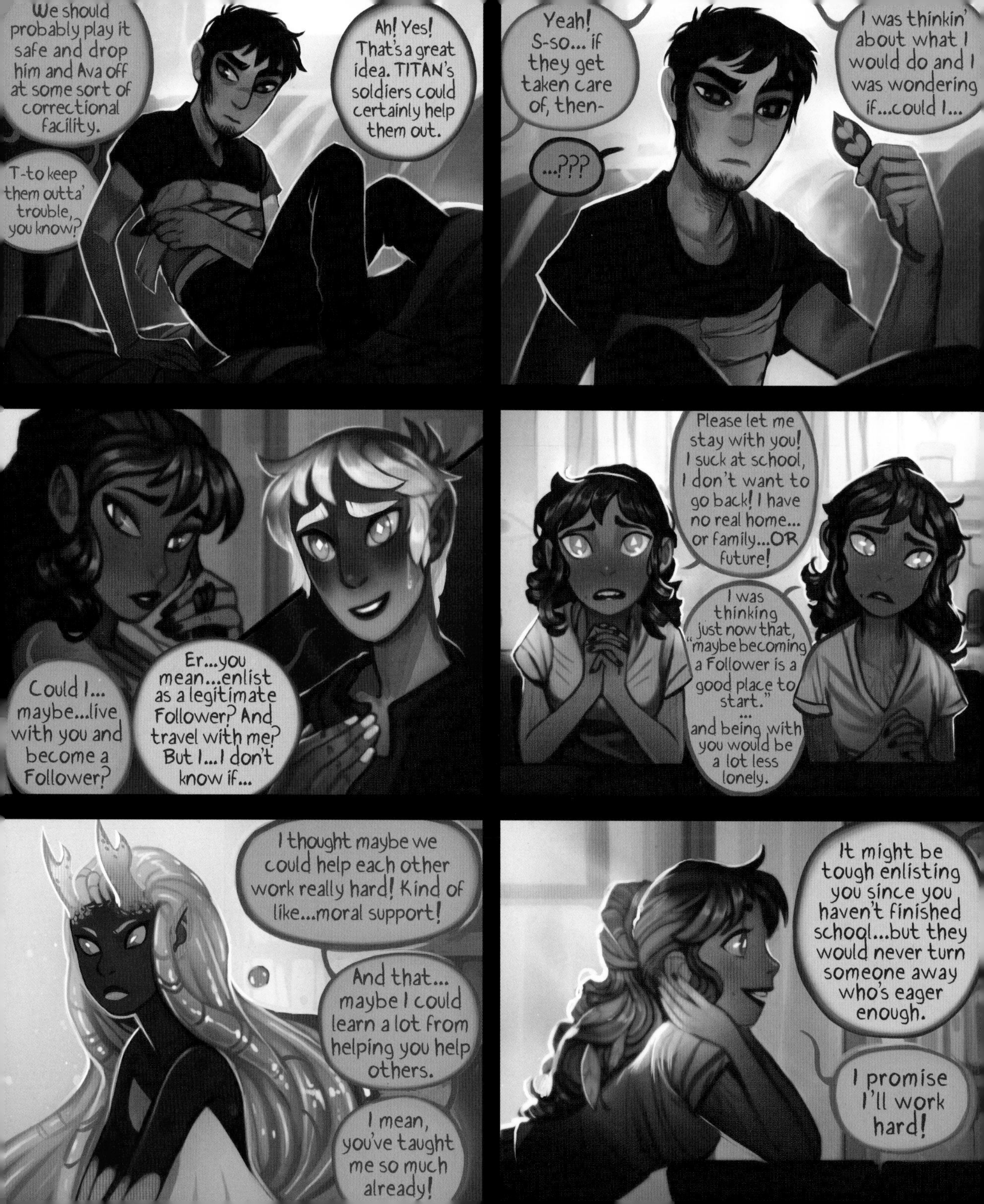
We should probably play it safe and drop him and Ava off at some sort of correctional facility.
T-to keep them outta' trouble, you know?
Ah! Yes! That's a great idea. TITAN's soldiers could certainly help them out.
Yeah! S-so... if they get taken care of, then-
...???
I was thinkin' about what I would do and I was wondering if...could I...
Could I... maybe...live with you and become a Follower?
Er...you mean...enlist as a legitimate Follower? And travel with me? But I...I don't know if...
Please let me stay with you! I suck at school, I don't want to go back! I have no real home... or family...OR future!
I was thinking just now that, "maybe becoming a Follower is a good place to start." ... and being with you would be a lot less lonely.
I thought maybe we could help each other work really hard! Kind of like...moral support!
And that... maybe I could learn a lot from helping you help others.
I mean, you've taught me so much already!
It might be tough enlisting you since you haven't finished school...but they would never turn someone away who's eager enough.
I promise I'll work hard!

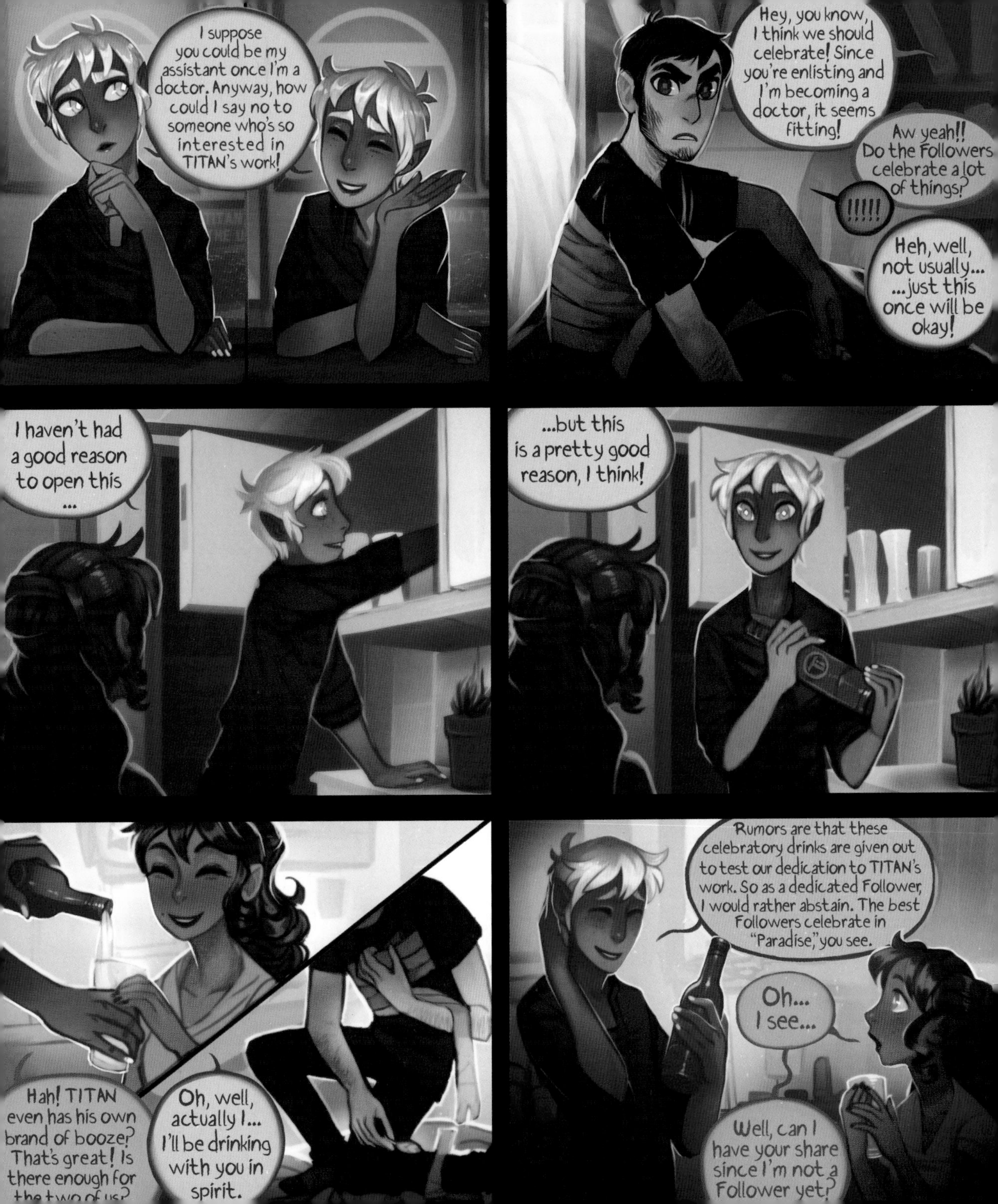
I suppose you could be my assistant once I'm a doctor. Anyway, how could I say no to someone who's so interested in TITAN's work!
Hey, you know, I think we should celebrate! Since you're enlisting and I'm becoming a doctor, it seems fitting!
Aw yeah!! Do the Followers celebrate a lot of things?
!!!!!
Heh, well, not usually... ...just this once will be okay!
I haven't had a good reason to open this ...
...but this is a pretty good reason, I think!
Hah! TITAN even has his own brand of booze? That's great! Is there enough for the two of us?
Oh, well, actually I... I'll be drinking with you in spirit.
Rumors are that these celebratory drinks are given out to test our dedication to TITAN's work. So as a dedicated Follower, I would rather abstain. The best Followers celebrate in "Paradise," you see.
Oh... I see...
Well, can I have your share since I'm not a Follower yet?

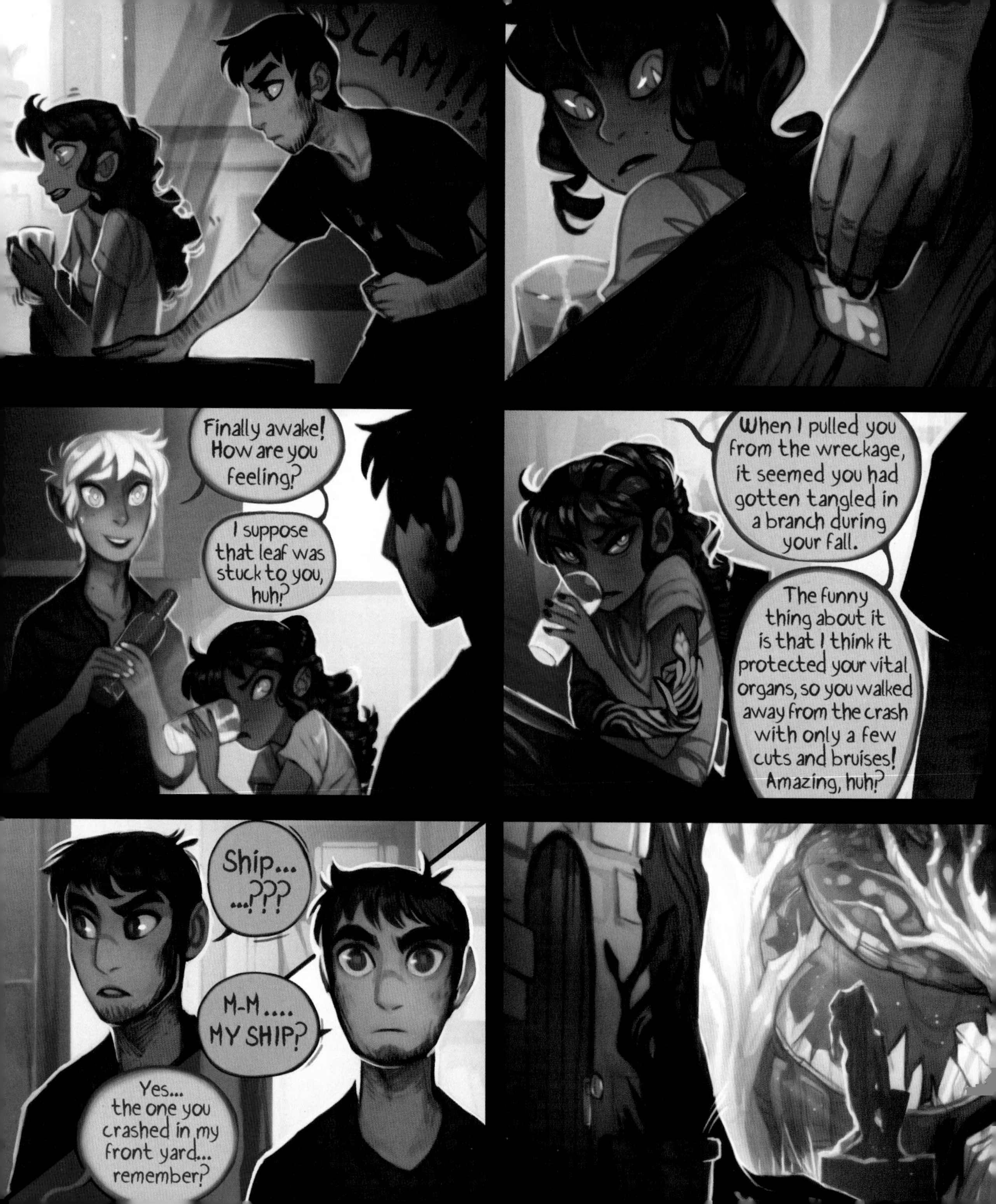
SLAM!!
Finally awake! How are you feeling?
I suppose that leaf was stuck to you, huh?
When I pulled you from the wreckage, it seemed you had gotten tangled in a branch during your fall.
The funny thing about it is that I think it protected your vital organs, so you walked away from the crash with only a few cuts and bruises! Amazing, huh?
Ship... ...???
M-M.... MY SHIP?
Yes... the one you crashed in my front yard... remember?

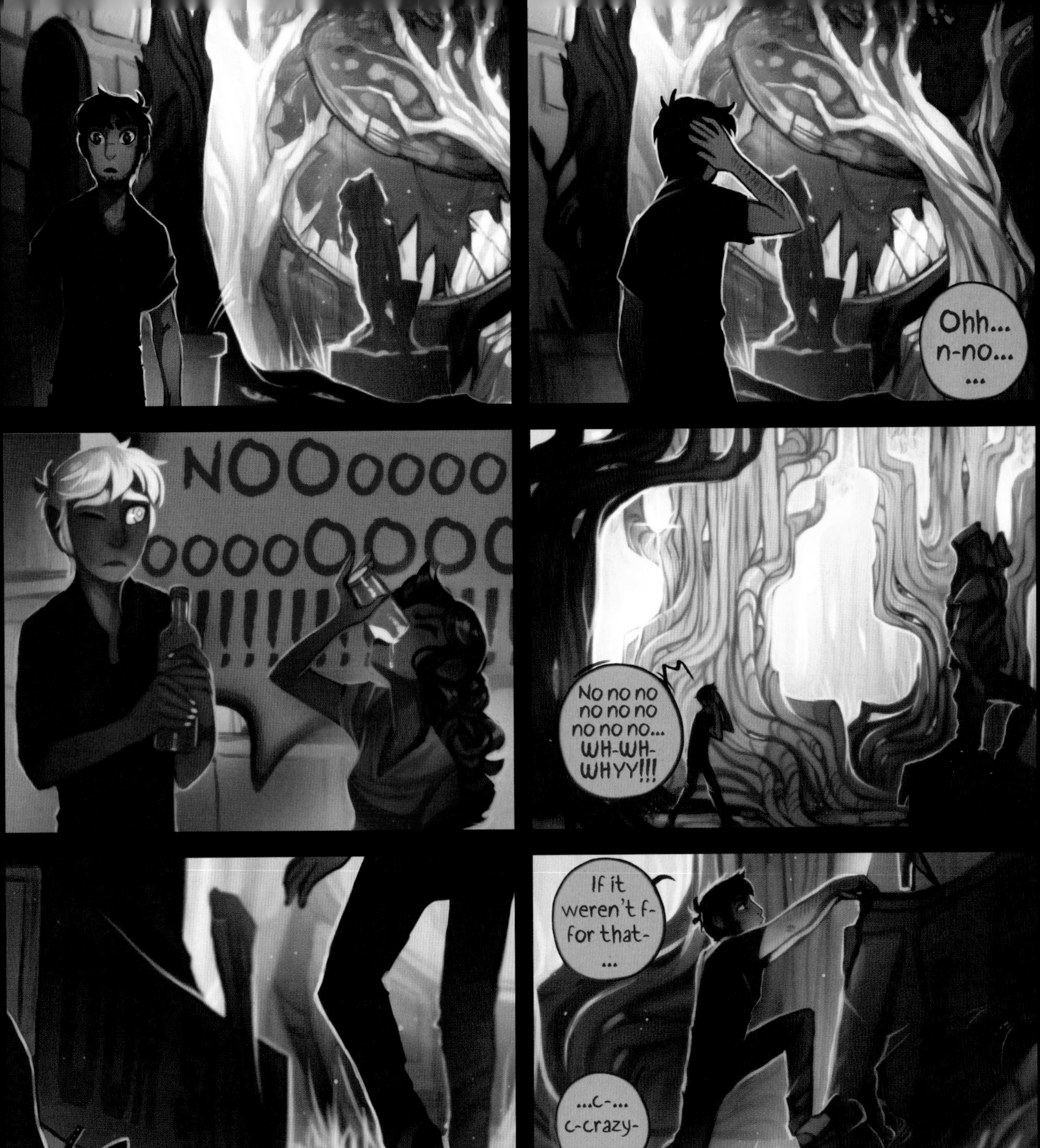
Ohh...
n-no...
...
NOOoooo
ooooOOOO
!!!!!!!!!
No no no
no no no
no no no...
WH-WH-
WHYY!!!
If it
weren't f-
for that-
...
...c-...
c-crazy-
...

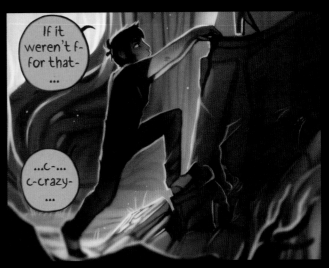

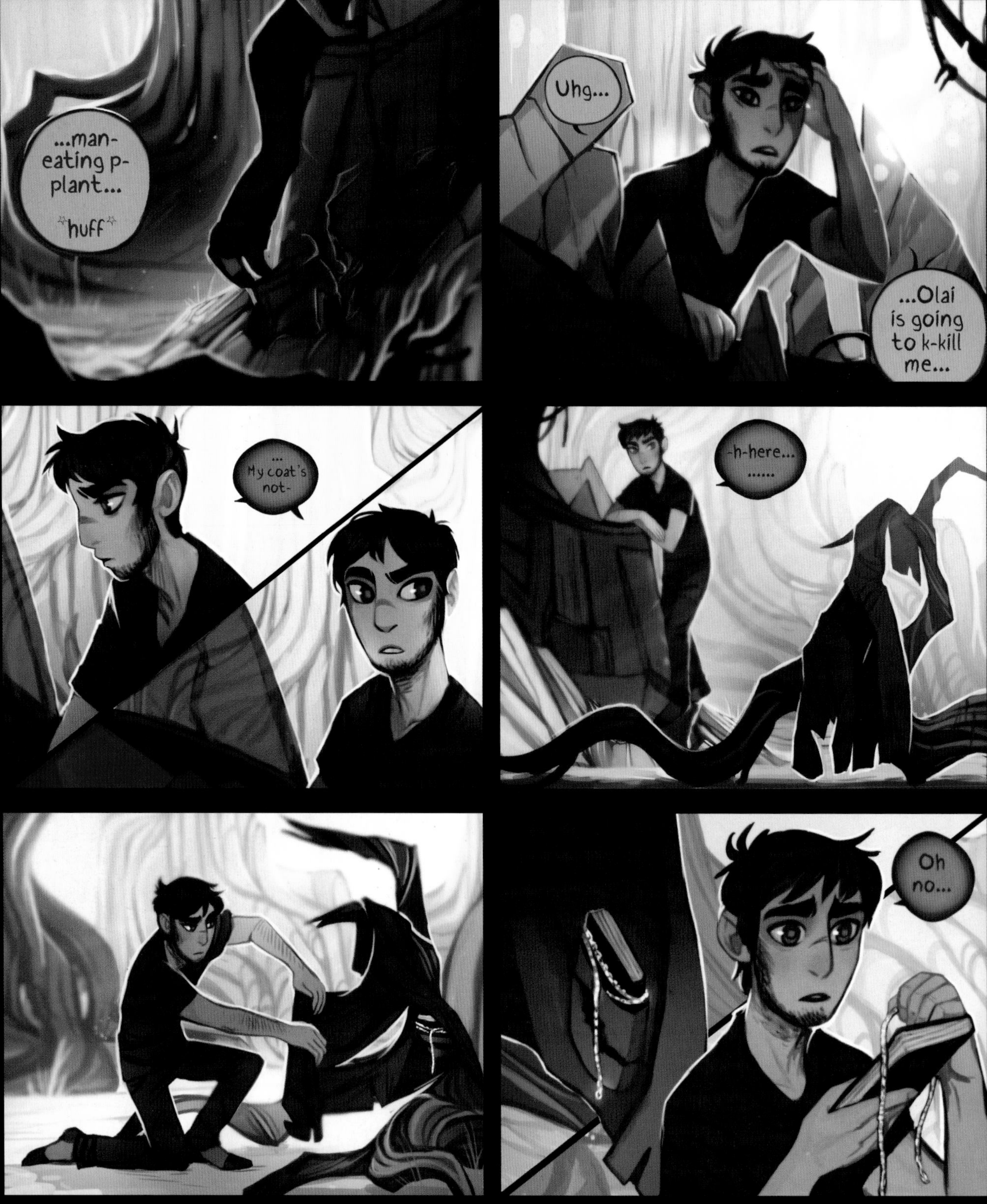
...man-eating p-plant...
huff
Uhg...
...Olai is going to k-kill me...
...
My coat's not-
-h-here...
......
Oh no...

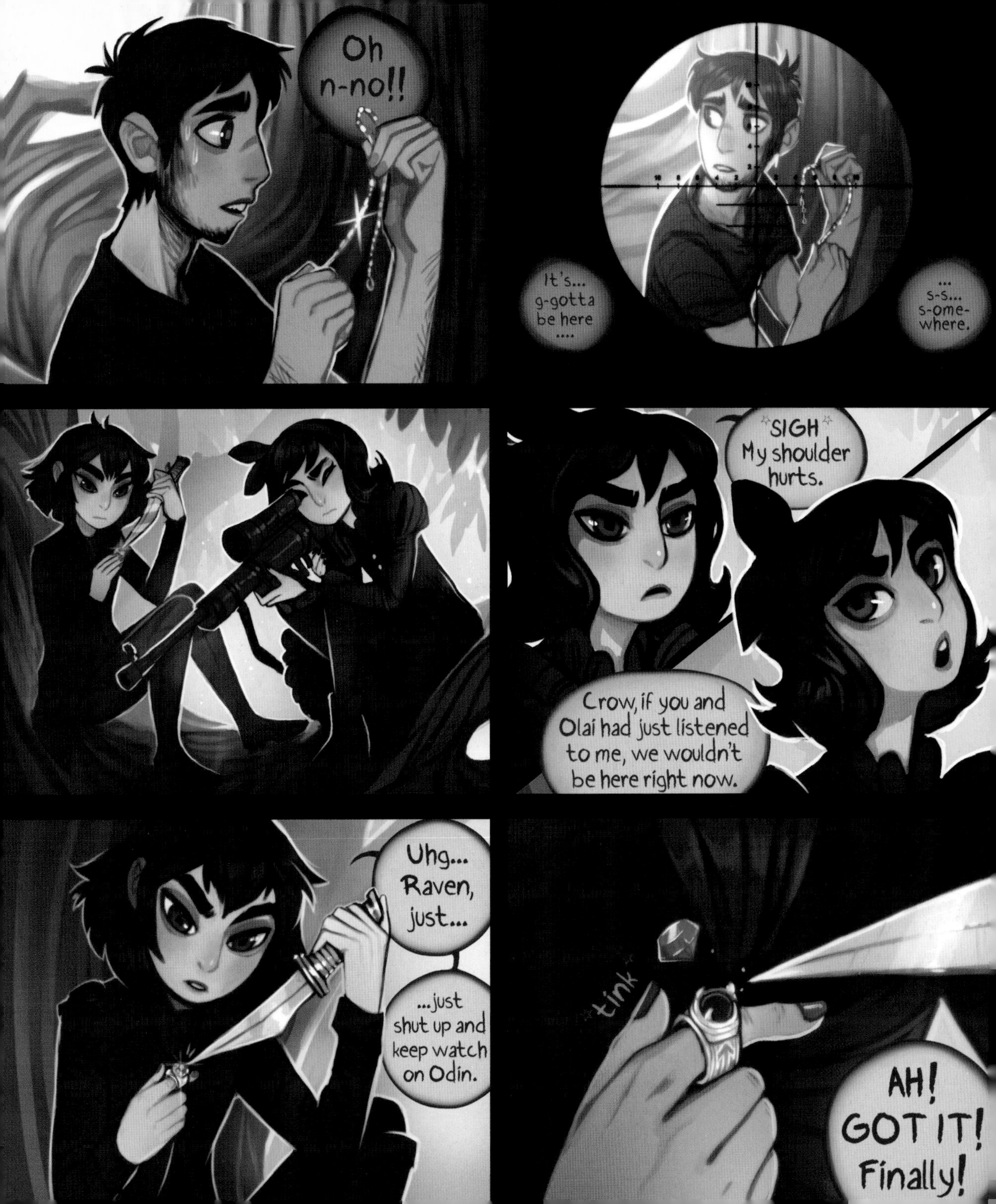
Oh n-no!!
It's... g-gotta be here ....
... s-s... s-ome-where.
SIGH My shoulder hurts.
Crow, if you and Olai had just listened to me, we wouldn't be here right now.
Uhg... Raven, just...
...just shut up and keep watch on Odin.
tink
AH! GOT IT! Finally!

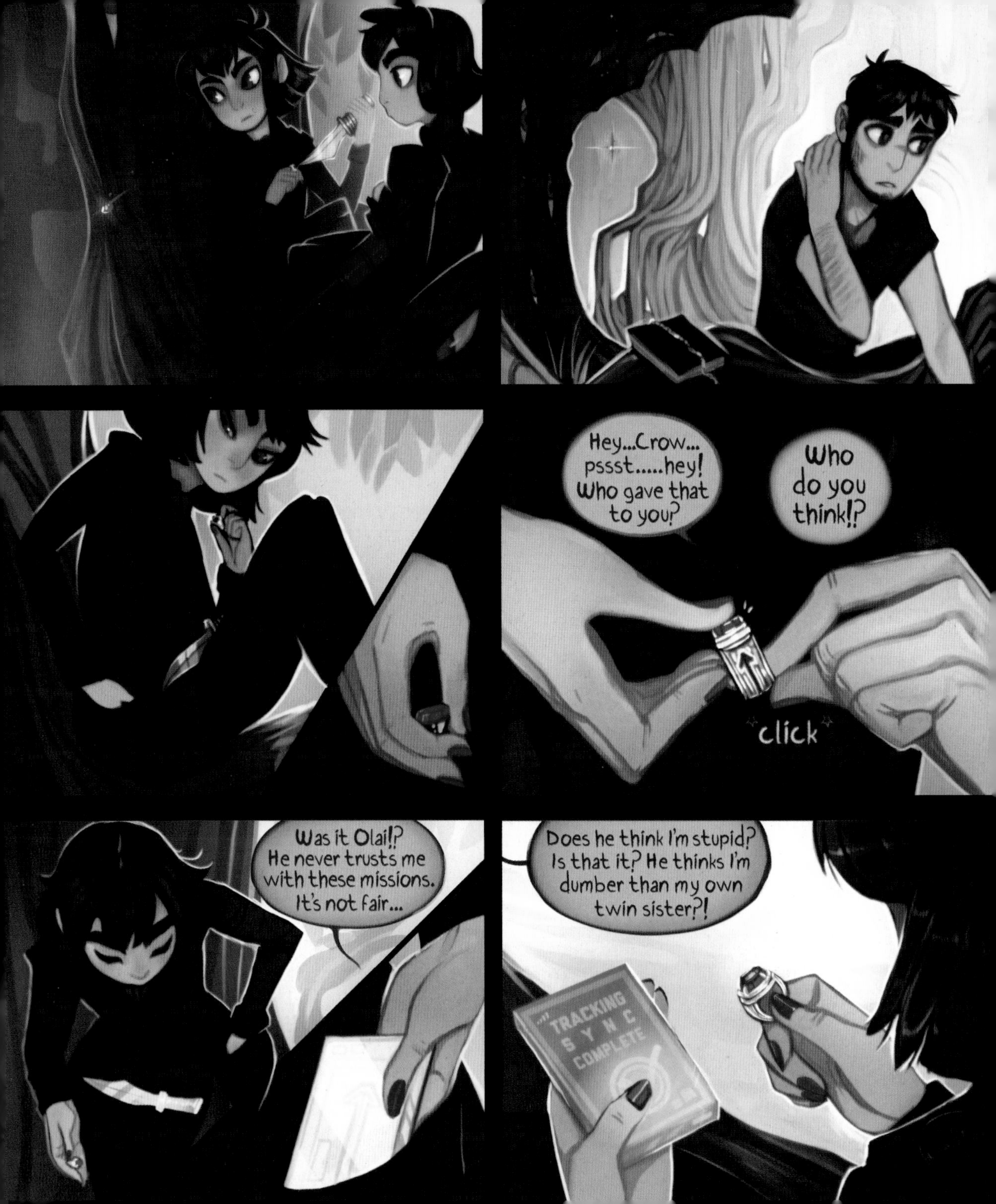

Hey...Crow...
pssst.....hey!
Who gave that
to you?
Who
do you
think!?
click
Was it Olai!?
He never trusts me
with these missions.
It's not fair...
Does he think I'm stupid?
Is that it? He thinks I'm
dumber than my own
twin sister?!
TRACKING
SYNC
COMPLETE

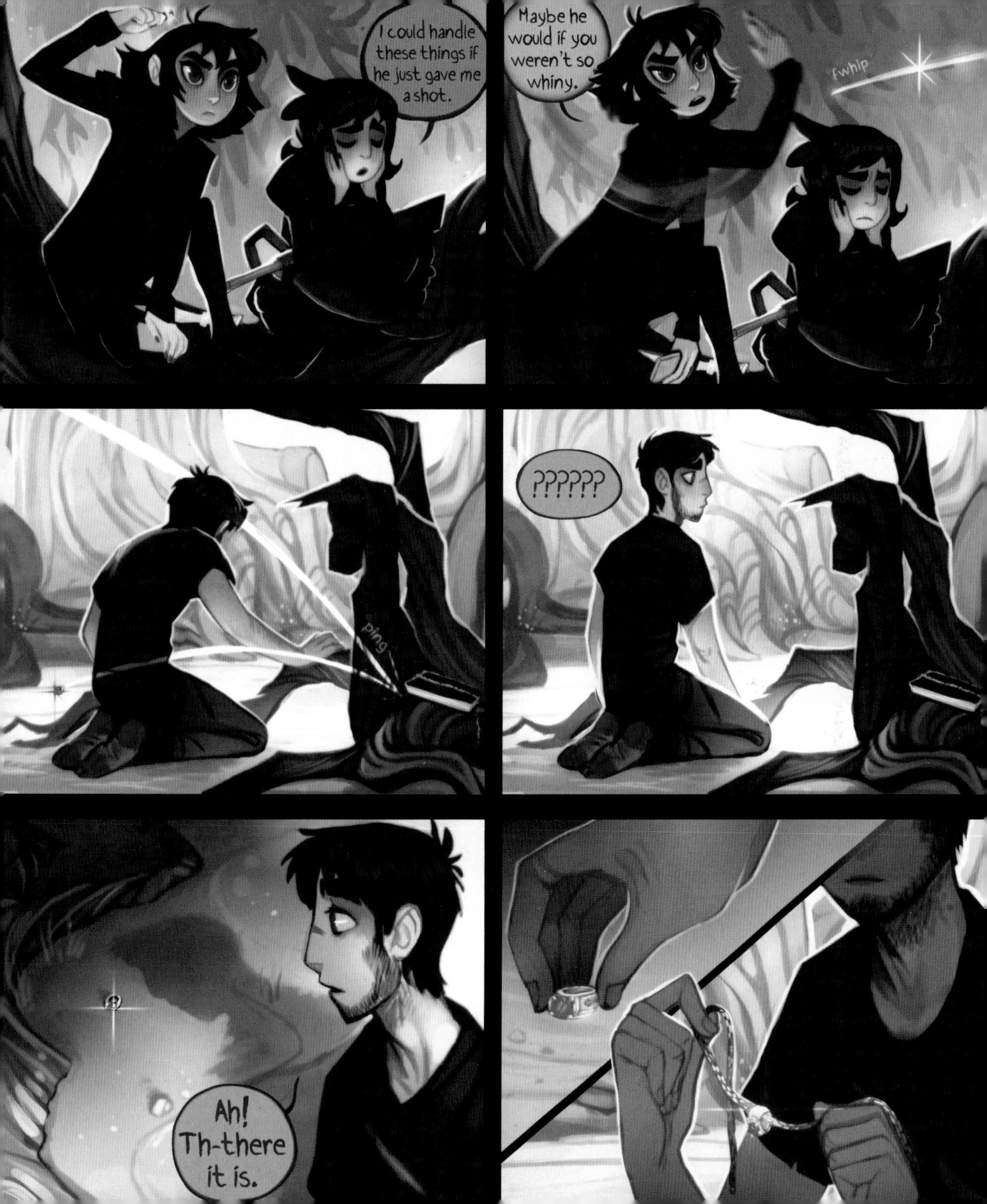
I could handle these things if he just gave me a shot.
Maybe he would if you weren't so whiny.
fwhip
ping
??????
Ah! Th-there it is.

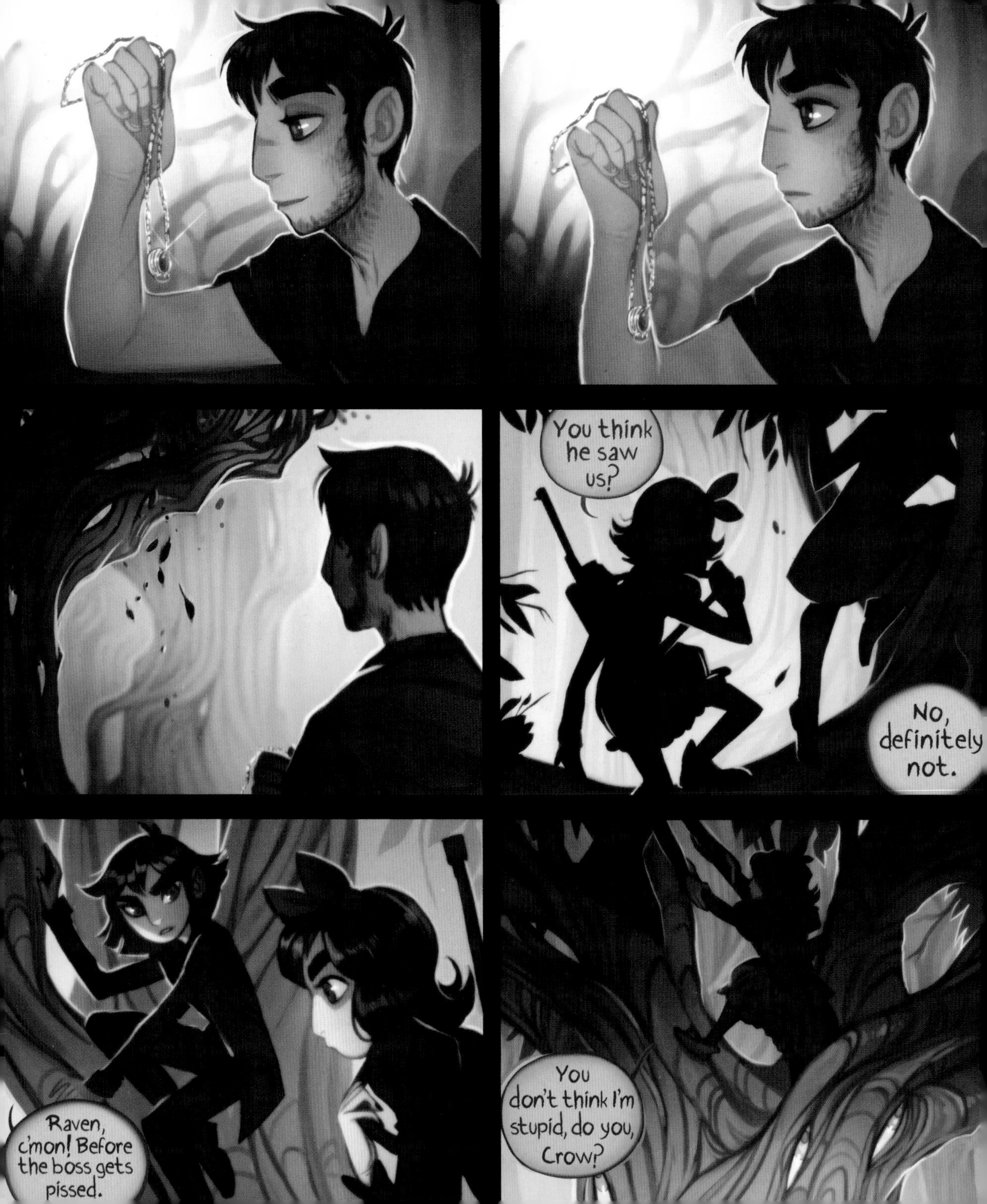
You think he saw us?
No, definitely not.
Raven, c'mon! Before the boss gets pissed.
You don't think I'm stupid, do you, Crow?

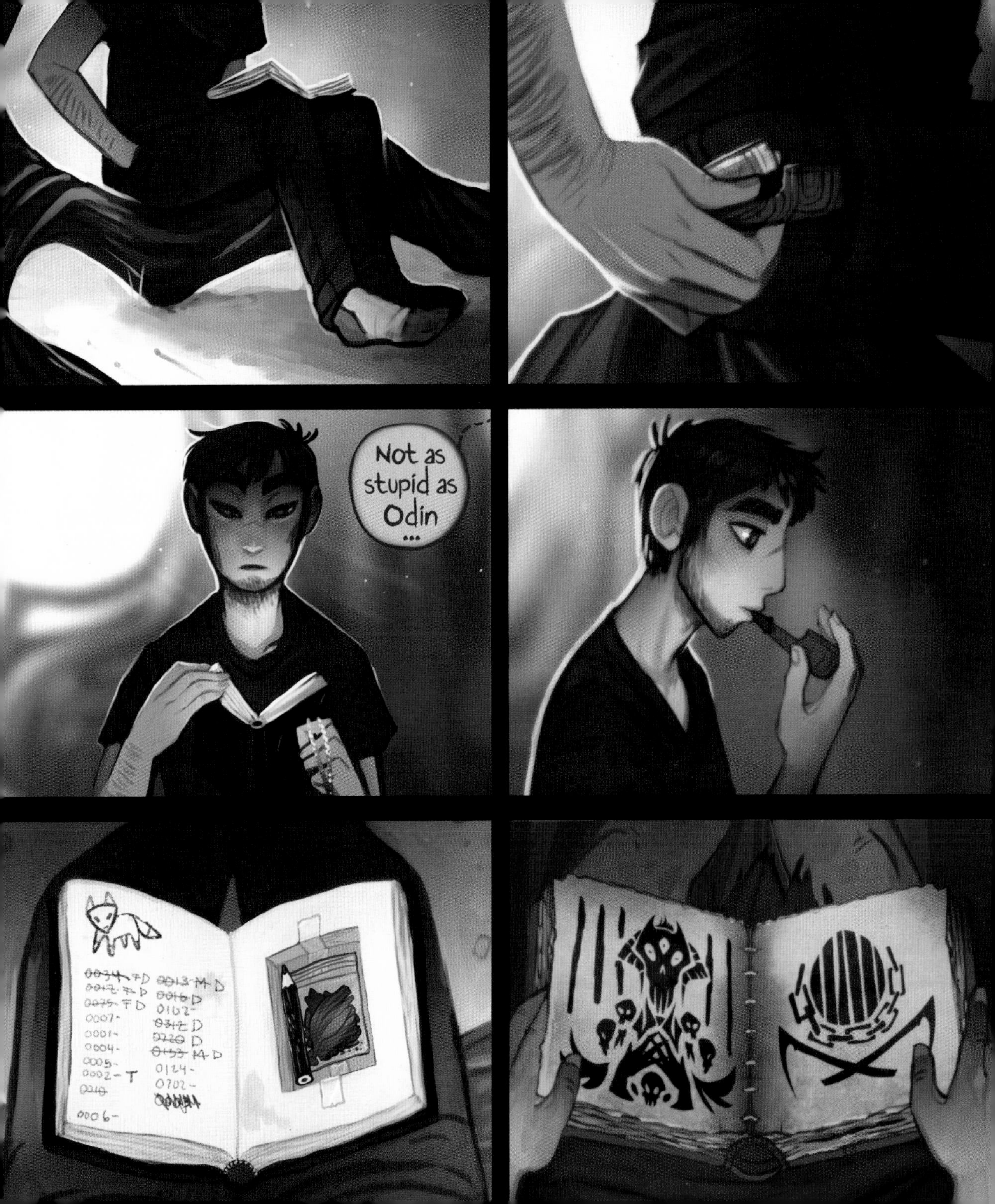
Not as stupid as Odin ...

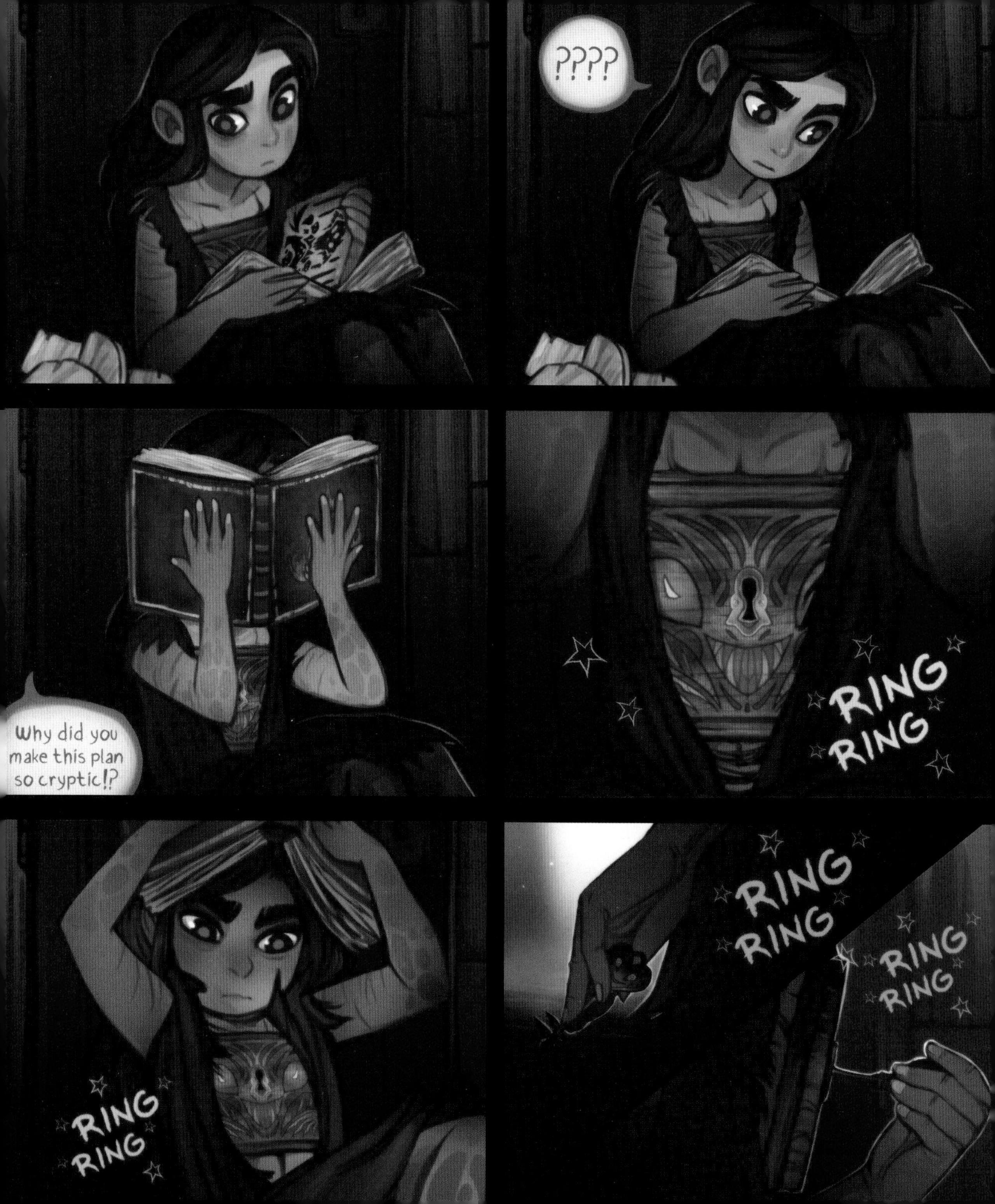
????
Why did you make this plan so cryptic!?
RING RING
RING RING
RING RING
RING RING

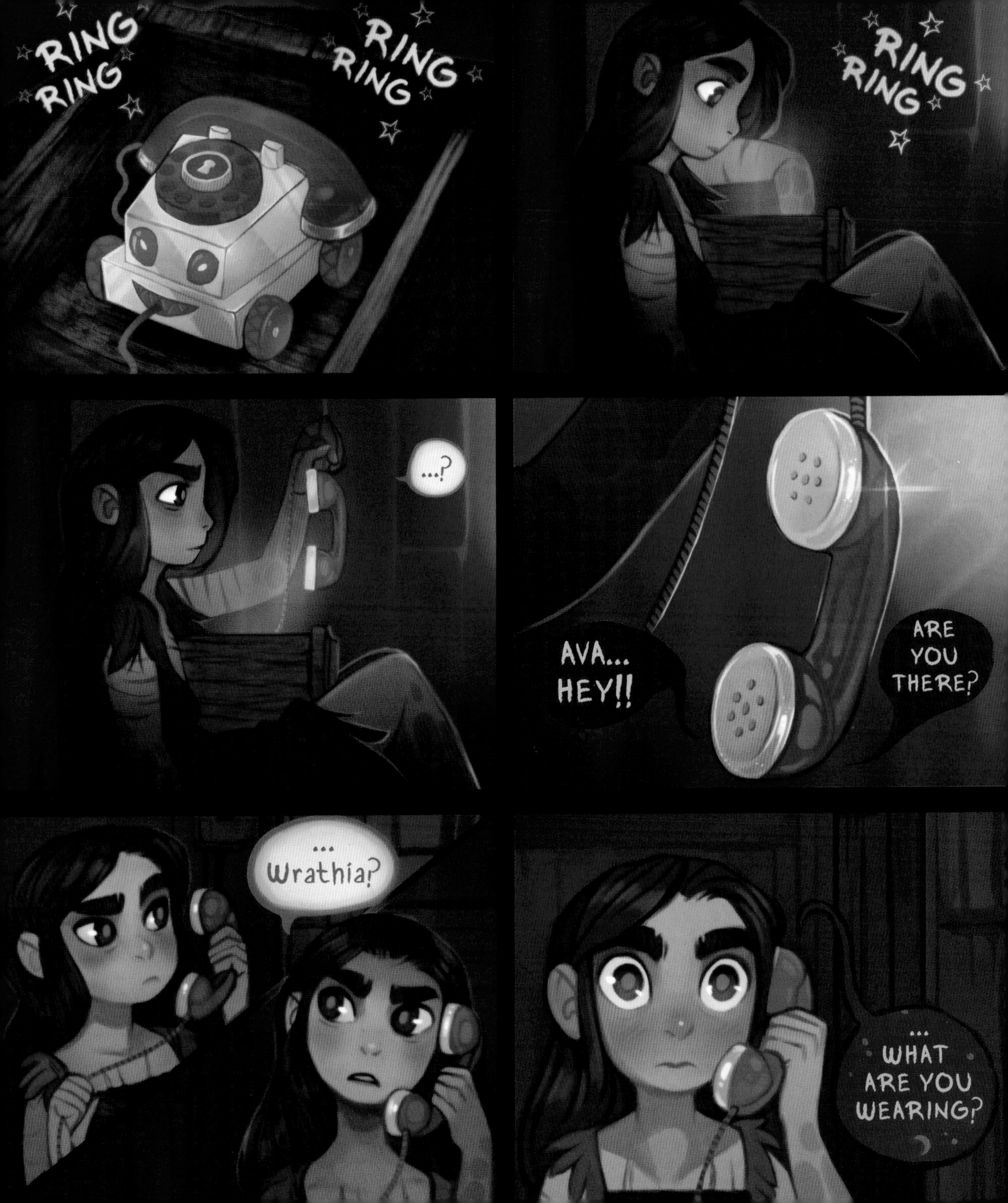
RING RING
RING RING
RING RING
...?
AVA... HEY!!
ARE YOU THERE?
...
Wrathia?
...
WHAT ARE YOU WEARING?

BECAUSE I'M NOT WEARING ANYTHING.

UHG!! Don't sound so proud of yourself!!

Wrathia, why is your plan a bunch of bad drawings?

I don't know what to make of this mess!

THOSE "BAD" DRAWINGS HAPPEN TO BE MY MOST POWERFUL WARRIORS, THANK YOU VERY MUCH...

...AND I DREW THEM MUCH PRETTIER THAN THEY ACTUALLY ARE... ...YOU CAN SEE FOR YOURSELF WITH THOSE LENSES.

Ah! The glasses?

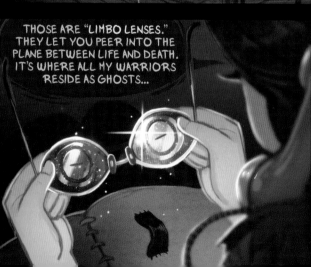

THOSE ARE "LIMBO LENSES." THEY LET YOU PEER INTO THE PLANE BETWEEN LIFE AND DEATH. IT'S WHERE ALL MY WARRIORS RESIDE AS GHOSTS...

...UNLESS THEY'VE MADE A PACT. IN THAT CASE ...

...I'M NOT QUITE SURE HOW THEIR SPIRITS WOULD MANIFEST.

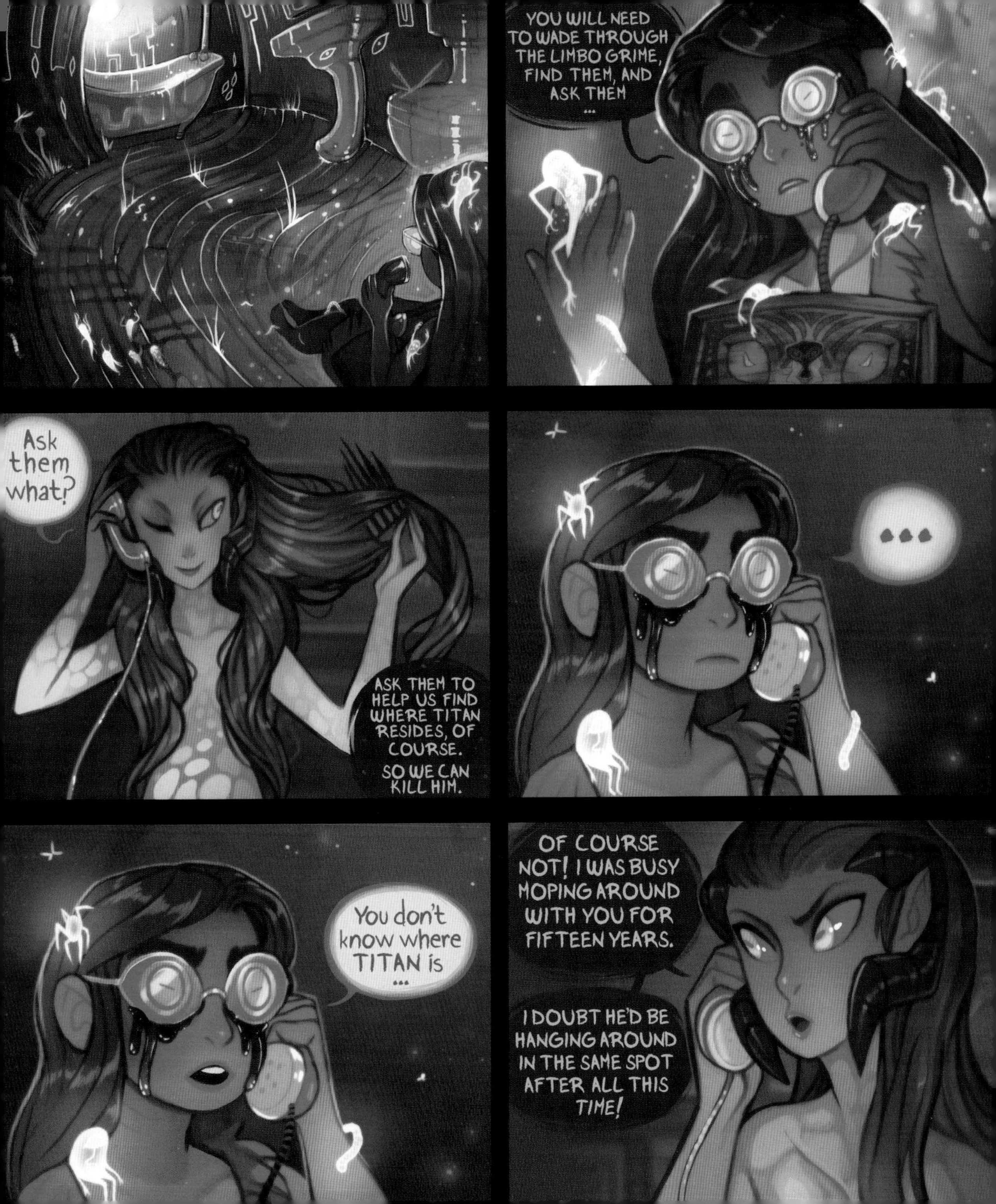
YOU WILL NEED TO WADE THROUGH THE LIMBO GRIME, FIND THEM, AND ASK THEM ...
Ask them what?
ASK THEM TO HELP US FIND WHERE TITAN RESIDES, OF COURSE.
SO WE CAN KILL HIM.
...
You don't know where TITAN is ...
OF COURSE NOT! I WAS BUSY MOPING AROUND WITH YOU FOR FIFTEEN YEARS.
I DOUBT HE'D BE HANGING AROUND IN THE SAME SPOT AFTER ALL THIS TIME!

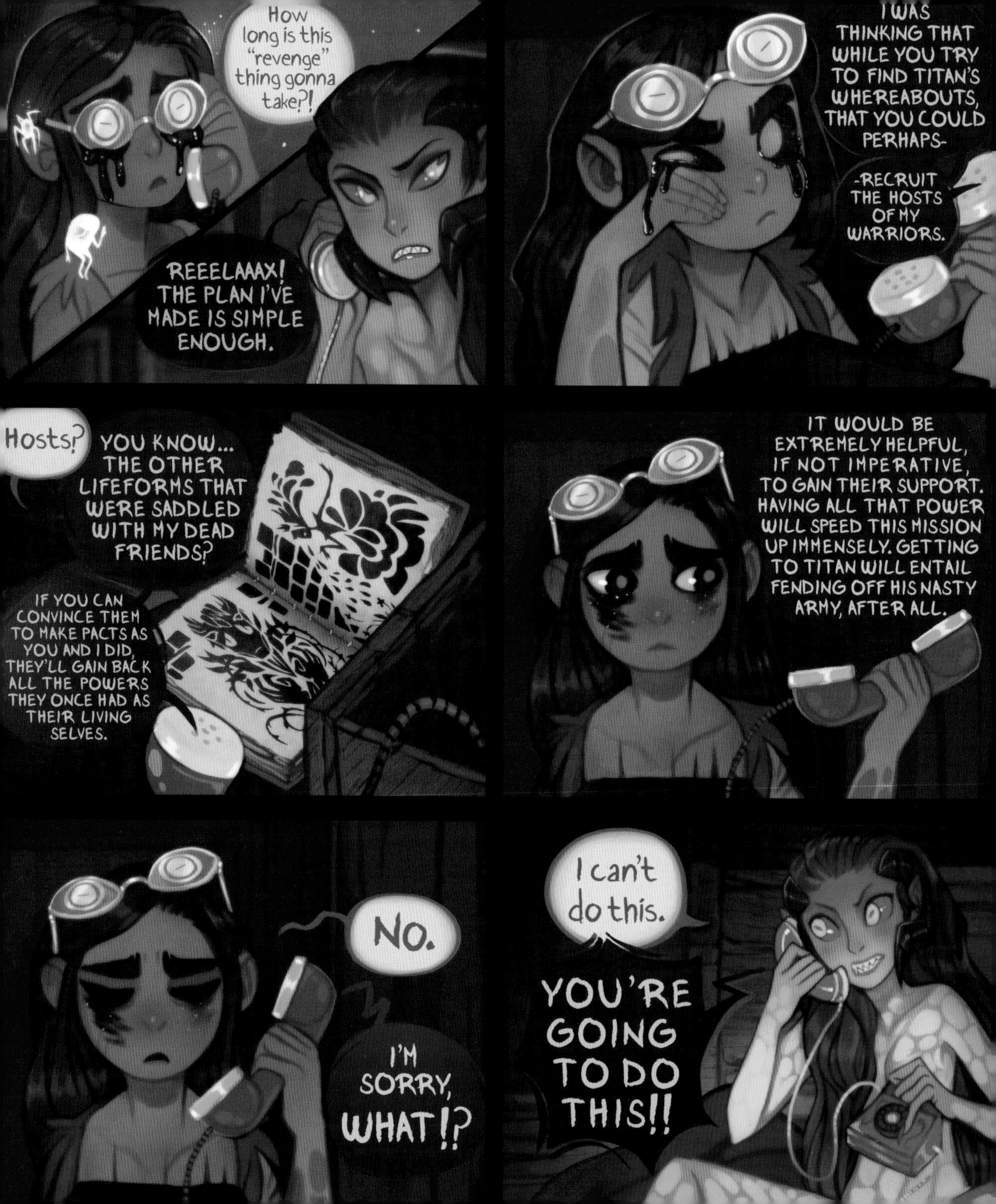

How long is this "revenge" thing gonna take?!
REEELAAAX! THE PLAN I'VE MADE IS SIMPLE ENOUGH.
I WAS THINKING THAT WHILE YOU TRY TO FIND TITAN'S WHEREABOUTS, THAT YOU COULD PERHAPS-
-RECRUIT THE HOSTS OF MY WARRIORS.
Hosts?
YOU KNOW... THE OTHER LIFEFORMS THAT WERE SADDLED WITH MY DEAD FRIENDS?
IF YOU CAN CONVINCE THEM TO MAKE PACTS AS YOU AND I DID, THEY'LL GAIN BACK ALL THE POWERS THEY ONCE HAD AS THEIR LIVING SELVES.
IT WOULD BE EXTREMELY HELPFUL, IF NOT IMPERATIVE, TO GAIN THEIR SUPPORT. HAVING ALL THAT POWER WILL SPEED THIS MISSION UP IMMENSELY. GETTING TO TITAN WILL ENTAIL FENDING OFF HIS NASTY ARMY, AFTER ALL.
NO.
I'M SORRY, WHAT!?
I can't do this.
YOU'RE GOING TO DO THIS!!

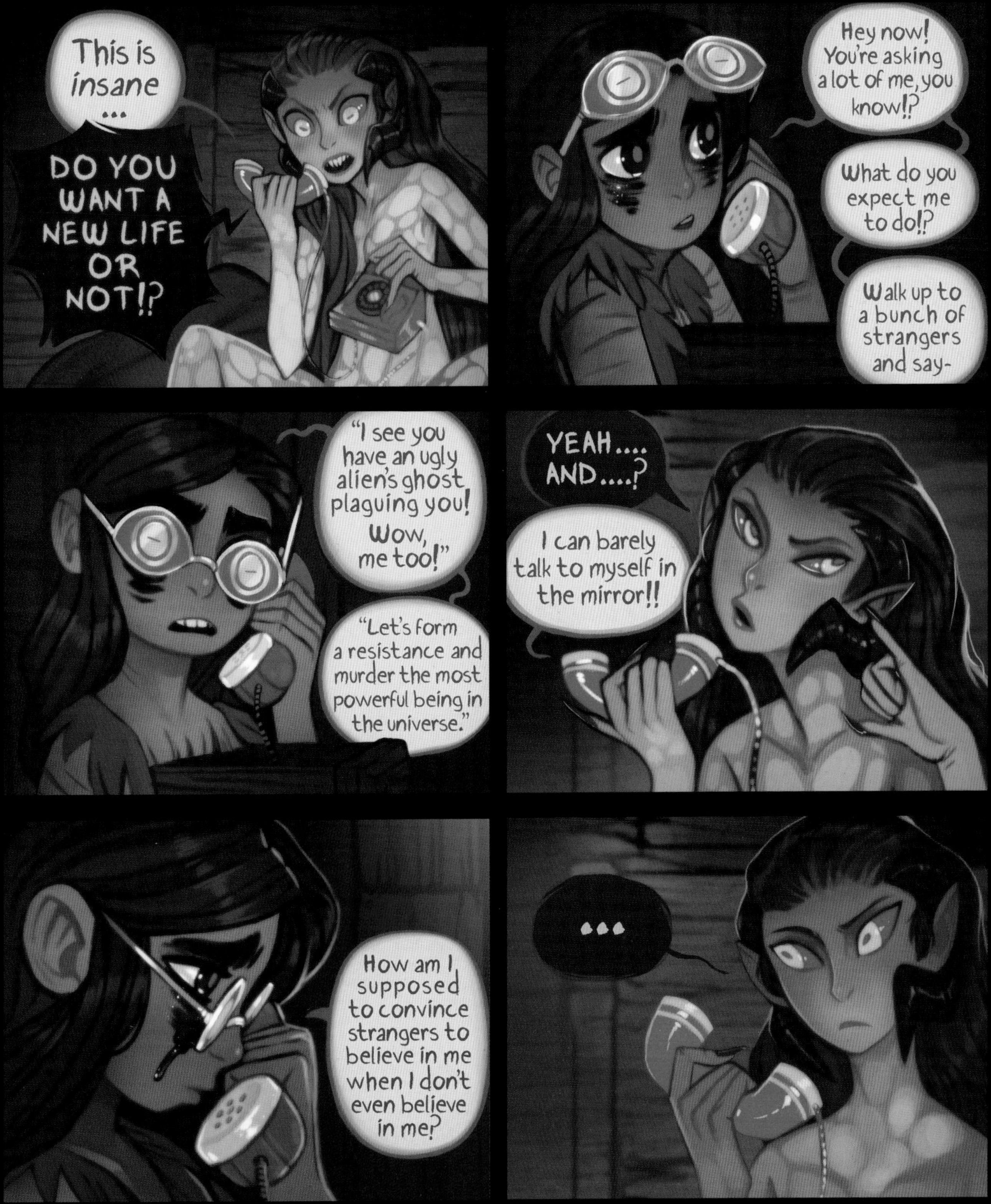
This is insane ...
DO YOU WANT A NEW LIFE OR NOT!?
Hey now! You're asking a lot of me, you know!?
What do you expect me to do!?
Walk up to a bunch of strangers and say-
"I see you have an ugly alien's ghost plaguing you! Wow, me too!"
"Let's form a resistance and murder the most powerful being in the universe."
YEAH.... AND....?
I can barely talk to myself in the mirror!!
How am I supposed to convince strangers to believe in me when I don't even believe in me?
...

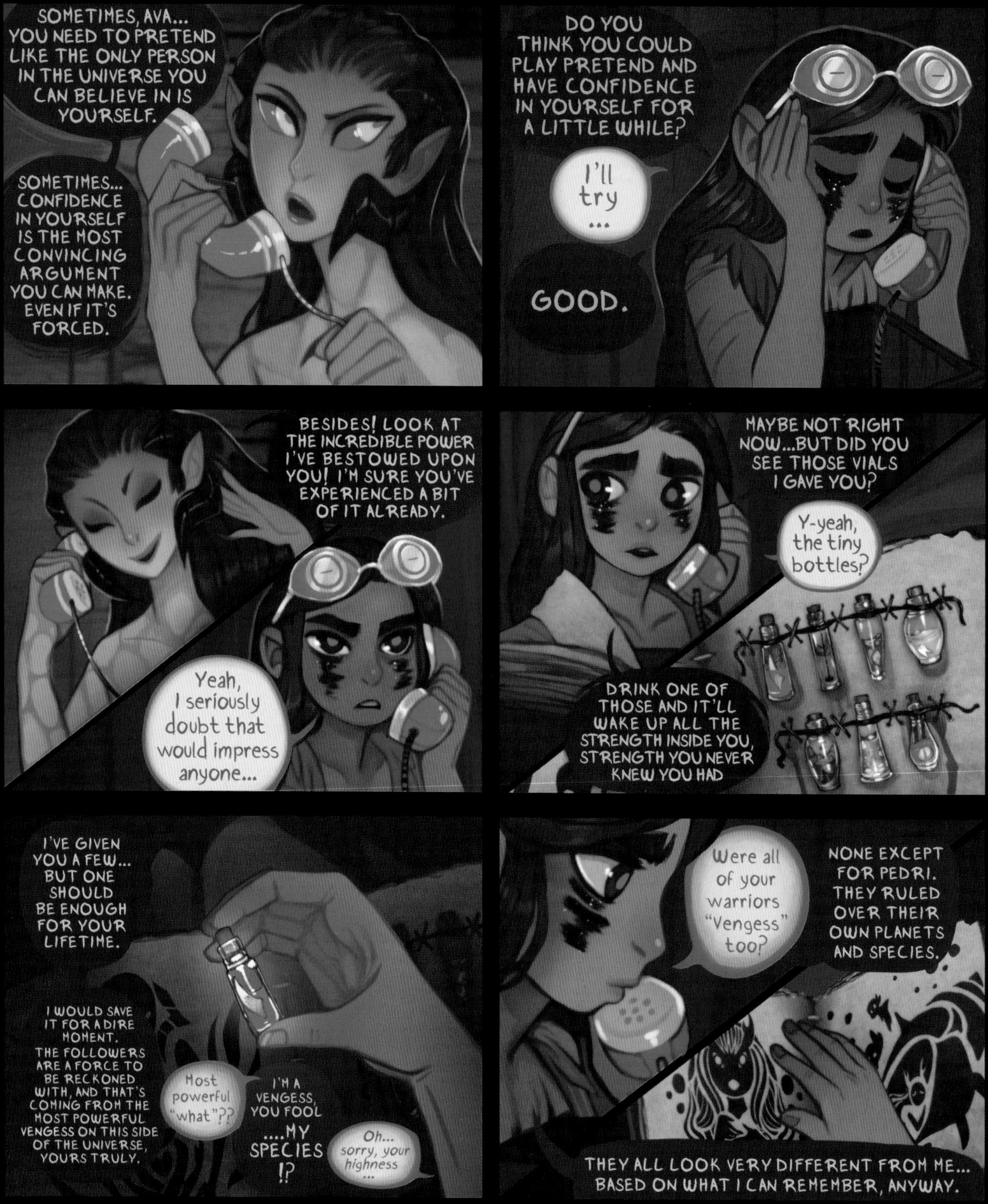

SOMETIMES, AVA... YOU NEED TO PRETEND LIKE THE ONLY PERSON IN THE UNIVERSE YOU CAN BELIEVE IN IS YOURSELF.
SOMETIMES... CONFIDENCE IN YOURSELF IS THE MOST CONVINCING ARGUMENT YOU CAN MAKE. EVEN IF IT'S FORCED.
DO YOU THINK YOU COULD PLAY PRETEND AND HAVE CONFIDENCE IN YOURSELF FOR A LITTLE WHILE?
I'll try ...
GOOD.
BESIDES! LOOK AT THE INCREDIBLE POWER I'VE BESTOWED UPON YOU! I'M SURE YOU'VE EXPERIENCED A BIT OF IT ALREADY.
Yeah, I seriously doubt that would impress anyone...
MAYBE NOT RIGHT NOW...BUT DID YOU SEE THOSE VIALS I GAVE YOU?
Y-yeah, the tiny bottles?
DRINK ONE OF THOSE AND IT'LL WAKE UP ALL THE STRENGTH INSIDE YOU, STRENGTH YOU NEVER KNEW YOU HAD
I'VE GIVEN YOU A FEW... BUT ONE SHOULD BE ENOUGH FOR YOUR LIFETIME.
I WOULD SAVE IT FOR A DIRE MOMENT. THE FOLLOWERS ARE A FORCE TO BE RECKONED WITH, AND THAT'S COMING FROM THE MOST POWERFUL VENGESS ON THIS SIDE OF THE UNIVERSE, YOURS TRULY.
Most powerful "what"??
I'M A VENGESS, YOU FOOL ....MY SPECIES !?
Oh... sorry, your highness ...
Were all of your warriors "Vengess" too?
NONE EXCEPT FOR PEDRI. THEY RULED OVER THEIR OWN PLANETS AND SPECIES.
THEY ALL LOOK VERY DIFFERENT FROM ME... BASED ON WHAT I CAN REMEMBER, ANYWAY.

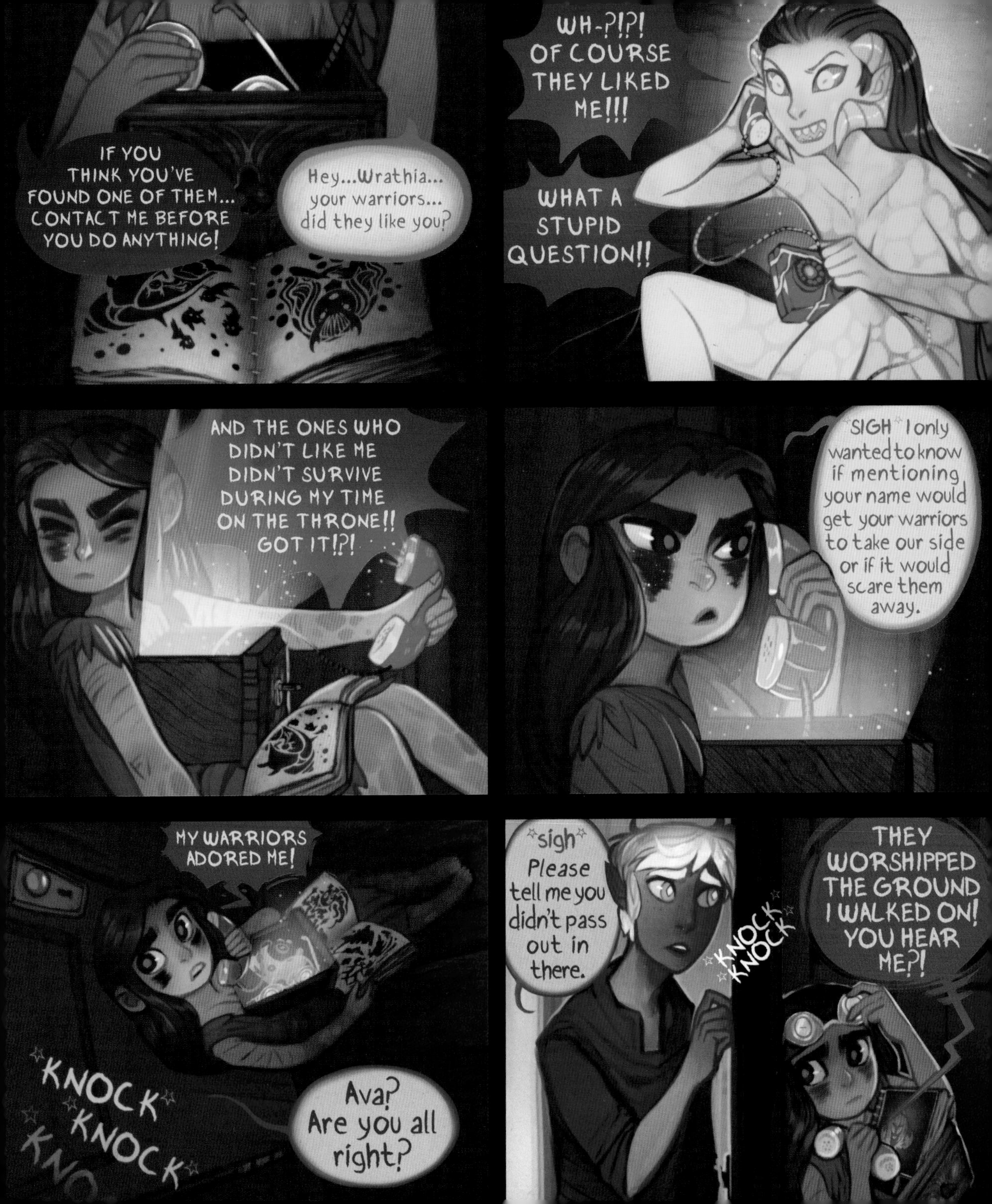
IF YOU THINK YOU'VE FOUND ONE OF THEM... CONTACT ME BEFORE YOU DO ANYTHING!
Hey...Wrathia... your warriors... did they like you?
WH-?!?! OF COURSE THEY LIKED ME!!!
WHAT A STUPID QUESTION!!
AND THE ONES WHO DIDN'T LIKE ME DIDN'T SURVIVE DURING MY TIME ON THE THRONE!! GOT IT!?!
SIGH I only wanted to know if mentioning your name would get your warriors to take our side or if it would scare them away.
MY WARRIORS ADORED ME!
KNOCK KNOCK KNO
Ava? Are you all right?
sigh Please tell me you didn't pass out in there.
KNOCK KNOCK
THEY WORSHIPPED THE GROUND I WALKED ON! YOU HEAR ME?!

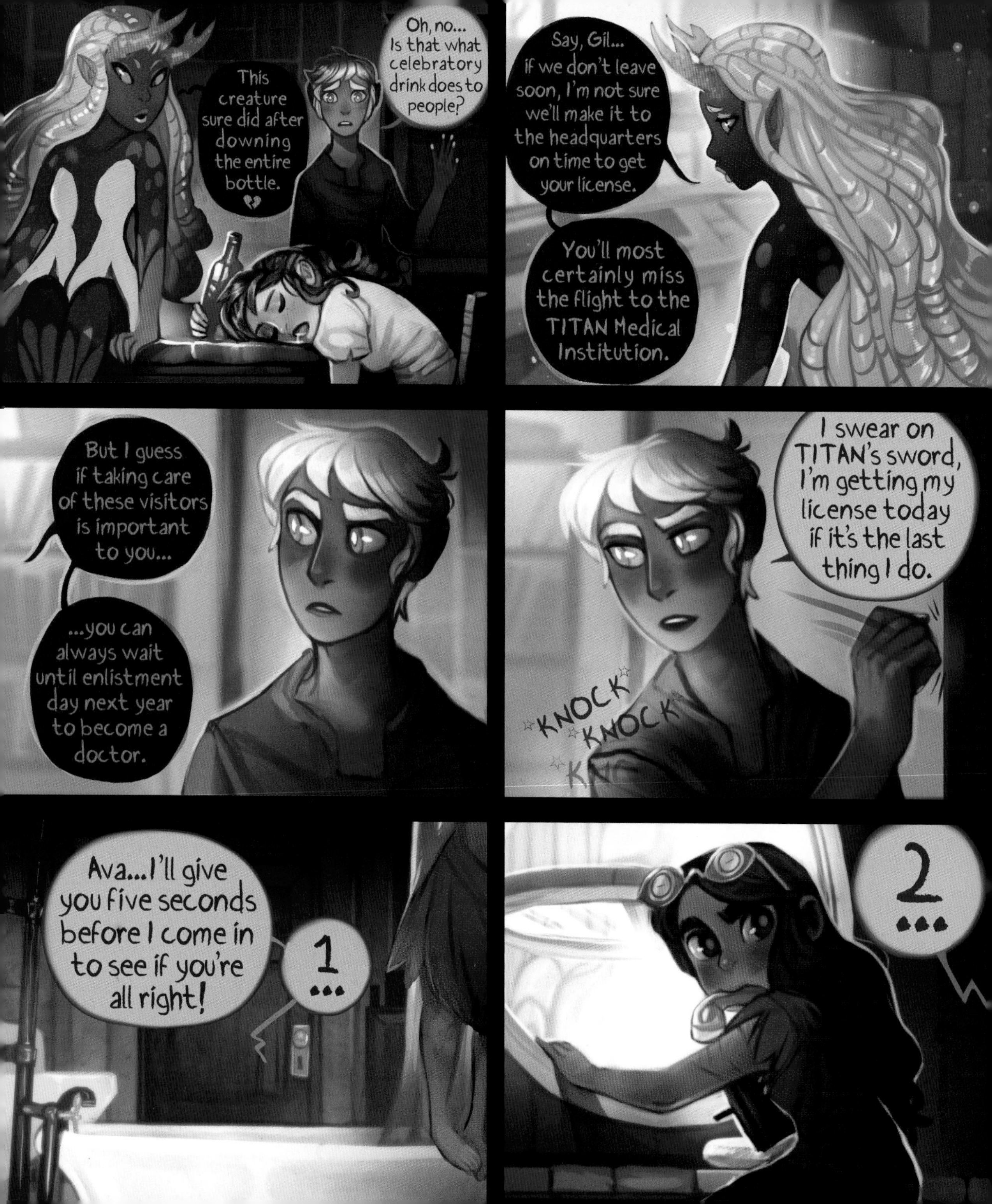

This creature sure did after downing the entire bottle.
Oh, no... Is that what celebratory drink does to people?
Say, Gil... if we don't leave soon, I'm not sure we'll make it to the headquarters on time to get your license.
You'll most certainly miss the flight to the TITAN Medical Institution.
But I guess if taking care of these visitors is important to you...
...you can always wait until enlistment day next year to become a doctor.
I swear on TITAN's sword, I'm getting my license today if it's the last thing I do.
KNOCK KNOCK
Ava...I'll give you five seconds before I come in to see if you're all right!
1...
2...

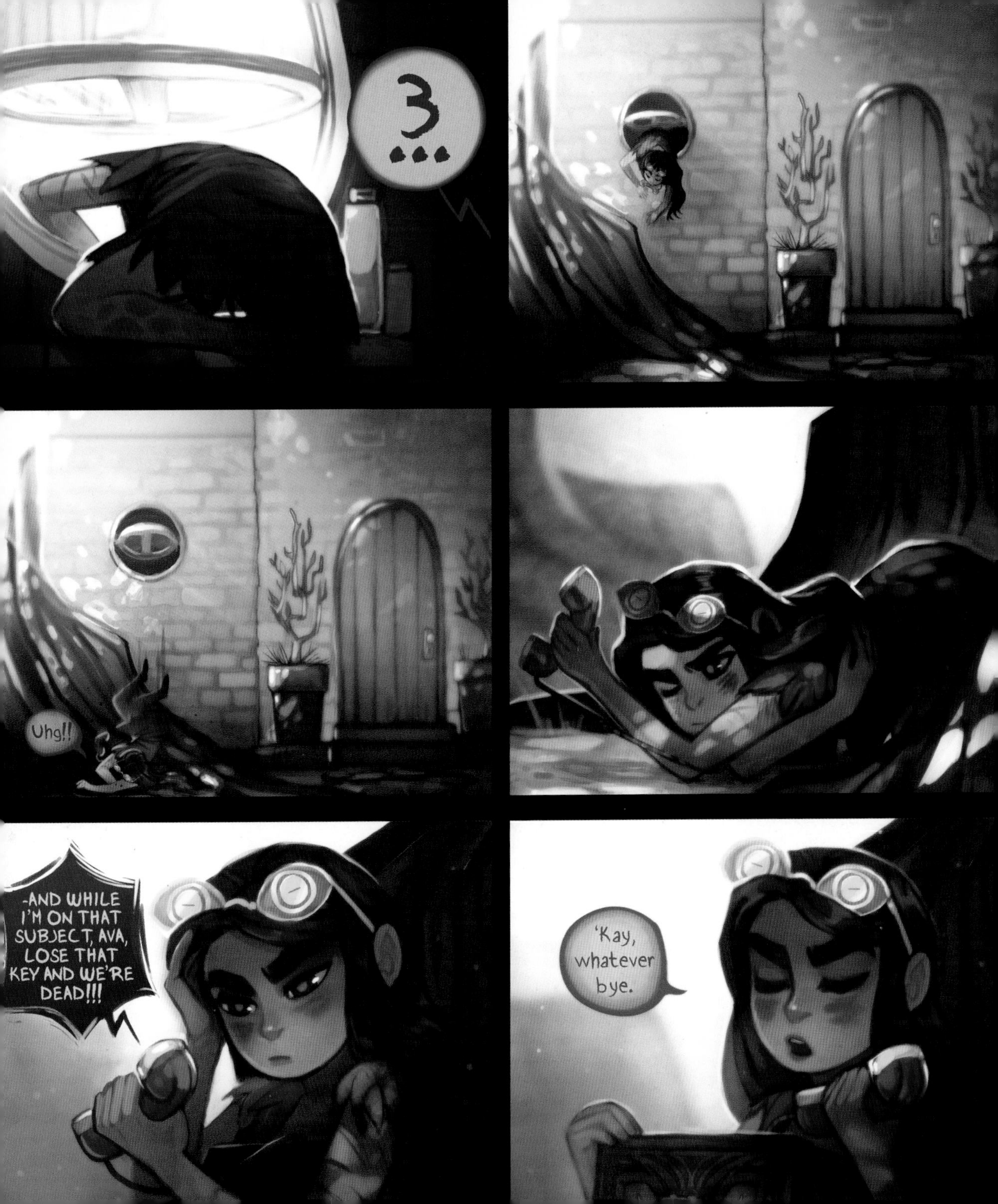
3...
Uhg!!
-AND WHILE I'M ON THAT SUBJECT, AVA, LOSE THAT KEY AND WE'RE DEAD!!!
'Kay, whatever bye.

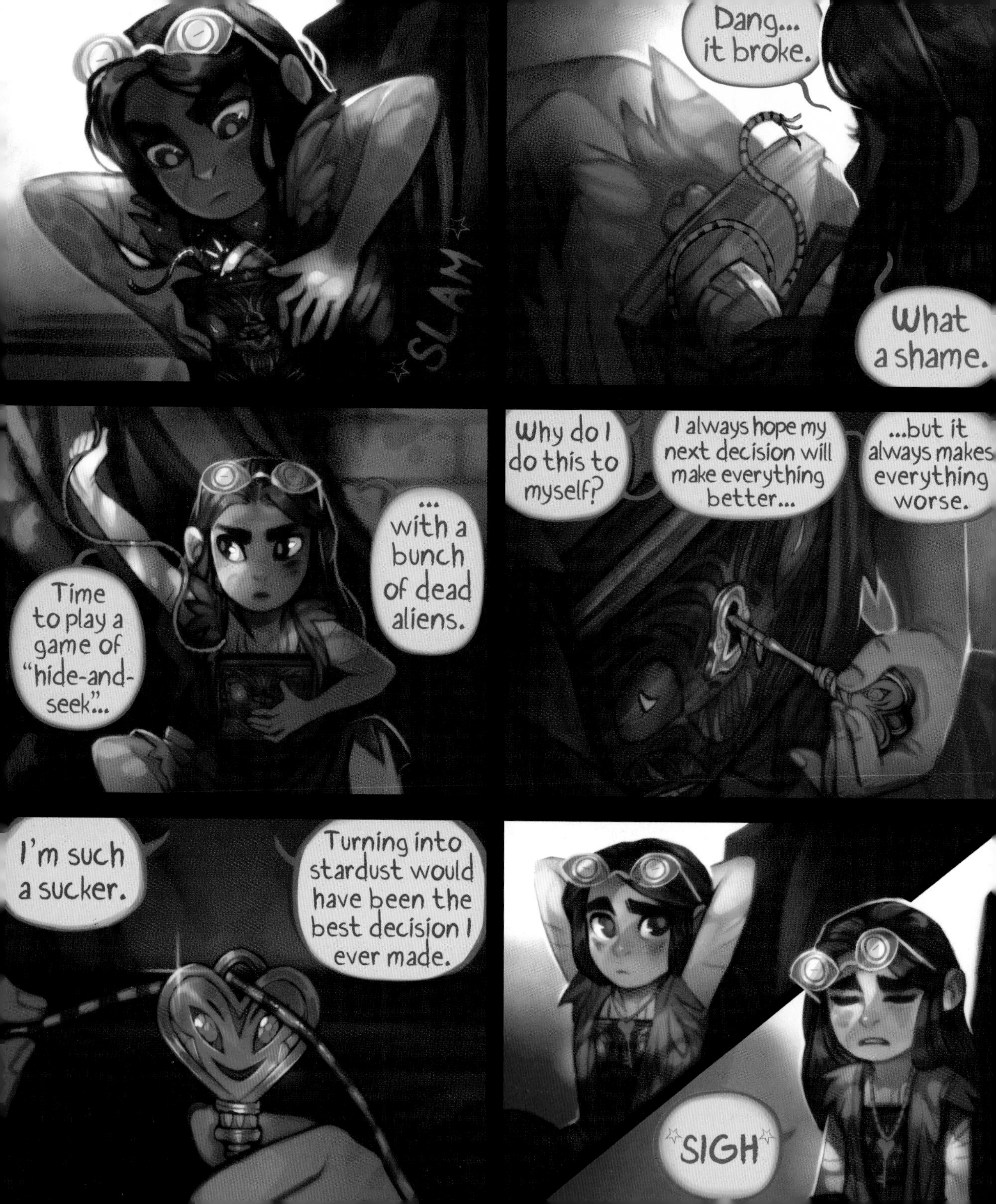
SLAM
Dang... it broke.
What a shame.
Time to play a game of "hide-and-seek"...
... with a bunch of dead aliens.
Why do I do this to myself?
I always hope my next decision will make everything better...
...but it always makes everything worse.
I'm such a sucker.
Turning into stardust would have been the best decision I ever made.
SIGH

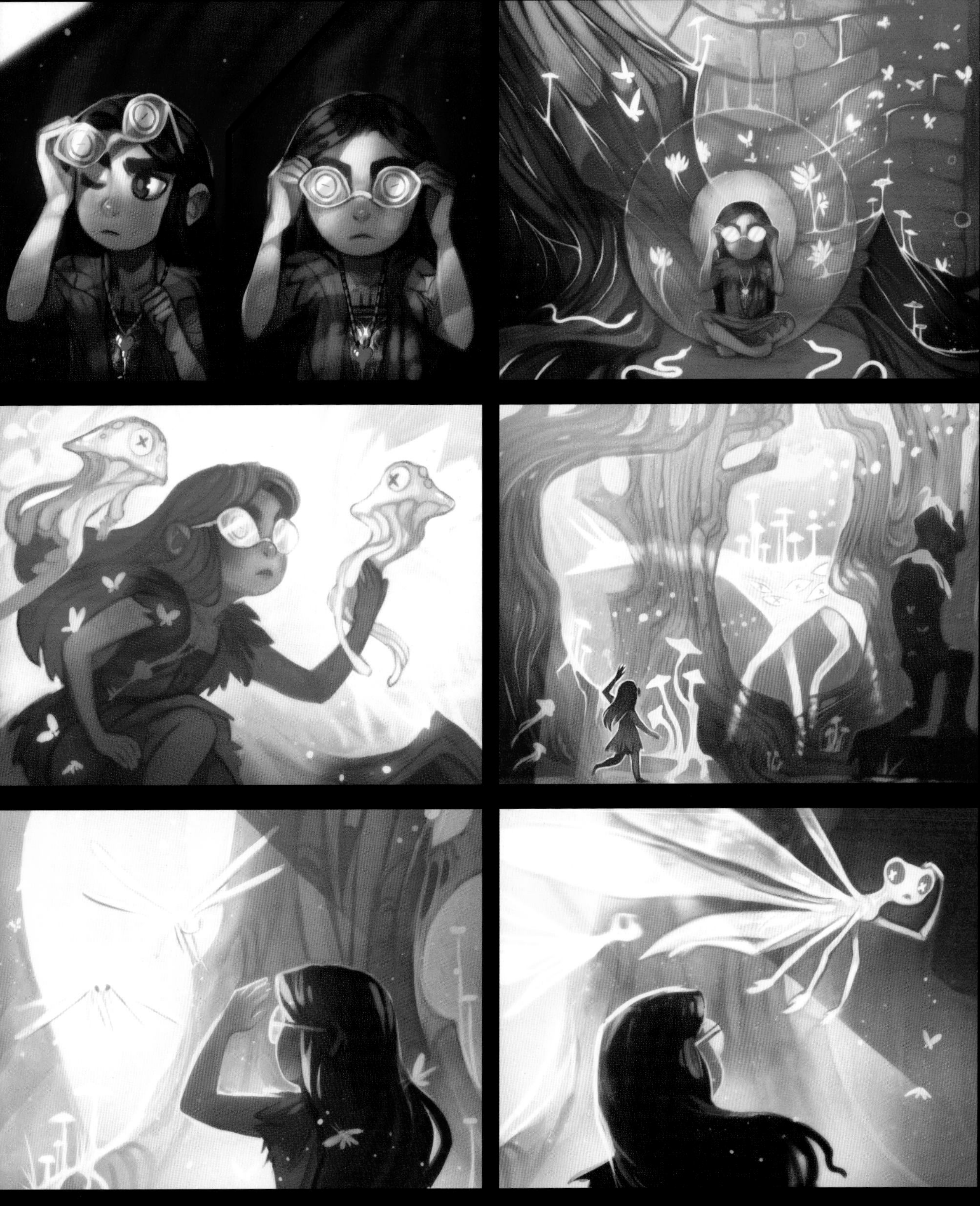

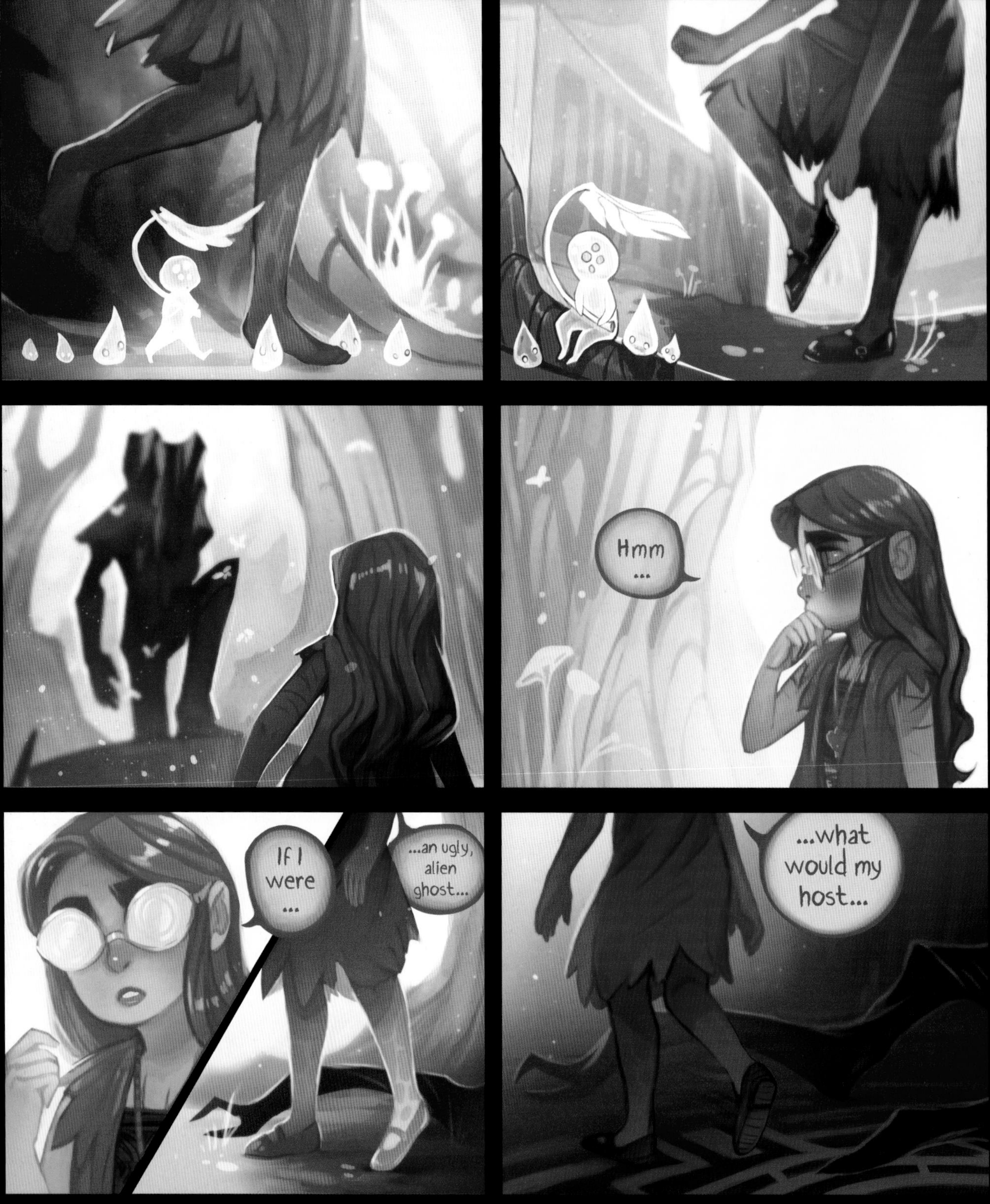
Hmm
...
If I
were
...
...an ugly,
alien
ghost...
...what
would my
host...

...look like?

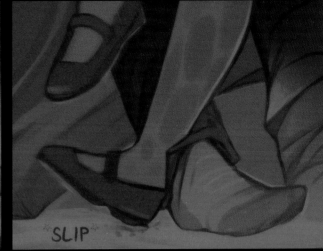

SLIP

AUHG!!

Ow, ow ow ow ow ...

H-Hey... it's the stowaway ...

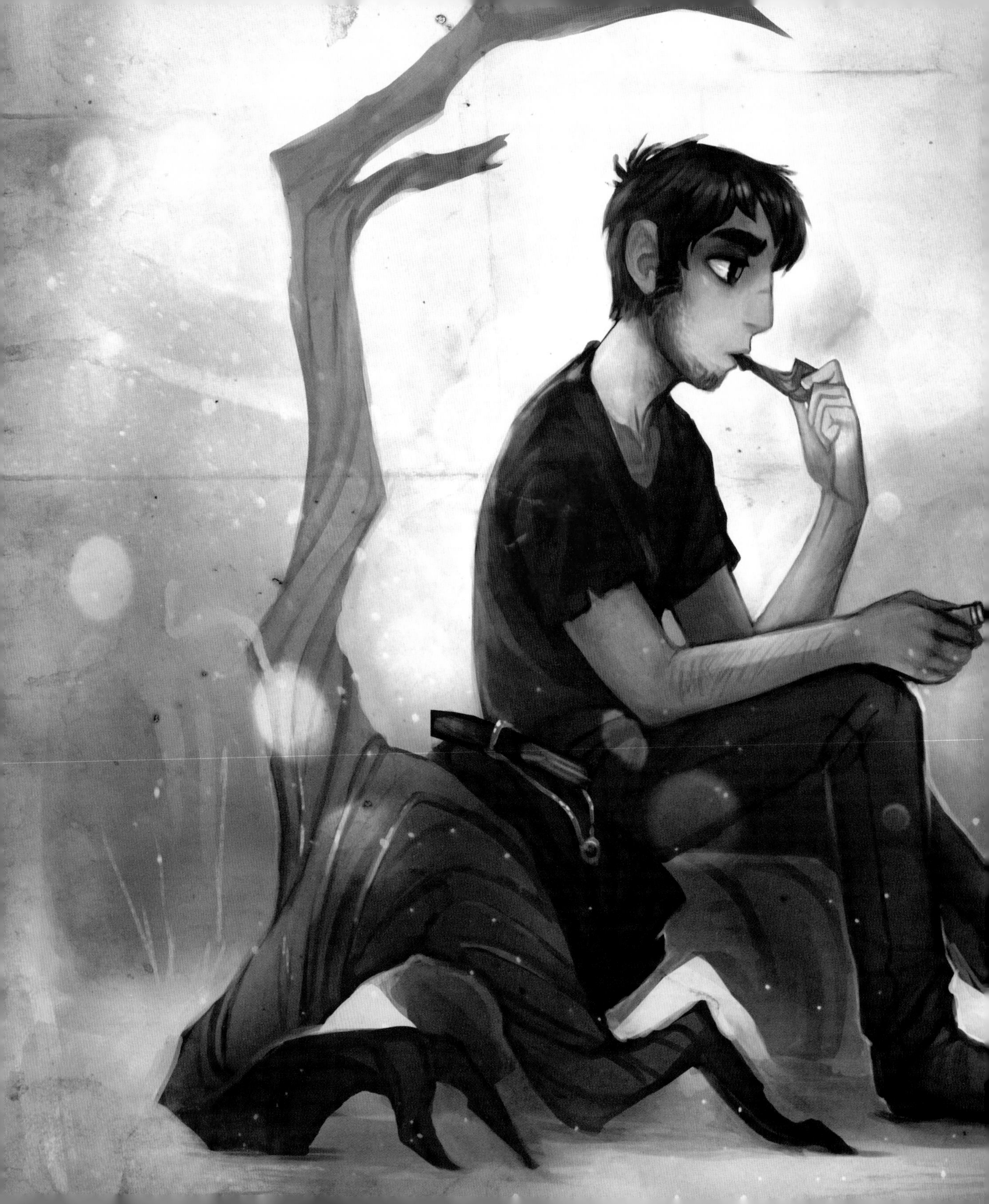

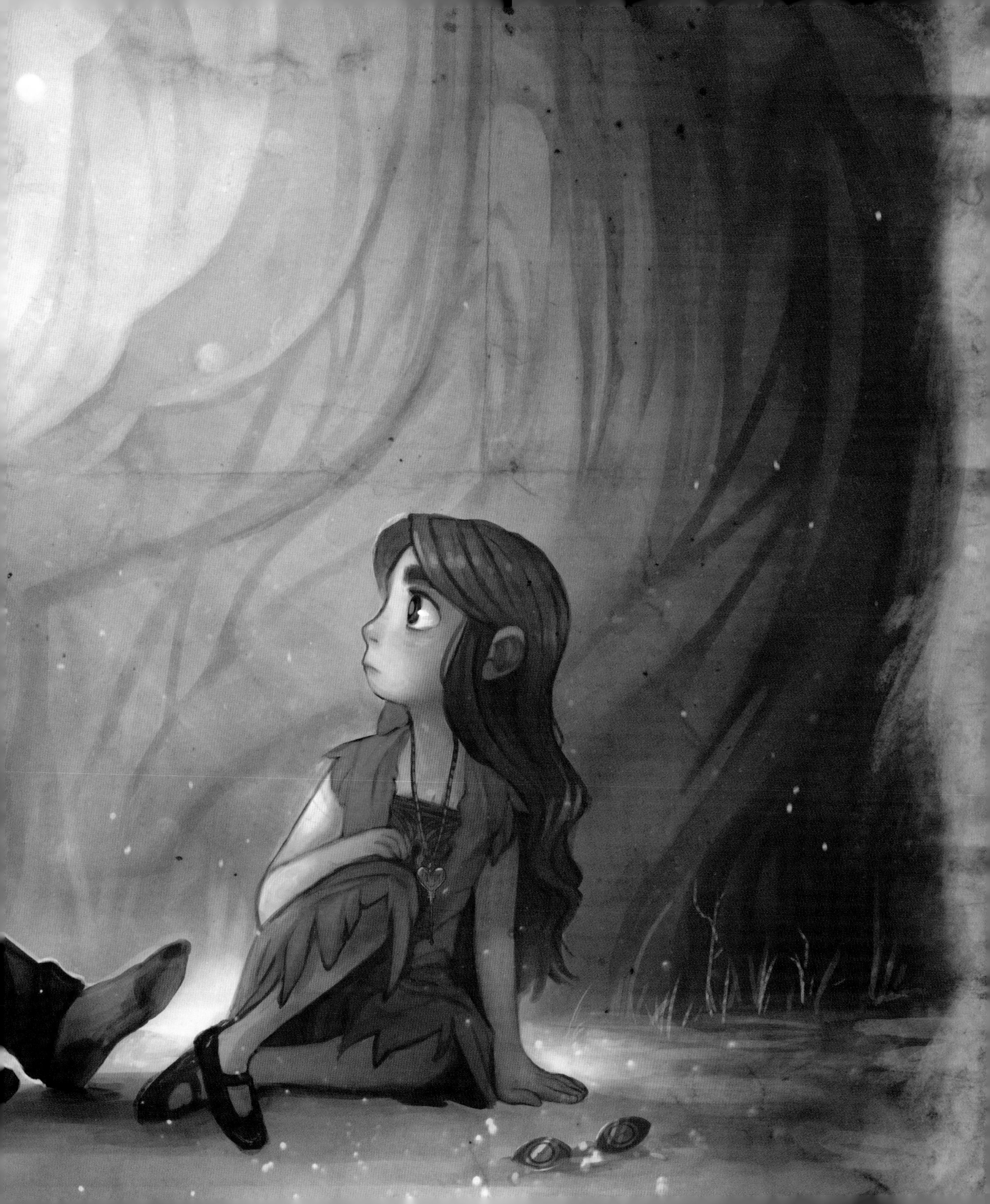

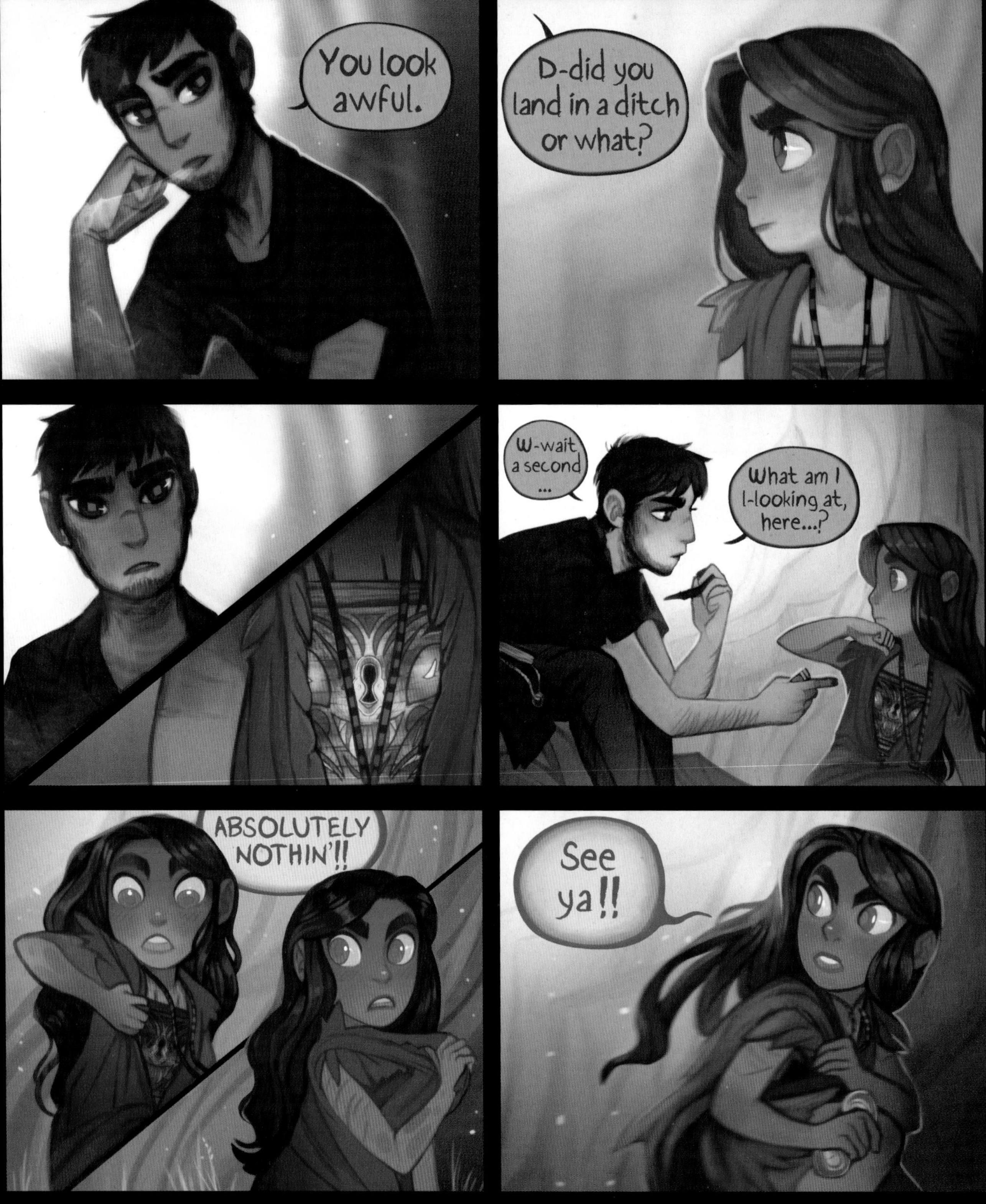
You look awful.
D-did you land in a ditch or what?
W-wait a second ...
What am I l-looking at, here...?
ABSOLUTELY NOTHIN'!!
See ya!!

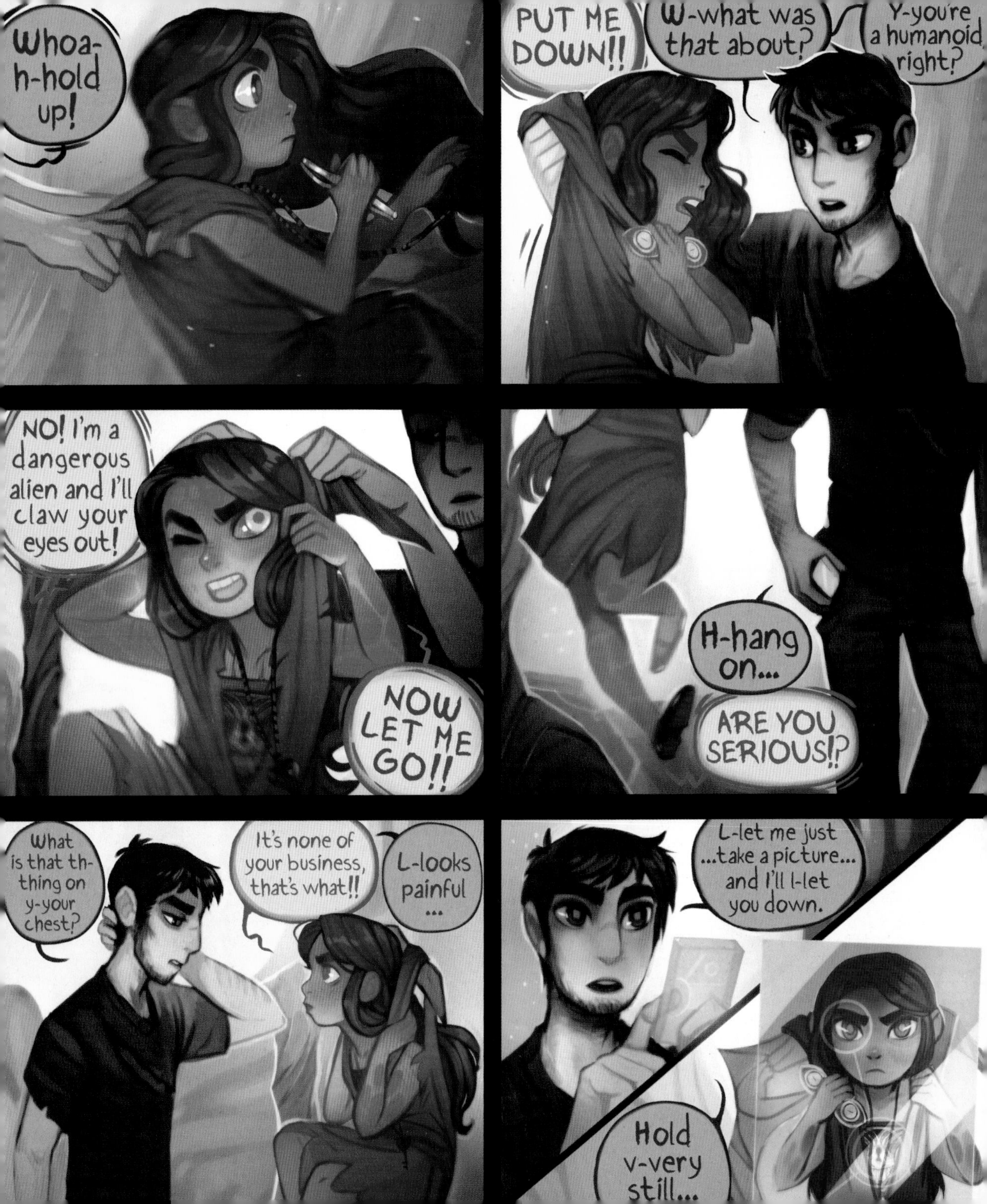
Whoa-h-hold up!
PUT ME DOWN!!
W-what was that about?
Y-you're a humanoid, right?
NO! I'm a dangerous alien and I'll claw your eyes out!
NOW LET ME GO!!
H-hang on...
ARE YOU SERIOUS!?
What is that th-thing on y-your chest?
It's none of your business, that's what!!
L-looks painful ...
L-let me just ...take a picture... and I'll l-let you down.
Hold v-very still...

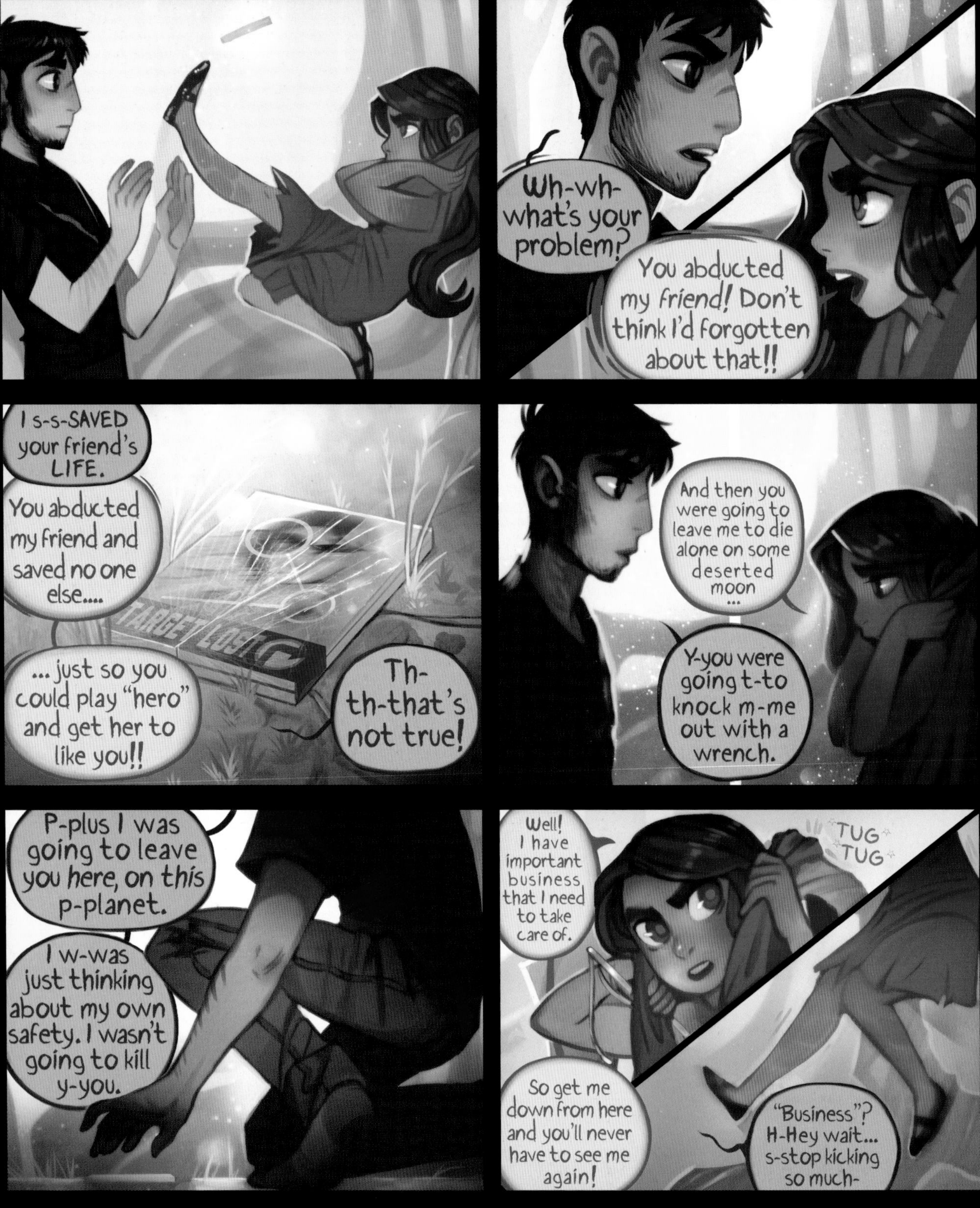
Wh-wh-what's your problem?
You abducted my friend! Don't think I'd forgotten about that!!
I s-s-SAVED your friend's LIFE.
You abducted my friend and saved no one else....
...just so you could play "hero" and get her to like you!!
Th-th-that's not true!
TARGET LOST
And then you were going to leave me to die alone on some deserted moon...
Y-you were going t-to knock m-me out with a wrench.
P-plus I was going to leave you here, on this p-planet.
I w-was just thinking about my own safety. I wasn't going to kill y-you.
Well! I have important business that I need to take care of.
TUG TUG
So get me down from here and you'll never have to see me again!
"Business"? H-Hey wait... s-stop kicking so much-

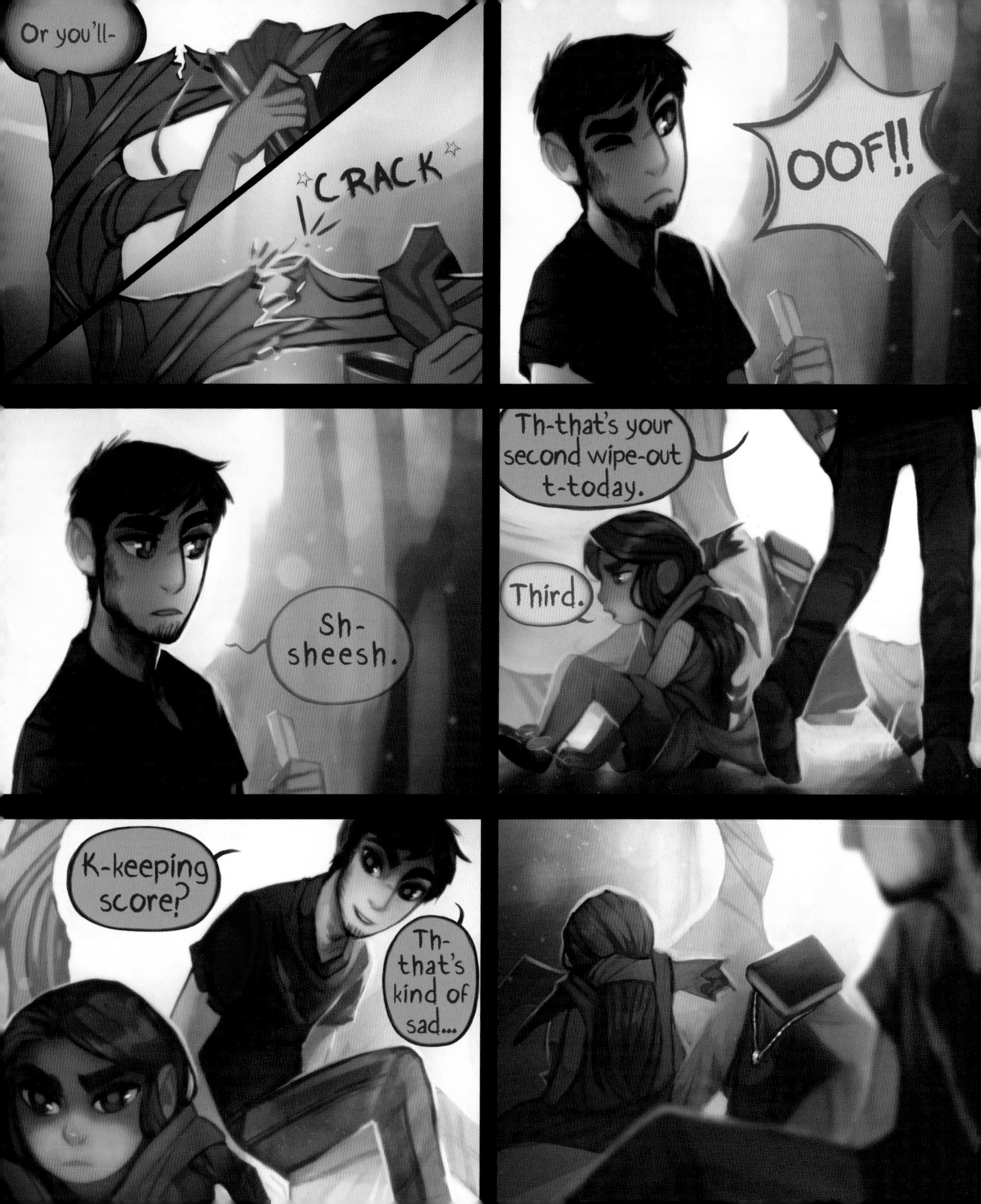
Or you'll-
CRACK
OOF!!
Sh-sheesh.
Th-that's your second wipe-out t-today.
Third.
K-keeping score?
Th-that's kind of sad...

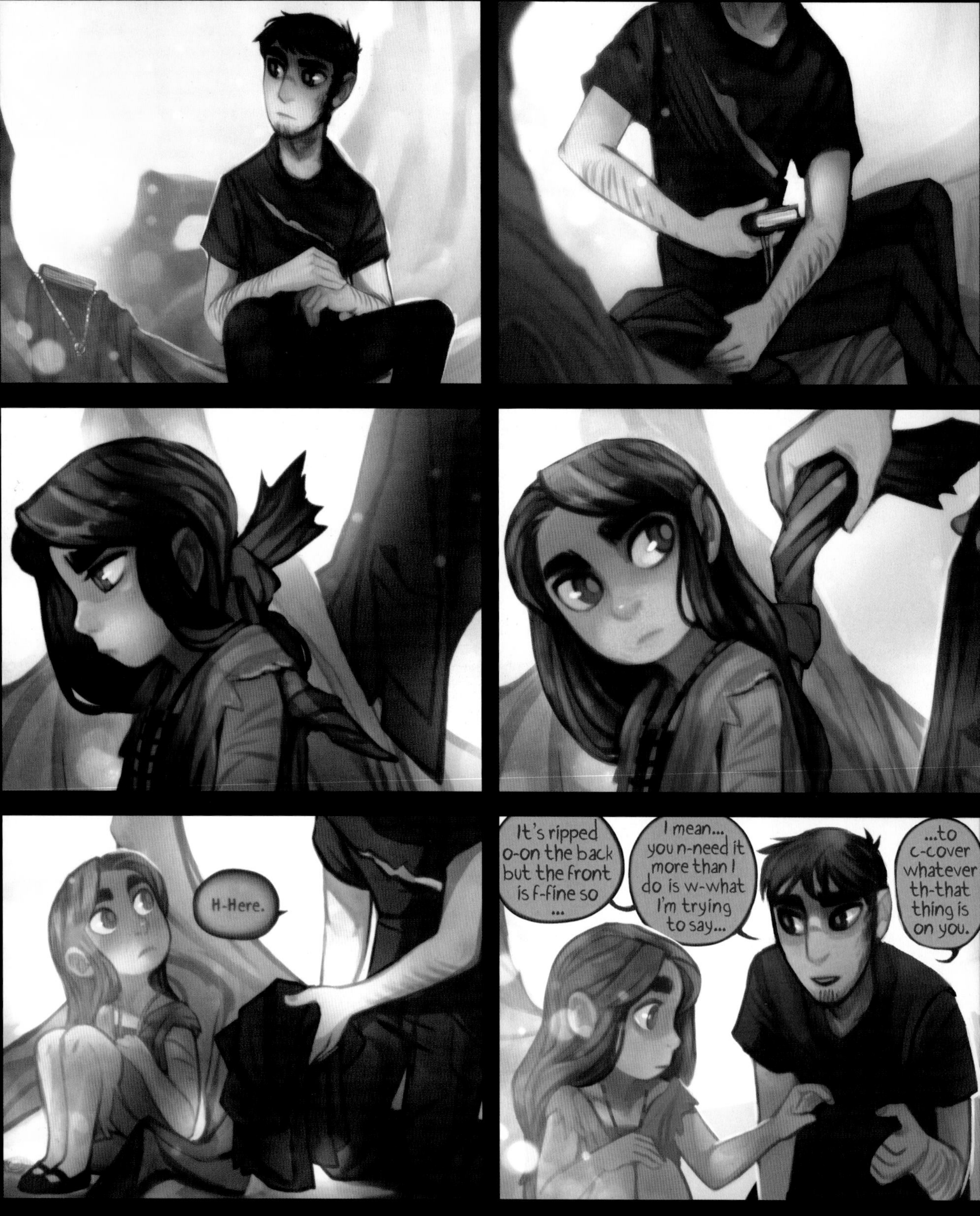
H-Here.
It's ripped o-on the back but the front is f-fine so ...
I mean... you n-need it more than I do is w-what I'm trying to say...
...to c-cover whatever th-that thing is on you.

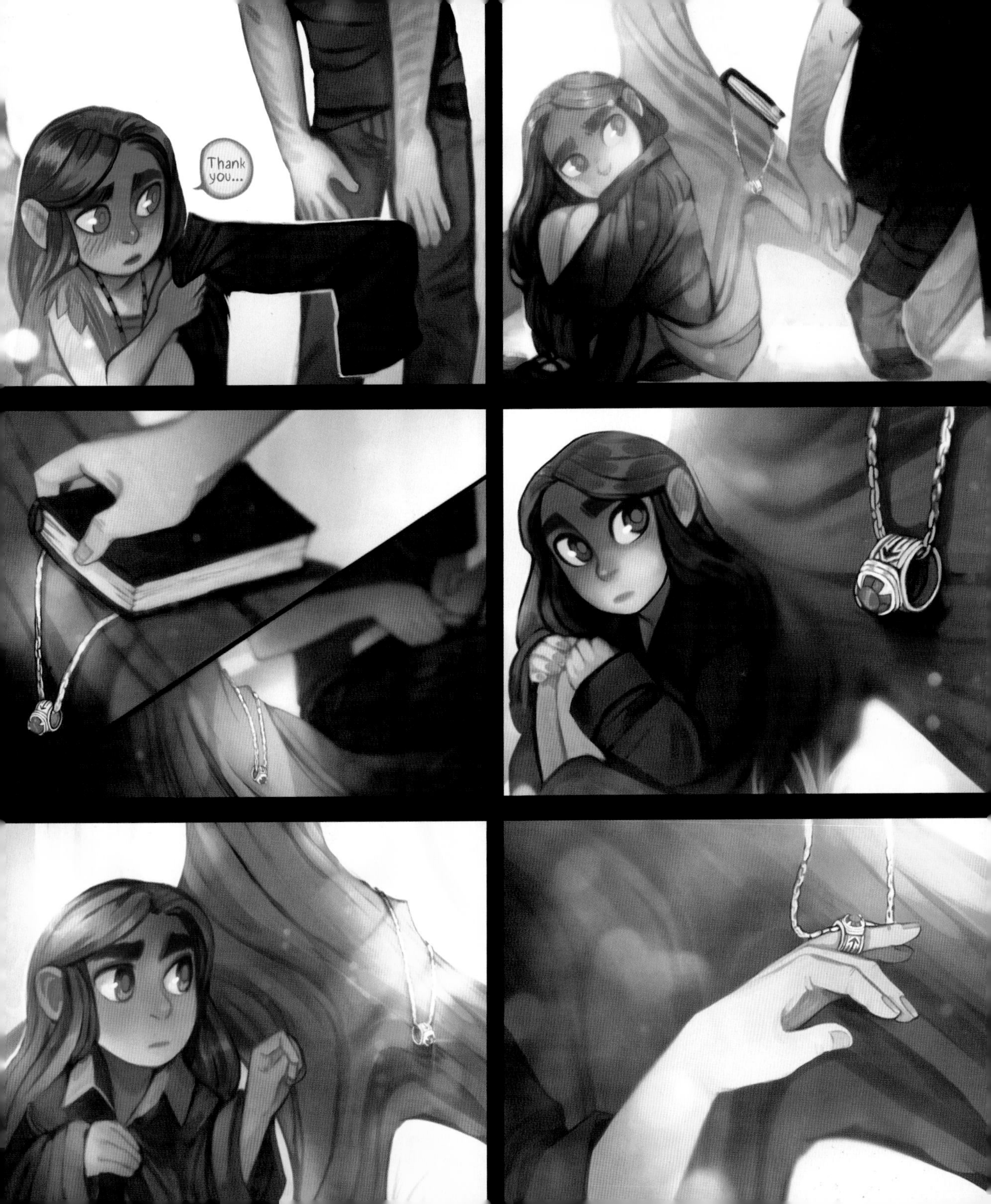
Thank you...

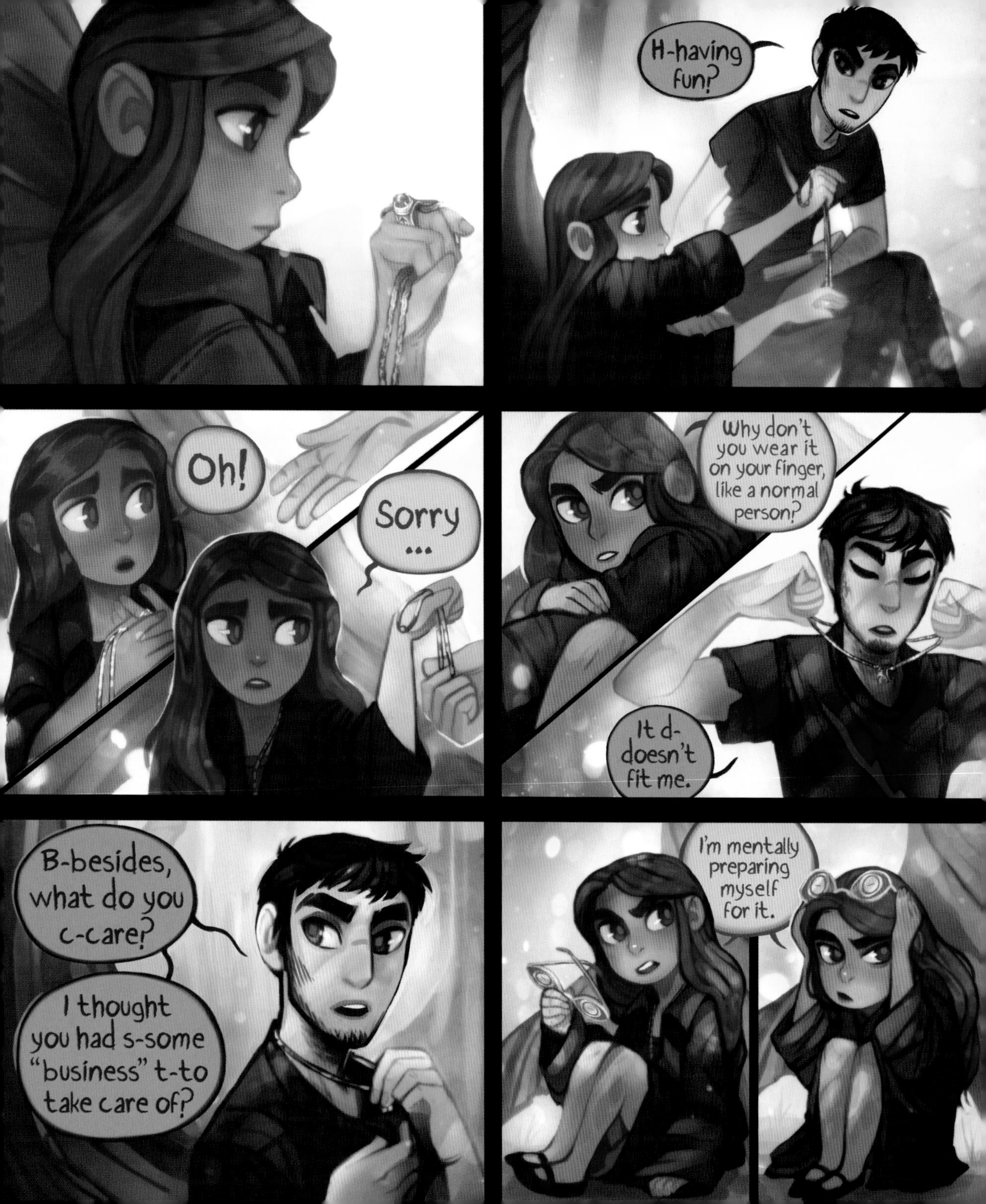
H-having fun?
Oh!
Sorry...
Why don't you wear it on your finger, like a normal person?
It d-doesn't fit me.
B-besides, what do you c-care?
I thought you had s-some "business" t-to take care of?
I'm mentally preparing myself for it.

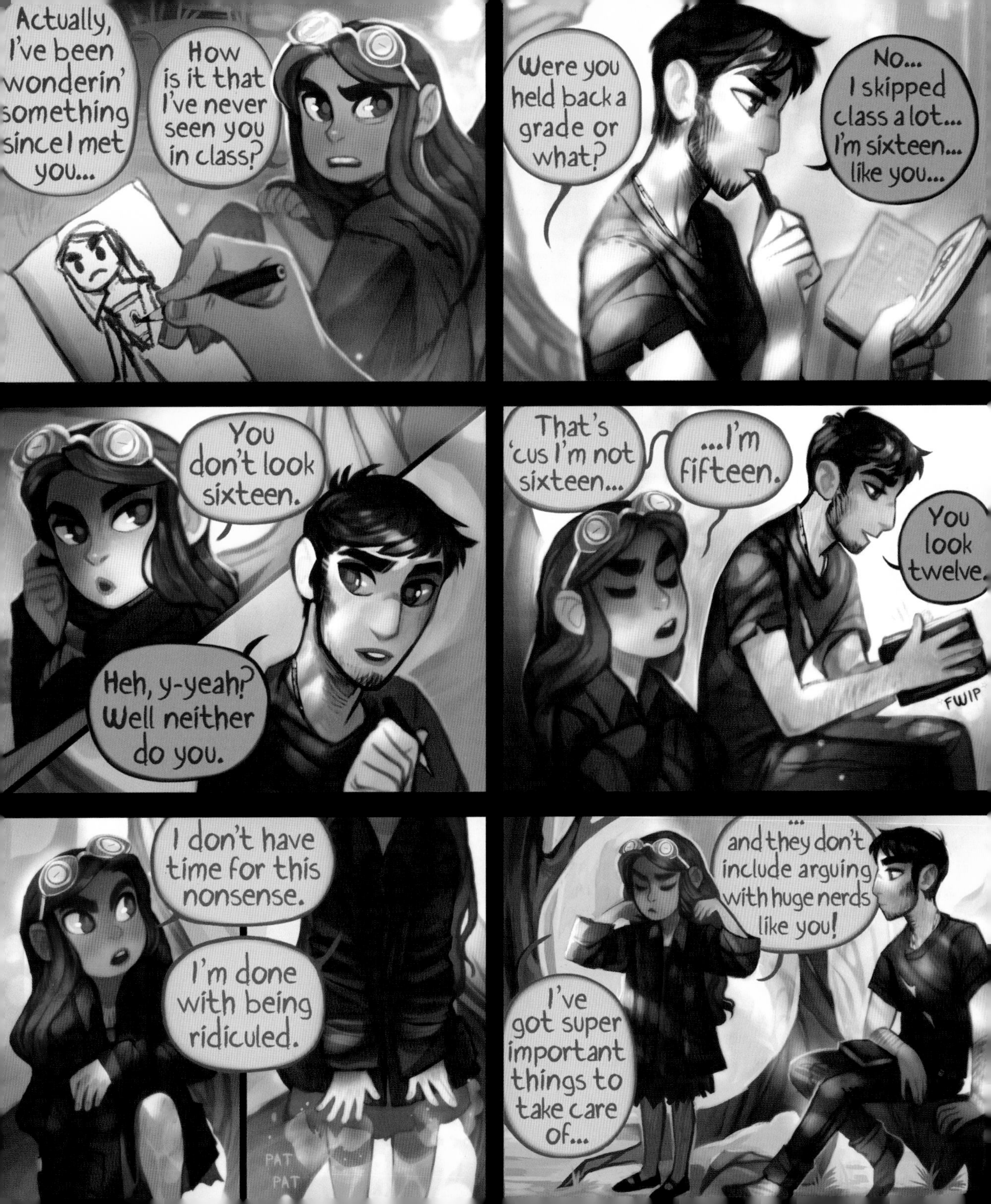

Actually, I've been wonderin' something since I met you...
How is it that I've never seen you in class?
Were you held back a grade or what?
No... I skipped class a lot... I'm sixteen... like you...
You don't look sixteen.
Heh, y-yeah? Well neither do you.
That's 'cus I'm not sixteen...
...I'm fifteen.
You look twelve.
FWIP
I don't have time for this nonsense.
I'm done with being ridiculed.
PAT PAT
I've got super important things to take care of...
...and they don't include arguing with huge nerds like you!

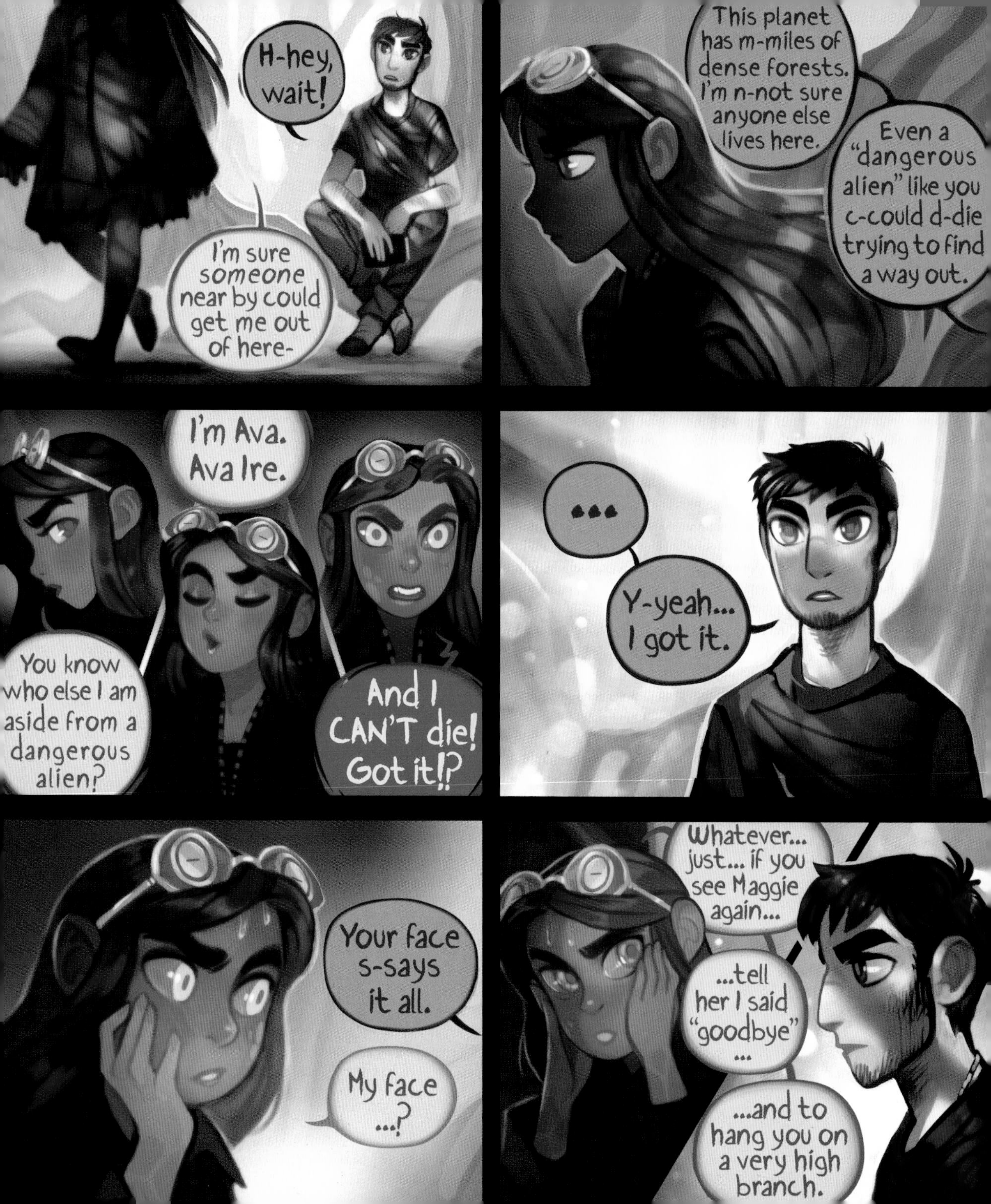
H-hey, wait!
I'm sure someone near by could get me out of here-
This planet has m-miles of dense forests. I'm n-not sure anyone else lives here.
Even a "dangerous alien" like you c-could d-die trying to find a way out.
I'm Ava. Ava Ire.
You know who else I am aside from a dangerous alien?
And I CAN'T die! Got it!?
...
Y-yeah... I got it.
Your face s-says it all.
My face ...?
Whatever... just... if you see Maggie again...
...tell her I said "goodbye" ...
...and to hang you on a very high branch.

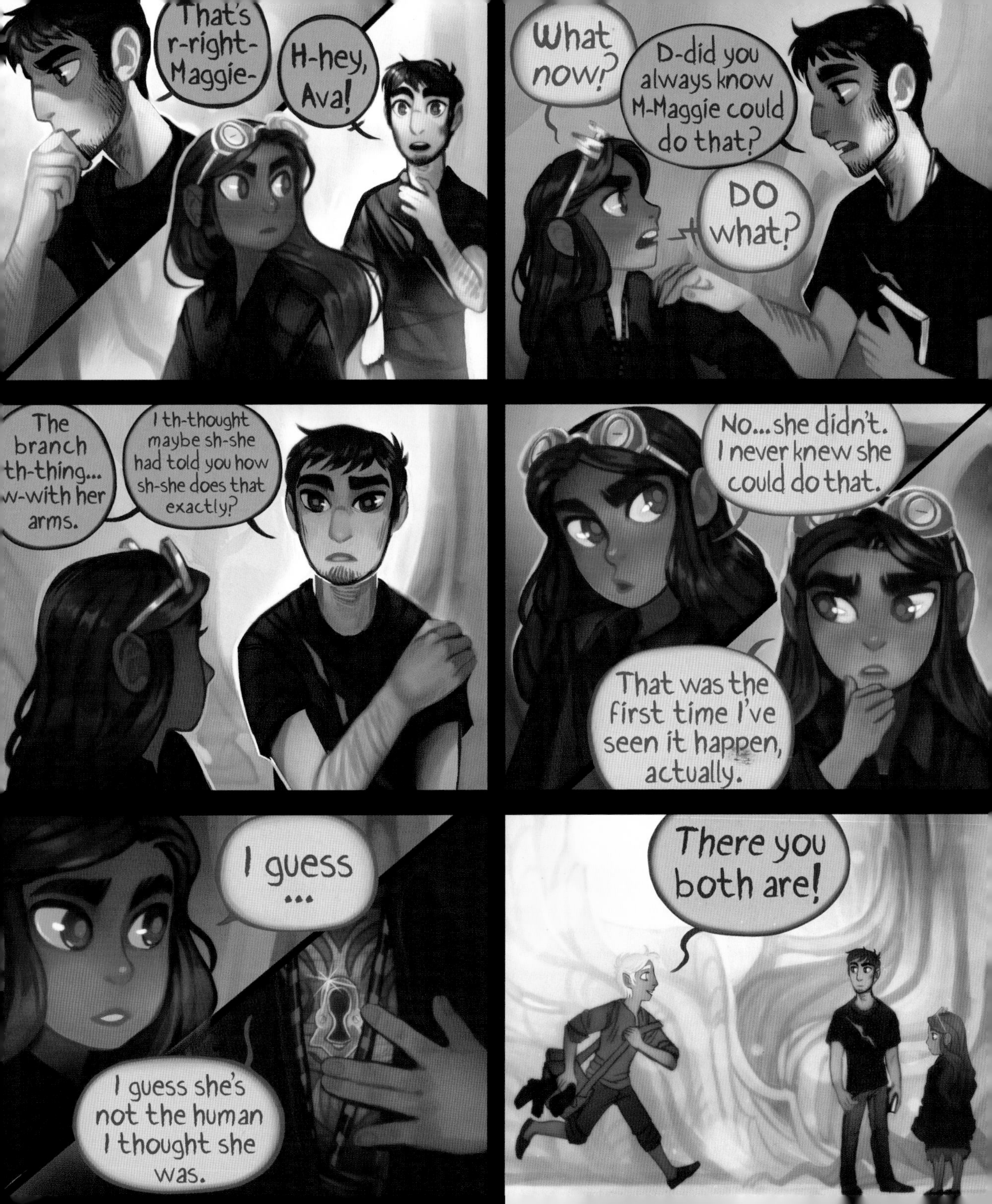
That's r-right-Maggie-
H-hey, Ava!
What now?
D-did you always know M-Maggie could do that?
DO what?
The branch th-thing... w-with her arms.
I th-thought maybe sh-she had told you how sh-she does that exactly?
No...she didn't. I never knew she could do that.
That was the first time I've seen it happen, actually.
I guess ...
I guess she's not the human I thought she was.
There you both are!

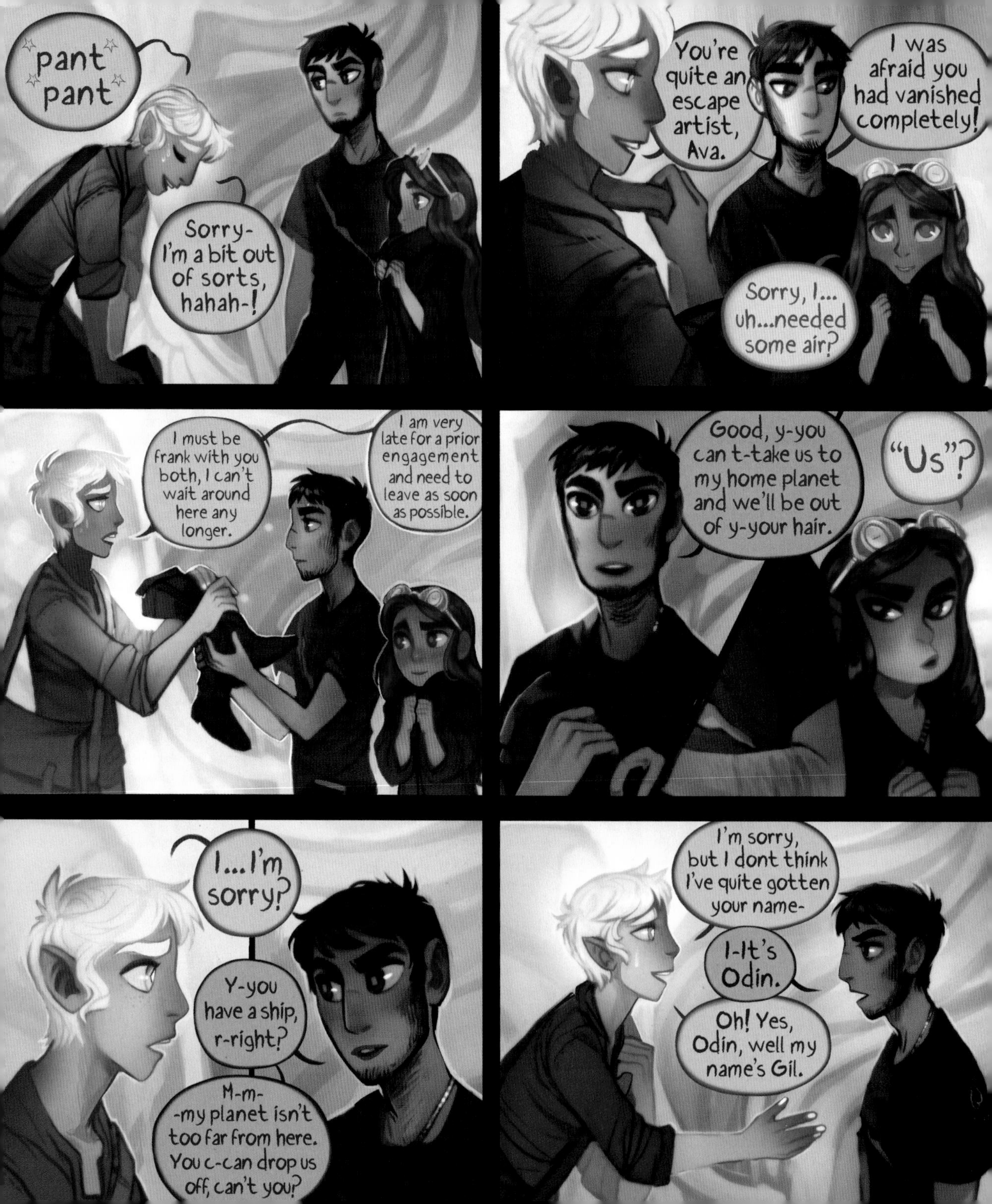
pant pant
Sorry- I'm a bit out of sorts, hahah-!
You're quite an escape artist, Ava.
I was afraid you had vanished completely!
Sorry, I... uh...needed some air?
I must be frank with you both, I can't wait around here any longer.
I am very late for a prior engagement and need to leave as soon as possible.
Good, y-you can t-take us to my home planet and we'll be out of y-your hair.
"Us"?
I...I'm sorry?
Y-you have a ship, r-right?
M-m- -my planet isn't too far from here. You c-can drop us off, can't you?
I'm sorry, but I dont think I've quite gotten your name-
I-It's Odin.
Oh! Yes, Odin, well my name's Gil.

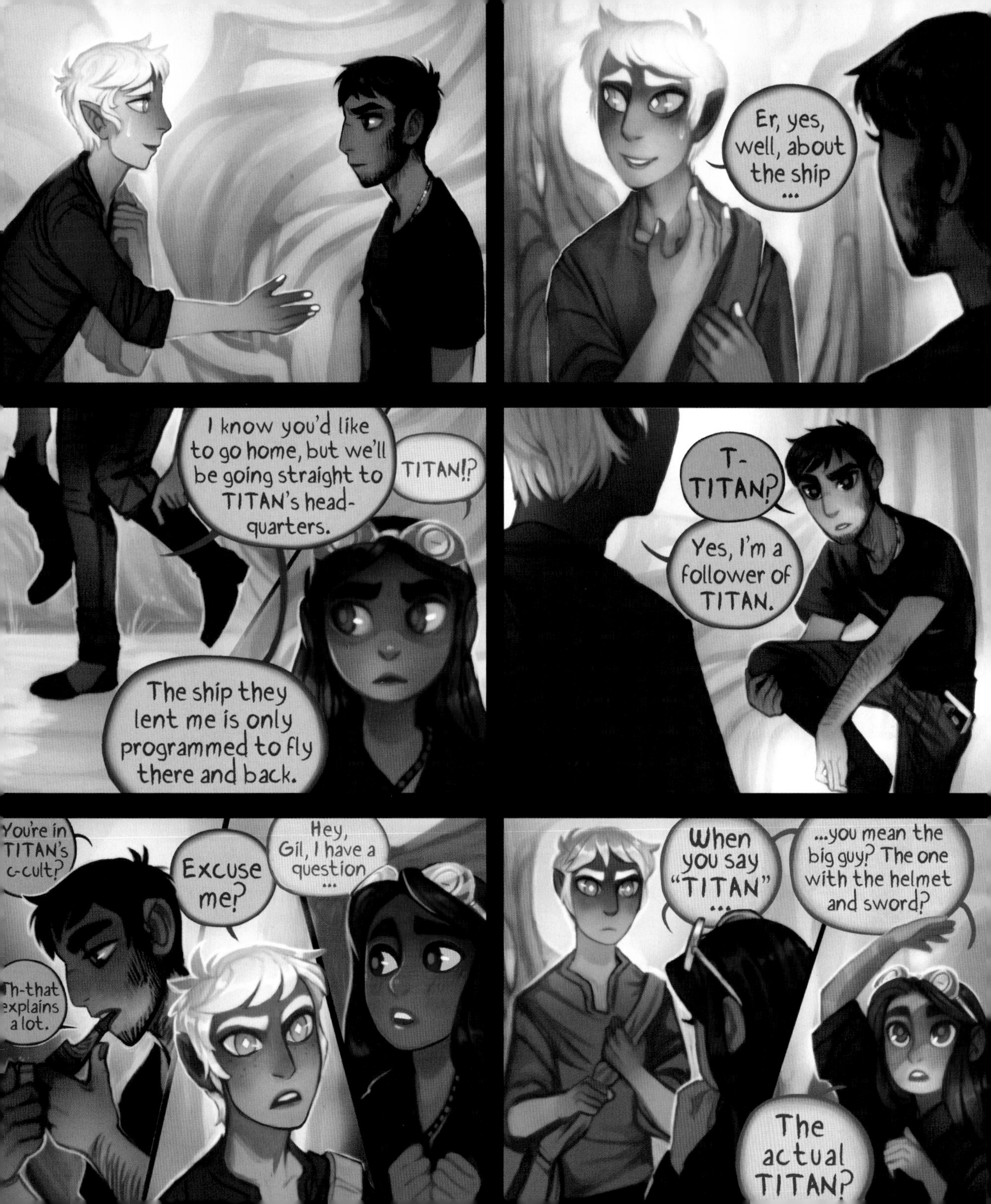
Er, yes, well, about the ship ...
I know you'd like to go home, but we'll be going straight to TITAN's head-quarters.
TITAN!?
The ship they lent me is only programmed to fly there and back.
T-TITAN?
Yes, I'm a follower of TITAN.
You're in TITAN's c-cult?
Excuse me?
Hey, Gil, I have a question ...
Th-that explains a lot.
When you say "TITAN" ...
...you mean the big guy? The one with the helmet and sword?
The actual TITAN?

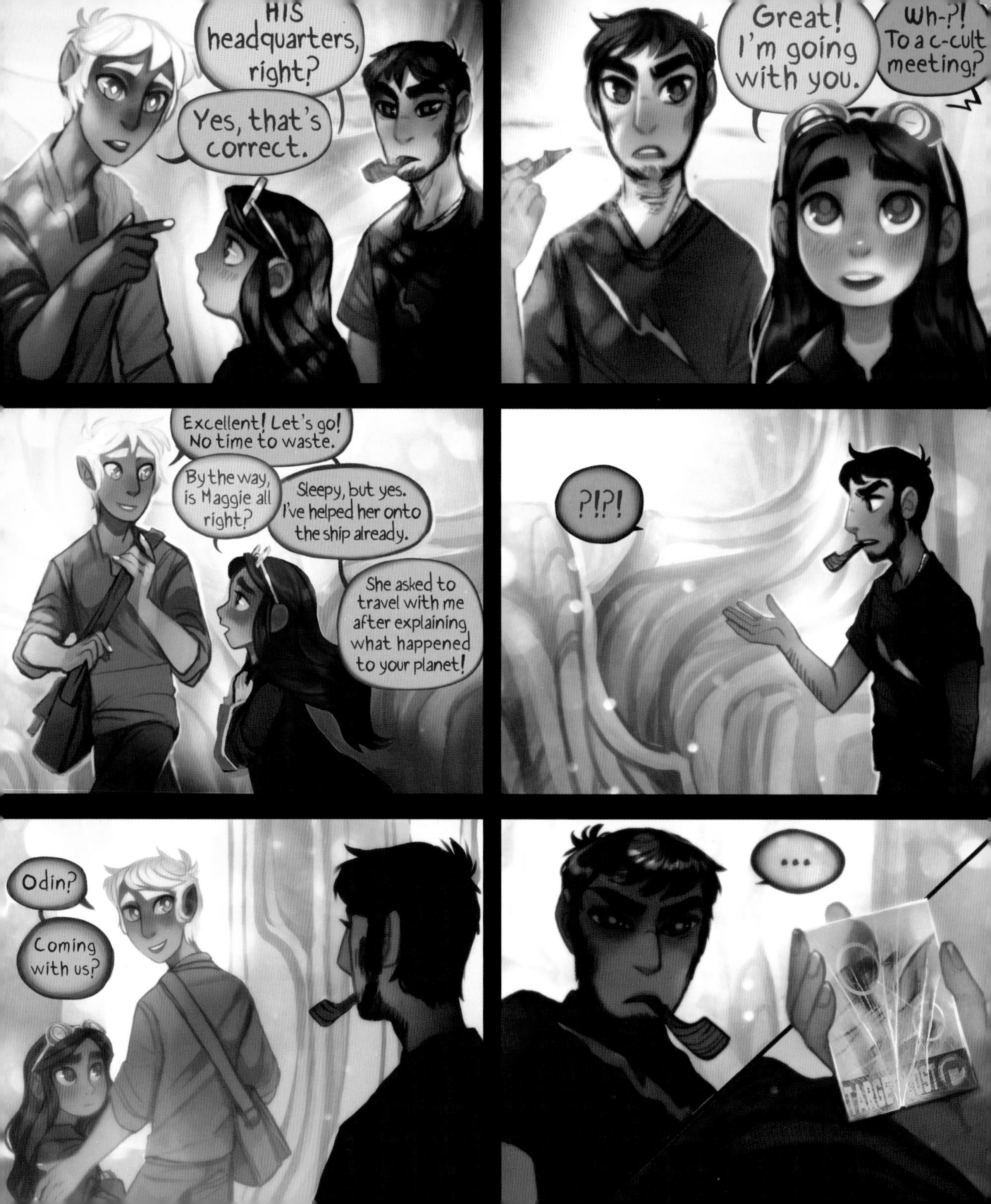
HIS headquarters, right?
Yes, that's correct.
Great! I'm going with you.
Wh-?! To a c-cult meeting?
Excellent! Let's go! No time to waste.
By the way, is Maggie all right?
Sleepy, but yes. I've helped her onto the ship already.
She asked to travel with me after explaining what happened to your planet!
?!?!
Odin?
Coming with us?
...

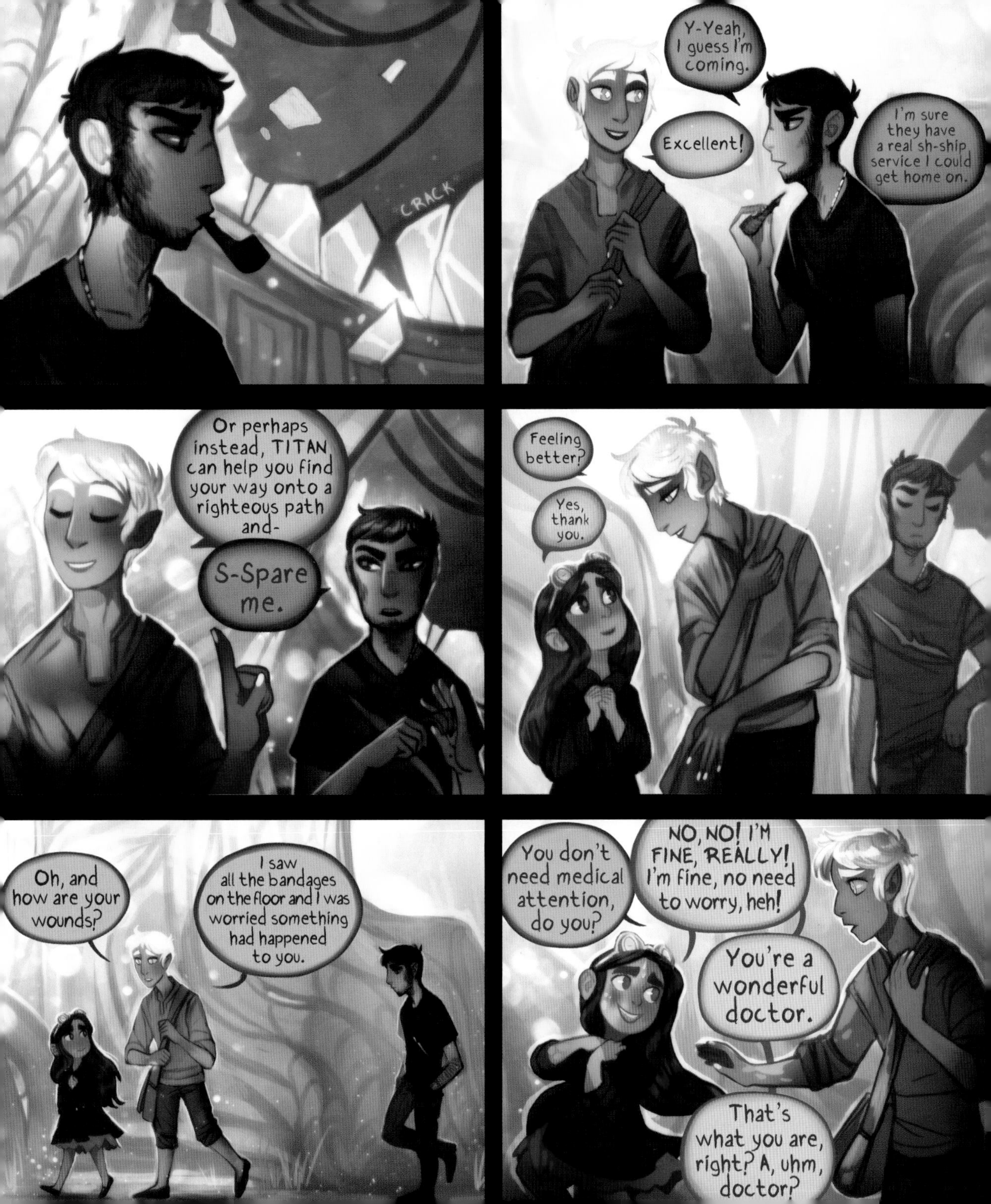
CRACK
Y-Yeah, I guess I'm coming.
Excellent!
I'm sure they have a real sh-ship service I could get home on.
Or perhaps instead, TITAN can help you find your way onto a righteous path and-
S-Spare me.
Feeling better?
Yes, thank you.
Oh, and how are your wounds?
I saw all the bandages on the floor and I was worried something had happened to you.
You don't need medical attention, do you?
NO, NO! I'M FINE, REALLY! I'm fine, no need to worry, heh!
You're a wonderful doctor.
That's what you are, right? A, uhm, doctor?

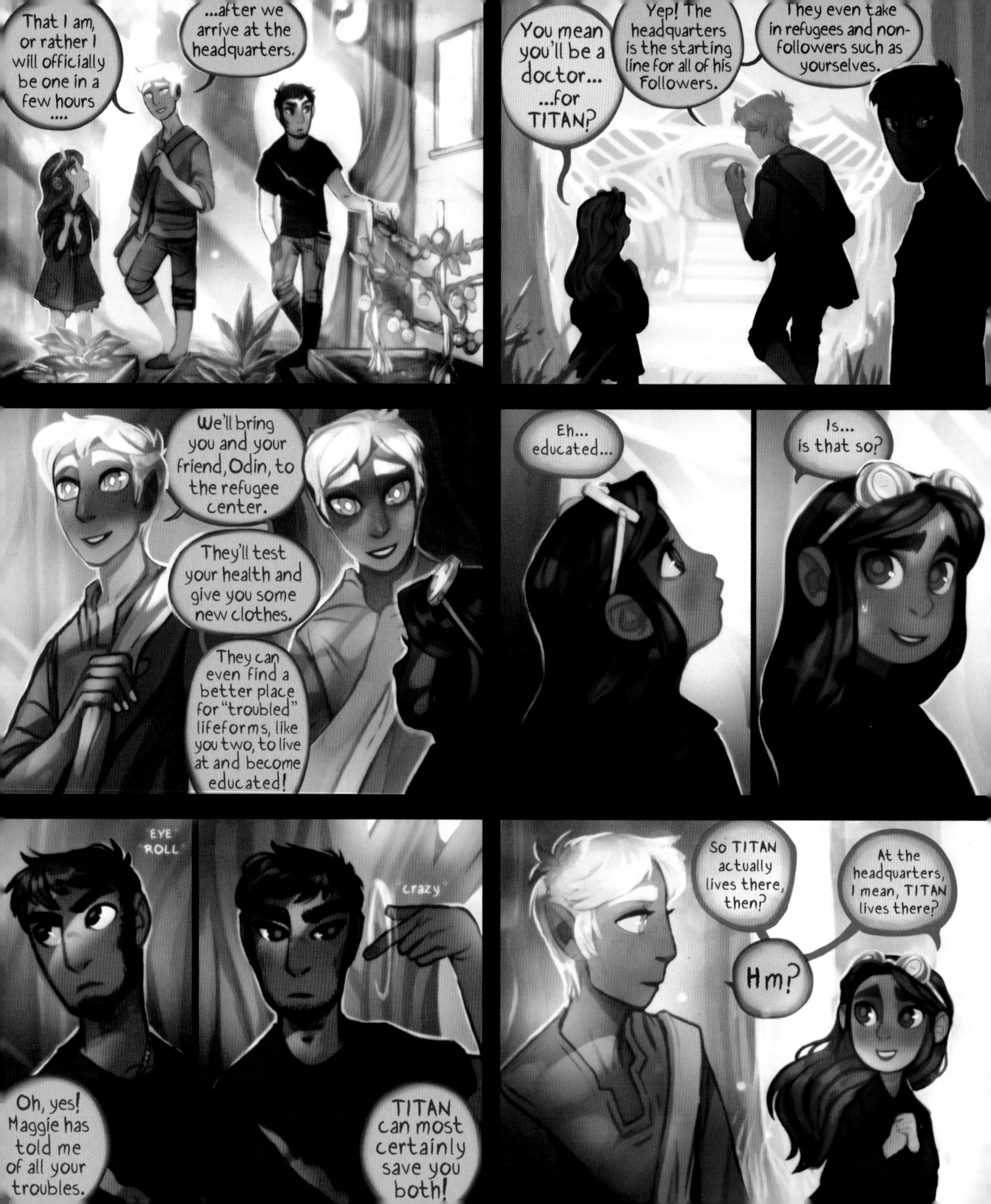

That I am, or rather I will officially be one in a few hours ....
...after we arrive at the headquarters.
You mean you'll be a doctor... ...for TITAN?
Yep! The headquarters is the starting line for all of his Followers.
They even take in refugees and non-followers such as yourselves.
We'll bring you and your friend, Odin, to the refugee center.
They'll test your health and give you some new clothes.
They can even find a better place for "troubled" lifeforms, like you two, to live at and become educated!
Eh... educated...
Is... is that so?
EYE ROLL
Oh, yes! Maggie has told me of all your troubles.
"crazy"
TITAN can most certainly save you both!
So TITAN actually lives there, then?
Hm?
At the headquarters, I mean, TITAN lives there?

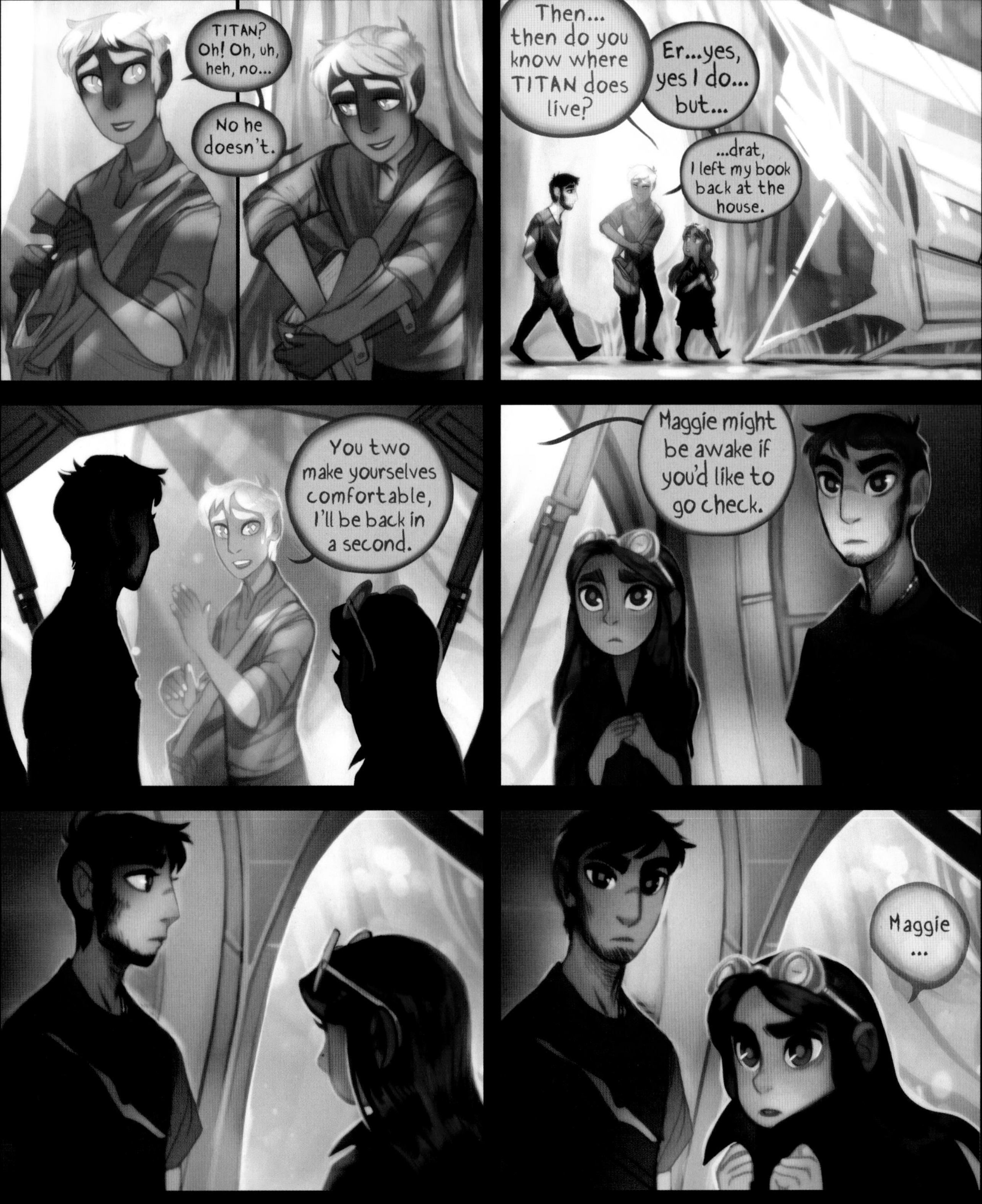
TITAN? Oh! Oh, uh, heh, no...
No he doesn't.
Then... then do you know where TITAN does live?
Er...yes, yes I do... but...
...drat, I left my book back at the house.
You two make yourselves comfortable, I'll be back in a second.
Maggie might be awake if you'd like to go check.
Maggie ...

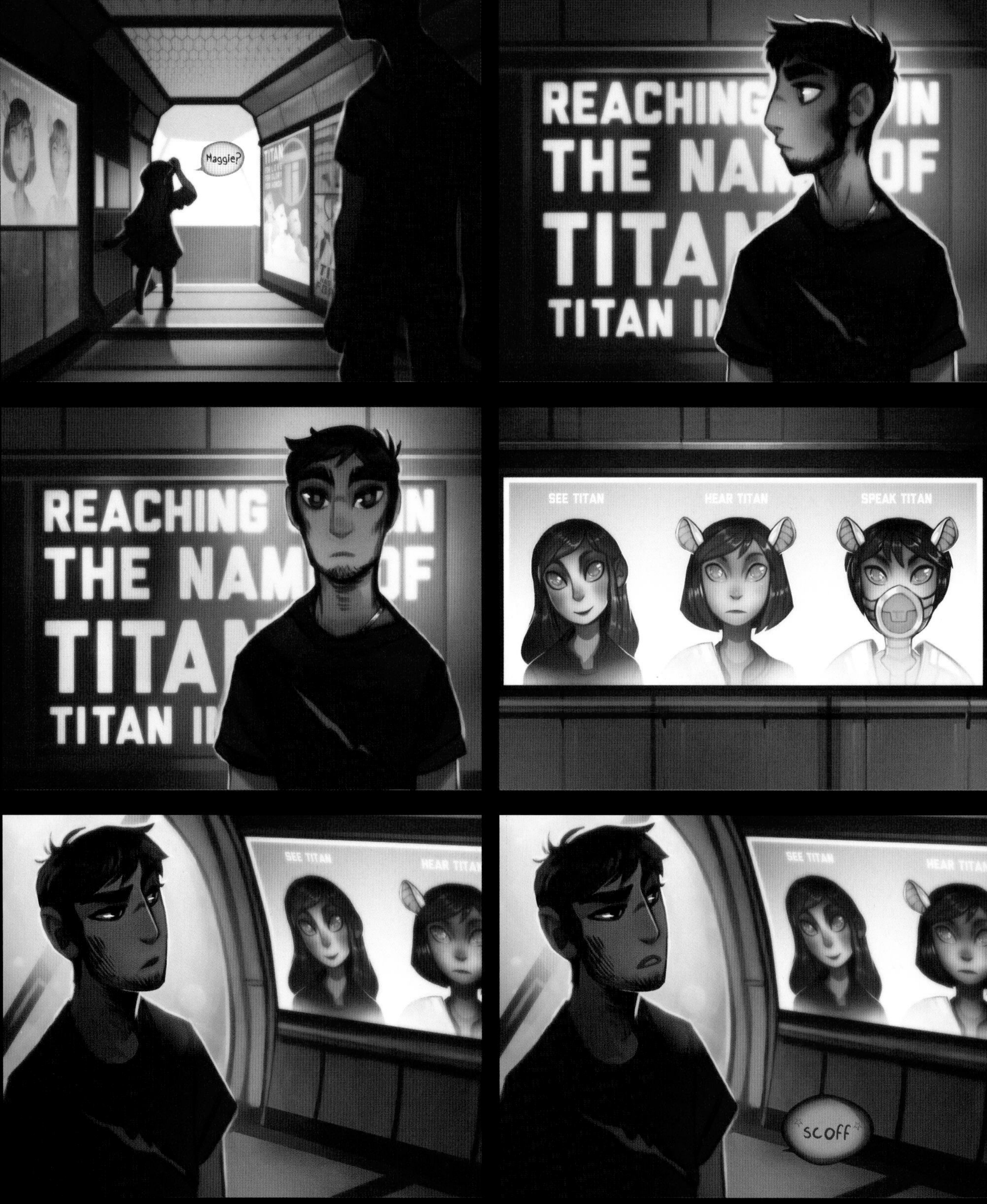
Maggie?
REACHING IN
THE NAM OF
TITAN
TITAN I
REACHING IN
THE NAM OF
TITAN
TITAN I
SEE TITAN
HEAR TITAN
SPEAK TITAN
SEE TITAN
HEAR TITAN
SEE TITAN
HEAR TITAN
scoff

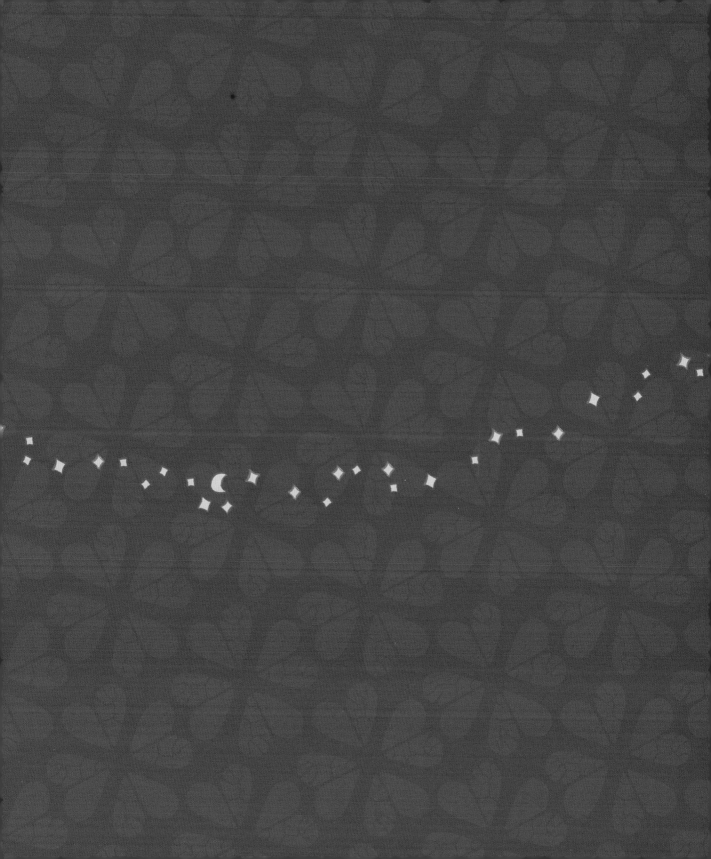

CHAPTER 4

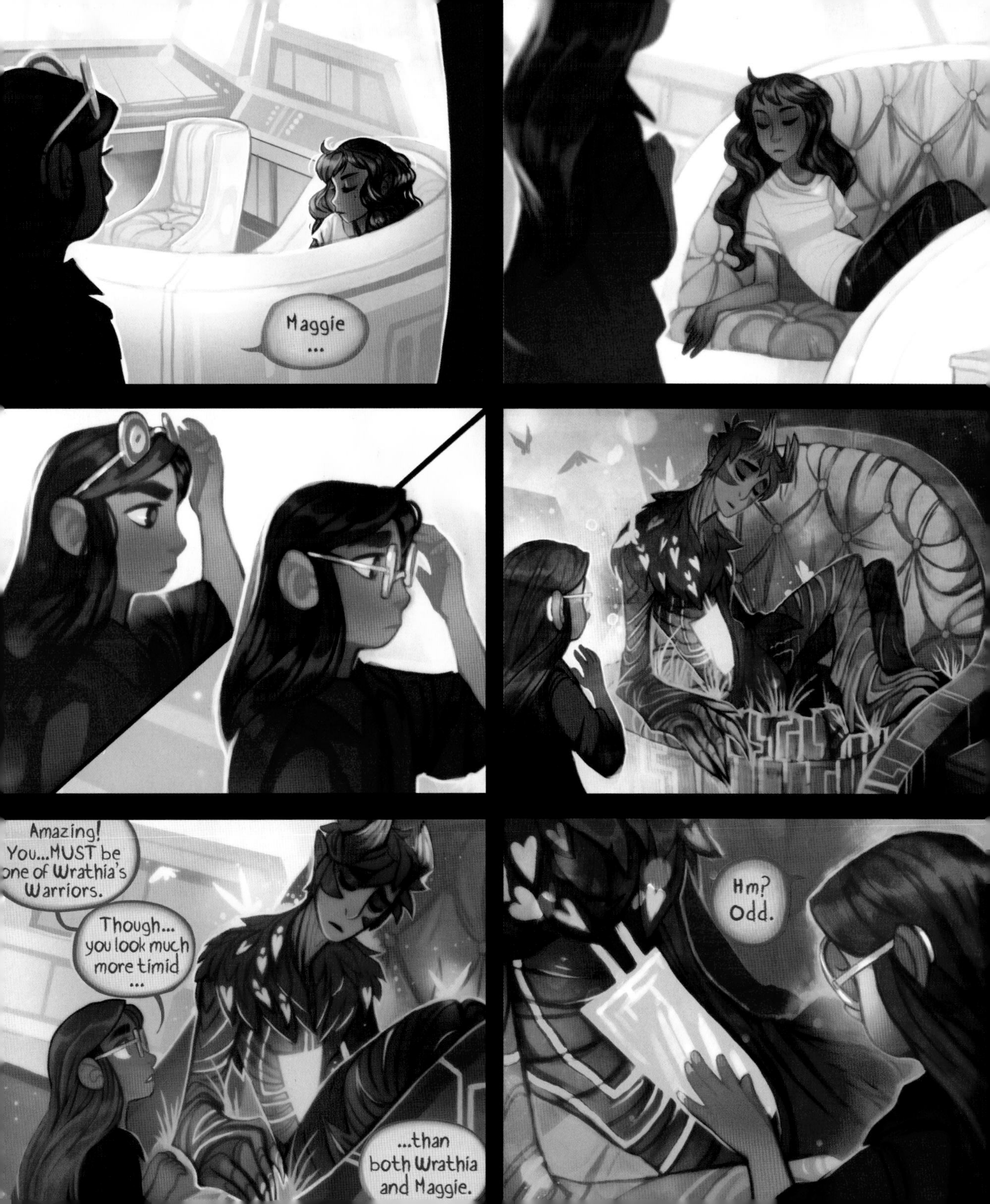
Maggie ...
Amazing! You...MUST be one of Wrathia's Warriors.
Though... you look much more timid ...
...than both Wrathia and Maggie.
Hm? Odd.

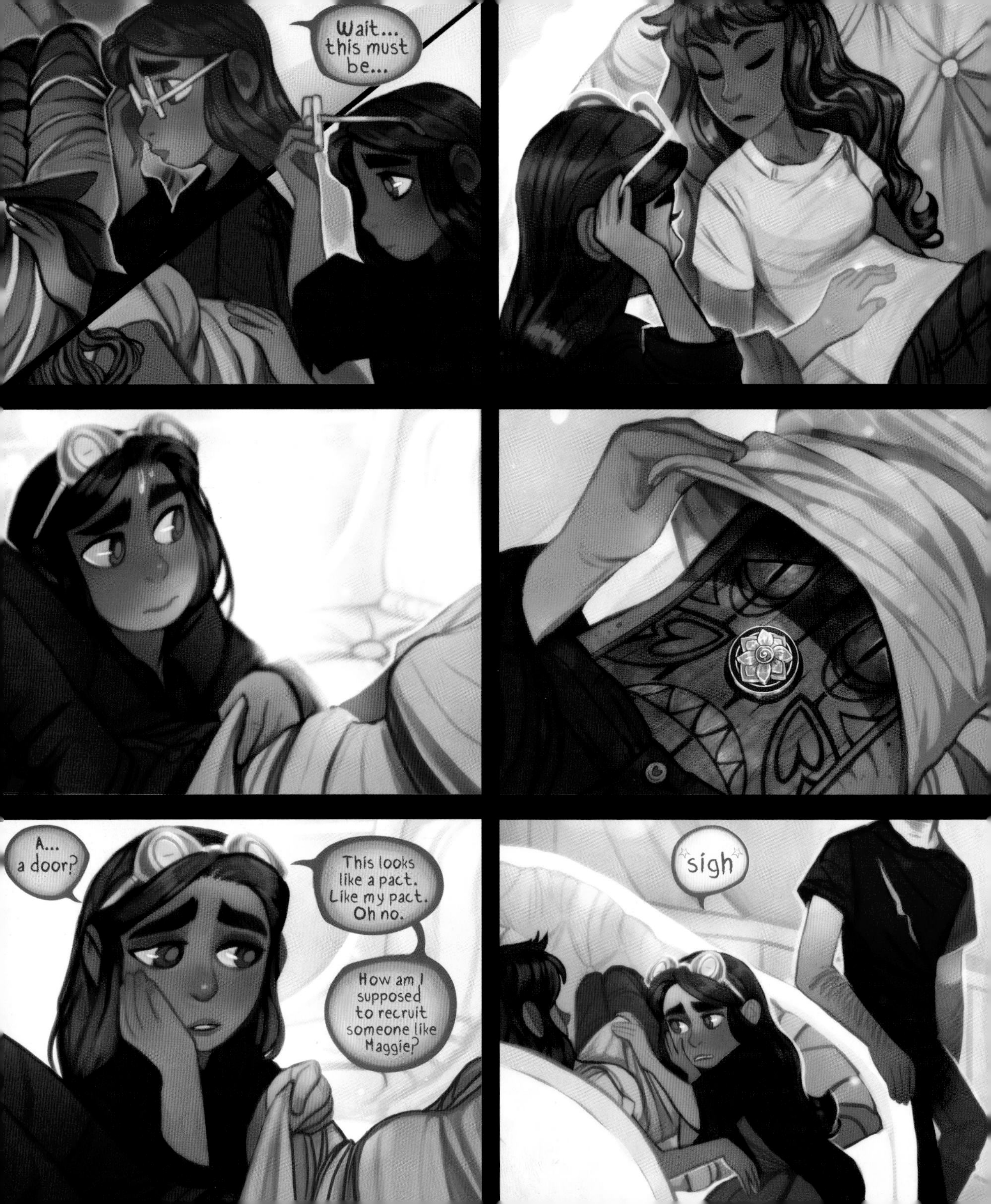
Wait... this must be...
A... a door?
This looks like a pact. Like my pact. Oh no.
How am I supposed to recruit someone like Maggie?
sigh

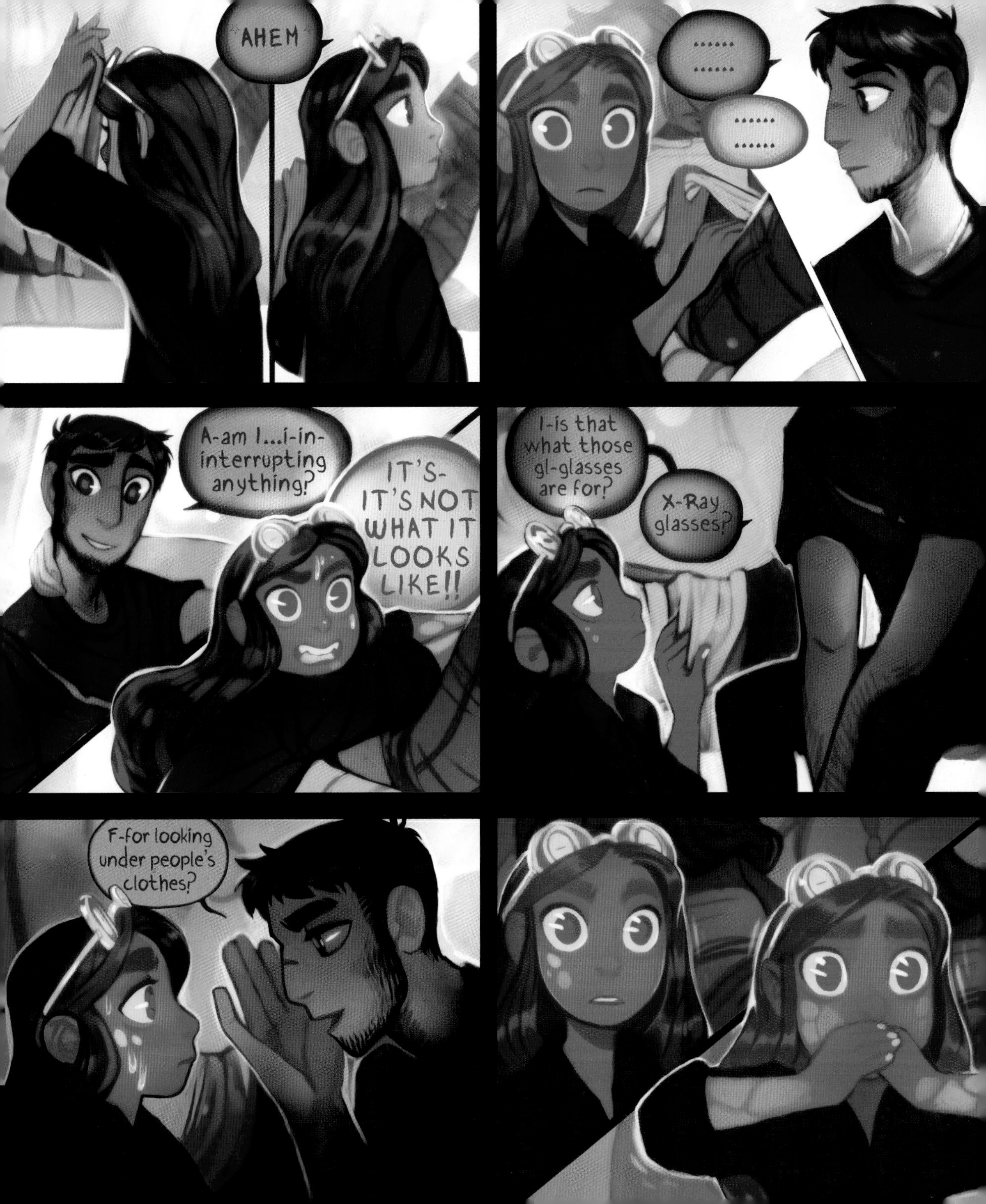
AHEM
......
......
......
......
A-am I...i-in-interrupting anything?
IT'S-IT'S NOT WHAT IT LOOKS LIKE!!
I-is that what those gl-glasses are for?
X-Ray glasses?
F-for looking under people's clothes?

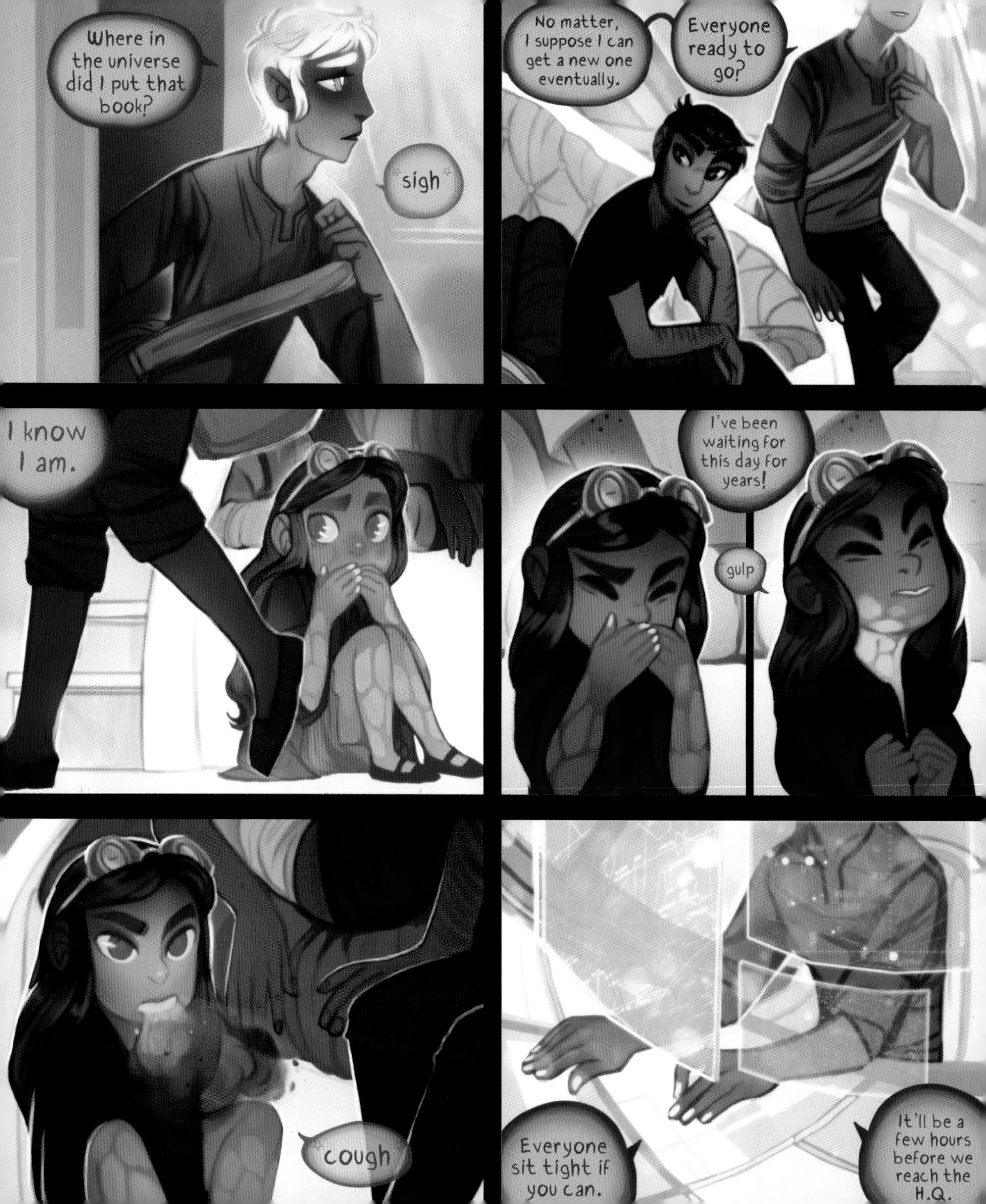

Where in the universe did I put that book?
sigh
No matter, I suppose I can get a new one eventually.
Everyone ready to go?
I know I am.
I've been waiting for this day for years!
gulp
cough
Everyone sit tight if you can.
It'll be a few hours before we reach the H.Q.

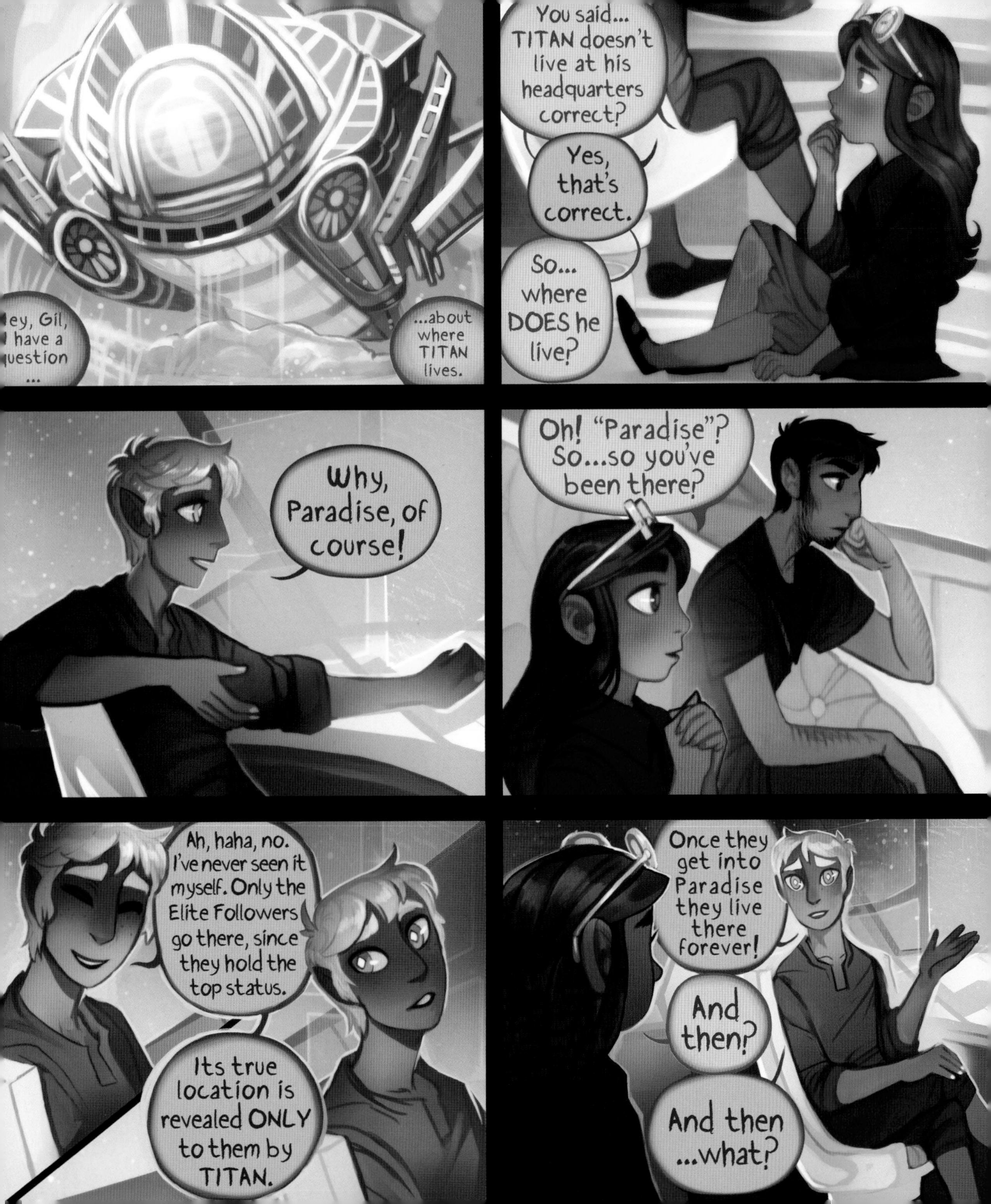

ey, Gil, have a uestion ...
...about where TITAN lives.
You said... TITAN doesn't live at his headquarters correct?
Yes, that's correct.
So... where DOES he live?
Why, Paradise, of course!
Oh! "Paradise"? So...so you've been there?
Ah, haha, no. I've never seen it myself. Only the Elite Followers go there, since they hold the top status.
Its true location is revealed ONLY to them by TITAN.
Once they get into Paradise they live there forever!
And then?
And then ...what?

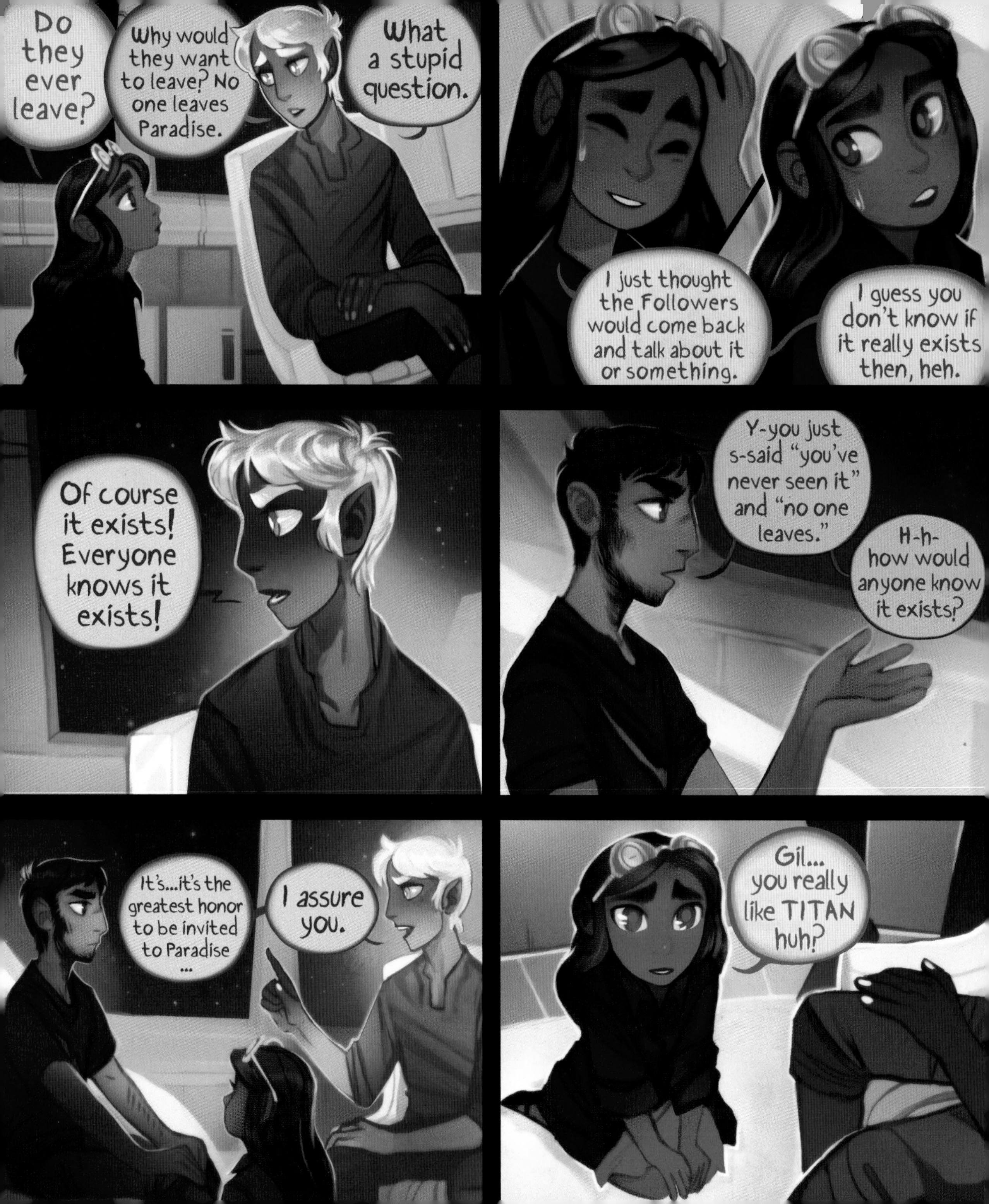
Do they ever leave?
Why would they want to leave? No one leaves Paradise.
What a stupid question.
I just thought the Followers would come back and talk about it or something.
I guess you don't know if it really exists then, heh.
Of course it exists! Everyone knows it exists!
Y-you just s-said "you've never seen it" and "no one leaves."
H-h-how would anyone know it exists?
It's...it's the greatest honor to be invited to Paradise ...
I assure you.
Gil... you really like TITAN huh?

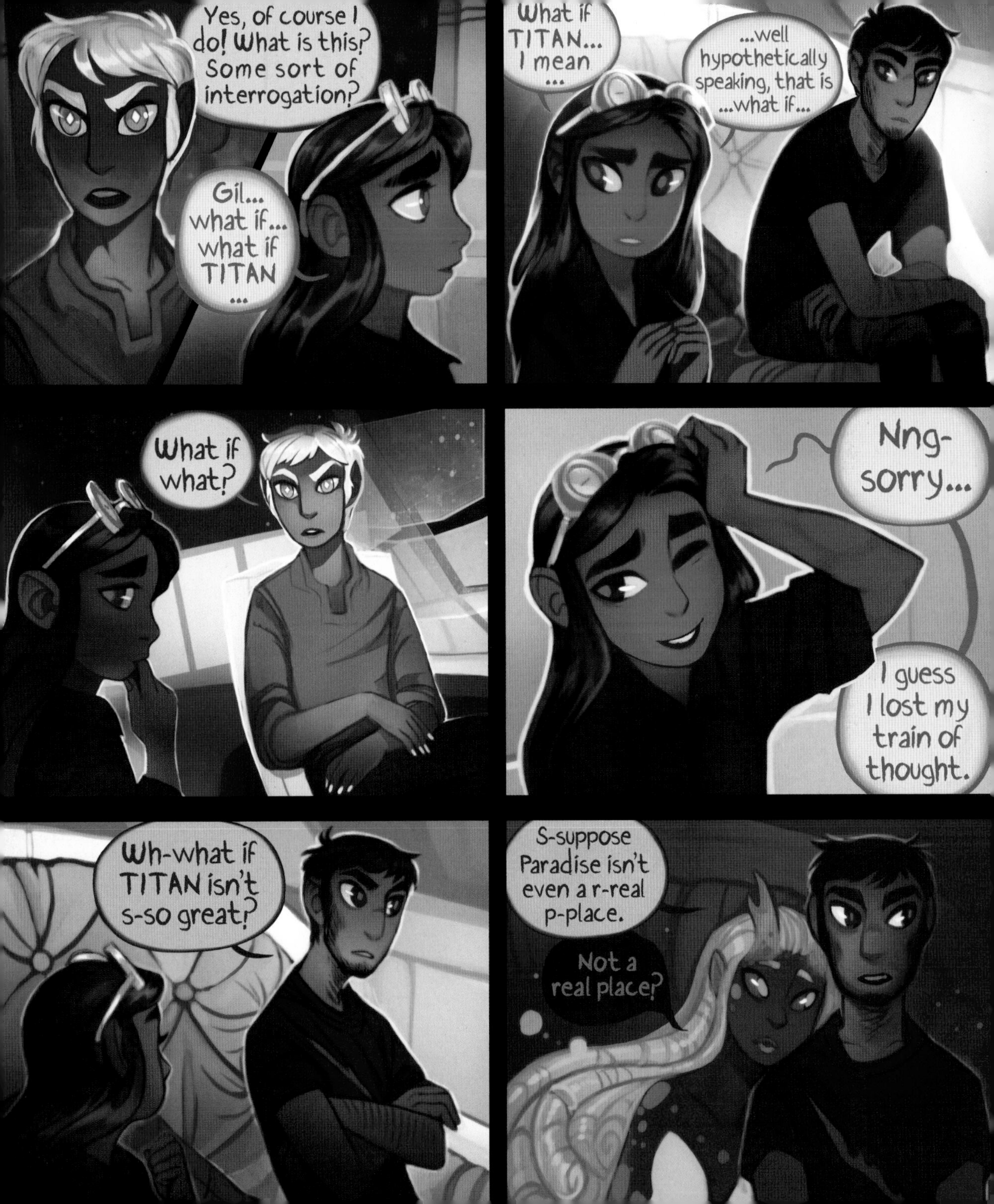
Yes, of course I do! What is this? Some sort of interrogation?
Gil... what if... what if TITAN ...
What if TITAN... I mean ...
...well hypothetically speaking, that is ...what if...
What if what?
Nng-sorry...
I guess I lost my train of thought.
Wh-what if TITAN isn't s-so great?
S-suppose Paradise isn't even a r-real p-place.
Not a real place?

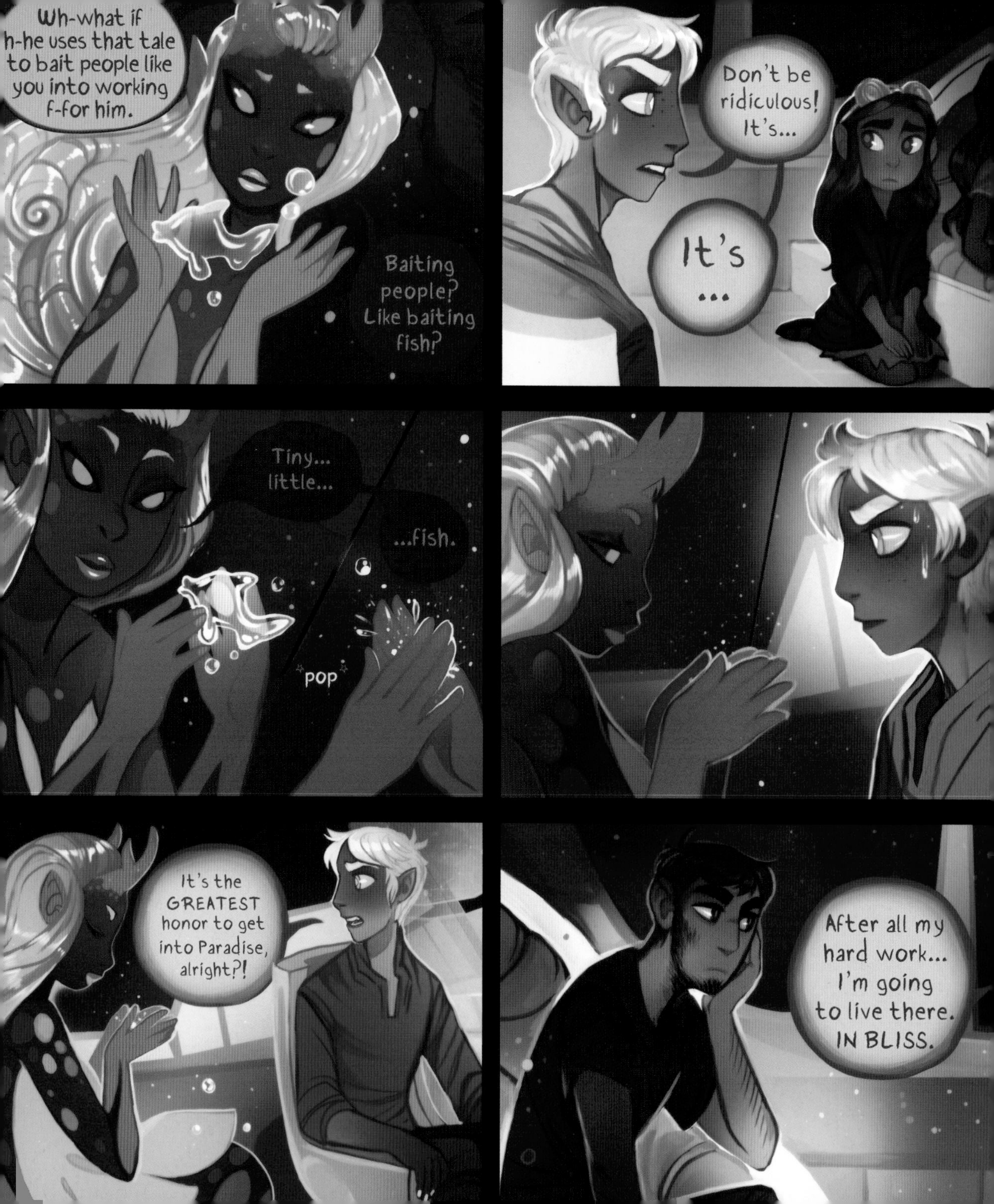

Wh-what if h-he uses that tale to bait people like you into working f-for him.
Baiting people? Like baiting fish?
Don't be ridiculous! It's...
It's ...
Tiny... little...
...fish.
pop
It's the GREATEST honor to get into Paradise, alright?!
After all my hard work... I'm going to live there. IN BLISS.

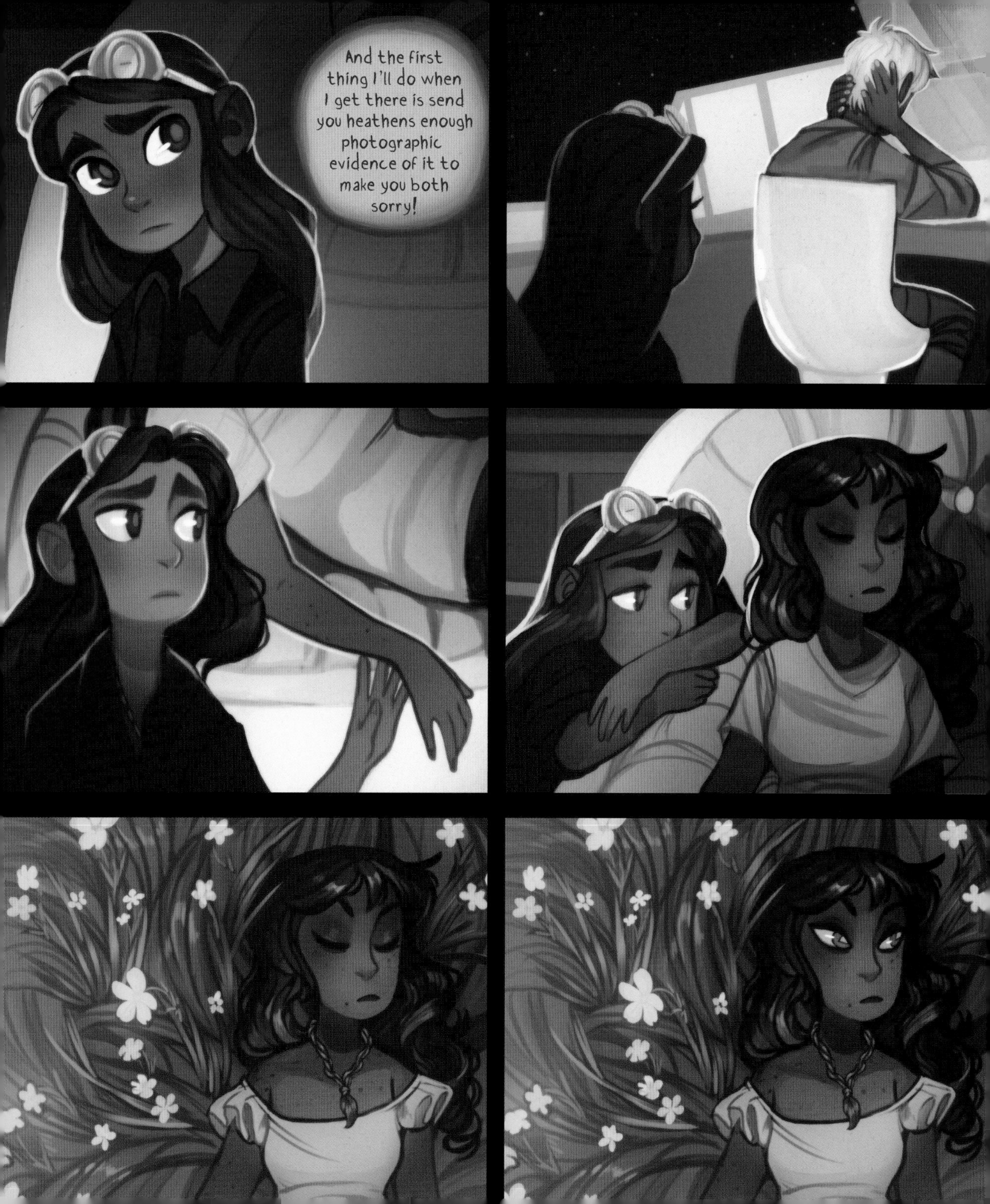
And the first thing I'll do when I get there is send you heathens enough photographic evidence of it to make you both sorry!

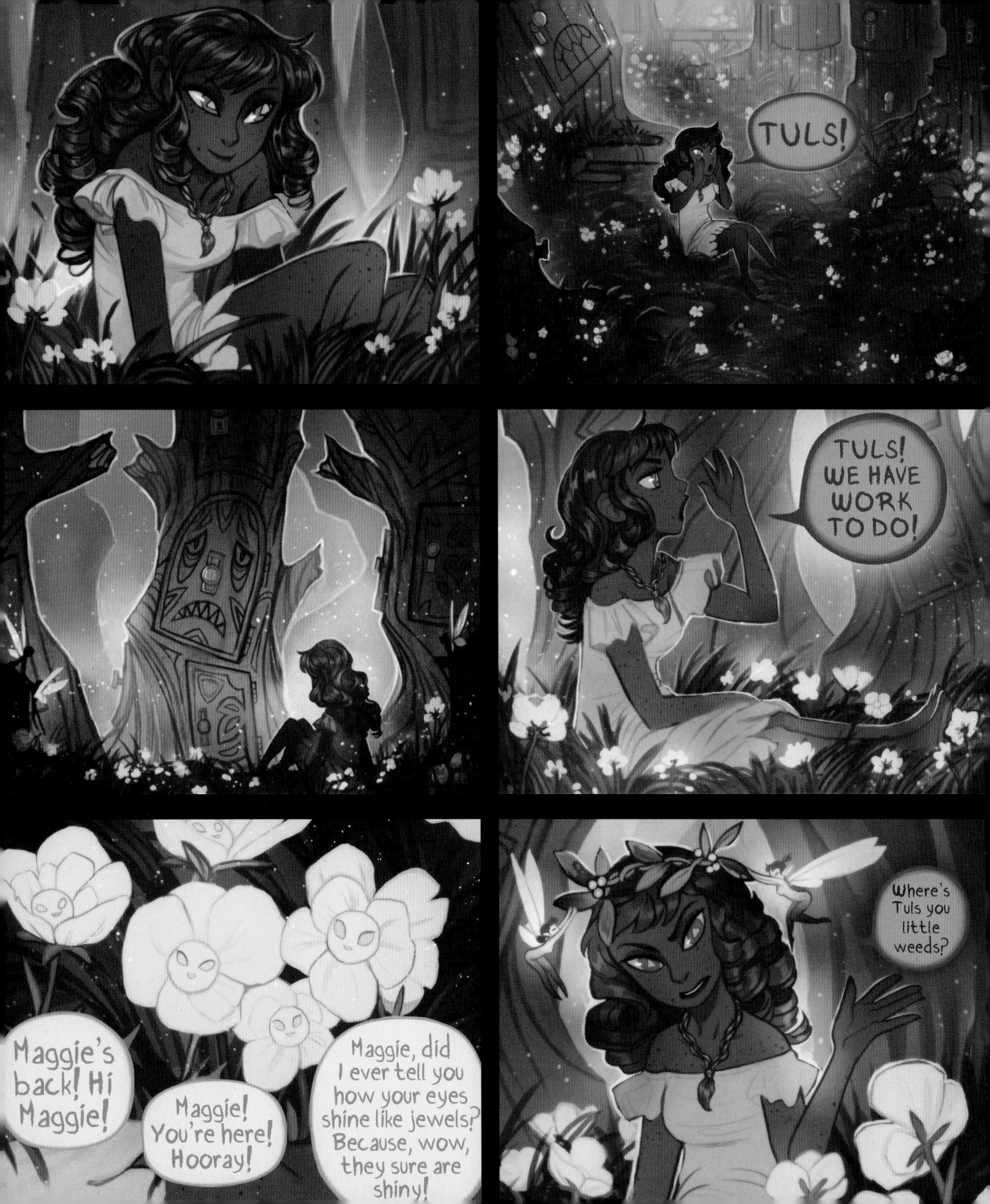
TULS!
TULS! WE HAVE WORK TO DO!
Maggie's back! Hi Maggie!
Maggie! You're here! Hooray!
Maggie, did I ever tell you how your eyes shine like jewels? Because, wow, they sure are shiny!
Where's Tuls you little weeds?

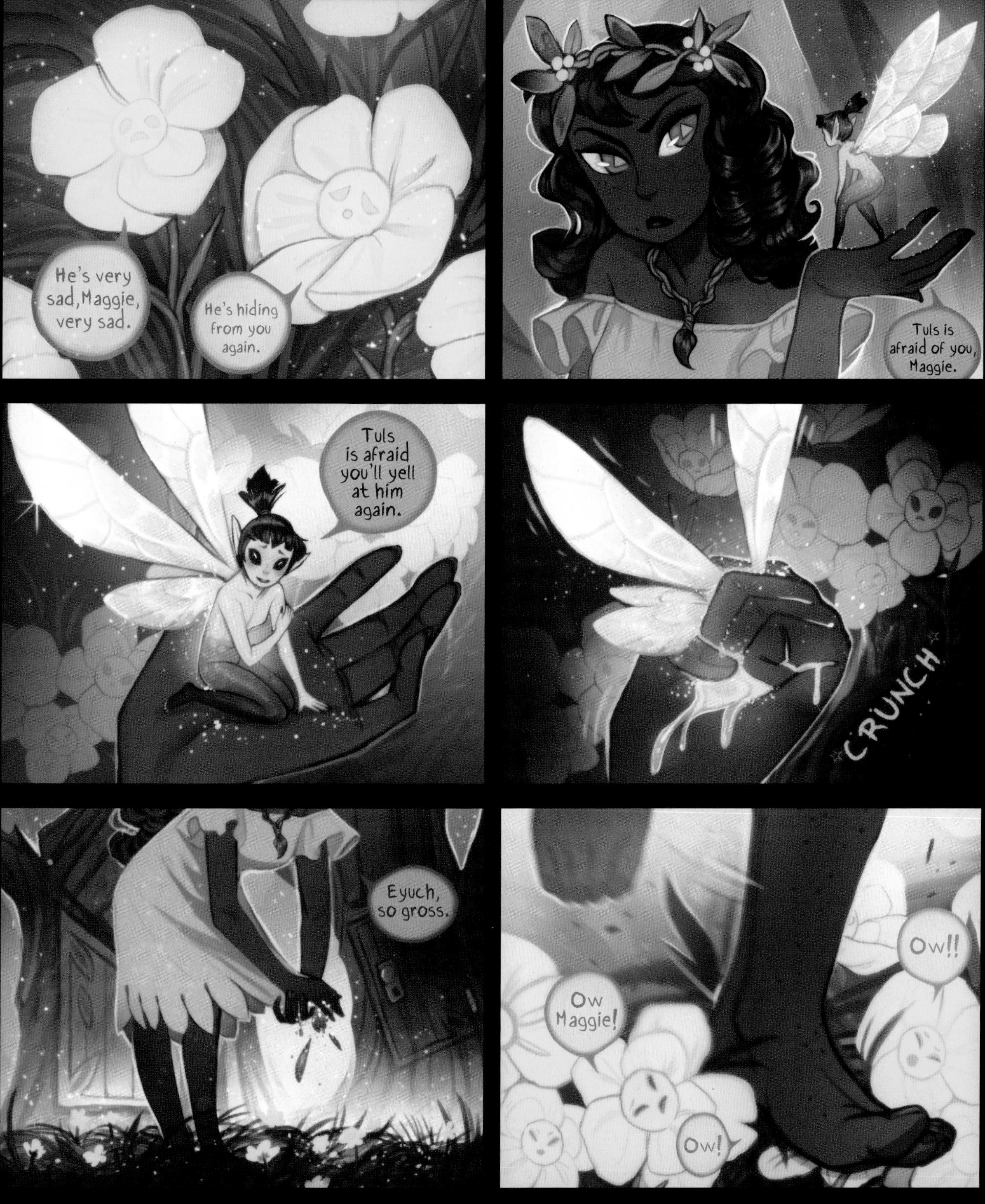
He's very sad, Maggie, very sad.
He's hiding from you again.
Tuls is afraid of you, Maggie.
Tuls is afraid you'll yell at him again.
CRUNCH
Eyuch, so gross.
Ow!!
Ow Maggie!
Ow!

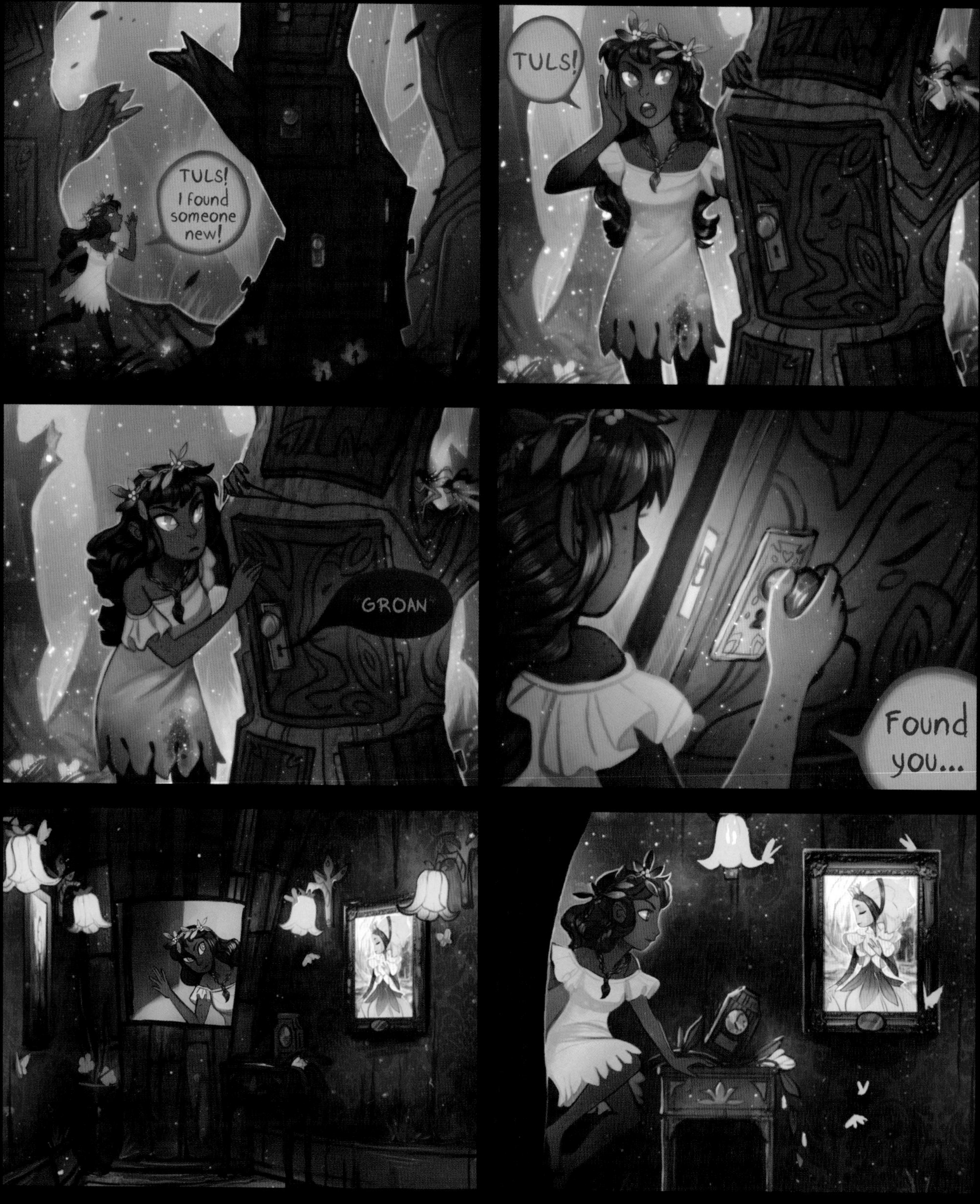
TULS! I found someone new!
TULS!
GROAN
Found you...

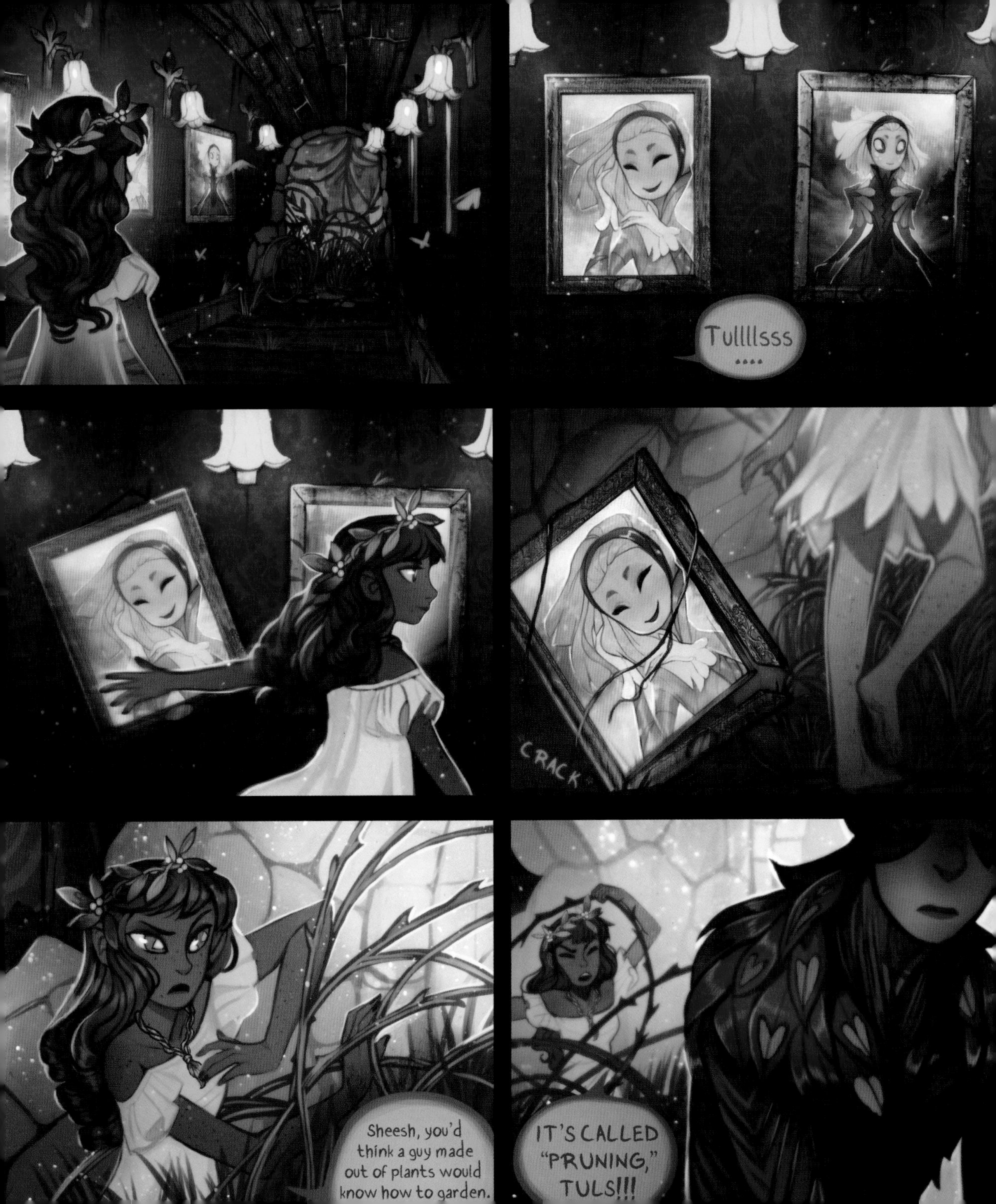
Tullllsss
....
CRACK
Sheesh, you'd think a guy made out of plants would know how to garden.
IT'S CALLED "PRUNING," TULS!!!

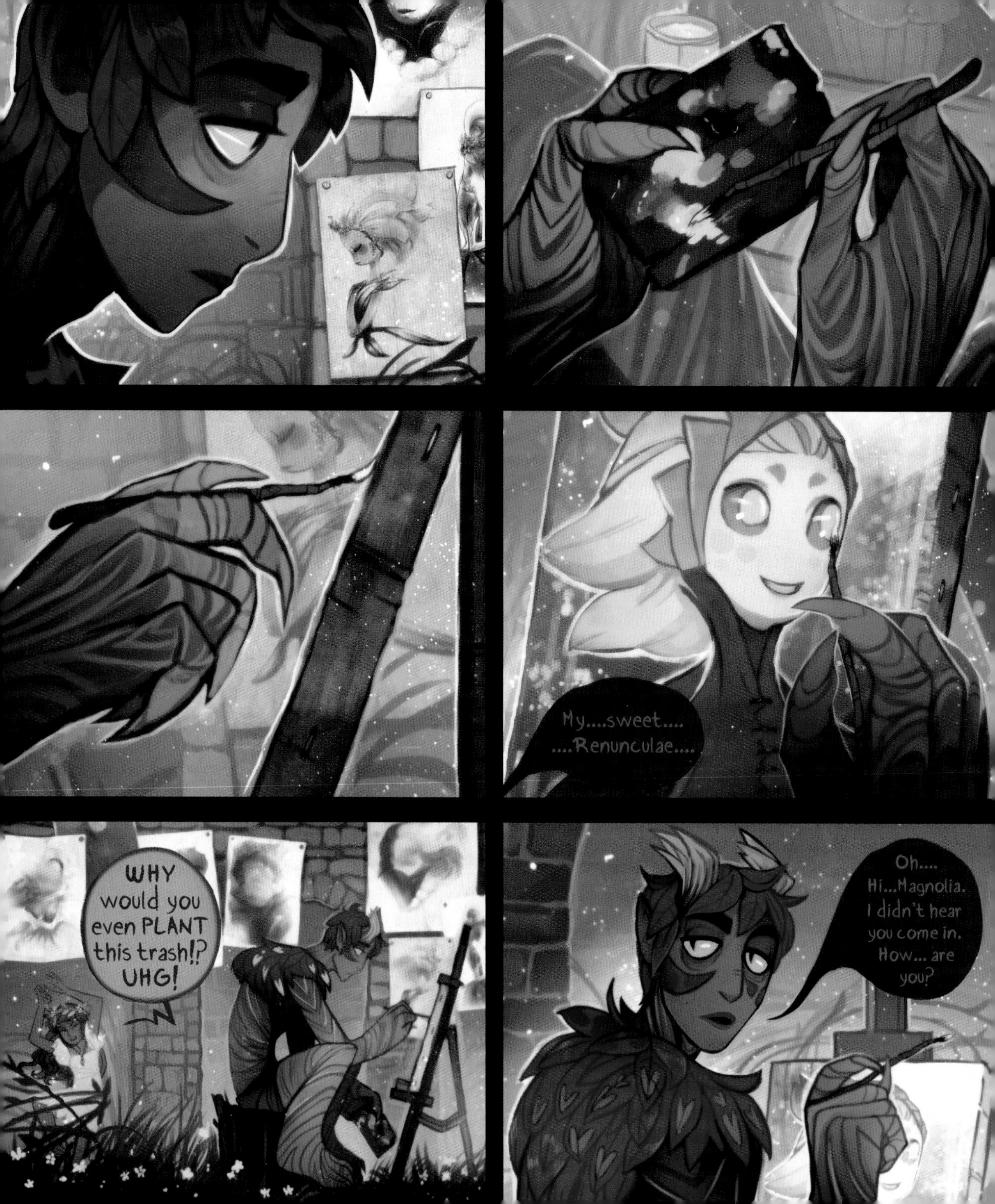
My....sweet....
....Renunculae....
WHY would you even PLANT this trash!? UHG!
Oh.... Hi...Magnolia. I didn't hear you come in. How... are you?

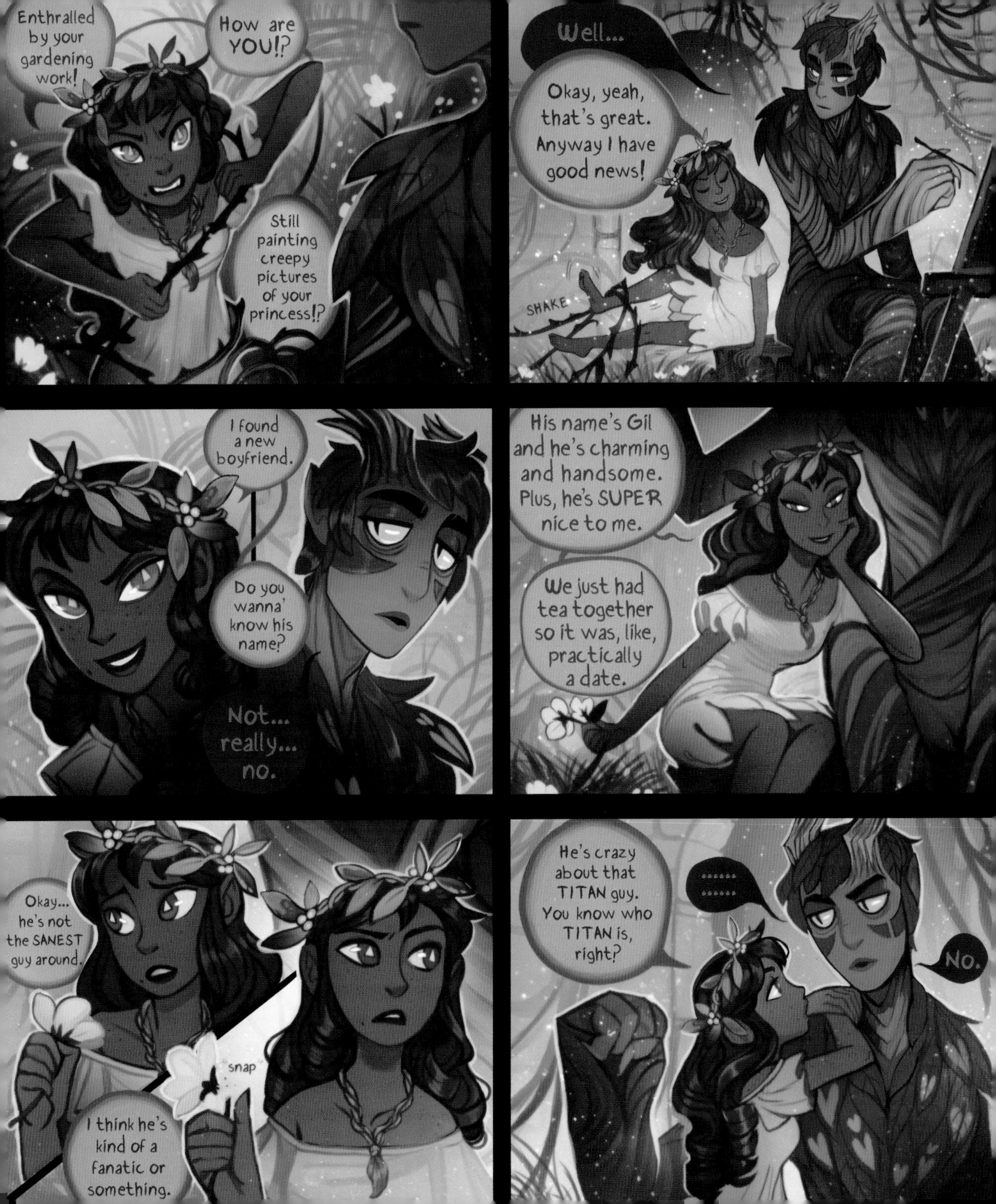
Enthralled by your gardening work!
How are YOU!?
Still painting creepy pictures of your princess!?
Well...
Okay, yeah, that's great. Anyway I have good news!
SHAKE
I found a new boyfriend.
Do you wanna' know his name?
Not... really... no.
His name's Gil and he's charming and handsome. Plus, he's SUPER nice to me.
We just had tea together so it was, like, practically a date.
Okay... he's not the SANEST guy around.
I think he's kind of a fanatic or something.
snap
He's crazy about that TITAN guy. You know who TITAN is, right?
....
NO.

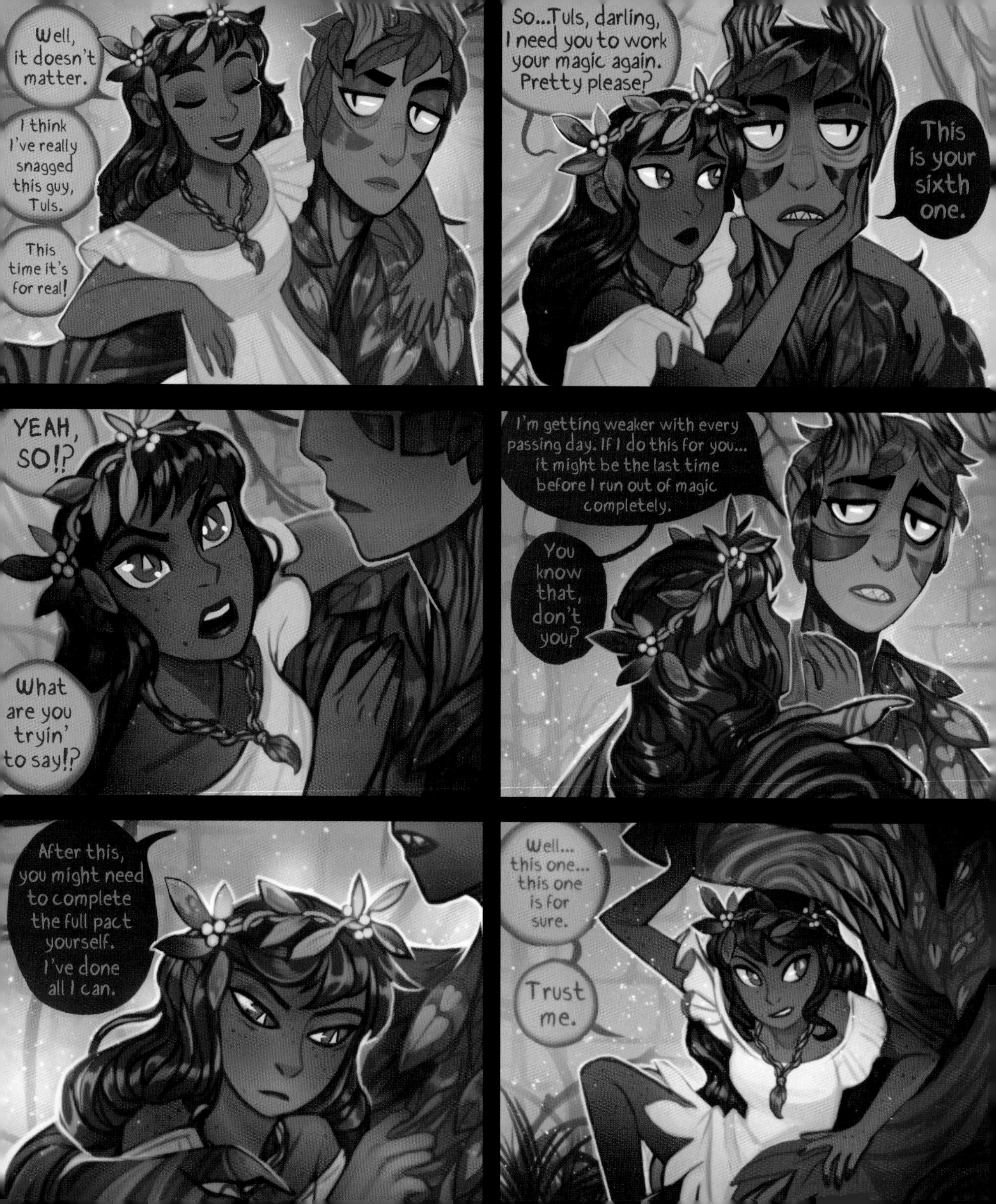

Well, it doesn't matter.
I think I've really snagged this guy, Tuls.
This time it's for real!
So...Tuls, darling, I need you to work your magic again. Pretty please?
This is your sixth one.
YEAH, SO!?
What are you tryin' to say!?
I'm getting weaker with every passing day. If I do this for you... it might be the last time before I run out of magic completely.
You know that, don't you?
After this, you might need to complete the full pact yourself. I've done all I can.
Well... this one... this one is for sure.
Trust me.

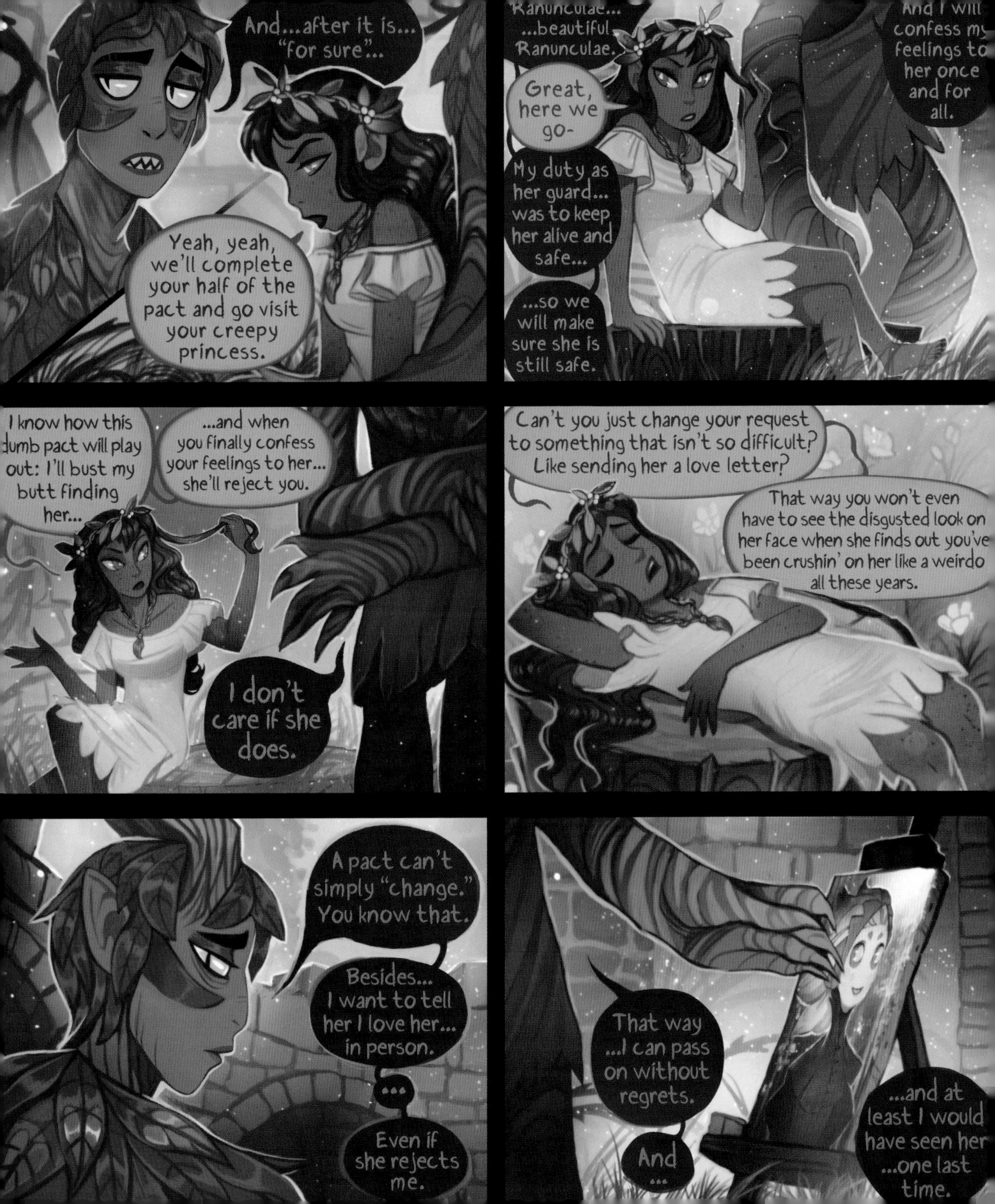
And...after it is... "for sure"...
Yeah, yeah, we'll complete your half of the pact and go visit your creepy princess.
Ranunculae... ...beautiful Ranunculae.
Great, here we go-
My duty as her guard... was to keep her alive and safe...
...so we will make sure she is still safe.
And I will confess my feelings to her once and for all.
I know how this dumb pact will play out: I'll bust my butt finding her...
...and when you finally confess your feelings to her... she'll reject you.
I don't care if she does.
Can't you just change your request to something that isn't so difficult? Like sending her a love letter?
That way you won't even have to see the disgusted look on her face when she finds out you've been crushin' on her like a weirdo all these years.
A pact can't simply "change." You know that.
Besides... I want to tell her I love her... in person.
...
Even if she rejects me.
That way ...I can pass on without regrets.
And ...
...and at least I would have seen her ...one last time.

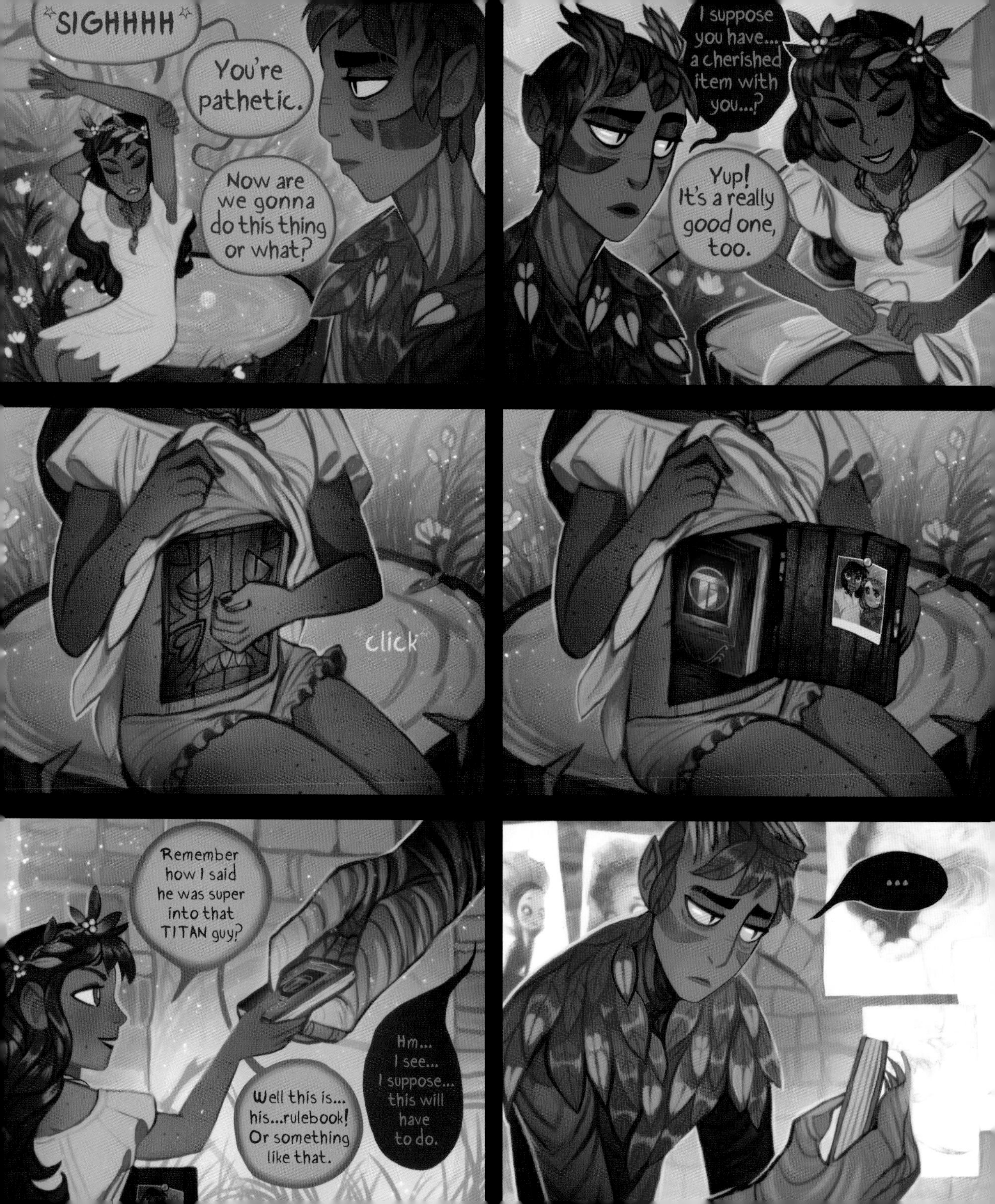
SIGHHHH
You're pathetic.
Now are we gonna do this thing or what?
I suppose you have... a cherished item with you...?
Yup! It's a really good one, too.
click
Remember how I said he was super into that TITAN guy?
Well this is... his...rulebook! Or something like that.
Hm... I see... I suppose... this will have to do.
...

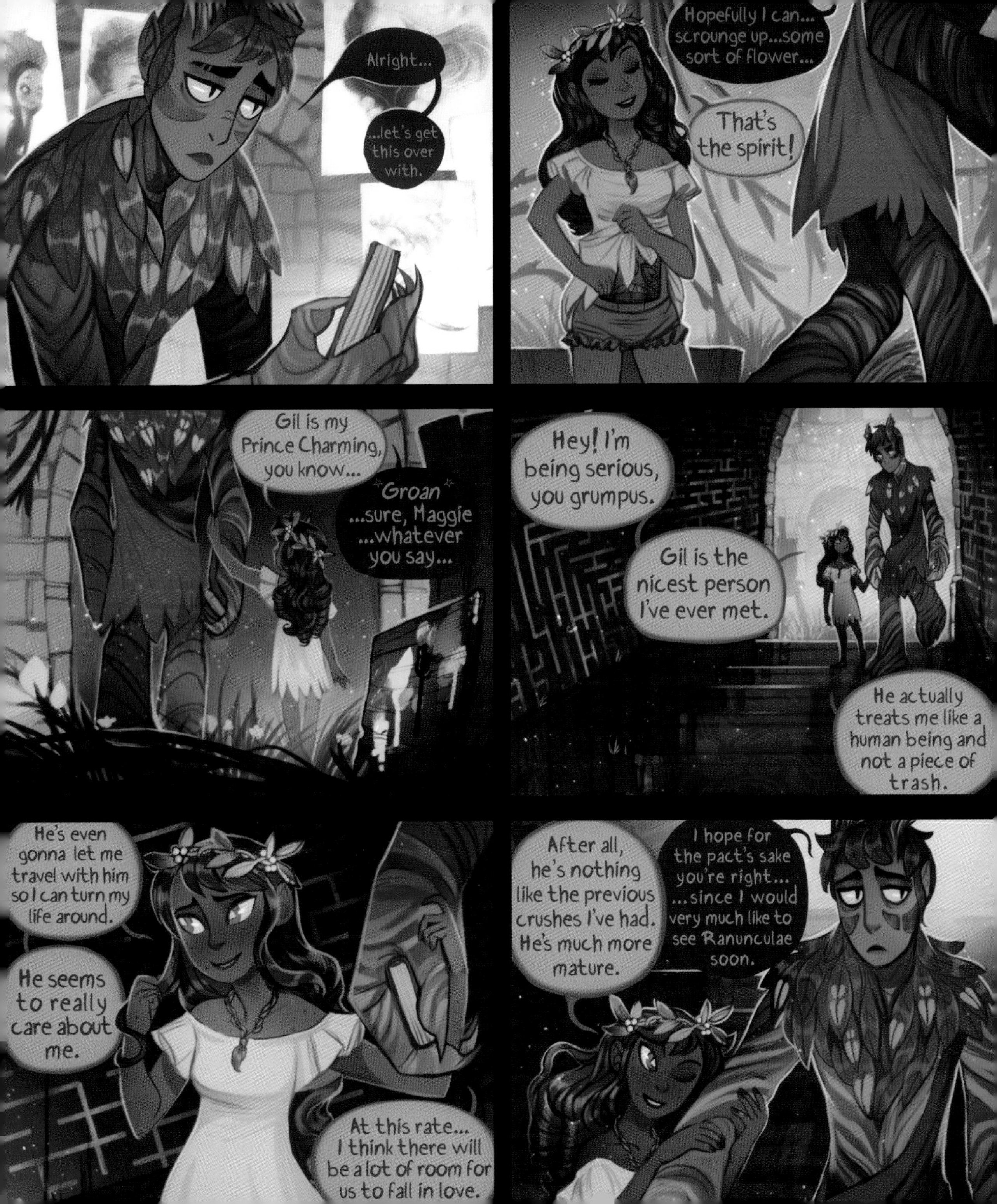
Alright...
...let's get this over with.
Hopefully I can... scrounge up...some sort of flower...
That's the spirit!
Gil is my Prince Charming, you know...
Groan
...sure, Maggie ...whatever you say...
Hey! I'm being serious, you grumpus.
Gil is the nicest person I've ever met.
He actually treats me like a human being and not a piece of trash.
He's even gonna let me travel with him so I can turn my life around.
He seems to really care about me.
At this rate... I think there will be a lot of room for us to fall in love.
After all, he's nothing like the previous crushes I've had. He's much more mature.
I hope for the pact's sake you're right... ...since I would very much like to see Ranunculae soon.

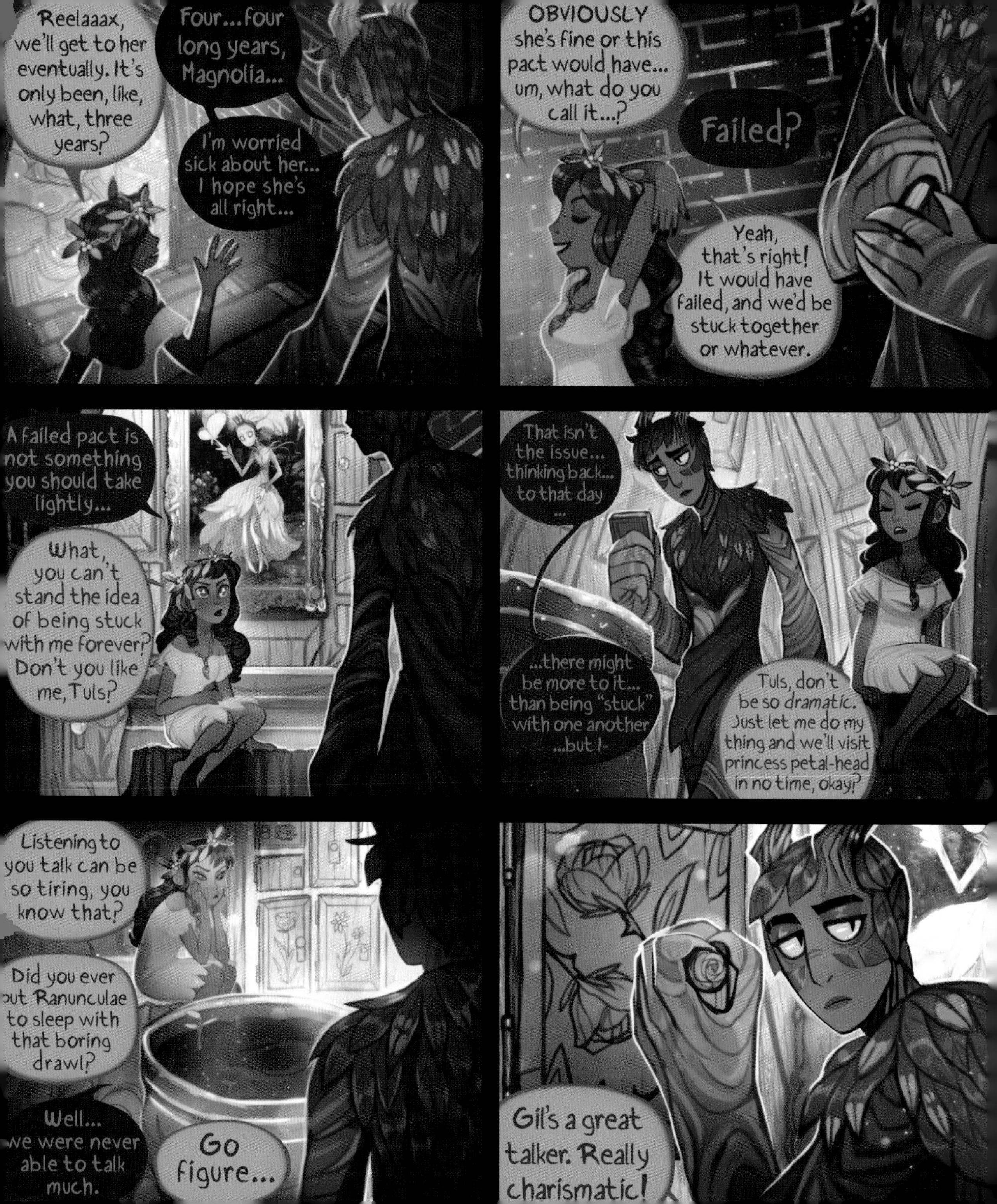
Reelaaax, we'll get to her eventually. It's only been, like, what, three years?
Four...four long years, Magnolia...
I'm worried sick about her... I hope she's all right...
OBVIOUSLY she's fine or this pact would have... um, what do you call it...?
Failed?
Yeah, that's right! It would have failed, and we'd be stuck together or whatever.
A failed pact is not something you should take lightly...
What, you can't stand the idea of being stuck with me forever? Don't you like me, Tuls?
That isn't the issue... thinking back... to that day ...
...there might be more to it... than being "stuck" with one another ...but I-
Tuls, don't be so dramatic. Just let me do my thing and we'll visit princess petal-head in no time, okay?
Listening to you talk can be so tiring, you know that?
Did you ever put Ranunculae to sleep with that boring drawl?
Well... we were never able to talk much.
Go figure...
Gil's a great talker. Really charismatic!

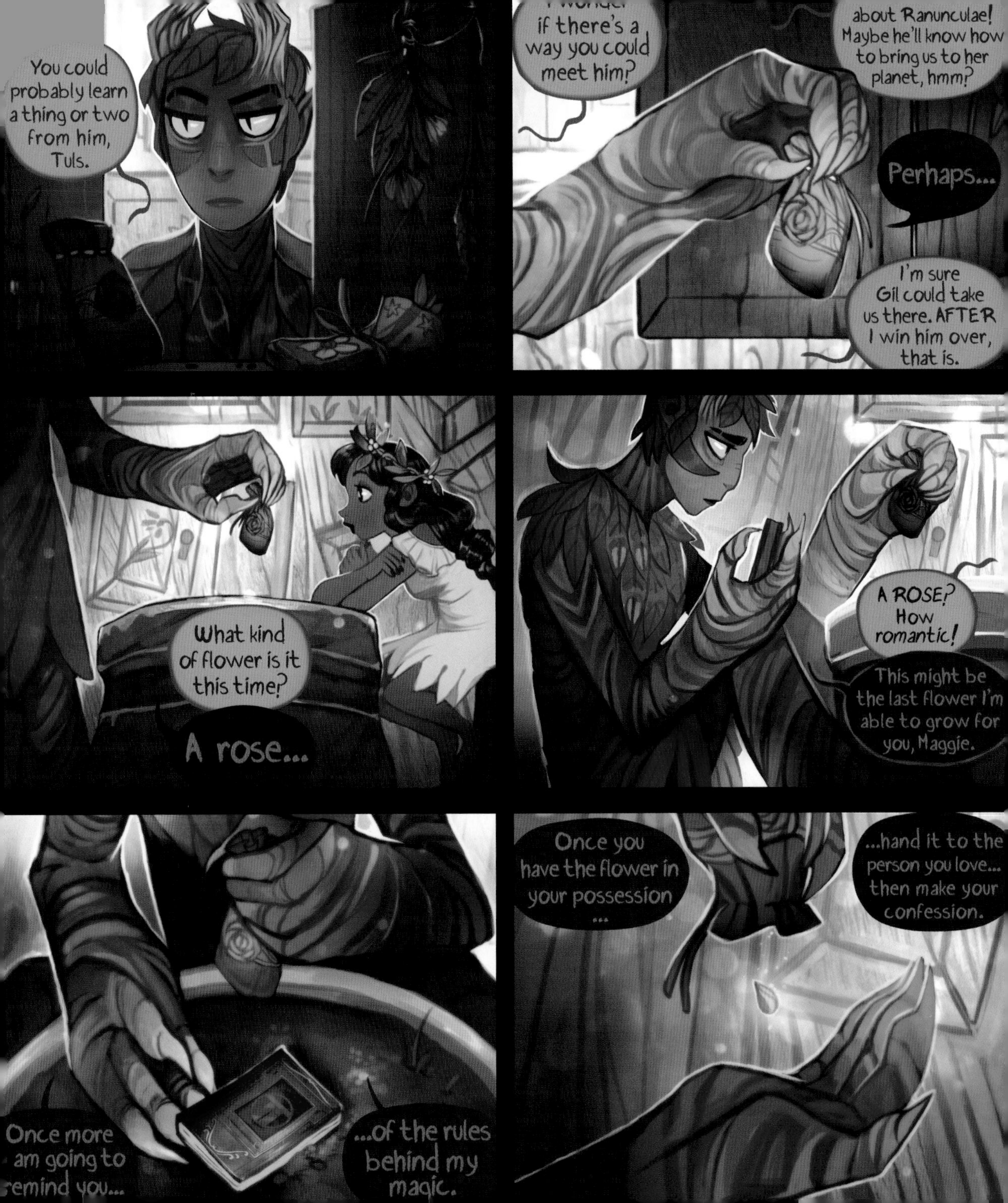
You could probably learn a thing or two from him, Tuls.
if there's a way you could meet him?
about Ranunculae! Maybe he'll know how to bring us to her planet, hmm?
Perhaps...
I'm sure Gil could take us there. AFTER I win him over, that is.
What kind of flower is it this time?
A rose...
A ROSE? How romantic!
This might be the last flower I'm able to grow for you, Maggie.
Once more am going to remind you...
...of the rules behind my magic.
Once you have the flower in your possession ...
...hand it to the person you love... then make your confession.

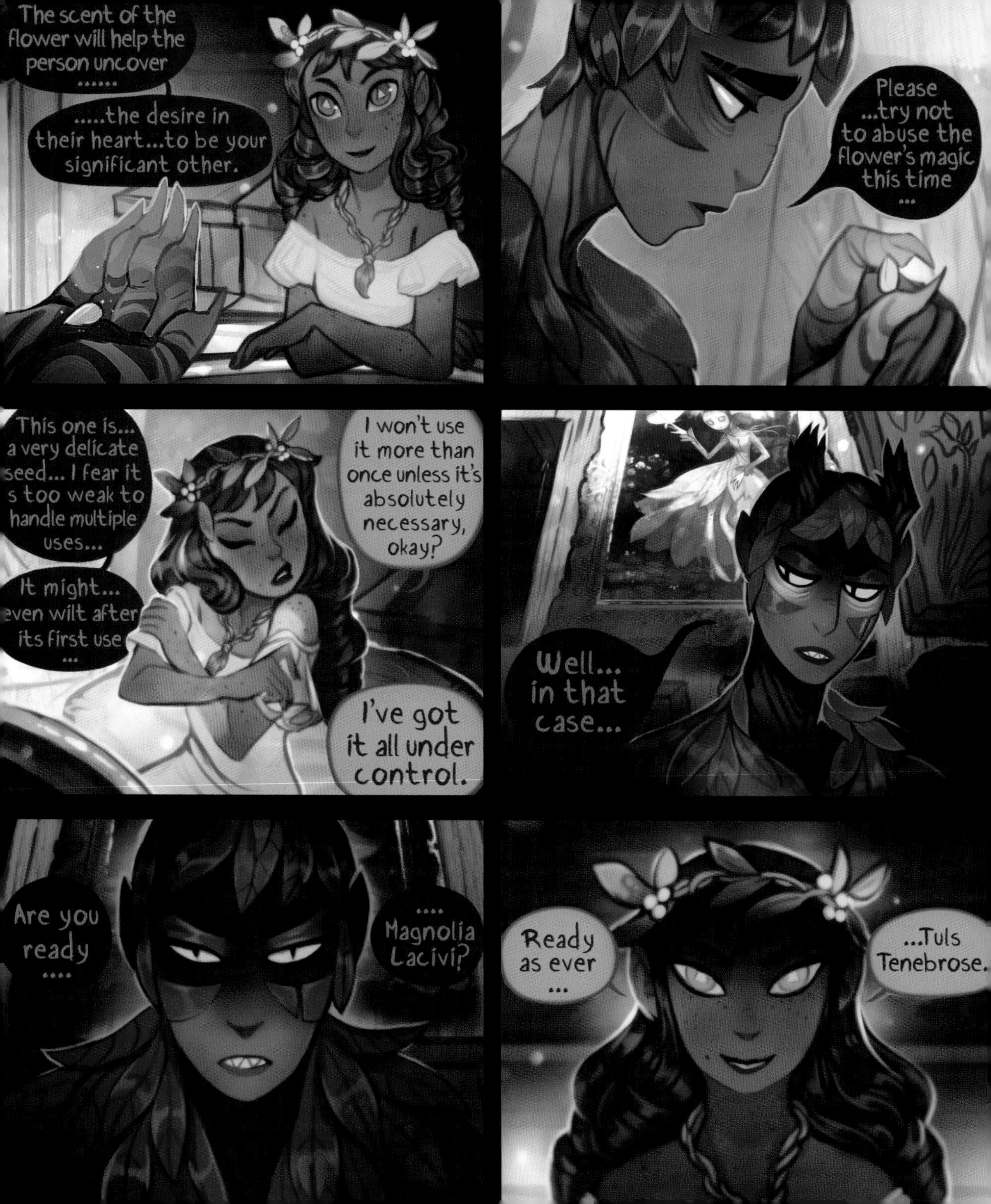
The scent of the flower will help the person uncover ......
.....the desire in their heart...to be your significant other.
Please ...try not to abuse the flower's magic this time ...
This one is... a very delicate seed... I fear it s too weak to handle multiple uses...
It might... even wilt after its first use ...
I won't use it more than once unless it's absolutely necessary, okay?
I've got it all under control.
Well... in that case...
Are you ready ....
.... Magnolia Lacivi?
Ready as ever ...
...Tuls Tenebrose.

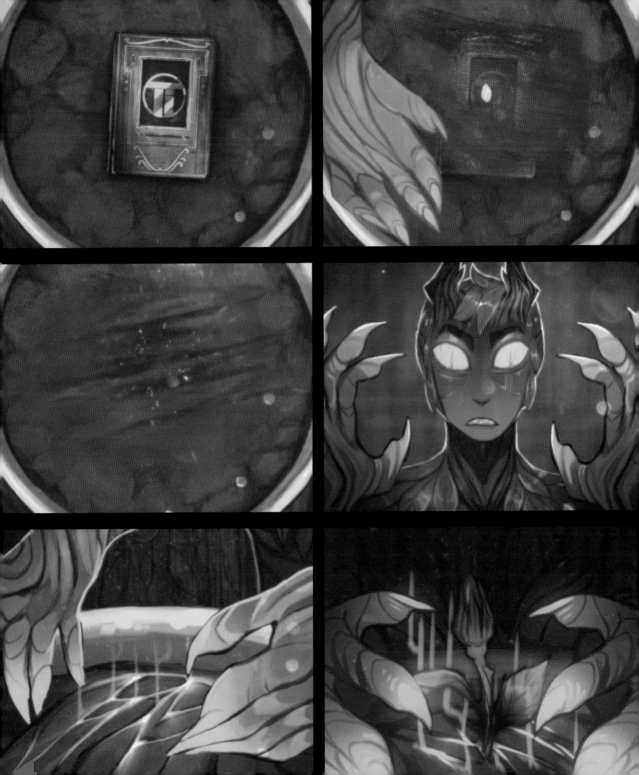

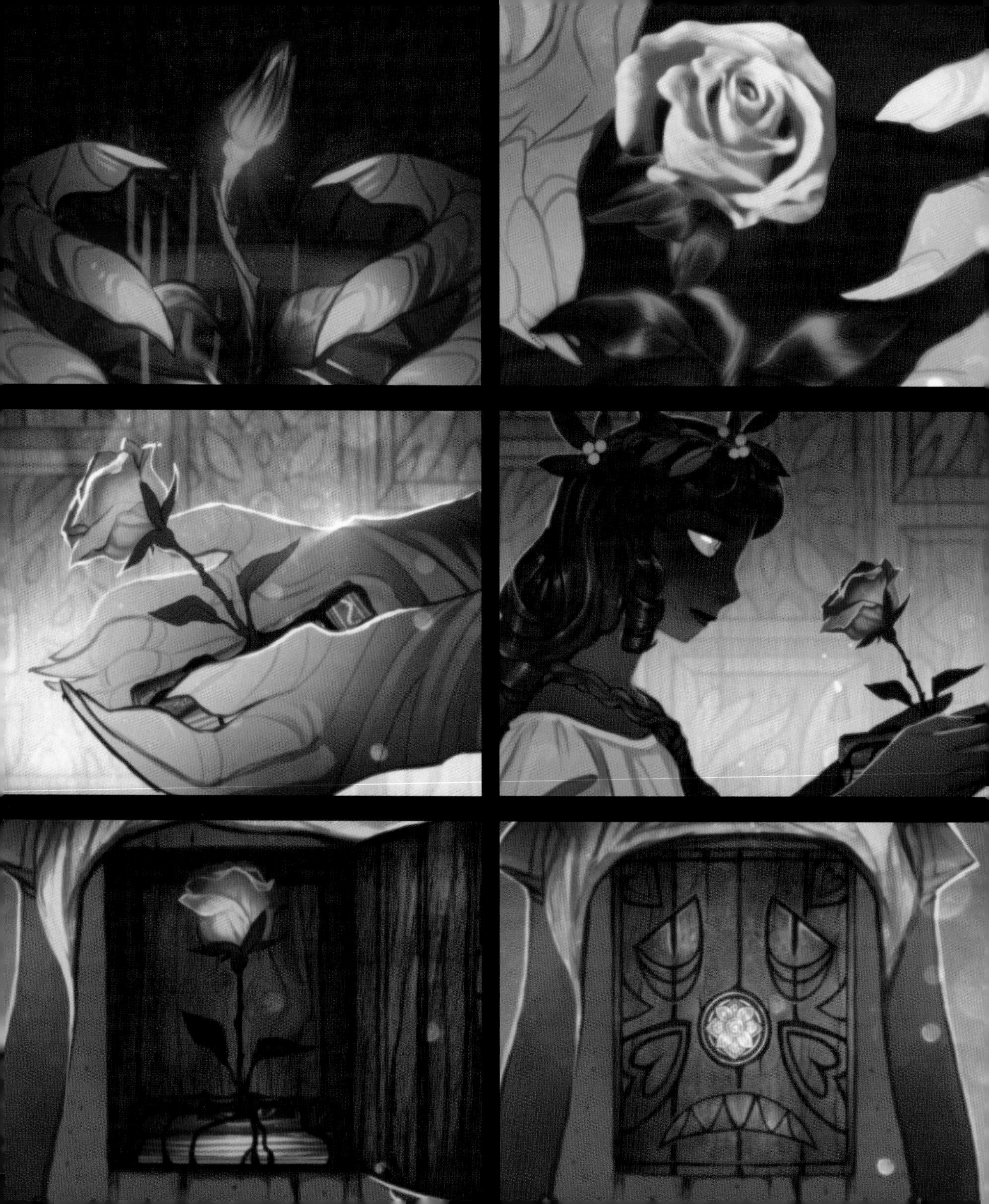

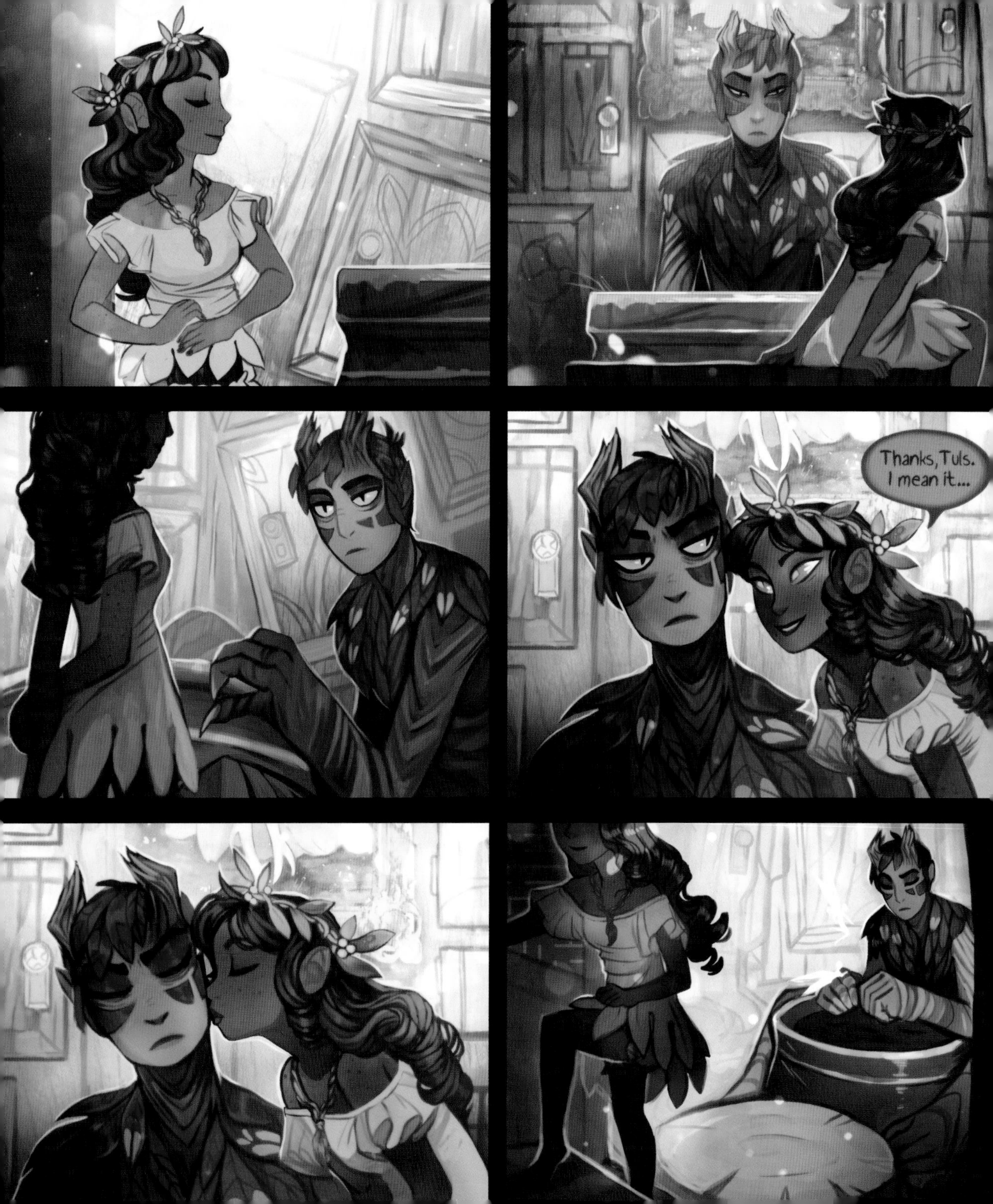
Thanks, Tuls.
I mean it...

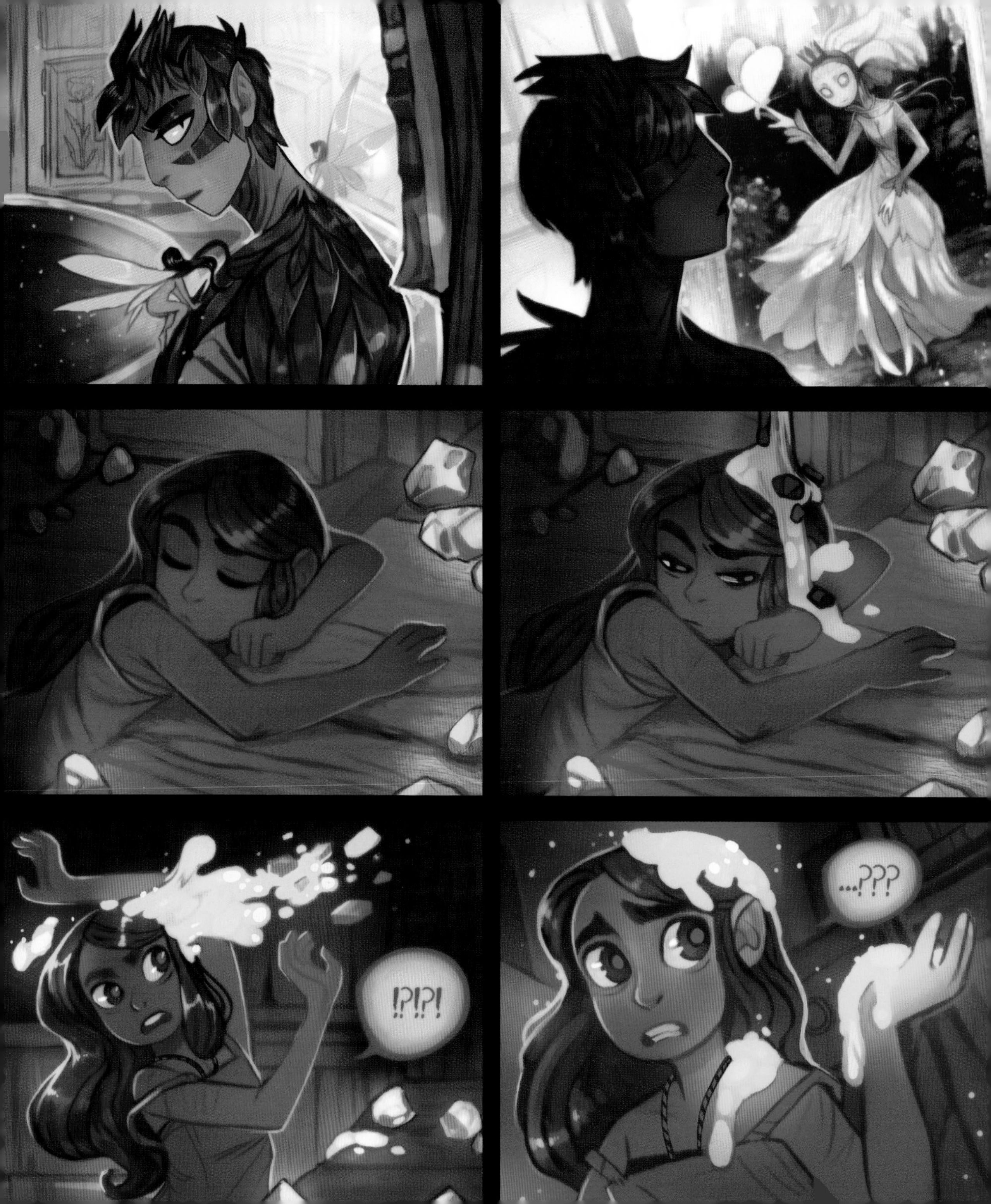
!?!?!
...???

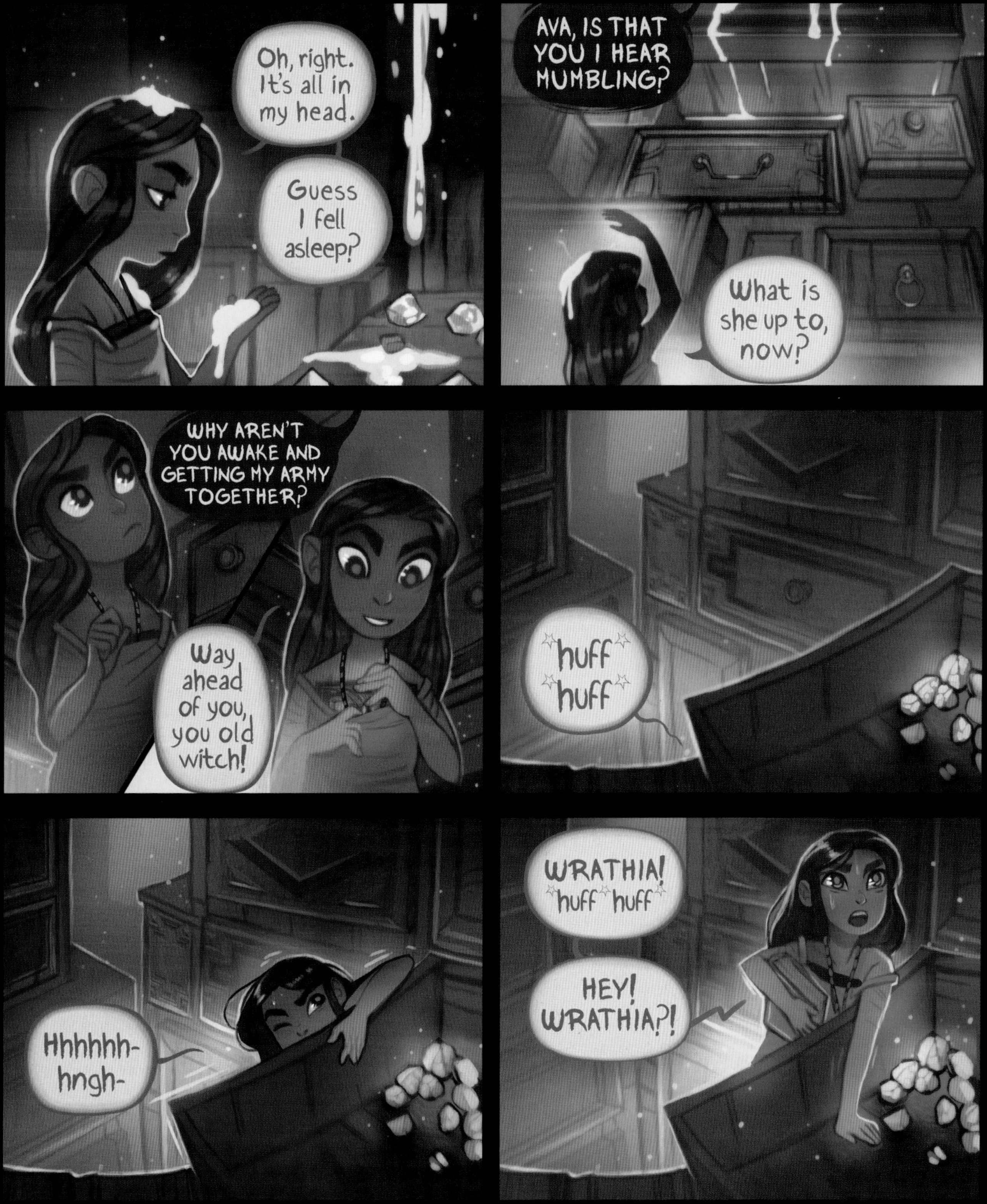
Oh, right. It's all in my head.
Guess I fell asleep?
AVA, IS THAT YOU I HEAR MUMBLING?
What is she up to, now?
WHY AREN'T YOU AWAKE AND GETTING MY ARMY TOGETHER?
Way ahead of you, you old witch!
huff huff
Hhhhhh-hngh-
WRATHIA! huff huff
HEY! WRATHIA?!

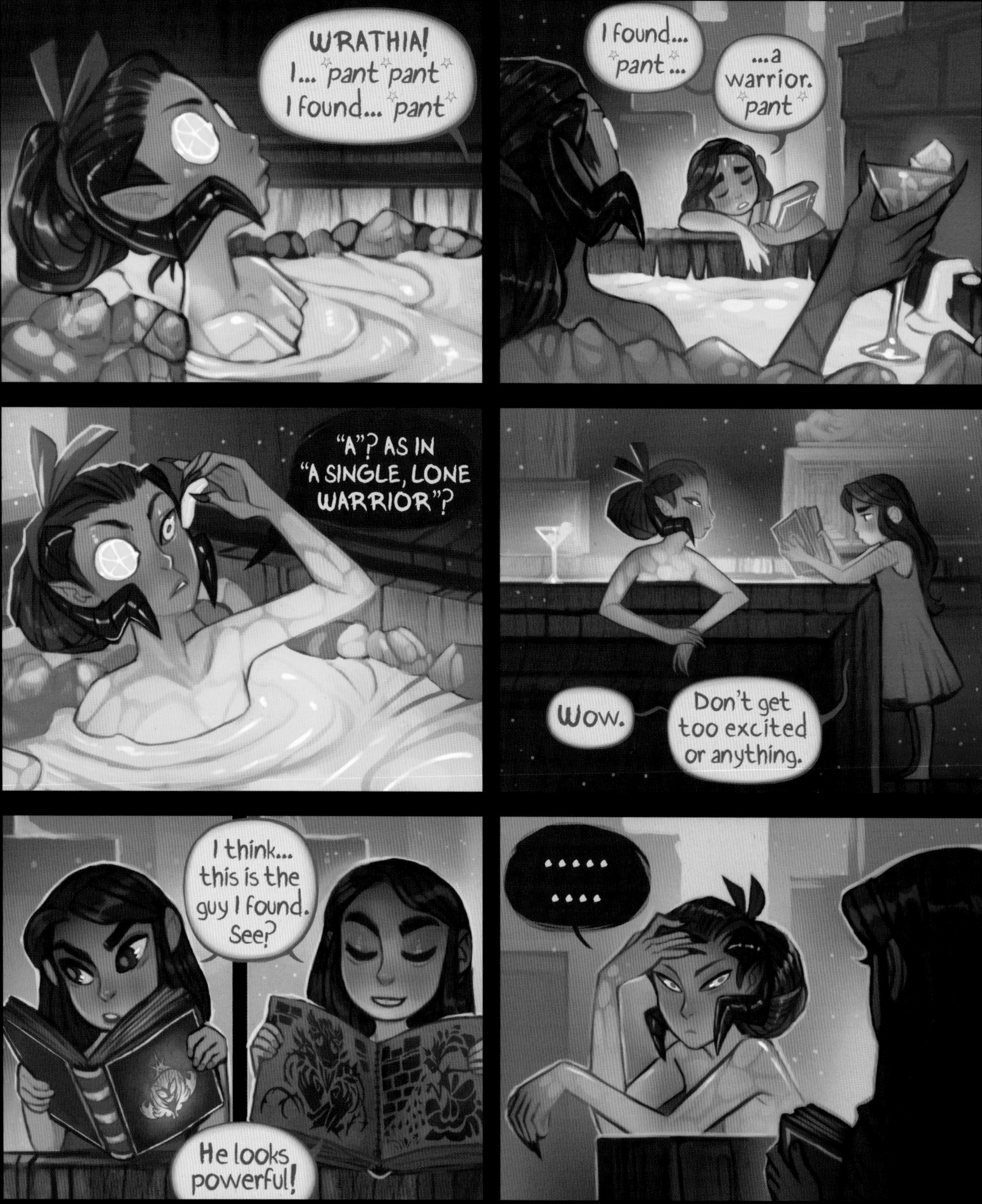
WRATHIA! I... pant pant I found... pant
I found... pant...
...a warrior. pant
"A"? AS IN "A SINGLE, LONE WARRIOR"?
Wow.
Don't get too excited or anything.
I think... this is the guy I found. See?
He looks powerful!

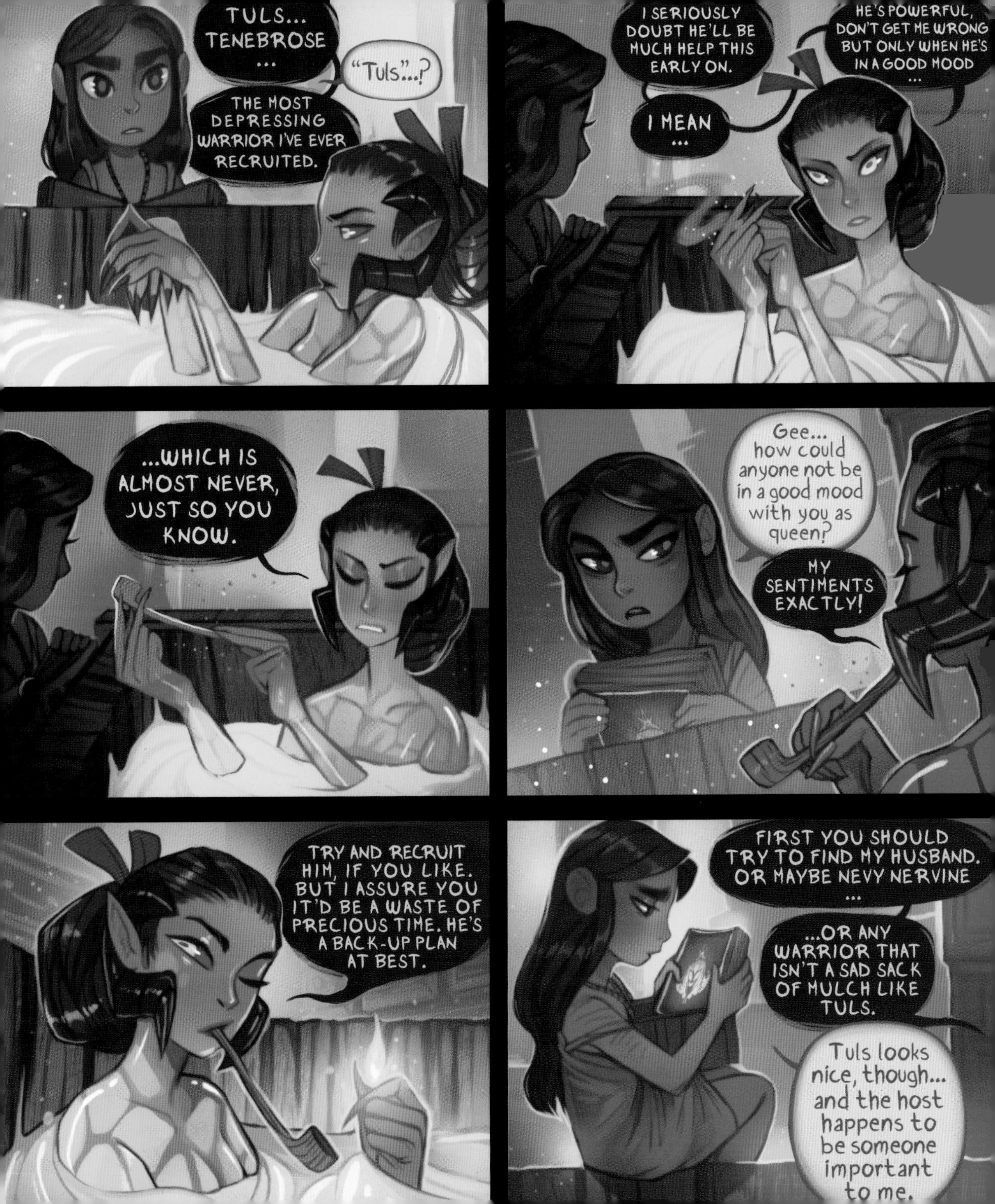
TULS... TENEBROSE ...
"Tuls"...?
THE MOST DEPRESSING WARRIOR I'VE EVER RECRUITED.
I SERIOUSLY DOUBT HE'LL BE MUCH HELP THIS EARLY ON.
I MEAN ...
HE'S POWERFUL, DON'T GET ME WRONG BUT ONLY WHEN HE'S IN A GOOD MOOD ...
...WHICH IS ALMOST NEVER, JUST SO YOU KNOW.
Gee... how could anyone not be in a good mood with you as queen?
MY SENTIMENTS EXACTLY!
TRY AND RECRUIT HIM, IF YOU LIKE. BUT I ASSURE YOU IT'D BE A WASTE OF PRECIOUS TIME. HE'S A BACK-UP PLAN AT BEST.
FIRST YOU SHOULD TRY TO FIND MY HUSBAND. OR MAYBE NEVY NERVINE ...
...OR ANY WARRIOR THAT ISN'T A SAD SACK OF MULCH LIKE TULS.
Tuls looks nice, though... and the host happens to be someone important to me.

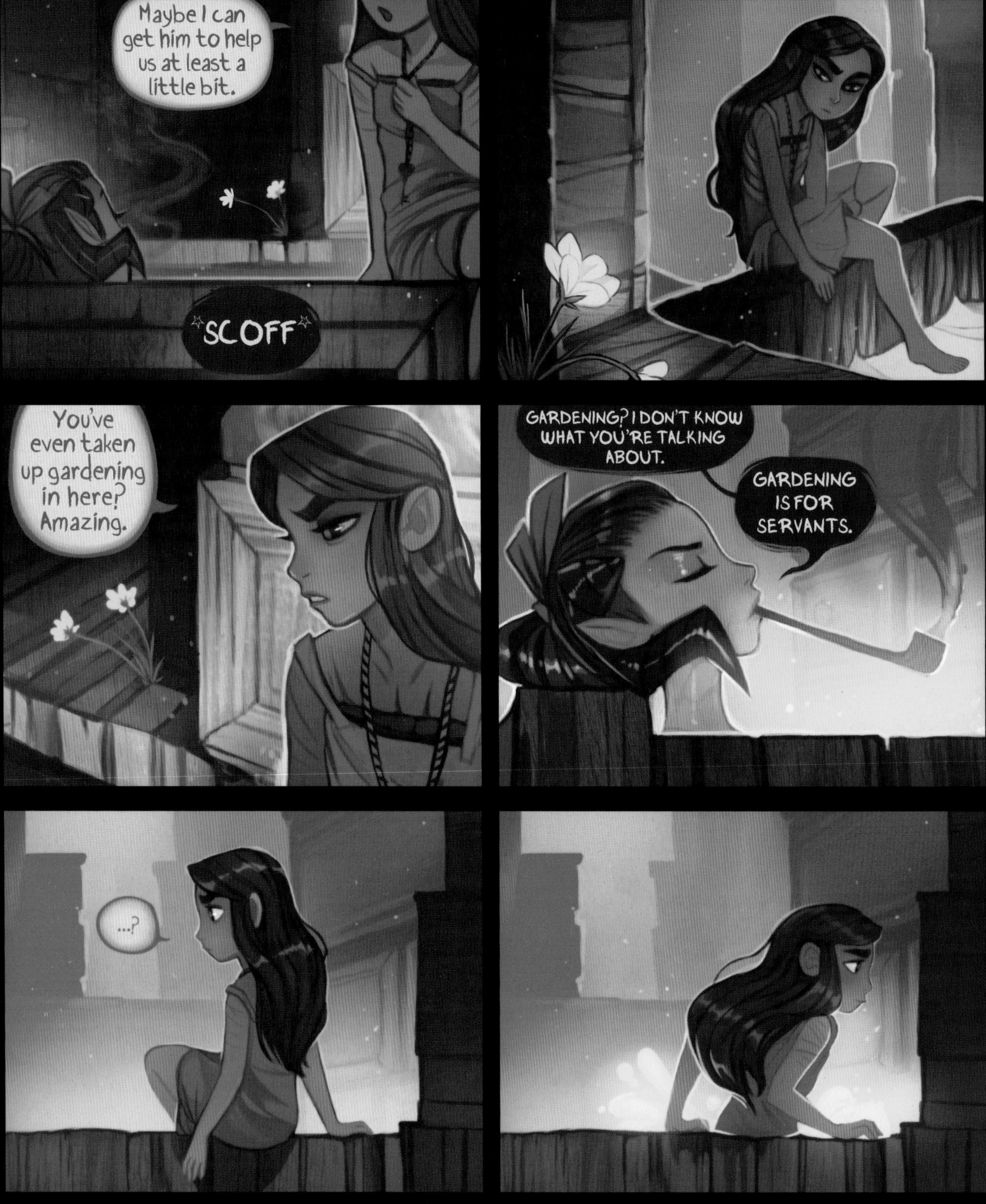

Maybe I can get him to help us at least a little bit.
SCOFF
You've even taken up gardening in here? Amazing.
GARDENING? I DON'T KNOW WHAT YOU'RE TALKING ABOUT.
GARDENING IS FOR SERVANTS.
...?

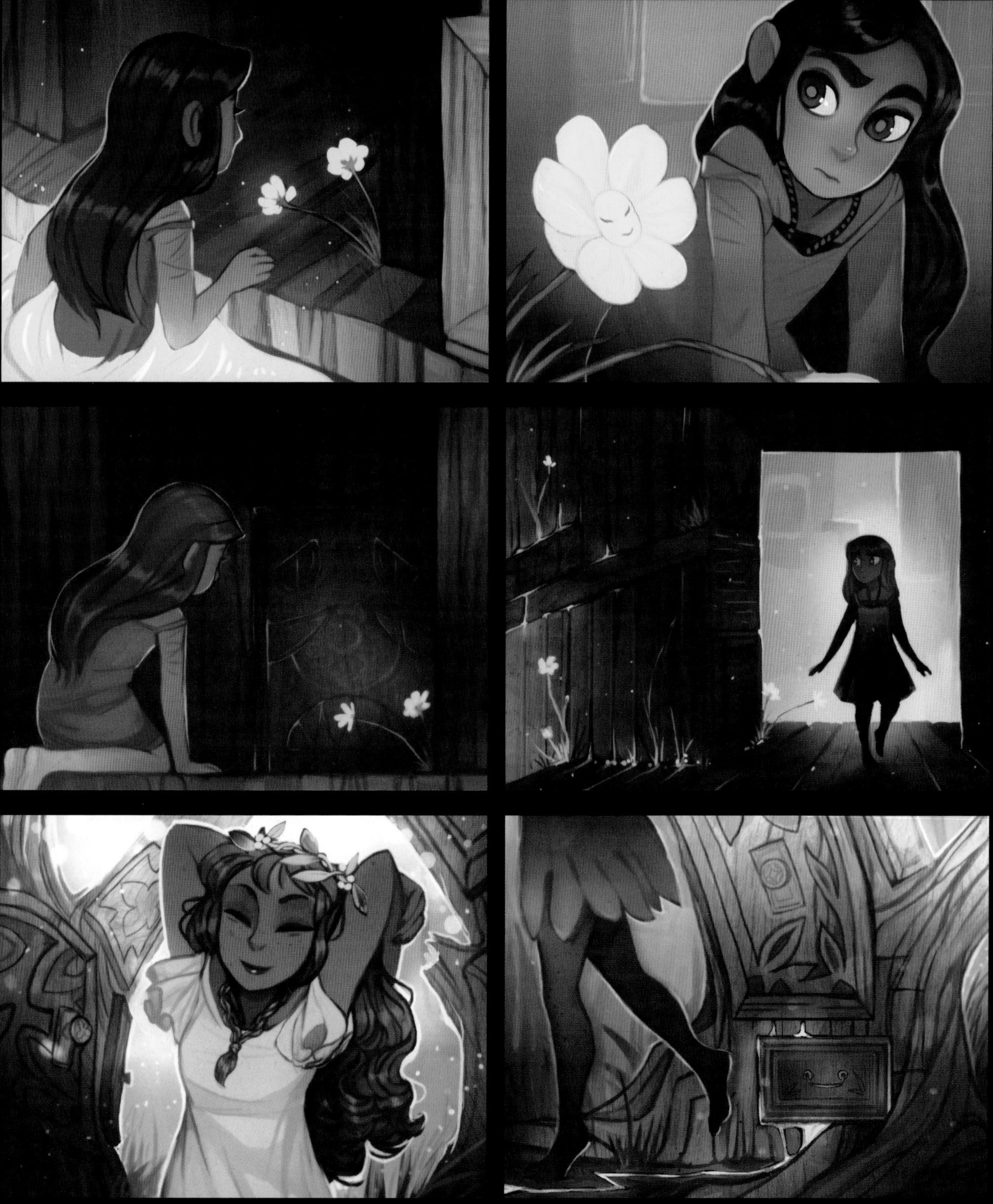

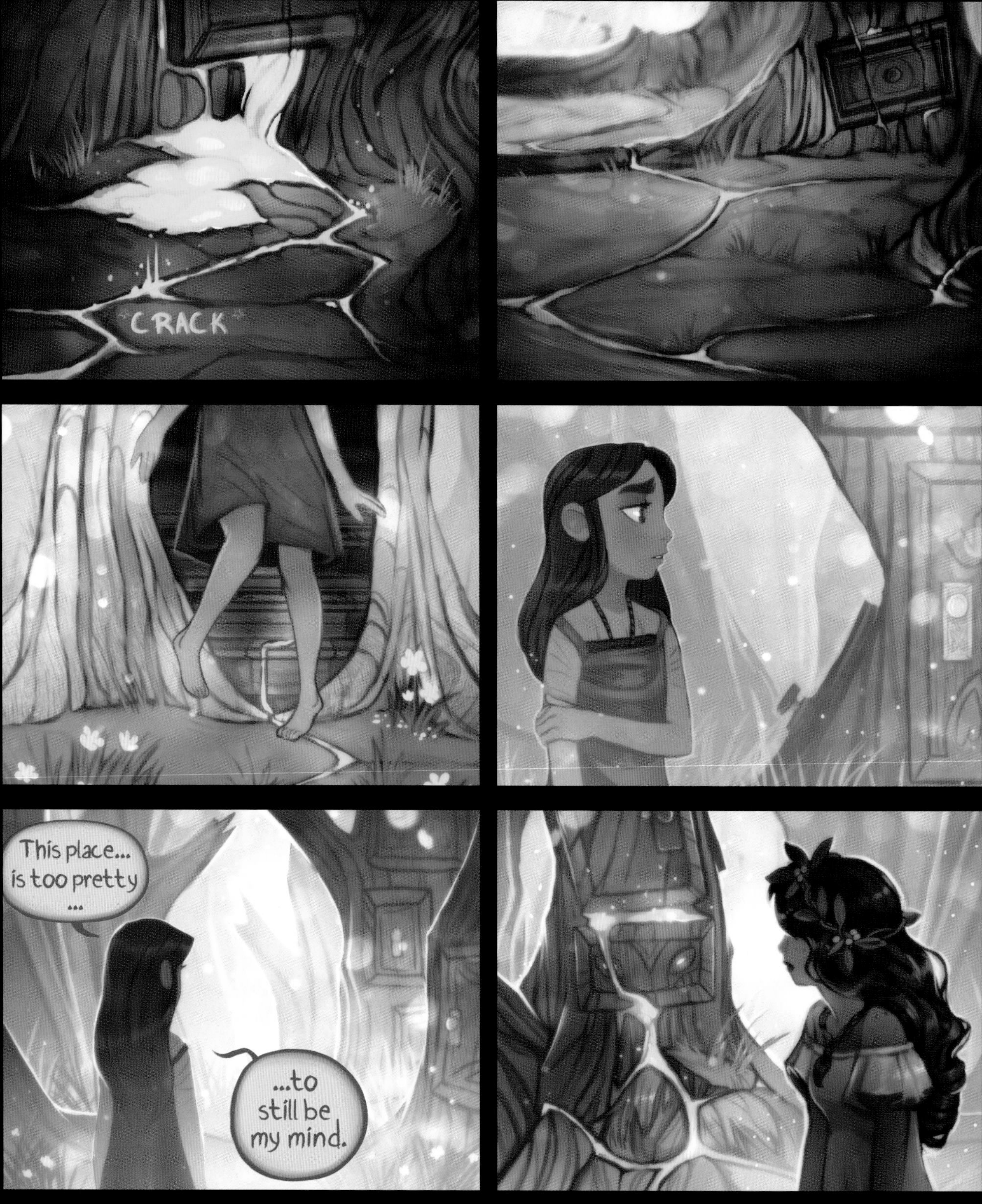
CRACK
This place... is too pretty ...
...to still be my mind.

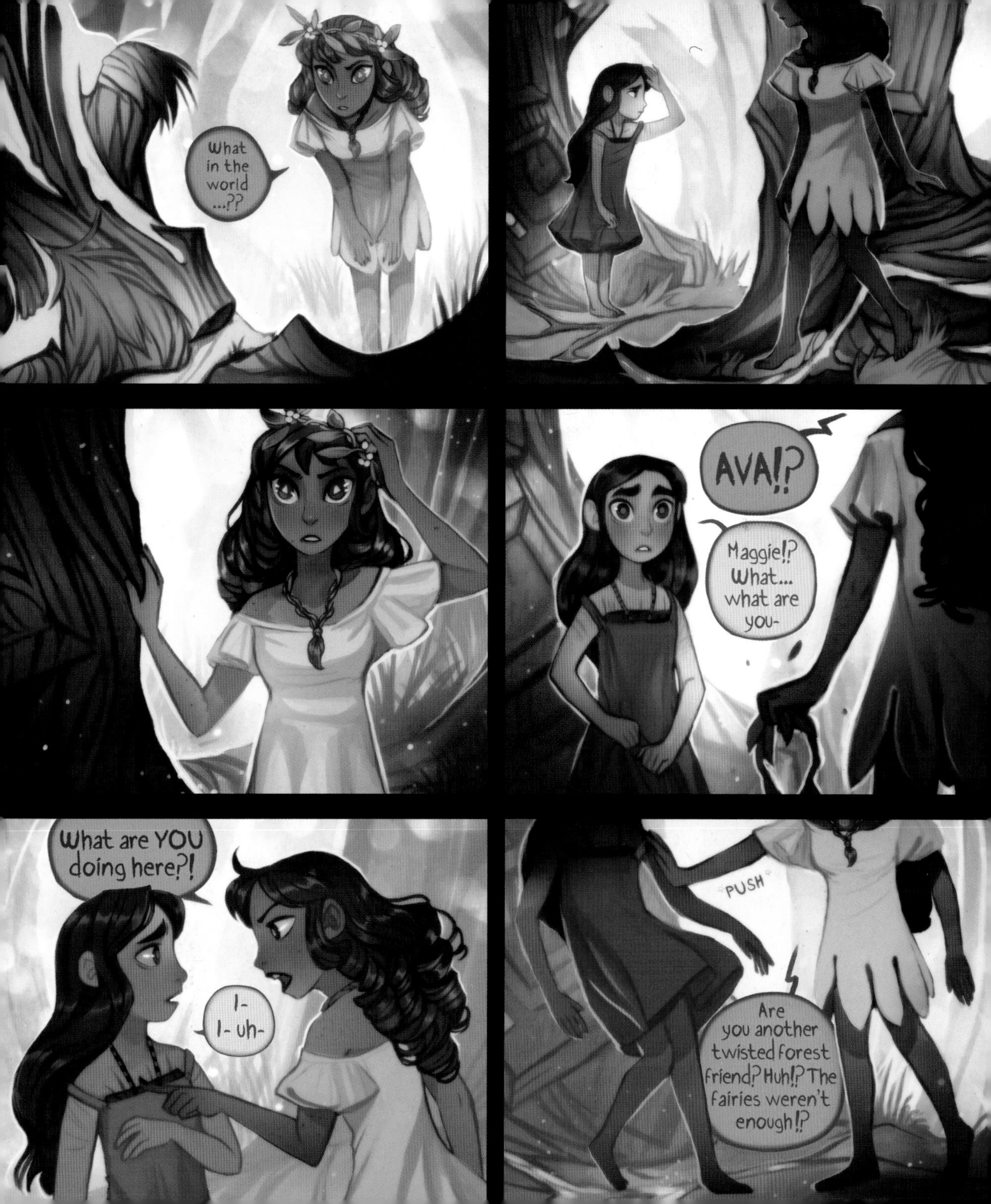
What in the world ...??
AVA!?
Maggie!? What... what are you-
What are YOU doing here?!
I- I- uh-
PUSH
Are you another twisted forest friend? Huh!? The fairies weren't enough!?

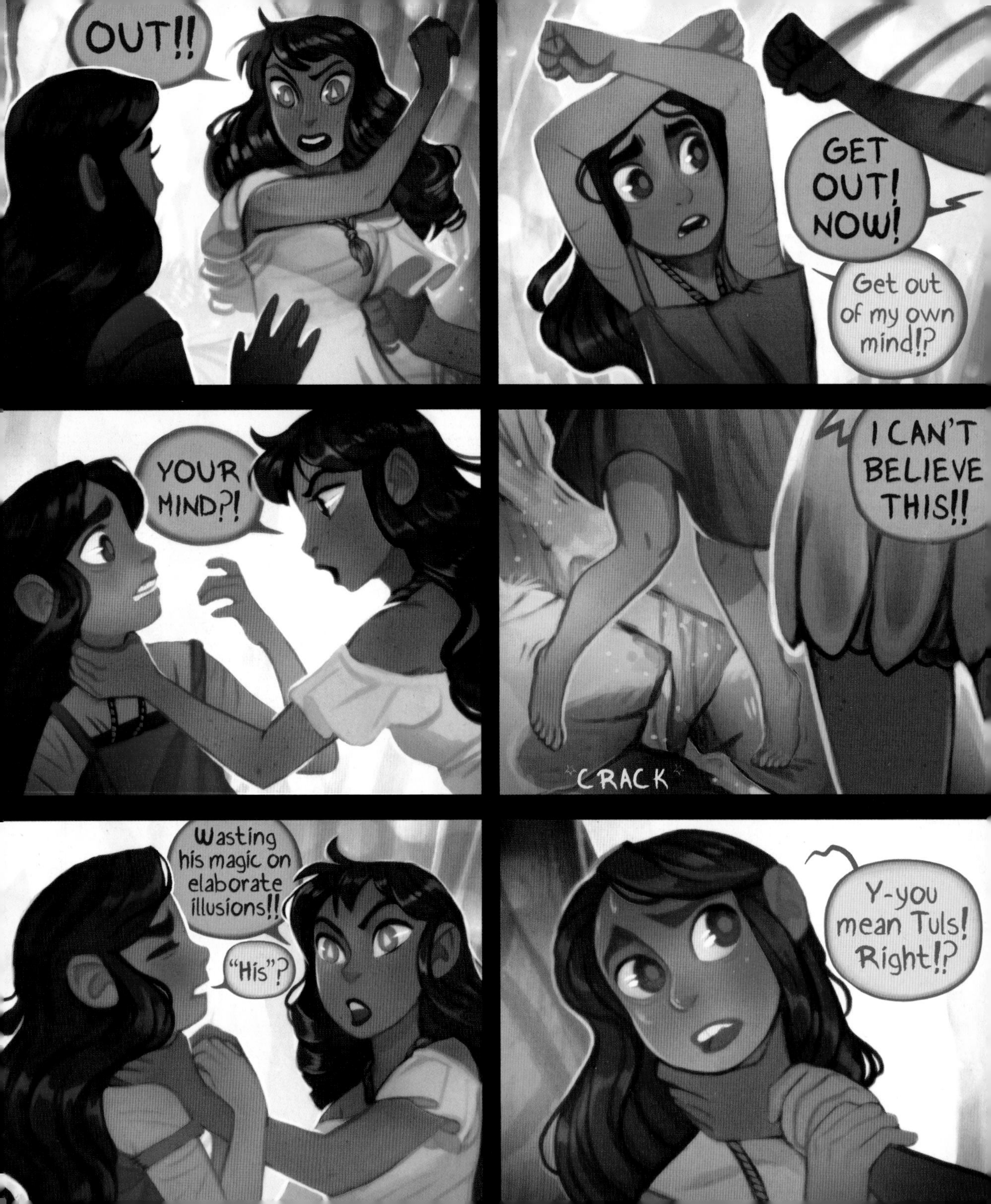
OUT!!
GET OUT! NOW!
Get out of my own mind!?
YOUR MIND?!
I CAN'T BELIEVE THIS!!
CRACK
Wasting his magic on elaborate illusions!!
"His"?
Y-you mean Tuls! Right!?

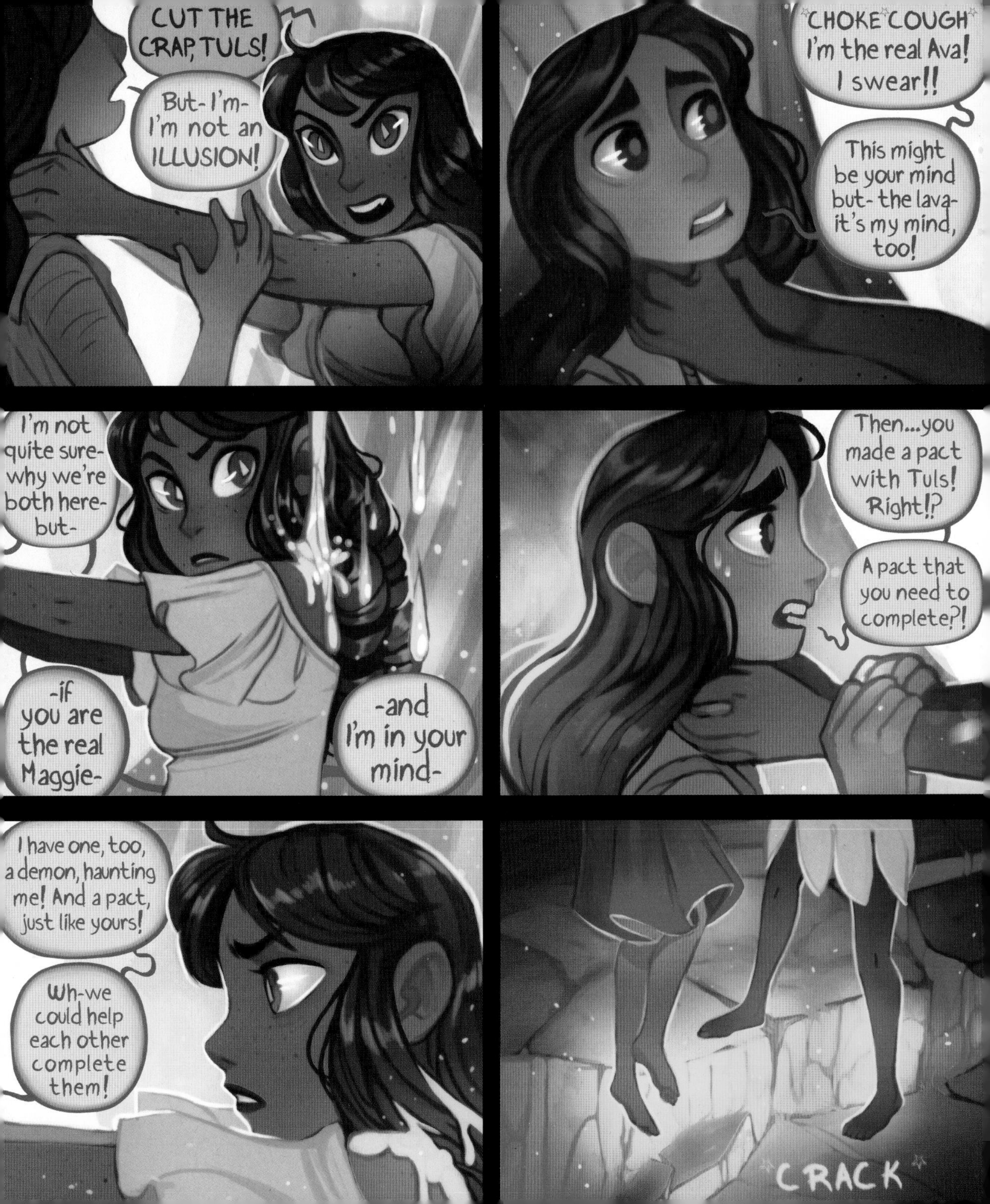
CUT THE CRAP, TULS!
But- I'm- I'm not an ILLUSION!
CHOKE COUGH I'm the real Ava! I swear!!
This might be your mind but- the lava- it's my mind, too!
I'm not quite sure- why we're both here- but-
-if you are the real Maggie-
-and I'm in your mind-
Then...you made a pact with Tuls! Right!?
A pact that you need to complete?!
I have one, too, a demon, haunting me! And a pact, just like yours!
Wh-we could help each other complete them!
CRACK

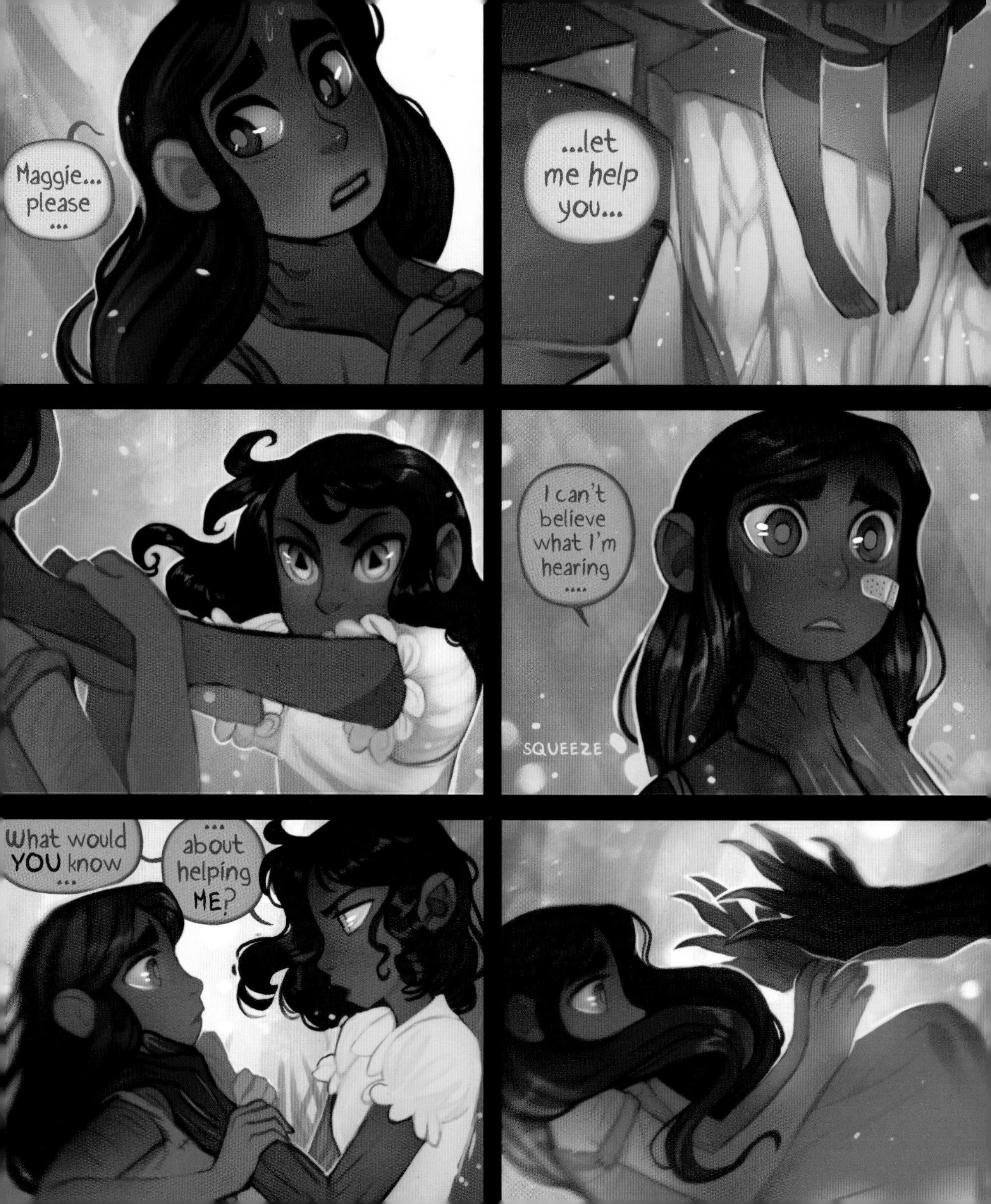
Maggie... please ...
...let me help you...
I can't believe what I'm hearing ....
SQUEEZE
What would YOU know ...
... about helping ME?

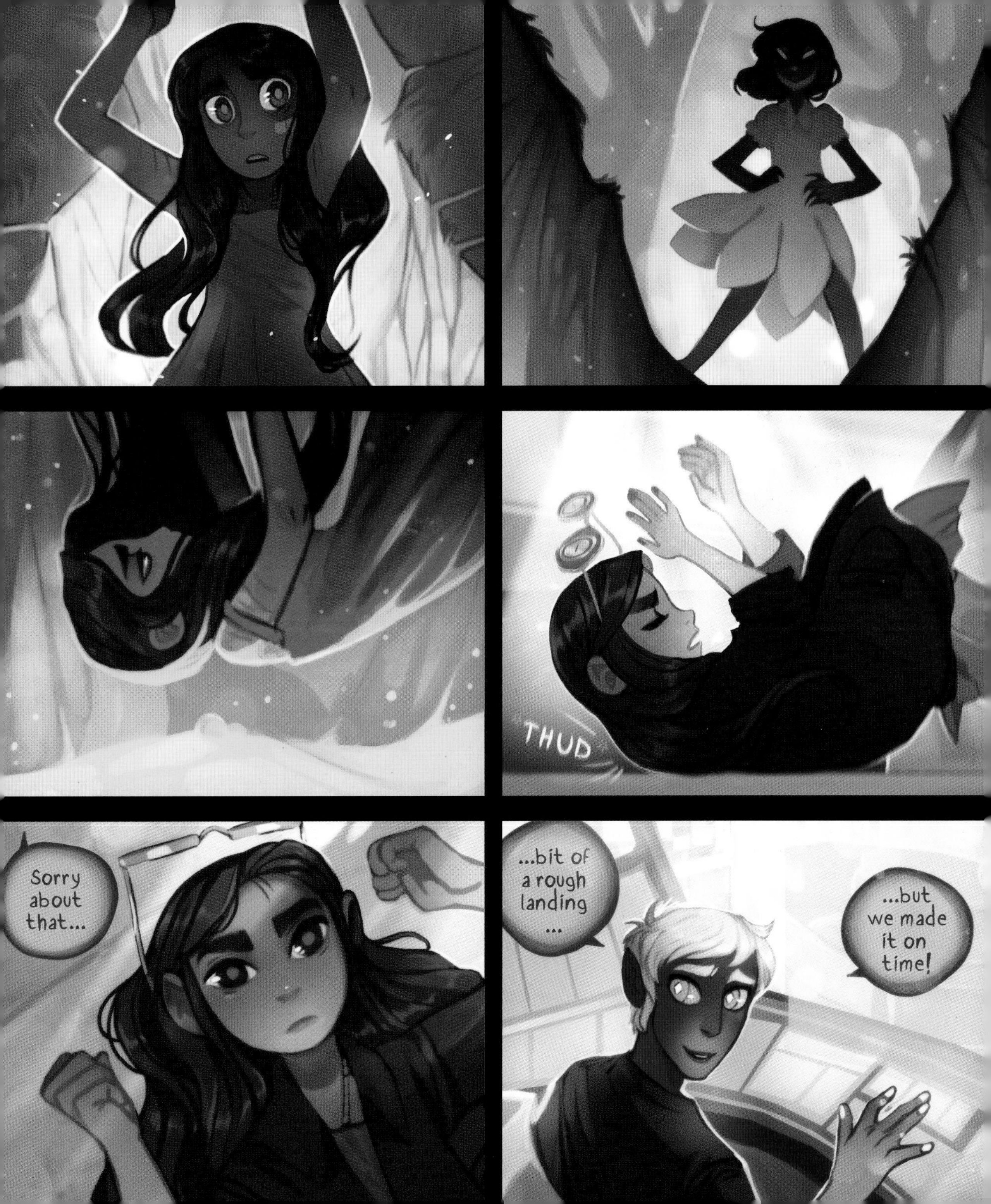
THUD
Sorry about that...
...bit of a rough landing ...
...but we made it on time!

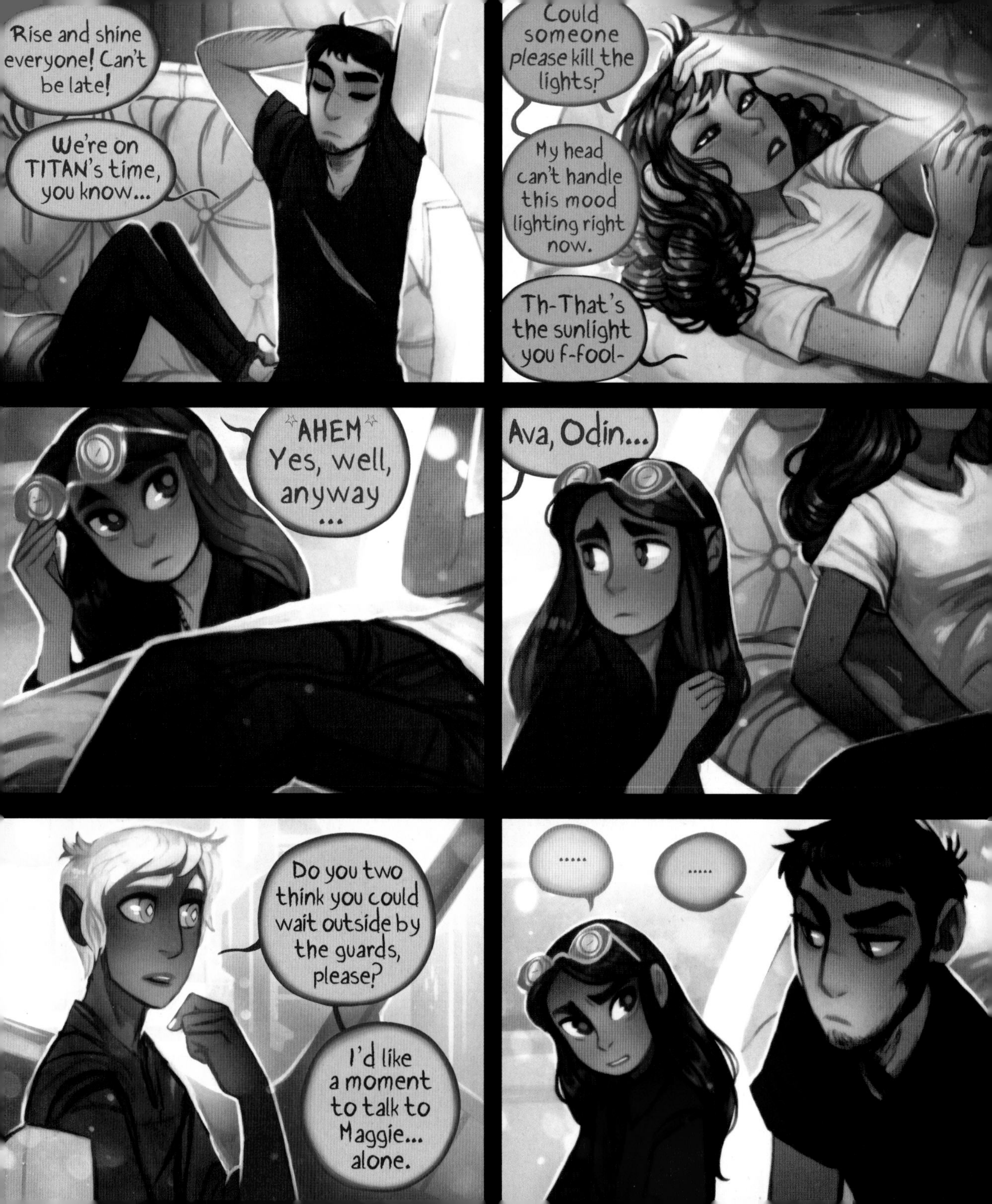
Rise and shine everyone! Can't be late!
We're on TITAN's time, you know...
Could someone please kill the lights?
My head can't handle this mood lighting right now.
Th-That's the sunlight you f-fool-
AHEM Yes, well, anyway ...
Ava, Odin...
Do you two think you could wait outside by the guards, please?
I'd like a moment to talk to Maggie... alone.
.....
.....

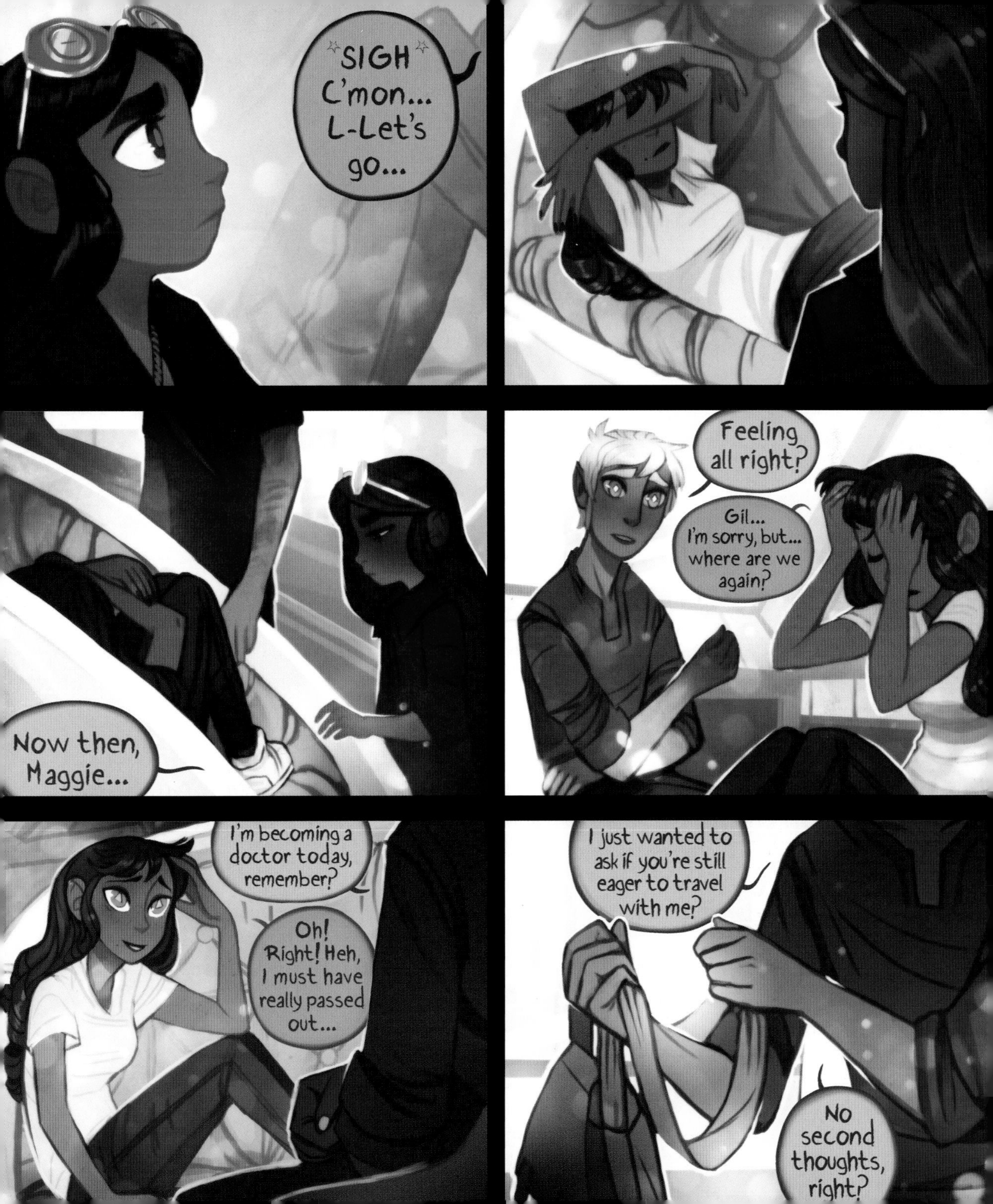
SIGH
C'mon... L-Let's go...
Now then, Maggie...
Feeling all right?
Gil... I'm sorry, but... where are we again?
I'm becoming a doctor today, remember?
Oh! Right! Heh, I must have really passed out...
I just wanted to ask if you're still eager to travel with me?
No second thoughts, right?

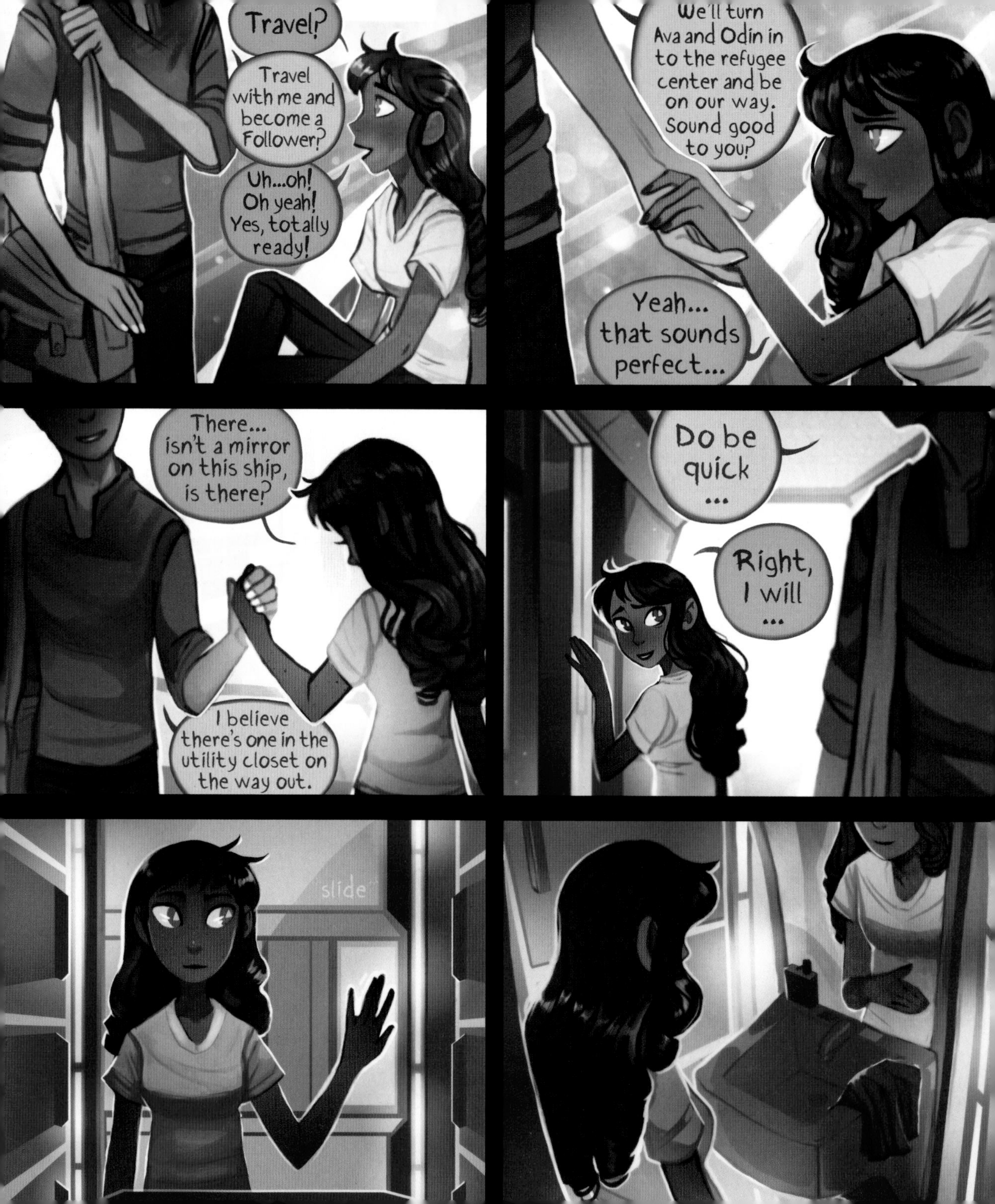
Travel?
Travel with me and become a Follower?
Uh...oh! Oh yeah! Yes, totally ready!
We'll turn Ava and Odin in to the refugee center and be on our way. Sound good to you?
Yeah... that sounds perfect...
There... isn't a mirror on this ship, is there?
I believe there's one in the utility closet on the way out.
Do be quick ...
Right, I will ...
slide

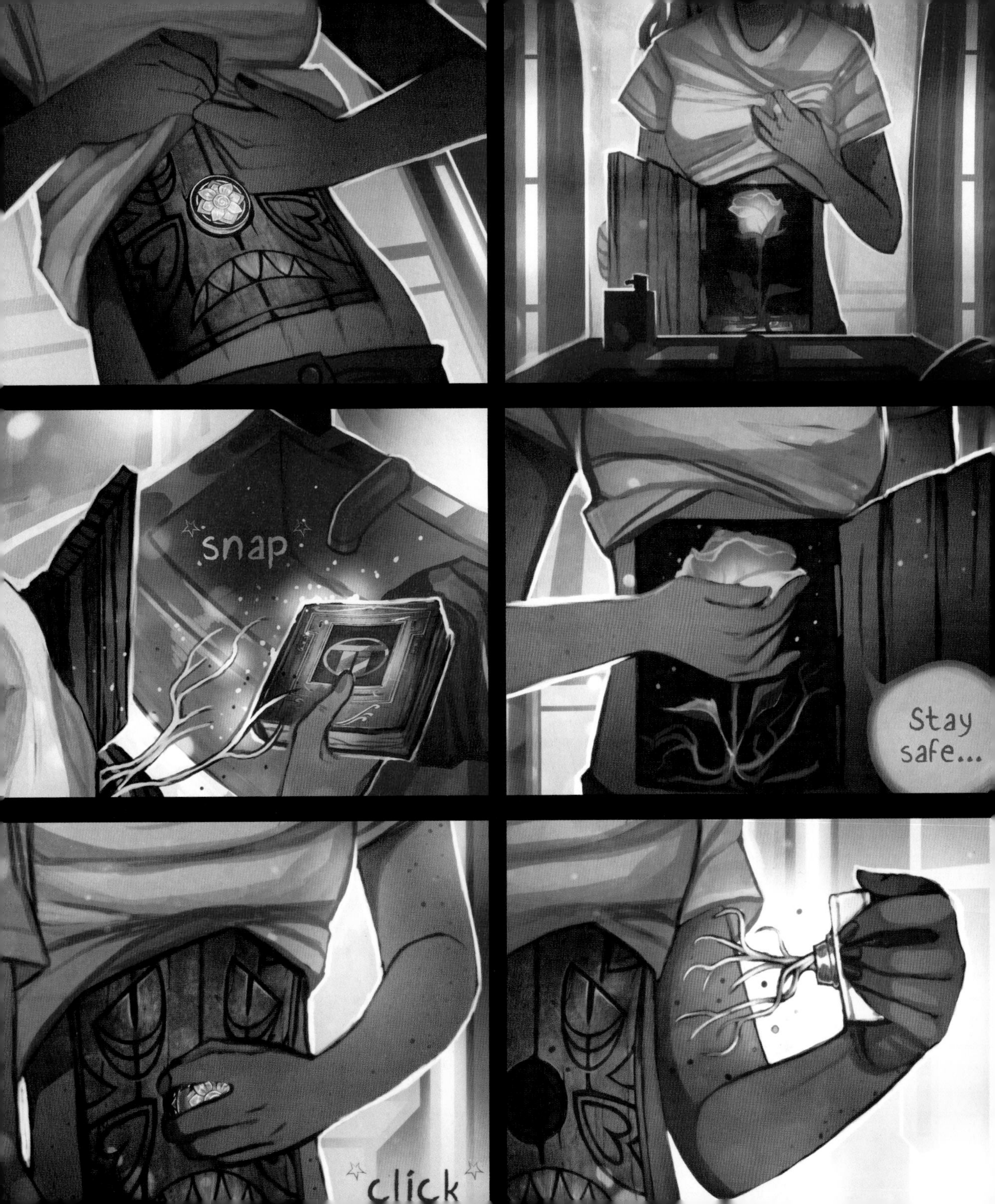
snap
Stay safe...
click

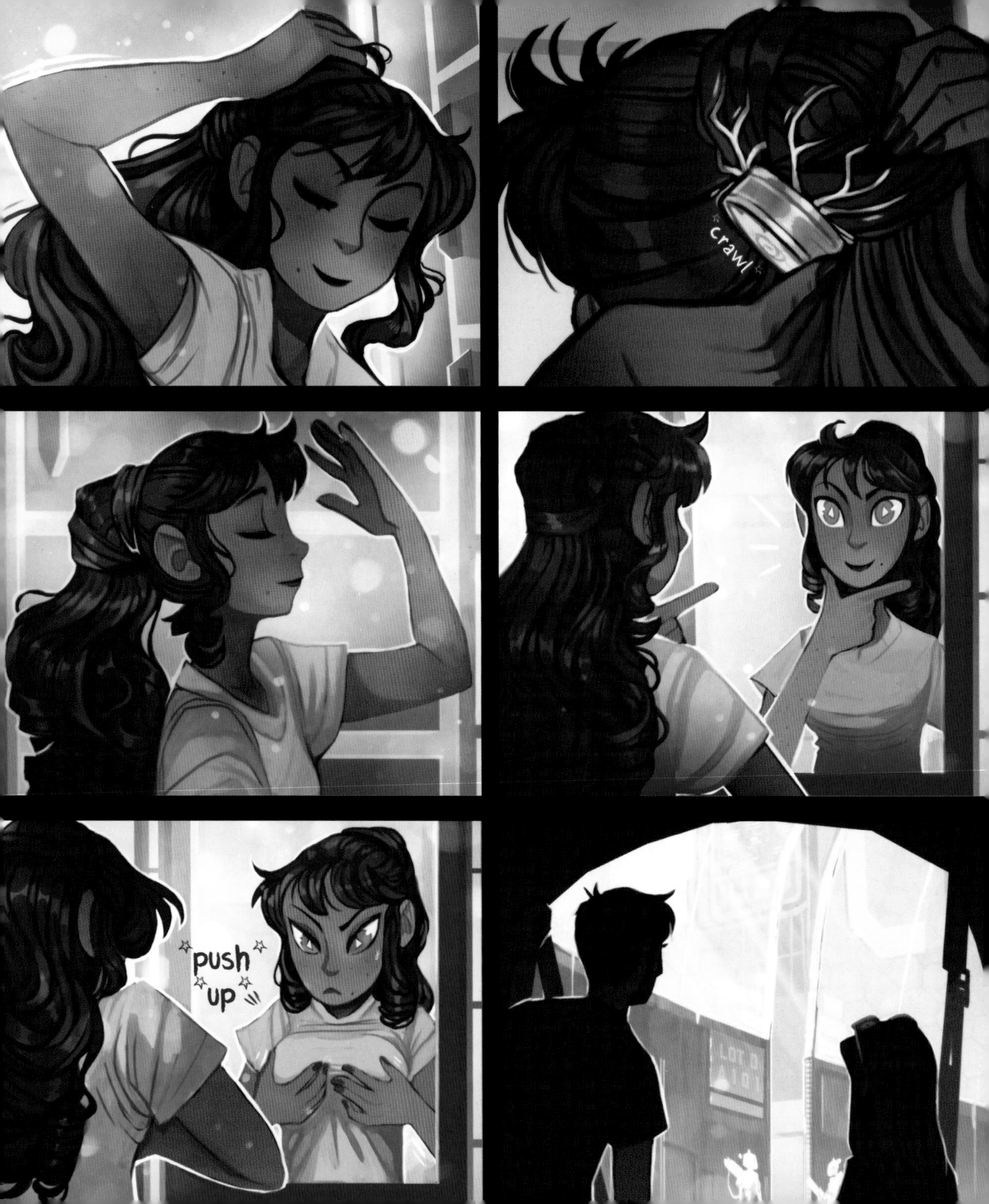
crawl
push up

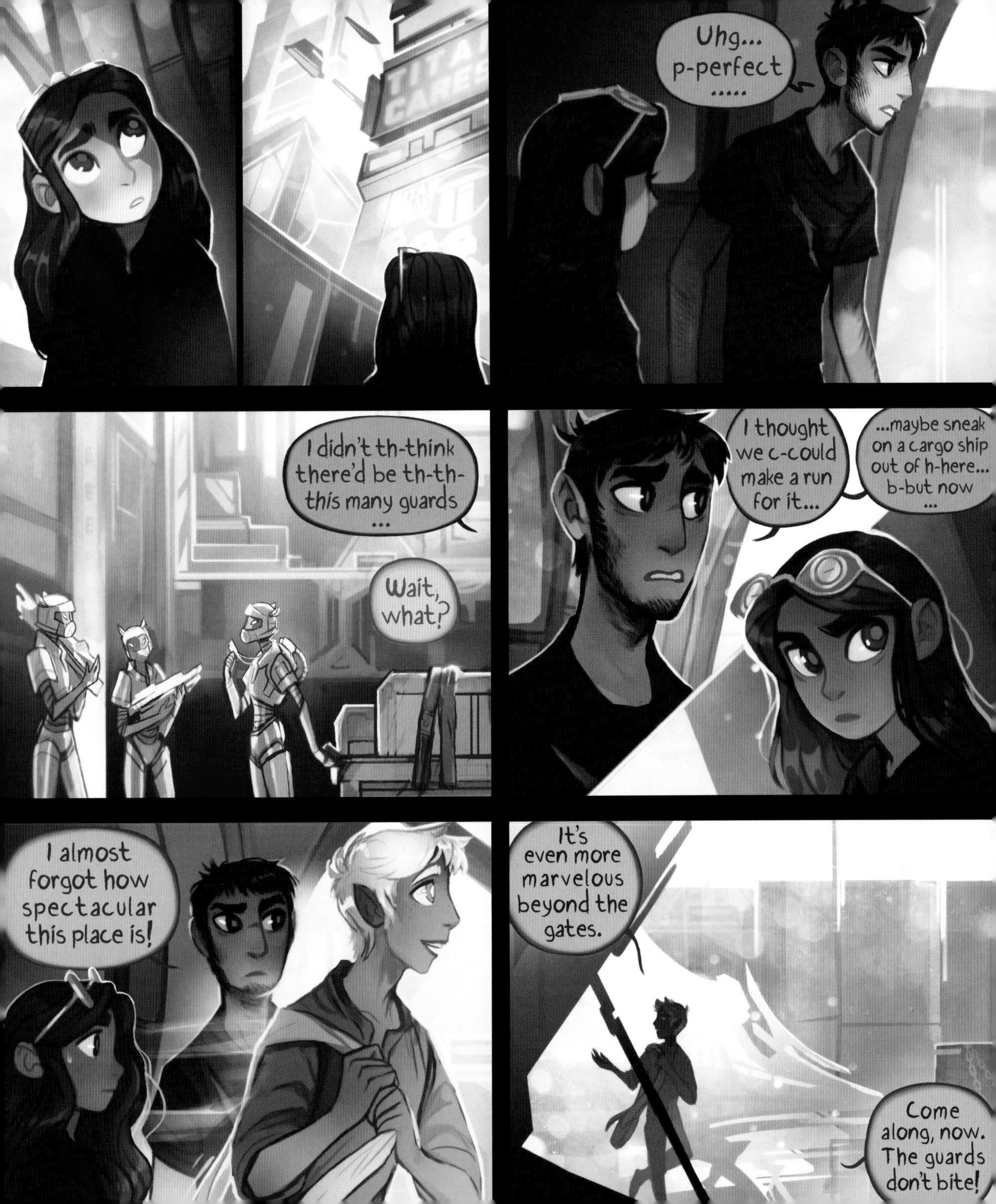

Uhg... p-perfect .....
I didn't th-think there'd be th-th-this many guards ...
Wait, what?
I thought we c-could make a run for it...
...maybe sneak on a cargo ship out of h-here... b-but now ...
I almost forgot how spectacular this place is!
It's even more marvelous beyond the gates.
Come along, now. The guards don't bite!

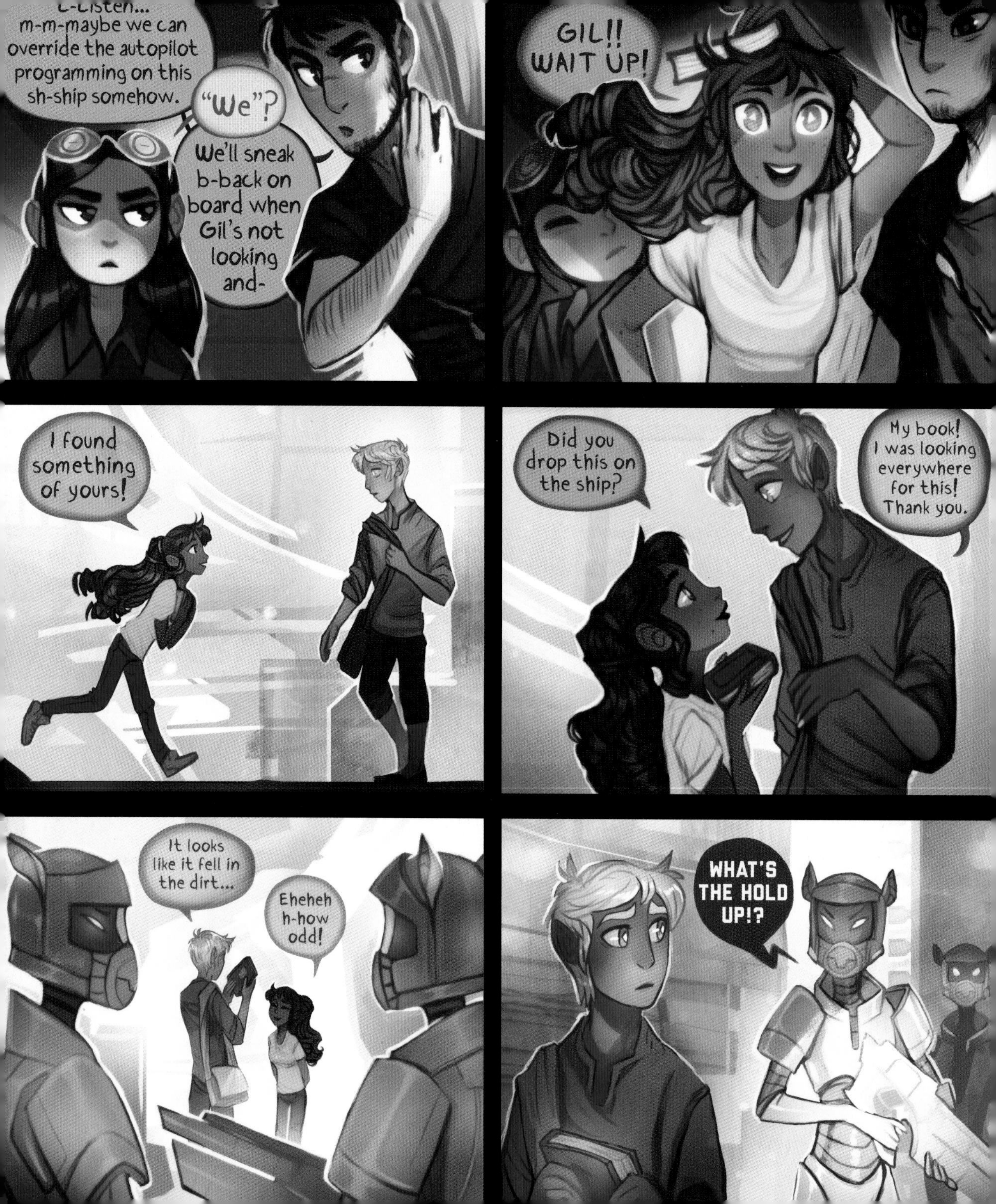
L-Listen... m-m-maybe we can override the autopilot programming on this sh-ship somehow.
"We"?
We'll sneak b-back on board when Gil's not looking and-
GIL!! WAIT UP!
I found something of yours!
Did you drop this on the ship?
My book! I was looking everywhere for this! Thank you.
It looks like it fell in the dirt...
Eheheh h-how odd!
WHAT'S THE HOLD UP!?

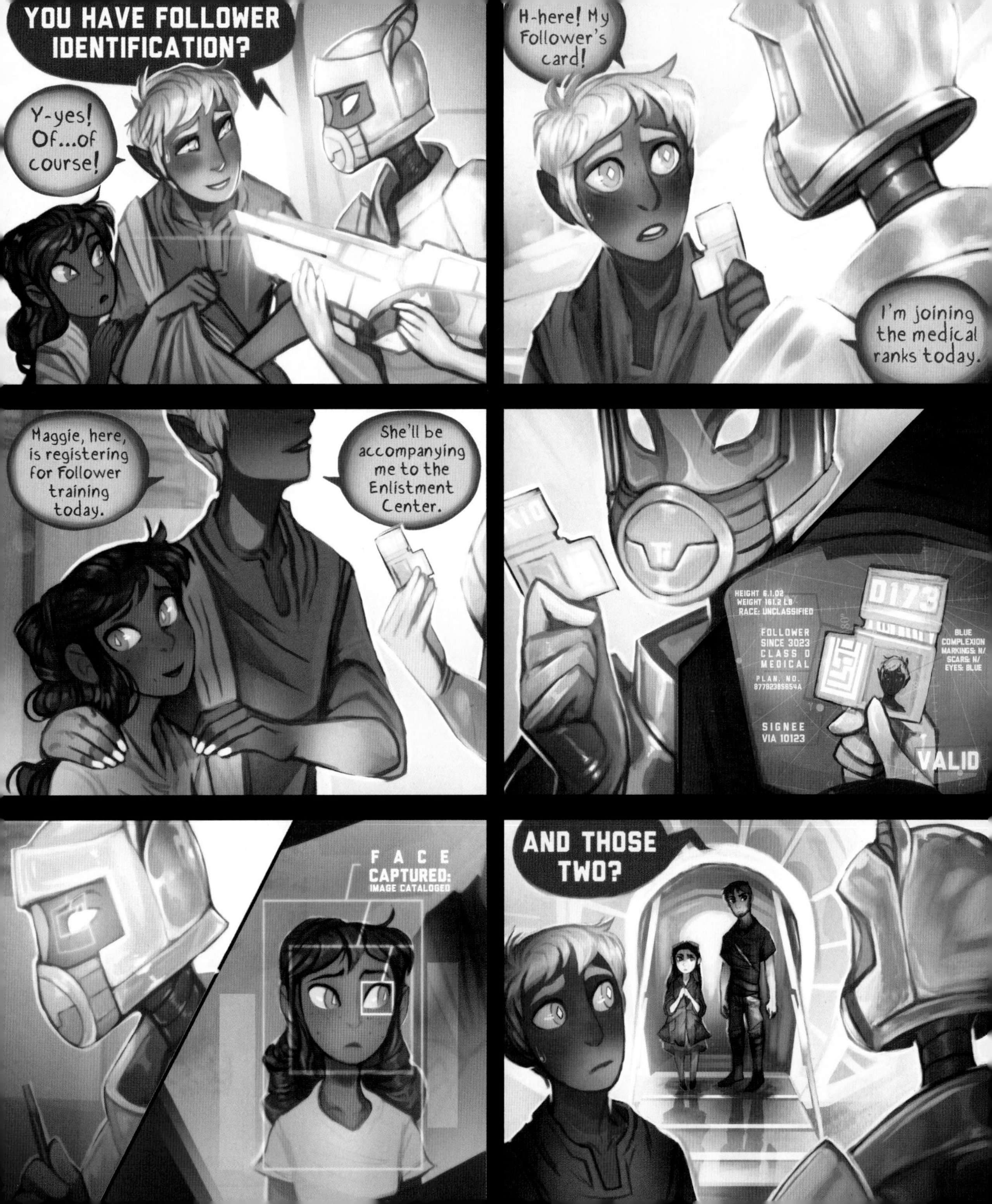
YOU HAVE FOLLOWER IDENTIFICATION?
Y-yes! Of...of course!
H-here! My Follower's card!
I'm joining the medical ranks today.
Maggie, here, is registering for Follower training today.
She'll be accompanying me to the Enlistment Center.
D173
HEIGHT 6.1.02
WEIGHT 161.2 LB
RACE: UNCLASSIFIED
FOLLOWER SINCE 3023 CLASS D MEDICAL
PLAN. NO. 877823BS654A
BLUE COMPLEXION MARKINGS: N/ SCARS: N/ EYES: BLUE
SIGNEE VIA 10123
VALID
FACE CAPTURED: IMAGE CATALOGED
AND THOSE TWO?

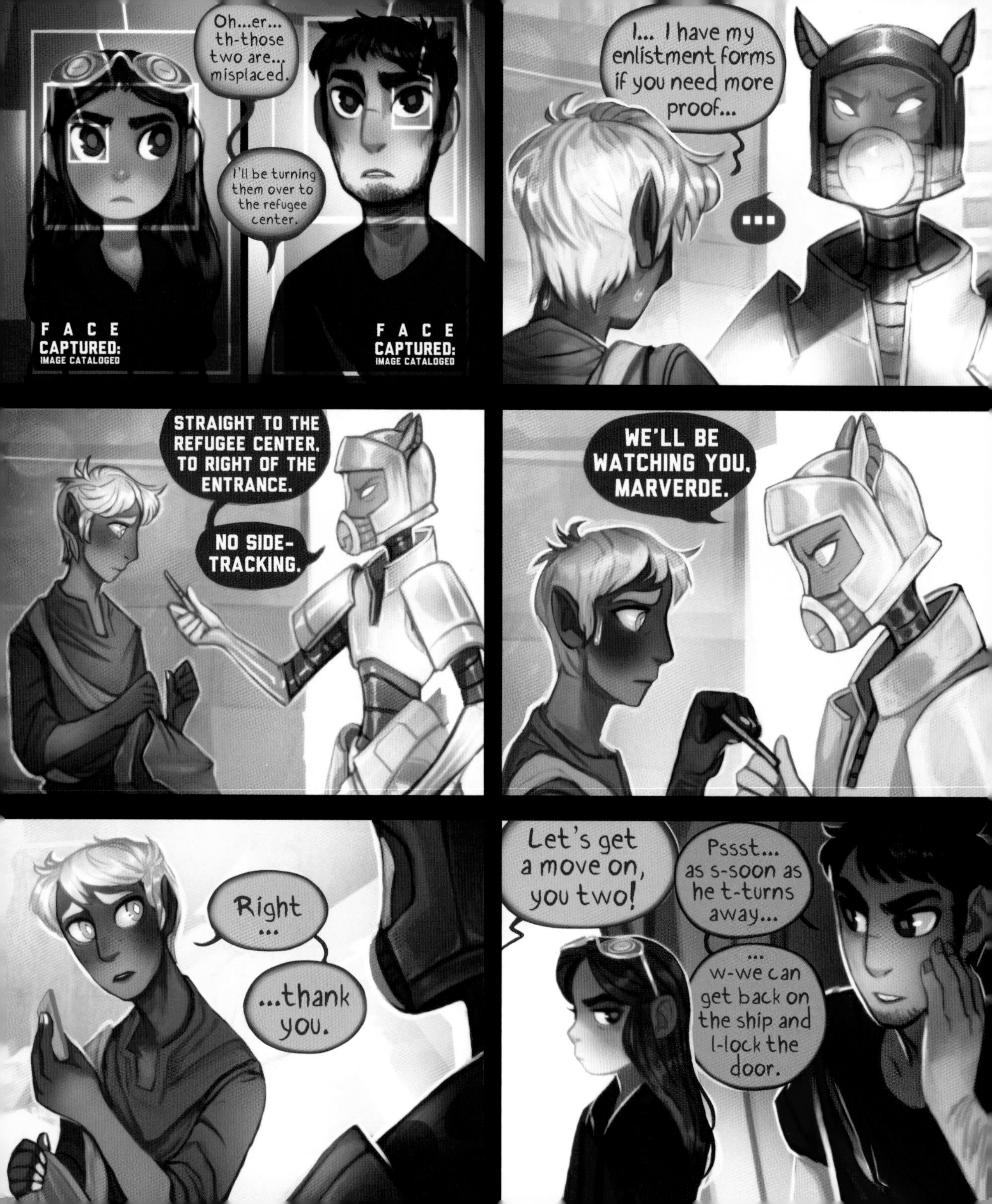
Oh...er... th-those two are... misplaced.
I'll be turning them over to the refugee center.
FACE CAPTURED: IMAGE CATALOGED
FACE CAPTURED: IMAGE CATALOGED
I... I have my enlistment forms if you need more proof...
...
STRAIGHT TO THE REFUGEE CENTER, TO RIGHT OF THE ENTRANCE.
NO SIDE-TRACKING.
WE'LL BE WATCHING YOU, MARVERDE.
Right...
...thank you.
Let's get a move on, you two!
Pssst... as s-soon as he t-turns away...
...w-we can get back on the ship and l-lock the door.

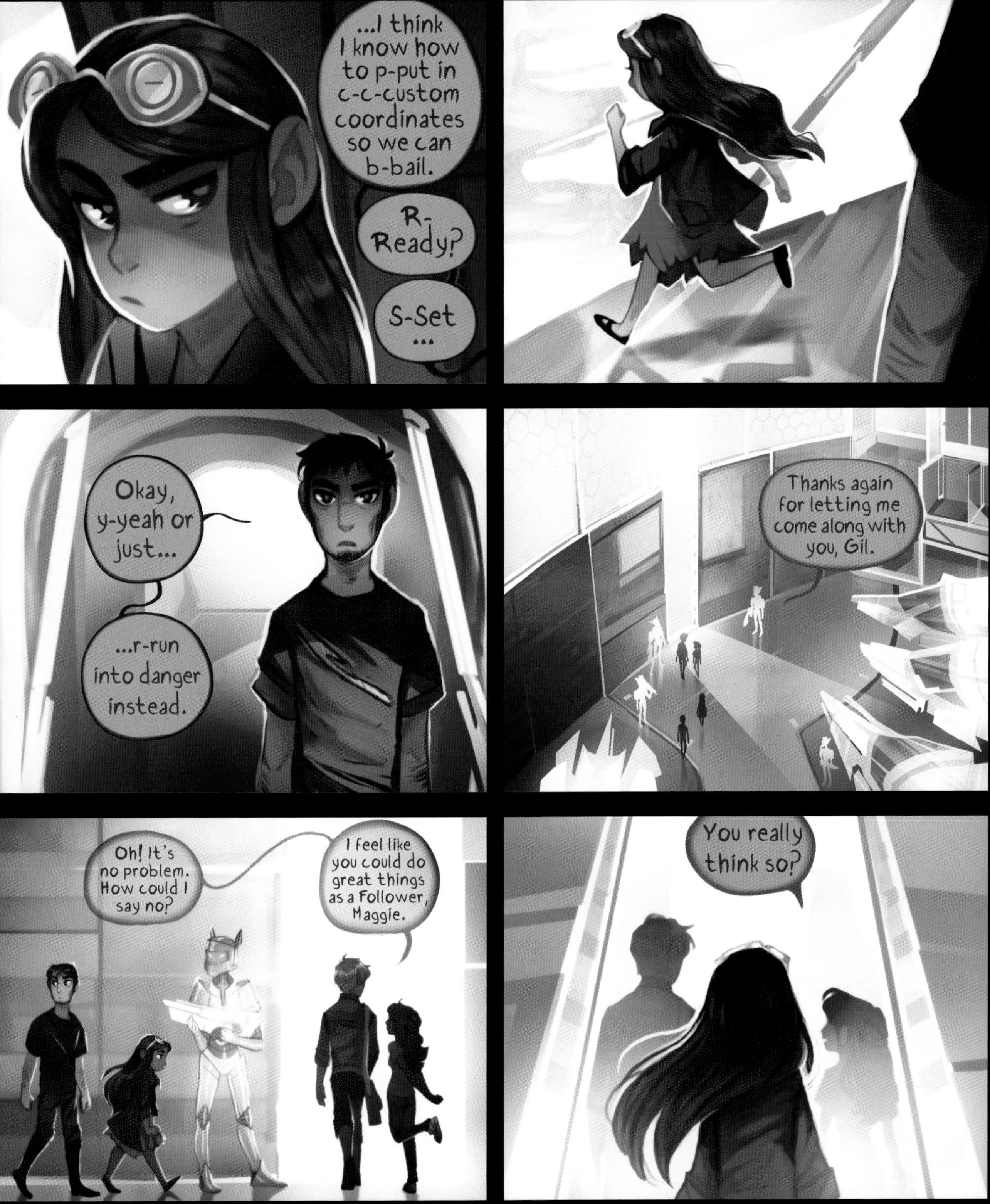
...I think I know how to p-put in c-c-custom coordinates so we can b-bail.
R-Ready?
S-Set ...
Okay, y-yeah or just...
...r-run into danger instead.
Thanks again for letting me come along with you, Gil.
Oh! It's no problem. How could I say no?
I feel like you could do great things as a Follower, Maggie.
You really think so?

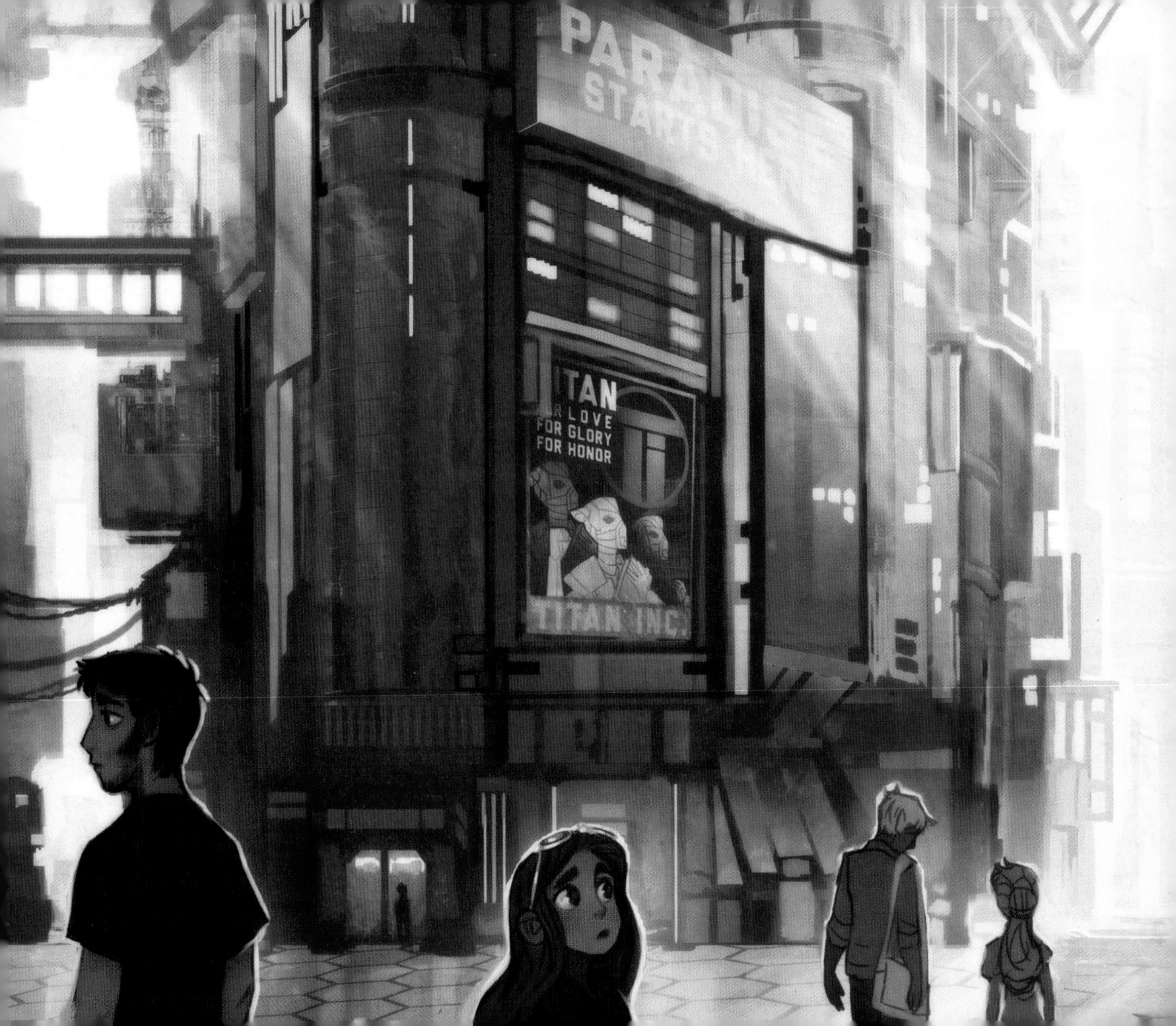
TAN
LOVE
FOR GLORY
FOR HONOR
TITAN INC

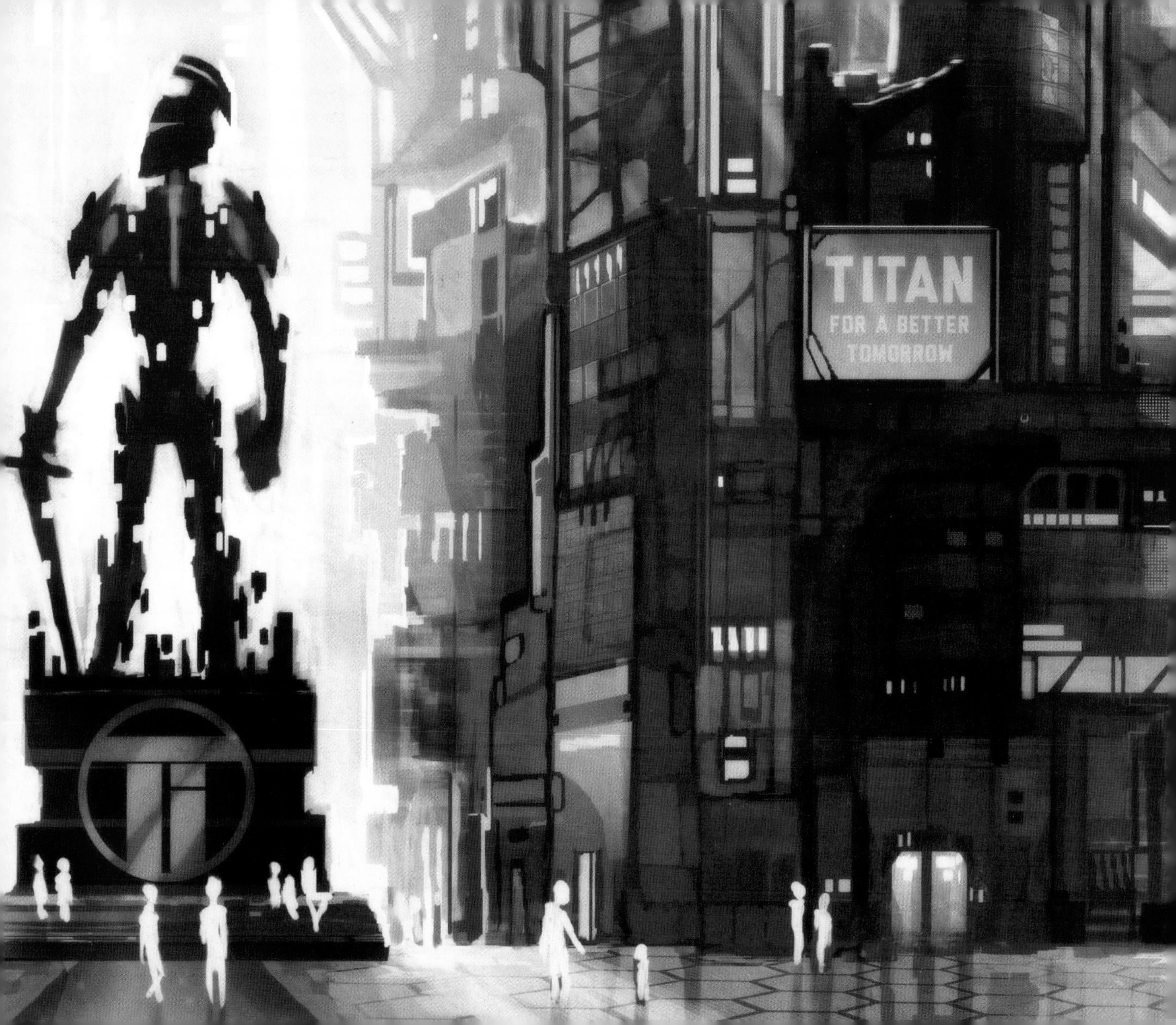
TITAN
FOR A BETTER
TOMORROW

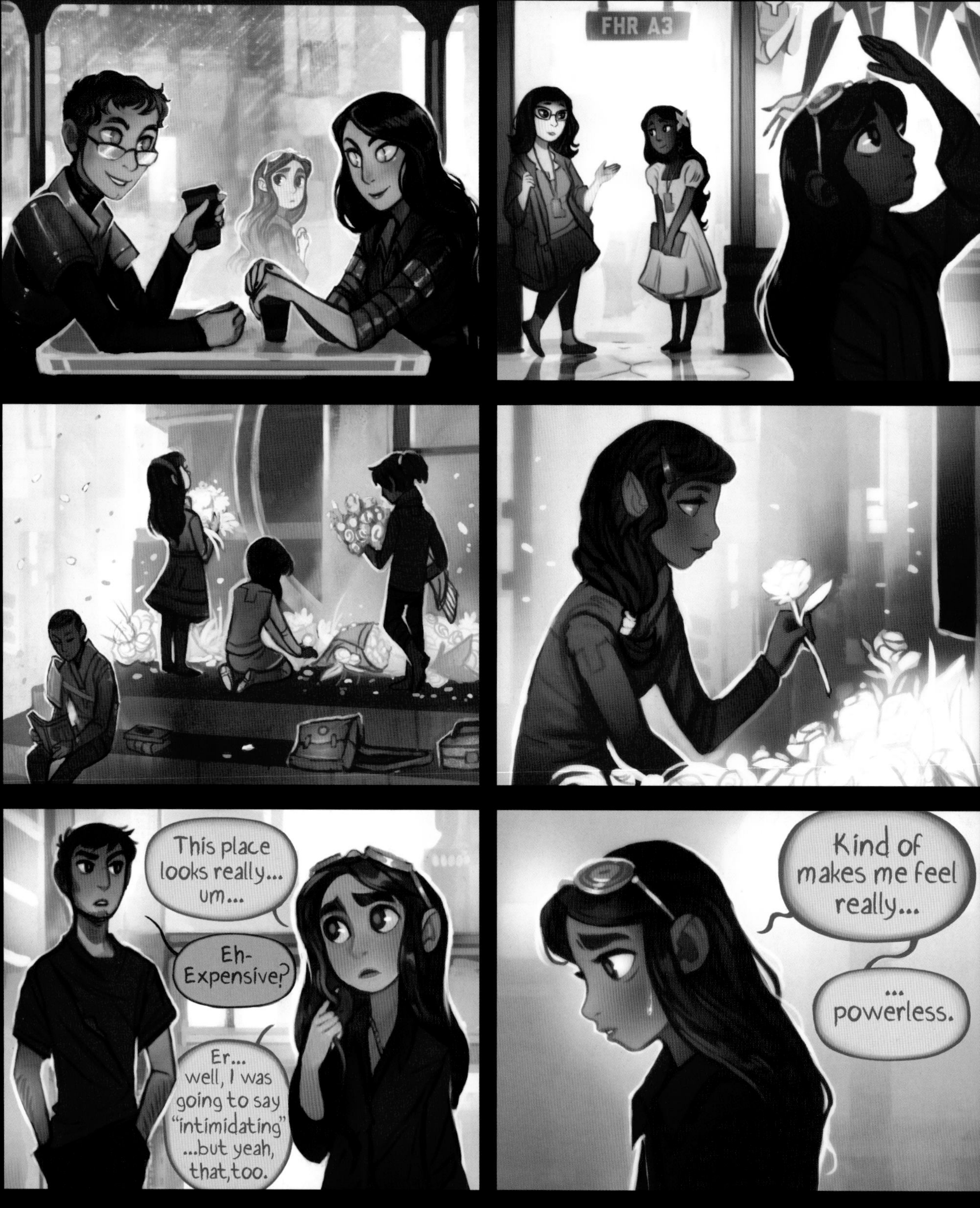
FHR A3
This place looks really... um...
Eh- Expensive?
Er... well, I was going to say "intimidating" ...but yeah, that, too.
Kind of makes me feel really...
... powerless.

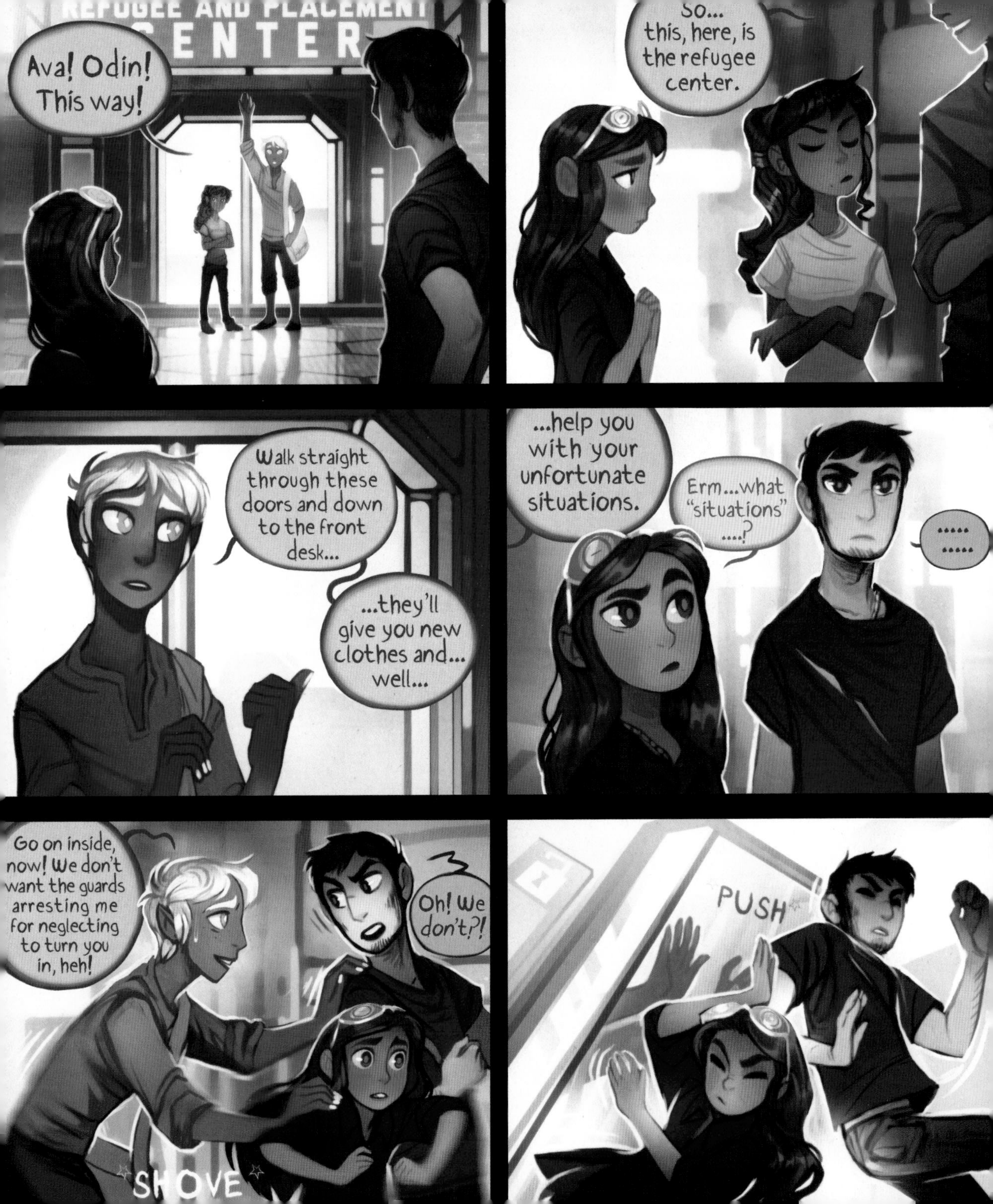
REFUGEE AND PLACEMENT
CENTER
Ava! Odin! This way!
So... this, here, is the refugee center.
Walk straight through these doors and down to the front desk...
...they'll give you new clothes and... well...
...help you with your unfortunate situations.
Erm...what "situations" ....?
....
Go on inside, now! We don't want the guards arresting me for neglecting to turn you in, heh!
Oh! We don't?!
SHOVE
PUSH

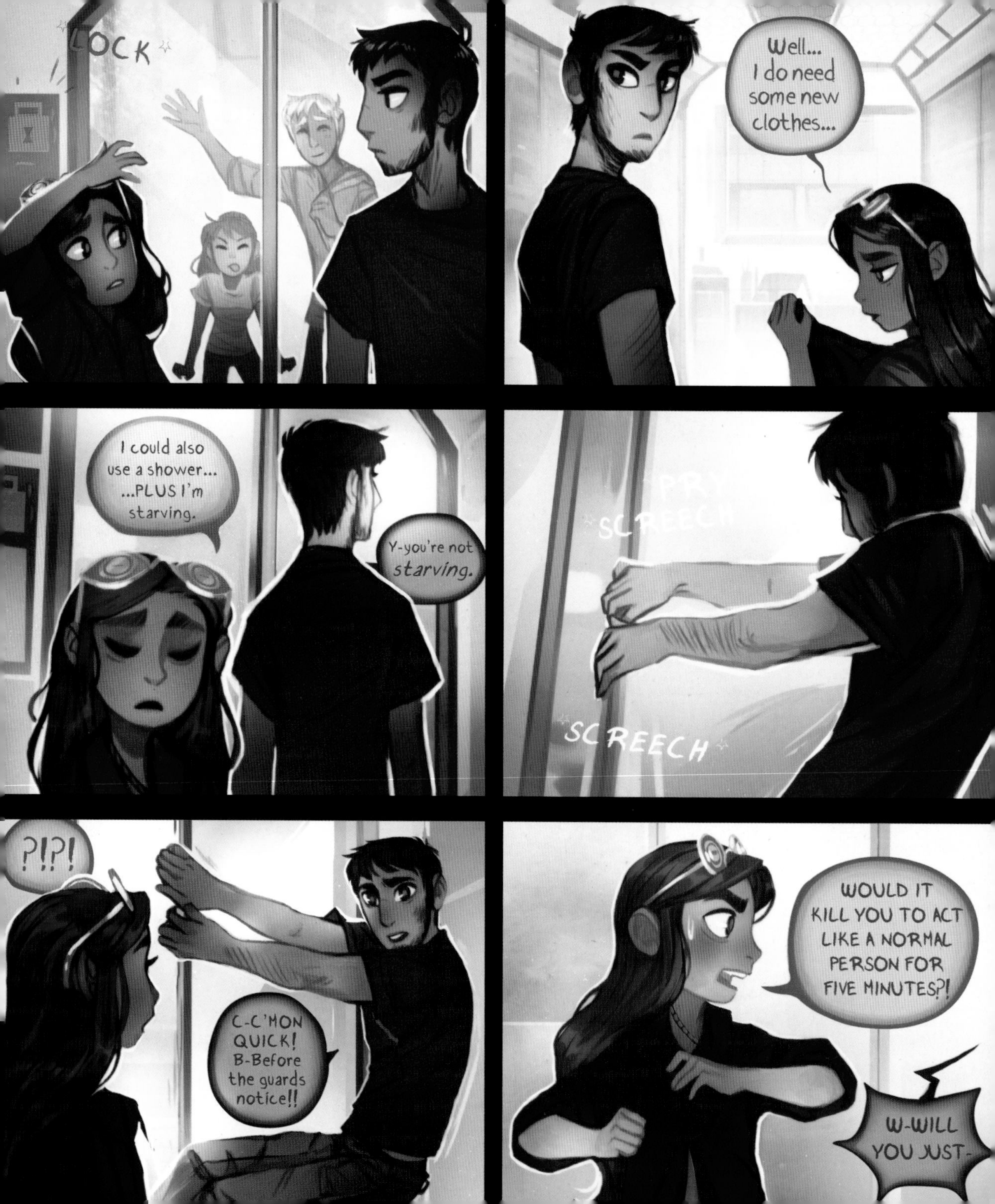
LOCK
Well...
I do need
some new
clothes...
I could also
use a shower...
...PLUS I'm
starving.
Y-you're not
starving.
PRY
SCREECH
SCREECH
?!?!
C-C'MON
QUICK!
B-Before
the guards
notice!!
WOULD IT
KILL YOU TO ACT
LIKE A NORMAL
PERSON FOR
FIVE MINUTES?!
W-WILL
YOU JUST-

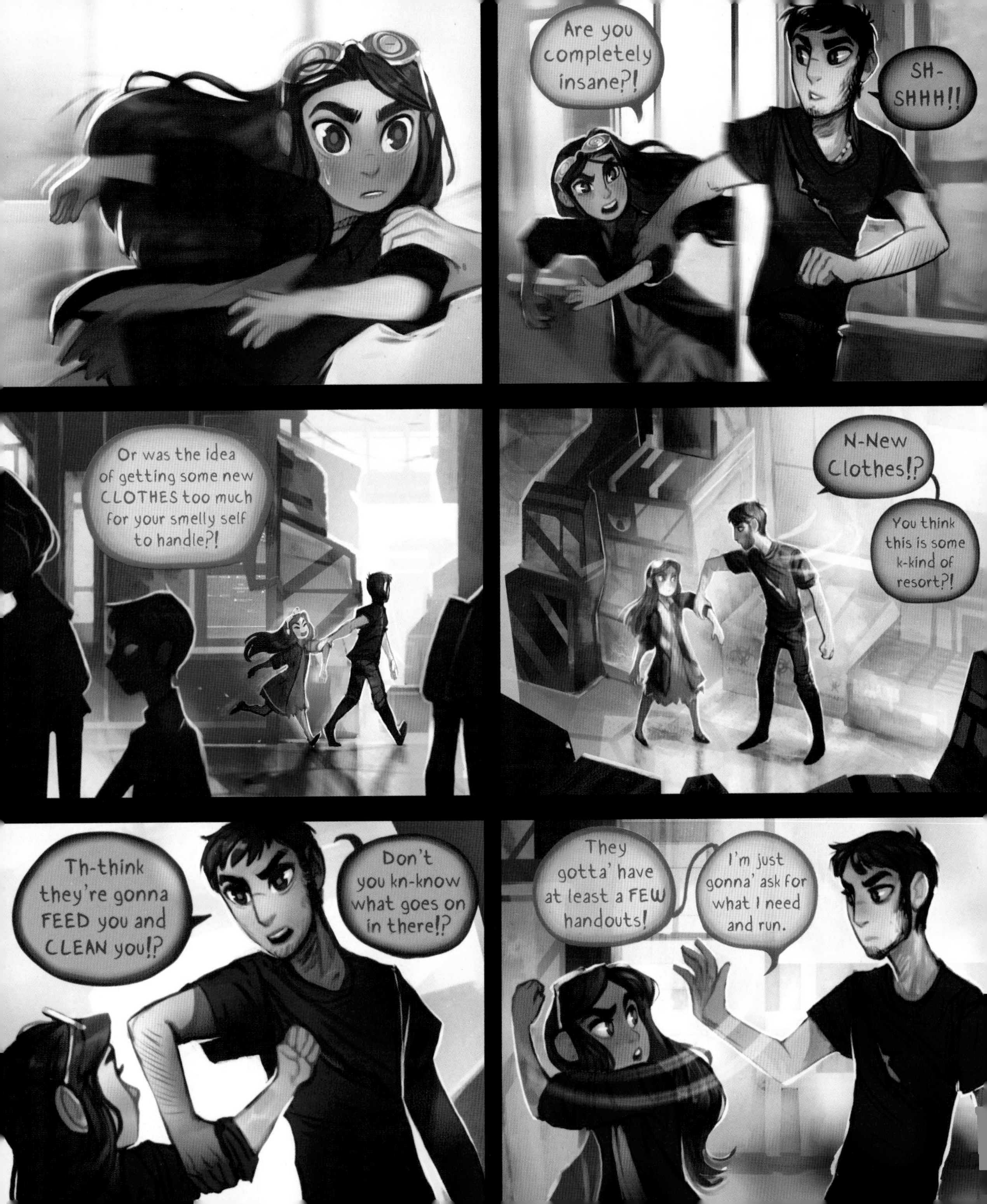
Are you completely insane?!
SH-SHHH!!
Or was the idea of getting some new CLOTHES too much for your smelly self to handle?!
N-New Clothes!?
You think this is some k-kind of resort?!
Th-think they're gonna FEED you and CLEAN you!?
Don't you kn-know what goes on in there!?
They gotta' have at least a FEW handouts!
I'm just gonna' ask for what I need and run.

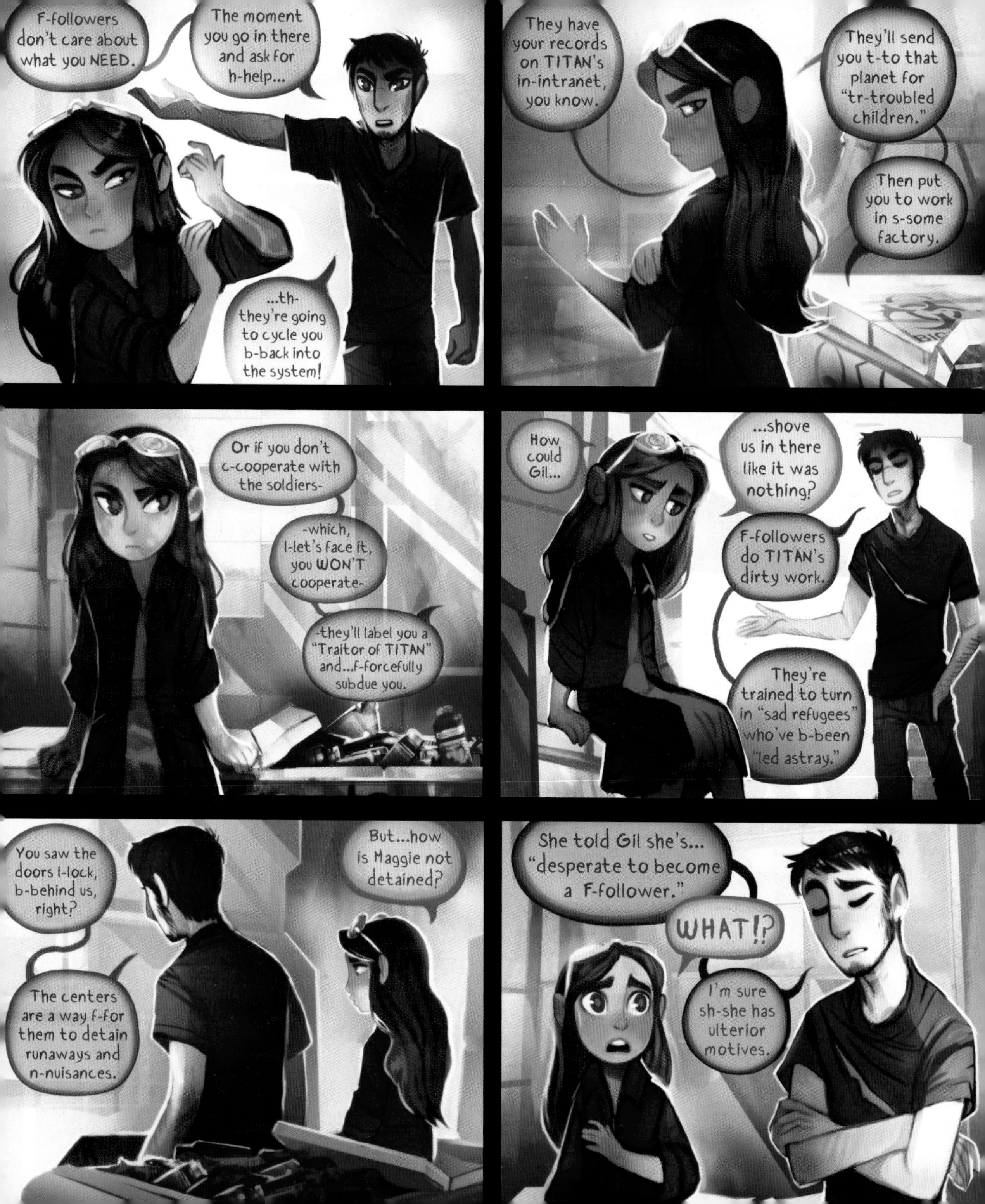
F-followers don't care about what you NEED.
The moment you go in there and ask for h-help...
...th-they're going to cycle you b-back into the system!
They have your records on TITAN's in-intranet, you know.
They'll send you t-to that planet for "tr-troubled children."
Then put you to work in s-some factory.
Or if you don't c-cooperate with the soldiers-
-which, l-let's face it, you WON'T cooperate-
-they'll label you a "Traitor of TITAN" and...f-forcefully subdue you.
How could Gil...
...shove us in there like it was nothing?
F-followers do TITAN's dirty work.
They're trained to turn in "sad refugees" who've b-been "led astray."
You saw the doors l-lock, b-behind us, right?
The centers are a way f-for them to detain runaways and n-nuisances.
But...how is Maggie not detained?
She told Gil she's... "desperate to become a F-follower."
WHAT!?
I'm sure sh-she has ulterior motives.

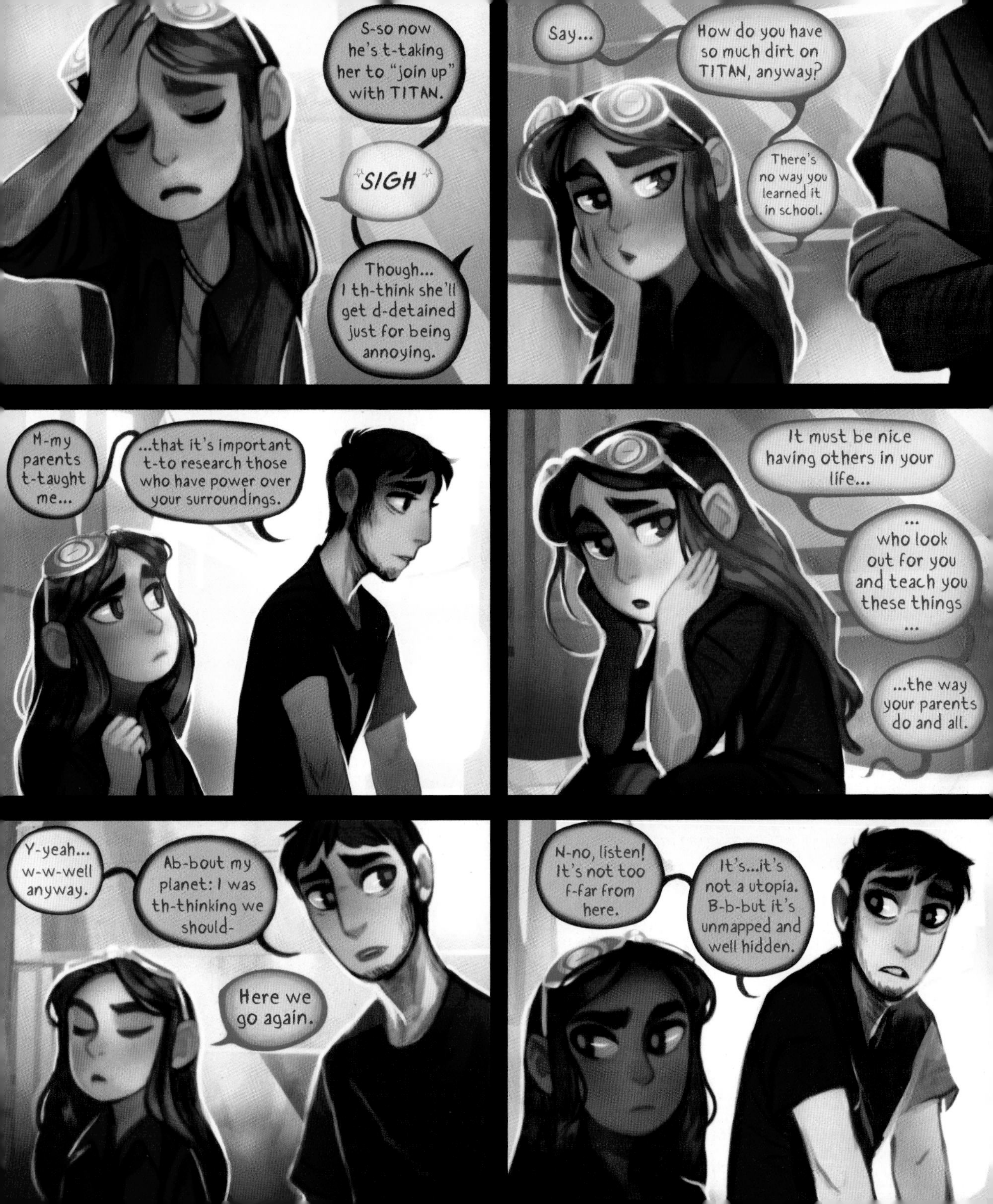
S-so now he's t-taking her to "join up" with TITAN.
SIGH
Though... I th-think she'll get d-detained just for being annoying.
Say...
How do you have so much dirt on TITAN, anyway?
There's no way you learned it in school.
M-my parents t-taught me...
...that it's important t-to research those who have power over your surroundings.
It must be nice having others in your life...
... who look out for you and teach you these things ...
...the way your parents do and all.
Y-yeah... w-w-well anyway.
Ab-bout my planet: I was th-thinking we should-
Here we go again.
N-no, listen! It's not too f-far from here.
It's...it's not a utopia. B-b-but it's unmapped and well hidden.

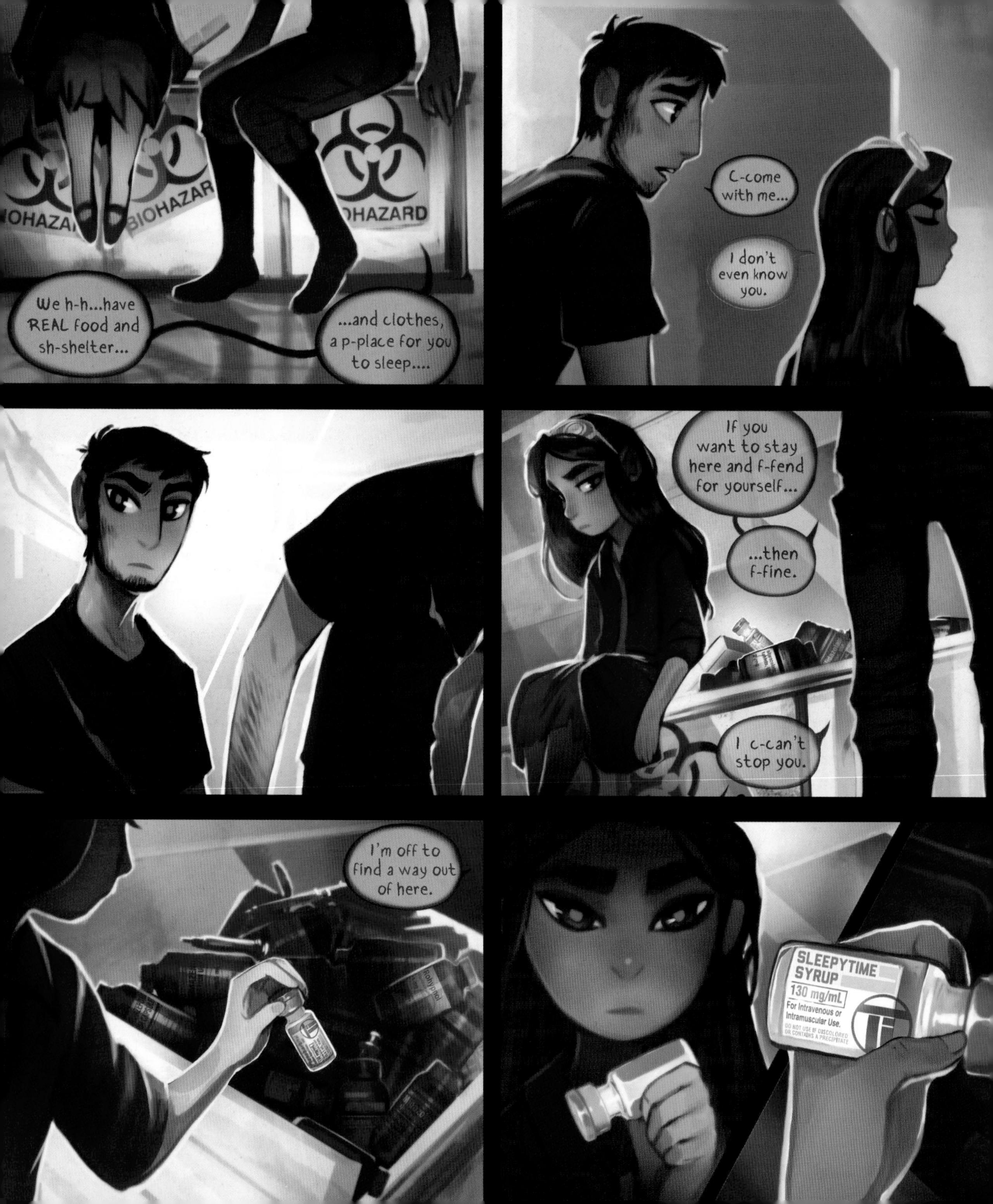
BIOHAZARD
BIOHAZARD
BIOHAZARD
We h-h...have REAL food and sh-shelter...
...and clothes, a p-place for you to sleep....
C-come with me...
I don't even know you.
If you want to stay here and f-fend for yourself...
...then f-fine.
I c-can't stop you.
I'm off to find a way out of here.
SLEEPYTIME SYRUP
130 mg/mL
For Intravenous or Intramuscular Use.
DO NOT USE IF DISCOLORED OR CONTAINS A PRECIPITATE

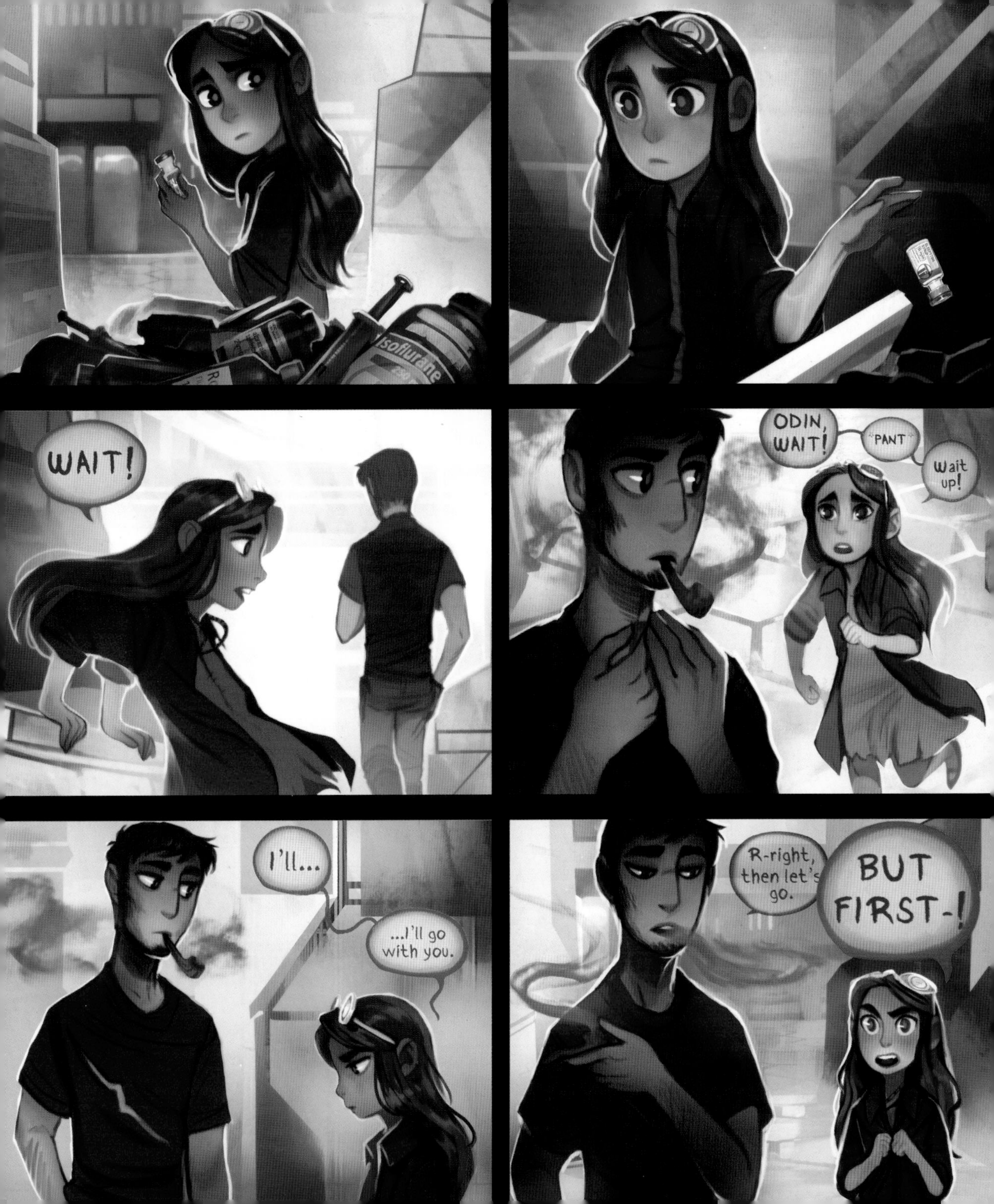
Isoflurane
WAIT!
ODIN, WAIT!
PANT
Wait up!
I'll...
...I'll go with you.
R-right, then let's go.
BUT FIRST-!

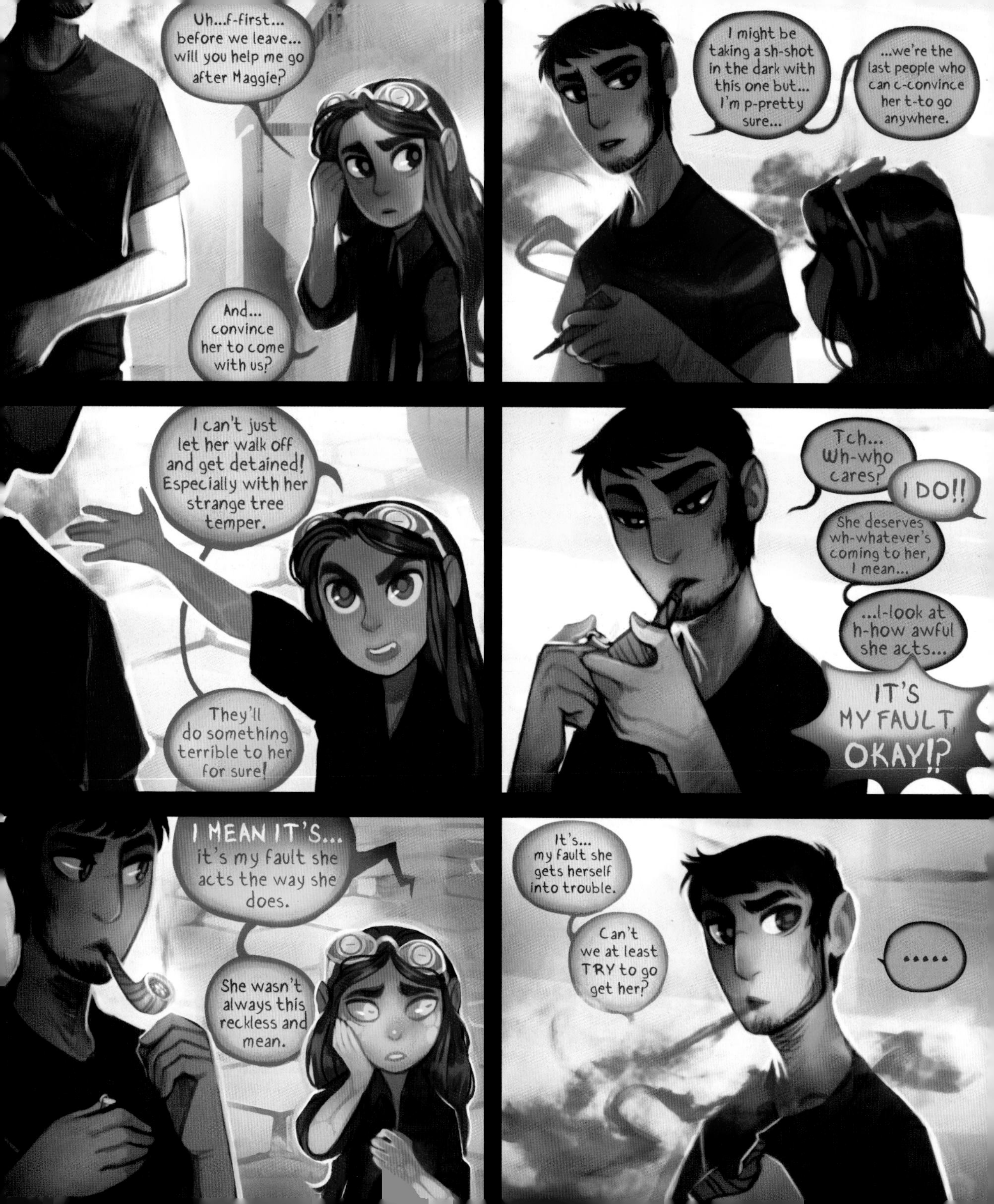
Uh...f-first... before we leave... will you help me go after Maggie?
And... convince her to come with us?
I might be taking a sh-shot in the dark with this one but... I'm p-pretty sure...
...we're the last people who can c-convince her t-to go anywhere.
I can't just let her walk off and get detained! Especially with her strange tree temper.
They'll do something terrible to her for sure!
Tch... Wh-who cares?
I DO!!
She deserves wh-whatever's coming to her, I mean...
...l-look at h-how awful she acts...
IT'S MY FAULT, OKAY!?
I MEAN IT'S... it's my fault she acts the way she does.
She wasn't always this reckless and mean.
It's... my fault she gets herself into trouble.
Can't we at least TRY to go get her?
.....

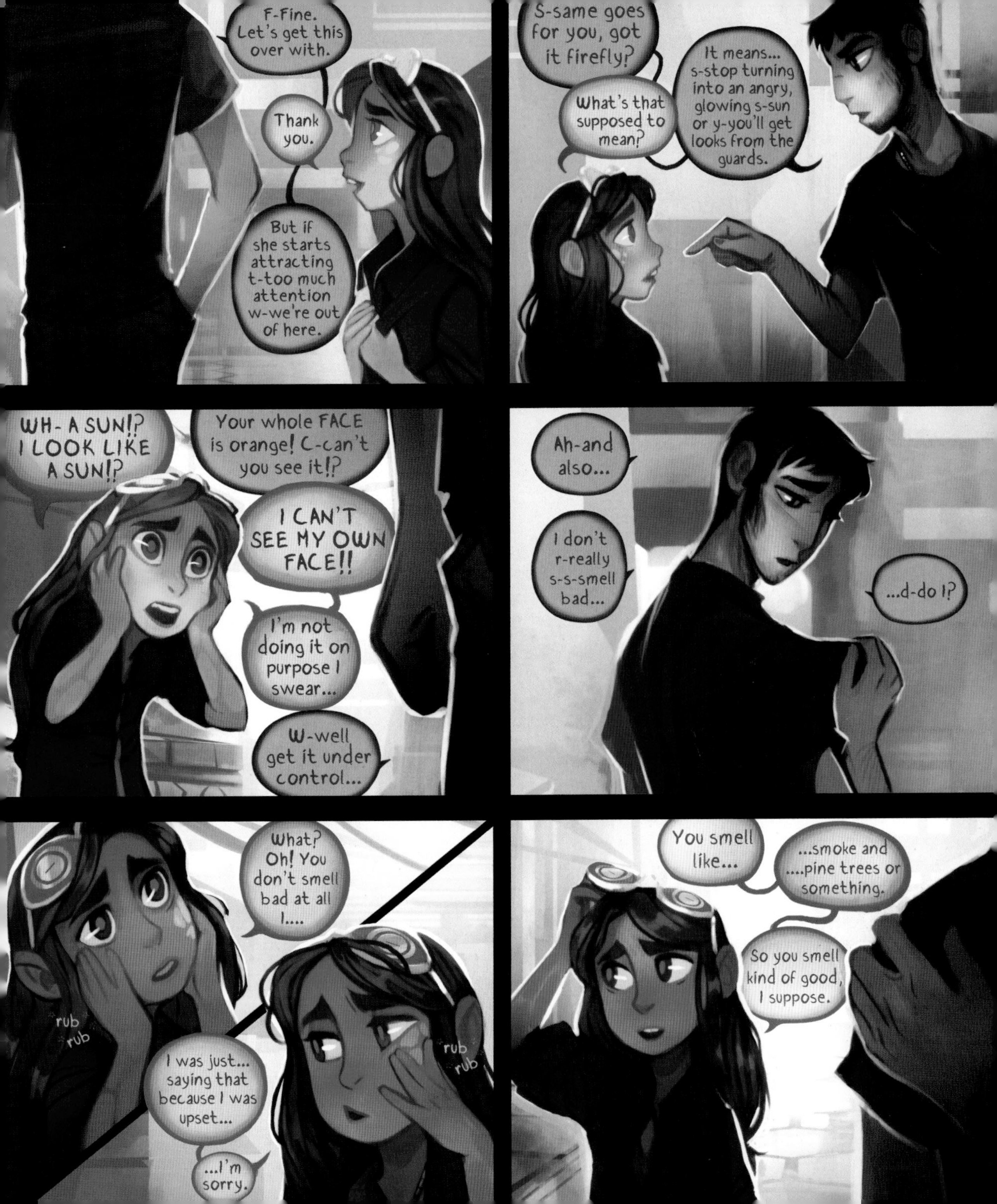
F-Fine. Let's get this over with.
Thank you.
But if she starts attracting t-too much attention w-we're out of here.
S-same goes for you, got it firefly?
What's that supposed to mean?
It means... s-stop turning into an angry, glowing s-sun or y-you'll get looks from the guards.
WH- A SUN!? I LOOK LIKE A SUN!?
Your whole FACE is orange! C-can't you see it!?
I CAN'T SEE MY OWN FACE!!
I'm not doing it on purpose I swear...
W-well get it under control...
Ah-and also...
I don't r-really s-s-smell bad...
...d-do I?
What? Oh! You don't smell bad at all I....
rub rub
rub rub
I was just... saying that because I was upset...
...I'm sorry.
You smell like...
...smoke and ....pine trees or something.
So you smell kind of good, I suppose.

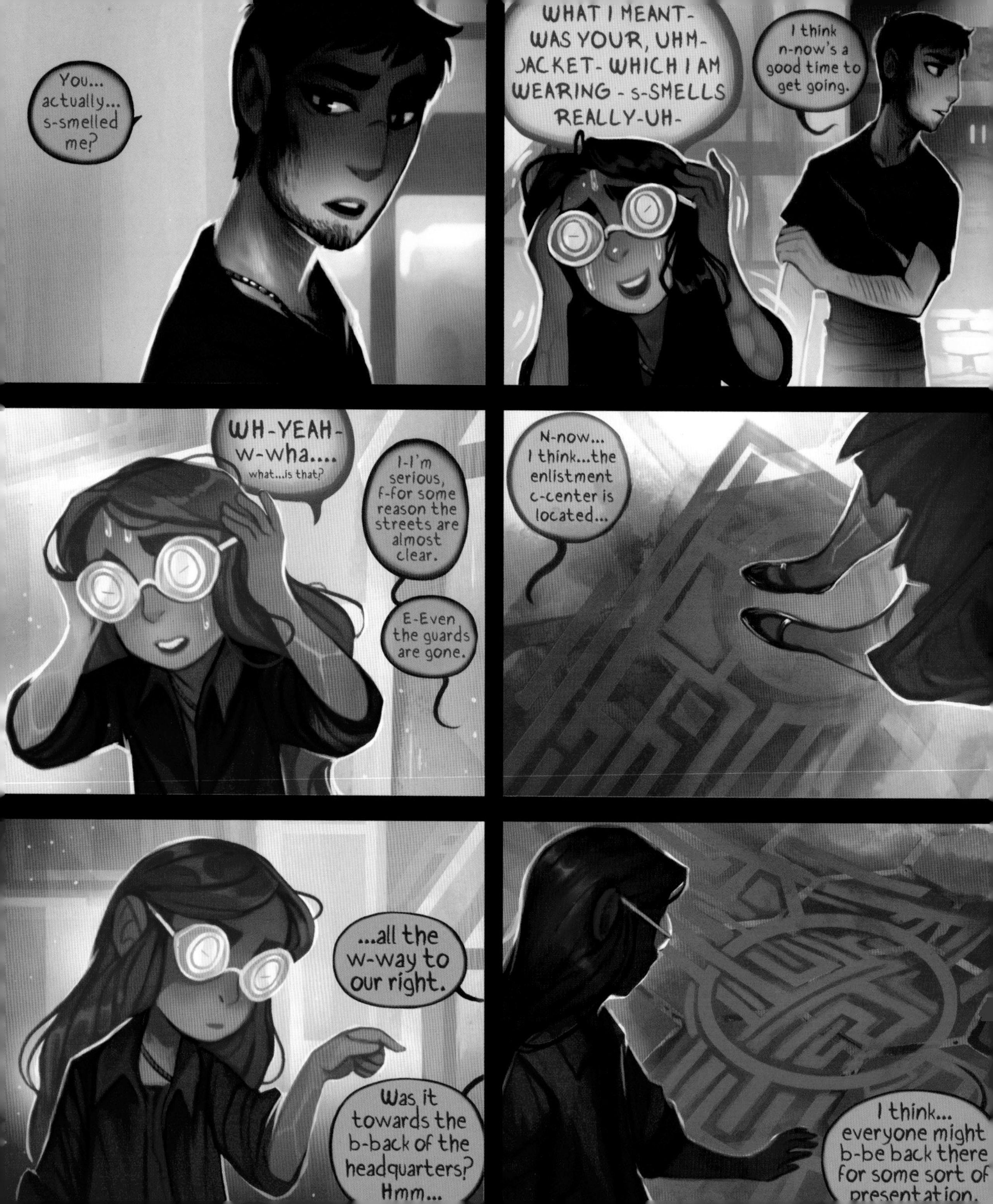

You... actually... s-smelled me?
WHAT I MEANT- WAS YOUR, UHM- JACKET- WHICH I AM WEARING - s-SMELLS REALLY-UH-
I think n-now's a good time to get going.
WH-YEAH- w-wha.... what...is that?
I-I'm serious, f-for some reason the streets are almost clear.
E-Even the guards are gone.
N-now... I think...the enlistment c-center is located...
...all the w-way to our right.
Was it towards the b-back of the headquarters? Hmm...
I think... everyone might b-be back there for some sort of presentation.

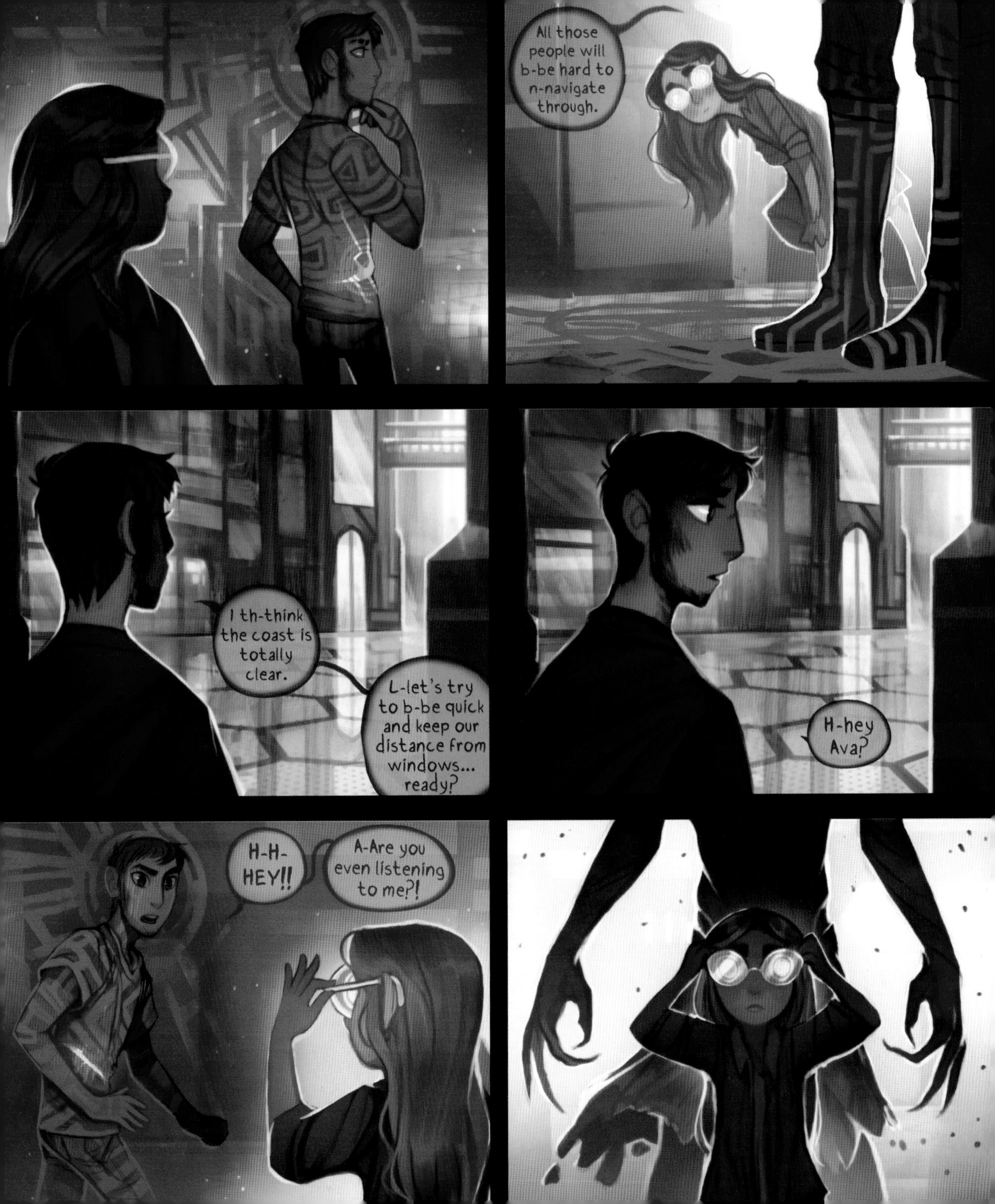
All those people will b-be hard to n-navigate through.
I th-think the coast is totally clear.
L-let's try to b-be quick and keep our distance from windows... ready?
H-hey Ava?
H-H-HEY!!
A-Are you even listening to me?!

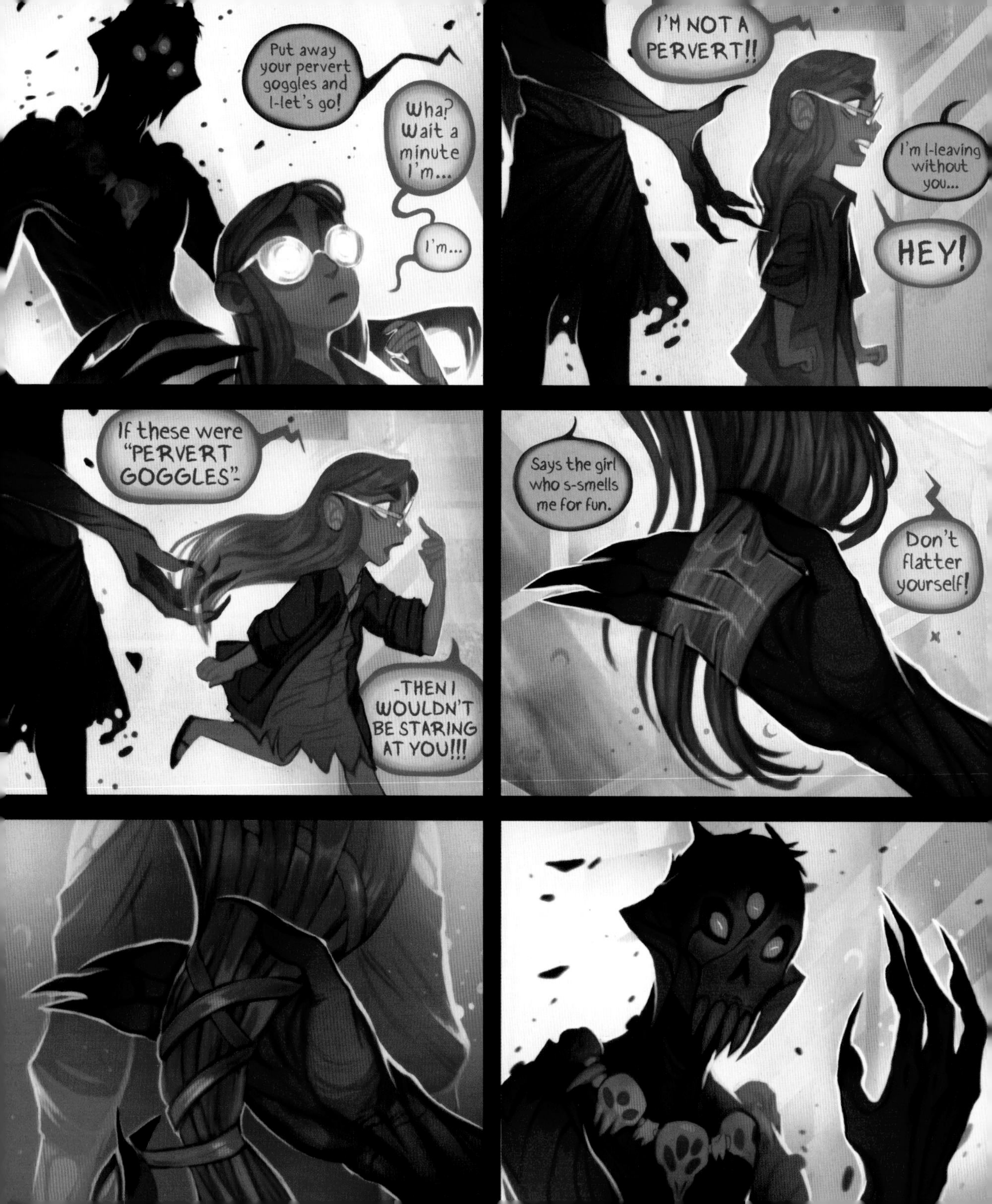
Put away your pervert goggles and I-let's go!
Wha? Wait a minute I'm...
I'm...
I'M NOT A PERVERT!!
I'm I-leaving without you...
HEY!
If these were "PERVERT GOGGLES"-
-THEN I WOULDN'T BE STARING AT YOU!!!
Says the girl who s-smells me for fun.
Don't flatter yourself!

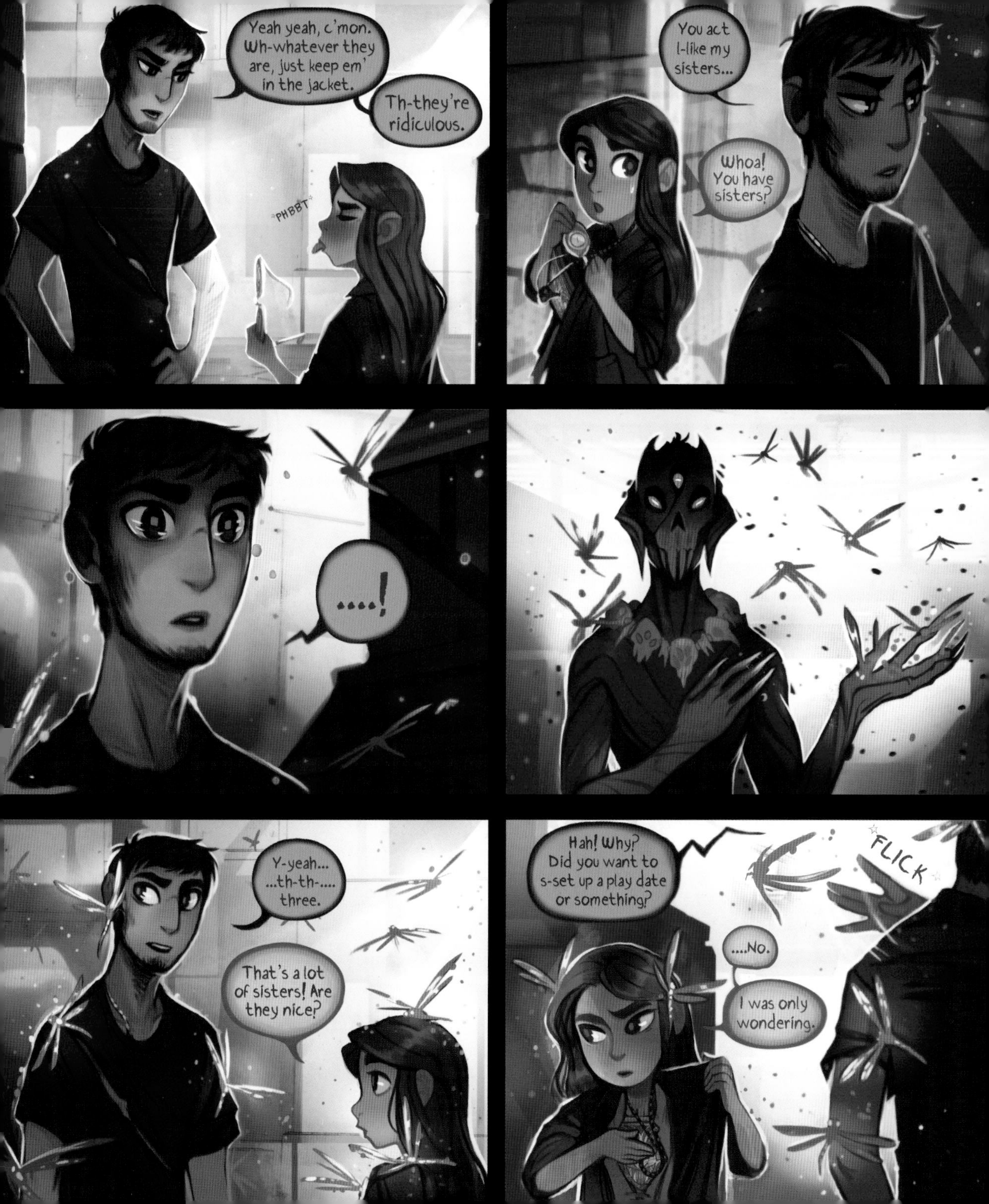
Yeah yeah, c'mon. Wh-whatever they are, just keep em' in the jacket.
Th-they're ridiculous.
PHBBT
You act l-like my sisters...
Whoa! You have sisters?
....!
Y-yeah... ...th-th-.... three.
That's a lot of sisters! Are they nice?
Hah! Why? Did you want to s-set up a play date or something?
FLICK
....No.
I was only wondering.

Well, anyway ...
...ready when you are.
R-right ...
I'm c-certain it's all the way at th-the back.
CAREER AND ENLISTMENT SERVICES
I don't like crowds. People make me so nervous.
All of these odd strangers staring at me ....
Uhg, j-just.... keep it together! We can't afford to s-stand out so stay cool.
This part of the headquarters is s-s-sealed off from the rest...
...s-so our entrance is also our exit.
If th-they close the doors then w-we're done for.
S-See them anywhere?

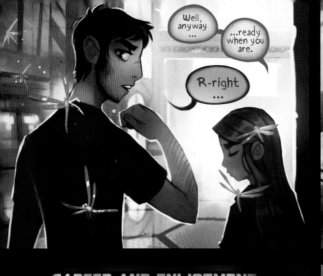

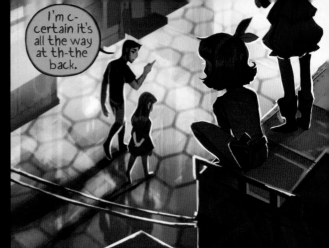

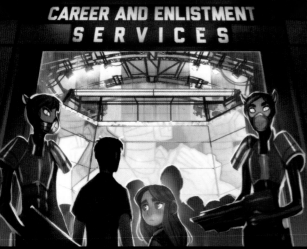

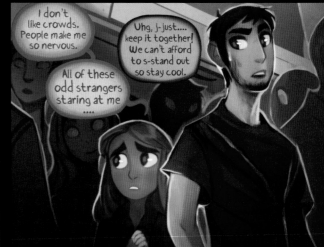

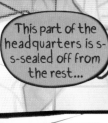

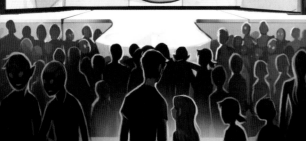

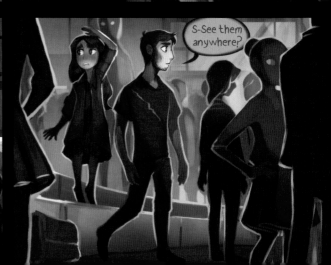

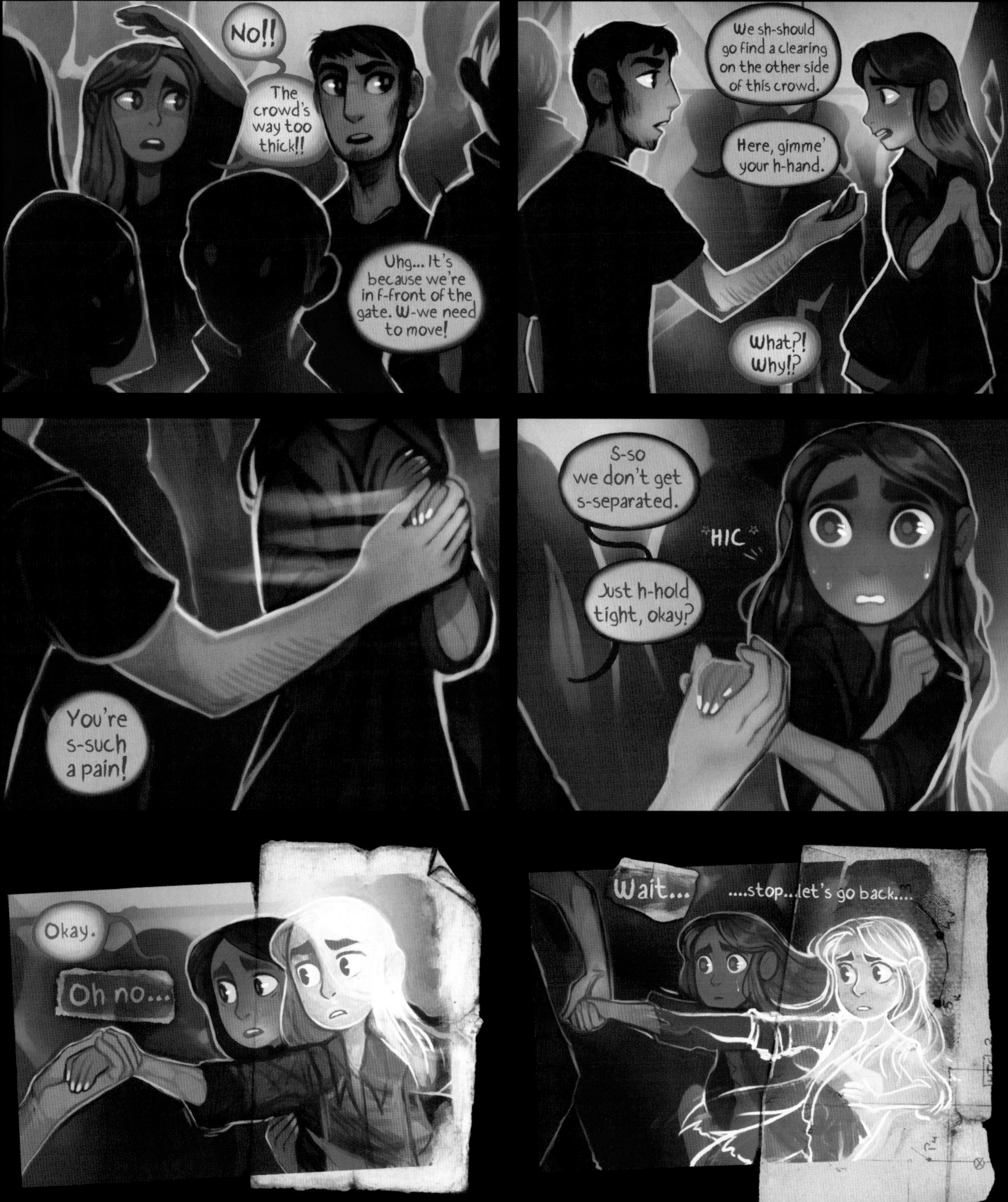
No!!
The crowd's way too thick!!
Uhg... It's because we're in f-front of the gate. W-we need to move!
We sh-should go find a clearing on the other side of this crowd.
Here, gimme' your h-hand.
What?! Why!?
You're s-such a pain!
S-so we don't get s-separated.
HIC
Just h-hold tight, okay?
Okay.
Oh no...
Wait...
....stop...let's go back....

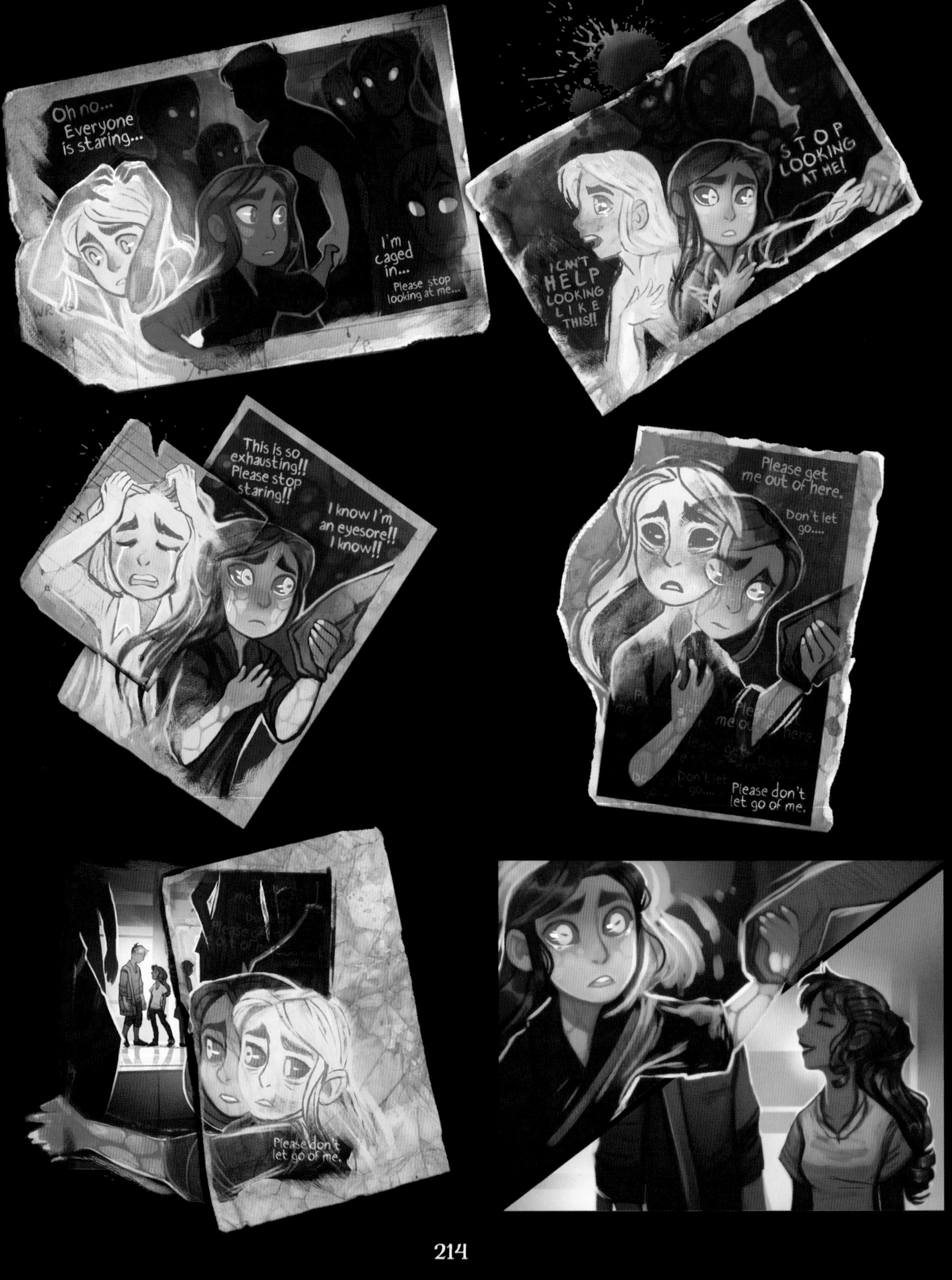
Oh no... Everyone is staring...
I'm caged in...
Please stop looking at me...
STOP LOOKING AT ME!
I CAN'T HELP LOOKING LIKE THIS!!
This is so exhausting!! Please stop staring!!
I know I'm an eyesore!! I know!!
Please get me out of here.
Don't let go....
Please don't let go of me.
Please don't let go of me.

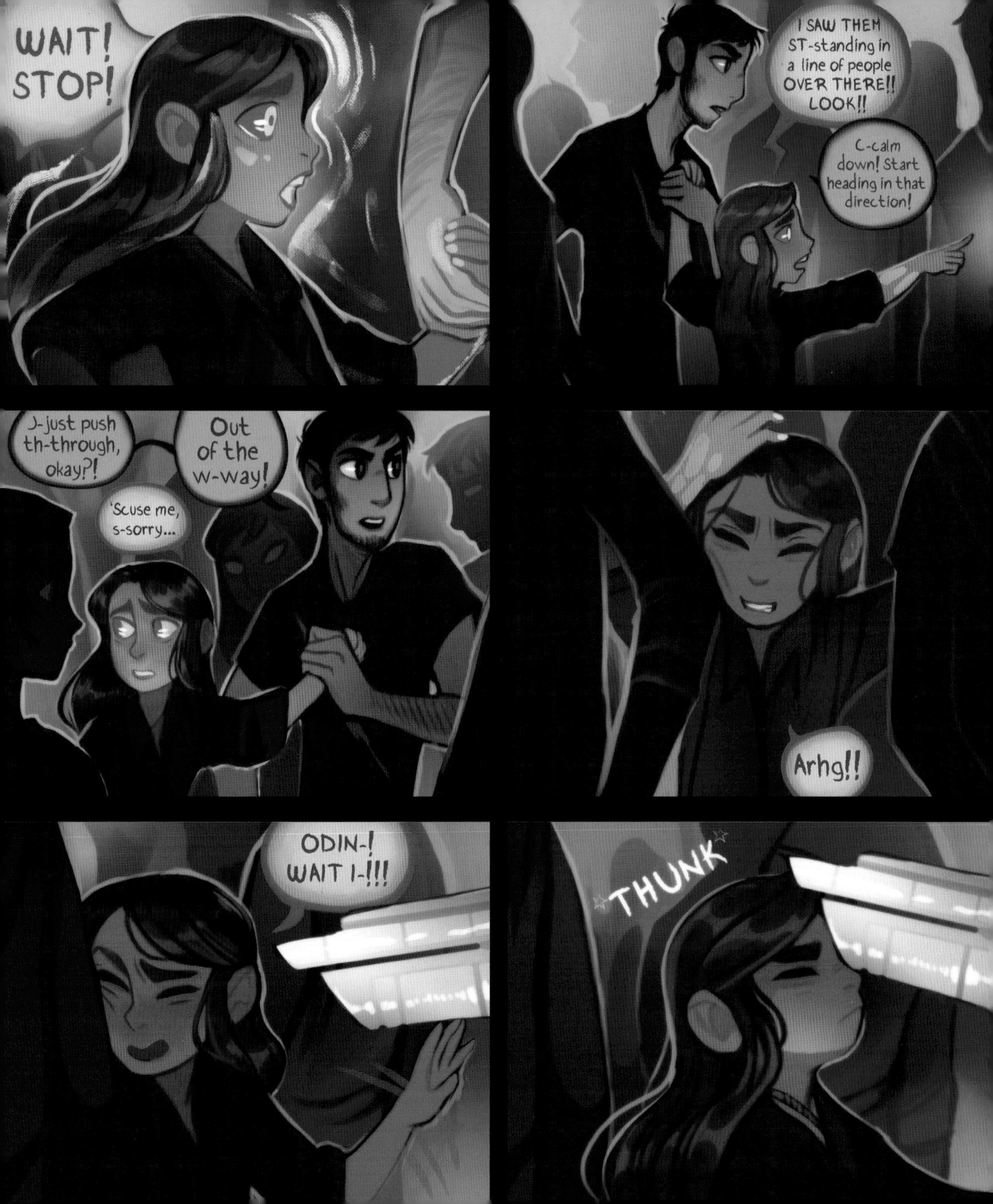
WAIT! STOP!
I SAW THEM ST-standing in a line of people OVER THERE!! LOOK!!
C-calm down! Start heading in that direction!
J-just push th-through, okay?!
Out of the w-way!
'Scuse me, s-sorry...
Arhg!!
ODIN-! WAIT I-!!!
THUNK

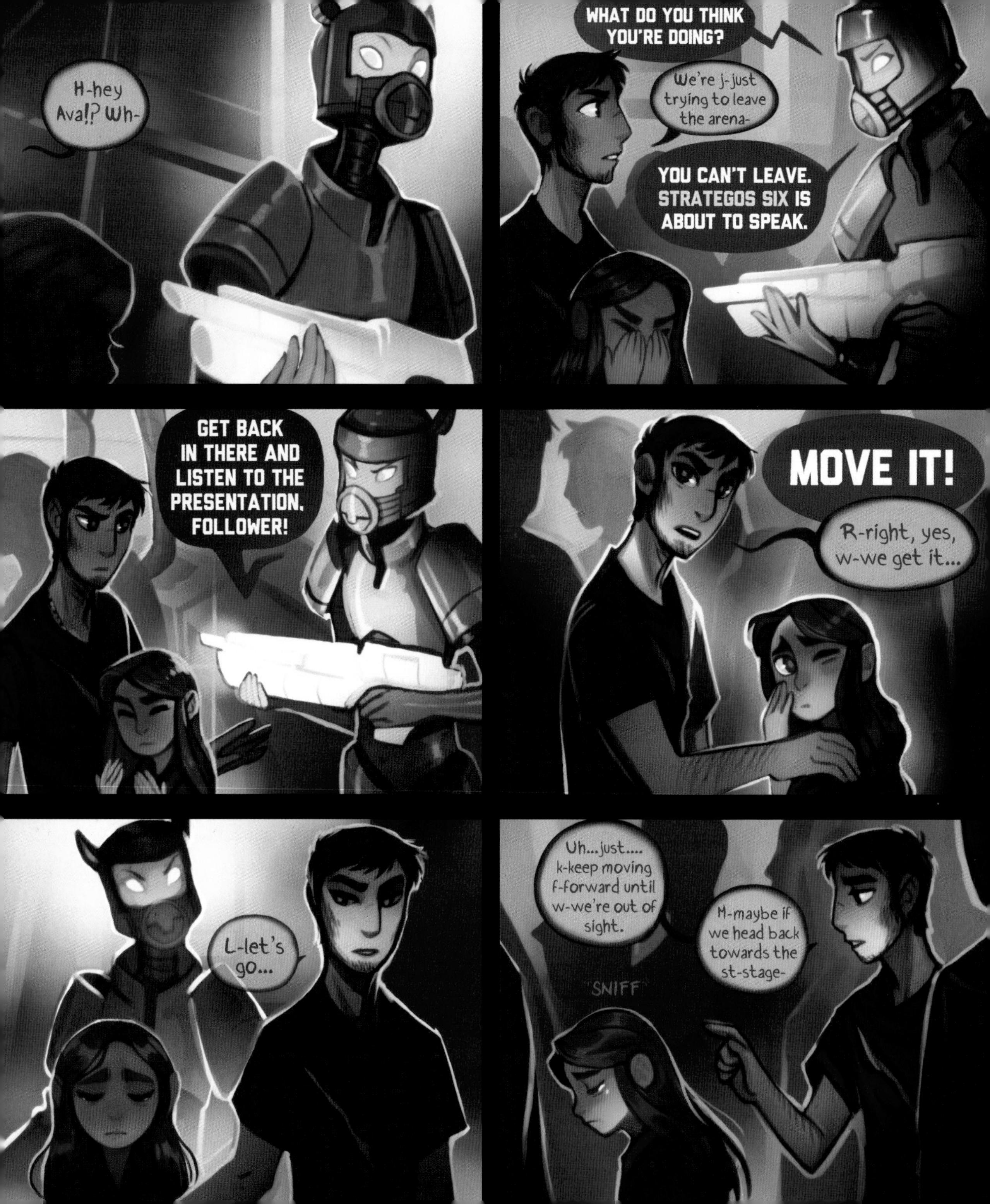
H-hey Ava!? Wh-
WHAT DO YOU THINK YOU'RE DOING?
We're j-just trying to leave the arena-
YOU CAN'T LEAVE. STRATEGOS SIX IS ABOUT TO SPEAK.
GET BACK IN THERE AND LISTEN TO THE PRESENTATION, FOLLOWER!
MOVE IT!
R-right, yes, w-we get it...
L-let's go...
Uh...just.... k-keep moving f-forward until w-we're out of sight.
M-maybe if we head back towards the st-stage-
SNIFF

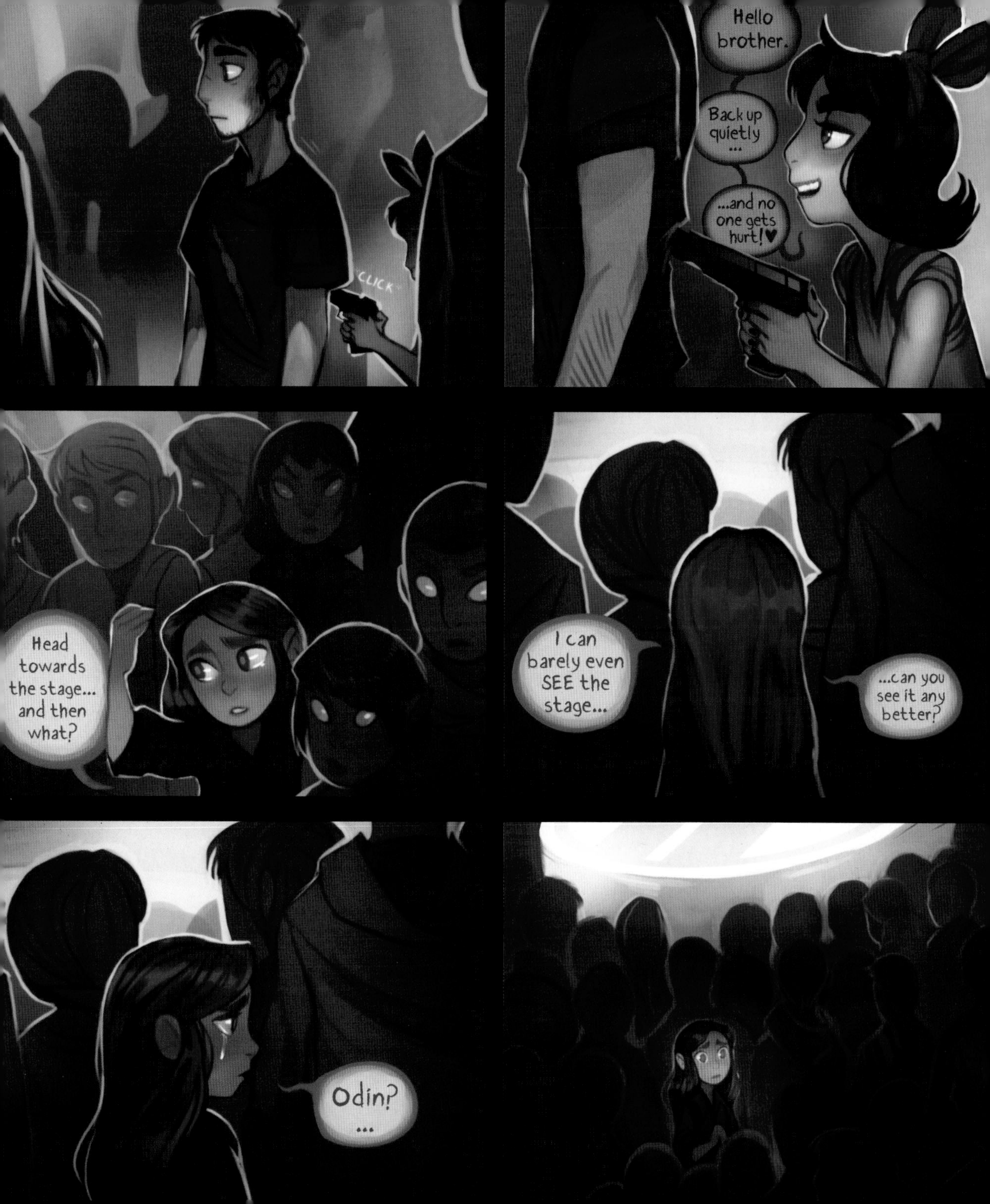

"CLICK"
Hello brother.
Back up quietly ...
...and no one gets hurt!♥
Head towards the stage... and then what?
I can barely even SEE the stage...
...can you see it any better?
Odin? ...

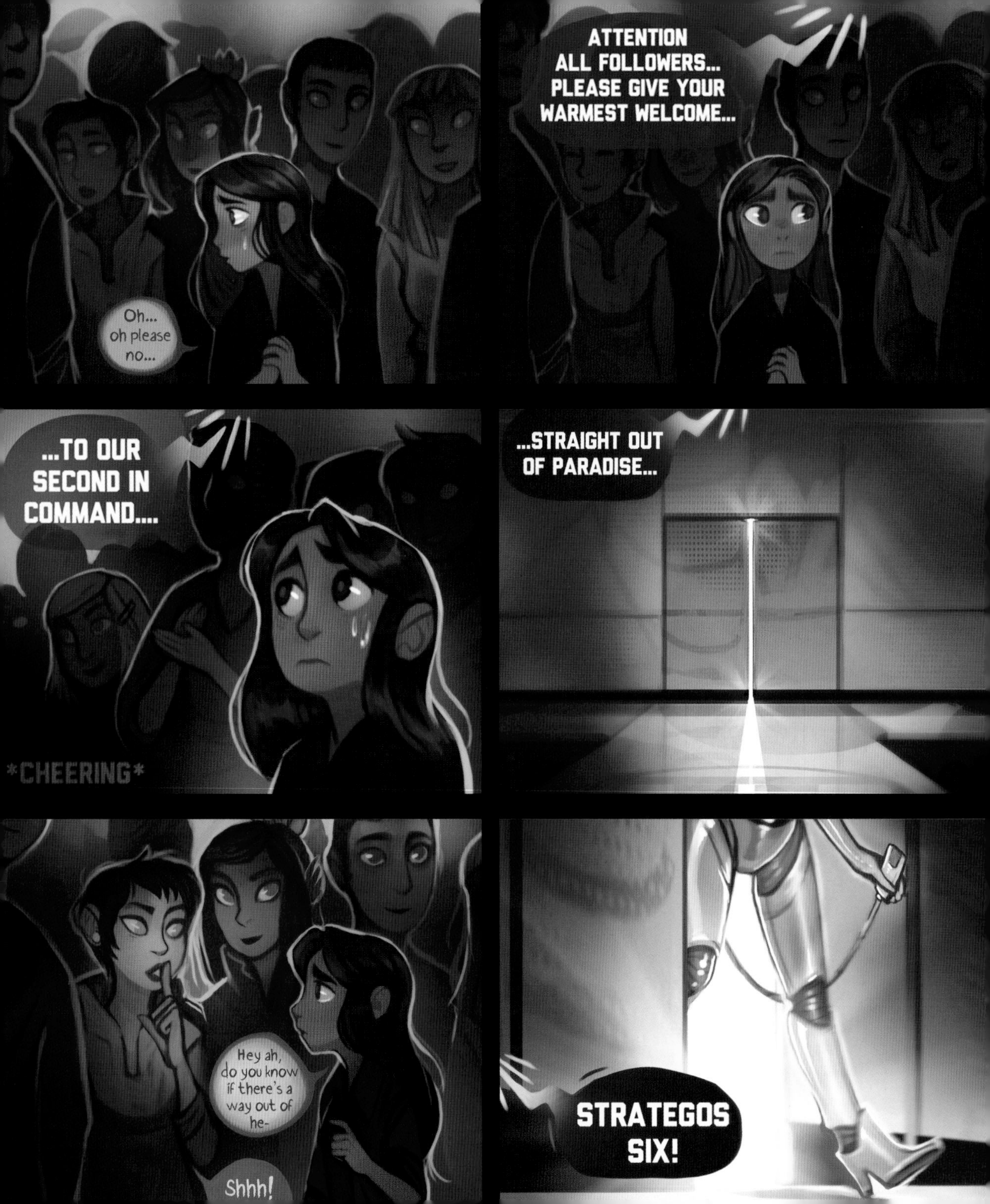
Oh... oh please no...
ATTENTION ALL FOLLOWERS... PLEASE GIVE YOUR WARMEST WELCOME...
...TO OUR SECOND IN COMMAND....
CHEERING
...STRAIGHT OUT OF PARADISE...
Hey ah, do you know if there's a way out of he-
Shhh!
STRATEGOS SIX!

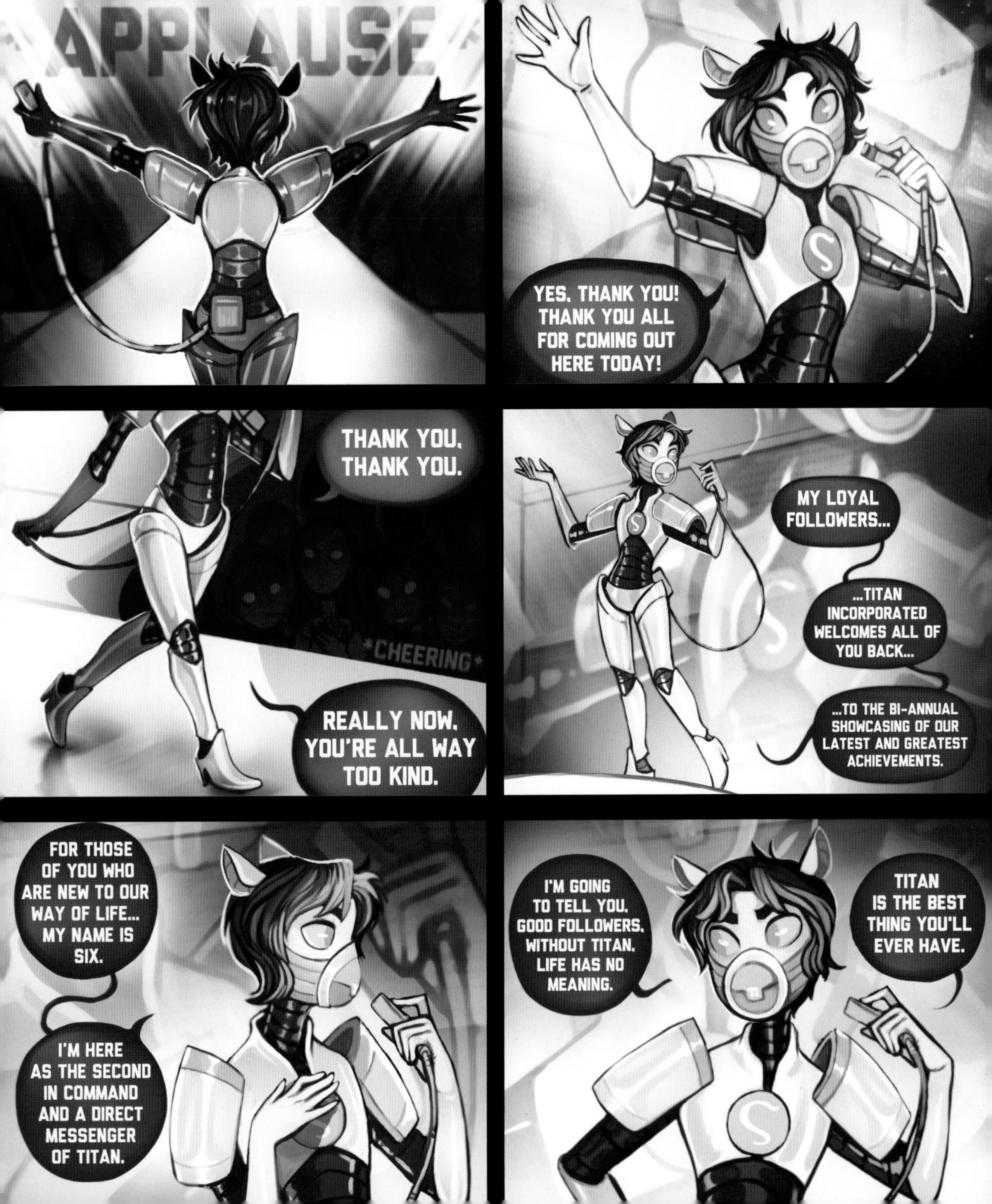
APPLAUSE
YES, THANK YOU! THANK YOU ALL FOR COMING OUT HERE TODAY!
THANK YOU, THANK YOU.
CHEERING
REALLY NOW, YOU'RE ALL WAY TOO KIND.
MY LOYAL FOLLOWERS...
...TITAN INCORPORATED WELCOMES ALL OF YOU BACK...
...TO THE BI-ANNUAL SHOWCASING OF OUR LATEST AND GREATEST ACHIEVEMENTS.
FOR THOSE OF YOU WHO ARE NEW TO OUR WAY OF LIFE... MY NAME IS SIX.
I'M HERE AS THE SECOND IN COMMAND AND A DIRECT MESSENGER OF TITAN.
I'M GOING TO TELL YOU, GOOD FOLLOWERS, WITHOUT TITAN, LIFE HAS NO MEANING.
TITAN IS THE BEST THING YOU'LL EVER HAVE.

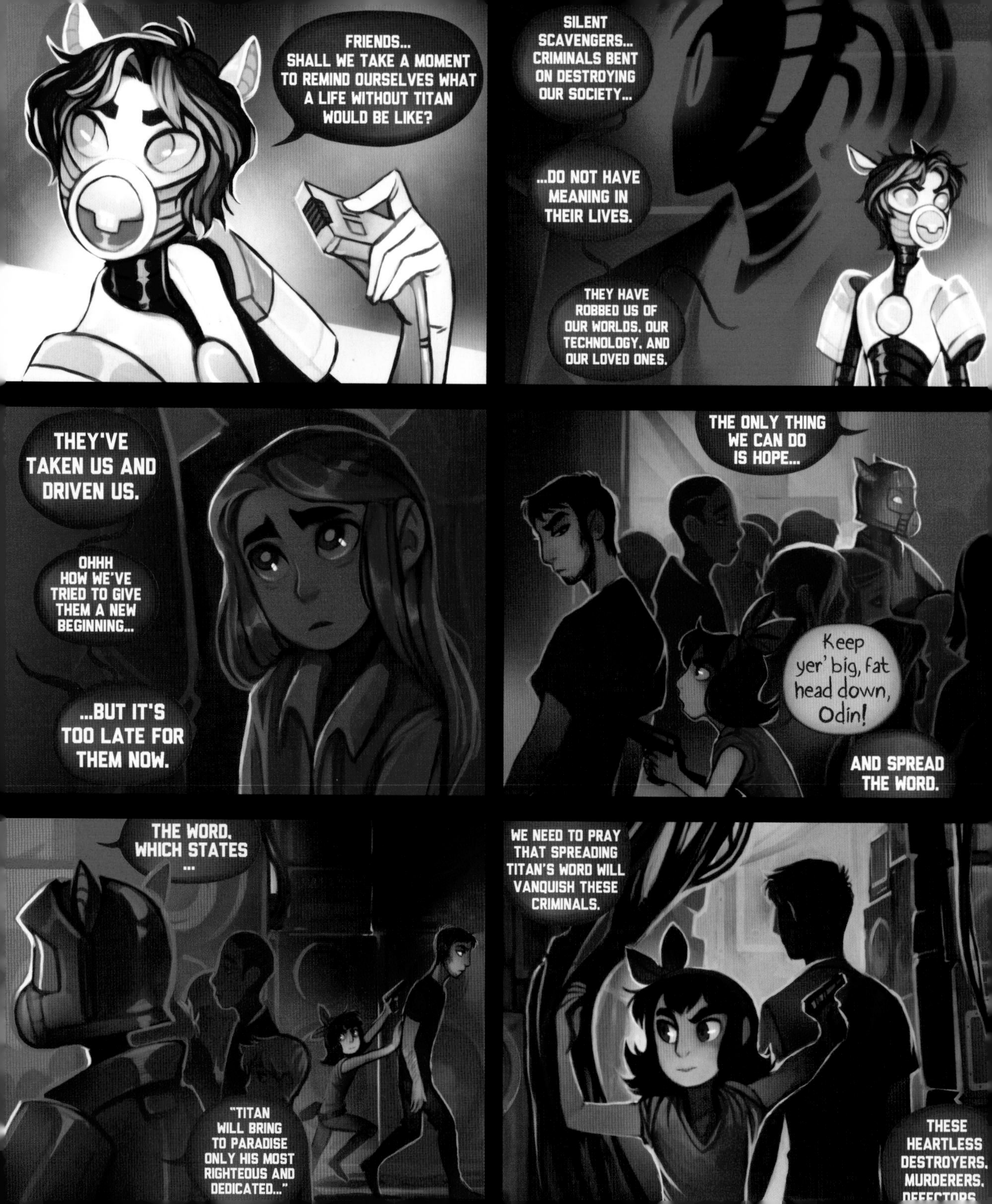
FRIENDS... SHALL WE TAKE A MOMENT TO REMIND OURSELVES WHAT A LIFE WITHOUT TITAN WOULD BE LIKE?
SILENT SCAVENGERS... CRIMINALS BENT ON DESTROYING OUR SOCIETY...
...DO NOT HAVE MEANING IN THEIR LIVES.
THEY HAVE ROBBED US OF OUR WORLDS, OUR TECHNOLOGY, AND OUR LOVED ONES.
THEY'VE TAKEN US AND DRIVEN US.
OHHH HOW WE'VE TRIED TO GIVE THEM A NEW BEGINNING...
...BUT IT'S TOO LATE FOR THEM NOW.
THE ONLY THING WE CAN DO IS HOPE...
Keep yer' big, fat head down, Odin!
AND SPREAD THE WORD.
THE WORD, WHICH STATES ...
"TITAN WILL BRING TO PARADISE ONLY HIS MOST RIGHTEOUS AND DEDICATED..."
WE NEED TO PRAY THAT SPREADING TITAN'S WORD WILL VANQUISH THESE CRIMINALS.
THESE HEARTLESS DESTROYERS, MURDERERS,

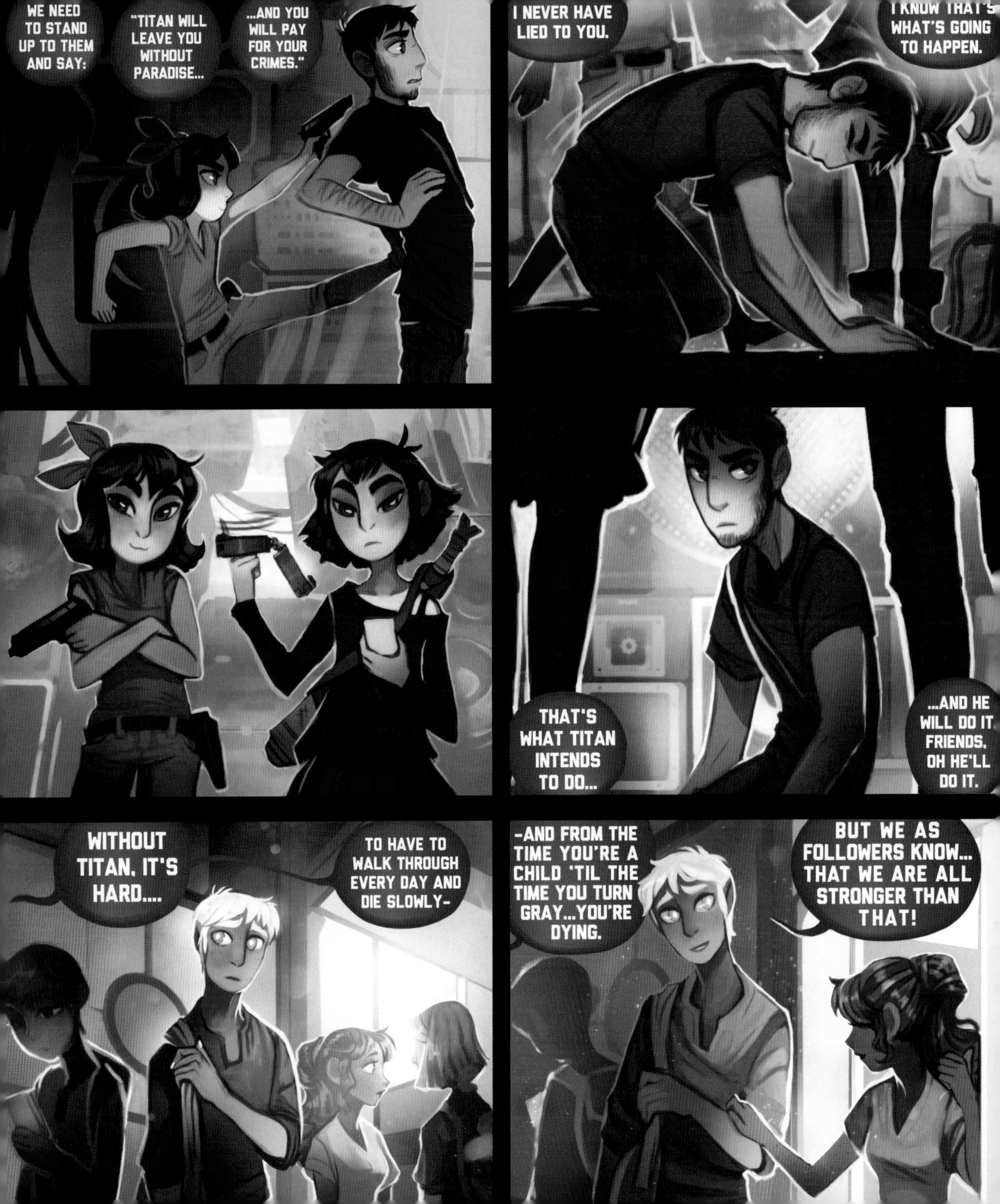
WE NEED TO STAND UP TO THEM AND SAY:
"TITAN WILL LEAVE YOU WITHOUT PARADISE...
...AND YOU WILL PAY FOR YOUR CRIMES."
I NEVER HAVE LIED TO YOU.
I KNOW THAT'S WHAT'S GOING TO HAPPEN.
THAT'S WHAT TITAN INTENDS TO DO...
...AND HE WILL DO IT, FRIENDS. OH HE'LL DO IT.
WITHOUT TITAN, IT'S HARD....
TO HAVE TO WALK THROUGH EVERY DAY AND DIE SLOWLY-
-AND FROM THE TIME YOU'RE A CHILD 'TIL THE TIME YOU TURN GRAY...YOU'RE DYING.
BUT WE AS FOLLOWERS KNOW... THAT WE ARE ALL STRONGER THAN THAT!

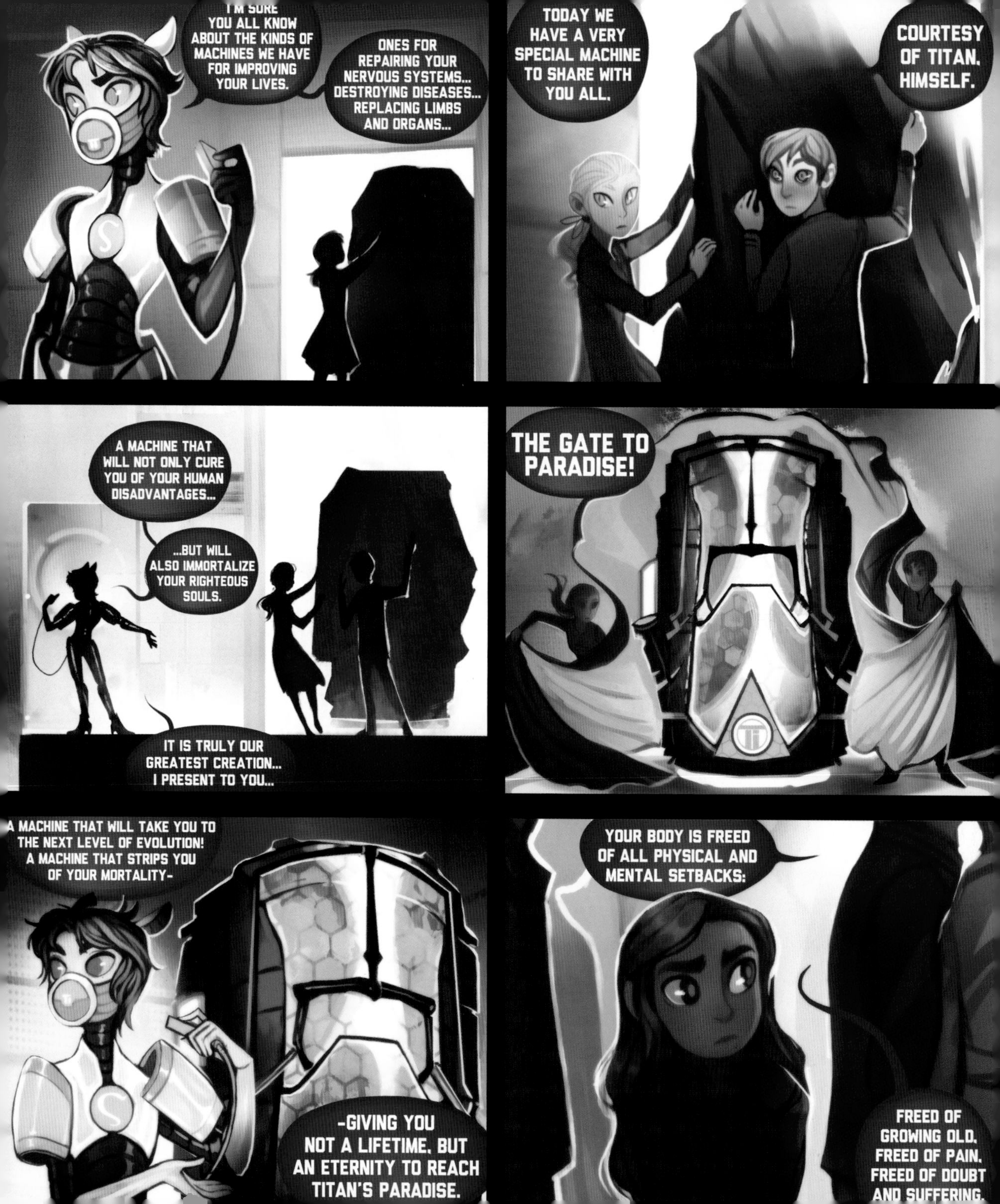
I'M SURE YOU ALL KNOW ABOUT THE KINDS OF MACHINES WE HAVE FOR IMPROVING YOUR LIVES.
ONES FOR REPAIRING YOUR NERVOUS SYSTEMS... DESTROYING DISEASES... REPLACING LIMBS AND ORGANS...
TODAY WE HAVE A VERY SPECIAL MACHINE TO SHARE WITH YOU ALL.
COURTESY OF TITAN, HIMSELF.
A MACHINE THAT WILL NOT ONLY CURE YOU OF YOUR HUMAN DISADVANTAGES...
...BUT WILL ALSO IMMORTALIZE YOUR RIGHTEOUS SOULS.
IT IS TRULY OUR GREATEST CREATION... I PRESENT TO YOU...
THE GATE TO PARADISE!
A MACHINE THAT WILL TAKE YOU TO THE NEXT LEVEL OF EVOLUTION! A MACHINE THAT STRIPS YOU OF YOUR MORTALITY-
-GIVING YOU NOT A LIFETIME, BUT AN ETERNITY TO REACH TITAN'S PARADISE.
YOUR BODY IS FREED OF ALL PHYSICAL AND MENTAL SETBACKS:
FREED OF GROWING OLD, FREED OF PAIN, FREED OF DOUBT AND SUFFERING.

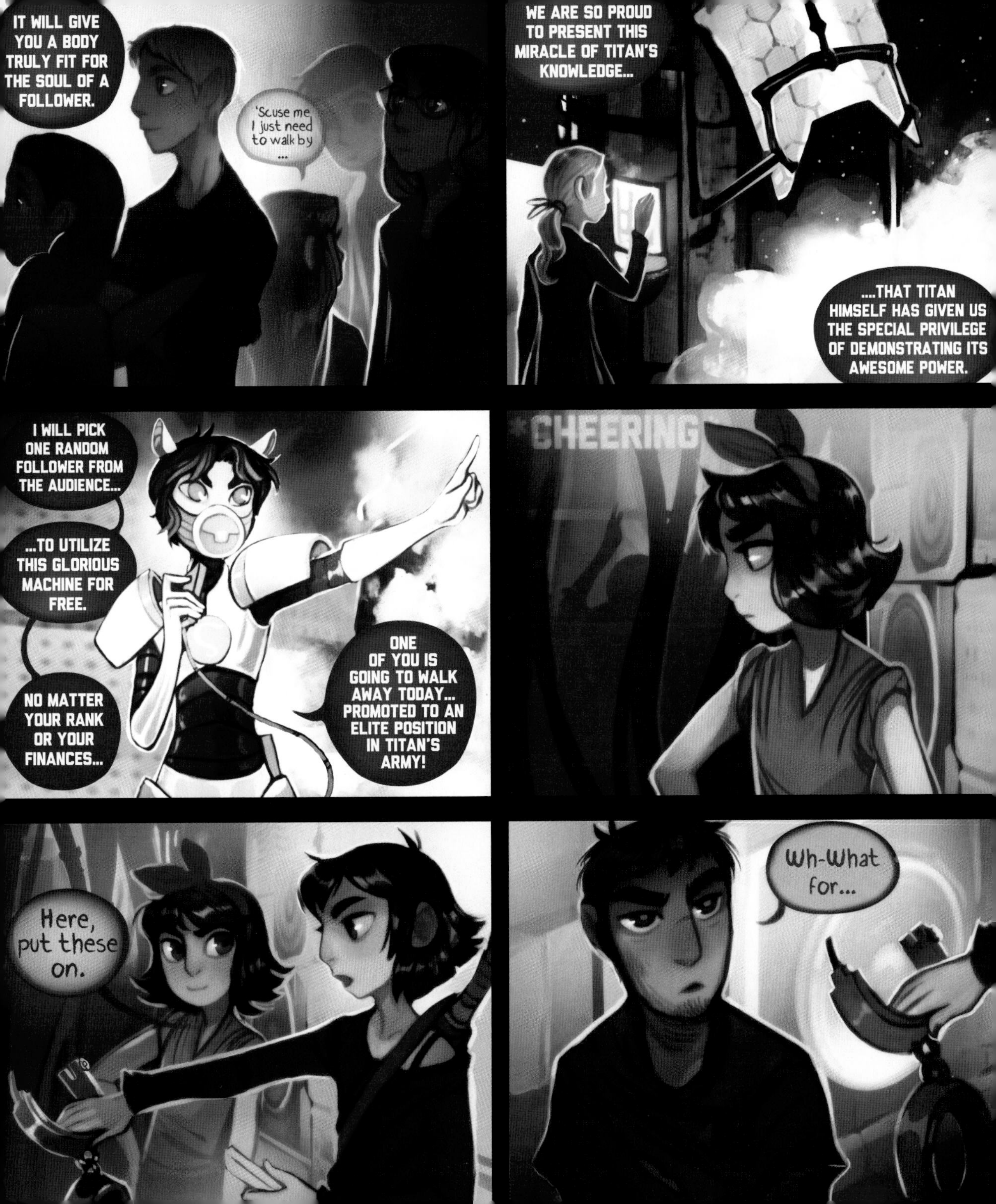
IT WILL GIVE YOU A BODY TRULY FIT FOR THE SOUL OF A FOLLOWER.
'Scuse me I just need to walk by ...
WE ARE SO PROUD TO PRESENT THIS MIRACLE OF TITAN'S KNOWLEDGE...
....THAT TITAN HIMSELF HAS GIVEN US THE SPECIAL PRIVILEGE OF DEMONSTRATING ITS AWESOME POWER.
I WILL PICK ONE RANDOM FOLLOWER FROM THE AUDIENCE...
...TO UTILIZE THIS GLORIOUS MACHINE FOR FREE.
NO MATTER YOUR RANK OR YOUR FINANCES...
ONE OF YOU IS GOING TO WALK AWAY TODAY... PROMOTED TO AN ELITE POSITION IN TITAN'S ARMY!
CHEERING
Here, put these on.
Wh-What for...

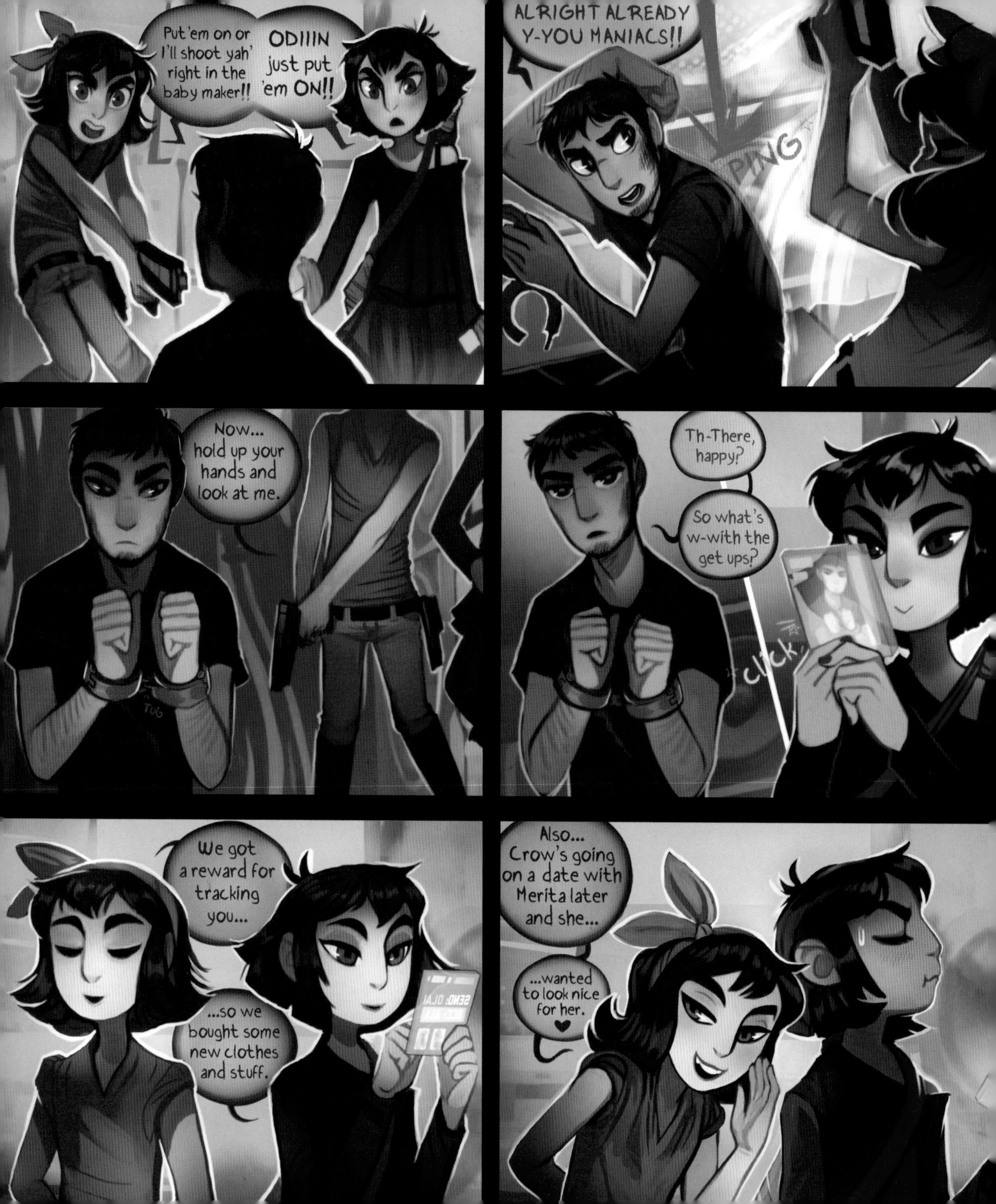
Put 'em on or I'll shoot yah' right in the baby maker!!
ODIIIN just put 'em ON!!
ALRIGHT ALREADY Y-YOU MANIACS!!
PING
Now... hold up your hands and look at me.
TUG
Th-There, happy?
So what's w-with the get ups?
click
We got a reward for tracking you...
...so we bought some new clothes and stuff.
Also... Crow's going on a date with Merita later and she...
...wanted to look nice for her.

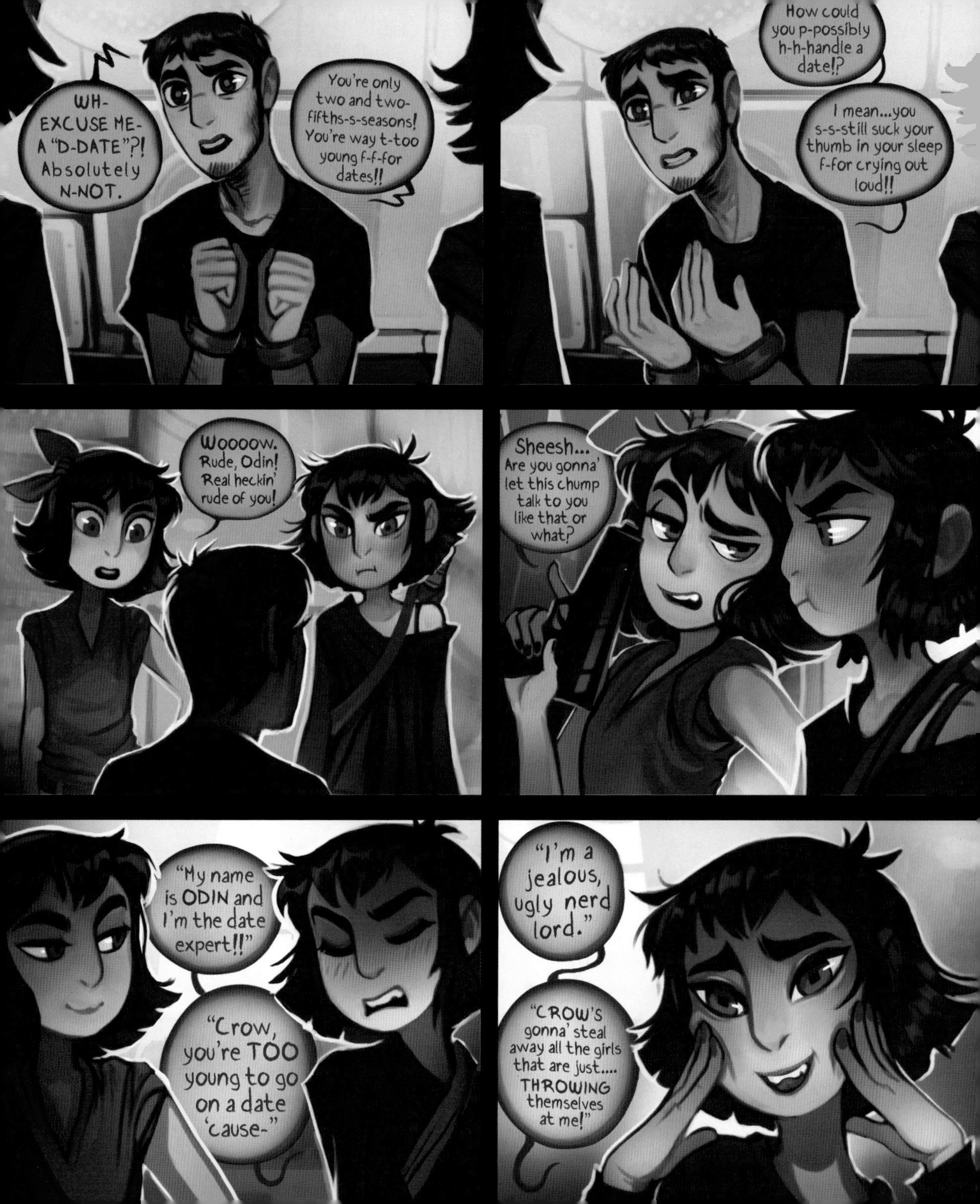
WH- EXCUSE ME- A "D-DATE"?! Absolutely N-NOT.
You're only two and two-fifths-s-seasons! You're way t-too young f-f-for dates!!
How could you p-possibly h-h-handle a date!?
I mean...you s-s-still suck your thumb in your sleep f-for crying out loud!!
Woooow. Rude, Odin! Real heckin' rude of you!
Sheesh... Are you gonna' let this chump talk to you like that or what?
"My name is ODIN and I'm the date expert!!"
"Crow, you're TOO young to go on a date 'cause-"
"I'm a jealous, ugly nerd lord."
"CROW'S gonna' steal away all the girls that are just.... THROWING themselves at me!"

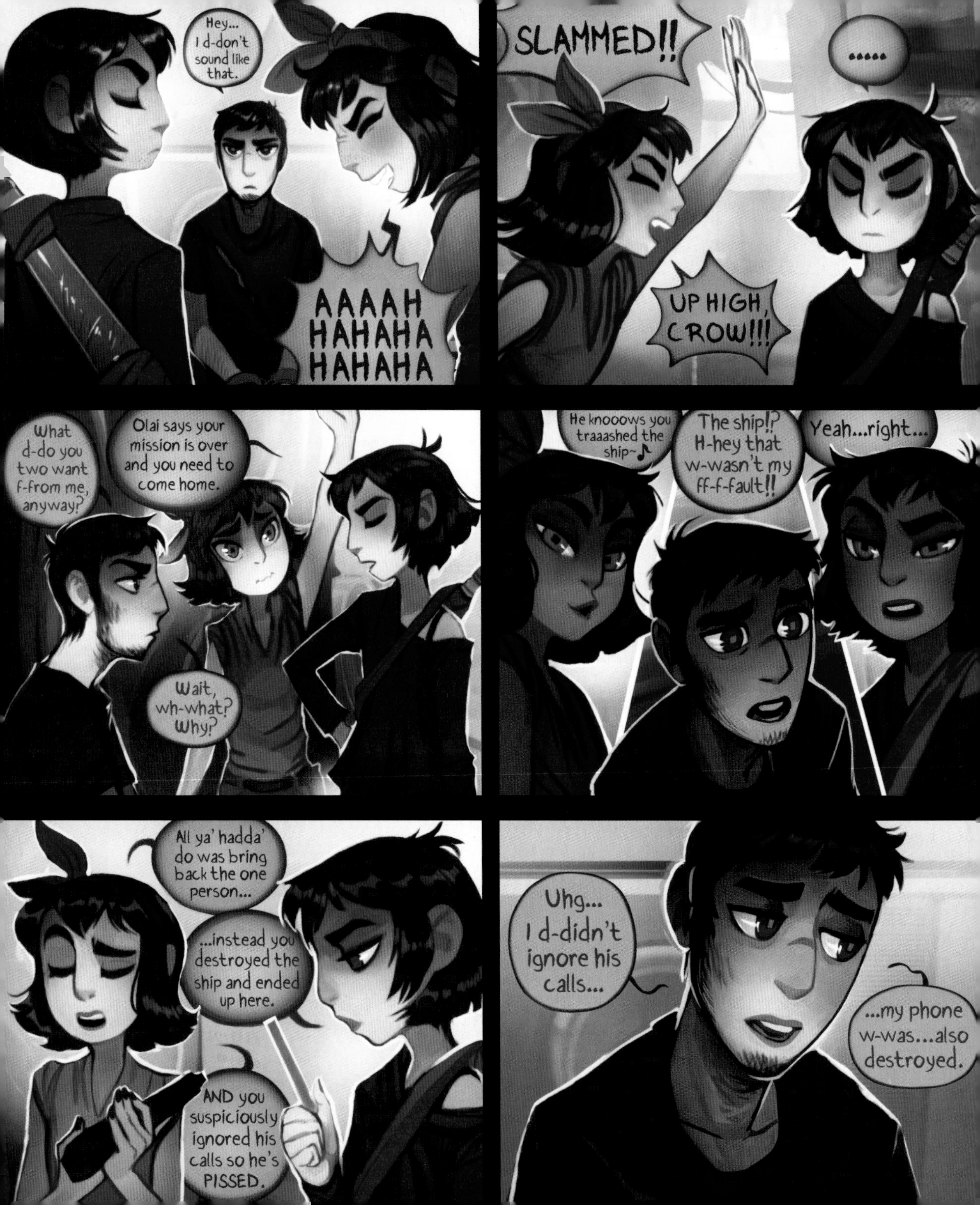
Hey...
I d-don't sound like that.
AAAAH HAHAHA HAHAHA
SLAMMED!!
UP HIGH, CROW!!!
.....
What d-do you two want f-from me, anyway?
Olai says your mission is over and you need to come home.
Wait, wh-what? Why?
He knooows you traaashed the ship~♪
The ship!? H-hey that w-wasn't my ff-f-fault!!
Yeah...right...
All ya' hadda' do was bring back the one person...
...instead you destroyed the ship and ended up here.
AND you suspiciously ignored his calls so he's PISSED.
Uhg... I d-didn't ignore his calls...
...my phone w-was...also destroyed.

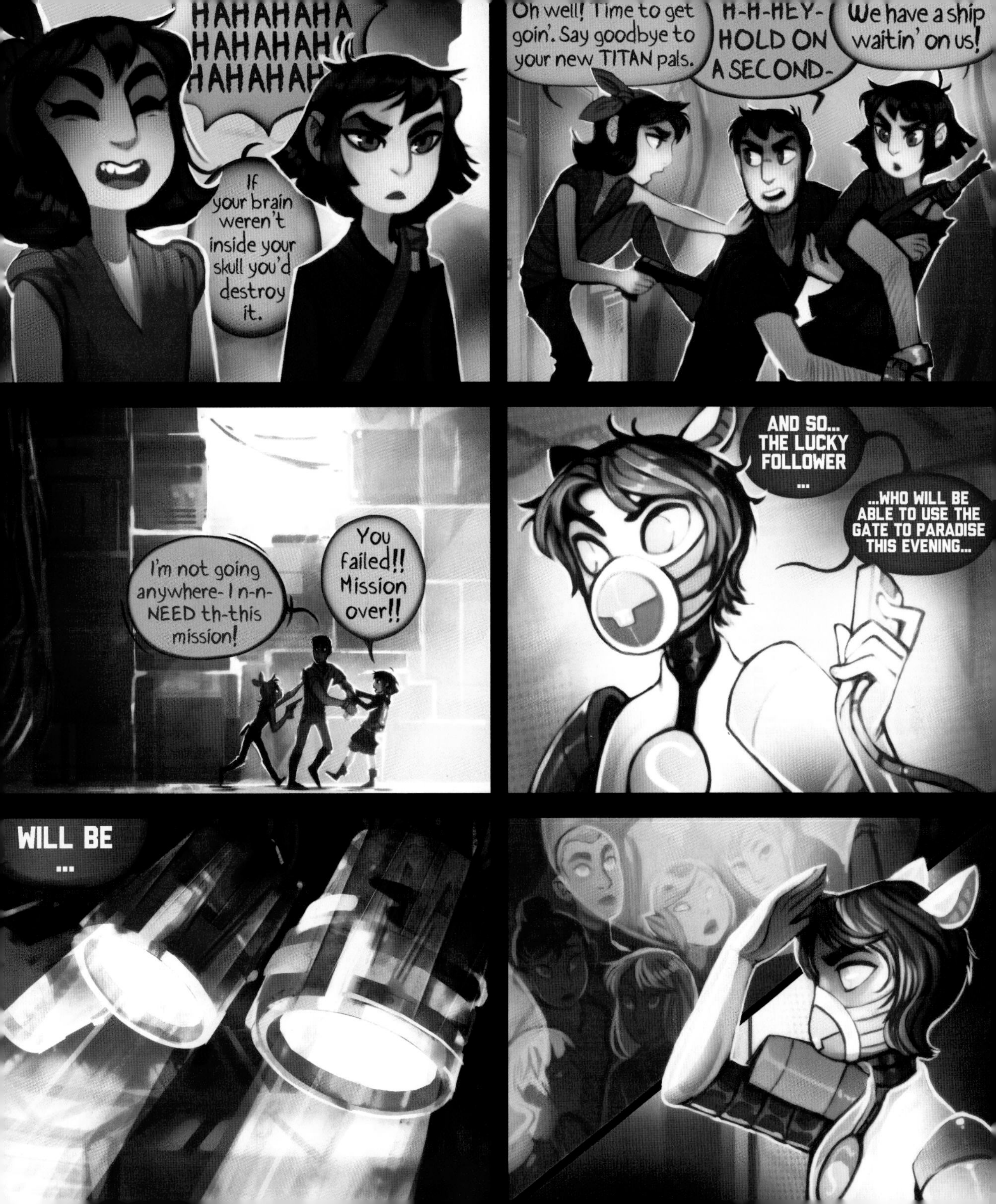
HAHAHAHA HAHAHAH! HAHAHAH
If your brain weren't inside your skull you'd destroy it.
Oh well! Time to get goin'. Say goodbye to your new TITAN pals.
H-H-HEY- HOLD ON A SECOND-
We have a ship waitin' on us!
I'm not going anywhere- I n-n-NEED th-this mission!
You failed!! Mission over!!
AND SO... THE LUCKY FOLLOWER ...
...WHO WILL BE ABLE TO USE THE GATE TO PARADISE THIS EVENING...
WILL BE ...

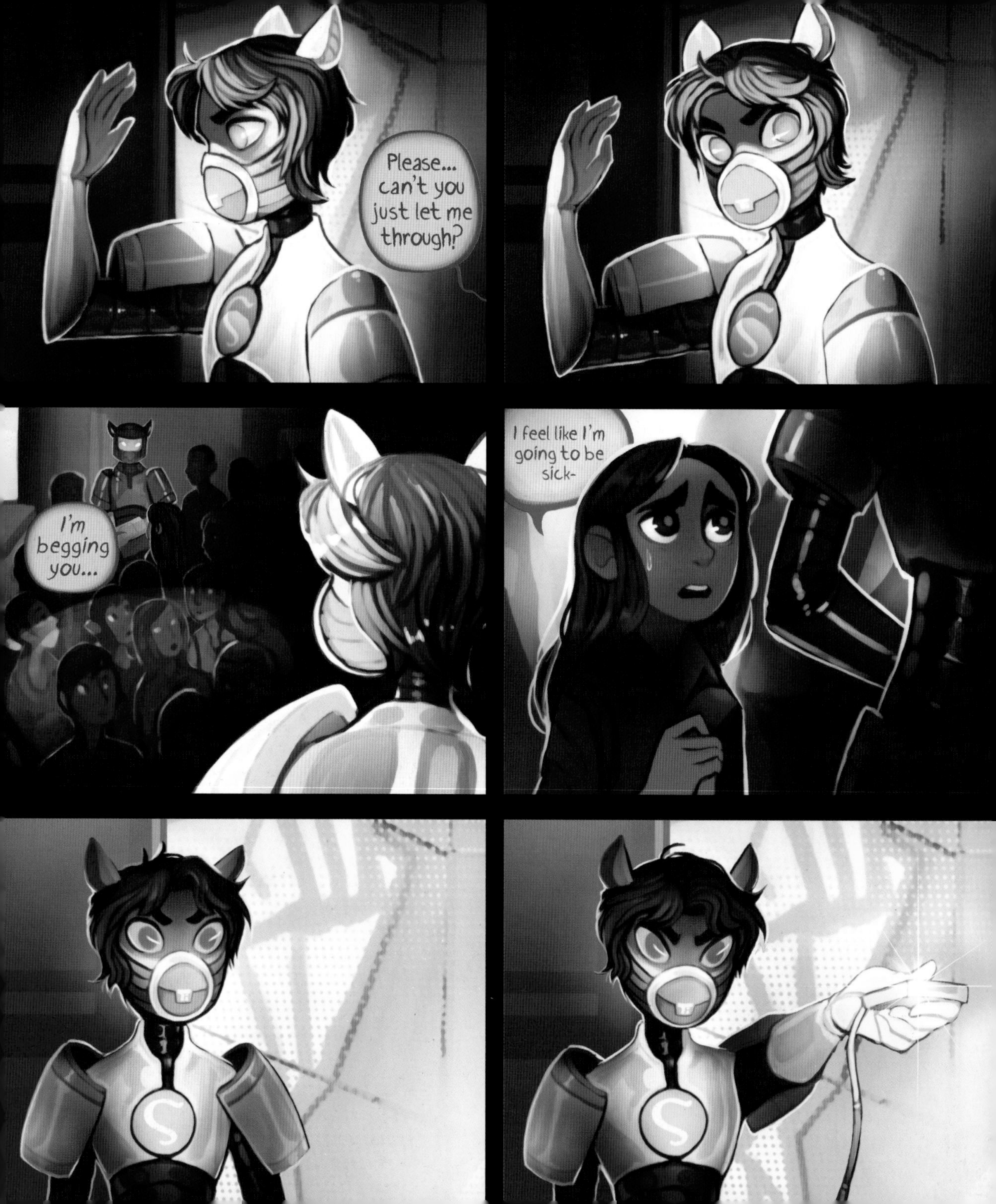

Please... can't you just let me through?
I'm begging you...
I feel like I'm going to be sick-

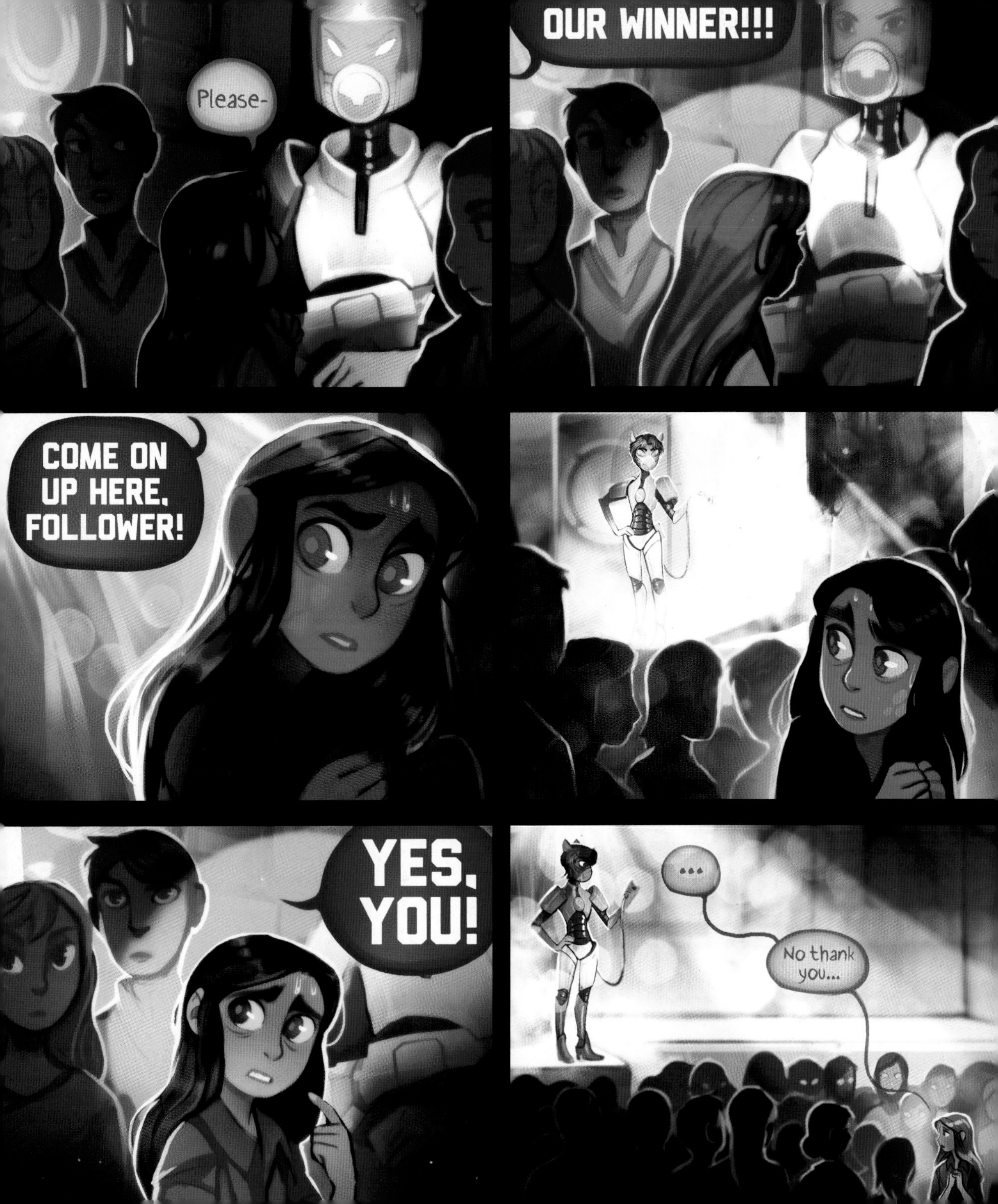
Please-
OUR WINNER!!!
COME ON UP HERE, FOLLOWER!
YES, YOU!
...
No thank you...

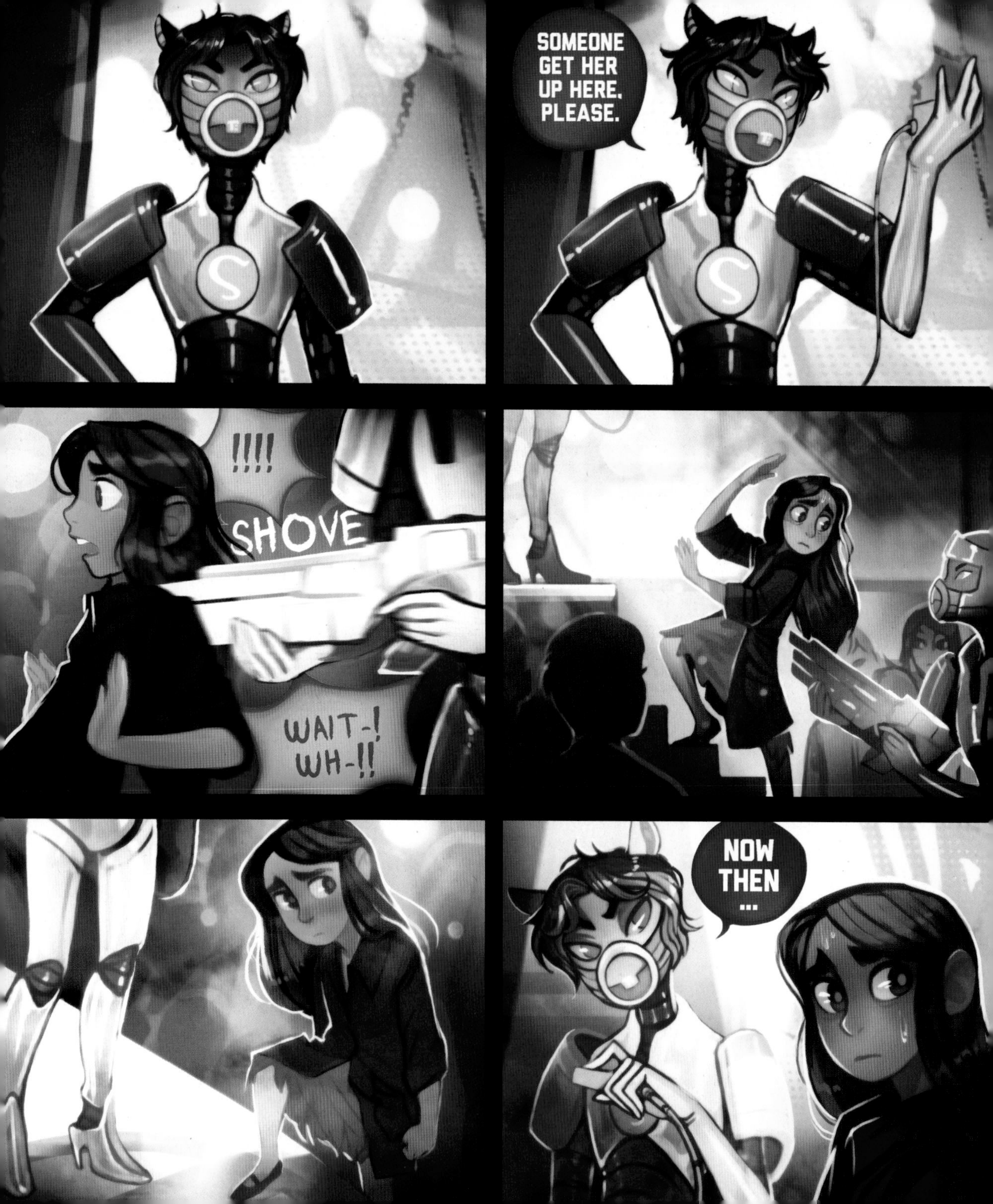
SOMEONE GET HER UP HERE, PLEASE.
!!!!
SHOVE
WAIT-! WH-!!
NOW THEN ...

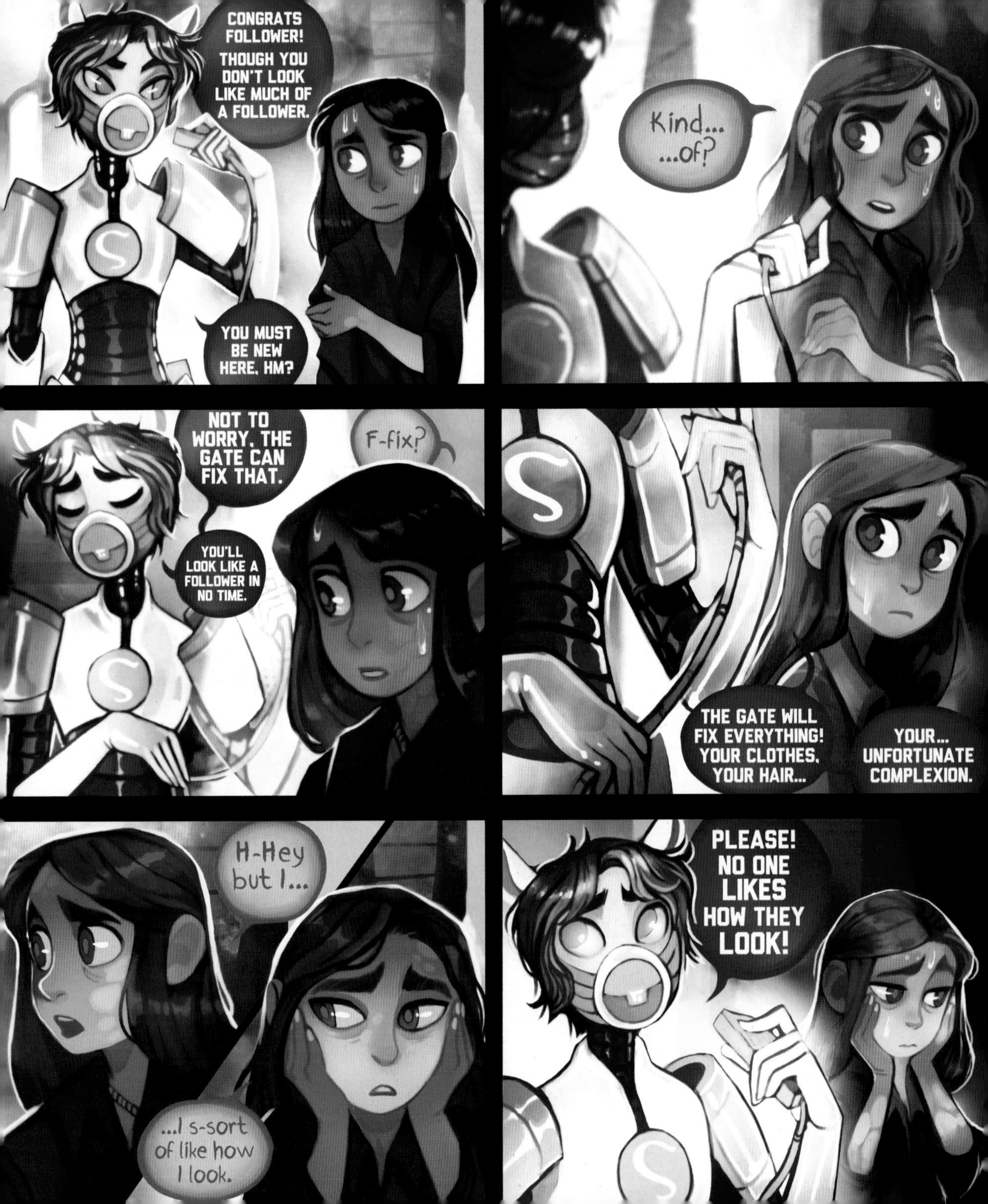
CONGRATS FOLLOWER!
THOUGH YOU DON'T LOOK LIKE MUCH OF A FOLLOWER.
YOU MUST BE NEW HERE, HM?
Kind... ...of?
NOT TO WORRY, THE GATE CAN FIX THAT.
YOU'LL LOOK LIKE A FOLLOWER IN NO TIME.
F-fix?
THE GATE WILL FIX EVERYTHING! YOUR CLOTHES, YOUR HAIR...
YOUR... UNFORTUNATE COMPLEXION.
H-Hey but I...
...I s-sort of like how I look.
PLEASE! NO ONE LIKES HOW THEY LOOK!

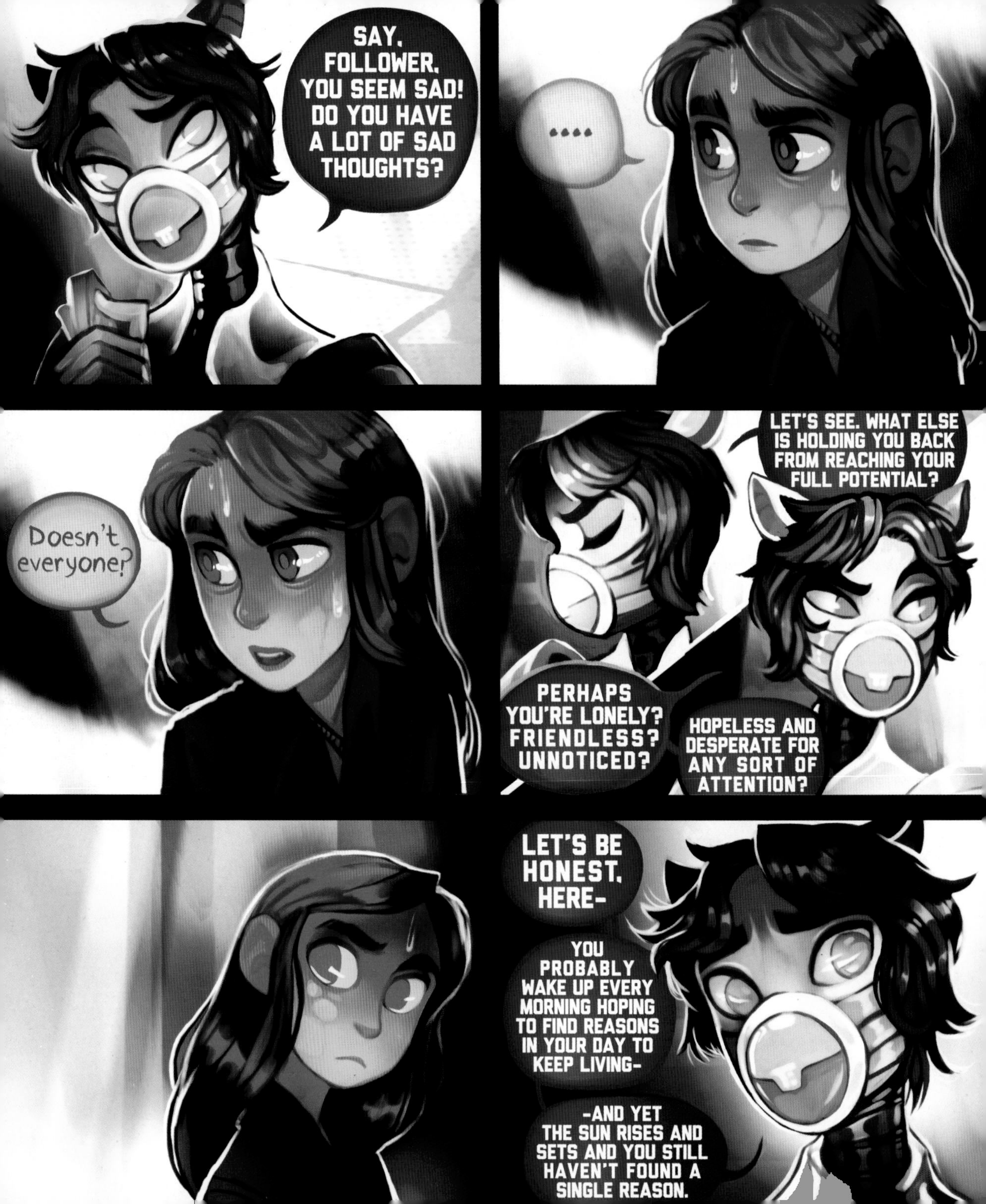
SAY, FOLLOWER. YOU SEEM SAD! DO YOU HAVE A LOT OF SAD THOUGHTS?
....
Doesn't everyone?
LET'S SEE. WHAT ELSE IS HOLDING YOU BACK FROM REACHING YOUR FULL POTENTIAL?
PERHAPS YOU'RE LONELY? FRIENDLESS? UNNOTICED?
HOPELESS AND DESPERATE FOR ANY SORT OF ATTENTION?
LET'S BE HONEST, HERE-
YOU PROBABLY WAKE UP EVERY MORNING HOPING TO FIND REASONS IN YOUR DAY TO KEEP LIVING-
-AND YET THE SUN RISES AND SETS AND YOU STILL HAVEN'T FOUND A SINGLE REASON.

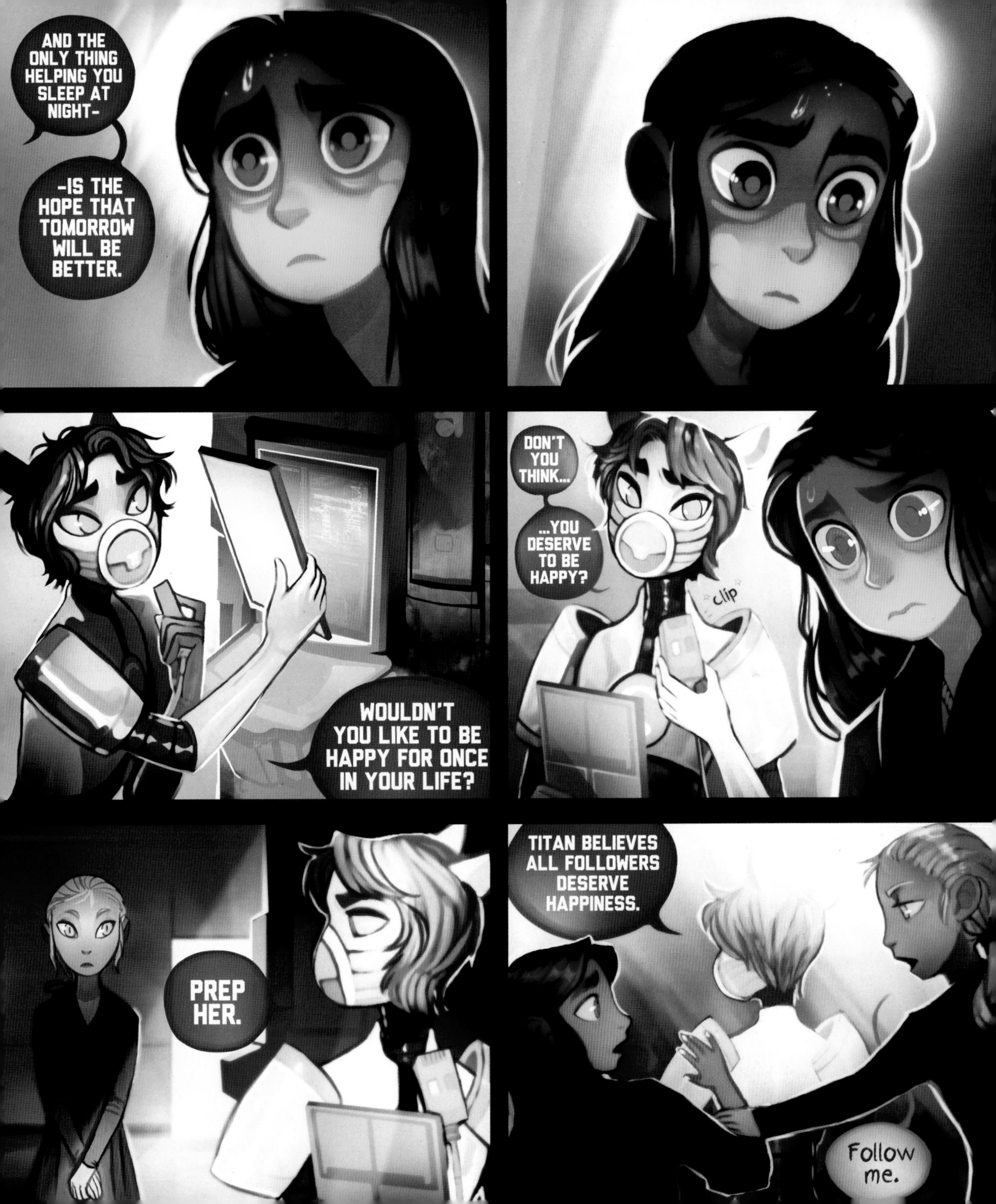
AND THE ONLY THING HELPING YOU SLEEP AT NIGHT-
-IS THE HOPE THAT TOMORROW WILL BE BETTER.
WOULDN'T YOU LIKE TO BE HAPPY FOR ONCE IN YOUR LIFE?
DON'T YOU THINK...
...YOU DESERVE TO BE HAPPY?
clip
PREP HER.
TITAN BELIEVES ALL FOLLOWERS DESERVE HAPPINESS.
Follow me.

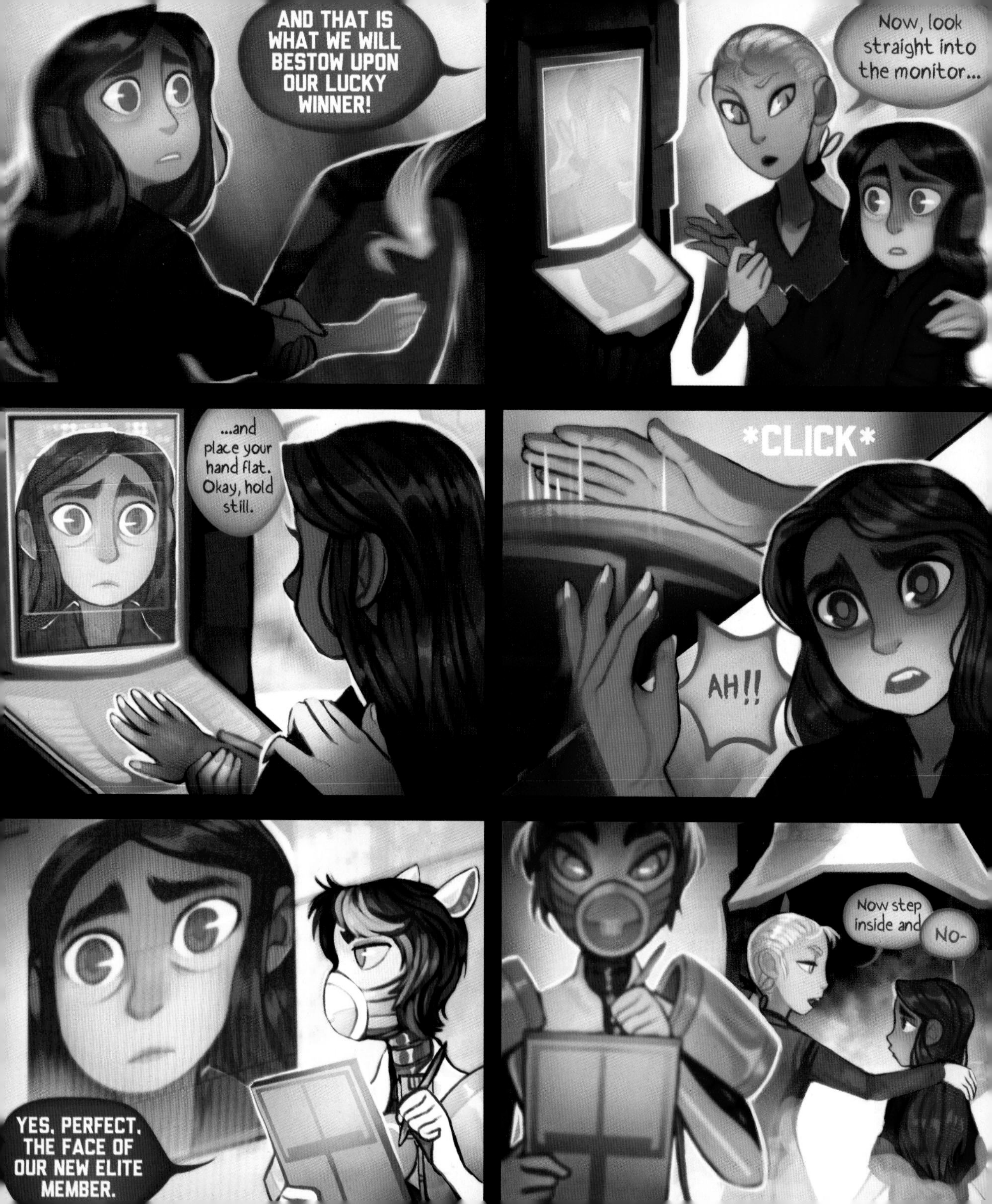
AND THAT IS WHAT WE WILL BESTOW UPON OUR LUCKY WINNER!
Now, look straight into the monitor...
...and place your hand flat. Okay, hold still.
CLICK
AH!!
YES, PERFECT, THE FACE OF OUR NEW ELITE MEMBER.
Now step inside and
NO-

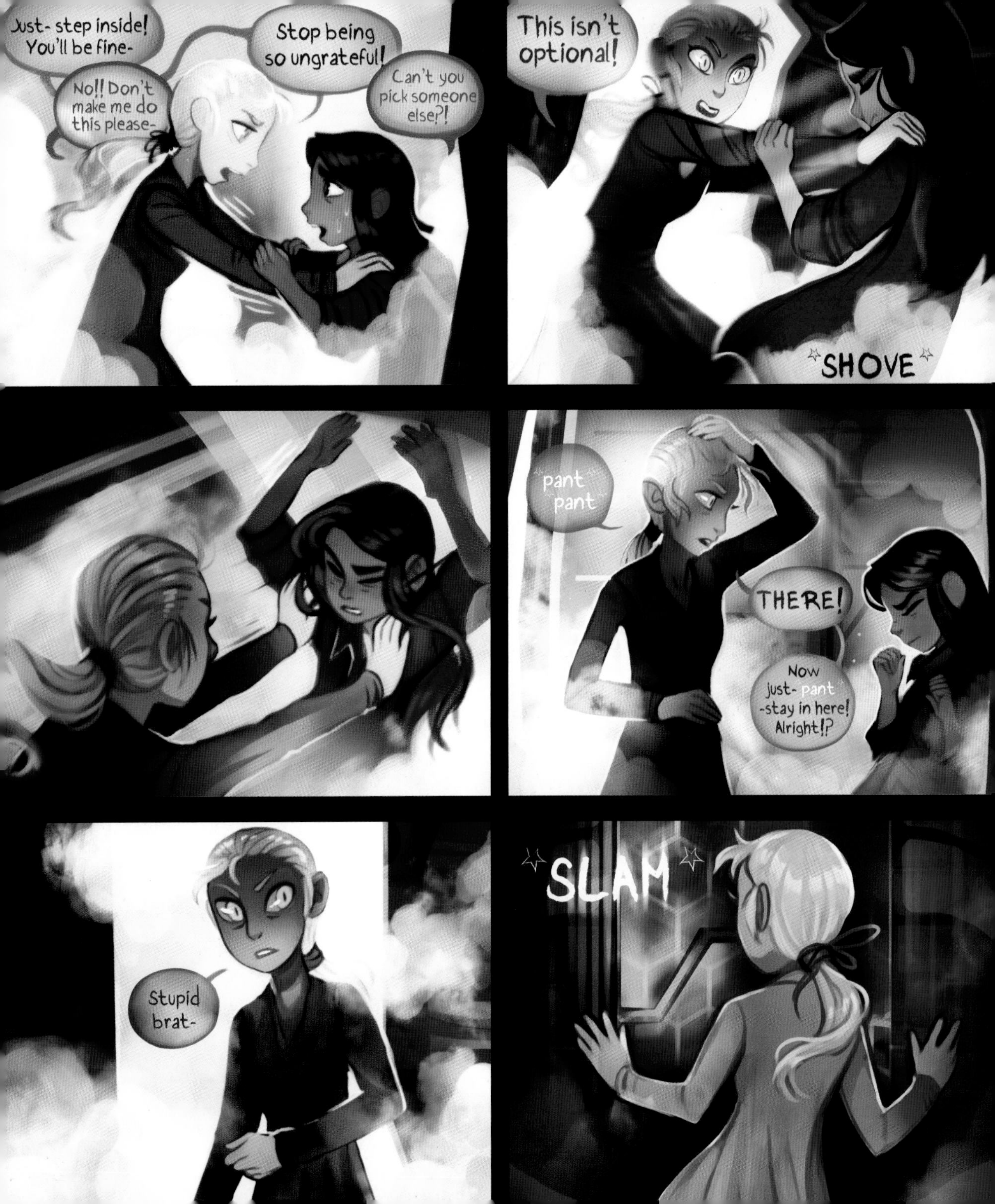
Just- step inside! You'll be fine-
No!! Don't make me do this please-
Stop being so ungrateful!
Can't you pick someone else?!
This isn't optional!
SHOVE
pant pant
THERE!
Now just- pant -stay in here! Alright!?
Stupid brat-
SLAM

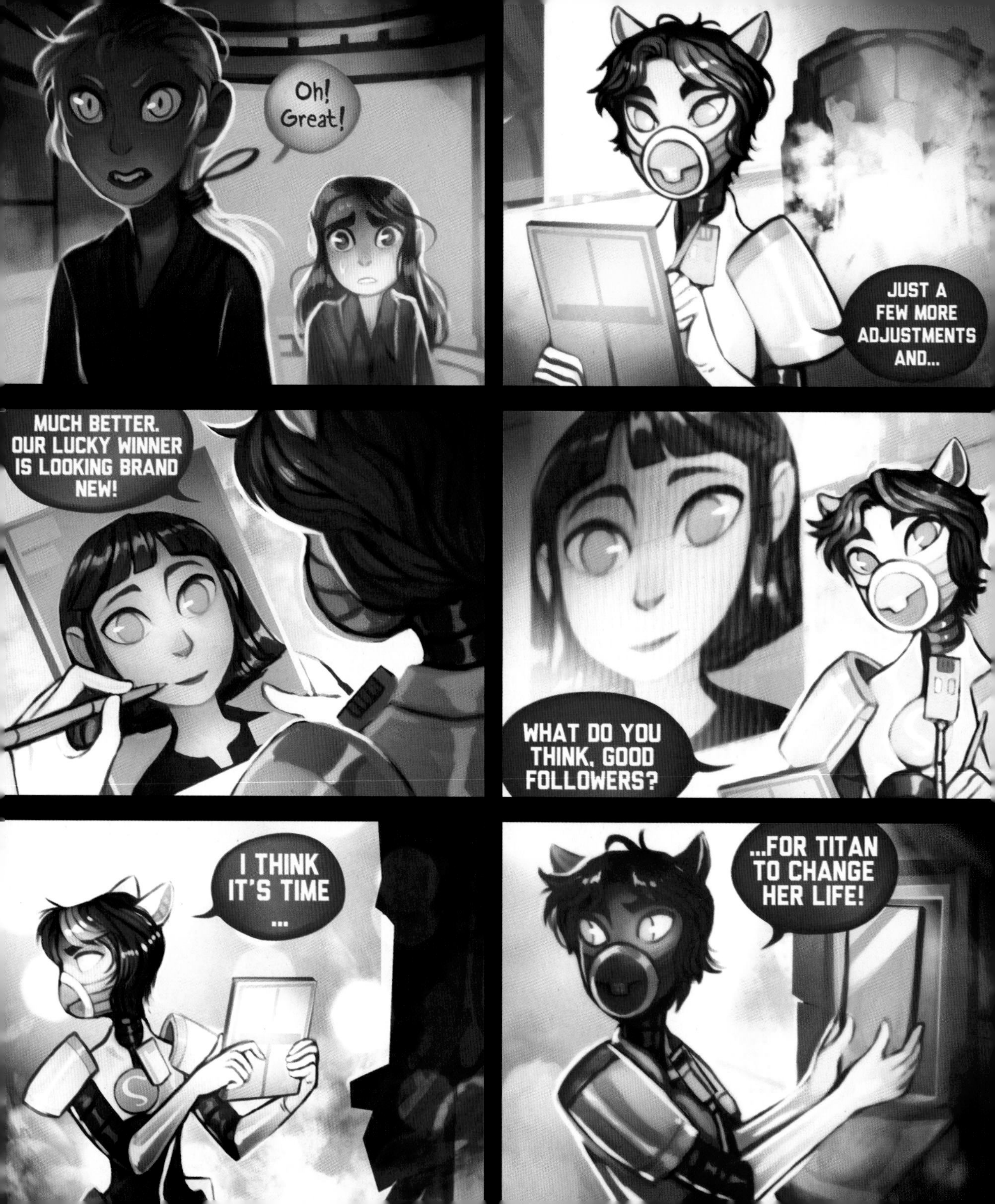

Oh! Great!
JUST A FEW MORE ADJUSTMENTS AND...
MUCH BETTER. OUR LUCKY WINNER IS LOOKING BRAND NEW!
WHAT DO YOU THINK, GOOD FOLLOWERS?
I THINK IT'S TIME ...
...FOR TITAN TO CHANGE HER LIFE!

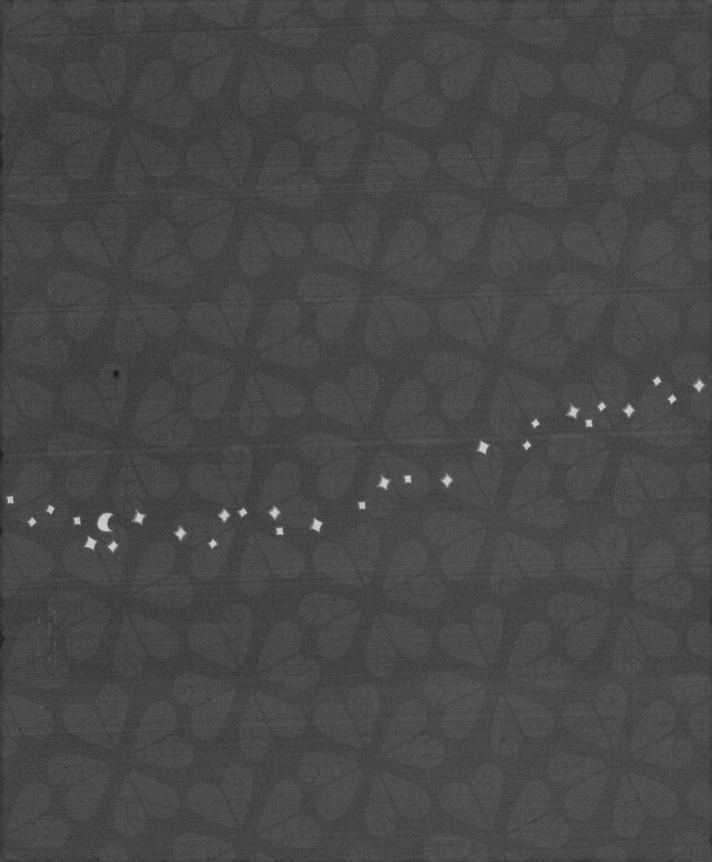

CHAPTER 5

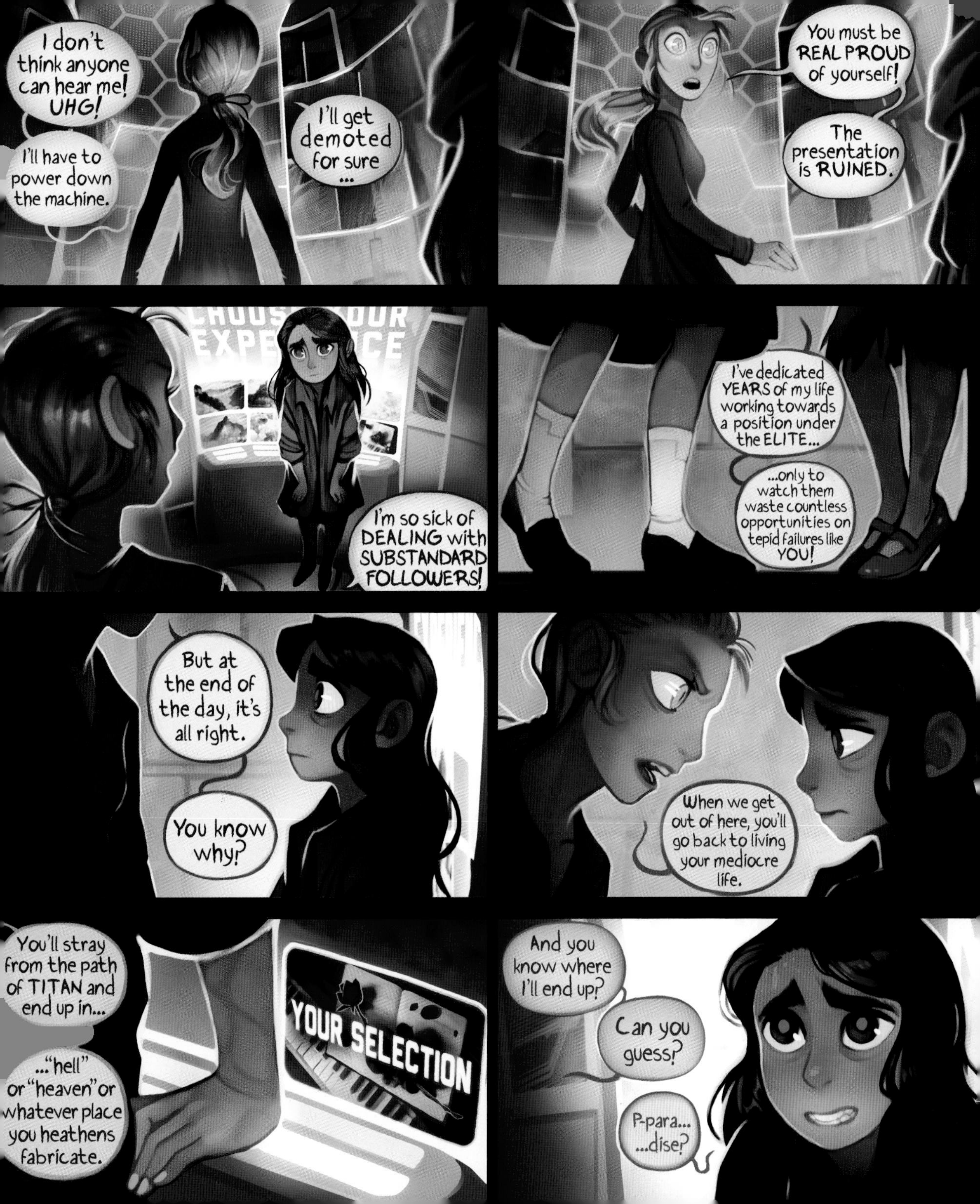
I don't think anyone can hear me! UHG!
I'll have to power down the machine.
I'll get demoted for sure ...
You must be REAL PROUD of yourself!
The presentation is RUINED.
I'm so sick of DEALING with SUBSTANDARD FOLLOWERS!
I've dedicated YEARS of my life working towards a position under the ELITE...
...only to watch them waste countless opportunities on tepid failures like YOU!
But at the end of the day, it's all right.
You know why?
When we get out of here, you'll go back to living your mediocre life.
You'll stray from the path of TITAN and end up in...
..."hell" or "heaven" or whatever place you heathens fabricate.
YOUR SELECTION
And you know where I'll end up?
Can you guess?
P-para... ...dise?

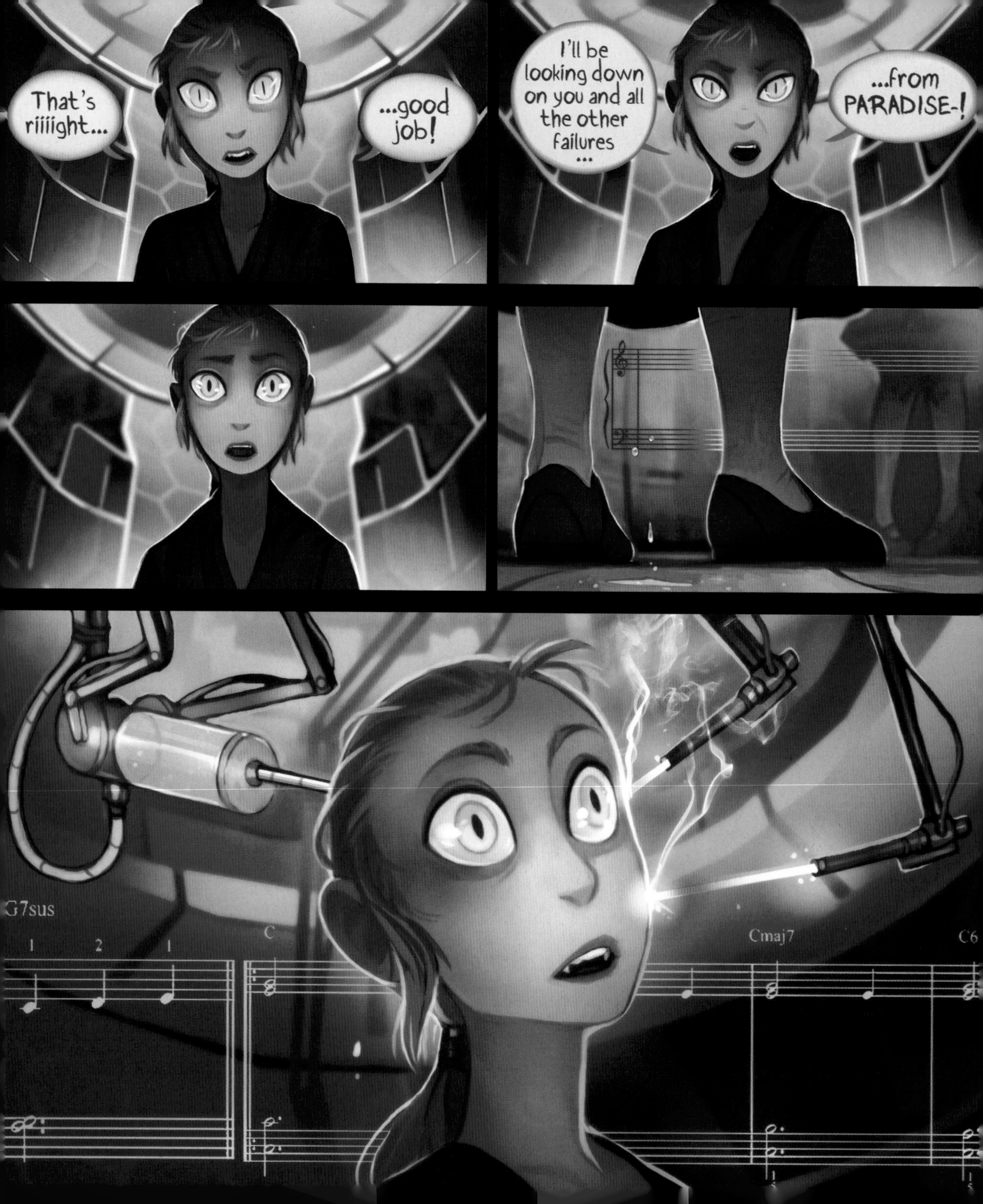
That's riiiight...
...good job!
I'll be looking down on you and all the other failures ...
...from PARADISE-!
G7sus
1 2 1
C
Cmaj7
C6

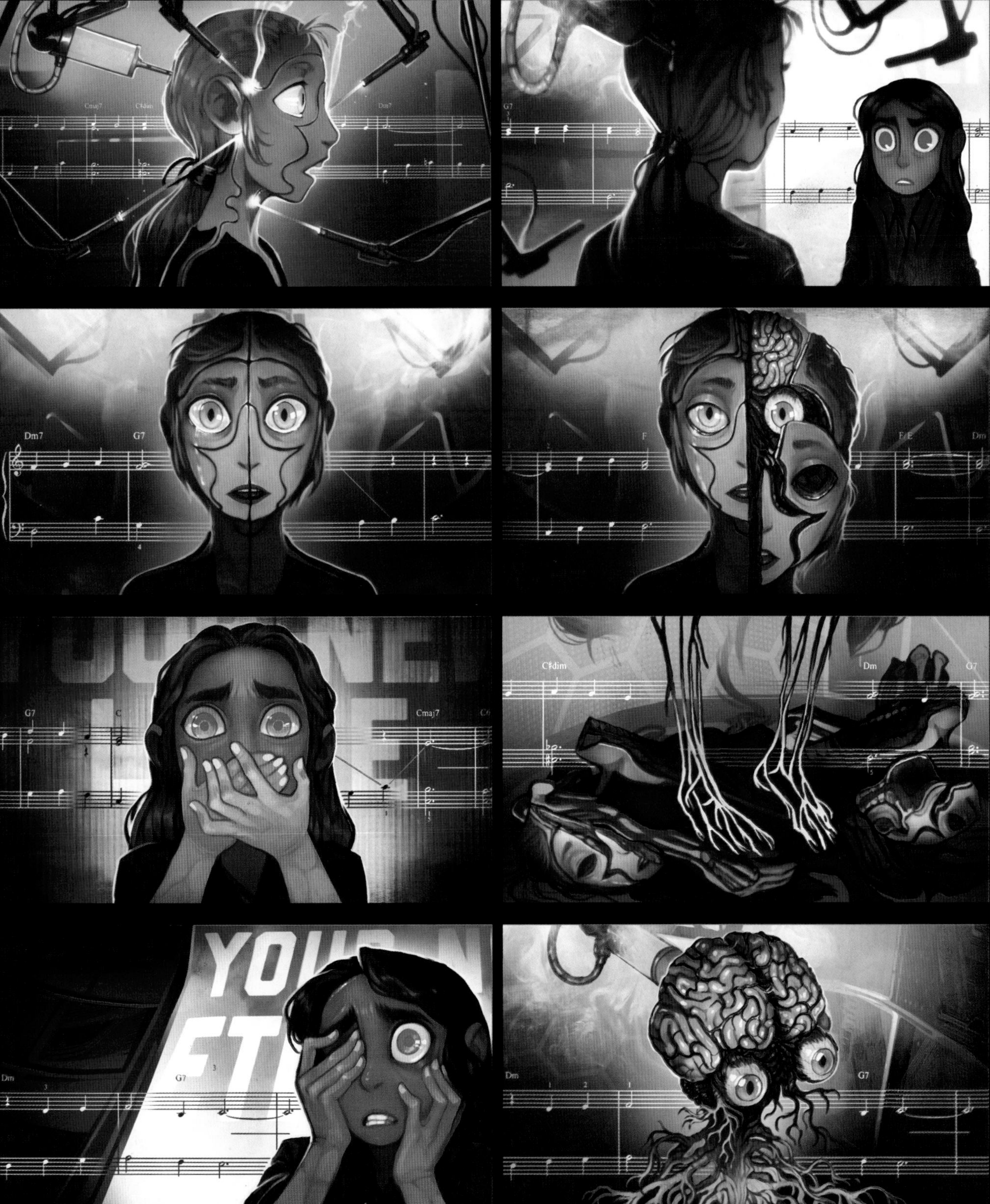
Cmaj7
C♯dim
Dm7
G7
Dm7
G7
F
F/E
Dm
G7
C
Cmaj7
C♯dim
Dm
G7
YOU
Dm
G7
Dm
G7

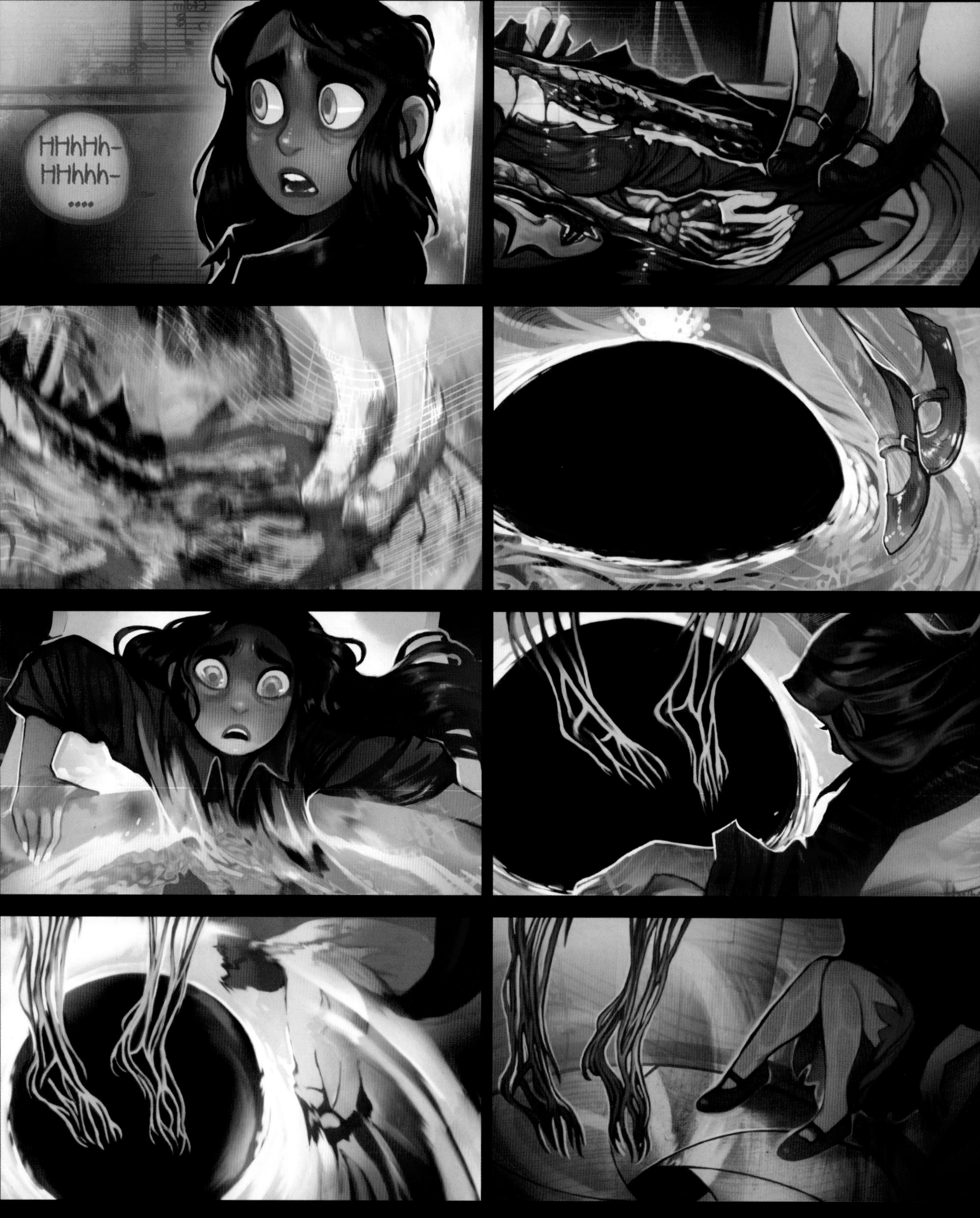
HHhHh-
HHhhh-
....

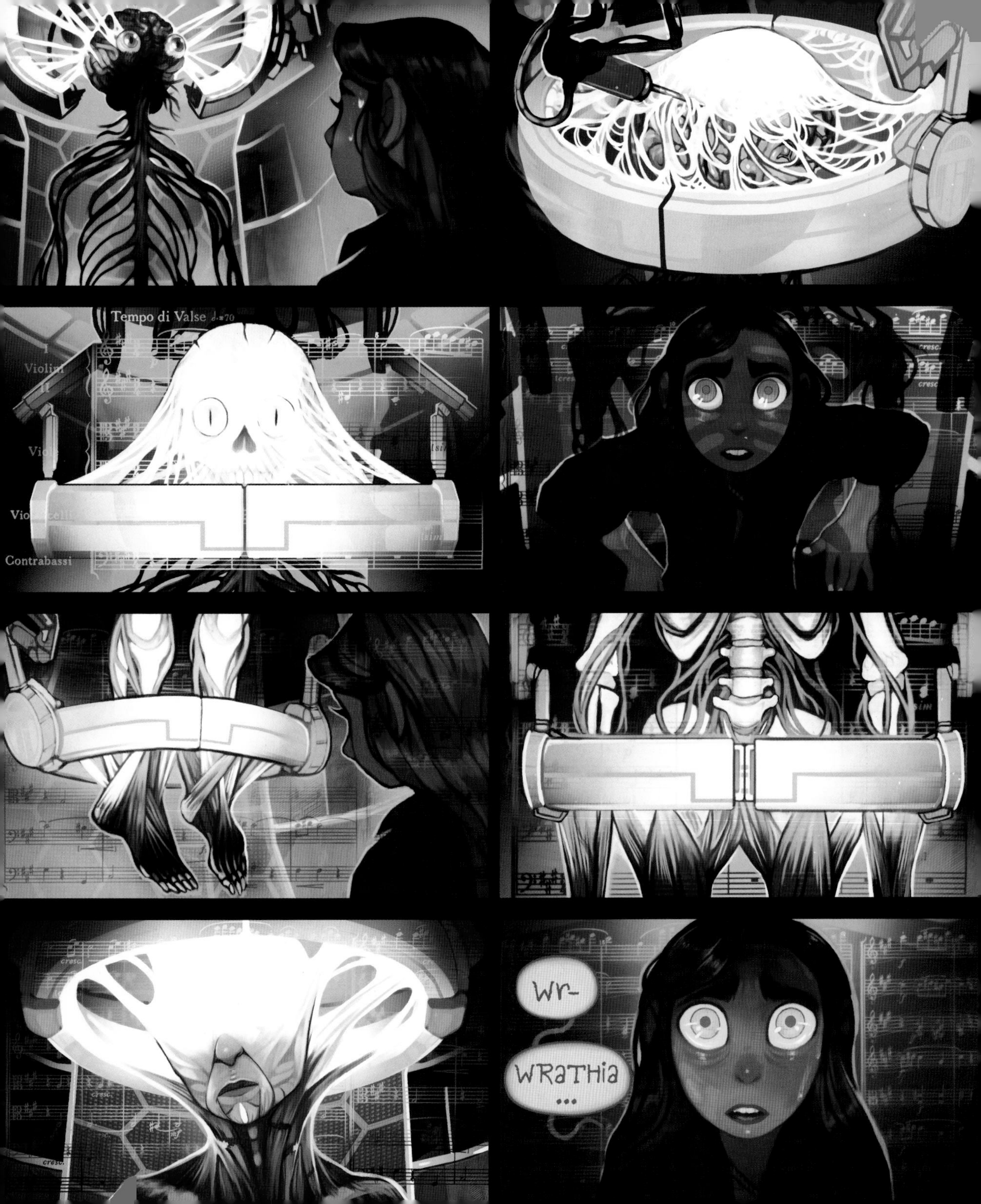
Tempo di Valse
Violini
Contrabassi
Wr-
WRATHIA ...

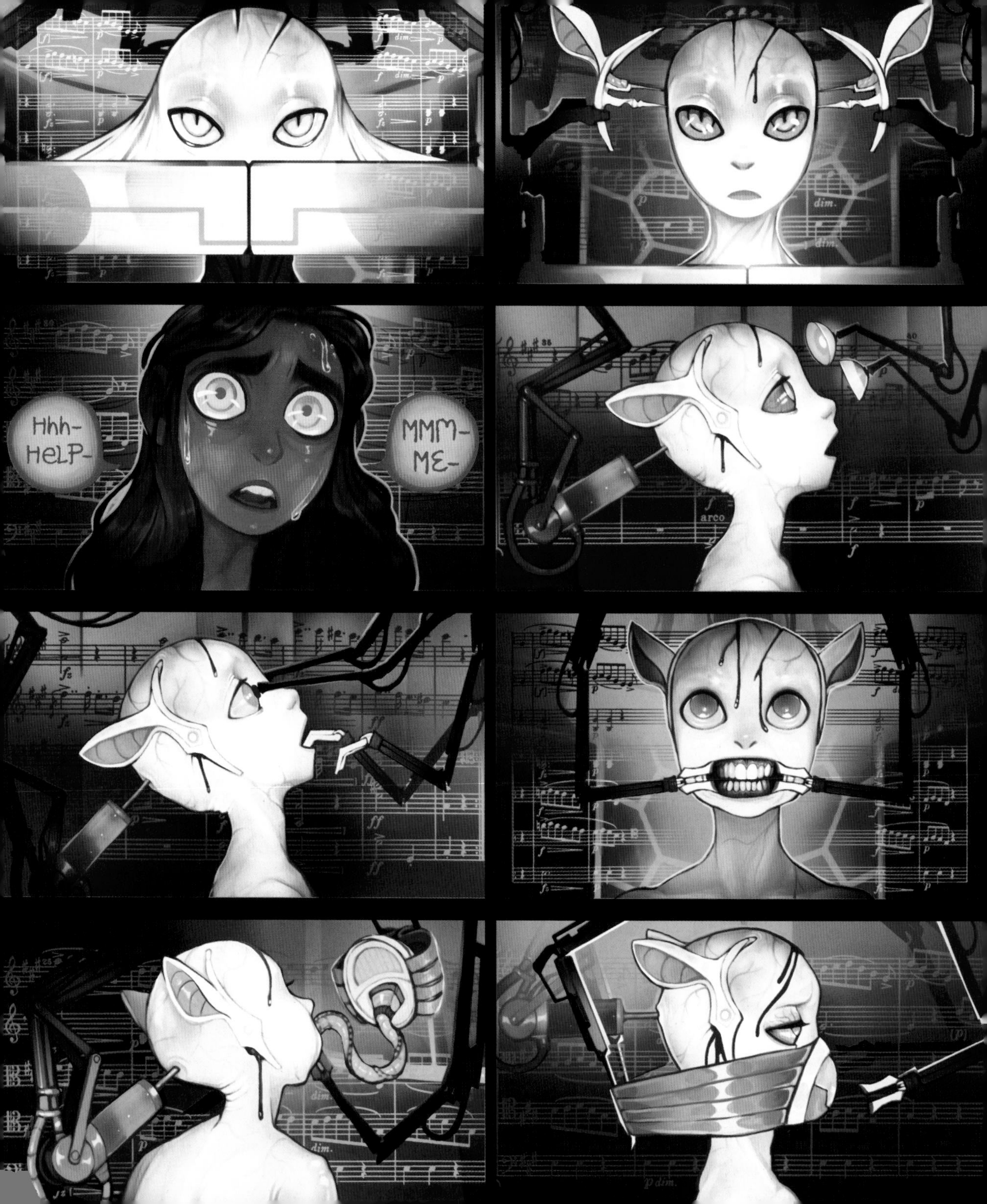
Hhh- HELP-
MMM- ME-

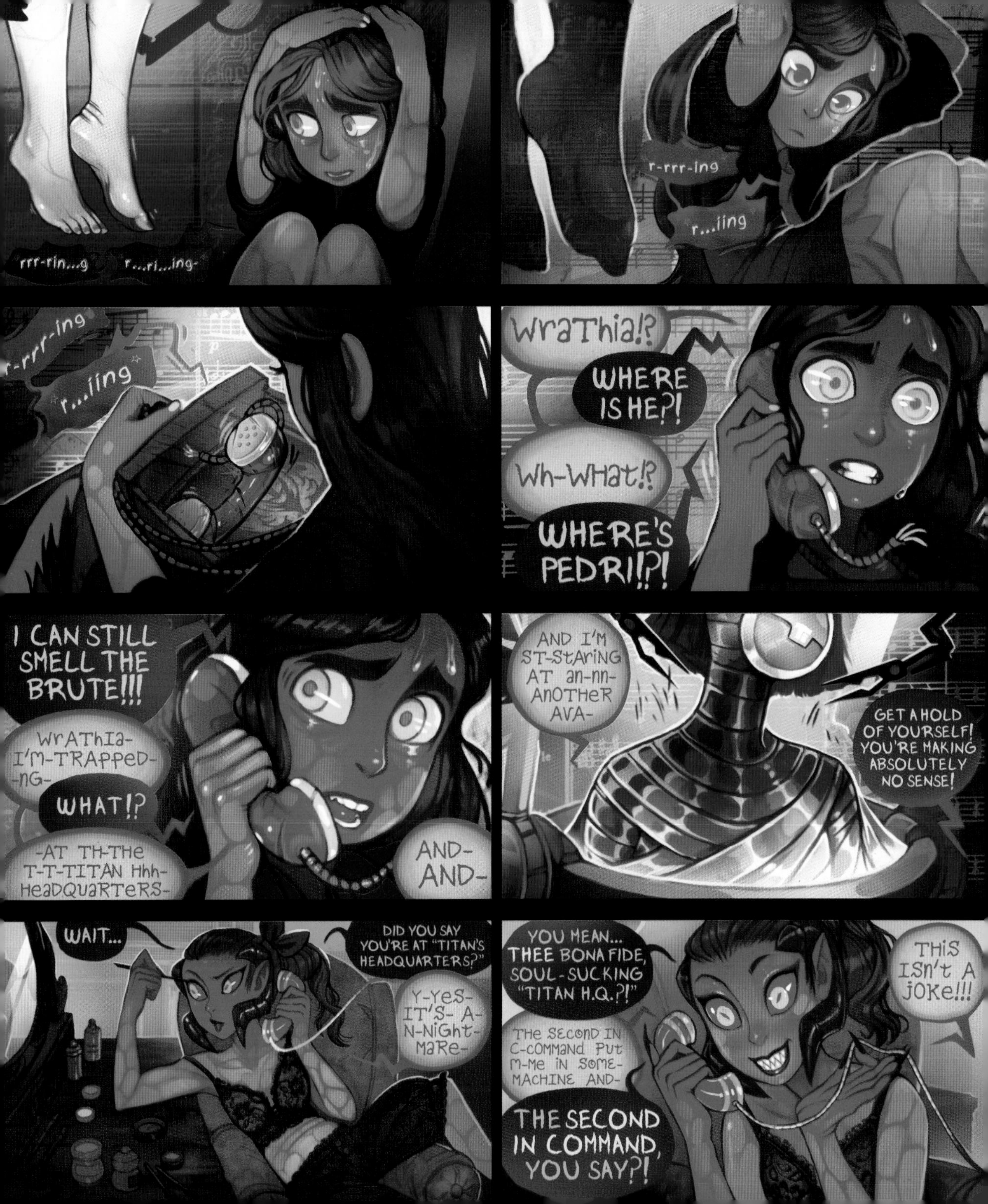
rrr-rin...g
r...ri...ing-
r-rrr-ing
r...iing
r-rrr-ing
r...iing
WraThia!?
WHERE IS HE?!
Wh-WHat!?
WHERE'S PEDRI!?!
I CAN STILL SMELL THE BRUTE!!!
WrAThIa- I'M-TRAPPED- -nG-
WHAT!?
-AT TH-THe T-T-TITAN Hhh-HeaDQuaRTeRS-
AND- AND-
AND I'M ST-StaRinG AT an-nn- AnOTHeR AVA-
GET A HOLD OF YOURSELF! YOU'RE MAKING ABSOLUTELY NO SENSE!
WAIT...
DID YOU SAY YOU'RE AT "TITAN'S HEADQUARTERS?"
Y-YeS- IT'S- A- N-NiGht-MaRe-
YOU MEAN... THEE BONA FIDE, SOUL-SUCKING "TITAN H.Q.?!"
THiS ISn't A JoKe!!!
The SEcOND IN C-COMMAnd PuT M-Me IN SOME-MACHINE AND-
THE SECOND IN COMMAND, YOU SAY?!

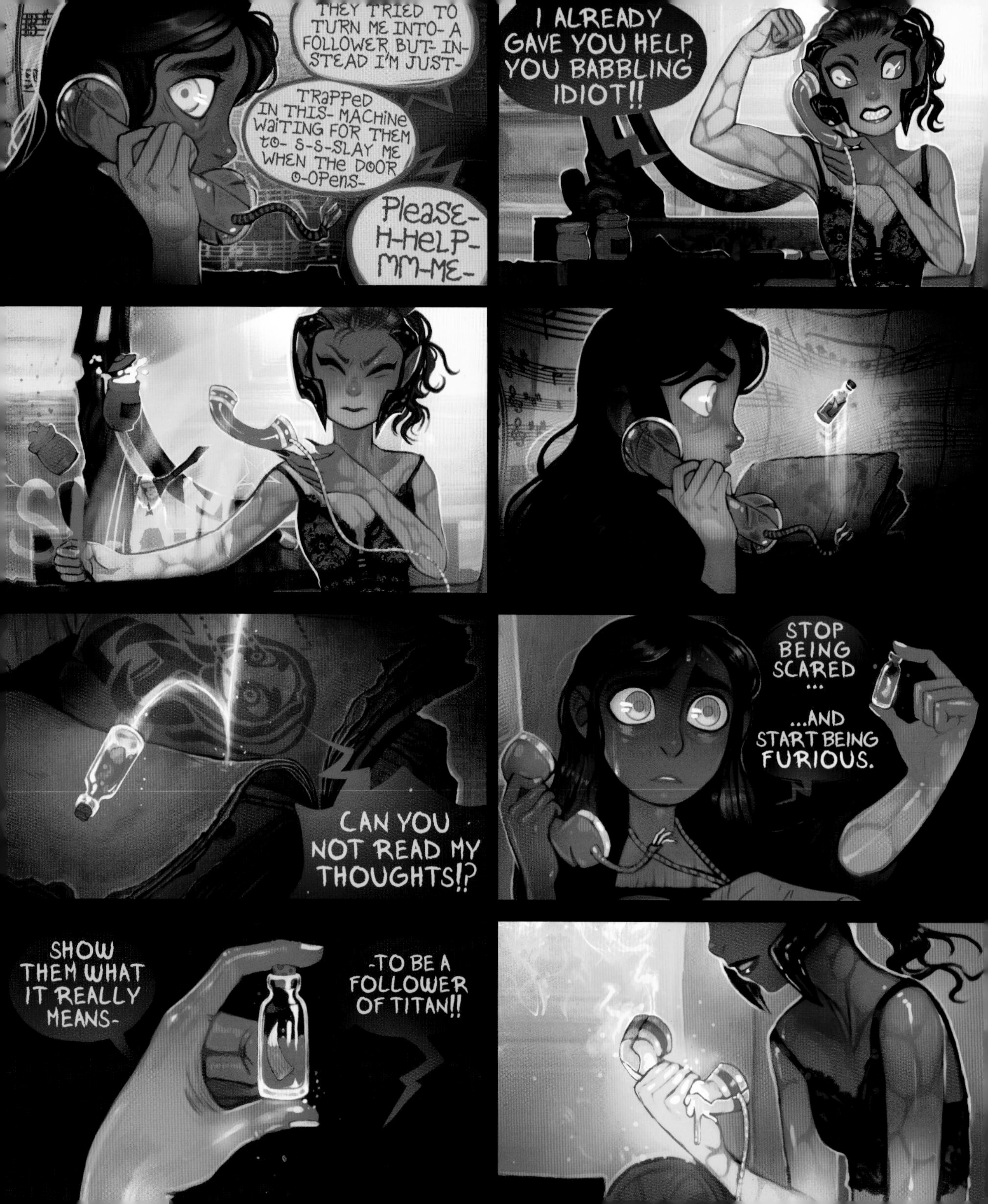
THEY TRIED TO TURN ME INTO- A FOLLOWER, BUT- IN-STEAD I'M JUST-
TRAPPED IN THIS- MACHINE WAITING FOR THEM TO- S-S-SLAY ME WHEN THE DOOR O-OPENS-
PLEASE- H-HELP- MM-ME-
I ALREADY GAVE YOU HELP, YOU BABBLING IDIOT!!
CAN YOU NOT READ MY THOUGHTS!?
STOP BEING SCARED...
...AND START BEING FURIOUS.
SHOW THEM WHAT IT REALLY MEANS-
-TO BE A FOLLOWER OF TITAN!!

FINALLY...

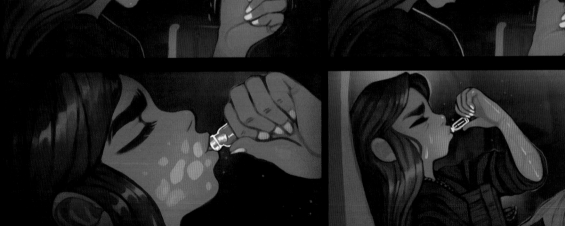

Here's to- a new- life-

Hhh- HHHHh!!!

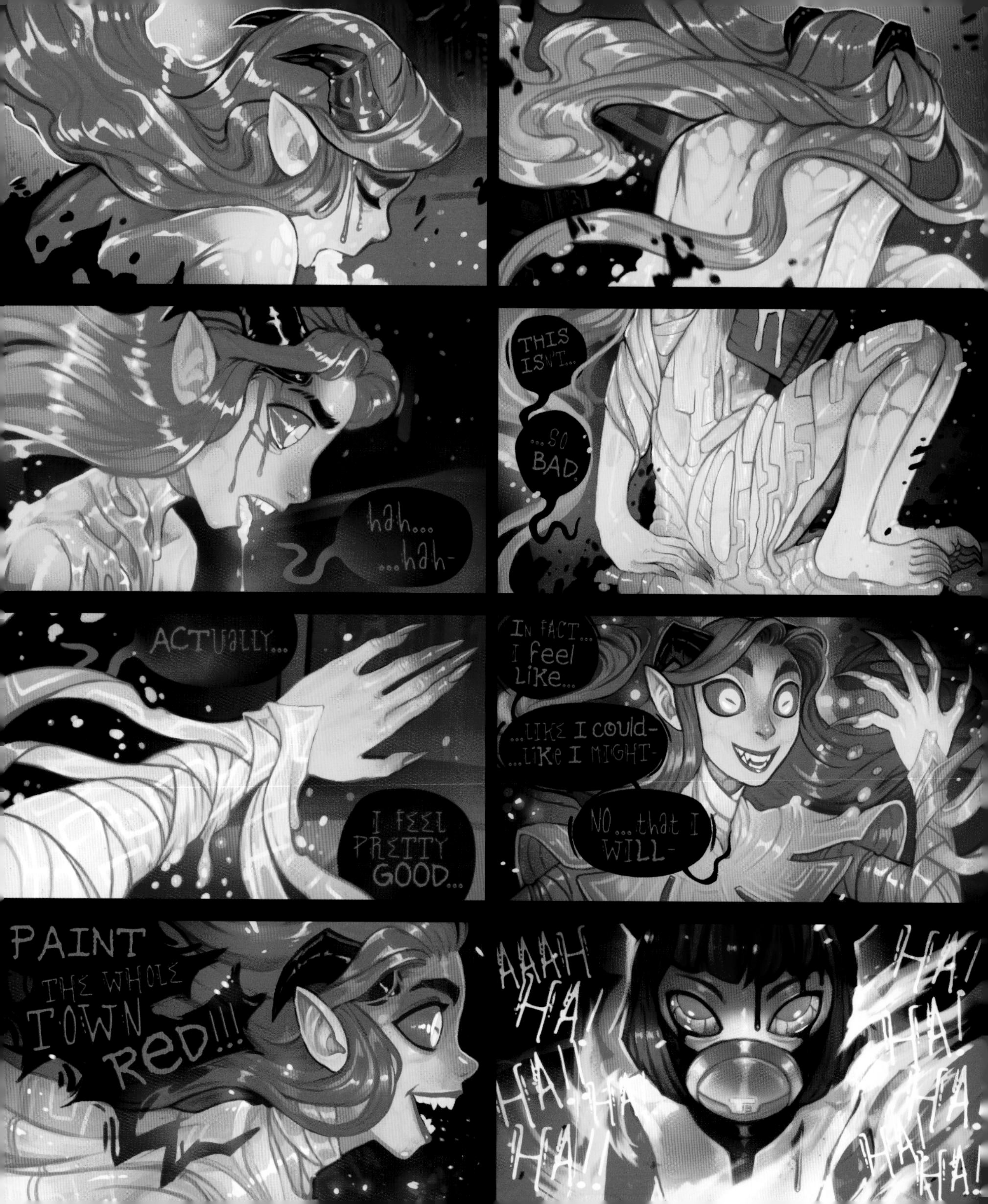
hah...
...hah-
THIS ISN'T...
...SO BAD.
ACTUALLY...
I FEEL PRETTY GOOD...
IN FACT... I feel like...
...LIKE I could-
...LIKE I MIGHT-
NO... that I WILL-
PAINT THE WHOLE TOWN RED!!!
AAAH HA! HA! HA! HA! HA!
HA! HA! HA! HA! HA! HA!

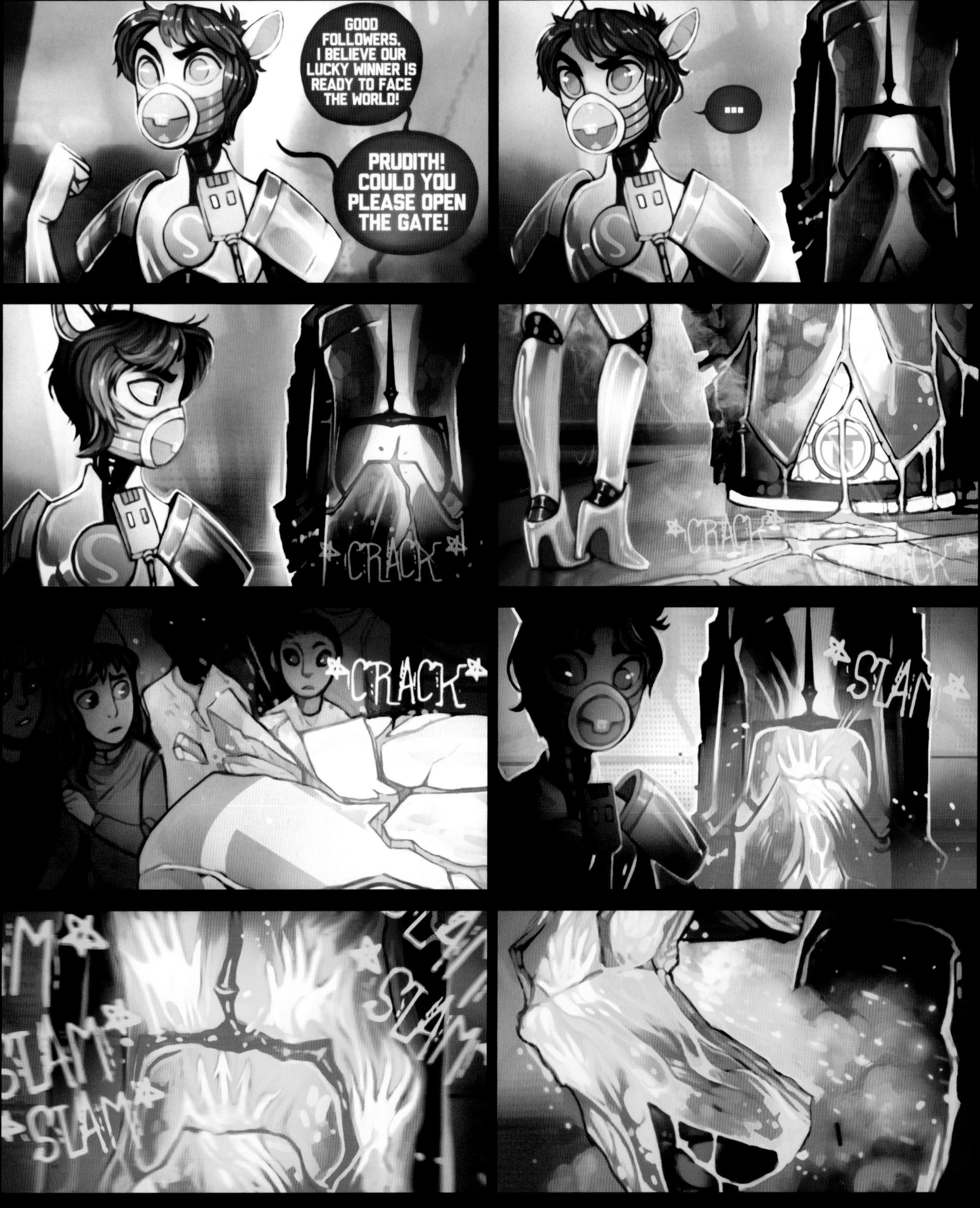
GOOD FOLLOWERS, I BELIEVE OUR LUCKY WINNER IS READY TO FACE THE WORLD!
PRUDITH! COULD YOU PLEASE OPEN THE GATE!
...
CRACK
CRACK
CRACK
SLAM

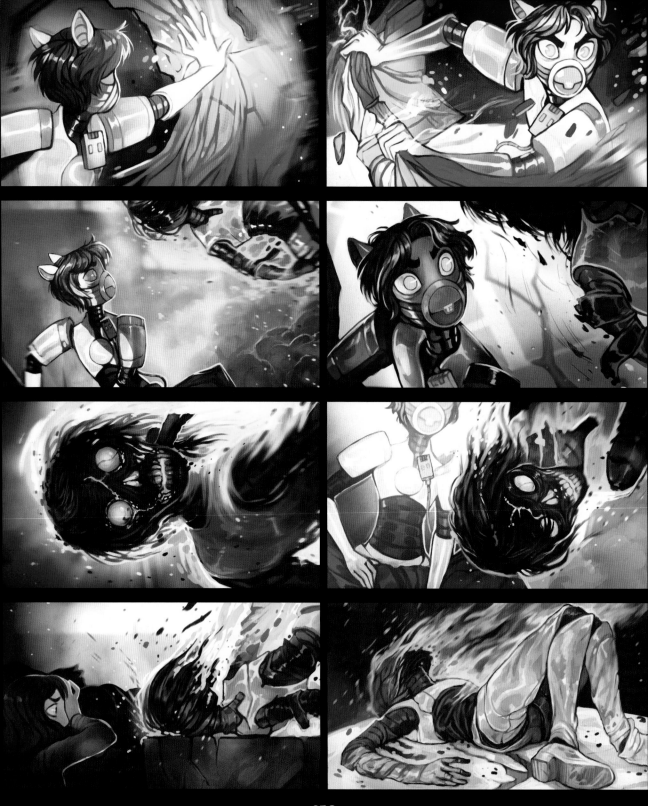

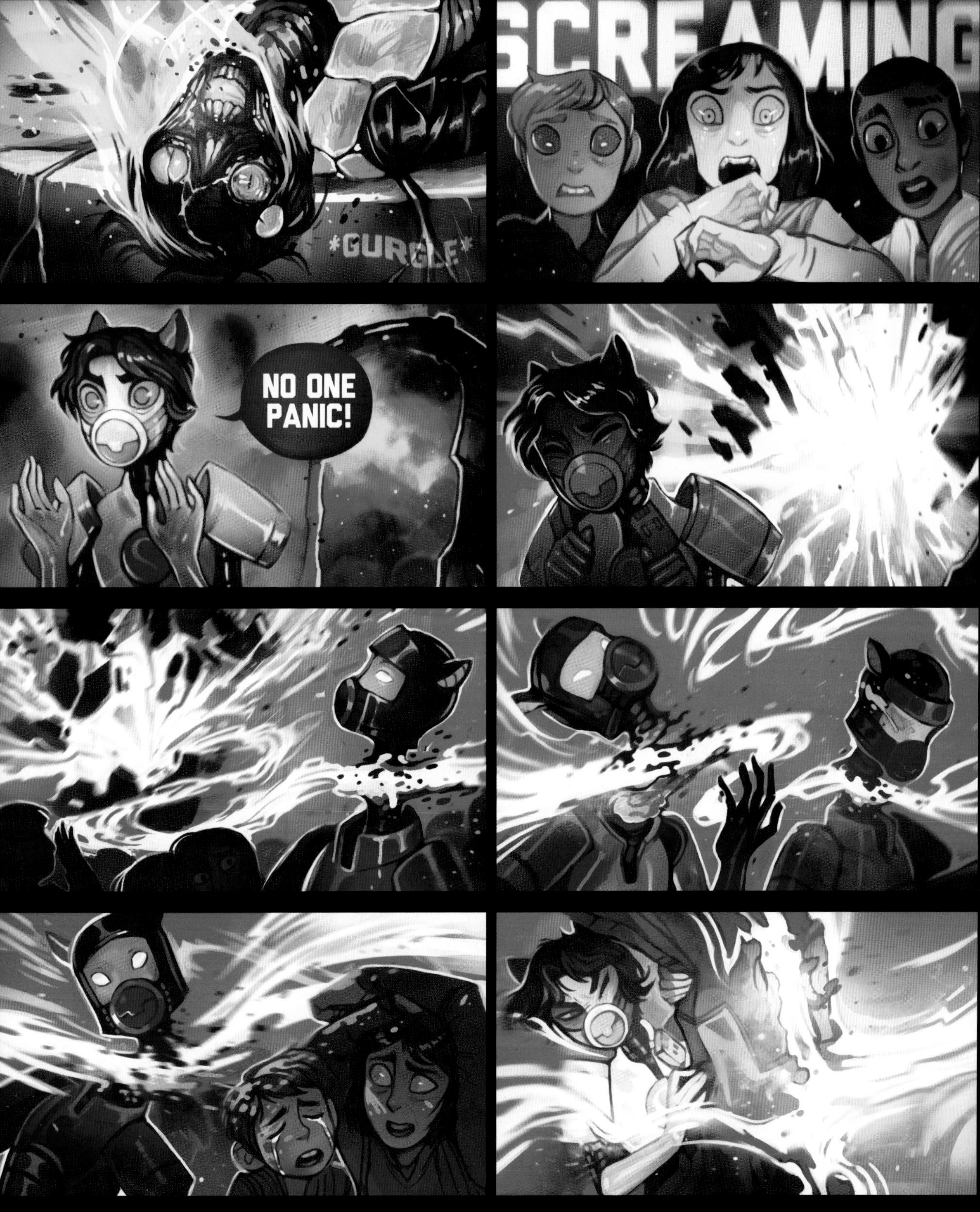
GURGLE
SCREAMING
NO ONE PANIC!

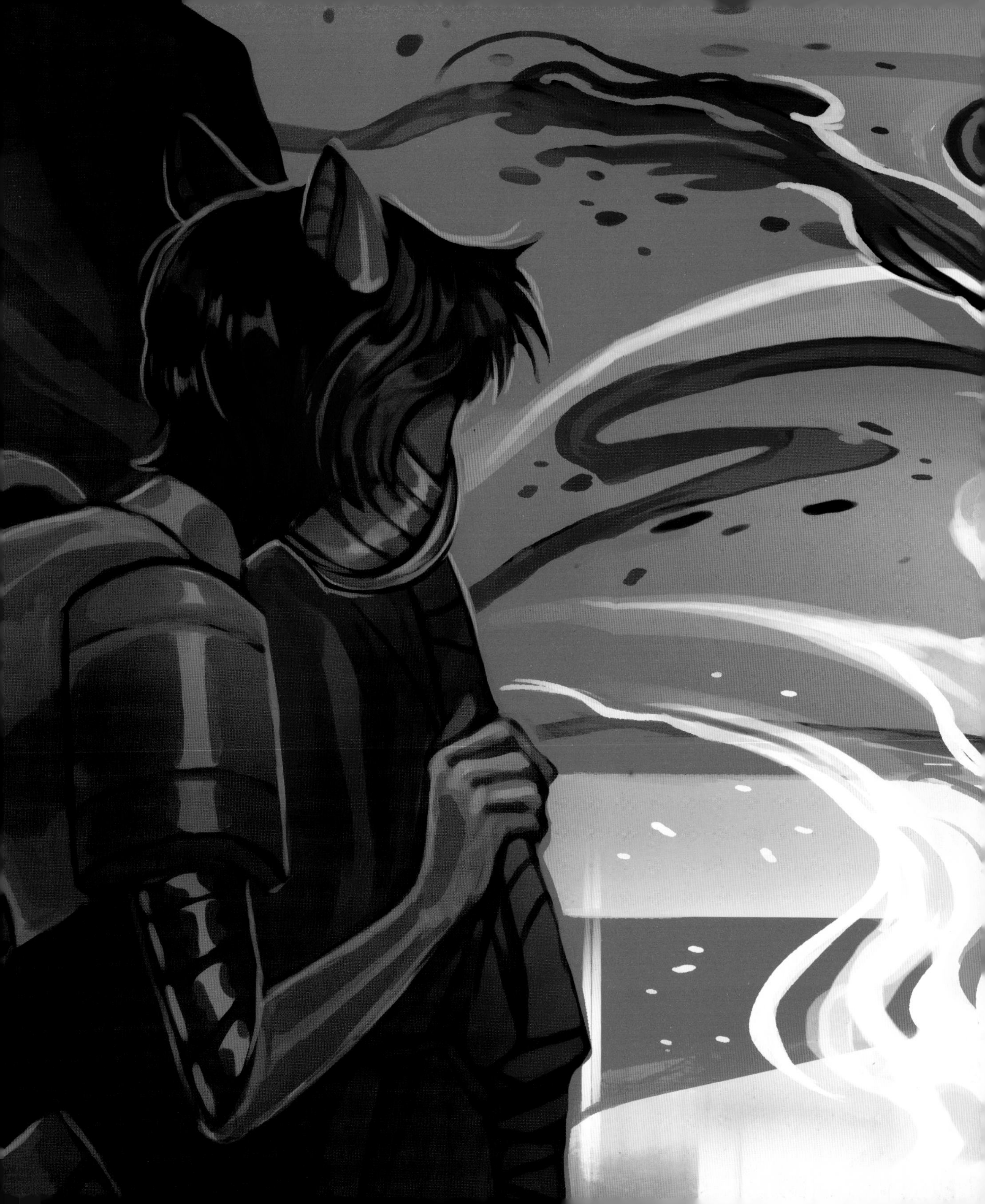

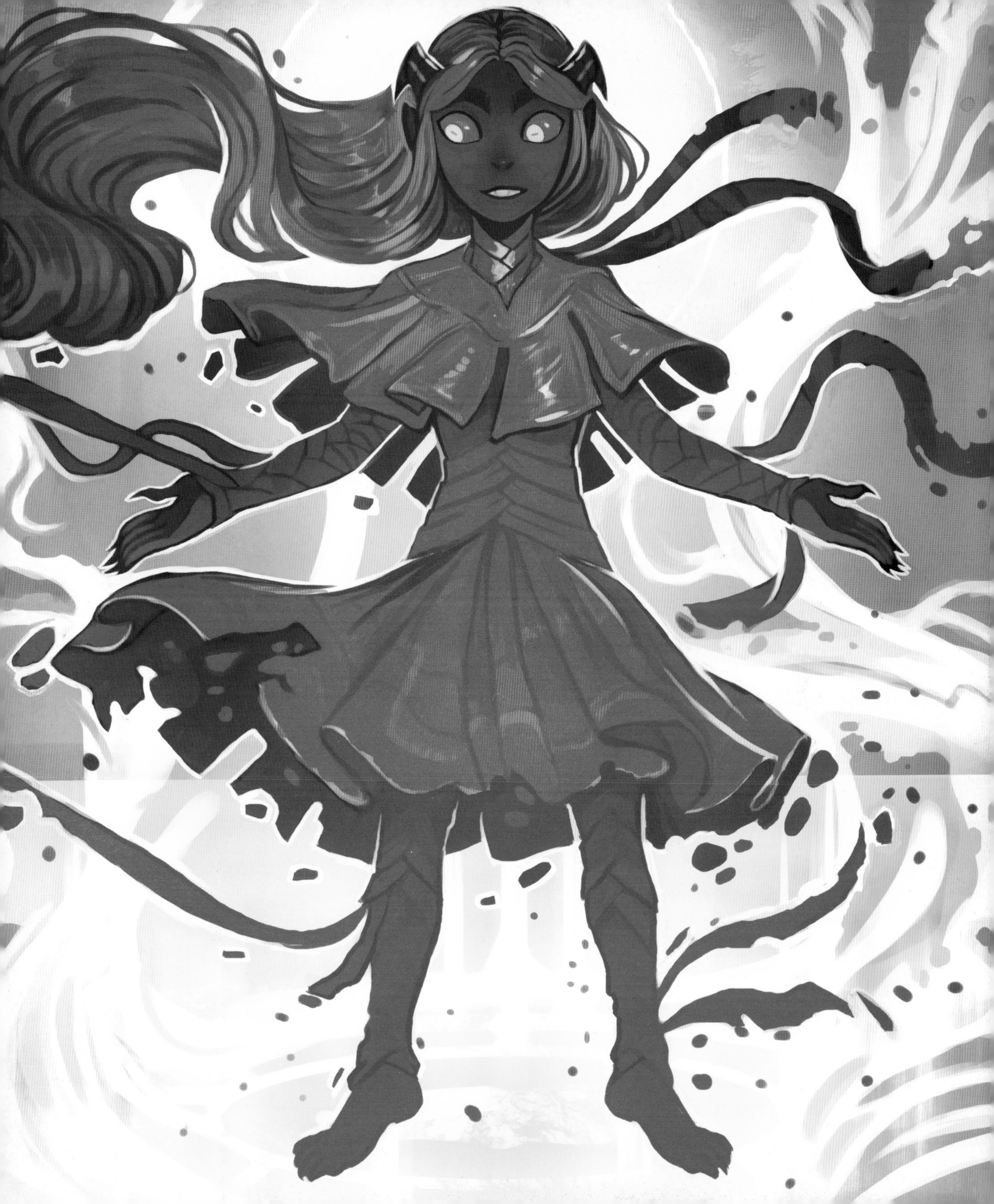

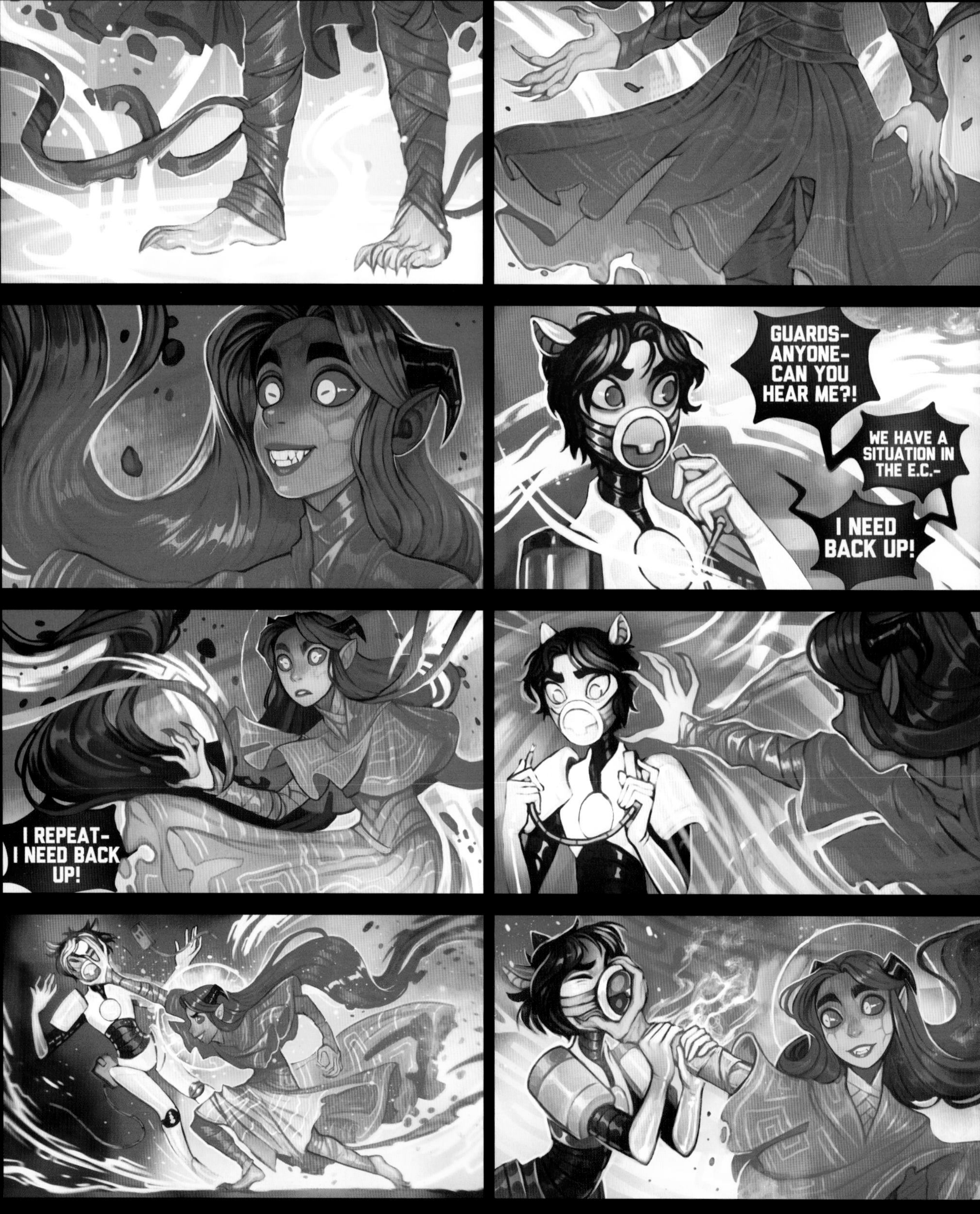
GUARDS- ANYONE- CAN YOU HEAR ME?!
WE HAVE A SITUATION IN THE E.C.-
I NEED BACK UP!
I REPEAT- I NEED BACK UP!

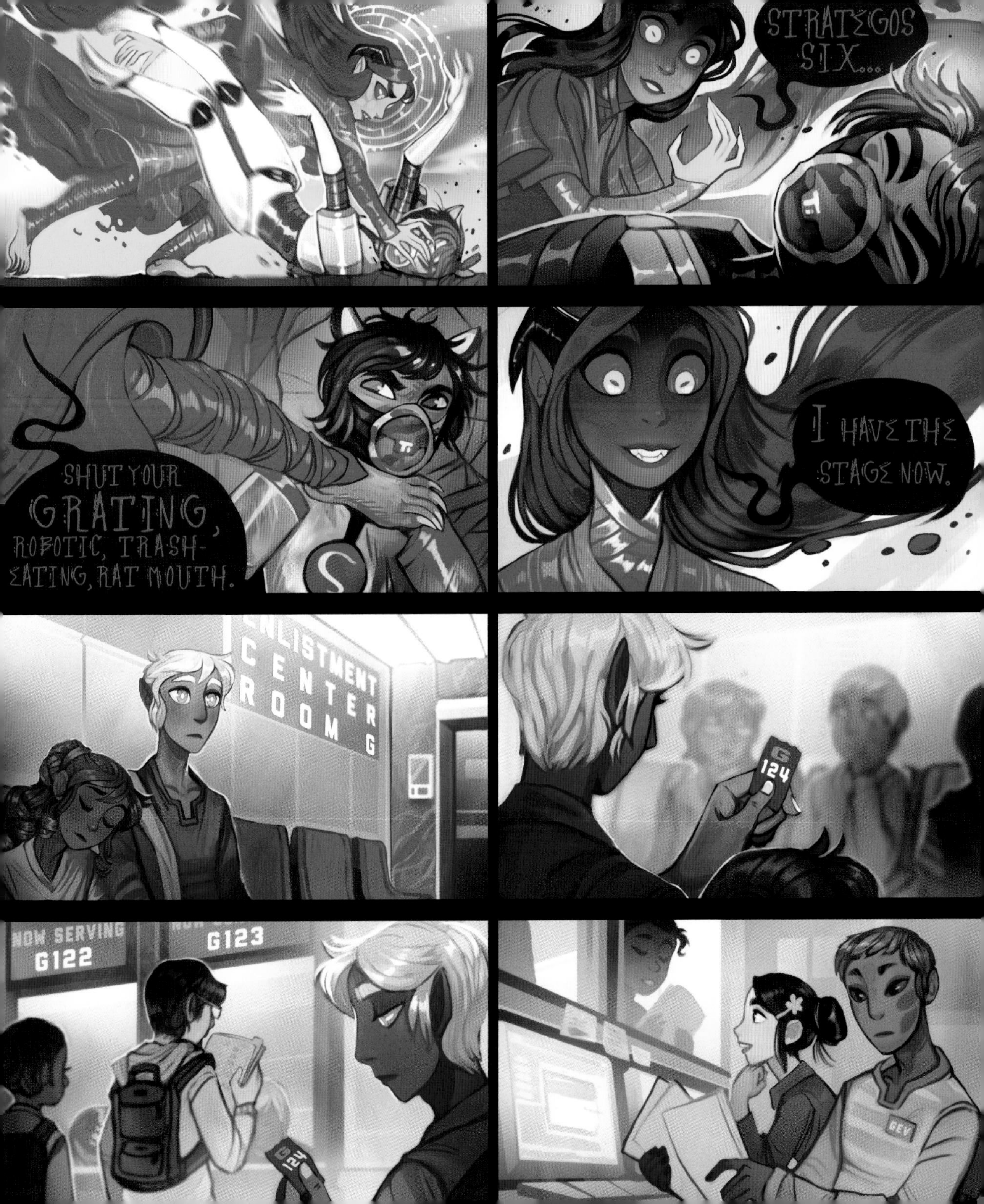

STRATEGOS SIX...
SHUT YOUR GRATING, ROBOTIC, TRASH-EATING, RAT MOUTH.
I HAVE THE STAGE NOW.
ENLISTMENT CENTER ROOM G
G 124
NOW SERVING G122
G123
G 124
GEV

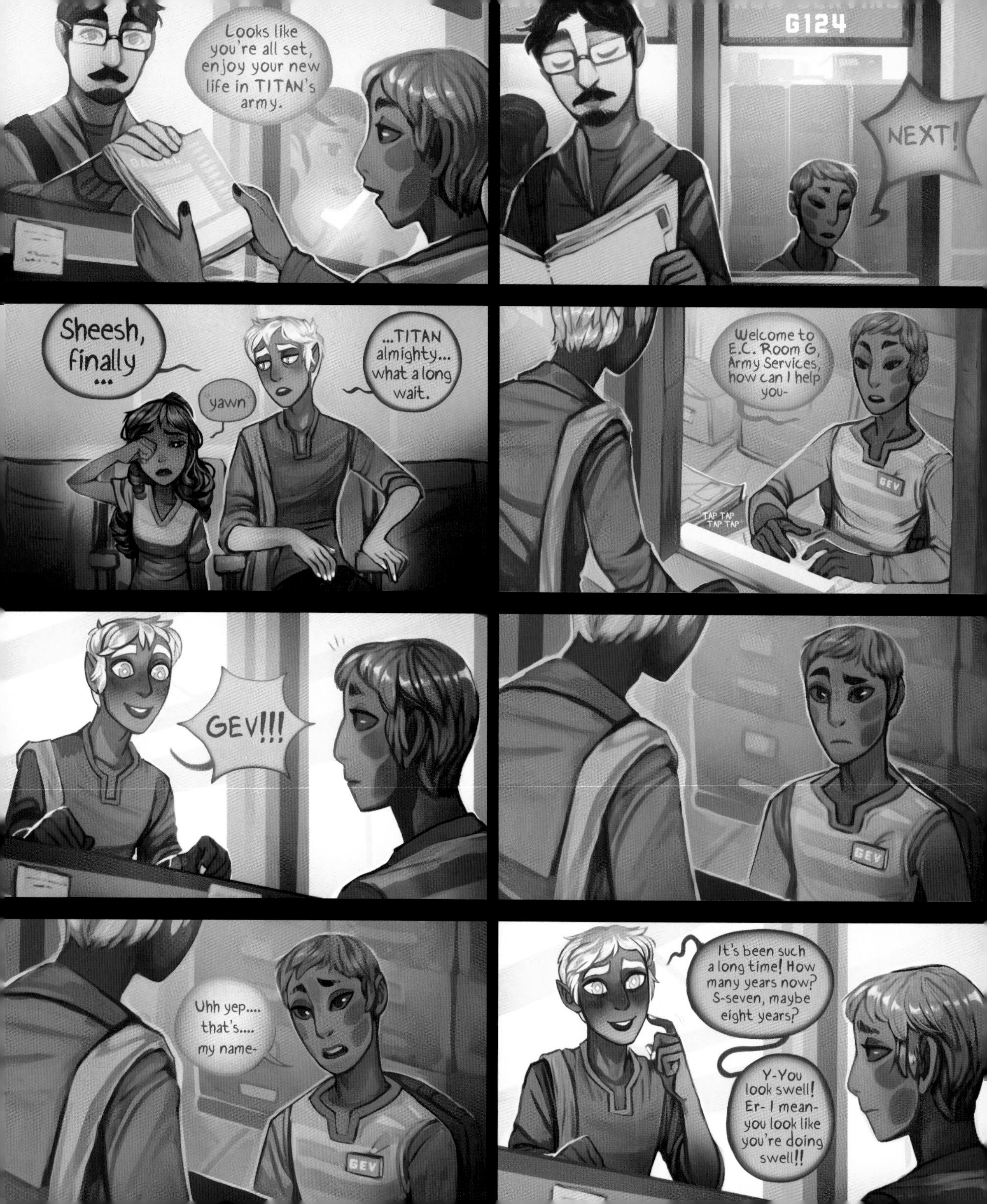
Looks like you're all set, enjoy your new life in TITAN's army.
G124
NEXT!
Sheesh, finally...
yawn
...TITAN almighty... what a long wait.
Welcome to E.C. Room G, Army Services, how can I help you-
TAP TAP TAP TAP
GEV
GEV!!!
GEV
Uhh yep.... that's.... my name-
GEV
It's been such a long time! How many years now? S-seven, maybe eight years?
Y-You look swell! Er- I mean- you look like you're doing swell!!

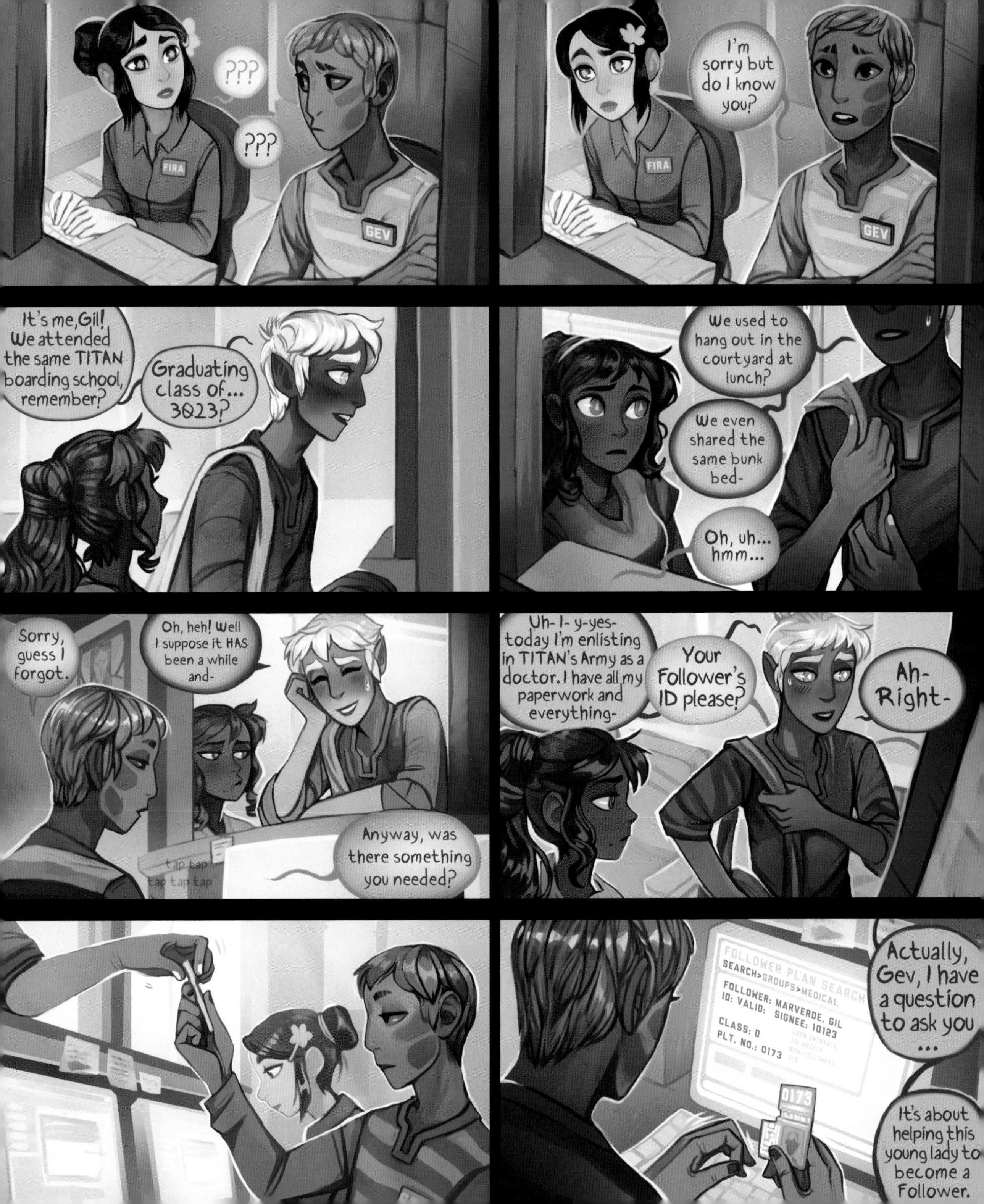
FIRA
???
???
GEV
I'm sorry but do I know you?
It's me, Gil! We attended the same TITAN boarding school, remember?
Graduating class of... 3Q23?
We used to hang out in the courtyard at lunch?
We even shared the same bunk bed-
Oh, uh... hmm...
Sorry, guess I forgot.
Oh, heh! Well I suppose it HAS been a while and-
tap tap
tap tap tap
Anyway, was there something you needed?
Uh- I- y-yes- today I'm enlisting in TITAN's Army as a doctor. I have all my paperwork and everything-
Your Follower's ID please?
Ah- Right-
FOLLOWER PLAN SEARCH
SEARCH>GROUPS>MEDICAL
FOLLOWER: MARVERDE, GIL
ID: VALID: SIGNEE: 10123
CLASS: D
PLT. NO.: 0173
0173
Actually, Gev, I have a question to ask you...
It's about helping this young lady to become a Follower.

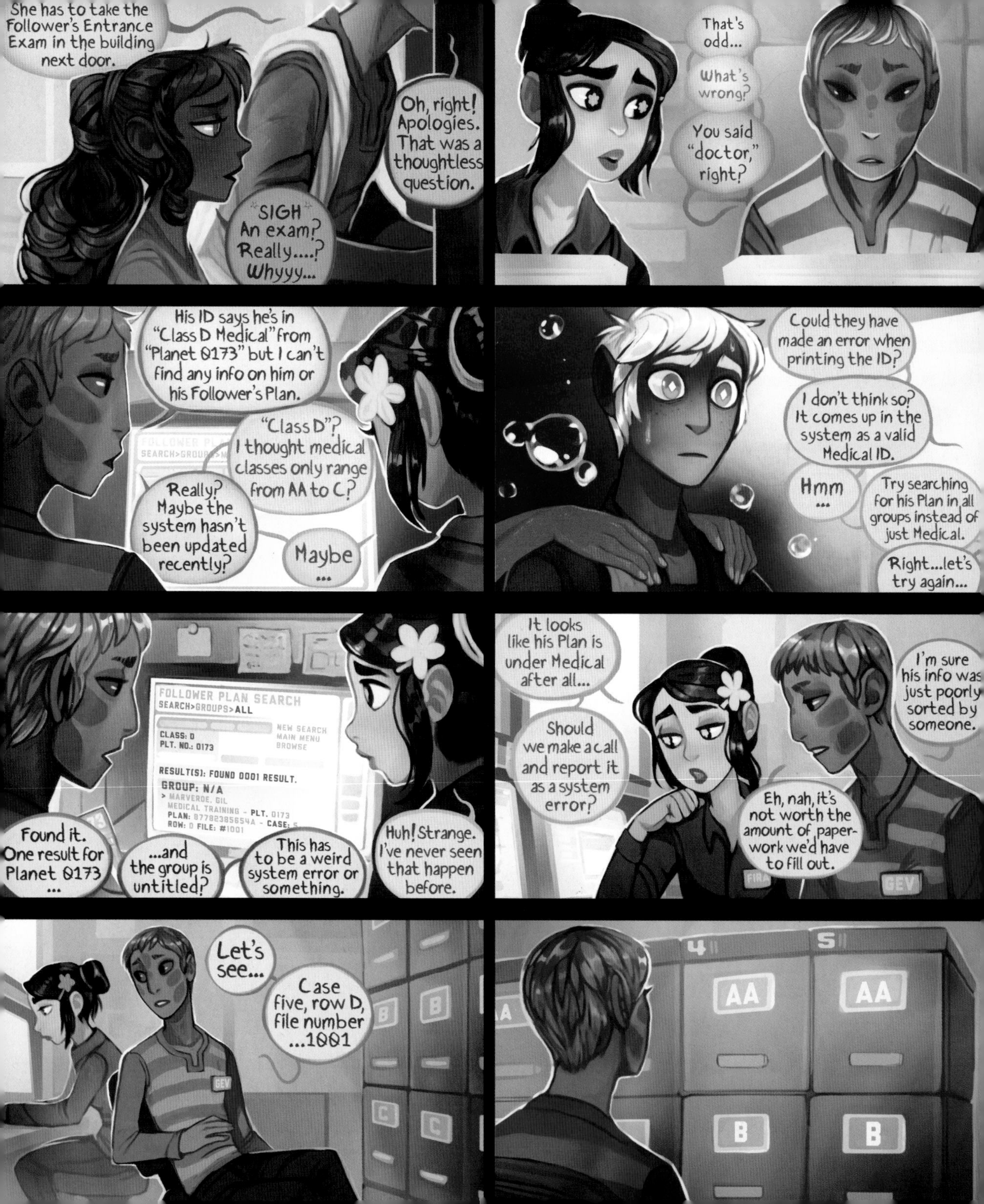

She has to take the Follower's Entrance Exam in the building next door.
SIGH An exam? Really....? Whyyy...
Oh, right! Apologies. That was a thoughtless question.
That's odd...
What's wrong?
You said "doctor," right?
His ID says he's in "Class D Medical" from "Planet 0173" but I can't find any info on him or his Follower's Plan.
"Class D"? I thought medical classes only range from AA to C?
Really? Maybe the system hasn't been updated recently?
Maybe...
Could they have made an error when printing the ID?
I don't think so? It comes up in the system as a valid Medical ID.
Hmm...
Try searching for his Plan in all groups instead of just Medical.
Right...let's try again...
FOLLOWER PLAN SEARCH
SEARCH>GROUPS>ALL
CLASS: D
PLT. NO.: 0173
NEW SEARCH
MAIN MENU
BROWSE
RESULT(S): FOUND 0001 RESULT.
GROUP: N/A
> MARVERDE, GIL
MEDICAL TRAINING - PLT. 0173
PLAN: 87782385654A - CASE: 5
ROW: D FILE: #1001
Found it. One result for Planet 0173...
...and the group is untitled?
This has to be a weird system error or something.
Huh! Strange. I've never seen that happen before.
It looks like his Plan is under Medical after all...
Should we make a call and report it as a system error?
I'm sure his info was just poorly sorted by someone.
Eh, nah, it's not worth the amount of paperwork we'd have to fill out.
GEV
Let's see...
Case five, row D, file number ...1001
GEV
AA
AA
B
B

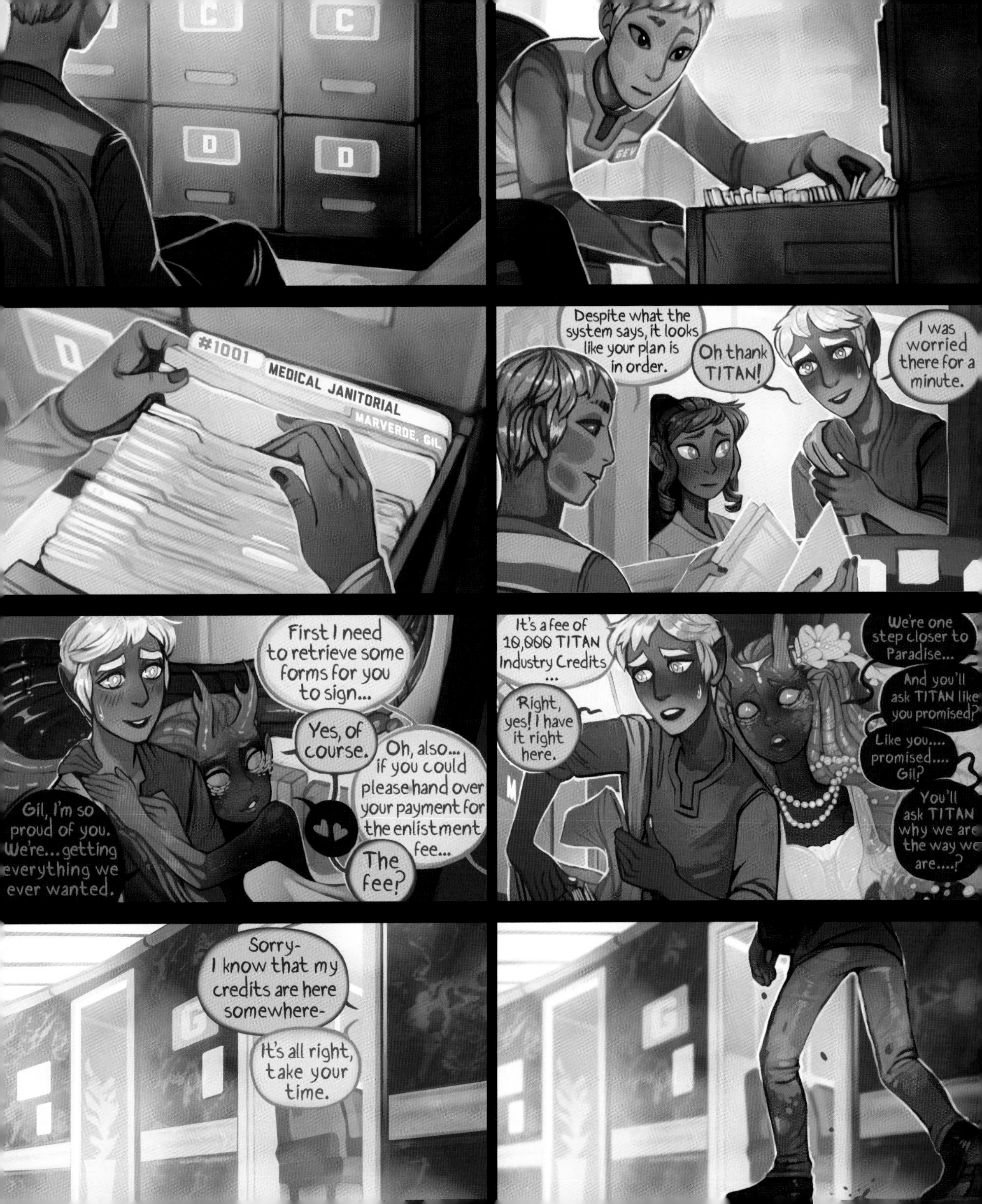
C
C
D
D
GEV
#1001 MEDICAL JANITORIAL
MARVERDE, GIL
Despite what the system says, it looks like your plan is in order.
Oh thank TITAN!
I was worried there for a minute.
First I need to retrieve some forms for you to sign...
Yes, of course.
Oh, also... if you could please hand over your payment for the enlistment fee...
The fee?
Gil, I'm so proud of you. We're... getting everything we ever wanted.
It's a fee of 10,000 TITAN Industry Credits ...
Right, yes! I have it right here.
We're one step closer to Paradise...
And you'll ask TITAN like you promised?
Like you.... promised.... Gil?
You'll ask TITAN why we are the way we are....?
Sorry- I know that my credits are here somewhere-
It's all right, take your time.

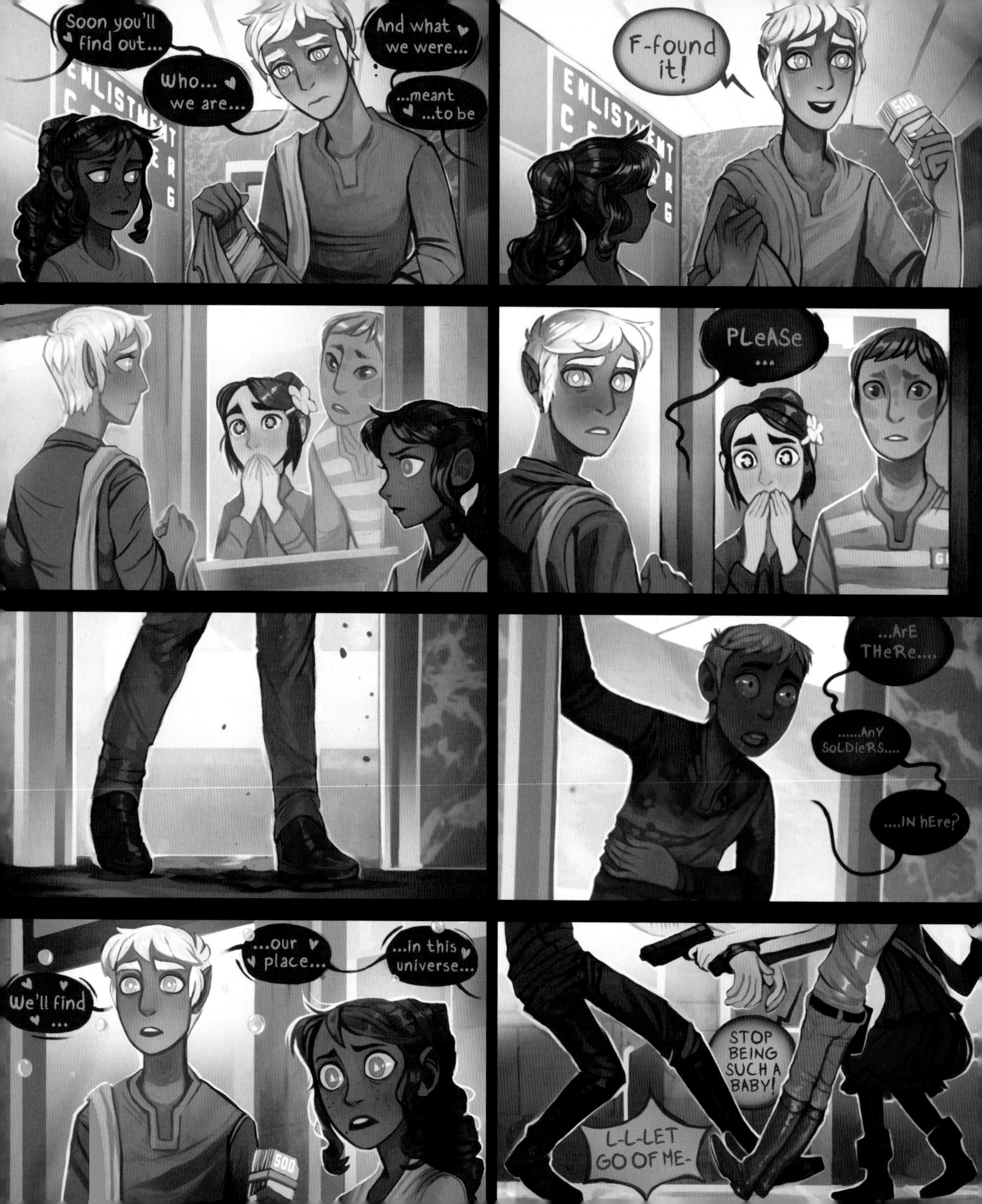

Soon you'll find out...
Who... we are...
And what we were...
...meant ...to be
ENLISTMENT
F-found it!
500
PLeASe ...
...ArE THeRe....
......AnY SOLDieRS....
....IN hEre?
We'll find ...
...our place...
...in this universe...
500
STOP BEING SUCH A BABY!
L-L-LET GO OF ME-

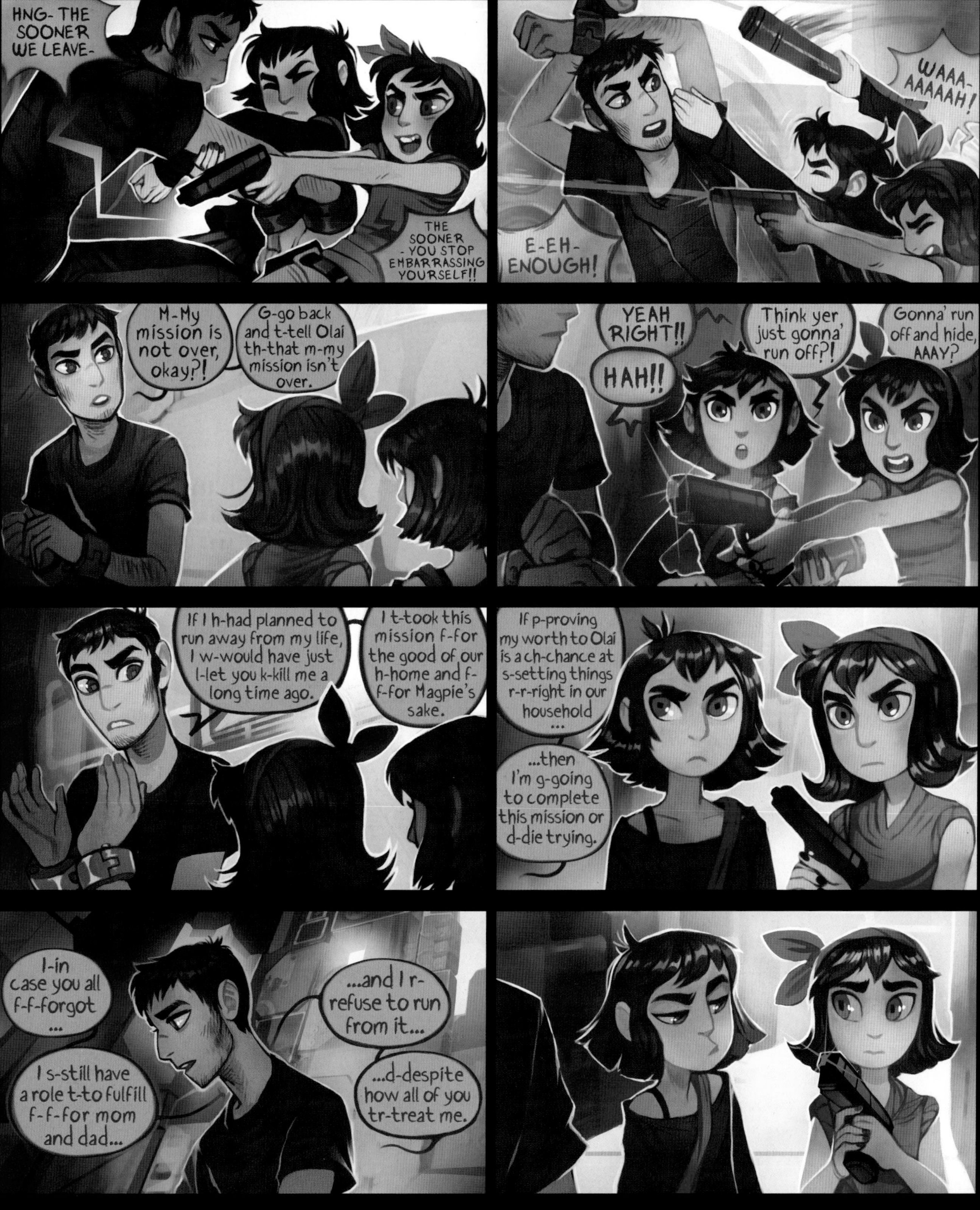
HNG- THE SOONER WE LEAVE-
THE SOONER - YOU STOP EMBARRASSING YOURSELF!!
WAAA-AAAAAAH!
E-EH- ENOUGH!
M-My mission is not over, okay?!
G-go back and t-tell Olai th-that m-my mission isn't over.
YEAH RIGHT!!
HAH!!
Think yer just gonna' run off?!
Gonna' run off and hide, AAAY?
If I h-had planned to run away from my life, I w-would have just l-let you k-kill me a long time ago.
I t-took this mission f-for the good of our h-home and f-f-for Magpie's sake.
If p-proving my worth to Olai is a ch-chance at s-setting things r-r-right in our household ...
...then I'm g-going to complete this mission or d-die trying.
I-in case you all f-f-forgot ...
I s-still have a role t-to fulfill f-f-for mom and dad...
...and I r-refuse to run from it...
...d-despite how all of you tr-treat me.

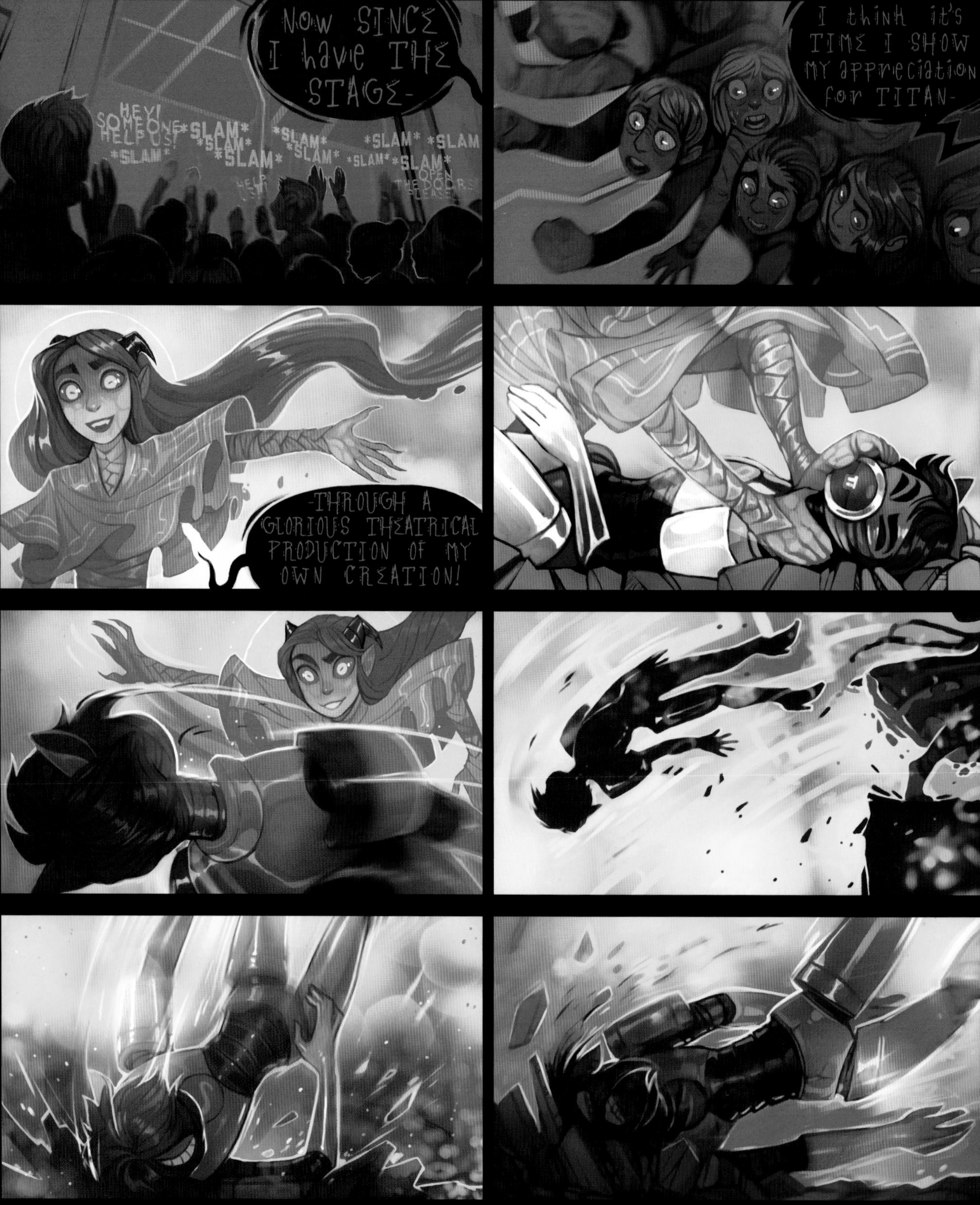
NOW SINCE I have THE STAGE-
HEY! SOMEONE HELP US!
SLAM *SLAM* *SLAM* *SLAM* *SLAM* *SLAM* *SLAM* *SLAM* *SLAM* *SLAM*
OPEN THE DOORS PLEASE!
I think it's TIME I SHOW MY appreciation for TITAN-
-THROUGH A GLORIOUS THEATRICAL PRODUCTION OF MY OWN CREATION!

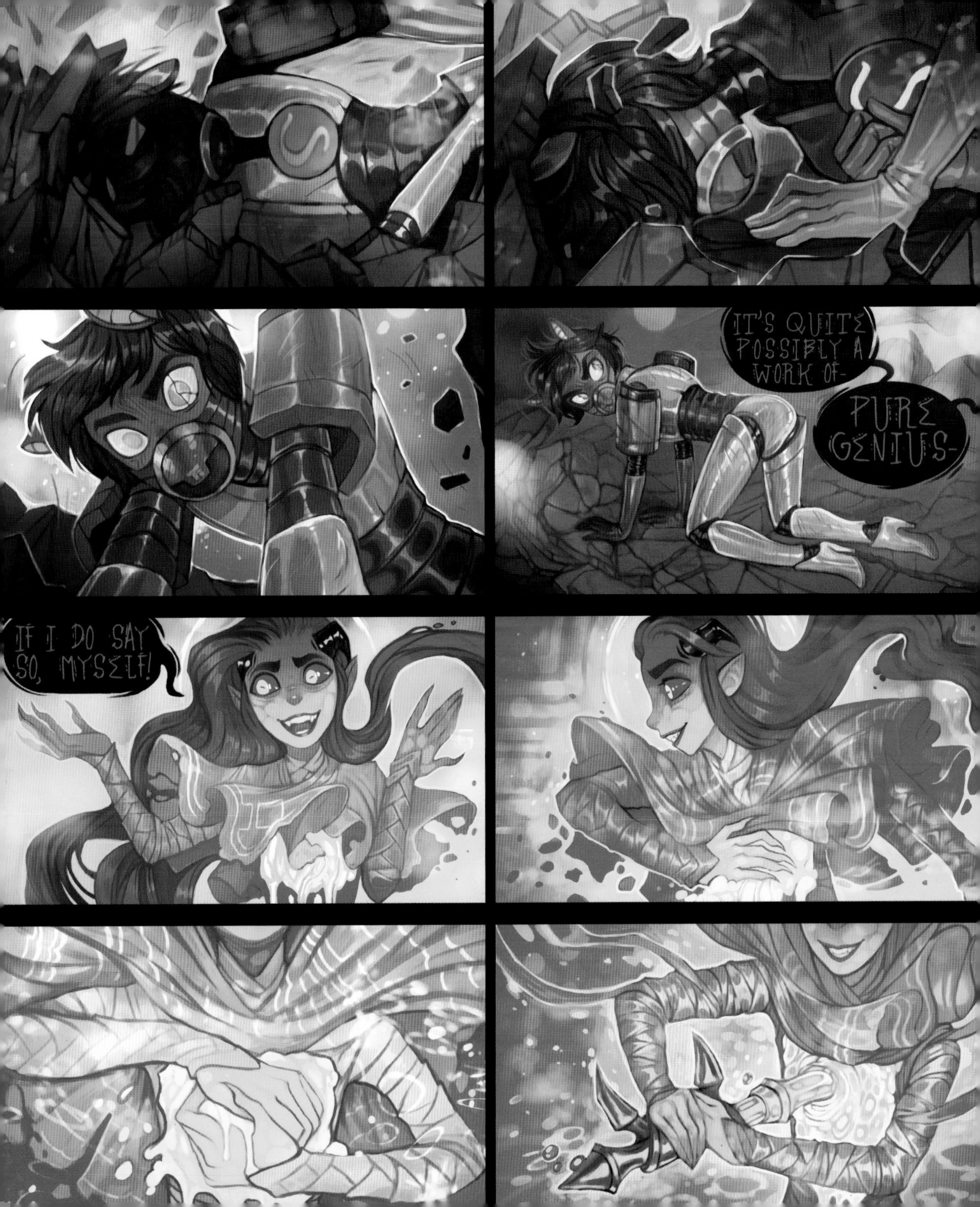
IT'S QUITE POSSIBLY A WORK OF-
PURE GENIUS-
IF I DO SAY SO, MYSELF!

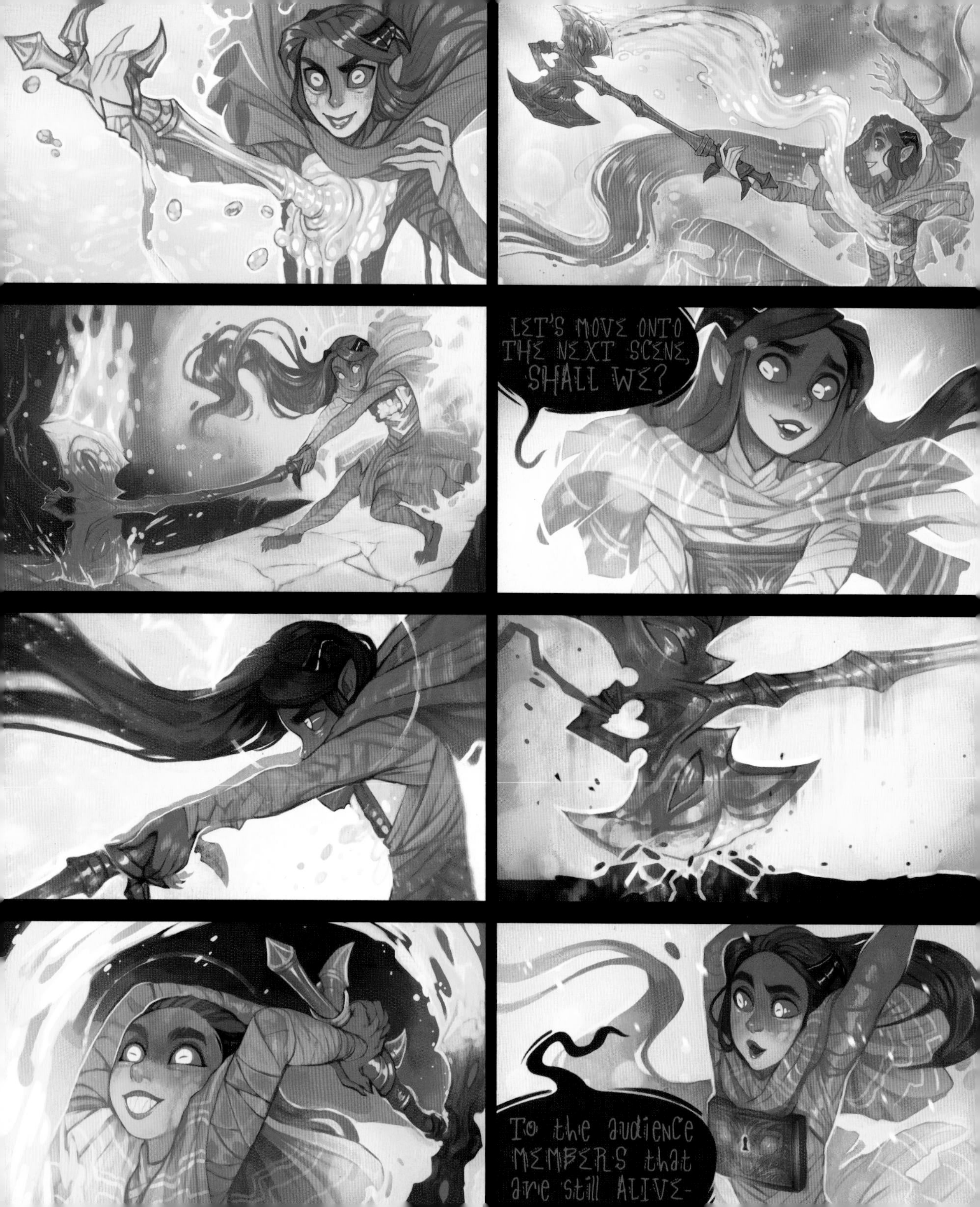
LET'S MOVE ONTO THE NEXT SCENE, SHALL WE?
To the audience MEMBERS that are still ALIVE-

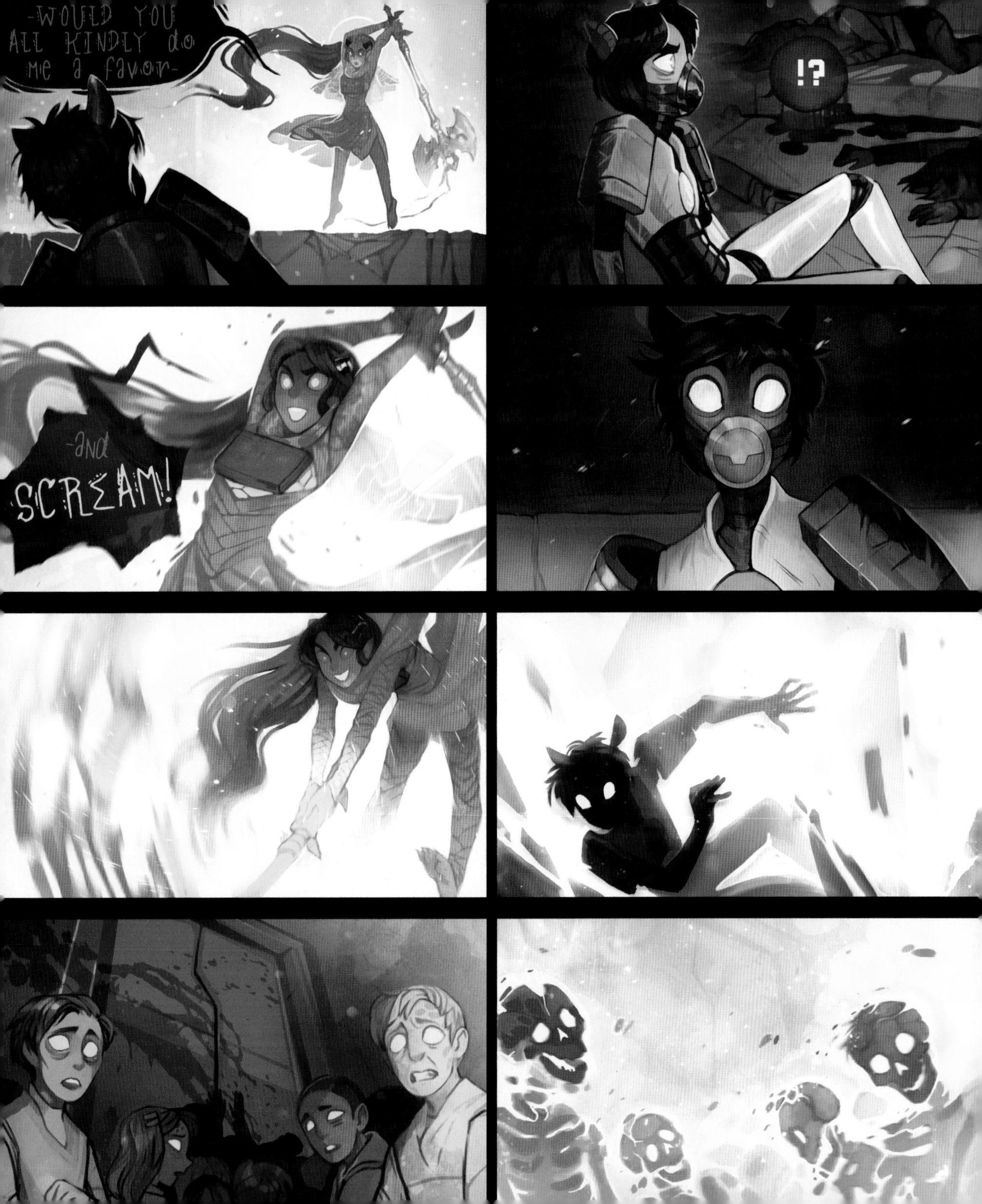

-WOULD YOU ALL KINDLY do me a favor-
!?
-and SCREAM!

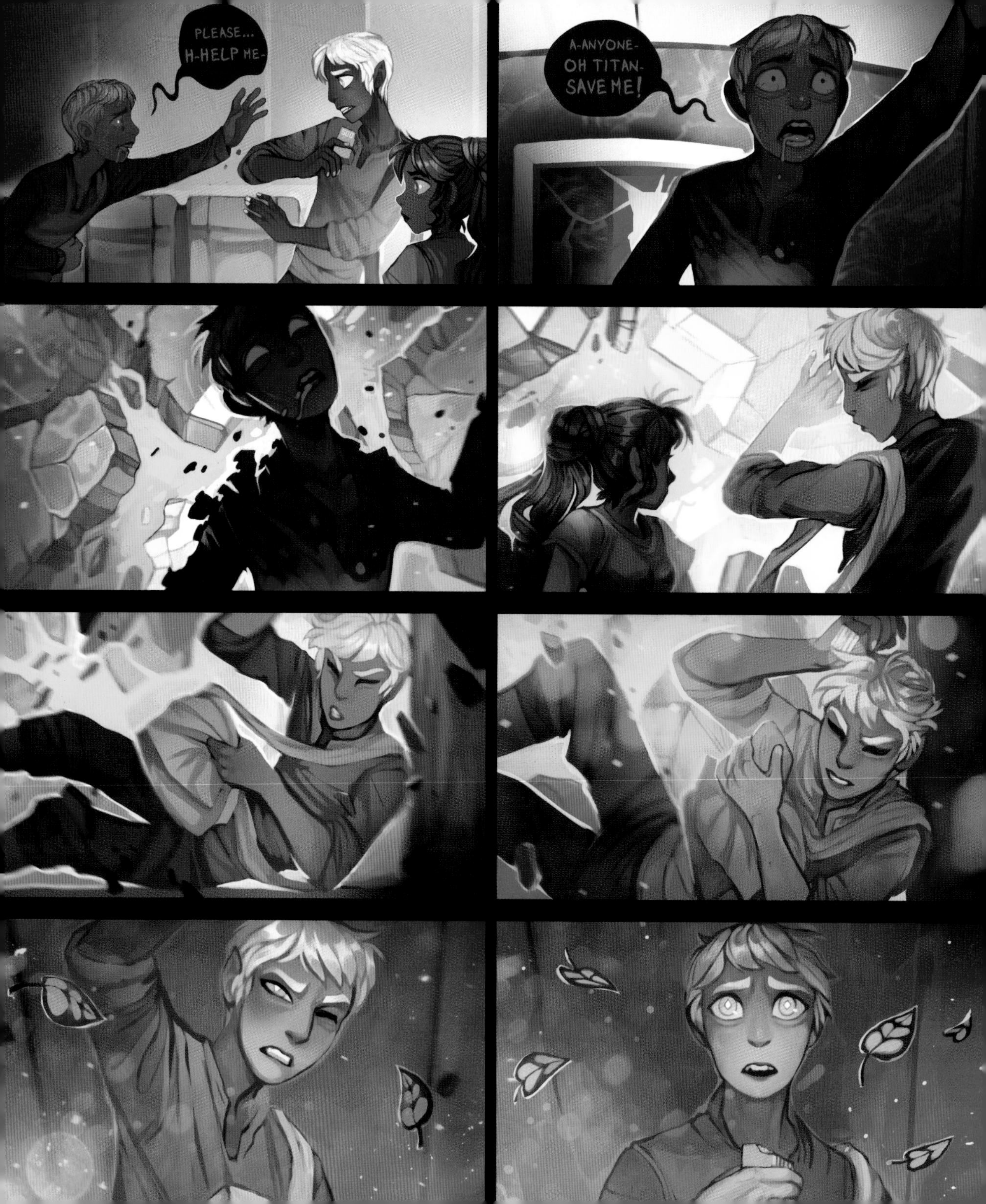
PLEASE...
H-HELP ME-
A-ANYONE-
OH TITAN-
SAVE ME!

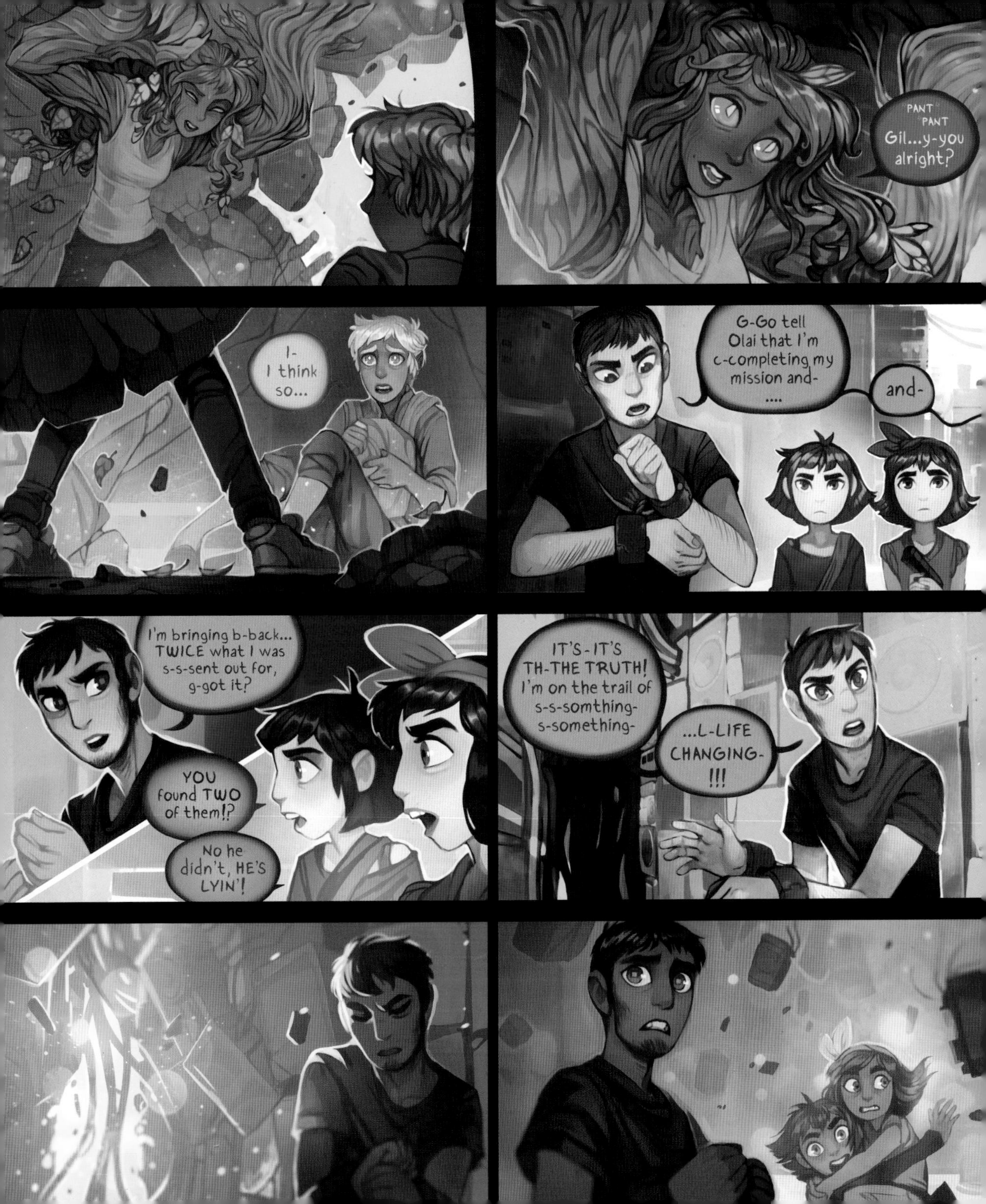
PANT PANT
Gil...y-you alright?
I- I think so...
G-Go tell Olai that I'm c-completing my mission and- ....
and-
I'm bringing b-back... TWICE what I was s-s-sent out for, g-got it?
YOU found TWO of them!?
No he didn't, HE'S LYIN'!
IT'S-IT'S TH-THE TRUTH! I'm on the trail of s-s-somthing- s-something-
...L-LIFE CHANGING- !!!

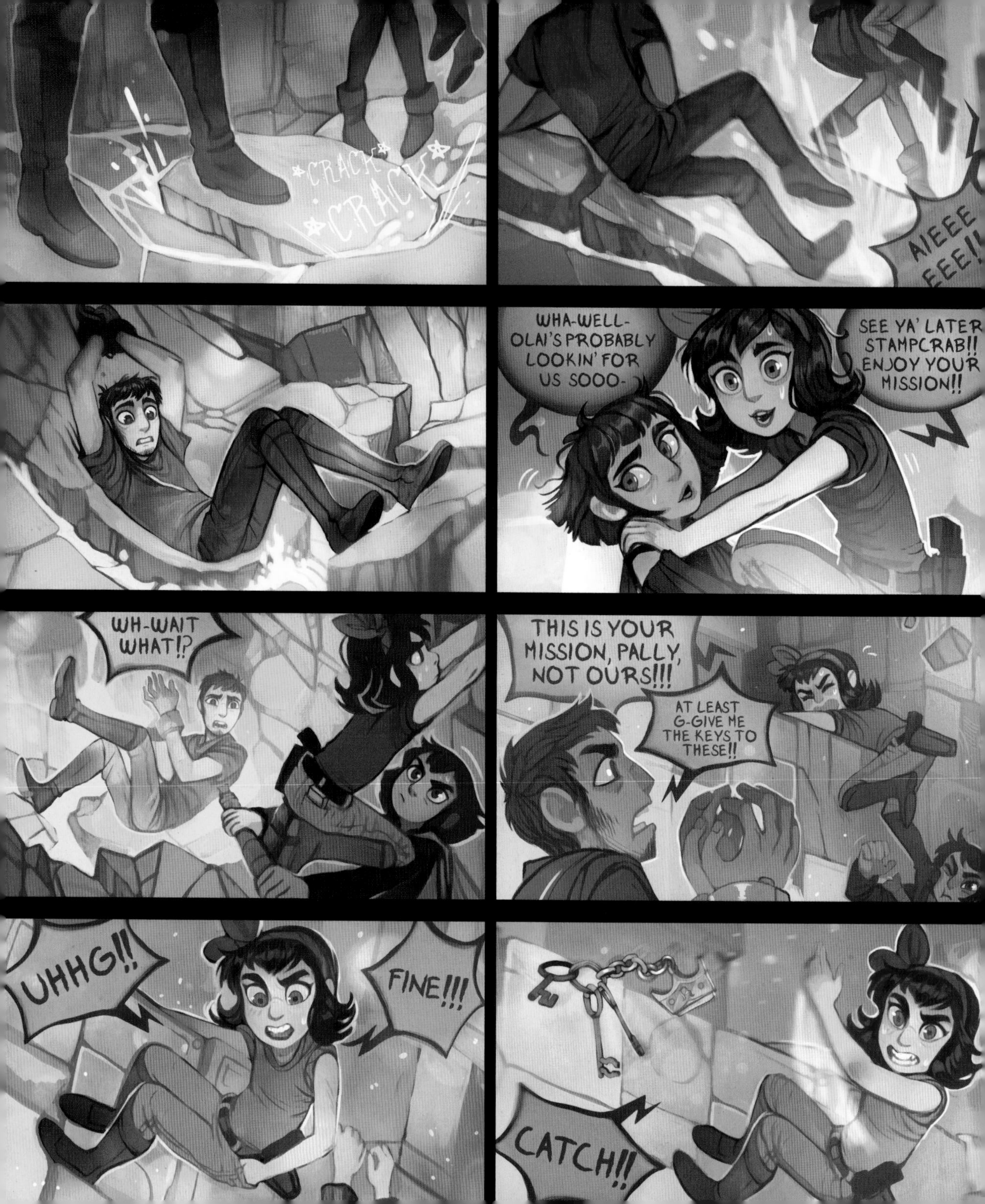
CRACK
CRACK
AIEEEEEE!!
WHA-WELL- OLAI'S PROBABLY LOOKIN' FOR US SOOO-
SEE YA' LATER STAMPCRAB!! ENJOY YOUR MISSION!!
WH-WAIT WHAT!?
THIS IS YOUR MISSION, PALLY, NOT OURS!!!
AT LEAST G-GIVE ME THE KEYS TO THESE!!
UHHG!!
FINE!!!
CATCH!!

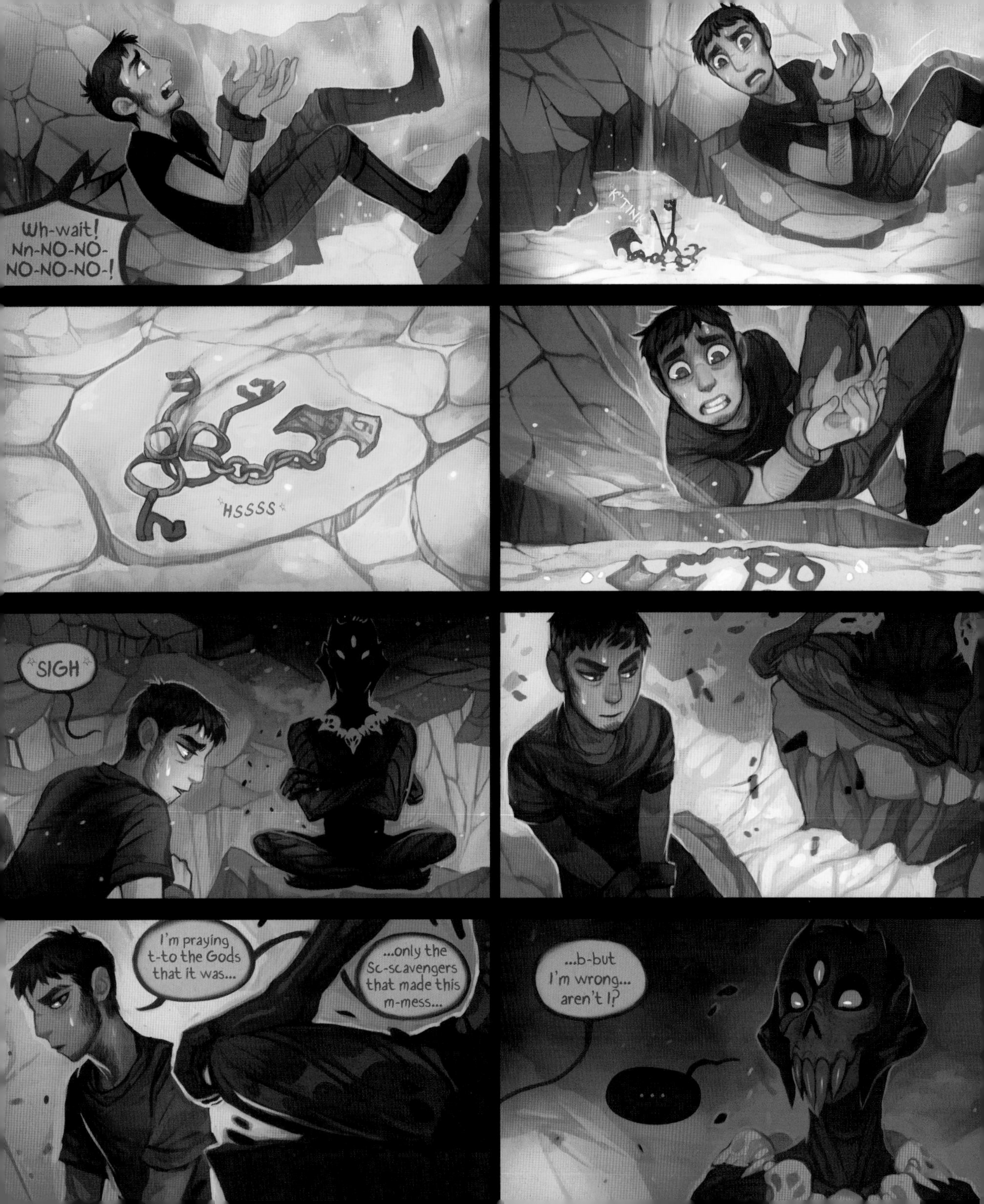
Wh-wait! Nn-NO-NO-NO-NO-NO-!
K'TINK
HSSSS
SIGH
I'm praying t-to the Gods that it was...
...only the Sc-scavengers that made this m-mess...
...b-but I'm wrong... aren't I?
...

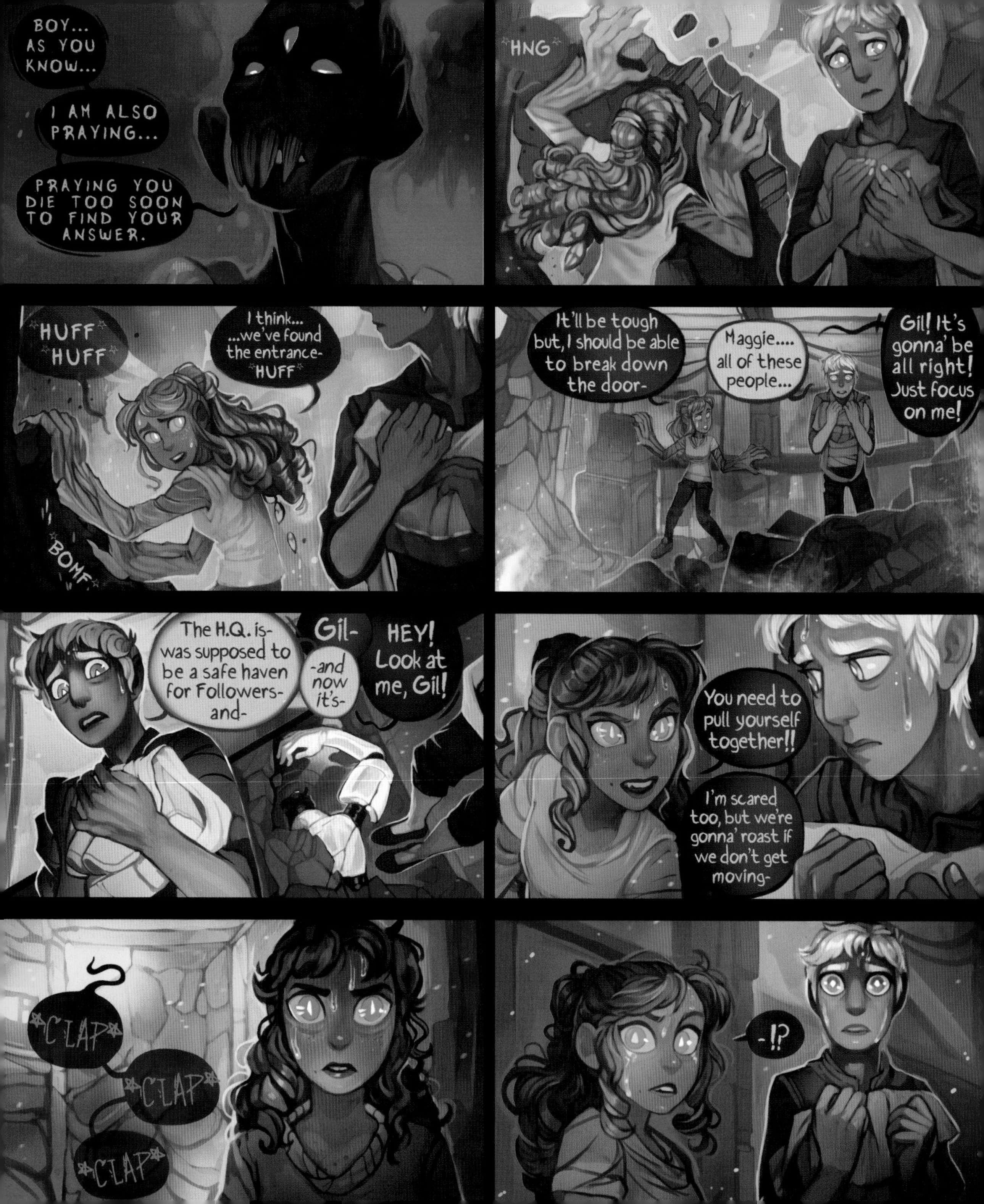
BOY... AS YOU KNOW...
I AM ALSO PRAYING...
PRAYING YOU DIE TOO SOON TO FIND YOUR ANSWER.
HNG
HUFF HUFF
I think... ...we've found the entrance- HUFF
BOMF
It'll be tough but, I should be able to break down the door-
Maggie.... all of these people...
Gil! It's gonna' be all right! Just focus on me!
The H.Q. is- was supposed to be a safe haven for Followers- and-
Gil-
-and now it's-
HEY! Look at me, Gil!
You need to pull yourself together!!
I'm scared too, but we're gonna' roast if we don't get moving-
CLAP
CLAP
CLAP
-!?

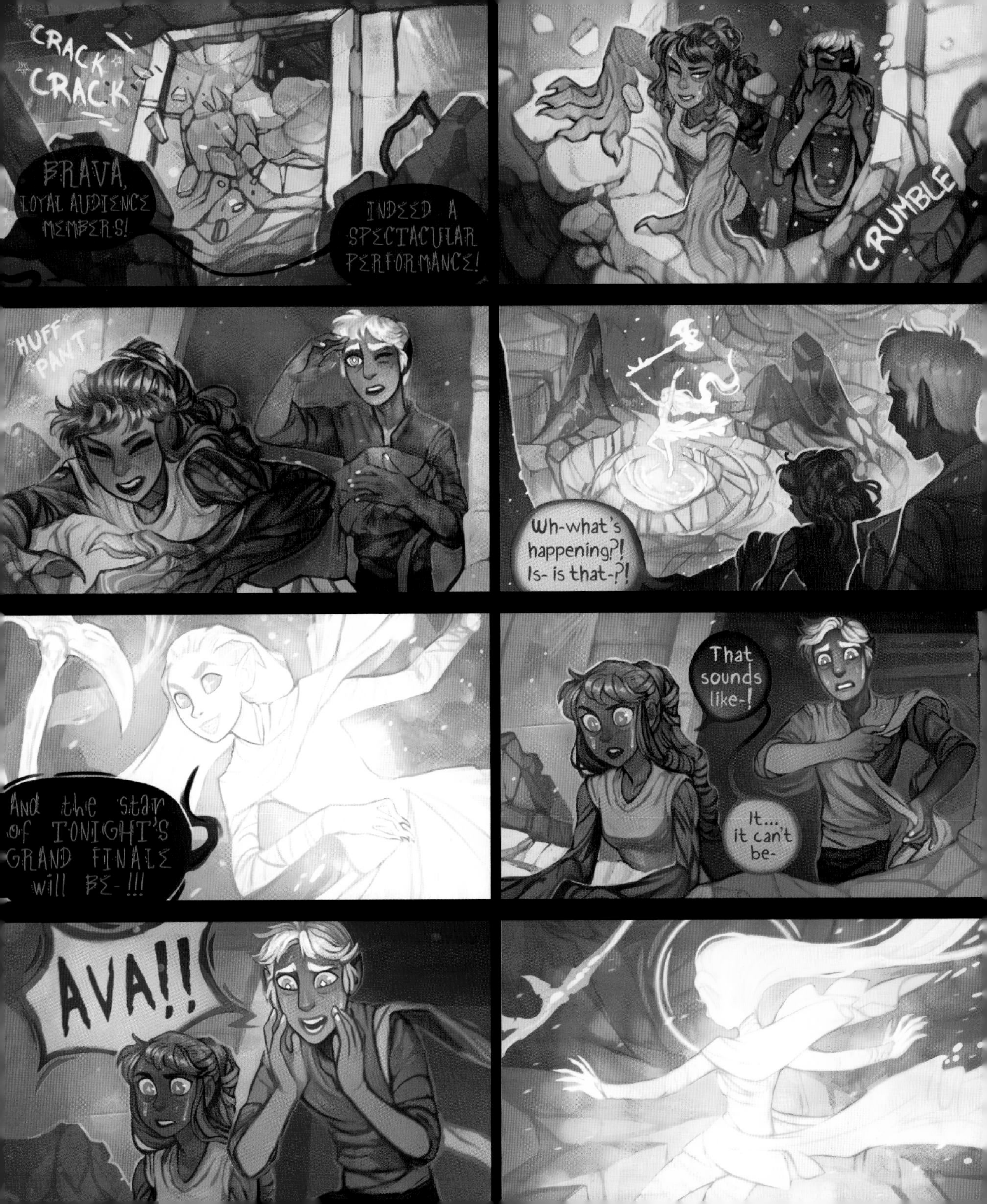
CRACK
CRACK
BRAVA, LOYAL AUDIENCE MEMBERS!
INDEED A SPECTACULAR PERFORMANCE!
CRUMBLE
HUFF
PANT
Wh-what's happening?! Is- is that-?!
And the star of TONIGHT'S GRAND FINALE will BE-!!!
That sounds like-!
It... it can't be-
AVA!!

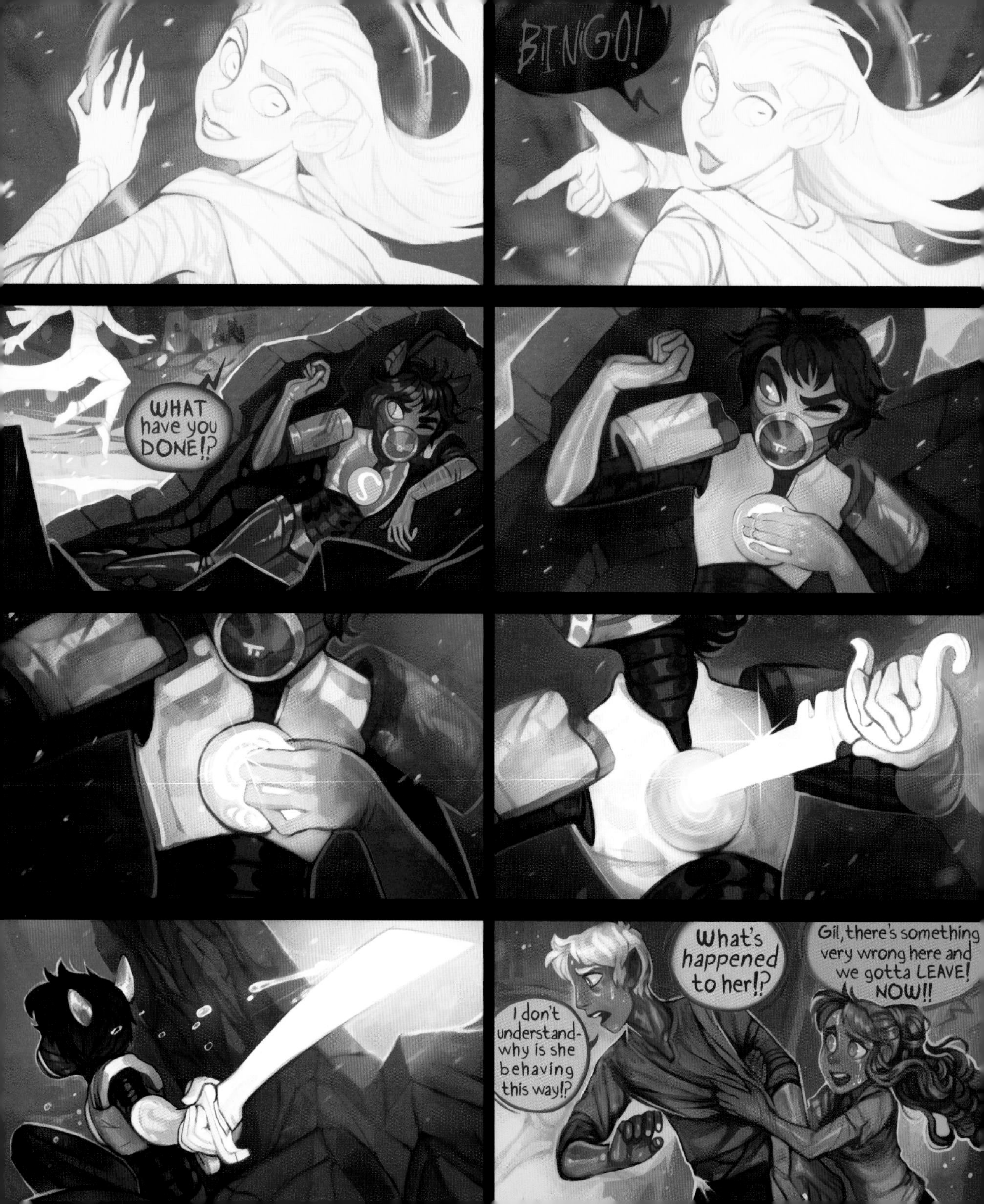
BINGO!
WHAT have you DONE!?
What's happened to her!?
I don't understand- why is she behaving this way!?
Gil, there's something very wrong here and we gotta LEAVE! NOW!!

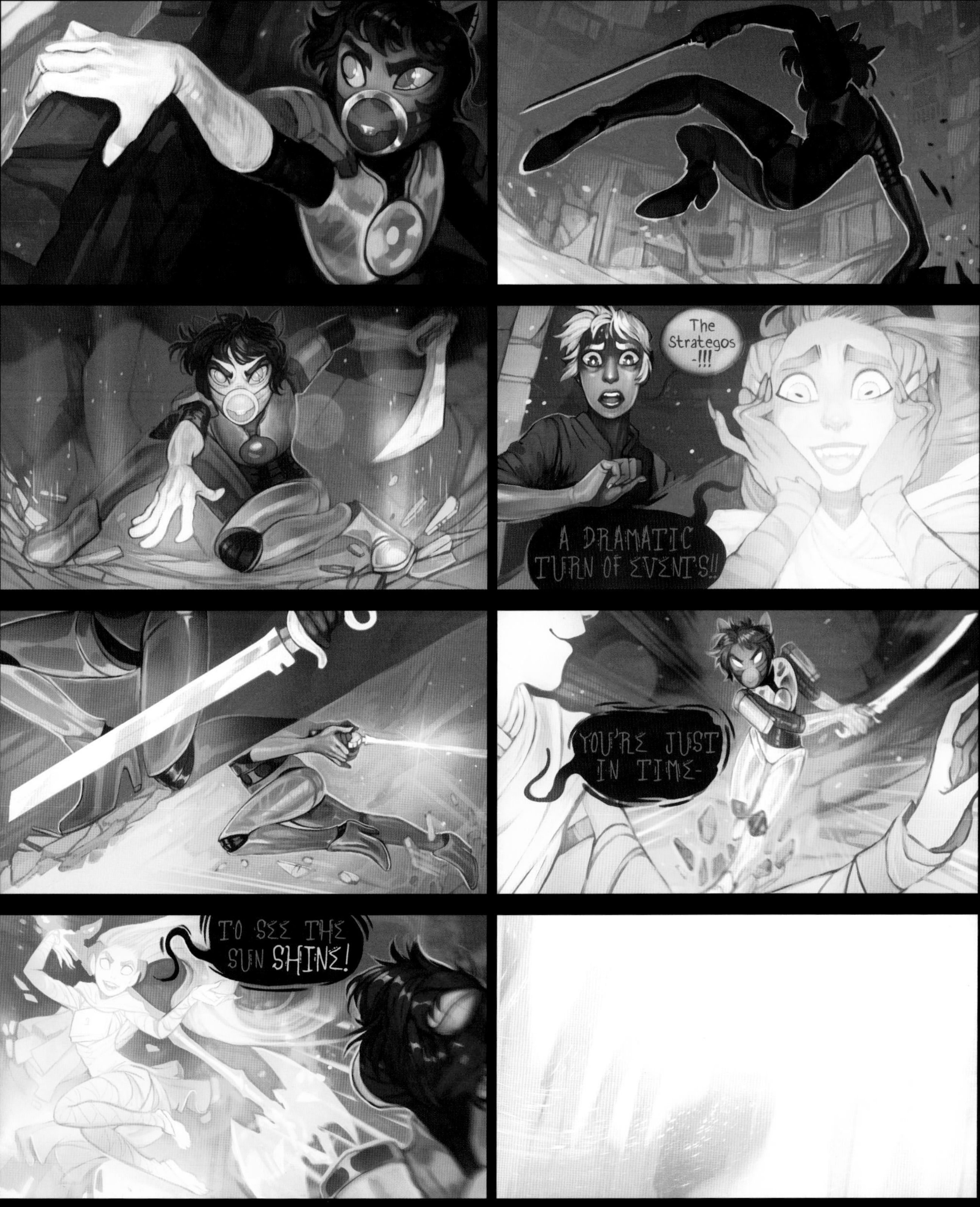
The Strategos -!!!
A DRAMATIC TURN OF EVENTS!!
YOU'RE JUST IN TIME-
TO SEE THE SUN SHINE!

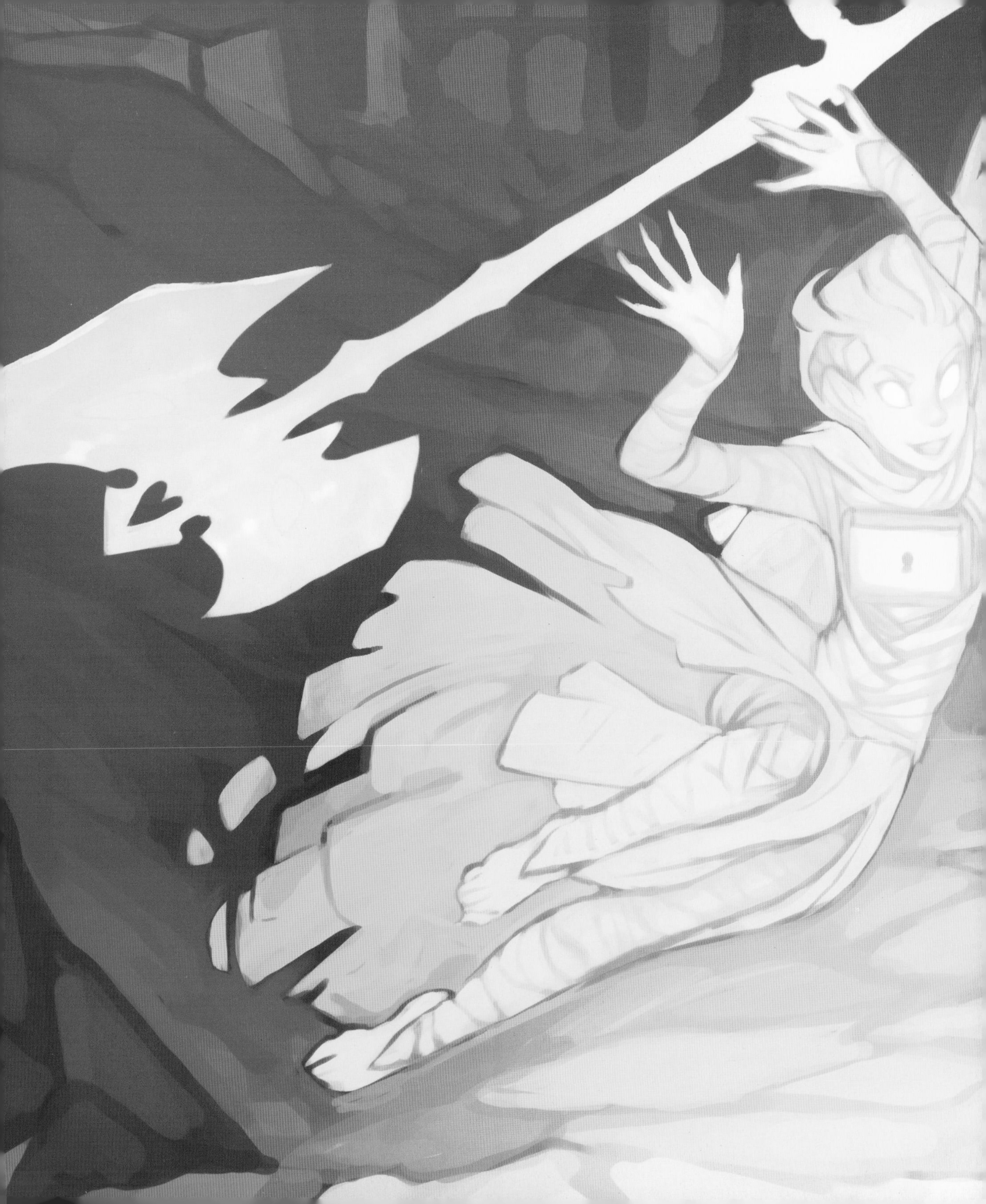

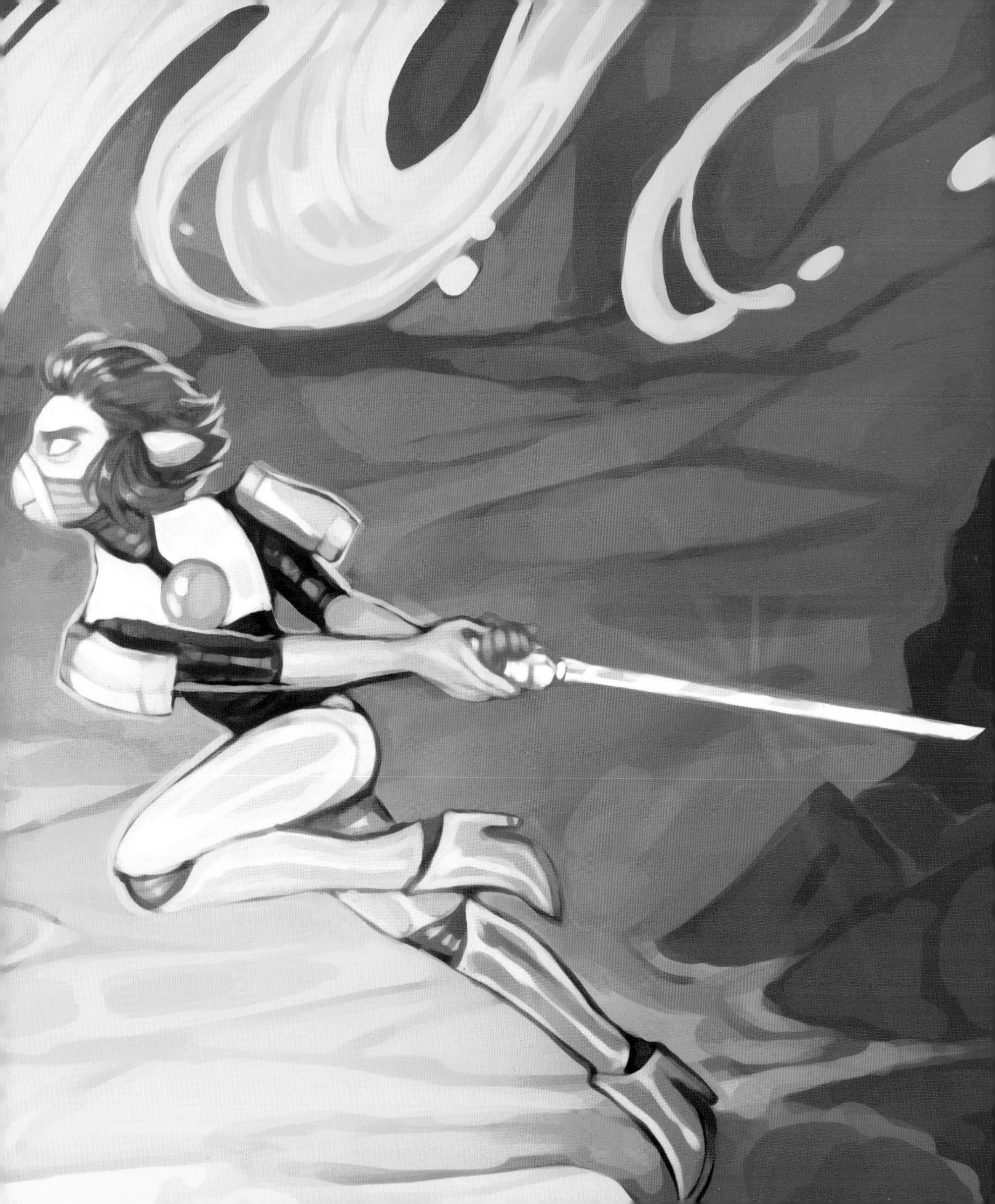

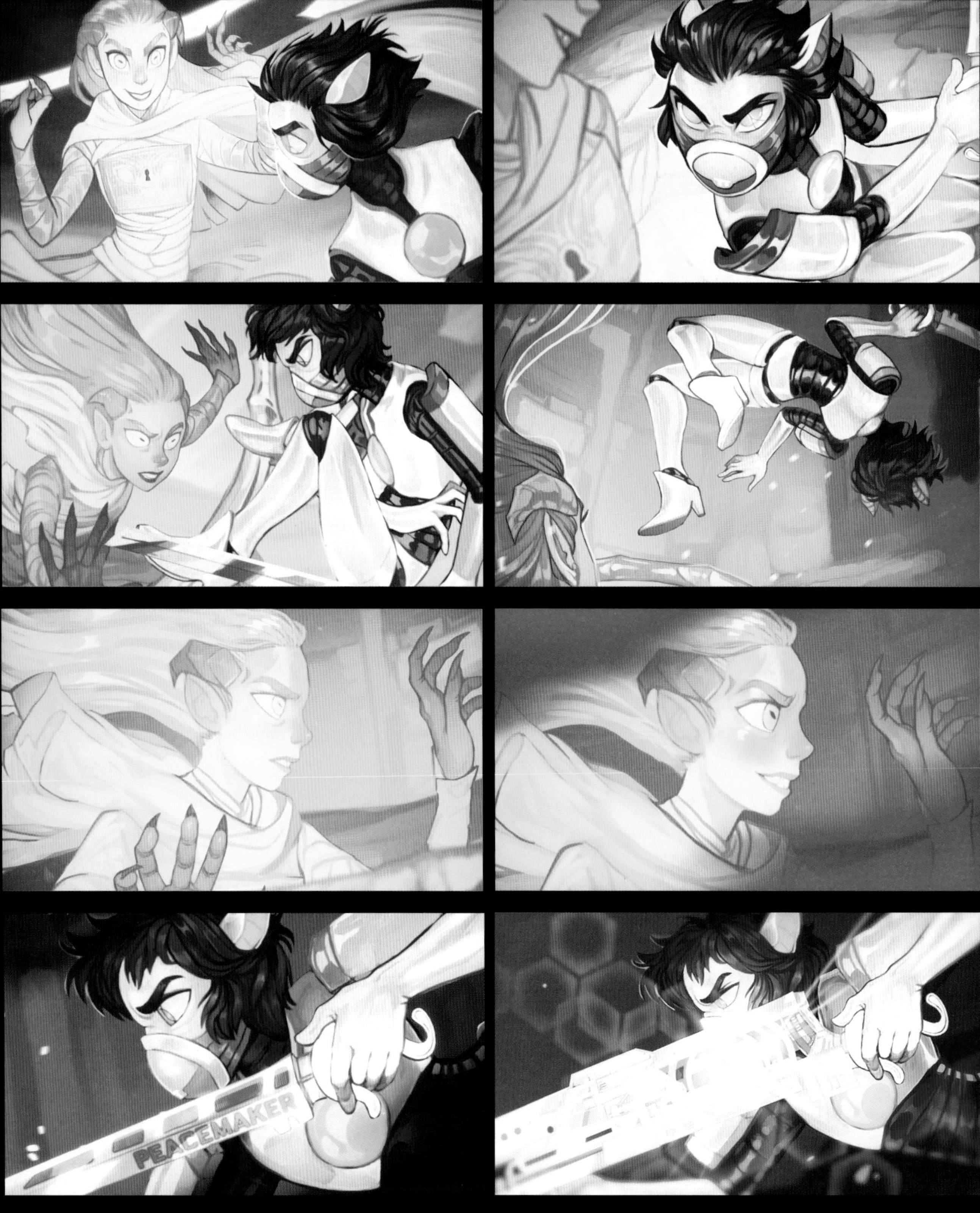
PEACEMAKER

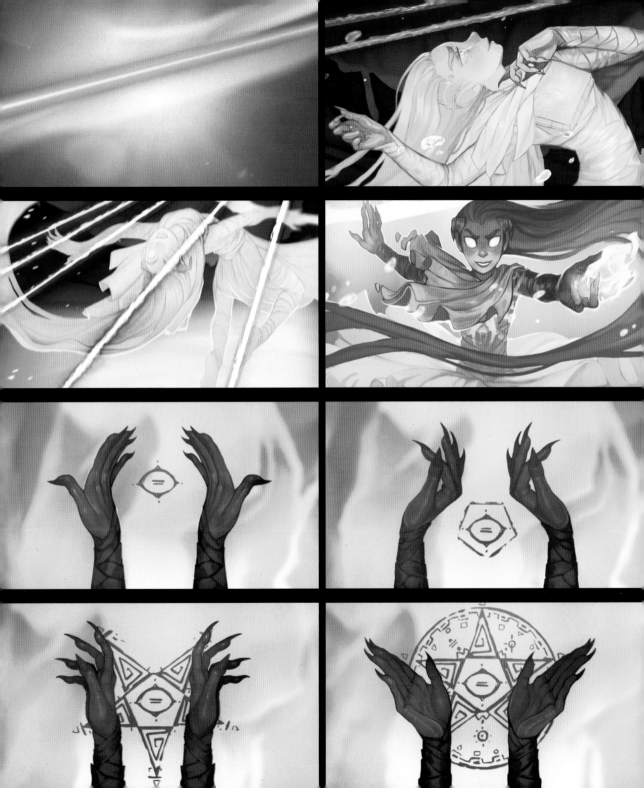

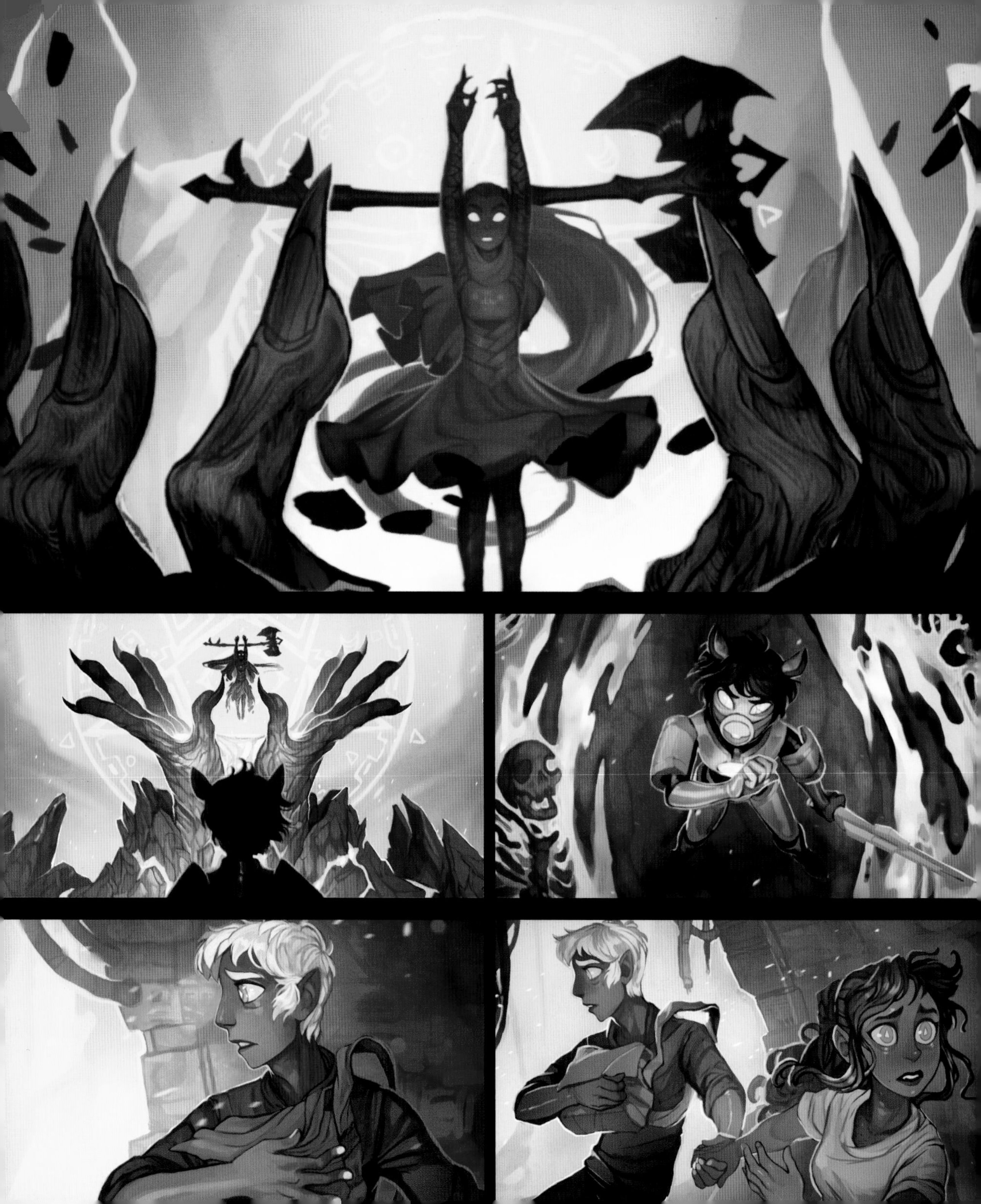

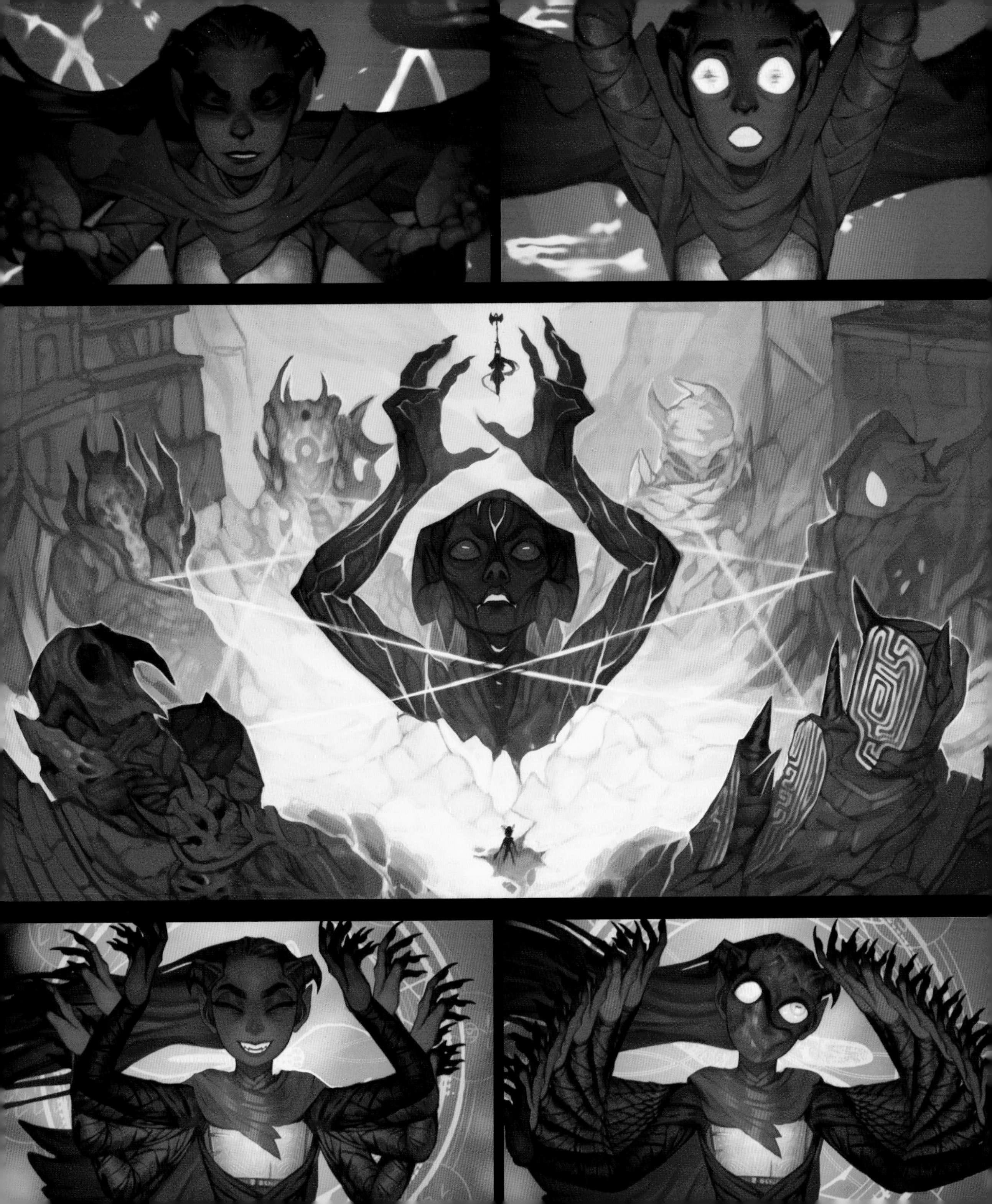

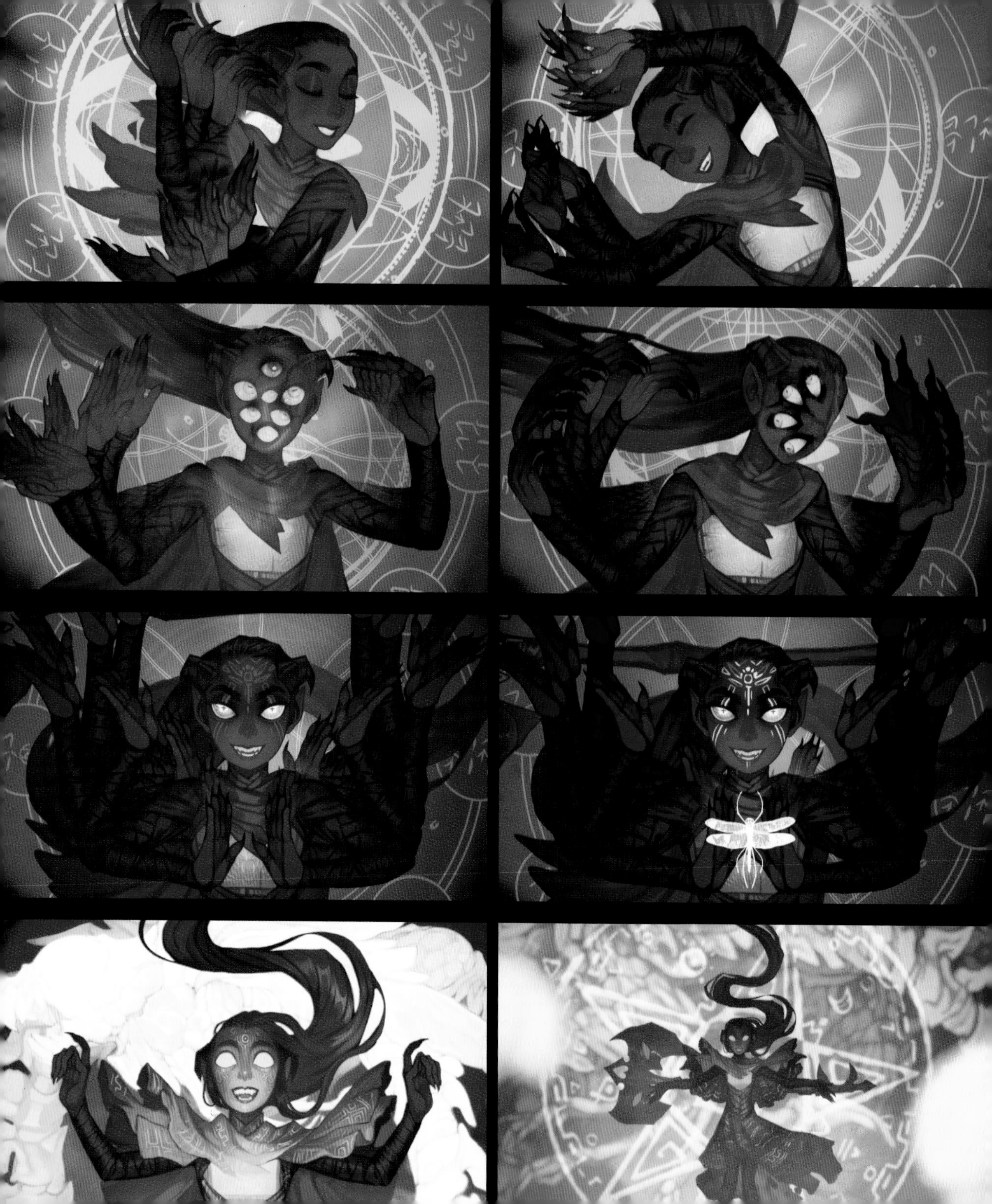

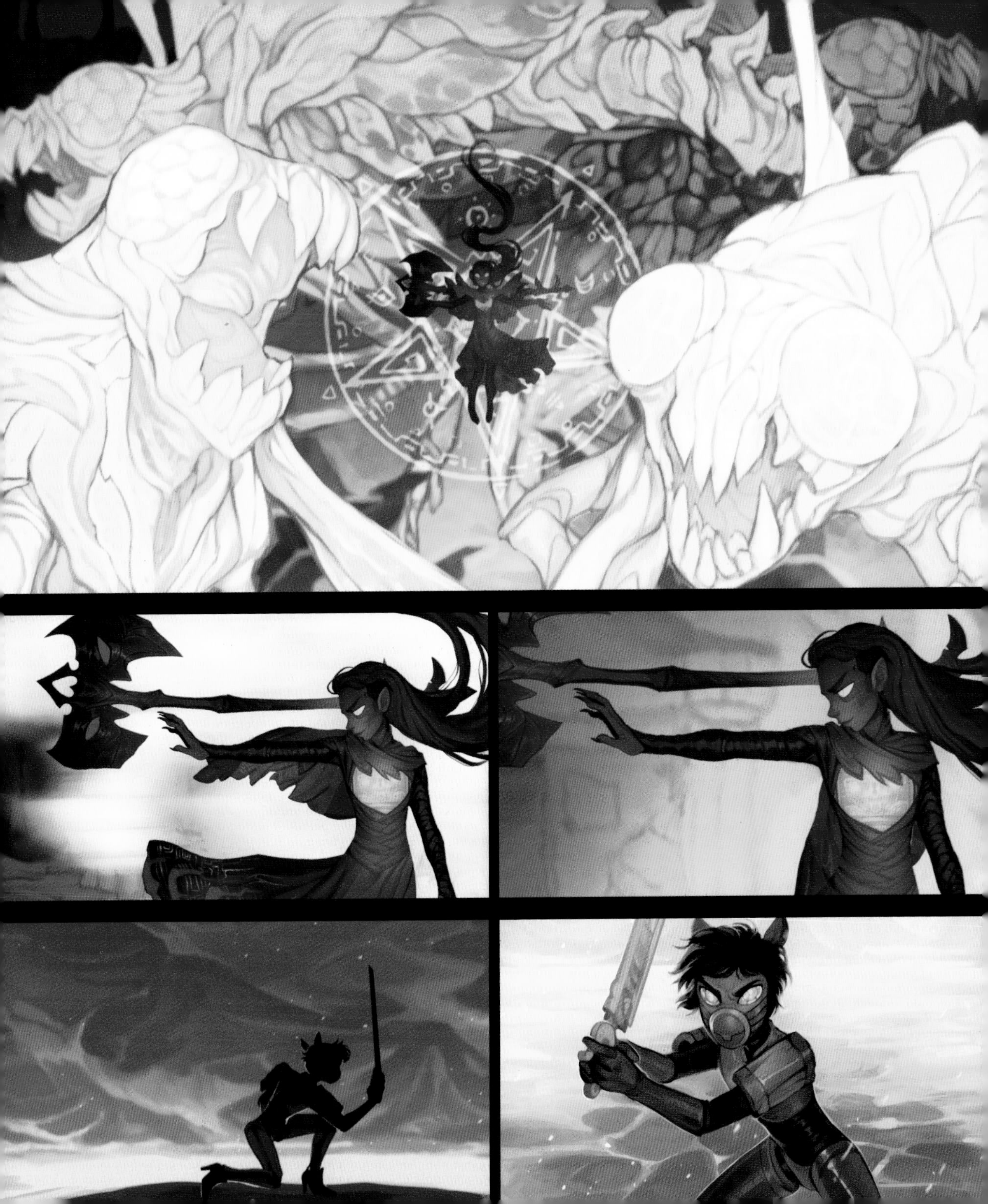

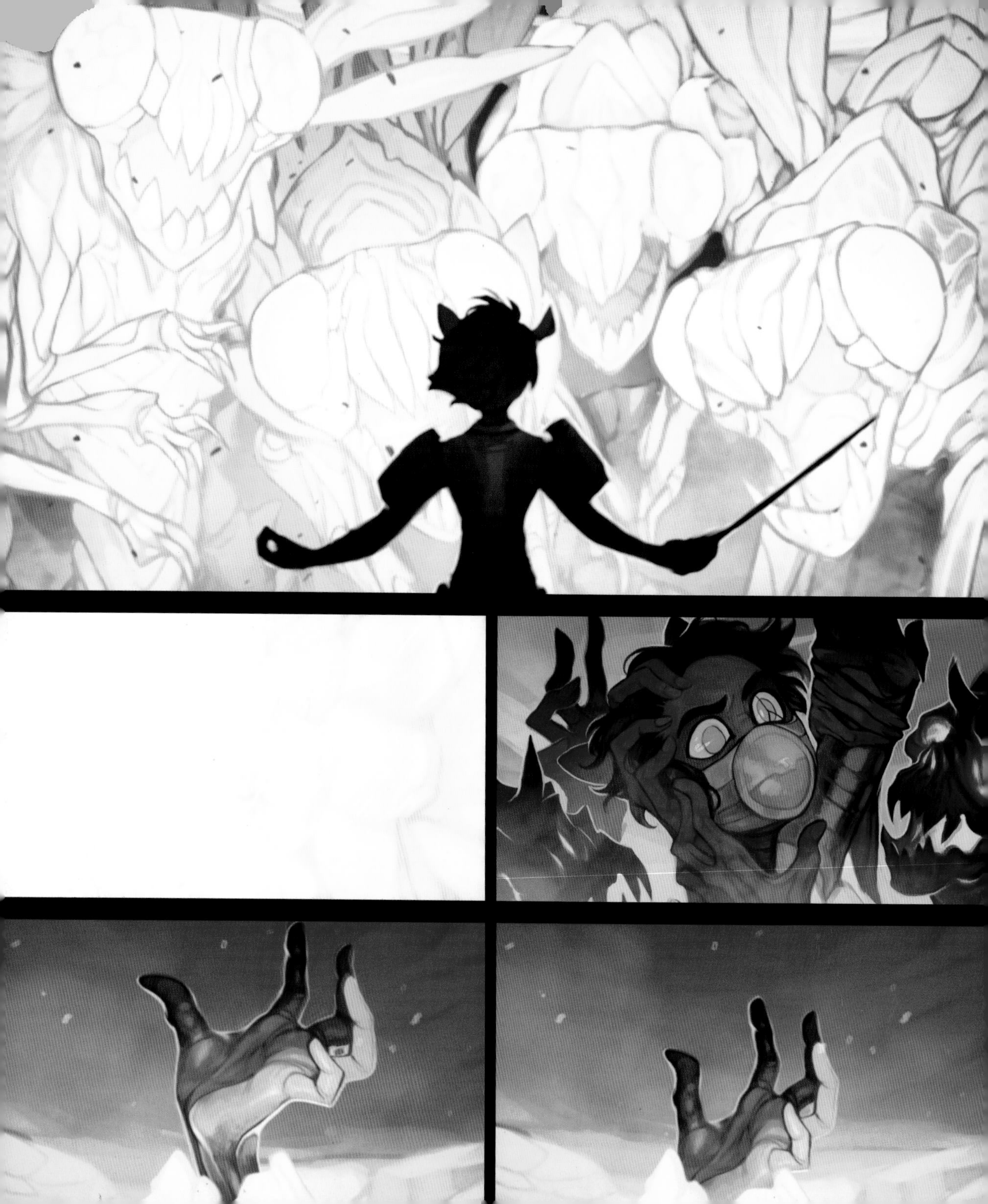

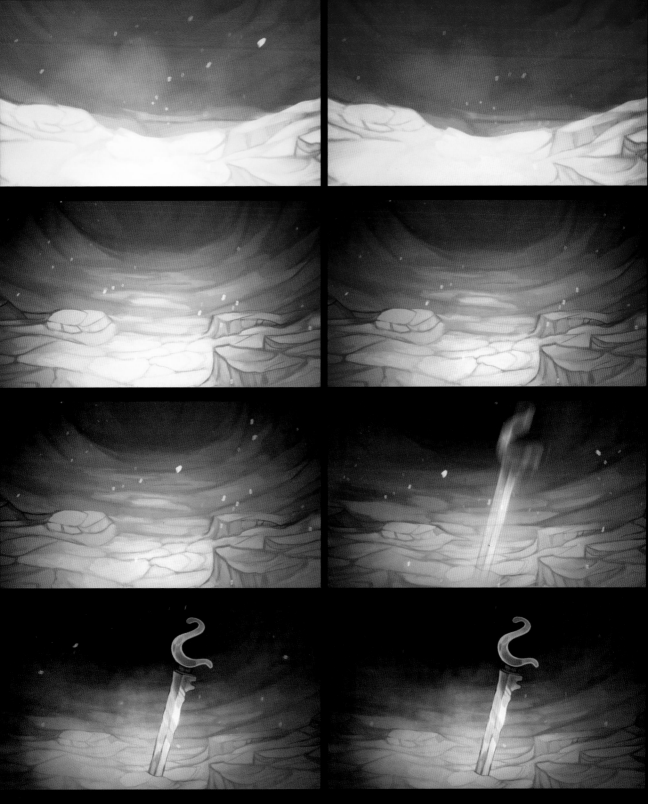

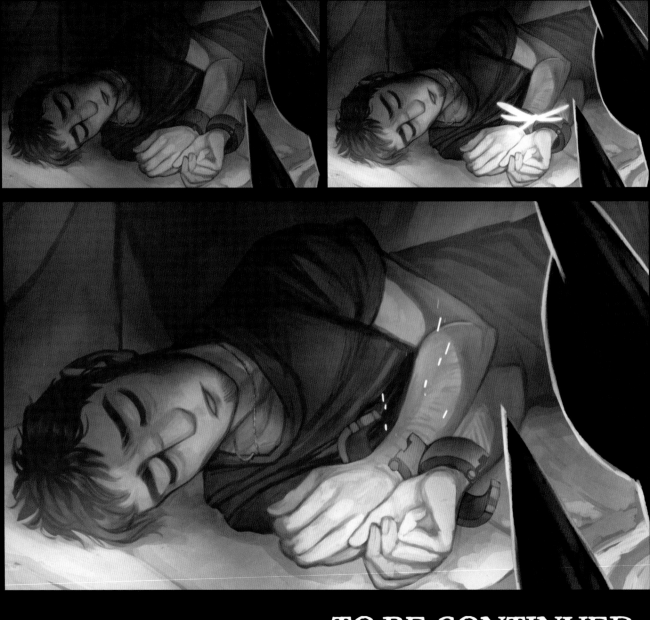

TO BE CONTINUED...

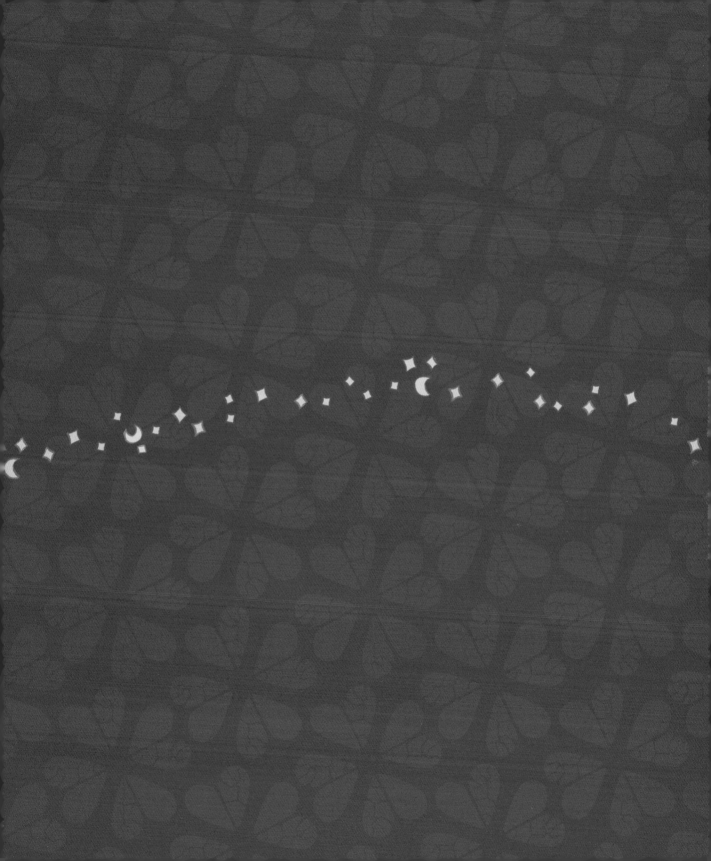

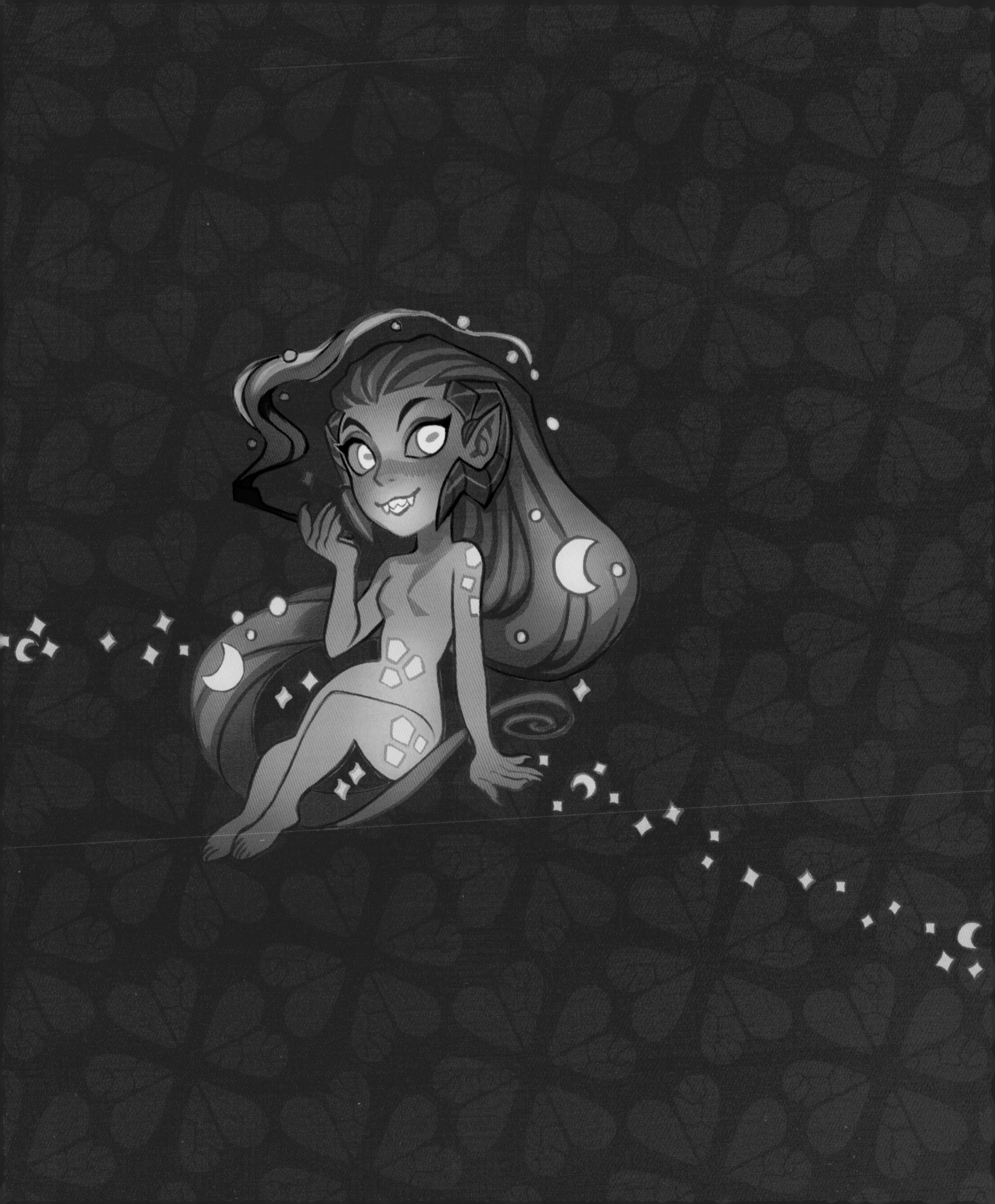

Michelle Fus graduated from the School of Visual Arts in 2011 for Computer Art and Animation. After interning at Pixar and working at DreamWorks Animation for two years, they decided to follow their dreams by telling stories and creating comics. Fus has been working on their sci-fi/fantasy epic, AVA'S DEMON, since 2012 and they hope to continue to add new and exciting installments to the story for as long as they can. They want to thank you for supporting their work and hope you thoroughly enjoy this book!

EXPLORE NEW WORLDS

For Young Adult & Middle Grade Readers in SKYBOUND COMET

Tiny heroes, epic adventures!

ON SALE NOW!
ISBN: 978-1-5343-2436-7 • $14.99
MIDDLE GRADE

Welcome to the smallest town in the universe.

ON SALE NOW!
ISBN: 978-1-5343-2437-4 • $17.99
YOUNG ADULT

Will you make the pact?

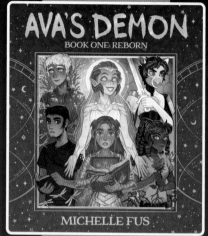

ON SALE NOW!
ISBN: 978-1-5343-2438-1 • $17.99
YOUNG ADULT

Tillie Walden enters the world of Robert Kirkman's THE WALKING DEAD!

ON SALE NOW!
ISBN: 978-1-5343-2128-1 • $14.99
YOUNG ADULT

Activate your heart. Be an Everyday Hero!

ON SALE NOW!
ISBN: 978-1-5343-2130-4 • $12.99
MIDDLE GRADE

What if you were destined to destroy the world?

ON SALE NOW!
ISBN: 978-1-5343-2129-8 • $14.99
YOUNG ADULT

SKYBOUND COMET

Visit **SkyboundComet.com** for more information, previews, teaching guides and more!

image